THE LONG COUNT

By Andrea Klosterman Harris

The Long Count

Copyright ©2010 by Andrea Klosterman Harris.

ISBN 978-0-557-53329-9

FIRST TRADE EDITION

Part I: The Black Road

For my part, I know nothing with any certainty, but the sight of stars makes me dream.

— Vincent Van Gogh

What can be asserted without evidence can also be dismissed without evidence.

— Christopher Hitchens

It's tough to make predictions, especially about the future.

— Yogi Berra

12.19.14.8.2

July 3, 2007 — Abby had been in Mexico for about eight weeks when she realized that she couldn't remember the last time she had thought of Simon. She sat up straight in her tent, almost shocked at the realization. While momentarily disturbing, it was a wonderful awakening, and she felt a slight, bewildered smile play over her lips. Tossing off her light blanket, she slid into a thin pair of sandals, then slipped out through the loose flaps of her tent and into the night. The small village of Xiba was located in fairly flat land, although she could see the dim rise and fall of the Sierra Madres in the distance. Every day, Abby gazed at these, wondering what lay beyond the tiny town where she was spending her summer, and tonight, she decided to go traveling.

Abby had set out toward the west and the ocean; she knew it was too far for her to make it on foot, but with the sky so clear and filled with stars, she just wanted to enjoy the cool night air.

Although they were done working by darkfall each night, Abby was always too exhausted to do much stargazing. She had broken out her telescope on a few occasions, but found herself spending more time explaining and giving demonstrations to the curious villagers than she had spent doing any actual viewing. Now she set out, wandering towards the sea, the wolves rumored to be in the area only a scant thought in the back of her mind. She had seen nothing larger than the town hounds in the eight weeks she had been in Xiba, and the romance of the night had her caught up in it. She felt strong and fearless; free, and alive.

Unbidden, however, thoughts of the night her world had fallen apart began to creep back into her mind, and as she walked, she thought back to ten o'clock on that Thursday night in April. As a PhD student, she'd been either in class, the lab, or tutoring students off and on since early that morning. She usually hit the library after her last class, but that night she'd been exhausted. All she wanted to do was get back to the house she shared with her fiancé and take a shower, grab something to eat and go to bed.

As she'd turned the key and pushed the door open, Abby was surprised to find the house in darkness. Simon, a mathematics professor at the university, should have been home hours earlier. His workload that semester was light, and he was usually home by dinnertime.

Abby had slipped off her light jacket, moving quietly through the shadowy living room. If Simon was in, he must be sleeping, and she did not want to wake him. As she neared the bedroom, however, her ears caught the sound of urgent whispers; quiet voices coming out of the darkness. She stopped in the hallway, listening closely, her heart pounding. Suddenly, he was there before her, still pulling a sheet around his waist as he stumbled wild eyed out into the hall.

"Hey, honey," Simon had said, managing a smile even while his eyes darted furtively into the dark bedroom. "What are you doing home? I didn't expect you for at least another hour."

Abby was speechless. The realization of what was happening, what *had* to be happening, was overwhelming, suffocating. She felt light headed as she tried to focus on Simon, the man she'd dated for four years and lived with for three. He was still blustering, blocking the doorway, reaching a hand towards her. She moved forward without thinking, zombie-like, her mind an absolute blank.

"Come on," Simon said, taking her by the arm and turning her away, back towards the living room. "It's okay," he soothed. For a moment she let him lead her away; then her numbness finally broke. Furiously, she turned on him, pushing past him and heading back to the bedroom. He was taken by surprise and she almost got by him, but he quickly grabbed her arms.

"No!" she cried, striking him on the chest and face. "I want to see her!"

Instead he picked her up, holding her fists tightly, her arms pinned against her chest as he carried her into the living room. She was sobbing now, her strength replaced by panic as it hit her; her relationship, her reality, her entire life had changed. One instant, and her world would never be the same.

Abby let herself be taken to the other room, sobbing uncontrollably. It barely registered a moment later when she caught a flash of long red hair as a female figure rushed past her down the hall. For the time being, all she felt was pain, and all she knew was the swirling dissolution of her life, her dreams, and her future washing away, leaving her empty and alone.

A few days later, Abby sat in her friend Amanda's apartment. There was still a month before the end of the semester, but Amanda would be leaving almost immediately afterwards for a three month charity project in Mexico. As a social work major, Amanda wanted to pad her resume before she graduated that winter.

Curled up tightly in the old armchair in her friend's living room, Abby's unmade-up face was still red and raw from her constant crying, her shoulder length dark hair pulled back into a messy ponytail. She hadn't been back to her house – actually *Simon's* house, as he often reminded her – since the wee hours of Friday morning, after they had sat up most of the night fighting. Abby had finally left, packing a bag for Amanda's small apartment, and she hadn't yet felt able to call or go back yet. She had asked Simon to pack up her things, which he'd refused to do; still, she couldn't bring herself to go do it.

Amanda climbed off the couch, a bounce in her step as she strode across the room to her friend. "Look," she said, crouching beside the armchair. "I don't know what you're feeling, and I can't tell you what to do about it. But I really think you need to get away for awhile. It's going to kill you to go back to that house and try to make arrangements to move, and to find a place to live for the next year. You need to get away from this whole situation for a while."

Abby nodded, holding a tissue up to her eyes as she answered. "I know," she said, her voice a bare whisper. "I don't want to go back there. I can't even stand the thought of walking through that house. *Four years*," she said, suddenly furious. "Four years I was with him; the rest of my life was planned around him – where I would live, where I'd work, even the names of our kids. Now I have to start over. I don't want to start over, damn it! I just want my life back."

Her friend was silent, watching as Abby tried to get control of herself. After a brief struggle, Abby finally wiped away the tears she had thought she was out of by now, cleared her throat and sat up a little straighter.

"I don't know," she said, her voice steadier. "I have one more year of work for my doctorate; I have to finish that. But right now I can't see past the next five minutes. I don't know what to do," she finished, her voice cracking.

Sensing her friend was about to break down again, Amanda put a hand on her arm. "You will get through this, Abby. It doesn't feel like it now, but you will. You need to start over; a change of address, a whole new outlook."

Abby nodded solemnly, sniffling. "I know. But where am I going to go? I just can't apartment hunt right now. I'm not in a state of mind to make any major decisions right now. Just finishing this semester is going to take every effort I can muster. I'm not going to have the time or the motivation to go out looking at places and moving right now – not to mention how to pay for it."

Amanda was silent for a moment. At last, she said, "You can store your things at your parents' house, can't you?"

"I don't know," Abby replied. "I haven't had the closest relationship with them since I started dating Simon. I don't think I could go back home."

"That's not what I was thinking," Amanda said. "I'm going to Mexico for ten weeks this summer with nothing to do but help the townsfolk build a septic system. It might just do your heart some good."

Abby was thoughtful. Finally, she shook her head. "First of all," she said, "I don't speak Spanish. Second, I have no money – you know Simon supported me through grad school these last couple of years. I can't spend ten weeks in Mexico."

"It's a Mayan Indian area," Amanda explained. "So none of us will probably speak the language. And we only have to pay a signup fee and our airfare to get down there. Although we have to buy our own food, we all take turns cooking and preparing it. They say that the villagers usually feed us, too. If you can handle living in a tent and bathing in a stream for ten weeks, there's not a lot of overhead."

For the first time in two days, Abby smiled, albeit faintly. "Damn, Amanda," she said. "Two and a half months with no plumbing or running water? How in the world are you going to survive?"

Her friend laughed. "I'll manage," she said. "It makes you appreciate things so much more when you realize that this is how these people live every day ... they're not on an adventure, or making sacrifices for ten weeks. This is their life. Being able to do something to improve that for them is the most incredible feeling in the world."

"I understand your point," Abby said. "But you're majoring in social work; this is what you want to do for the rest of your life. I'm going to be an astrophysicist, studying the universe; I can't see me planting corn in rural Mexico."

Amanda smiled and rose to her feet. "All I'm saying is think about it," she said. "You need something to take your mind off of poor you for awhile. Thinking about others is the best way to do it. Maybe it'll make you see how lucky you are – with or without Simon."

Abby looked up at her friend. "An entire summer living in third world conditions *would* give me some perspective, some time to think about everything," she said.

"Good girl," Amanda answered with a wide smile. "I'll get you a sign up form and a list of costs."

"Well, that might be a problem," Abby said. "I'm pretty much flat broke."

Amanda had returned to her place on the couch. "It's not a lot; just a couple hundred bucks. You don't have anything saved up?"

Abby shook her head. "Simon wouldn't let me work these last few years except for student teaching. I was completely dependent on him – even my car is in his name."

Amanda was silent for a moment, twisting a long strand of hair and thinking. Finally, nodding toward Abby's left hand, she said, "Well, what about that?"

Abby looked down at the sparkling ring on her finger. A sharp pain caught in her chest and she felt tears well up again as she remembered Simon's proposal almost two years ago. He said he had begun putting aside money for the ring soon after he had met her, because he "was that sure."

A tear rolled down her cheek as the solitaire caught the light, flashing brightly, and she was struck with a fresher memory: the redhead rushing out of their house while Simon held Abby down in the hallway as she shrieked and wailed like a hurt child.

She raised her hand over her head, turning it to let the stone catch the light again. After a long moment, she said, "I guess it might be worth a few bucks."

Slightly over a month later, she was on a plane to Mexico.

Now, walking slowly under the ancient constellations in the night sky, she was again troubled. It had been more than two months since she had last spoken with Simon, and she had left with their relationship status open-ended. He had apologized profusely for what he had called a "dire mistake." He blamed her long hours of studying; her work towards her doctorate took the majority of her time and attention. When she wasn't in class, she was studying; when she wasn't studying, she was sleeping. She hadn't spent a full evening with him in the months leading up to his infidelity and, he claimed, he was lonely.

Abby hadn't bought his loneliness as justification for cheating, but she had felt a pang of guilt all the same. She had essentially abandoned him both physically and emotionally long before she had caught him with the redhead. Her research monopolized all her time and energy, and she knew he had a valid point.

Abby had left after this discussion, torn about what direction to take. While she couldn't excuse or forgive Simon's infidelity, she still felt guilty, knowing that what he said was true. She'd simply counted on him hanging in there until she was finished with her PhD; she'd forgotten that he needed her, too.

The fresh air rolling in from the ocean beyond the mountains was clearing her head, giving her an opportunity to think, and to consider. She thought that when she returned to Boston, she would try to work things out. She had too much invested in Simon and their relationship to end it over something he seemed honestly sorry about. Besides, Abby thought; she knew that she still loved him, and she couldn't imagine her life without him.

Abby had been walking for nearly an hour, knowing she should turn back soon, when she realized that the darkness up ahead was a little blacker than the surrounding area. A chill passed over her briefly, like a cloud across the moon, and her steps faltered. Suddenly she realized how far she had come, and that she not seen another sign of human life at all in the darkness. Alone in the rural countryside of southern Mexico, just north of the Guatemalan border, fascinated by the hugeness of the sky, she had wandered far from their camp, and up ahead she saw the deep shadows of something large looming in the darkness.

She stopped, listening to the deep quiet surrounding her. There was a flutter of wings as some night bird soared overhead, and the grasses at her feet rustled softly in the slight breeze. Abby peered ahead at the mass of shadows a few hundred yards away, scanning her memory for her geography. Her night vision sharpened a bit as she focused upon the darkened area, and she drew her in breath as her mind caught upon a remnant of thought and her eyes cleared.

"My God," she whispered in awe as she realized where she might be, and that the shadows she had been heading towards were actually monuments, tall ruins of buildings shadowed deeply against the night sky. Her eyes had adjusted to the perfect, star-filled firmament, but she had been almost upon the ancient ruins before she saw them for what they were.

One of the few ancient Mayan cities this far to the south of Mexico, Izapa was a site she had learned about in an astronomy course during her graduate work. Izapa, the Ceremonial City of the Ancient Skywatchers, stood now in ruin, picked over by generations of archaeologists, tourists and treasure hunters. Several relics still stood – broken monuments and thrones, stela and statues, the last representation of skywatchers and ancient astronomers from time immemorial.

Abby approached in wonder, her reverence overwhelming as she carefully descended the stone steps, studying the old altars as she passed. She moved slowly through the ancient grounds, examining old artifacts and stopping more than once to watch the sky, gazing upon the vast starred universe as the creators of this site had done thousands of years before. It was as if time had stood still here, the stone ruins alit only by the natural light of the moon and stars, which bathed the ancient site with their misty, long-dead light.

10

The night had grown cooler, and she hugged her arms around her as she threaded her way through the old settlement. The stark beauty of the stars stood out like diamonds against the velvet blackness of the sky, holding her attention captive as she wandered. For once the shrill voices in her head were still, and her heart no longer bore the leaden heaviness which she had carried around in her chest like a sharp stone. Instead, her mind was clear, and the cold, still light of the stars filled her eyes and her spirit, and for the first time in a long time, her soul felt at peace.

"Watch out for that stela," a bodiless voice cautioned, and Abby stumbled, startled out of her meditation. Her heart pounding wildly, she glanced around frantically to see from where the voice had come.

"Over here," the voice said, calm but amused. She saw motion in the shadows, and from only a few yards away a tall, broad-shouldered figure rose to greet her. He stood in a pool of moonlight, and Abby could see the outline of long, tangled black hair and a scruffy beard. His features were impossible to discern, but even in spite of her diminished night vision she could see that his clothes were rumpled and apparently, unwashed. She took an unconscious step back, but the man immediately put out both hands to her, palms up. Even from a distance, she could see that they were empty. "It's okay," he said, his voice quiet and deep. "Do you speak English?"

"Yes," she answered, trying to sound brave and confident, but her voice was a strained whisper. Her skin began to tighten, a chill running up her spine, and she could feel the goosebumps on her bare arms even in the warm night. The surprise of finding someone else out here in the ruins was quickly chased by the realization that she was alone in the darkness, miles from camp, with a wild looking male stranger. He seemed to sense her trepidation and stayed where he was. Continuing to hold his hands out where she could see them, he said in a quiet, calm voice: "My name is Dominic Ciriello. I'm an anthropologist."

"What are you doing out here?"

"Star gazing," he said quietly. "From an ancient observatory."

Abby stood back, watching him, as a shadow passed over the full moon. Again, she noticed how chilly the night had become, and a small shiver passed over her. "It looks like these ruins have been well-trampled," she said. "Haven't they pretty much found everything they're going to find here?"

Dominic lowered his hands, but did not make a move towards her. Instead, he lowered himself slowly to the ground, where he sat in the thick grass and looked around at the stone monuments.

"Yes," he said, "and no. These ruins are an ancient Mayan site called Izapa. It has probably already given up all its artifacts ... but that's not what I'm here to find." He glanced up at her as the moon cleared once again, illuminating the structures around them. She tensed as she sensed him taking in her face and figure, but he didn't pause, continuing instead in his quiet, almost meditative voice.

"People didn't stop visiting the tombs in Egypt when they had been cleared out. They didn't stop studying the Inca and Aztecs after they'd uncovered their temples," he said, looking around again at the stone heaps, all that remained of the prehistoric Mayan ceremonial grounds. "This place could be a useless pile of rocks; all catalogued and marked, but worthless. But it isn't. There is still much to be found here. There is always history. There is always information. And there are always answers. That is, as long as you still have questions."

He fell silent for a moment, and Abby peered at him intently through the darkness, unable to read his expression. After a considerable silence, she finally asked, "So — what is your question?"

He turned to her again, his dark eyes glittering with starlight. "Have you ever heard of the Long Count?"

Abby frowned. "I'm not sure. It sounds vaguely familiar, but …" Her voice trailed off as she noticed him looking away again, up at the stars above them, as if distracted. She leaned against a tall stone, keeping distance between them. She still could not see his face and features, and although she didn't feel threatened by him, she couldn't relax. The stranger had shown no interest in her other than talking, however, and his low voice was calming, his words belying an intelligence that comforted her.

"I don't know much about Mayan history," she finally continued. "I've heard of the Long Count, but the only reason I remember it is because it was the first calendar, wasn't it?"

"It's *a* Mayan calendar," Dominic corrected gently. "The Sumerians were the first to actually create a calendar. The Long Count isn't the first one, but the most enigmatic." He smiled briefly in the darkness. "The ancient Maya had two calendar systems, independent of one another. The first was the Tzolkin; it was a 260-day calendar fairly similar to ours. The other one was the Long Count." He weighed his words, running a hand absently through the grass before he continued. "The Tzolkin is considered the *real* calendar by modern anthropologists. It's important to the historical and scientific communities because of the concept and recognition of celestial cycles. The Tzolkin, or Calendar Round, is roughly 52 years long and was used to track World Ages."

Abby nodded, not really understanding, but Dominic continued. "The Long Count is also made up of cycles like the Calendar Round," he said, "and it breaks up into segments similar to our days and weeks and months. Only it's much, well … longer." He glanced up at her with a wry smile. Abby found herself smiling back, and she let herself relax a bit more. Still, she stayed on her side of the tall stone, and he seemed content to remain sitting in the dirt.

"The Long Count is made up of a cycle of 13 baktuns, which are broken into smaller cycles of katuns, tuns, uinals, and kins," Dominic continued, his finger tracing abstractly in the grass in front of him. "These would be like decades, years, months, weeks, and days. But they aren't a direct correlation to the Gregorian calendar that we use … a baktun is a period of 144,000 days."

"Damn," Abby commented with a small laugh. "They sure named it right."

Dominic smiled again before he continued. "The funniest thing about the Long Count, though, is that they didn't just start at one point and then cycle up through 13 baktuns. The Long Count was created sometime around 104 BCE, but they didn't start it on that date. Instead, they counted backwards … and began with a start date of August 11, 3114 BCE."

"I don't understand," Abby said.

"It didn't start on the day, or the year, or even the century that it was created," Dominic said. "It begins thousands of years before the day they created it. They backdated it. So the Long Count begins in 3114 BCE, over 3,000 years earlier than it was conceived."

"What's significant about that year?"

"No one knows," he explained. "That's the thing about the Long Count — no one knows why the Maya started it when they did, or why it spans over 5,125 Years. No one knows why they were measuring that set period of time."

He went on. "The creators of the Long Count counted up through the cycles from the beginning date, the Zero Point, up to 13.0.0.0.0. … the end of the Great Cycle." He fell silent, and Abby turned her questioning eyes to his. He shrugged, then mused, "Why choose that end date? Is it just arbitrary? Is the Zero Point, the beginning date, the important date? Or is the End Date the significant date, where they chose *that* date and counted backwards through the 13 Baktuns? Is it the end of some great cycle that they mapped out thousands of years ago? A future that they knew about long before we did? There are so many questions about what it's measuring, and why. But the biggest question of all is this:

"What happens when the Long Count ends?"

Unbidden, a chill passed over Abby, and she shuddered. Dominic smiled up at her, his dark eyes warm again, and Abby smiled apologetically. "It's getting cold," she said, knowing as she said it that her words sounded empty, but the man on the ground only nodded. "Yeah," he said as he rose to his feet, brushing dirt off his rumpled jeans. "It's getting cold and it's getting late."

Abby felt a shiver run down her spine, but she was still intrigued. "Do you think it's predicting something?" she asked.

Dominic shrugged. "That's what I'm trying to find out," he said. "The Long Count was created to represent something, or to count something. I think they started at a specific important event in their history, and counted out to when that event would repeat, like Haley's Comet. Whatever the event is, the Long Count is a measure of that."

"But 3114 BCE?" Abby questioned. "The Maya weren't around then, were they? Few cultures were."

"That's right," Dominic agreed. "They were documenting an event that happened long before their time; an event that even then was pre-historic. And whatever it is, it's going to come around again, but the old Maya aren't here anymore to tell us what it is. Whatever's going to happen, if we're going to figure it out before it gets here, we're on our own."

"What about the modern day Maya?" Abby asked. "There are still small pockets of the native Indian cultures in this area."

"Sure there are," he agreed. "But that's like asking modern day Egyptians how the pyramids were built. Or asking the British what Sillsbury Hill means. The past is passed. It's up to us in the present now to figure out the future."

"So you'll just keep studying ruins until something comes to you?" she asked.

Dominic sighed. "No," he said. "I can't. It's not getting me anywhere. What I'm planning to do," he said as he perched on the edge of an altar, "is gather a team of scientists — mathematicians, astronomers, geologists, theologians, archaeologists and anthropologists. I want to set up a lab here near Izapa, where the Long Count was created. Use all the data that's been gathered since its discovery, put it together in the location of its birth, and figure out what this damn thing means!"

"So what's stopping you?"

"I need a team that'll work for the love of the work. I've spent most of my life living off of a trust fund my parents left me. I can't pay anyone for their research, but I can rent the land, probably out where I'm camping now. I'll have a small lab built. Nothing elaborate, just one man's dream, you know?"

"Where are you staying?" Abby asked, stepping back as he rose to his full height, well over six feet tall. She couldn't help but to again feel uneasy.

"About two miles from here," he said, making no motion to move towards her. "A few colleagues and I have set up a camp ... we usually study this place during the day, but my mind keeps coming back to the astronomy. The Maya were skywatchers; this place was an observatory. The calendar revolves around the constellations, around the night sky from the celestial views that they had from this point … the answer *has* to be here, somewhere."

"Is that what you're doing?" Abby asked, glancing up again at the expanse of star filled sky. "Trying to figure out what the Long Count has to do with *this*?" She gestured at the ruins surrounding them.

Dominic ran a hand through his tangled dark hair and nodded again. "The Long Count was created here," he explained, glancing around almost lovingly at the lifeless stone. "I believe the answer is here, too." He looked up, the stars glittering brilliantly above in their set patterns across the sky. "Why did they create the Long Count? What were they counting? What was so big as to justify the end date of a cycle of more than 5,000 years? I mean, the implications of what is going to happen at the end of this cycle are incredible … I *have* to find out. I *have* to know." He glanced over at her, and she saw an almost fanatic shine in his eyes. She took an involuntary step back, then a more purposeful one.

"It looks like you sure have your work cut out for you," she said, backing away slowly. She felt for the steps behind her.

Dominic paused, then sat back. "You're running away from me," he said.

"No." She shook her head, crossing her arms tightly over her chest, fighting the urge to retreat another step.

"You think I'm crazy, don't you?"

Abby looked at him, taking in his dirty clothes, his tangled hair and beard. "I think you're a little obsessive, maybe," she conceded. "But I don't think you're crazy."

"It's okay," he said, and she could hear the humor in his voice. "You're in the middle of nowhere, alone in the ruins, and you come across me." He laughed self-deprecatingly under his breath.

"I've been camping out for four weeks now," he said. "Haven't taken a bath – except for washing in a small cenote nearby – in a month; ran out of soap three days ago. I'm surprised you couldn't smell me before you almost tripped over me."

Abby smiled. "I think you're downwind."

Dominic laughed, a surprising sound, low and deep. Abby put a hand to her chest, feeling that her heart was still racing nervously. "So what do you think you'll find at Izapa?" she asked.

Dominic pushed off the altar, coming towards her. She tensed, but saw as he approached that he wasn't even looking at her; he was watching the sky. "The ancient Maya had a rich mythical history, and much of their mythology was based on astronomy. They recognized patterns in the sky, constellations, and they observed cosmic events. The Maya created mythologies to describe these events. Izapa is an observatory. I'm trying to find what they would've seen."

"Well, what was one of their myths? Maybe I can help."

Dominic stopped beside her, looking at her strangely, and she fought the urge to step away. Still, she watched him out of the corner of her eye as he spoke.

"Well," he said, "they speak a lot of a cross, or of a cross-roads. They have a myth about a Sacred Tree, from where all life on Earth came. It wasn't just mythology; it was directional, used for navigation. I'm trying to figure out what would have resembled a celestial tree, or cross-roads, or cross."

"How about the Southern Cross?"

"Steve, one of the guys I'm traveling with now, mentioned that too. That's it right there, isn't it?" Dominic pointed.

Abby shook her head. "That's the false cross," she said. "It's larger, and most people mistake it for the Southern Cross. Look to the left of it, maybe 10 degrees higher."

"How do I know degrees?"

She smiled. "Make two fists. Hold one up at arm's length against what you're measuring. That's 10 degrees. Put your other fist on top of it for another 10 degrees. Stack your fists, one for every 10 degrees you want to measure."

Dominic did as she instructed, measuring upwards. "Okay," he said, "I see it." He studied it for a moment, the stars twinkling high above them in the southern sky. He tilted his head. "How is that used for navigation?"

"Follow the longest line of the cross," she gestured. "About four and a half times the length of it. Then, drop straight down to the horizon. That's due south."

"Cool," Dominic said, sounding impressed. "I've traveled a lot by the sun — hiking, climbing, sailing, you name it — but not much by the stars. I can tell general directions, but not distances." He looked at the sky a moment longer, then dropped his hands.

"The Maya were sun astronomers," he said. "Look at their ruins; the Plaza of the Sun in Copan, for example. The ceremonial center has alignments with the sun's movements. Equinoxes, zeniths, solstices, you name it. All their observation points exactly coincide with dates on the Tzolkien and the Haab."

"What's the Haab?"

"Another of the original Mayan calendars. Taken together with the Venus calendar, they're considered the Short Count. The Tzolkien is a 260-day calendar, the Haab is 365 days."

"It doesn't sound like they were so sure. So much for expert astronomers."

He laughed. "The first calendars weren't mistakes, they were just different. They were among the first calendars created by man, remember: they weren't necessarily measuring a full year at first. They were creating a calendar that meant something to them at the time. For example, the 260-day calendar is thought to be the gestational cycle of a human being. But the Long Count was something else entirely. It was based on the movements of the Sun."

"A five thousand year cycle of the Sun?"

Dominic shrugged. "Just repeating cycles, that's all. Just like we might make a calendar of seasons into a year or a decade, or maybe a century. It's all just a series of cycles; the moon around the Earth, the Earth around the sun. Over and over to make up a month, to make up a year, to make up a decade. Just repeating cycles."

"So they knew the orbit of the Earth around the sun was about 365 days. And that's what they based their calendar on — the sidereal, or solar, year?"

"It looks that way," he said, "Not so much from the calendar data itself, but the clues the Maya left. Come here, I want to show you something," he said, reaching out a hand. Abby stood back, reluctantly, and Dominic dropped his hand. "Well, maybe in the daylight," he said with a smile. "I'm coming back tomorrow. If you can come back out this way, I'd like to show you what some of these structures mean."

Abby deliberated. "We're doing a lot of work tomorrow … "

Dominic shrugged again. "It's my last day," he said. "I'm heading back to Chicago tomorrow night. I plan on coming back next spring to stay for awhile, but I don't imagine you'll be here then."

She smiled. "I don't believe I will," she said. "What is it you want to show me about this site? I've got a pretty good hike to get out here."

"It'd be worth it," he said. "If you like astronomy, you'll love this."

Abby studied him as closely she could under the starlight, and she could see the sincerity on his face. "Ok," she said. "I'll try."

He broke out into a genuinely happy grin, and she couldn't help but smile. "I'll see you in the morning, then," she said.

"I'll look for you," he answered. He gave her a slight wave, and she retreated, not turning her back on him until he was no longer in her sight. When he had faded into the darkness, Abby finally turned away. As she headed back to camp, following the stars as her map and wondering what she was getting herself into, she was surprised to find she was smiling.

July 4, 2007 — Abby was apprehensive as the first grey stones of Izapa came into view. Her meeting last night with Dominic seemed surreal now in the daylight. The brilliant sun glinted off the whitewashed stone, and the monuments, which had loomed eerily over her in the previous night's gloom, now rose lonely and forlorn from the jungle floor like long forgotten tombstones.

There was no sound as she entered the clearing; not a bird sang nor a creature moved. Abby felt as if she'd stepped into a mystical time warp, where she was the only living creature among the stones.

"Hey, you made it."

The deep voice startled her; she turned to see Dominic lounging against the steps of the temple. Unlike the site itself, her new companion had not changed under the daylight. He was wearing the same outfit he'd had on the night before, but in the brilliant sunlight she saw the bright colors of the hemp shirt that covered his slender frame and broad shoulders. Even seated, he was obviously tall, his long blue-jeaned legs stretched out in front of him and crossed casually at the ankle.

Slowly, Dominic pulled himself to his feet, brushing the dirt from his legs as he stood up. "Thanks for coming out," he said, strolling towards her.

Abby fought from taking an involuntary step back. She could not see his face well, as he wore a thick beard, and that made her nervous. His hair was long and curly, as black as his beard and heavy eyebrows, and she couldn't help but think he looked like a madman.

As if reading her mind, he stopped. "Sorry about my appearance," he said, reaching up to stroke his beard. "I know I'm a little disheveled right now, but don't let that scare you. Since my buddies don't care what I look like, and I didn't plan to run into anyone out here …" his soft voice trailed off.

Abby nodded, relaxing a bit. Although she had no reason to believe or to trust him, she found the sound of his voice comforting.

"Anyway," he said. "Quick history lesson: Izapa is one of the oldest surviving sites. It's Late Formative, reaching its height between 300 BCE and 250 CE, and used to be the center of Mesoamerica. Westerners started investigating it in the 1930's. They've identified over fifty carved monuments, including thrones and altars. Everything was found pretty much exactly as it was left.

"It was occupied from about 1500 BCE to 250 CE. Then for some reason, it was abandoned. By the time Mayan culture was running wild around 400 CE, Izapa was grown over by the jungle. Part of a lost, prehistoric civilization."

"Prehistoric," Abby mused.

Dominic nodded, approaching her. "Izapa was before the beginning of western recorded history. No one knows much about the people who were here then, or what happened to them. The modern day Maya – the Quiche Maya – live in small towns and villages around here, but no one knows why they left these ancient cities and moved on."

Abby looked around the site. "There are a lot of — what do you call them? Stelae?"

"Yes. That's what Izapa is most famous for," Dominic explained. "Even though many of them are gone now, locked away in museums, there are still quite a few standing. Stela 4 shows man's transformation into a bird — it's a common Mayan mythology. Stela 25 is a page right out of the Mayan creation story: it shows the Hero Twins trying to usher in the new world age; they have to knock Seven Macaw, the bird deity who ruled the previous age, out of the tree. The bird is represented in the night sky by the Big Dipper. So the stela, and their astronomy, are based on a Mayan myth."

"Everything seems to be," she commented.

Dominic smiled. "Come on," he said. "There's something I want to show you."

Abby followed as he led her across the open plaza. As they went, he explained the various stelae and their significance. "Some of these haven't been interpreted yet," he said. "As much work as has been at Izapa, there's still as much that remains a mystery."

"Is this a popular site? I've only heard of it because of the astronomy. I haven't seen it advertised in any tourism ads."

Dominic shrugged. "It's not one of the most popular, maybe because it's so far out. It can be reached by highway, though, and it gets its share of visitors. But it's not like Chichen Itza or Tikal or any of the big ones; I've always found it relatively quiet."

They strolled through the site, and Abby paused at the base of the pyramid. "What are these?" she asked. "These three columns with the round balls balanced on them?"

"They represent another Mayan myth," he explained. "They're called the Hearthstones. They say the world before this one ended in fire, marked by three hearthstones that shot out of a fireplace and made a place in the sky," Dominic said.

"And that means …?" Abby asked.

"Not sure," Dominic admitted. "I suppose it could be meteors, asteroids, something like that. Mayan fireplaces are always made with three hearthstones in the shape of a triangle." He quickly drew a triangle in the air. "Like that," he said.

"Like Orion," Abby said.

Dominic was unsurprised. "That's what they say," he said. "Another sign that Mayan mythology mirrors astronomy."

Abby nodded, looking over the Hearthstones. "Amazing," she said, looking around. "Absolutely amazing."

Dominic watched her climb the bleached stones of the pyramid. Her small rear was clad in a pair of faded jeans shorts, and he admired it as she climbed. He had been unable to see her face clearly in the darkness the night before, but this afternoon he had been transfixed by her tawny eyes under the dark, arched brows. She appeared at least in part Native American; her ancestry still showed in her tan skin and dark, fluid hair, rich as coffee and silky as water. It bounced on her shoulders as she moved, dark and sleek as sealskin, with rich deep highlights shining like embers within. She glanced back at him now, catching his eyes.

"This whole site is aligned with the volcano Tajumulco," Dominic said, pointing in its direction. "That's the tallest mountain in Central America. All of Izapa is aligned with the sun and the stars on certain dates. The temples, the pyramids, even the ballcourts are all aligned with the solstices. The ballcourt was for gaming, but it was also very symbolic. It symbolized victory and defeat, life and death."

Abby paused on the steps and looked out across the ballcourt behind it. "Which solstice is the ballcourt aligned with?" she asked, noting that it ran perpendicular to the general direction of the Izapan site.

Dominic held up a hand to her and she climbed back down. He took her hand and helped her off the monument, releasing her as she set foot once again on solid ground. They strolled around to the rear of the pyramid, towards the ball court.

"Stand at this end," he advised as they came upon the court. They situated themselves at the western end, scanning down the long length of the court.

"We're now facing the southeastern horizon – the December solstice horizon. He jogged over to a worn stone throne. "This is Throne 2."

Abby followed him as he pointed out the inscription. "This is a marker stone. The glyph on it is of a ring and ball, the symbol of the ball game. The serpent with an open mouth is a significant symbol in the Mayan world. It's too bad the colors are gone; the Maya used a lot of symbolism for representation, including the colors used in their paintings. North was white, East, red; South, yellow, and West, black. Green was the color of the Earth's center, where the World Tree was. The Earth revolved around it."

20

He walked up to a pillar with a sitting figure on it, which also faced the southeastern horizon. "The whole court is aligned to face the winter solstice," he explained. "There has to be some meaning to it — the winter solstice is the end date of the Long Count,"

"So, what's aligned on the end date?"

"The whole Earth."

Dominic waved her along as he headed towards another stela, explaining as he went. "This is one of the Hero Twins," he said. "He's standing over the body of Seven Macaw, ruler of the previous age and 'false god.' Legend has it that they had to destroy him before their father could be reborn and usher in the new age."

"How does that fit into the alignment?" Abby asked.

"I'm not sure," Dominic admitted. "Like I said before, Seven Macaw is said to represent the Big Dipper, but I don't know of any astronomical connection that would explain the myth."

Abby's interest was piqued. "I'd have to run the numbers and check the astronomical alignments, comets and stellar events," she said. "Do you know what date this was carved?"

"We don't have exact dates," he said. "The whole site is estimated at first or second century CE, but the dating on most stelae isn't very specific. If you look over here," he said, setting off towards another one, "This one depicts the solar god sitting in a canoe, arms outstretched. The canoe symbolizes the Milky Way. The way he's stretching out his arms is a time marker; it indicates a period-ending event."

"What about that end of the court?" Abby asked, nodding towards the far end, where the December solstice would rise.

Dominic walked that way and Abby followed. At the end of the court was a heavily eroded sculpture; only the bottom was clear enough to determine the original glyph. "It's the sky-lifter," Dominic said. "But it's impossible to know what else was depicted here. I believe it was of extreme importance, though – with the whole ball game facing this direction, they were looking at something."

"Maybe the sky lifter uplifts the December solstice sun?"

"Could be," Dominic said. "I know what the symbolism of the different stelae and monuments are, but I don't know the astronomy that might connect them or give them meaning. To me, they're mythology with no base in the real world; to the more educated, they're detailing actual astronomical events or passages. I'm hoping to find out how it all relates."

Abby nodded. "I'd love to know, too," she said. "Most of my studies have been on the astronomical past of the universe. Since our planet's creation, events have affected the Earth, from meteor showers to exploding supernovas; everything that occurs around us has helped to shape the evolution of this planet. But I don't know of anything recent, anything small, that the Maya could have been recording, or counting down to. It'd be fascinating to try to find out."

Dominic smiled. "I think so, too. That's why I want to put a team together. I want to find out what all this means."

She paused, then said: "You said the Maya were sun astronomers."

"Yes. Are there any solar changes that might influence the Long Count?"

"It's hard to say," Abby admitted. "Scientists have only been seriously studying the sun for about one hundred years, and we haven't had the equipment to get an accurate look at it until the last half of that."

"But could there be something? Anything?"

"There are always sunspots," she said. "Storms on the sun in pretty random patterns and duration." She knelt to study the stone monument, running her fingers along its rough surface. Most of it had been worn away, lost to almost twenty centuries of wind and rain.

"Nothing that goes in cycles?" he asked, somewhat disappointed.

"Again, that's hard to say," she explained. "We're talking about the sun; something that's at least four and a half billion years old. We've been looking at it for about a century. Any cycles that small wouldn't much matter to your Long Count unless the cycles were building up to something. Anything longer than that and we wouldn't have the observations to notice it yet."

"It is possible, then, that they could have been recording some solar event."

"It's possible," Abby answered. "But not likely. There is some evidence that sunspot activity has been greater more recently than in all our recorded history of it. The sun's magnetic field appears to have grown stronger, too — by over two hundred percent. But again, what can that mean? If the sun was going to shoot out a solar flare or a burst of radiation that might endanger the Earth, if it has done so in the past, there'd be some record of it. There'd be terrestrial signs of it, especially if it was damage done only 5,125 years ago. Anything in that time period would have left a definite scar on the Earth. I don't think your Long Count is predicting any repetitive catastrophic solar event – five thousand years is just too recent for that."

"Not if you believe in the Biblical record," he said. "If you follow a literal interpretation, the Earth was covered in a deluge only a few thousand years ago, destroying all life on the planet."

"And the Earth was created in six days," she countered. "Sorry, Dominic, but it's just not possible. If there was a flood 5,000 years ago that the Maya counted from, it couldn't have destroyed all life on Earth.

There are over a million known species of life on this planet — they couldn't have repopulated to their present numbers in so few millennia. And you'll never convince me that Noah or anyone else got millions of animals, fish, birds, insects, and bacteria on a 450-foot boat."

Dominic smiled. "Even in jest, a scientist," he observed. "I like that. I'd like to have you work with me."

Abby glanced up at him. "Really?" she asked.

"I'm gathering a team of experts," he said, "mostly friends of mine; a few people I don't know. Friends of friends, colleagues of people I've worked with. I'd like at least one astronomer, a physicist, a couple historians and archeologists, anthropologists, geologists, a linguist — just a solid group of people dedicated to studying the Long Count." He paused. "You are an astronomer, aren't you?"

Abby nodded silently. She was actually still a post-graduate student — Simon hadn't wanted her to find a job until she finished her PhD — but she'd been studying astronomy since she was a child, and held a dual bachelor's degree in astronomy and physics, a master's in cosmology, and was less than a year away from her doctorate in celestial mechanics.

"I can't pay," Dominic continued. "I can provide free room and board and whatever research equipment we'd need, but that'll just about wipe me out. I have enough money to take care of that, but not to pay anyone for their time and effort. I need people who'd work for passion, not money."

"How many do you already have signed on?" she asked.

He shrugged. "Me. An archeologist buddy of mine; he also teaches theology. Another friend who's an archaeologist and does anthropology research. She and I are both fascinated by Mayan culture."

Dominic sighed, staring out at the ruins. "The three of us have been across Central America a dozen times to different sites. We have the drive to figure it out, but not the background to put it all together. What we really need is a cumulative effort, and people with the academic background and knowledge base to help us fill in the blanks, tie things together. There have been a lot of theories thrown out there, but none that get all the different disciplines to agree. Geology, physics, astronomy, archaeology — all these different fields must concur."

Abby was quiet, and after a moment, Dominic knelt beside her. "You okay?" he asked apologetically. "I'm sorry if I'm boring you — every time I talk about this I start babbling. Don't listen to me, let's have a look at the site. I can show you some great structures off to the west there; you won't believe the stonework."

Abby smiled and shook her head. "It's not that," she said. "Actually, you've gotten me interested. But it's something I need to think about."

Dominic looked surprised. "Would you really be interested in working with us?" he asked. "It's been hard finding someone knowledgeable who'll work for free who isn't ... well, 'out there.'"

Abby rose to her feet. "Like I said, I need to think about some things. If it was just me, I think I'd say yes. Or at least I'd seriously consider it. But I can't just pack up and come to Mexico, either. I'd have to talk it over with my fiancé."

Dominic paused briefly, almost imperceptibly. "I can see where that'd be a problem," he said. "I can't tell you how long this project will take. I'd like to aim for less than two years, but there are no guarantees. And I'd like to keep the same team throughout — I've worked with research teams on projects before where there was so much turnover that we never got far beyond bringing the new people up to speed. So when I build my team, I'd like to make sure we're all serious, and we're in it for the long haul."

Abby smiled. "Considering we just met, you have a lot of faith in me."

"I have a lot of faith in *me*," he said. "I believe I can make the connections; I just don't know the astronomy, and I don't have time to learn it. I need a walking encyclopedia so when I need a number, or a distance, or a location, you'll be there. I need you there for what you know, Abby. I can reference the constellations, but not what they mean. I don't know what the Maya could have seen with the naked eye, or what they might have been measuring. You do."

Abby thought for a moment. "You said you need a mathematician. My fiancé, Simon, is a PhD, a professor of advanced mathematics in Boston. He's excellent at what he does; his work has been published in several scientific journals."

"Would I know anything he's published?"

"If you read mathematical journals, maybe. They'd be under Simon Thomas Nieson."

"Isn't using your full name a designation usually reserved for assassins? Lee Harvey Oswald. Mark David Chapman. John Wilkes Booth."

Abby smiled uncomfortably. "I never thought of it that way. Simon just thinks it sounds more professional, I think."

Dominic nodded, considering. "Do you think he'd be interested in this project?"

"I honestly can't say. It sounds like something he'd find intriguing, but he probably can't just take two years off work. I'd like to run it by him, though."

"I'll look up his work," Dominic said. "I'd like to see what he can do. I could do much of the mathematical work on my own; I just want to bring others in to make it easier on me. People who'll pick up the bulk of the work in their individual field while I'm working on other angles; people who can fill in the blanks for me, who I can bounce things off of."

"I'd love to be there," Abby said. "I'll definitely think about it."

"Perfect," he smiled. "Now — let me show you the plaza."

12.19.14.10.6

August 16, 2007 — Abby had been back in Boston for several weeks before she broached the subject with Simon. Their initial meeting had been tentative; since then, they'd been through arguments and tears, accusations and shouting matches, and it had only been within the last few days that things had settled into some semblance of normalcy again. She had done a lot of thinking in the nearly three months she had been away from him, and had decided to give him a second chance. The pain had faded with time and hard work, and by the time she returned to Boston, Abby was weary of the whole situation. She only wanted things to be normal again. So with Simon's promise to never repeat his indiscretion, and an increased openness of communication between them, Abby was finally ready to move on, if not to forgive.

Now she found her way to his office, where he was preparing his notes for classes to start the following week.

"Hi sweetheart," Simon said with a smile when she came in. While he was a dozen years her senior, his blond hair, young face and sparkling blue eyes gave him a youthful demeanor, both movie-star handsome and impishly attractive at the same time. He looked as he always had, in fact; and for a moment, Abby was troubled. Upon her return, Simon had been ready to pick right up where they'd left off, as if his infidelity had never happened. She still didn't know how far she could trust him, or how far he was willing to go to make it up to her. She supposed the conversation about Dominic's project might tell her all she needed to know.

She gave him a quick kiss, then pulled up the chair next to his desk. After sitting down, she watched him for a moment.

"To what do I owe the pleasure?" he asked.

"Well," she said slowly, "There's something I wanted to talk to you about. Something I want to do after I finish my PhD."

Simon set down his pen, giving her his full attention.

"When I was in Mexico, I met a researcher. He was studying Mayan astronomy and the end of a Mayan calendar, the Long Count. He's putting together a research team in the spring, and I'd like to join them. Actually, I'd like for both of us to join them."

Simon stared at her for a long moment, and Abby inwardly cringed, afraid he was going to yell. Instead, he spoke slowly, as if to a child.

"And I'm supposed to do what? Give up my teaching position?"

"Can't you take a year sabbatical?"

"For what?" he asked. "To watch you study Mayan astronomy with some guy? Who the hell is this guy, anyway?" he asked, suddenly suspicious.

She shook her head. "He's just some random guy; I ran into him in the ruins near where we were working." She thought it best to leave out the late night circumstances of their meeting. "We got to talking, and I found his research subject fascinating. Have you ever heard of the Long Count, Simon?"

He shook his head impatiently.

"It's a Mayan calendar, but it's a puzzle. I've read more about it since I've been back here, and it's fascinating. Archaeologists, mathematicians, astronomers, all kinds of researchers have been working at it for decades, but no one really understands it. It's supposed to measure time cycles, and some believe it even predicts the end of the world."

Simon folded his hands, suddenly interested. "Who has been working on it? Who's the competition?"

"I don't know specifics," she admitted. "It's kind of like the Dead Sea Scrolls; a select group of people worked to decipher them, but the whole world wanted to know what they said."

"It sounds like pseudo-scientific bullshit to me. I don't have time for that."

Abby tried to maintain her calm. "Well, I do."

He stared at her. "And I'm supposed to just do whatever you want with no thought to my own career? Have you thought about what this would do to me? What I'd be giving up?"

"Simon, I've always thought about your career. That's why I'm here studying for my PhD instead of working at the observatory in Arecibo like I wanted to after I got my Masters. I turned down several great jobs for you."

"And I bought you an engagement ring, even though you knew I wasn't ready to get married."

Abby's mouth fell open, but before she could speak, Simon held up a hand. "An engagement ring that you sold like it was a piece of worthless junk, and not my heartfelt promise — my very expensive heartfelt promise — to commit to you, forever. I haven't mentioned it because I want us to put that whole ugly argument behind us, Abby. But I sure as hell haven't gotten over it yet."

Abby was speechless, but Simon didn't give her a chance to find her words.

"In the spirit of wanting to put the past behind us, I'm willing to hear you out. I'd certainly like to know what you and this guy were up to down in Mexico." Abby remained silent while Simon thought for a moment.

"You said it predicts the end of the world," he finally said. "Does this buddy of yours have any idea when that's going to be?"

"Apparently this Count spans a period of just over 5,000 years before it ends."

"That's about the length of recorded civilization up until now," Simon commented. Abby saw his interest was growing and didn't answer. "Does this Count say anything about signs leading up to the end? Any precursors to the apocalypse?"

"None," she said carefully. "In fact, the Long Count is exactly that: A count. It's just numbers. That's why people are having such a hard time putting any sort of reference to it; they're just trying to break the numerical code."

Simon thought about it again, leaning back in his chair. "Biblical prophecy puts us close to Armageddon," he said. "If you read the signs — the atomic bomb; the creation of Israel; the millennium; the continuing and expanding wars in the Middle East ... "

"The plague of locusts," she joked, but Simon didn't smile.

"A lot of evangelical groups have been predicting the end times are coming for the last ten years or so," he said.

"Simon, people have been predicting the end of the world for a thousand years. I don't think we're any closer to it now than we have been at any point in history."

"Then why are you interested in hooking up with this guy in Mexico?"

Abby paused, thrown off guard again. "Well ... because this is fascinating. I don't have a job lined up for after graduation yet — I'm sure you'll want to stay around here, and I haven't found anything locally — and after this year and how hard I've worked ... well, I'd kind of like to take a little break. Dominic says the Long Count is based in astronomy. It'd be great research work, and if we actually broke the code — well, damn, wouldn't that look great on my resume?"

"And mine," Simon mused. He caught her eye and smiled. "Why don't we get a hold of this Count ourselves and work on it? Why do we need this guy?"

"Dominic Ciriello is an expert on Mayan culture — an anthropologist and, I recently discovered, an author. He's published several books on the ancient Maya — books we could read and try to fit into the Count, I guess, but we'd never have the knowledge base Dominic does. He says the Long Count is such a deeply entwined part of Mayan history and mythology that he thinks the answer lies there; whatever event they were predicting, he'll find the answer based in their myths, history, and legends. Maybe in some recurring Mayan event, or a huge catastrophe based on their creation myths."

"Our concept of the end of the world comes from our creation myths," Simon commented. "From Genesis to Revelation, the beginning and the end, all rolled up in one. Is that what the Long Count is?"

"I think it's something like that," Abby said. "It's not a religious text or philosophy book; it's an actual count with a definite beginning, and it counts down, cycling through thousands of years, to a definite and distinctive end."

"I have to admit, it's interesting," Simon said. "I can see why you'd be willing to sacrifice a year to work on it. But I can't do it. Just because I have tenure doesn't mean I can just drop out of sight anytime I want. This is no time for a sabbatical."

"I know," Abby said quietly.

He looked at her carefully. "You're planning on going anyway, aren't you?"

Abby took a deep breath, and then nodded.

He sighed. "I don't think that'd be good for us, Abby. I mean, if you go away for a year, how much longer do we have to put off the wedding?"

She stopped, startled. It had always been Simon who had avoided setting a date. She wondered if he would do so now, just to keep her from leaving.

"Simon …"

He put up a hand. "Let's take some time and think about it," he said. "We could do one of two things next spring: We could get married, or you could run off to Mexico."

"Simon — I want to do this. I'm really, really interested in it. I don't want to go alone, but I will if I have to. I'd rather you come along. Dominic needs a mathematician, and I wouldn't want to work with anyone but you. And if we find the answer to this, Simon — well, I can't even begin to think about the publicity that would go with it."

He didn't answer, just studied her earnest face for a moment. Finally, he asked, "Will he pay us?"

Abby smiled, visibly relieved. "Doubtful," she said carefully. "The man didn't look like he had enough money to get himself back to Chicago. He said he'd finance the research facilities, though."

"No shit," he said, flipping open the notebook on his desk, picking up his pen again. "Bad enough this guy wants us getting caught up in his wild goose chase; he wouldn't have the nerve to ask us to pay for it, too." He paused, then looked up at her sharply. "Unless this is some kind of scam."

Abby shook her head quickly. "It's not," she insisted. "This guy is obsessed. And the more I looked into it, the more excited about it I became. I can see why he's so crazy about it. There are a lot of people working on this. And if someone figures out what it all means, and it actually predicts some great catastrophe — my god. This could be one of the most important discoveries in the history of the world."

He sat back, chewing his pen thoughtfully. He spit out a chip of plastic and looked up at her, a sly smile growing around his lips. "Which would make me the most brilliant scientist in the world."

"I guess so. You'd be famous, anyway."

Simon nodded. "Let me think about it. I want to know more about this guy and what he's up to before I do anything."

"Ok," Abby said. "I'm heading home, then. I'll see you tonight." She leaned over and gave him a quick kiss on the cheek before she left. She knew she'd have to leave the decision up to him – no amount of talking on her part had ever done a thing to convince him.

Simon didn't mention it again for several days. When he did, he brought it up nonchalantly over dinner.

"I looked up the Long Count and didn't find a whole hell of a lot," he said. "There have been some books written, but the little online research I could find seems to be mostly wacko theories about UFOs, time travel, or some other sort of craziness. The research is ridiculous. The Long Count is for real, though."

Abby knew enough to not comment; Simon had already made his decision. She just had to wait for it.

"I wasn't overly impressed by what I found," he continued. "There's not as much interest or published research as you've insinuated." He set down his fork and locked eyes with her across the table. "What I *did* find interesting, though, was your new friend. Seems he's a fairly celebrated researcher in his field. He's written numerous books on Aztec, Incan, and Mayan history. I also found a few articles by him in archaeological journals, and his name is pretty well-respected. He does seem to know his shit. It makes me think that he may have stumbled onto something that a lot of people don't know about yet."

"So …," Abby finally said. "What do you think?"

"So," he responded, picking up his fork again. "Count me in."

12.19.15.6.4

May 20, 2008 — Abby laughed when she saw Dominic. He stood by the large windows of the small airport, a big bear of a man with his back to them, hands buried deep in the pockets of his blue jeans. Abby never would have recognized him except for the bright hemp shirt he wore. His long tangled hair had been cropped to short dark curls; only the tousled front of it fell across his forehead. The thick beard was gone now, and she was startled by his profile; sensitive, if not quite handsome.

The airport wasn't crowded, and her laughter carried. Dominic turned towards the sound of her voice, and when he saw her, he broke into a grin. Crossing the room in a few long strides, he opened his arms wide.

"Abby! How great to see you again." He embraced her warmly, then released her and turned his attention to Simon.

"And you must be the professor," he said, extending a hand. Simon shook it stiffly, studying the larger man carefully. Dominic was at least six inches taller and much broader across the chest and shoulders.

"I'm Dr. Nieson," Simon said. "Good to finally meet you, Dominic."

"Great," Dominic said, clapping his hands together. "Let's get going then."

After collecting their bags, they finally made it out to the parking lot, where Dominic threw all their bags into the back of a late model pickup truck. They all loaded into the cab, the threesome squashed uncomfortably together, with Abby in the middle.

"So we're staying outside Izapa," Abby said.

"That's right," Dominic responded. "The closest we were allowed to set up is about six miles away. It's kind of a haul by car, since there's no direct road from the worksite to the ruins, but it's not a bad walk. We're close to the jungle, and you have to walk about two miles before you get out from under the tree canopy, but from there is nothing but clear night sky."

"That's fantastic," Abby said.

"I'm not sure I like the sound of this 'camp'," Simon interrupted. "We're six miles from Izapa — so what is that, a hundred miles from nowhere?"

Dominic shrugged. "It's pretty isolated, but that's one of the reasons I chose it. I didn't want to be tripping over other people, or dealing with a lot of distractions. I prefer if no one even knew we were out there. And they probably won't; most researchers are working on the big cities; Chichen Itza, Tikal, Palenque. We can visit there, but I still think the real work to be done is Izapa. I found a good site, though. There used to be an old village there, so there's still a well."

"Holy Christ," Simon muttered. "Thank god I'll be at the university most of the time."

Dominic glanced over at him, but Simon had turned to look out the window. Dominic caught Abby's eye, and she smiled apologetically.

"Simon couldn't take any time off work, so he set up a visiting professorship with the University of Chiapas. He'll just be teaching a couple classes three days a week, so he can come back in between, and on weekends."

"That's cool," Dominic said. "It's going to be mighty crowded out at the house, anyway."

Simon turned to him warily. "Who else did you invite?" he asked.

"Just three more of us," Dominic answered, oblivious to Simon's tone. "Tina is another cultural anthropologist — I've known her for a long time; we met in Mayan studies in school about a million years ago. She's not as fascinated with the Long Count as I am, but she's a good friend and offered to help me out. She'll be good to have on the team.

"Steve is an archeologist; he's good at reading the stelae and making sense of the layout of the cities. He's fluent in Spanish and also knows some of the Indian languages of that area. He'll be good to have along; he can help us interview some of the modern-day Maya, or at least help us if we get into some kind of trouble out there.

"The last guy I don't know too well," he admitted. "He's a geologist." He turned to Abby with a smile. "So there'll be six of us out there in the jungle. Six humans, and a hell of a lot of snakes and bugs."

She looked at him nervously. "Is it dangerous?" she asked.

Dominic smiled. "Not to worry," he said. "You're in good hands."

"How can you know it's not dangerous?" Simon asked. "I'm entrusting my fiancée to you and a bunch of strangers, stranded out in the middle of nowhere, surrounded by indigenous peoples that don't speak the language of their own god-forsaken country. And didn't the Mayans believe in human sacrifice?"

Dominic laughed. "That's the last thing you need to worry about. These people are farmers. I've lived among them. They're harmless as butterflies, and just as colorful. Trust me, they'll stay to themselves as long as we do. We'll be fine. Besides, the ancient Maya believed in resurrection and rebirth through sacrifice — it wasn't done out of malice."

Simon muttered something under his breath and turned to look out the window again. Abby glanced over at him uneasily. He prided himself on taking care of her, and now, much of the time, he would be leaving her alone with virtual strangers.

She glanced over at Dominic's unexpectedly attractive profile, but he was no help; he whistled merrily as he drove them further and further into the ancient lands of Mayan country.

They followed a long dirt path for miles after they pulled off the main road. Abby had taken a similar route to the tiny village she'd worked in most of the summer, so she didn't start to worry until Dominic pulled off the dirt road and drove across a jarring, uneven field.

"Uh, I think you ran out of road there, buddy," Simon said uncomfortably.

Dominic laughed. "Short-cut," he said. "Our base is at the bottom of a mountain, near the edge of the jungle. There was nothing there before I showed up, and there's not much there now but for our house and lab. The ground is hard and dry enough to drive over, so there wasn't much point in building a road."

"What about when it rains? Are we going to get bogged down out here?" Simon asked.

Dominic shrugged. "A dirt road wouldn't make a lot of difference. And I can't lay down twenty miles of gravel or blacktop. We'll be fine."

Neither of his passengers responded, and they drove on in silence, bouncing and jostling over the uneven terrain, following faint tire tracks left over from hauling wood, stone and equipment to the site. The surrounding area was mountainous, and in the distance Abby could see a high mountain rising from the trees. As they closed in on it, she thought it looked familiar.

"Don't worry, the volcano is dormant," Dominic said, catching her look. "It's called Tacana. Izapa is in ruins at its foot, on the other side of the mountain from us, through the jungle."

"This is it?" Simon asked doubtfully. A tile roof rose up around the bend where the rutted path turned.

As they came over a final hill, they could see buildings in the distance. The clay roof was attached to a small two story stone structure, with a long, low wooden building stretched out below it. A small shed on the other side of the two story building housed a generator, Dominic informed them.

They pulled up out front, unfolding themselves from the truck's cab and stretching stiffly in the makeshift driveway.

"What the hell is that? A flagpole?" Simon asked, looking up.

"Lightning rod," Dominic answered. "We get a lot of storms in this area. Last thing I want is this place burning down in a lightning strike."

"No shit," Simon said. "I'd prefer not to be stranded out here in the middle of nowhere with no shelter." He looked up at the house, which was small but well built. "What's with the two story building? All the villages around here only have one story structures. What do the locals know that you don't?"

"The locals know the same thing I do: That you can only build on flat ground. The landscape here is so hilly and rolling that there was no way to build a three bedroom addition onto the kitchen and bathroom area; the flat space was too small. It was better to stagger the second floor and put the bedrooms up top."

"But you wasted no space on the lab."

"What do you think we're here for, Simon? Vacation?" Dominic's words were sharp, but his tone remained carefully modulated. "We're here for the lab. Hell, we should be living, eating and sleeping in the lab. The house is a luxury."

Simon didn't answer, and Dominic shrugged. "Besides, the locals live in huts made of mud, stone and grass; there isn't much made out of wood. They don't have the technology or the capability to build a second floor."

"It's perfect," Abby said, looking up at the house. "Beats a tent any day. Really, the conditions are the same as those that Galileo worked under. I only hope that we can do as well."

"Well, it's not much," Dominic shrugged. "But for being in the Mexican highlands, bordering a Guatemalan jungle, miles away from any modern city, I think we did pretty well."

"Is there running water?" Simon asked.

"There's a well with a pump out back that brings water up to the house, and we've dug out a septic tank. There's a shower out back."

"You are absolutely kidding me," Simon said in a flat voice.

"Afraid not," Dominic answered. "We're lucky to even have a well. When there was a village here, they used to drink out of the cenote – a 'sacred well,' or natural sinkhole. They did laundry in it, used it as a latrine, cooked with the same water. The well was dug shortly before most of the people left; it isn't much, but the water's clean and clear and fresh any time we need it."

"Why'd they leave?" Simon asked.

"The land is no good for agriculture or animal farming. The real question is why anyone ever settled here in the first place."

Simon turned away with a scowl, looking out over the landscape.

"We'll be banging our laundry clean on rocks, I take it?" Abby asked, trying to muster some humor.

"That'd be about right," Dominic smiled in return. "There's actually a tub and a washboard on the back porch, if you want to give that a try."

"Holy shit," Simon said. "Abby, you're going to be a real pioneer woman. I hope you can figure out how to keep my shirts crisp and clean with that thing."

"Screw that," she said. "I'll do my own laundry, you boys are on your own."

Dominic laughed, but Simon was silent. Abby glanced at him out of the corner of her eye and saw his mouth was a tight drawn line.

"I'm just kidding, sweetheart," she said quickly. "You know I'll take care of you."

"Damn straight you will," he muttered, setting off for the house.

Dominic glanced to Abby questioningly, but she didn't look his way. She tagged along on Simon's heels while their host followed along slowly behind her. Something had changed, but he wasn't quite sure what it was. He only knew that he felt uneasy.

"Well, what do you think?" Dominic asked. They'd moved quickly through the small house, checking out the three bedrooms upstairs. Dominic had explained their sleeping arrangements: "Simon, you and Abby get the room with the full bed; the other two rooms each have a pair of twin beds. Tina and I will share a room, Dante and Steve will share a room. There's one bathroom on the first floor by the kitchen, with a shower stall around back. I wish I could do better, but I think we'll be pretty comfortable here."

They'd descended the steps to kitchen and went out the house's only door, coming out to cross through a small courtyard to the wooden building. The sky between the two structures was growing darker; Abby had forgotten how early – and how suddenly – night fell so close to the equator.

Through a screen door, they entered the lab, which was large but sparsely decorated. The far wall was covered with wooden shelves crowded with books and notebooks, and a lab table sat in the middle of the room, stretching most of the length of the room. In front of it was a long, low bench.

In the corner closest to them, to the right of the doorway, was a desk with a notebook computer; a printer rested on a table beside it. Across the room, the outside wall was mostly windows, all partially open, their expanse broken up only by a flimsy screen door. Gauzy white curtains blew lightly in the early evening breeze.

"It's not much," Dominic said with a self-conscious smile, glancing around the makeshift lab, "but it's home."

"Jesus, it's a dump."

Simon had paused in the doorway, hands on his hips, surveying the room.

"Honey, there's nothing wrong with it," Abby said. She glanced over at Dominic, who turned away. Too late, however; Abby had already caught his expression.

"Shit," Simon said, giving the room a quick once-over. The disgust in his voice was apparent. "You're talking about predicting the end of the world. We're supposed to be working on what could be the biggest event in the history of everything," he said. "And this is what we have to work with? You called us all here, and you aren't even going to give us the means to work it out?"

Dominic sighed, running a hand through his short cropped curls. He crossed to a window, leaning against the sill, palms flat on the thin wood. Abby could see that his eyes were closed.

After a moment, he said quietly, "This is my life's work. I've spent every cent I've ever earned, been given or saved to come here and work on this, to assemble the team I have. I'm sorry if it's not up to your usual standards, but it's the best I could do with the resources I had."

There was silence for a moment, then Simon shrugged. "It'll work for you guys, but I don't have to be here," he said. "I'm working with numbers; I'll be damned if I sit in this cramped room on that hard-ass bench. I'll be back up at the house in my cozy little room or even better, at the university."

Abby looked up at him pleadingly. "Simon, we need you with us."

"Don't worry, I have no intention of leaving you alone here. I'll be around. I'm not trusting my numbers to either of you. It might be your life's work and all, big guy, but it's my ticket to immortality. I'll be on top of this shit every step of the way."

He looked over at the computer in the corner. "I assume there's no internet service, right? So I'll have to do any computer research at the university, too."

"We have a Sat-phone and Wi-Fi," Dominic replied. "There's been a lot of interest in Izapa lately; another group of researchers paid to have a station set up so they could run their cell phones and laptops. We're just close enough to get in on it. It's a strong one – they were relaying stations all the way to Mexico City."

Abby turned her attention back to her fiancé. "I'm going to look around here, and get set up. I want to head out and see what kind of sky there is out here. I'll be up in a little while."

"Take your time," he said, shrugging. "I'm going up to unpack and take a hot shower. I assume there's hot running water?" he directed this last at Dominic. Without a word, the dark haired man nodded.

"Is it all right with you if I stay?" Abby turned to Dominic. "I'd like to explore a little and check out the area."

He shrugged. "I'll be out here late. I need to get some things organized. You can stay out here with me or go explore. This place is as much yours now as it is mine; you both have the freedom to move around as you will."

Simon laughed. "How gracious of you." He directed his attention back to Abby. "Well, your choice, babe. You can come upstairs to a shower and a clean bed with me, or you can sit out here with our gracious benefactor."

A cross look passed over Abby's face, but she covered it quickly. "As tempting as it is, I want to get started here," she said.

"Suit yourself," he said, and turned and left the building.

Abby let out the breath she didn't know she'd been holding and lowered herself to the bench. She closed her eyes for a second, and when she opened them again, Dominic was standing beside her.

"What exactly do you see in him?" he asked.

Abby looked up sharply, but bit back her sharp retort when she saw the concern in his eyes. She shrugged.

"He's not really this bad," she apologized. "He only acts this way when he's stressed."

"So he reacts to stress by taking it out on everyone else?"

Abby stood up, brushing past him to head for the bookshelves across the room. "Look, Dominic, I don't want to talk about Simon, okay? He is who he is. Life goes a lot easier if you just let him be and go about your business."

"Let him be what? An asshole?"

Abby turned to him, and this time her anger showed in her eyes. Before she could speak, though, Dominic raised his hands in front of him, palm out.

"Hey," he said. "I'm sorry. It's your business."

"You're right, it is," she snapped, turning back to the shelves again.

"It just makes me sad — you say things are easier when you let him act out, but you don't say they're better. You only get one life, as far as we know it. Why waste it for somebody else?"

"Because I love him?" she responded. "If I can let him be happy, then I'm happy."

"Suit yourself," he shrugged. "I'm just concerned about the rest of us working with him. You've voluntarily attached yourself to him, so you'll willingly put up with him. But there are other people here besides us, and I guarantee you they aren't going to take that kind of attitude from him. We'll all be working together very closely for what might end up being a very long time, so he'd better settle in quick."

Abby looked stricken, and Dominic suddenly smiled. "Hey," he said. "It's been a long flight from Boston, and a long drive. Why don't you head on up to the house and rest? The others will be back soon, and I'll introduce you to them when you come down for dinner."

"Where is everyone?" she asked.

Dominic shrugged. "Probably drove into town for supplies. Most of us have been here for a few days already, and there's been some arguing about the best foods to keep out here. We have a small refrigerator, but since it runs off the generator we don't want to overload it. We've found we can keep beverages cool in the cenote down the hill there — it's fed by a natural spring, and the water stays about fifty degrees year round. Anyway, they probably made a run to the store, or to a local vegetable stand or something. Either way, with no roads here in the highlands, it'll take them a couple hours round trip, so I can't guess when they'll be back."

"Okay," Abby said, "maybe I will head up to the house and freshen up. Although I'd love to take a walk around and check this place out."

Dominic smiled, walking her to the door. "No hurry," he said. "You might as well wait until it cools down. Besides, you'll have plenty of time for exploring — none of us are going anywhere any time soon."

Abby was upstairs lying down beside a sleeping Simon when she heard a vehicle pull up. She went to the bedroom window to see a silver SUV come to a stop, and then three people spill out. There were two men, one dark and one light, and a red-haired woman. All three were laughing and talking, and as they unloaded paper bags of groceries from the back, Dominic joined them.

Abby glanced back at the bed were Simon was still sleeping, then quietly slipped out the door. Their room was at the top of the stairs; the other two bedrooms were across from each other toward the back. She went down the stairs into the kitchen, almost running into the others as they came in.

"Abby Bowman," Dominic said, setting a bag down on the table, "I'd like you to meet the rest of our crew. This is Dante Perkins," he said, nodding at the man closest to him. Dante was not a purebred of any race, but it was hard to determine his mix. He had sun-dark skin and black hair, worn in short tight curls. His dark eyes tilted up slightly at the corners, and he could have been black, Latino, Asian, or even all three.

"Hi, I'm Christina Warner. Tina," the woman spoke up as she came through the door. She was petite, a small freckled girl who appeared to be a few years older than Abby. Abby introduced herself as Tina set her grocery bag on the counter.

"This is Steven Cooper," Tina continued, nodding towards a plain-faced, sandy-haired man a little ways behind her.

"Hi, Abby," the man called, offering a little wave and a friendly smile, then set his own bag on the counter beside Tina's.

"Do you guys need any help?" Abby asked.

Tina smiled. "Why don't you help me unpack this stuff and let the boys bring in the rest."

"How much did you buy?" Dominic asked, glancing at the grocery bags on the counter and kitchen table.

"Not any more than we'll go through," Steve said. "We figured we'd load up on dry goods; pasta and tuna and stuff that will keep, so we won't have to run into town that often. We got some powdered milk and other things that we just have to add water to. Then Tina wanted to stop at a farmer's market, so she's got a basket of fruit out there that needs brought in."

"You guys would live on macaroni and cheese if I didn't come along," Tina said, unpacking a bag of boxes onto the counter. "We'd all end up with rickets or scurvy or something."

Abby smiled at their banter, happy to be among cheerful, friendly people. She'd been worried about how they'd all get along, but so far they seemed like good company. She helped Tina unload the groceries, finding cabinet space for storage, trying to ignore the thought that kept trying to push itself to the front of her mind —wondering how they'd react to Simon.

Simon was still asleep upstairs when the others finished unpacking the groceries and went their separate ways. Abby headed out to the lab, where, out the back door into the field behind it – a good sized clearing surrounded by bushes and large boulders – Dominic pointed to a break in the trees at the far end, barely visible in the deepening darkness.

"There's a path through there that goes out towards the mountain," Dominic explained. "In between us and the mountain is the spring-fed pond I was telling you about."

Abby nodded, looking around. The house and lab were built on a hillside, and the ground flowed downwards towards the pond, then began rising again. It looked as if there was another fairly large clearing at the base of the mountain, flat and surrounded by trees.

"That mountain top would be perfect for me to set up my telescope," she observed. "No need for pollution filters, no extraneous light."

"You'll have that down here on the ground, too. No light pollution at all."

"For a telescope, there's nothing like rarified mountain air," Abby said. "Turns a fuzzy image crystal clear. How high is that mountain, do you know?"

"To the top? Well over 13,000 feet. But it has quite a few large outcroppings much lower than that."

"It's perfect. Any roads up that far?"

Dominic laughed. "There isn't so much as a burro trail up that hillside," he said. "Although it's not that steep. How are you at mountain climbing?"

"With an expensive telescope strapped to my back?" she shook her head, then looked back towards the house. "I wonder if I'd get too much heat shimmer off the roof?"

"You'd be better off taking your chances climbing the mountain. I've been up there before, and there *is* a way, although it's rough. But that's a thin clay roof, intended to keep the sun off and the rain out. If you didn't slide right off of it, you'd probably bust through."

"Well, damn," Abby said. "I guess I'll have to trek out past the pond later on and see what kind of viewing station I can find."

"Is this field too close to the lab?" Dominic asked, glancing back at the building behind them.

"I don't know how many lights you'll be running off the generator, but I saw that the lab had fluorescents. The light will be pouring out of it, and maybe even from the house. For optimal viewing, it needs to be pitch black, without any other light source than the reflection off the stars and planets. Even when I take a flashlight with me, it has to have a red bulb or filter."

"Well, you're welcome to walk out there and see if you can find someplace you like. I have to go in and get some things together for tomorrow, when we start our first official day of work. I can see if Tina or Steve will go with you, if you want company."

Abby shook her head. "That's okay," she said. "I'm sure I won't do much observing tonight anyway. I'm going up to the house to unpack and see if I can wake Simon up. I'll have plenty of time to set up my scope."

As they headed back into the lab, Abby took a last glance around the clearing, down the hill where the path disappeared into the trees. They were completely isolated out here, she thought; yet, she'd never felt more at home.

12.19.15.6.5

May 21, 2008 — A few minutes after eight the next morning, Abby slipped through the doorway of the lab. Although she tried not to make any noise, the rest of the group turned to look at her as she slid into the room. She sat on the bench by the lab table, silently willing the others to turn back around. "Sorry," she said under her breath.

"Not a problem," Dominic responded with a smile. He was standing to her left at the short end of the long room, where the wall was covered with a green chalkboard and white dry erase board. "Will Simon be joining us this morning, then?"

Abby felt her face flush. "He got up before I did. I thought he'd be here already." She'd had to wait her turn while Simon showered, then had to prepare his breakfast before she could get ready herself. He was gone when she had finished dressing, and she had assumed he'd already left for Dominic's scheduled eight o'clock meeting.

Abby blushed, and Dominic smiled again, admiring the pink blossoms forming under her toffee skin. "Well, I'm sure he'll find us," he said, turning back to the chalkboard.

"We all know why we're here," he said to the group. "This is what we're looking at: The Long Count of Days, as you all know, is a Mayan calendar. The earliest found monuments with Long Count dates go back to the first century BCE, but that's not the beginning." He turned to face them, pointing at the white board that he'd covered with numbers.

"This," he said, indicating a five digit number series, "is the beginning of the cycle. Zero point zero point zero point zero point zero," he read across. He pointed to the next set of numbers. "About three thousand, one-hundred fourteen BCE. The beginning of the Long Count."

"Explain that," Simon said. Dominic glanced towards the sound of his voice; the mathematician was leaning against the doorframe,

40

chewing on his pencil eraser. He spit out a piece of it. "Explain to us how 0.0.0.0.0 denotes 3114 BCE."

"Okay," Dominic said. "Without going into too much detail — Tina and Steve already know this, but Simon, I'll sit down with you, Abby, and Dante later if you want the whole story with examples. Basically, the dating involved the interpretation of glyphs found on stelae in Mayan ruins throughout Mesoamerica, kind of like interpreting Egyptian hieroglyphics. When those events were interpreted, the Long Count dates were matched against the Gregorian calendar, lining up matching events until the time frame was established. There's always been some disagreement as far as the true start date, but the most common dates agreed upon are only a day apart. I think we'll be okay with that, because if we can find out what the Long Count is measuring, we'll find out the true date.

"The Maya recorded days, months, years, like we do." He began writing again. "One day equals one 'kin.' A month consisted of twenty days. This gave them a 360 day year. That wasn't a mistake though," he said, glancing back at them. "They knew there were 365 days in a year. They just considered the last five days an unlucky period of time, something they avoided until it was over and they could celebrate the coming of the new year.

"Anyway," he continued, "Twenty kin equal one 'uinal,' which was a Mayan month. 18 uinal equal one 'tun', which is one year. Twenty tun, or twenty years, equal a 'katun'. Twenty katun equal one 'baktun,' a measurement kept by the Maya, but for which we don't have an equivalent – the Western world tends to use a base-10 counting system – years, decades and centuries – while the Maya used a base-20 system.

"Finally," Dominic concluded, "twenty baktun are equivalent to 8,000 years, or 2,880,000 days. This is a full cycle."

"So we're here to figure out the end of the cycle?" Simon frowned. "Eight thousand years? Almost three million days? That isn't even in our lifetimes, Ciriello, or even in the remote future. The calendar would end in about 4- or 5,000 CE. So why do we care about working on it?"

Dominic shook his head. "That's just it, Simon. The Long Count doesn't end with a full cycle. It doesn't count from the beginning and cycle up through twenty baktuns. A Great Cycle is only 13 baktuns." He turned and wrote again on the board: 13.0.0.0.0.

"Mayan time, 13 baktun, zero katun, zero tun, zero uinal, and zero kin. That's when the Long Count ends."

"Which is equal to what in American time?" Simon asked.

"The Long Count ends on December 21, 2012."

There was silence in the lab as they digested this. It was Simon who finally spoke. "That's only a little over four years from now," he said.

"That's right," Dominic responded. "And that's why it's so important right now that we figure out what it means."

After a moment, he spoke again. "The Maya marked certain repeating cycles, like the Venus Round. Some dates were based on sacred numbers, others on astronomical cycles. They all come together to form the Long Count.

"The Long Count actually ends at 1,870,990 days," he continued. "These are enormous numbers. Huge periods of time. With the Long Count, they weren't mapping events in their lifetime, or even *a* lifetime; not even a century or millennium or two."

"So how does it fit into the notation, Dominic?" Abby asked, a hand half-raised.

"Simple," he said, turning to the board again. "There are five cycles, rotating within each other, like clockwork. You write each date as a set of five numbers, one for each sub-cycle. You start the notation from right to left, starting with the smallest unit of measure — of time, I mean."

He scrawled a date quickly on the board. "12.19.15.6.5. You read it from right to left, from kin to baktun. In Mayan time, that's today's date — May 21, 2008. That's 1,870,325 kin that have elapsed since the beginning of the cycle."

"How do we know the dates start and end when you say they do?" Simon asked.

"By the work of dozens, if not hundreds, of researchers before me. There's no doubt on the dates, except for some researchers there's a correlation problem that puts the start and end dates either one day before we do, or one after. This is a minor point that doesn't affect the Count. The dates have been checked and re-checked, but I'll give you the numbers and the correlation date so you can look into it yourself, if you're so inclined."

"I think I am," Simon said. "I don't like to just trust the words of someone I don't even know."

"You do it all the time as a mathematician, don't you?" Dante suddenly spoke up. "I mean, you're using other people's theorems all the time. Do you question those, too?"

Simon turned to Dante, eyes narrowing. "Tell me again what you do?" he asked.

"I'm a geologist," Dante answered evenly. "And I tend to trust the work of other scientists before me, as long as it's been cross-checked and verified, put up for debate through peer review, predicted and tested, and all come out fine."

Simon turned away from him, back to Dominic. "I'll need those dates and numbers," he said. Dominic simply nodded, then turned to the board again.

"Just a little Mayan history for you, before we get started," Dominic continued. "The first calendar was the Haab. It was the first 365-day calendar, the first calendar that used the moon as a timekeeper. The next calendar was the Tzolkien – the Sacred Calendar – a calendar of 260 days that fit into the Haab like a pair of cogs. Those two calendars were cyclical, meshing together and rotating to return to the same place every 52 years. The time-measure where they coincided was a marker date, like our century.

"The Long Count was a calendar of a very different nature. It still kept time in days, months, and years, but it wasn't the type of calendar you could use year after year. It was cyclical, sure; many rotating cycles inside itself. But it was also linear. It wasn't so much a calendar as a map — a map that charts a set period of time.

"It was a system of reckoning. You've probably all seen pictures of the great calendar, the Aztec sun-stone, but the record of the Long Count is found on stelae across Latin America. It's not a single piece that's been excavated, but a system of timekeeping throughout the Mayan world. Long Count dates have been found in glyphs at nearly every Mayan site. It was their system of dating, of recording."

"So the Long Count was actually in use at some point?" Abby asked.

"Actually," Steve spoke up, "The Long Count is *still* in use. The Quiche Maya still use the Count."

"Why the hell would they do that?" Simon asked. "It's long and complicated. I thought these people weren't complex enough to build wooden houses. Why don't they use what everyone else is using?"

"Well, that's just it," Dominic said. "There really *is* no universal calendar. We use the Gregorian calendar, based on the birth of Christ. But Christians are still a minority in many parts of the world. So, there's the Julian calendar, the Hebrew calendar, the Islamic calendar, the Persian, the Indian, Chinese, Buddhist, old Roman and French Republican calendars. I won't even get into how many different ways there are of keeping time among the different tribes of Africa, Australia and the Middle East; of the gypsies and various peoples of Eastern Europe ..."

"Fine," Simon interrupted, holding up a palm. "Just tell us about the Long Count."

"Ok," Dominic continued, unfazed. "It was used by the Maya in their classic period as their time-keeper. That was around 200-900 CE."

"The Mayan Golden Age," Tina added.

"Yes," Dominic replied. "Most of our glyphs came from that period. They had about another fifty years after that before their culture went into pretty steep decline. No one knows why the Long Count started when it did, and no one knows why it ends. But the dates weren't just arbitrarily picked and set; there's significance to the beginning and the end. Our job here is to find out what that significance is — hopefully, before it's too late."

The group spent most of the morning familiarizing themselves with each other and the work that Dominic, Tina, and Steve had already done. The three archeologists and anthropologists had studied the ruins at Izapa and accepted it as the birthplace of the Count, but had made no progress in figuring out why it was created or what it meant. They shared their notes and work, trying to bring the others up to speed — at least, Dante and Abby. Simon had insisted that Dominic provide the correlation numbers immediately, and he'd retreated outside to look at them.

Steve was debating the importance Dominic set on the specific dates. "The dates don't really mean that much, I don't think, as far as the starting point goes. It's not the start of everything, the beginning of time or anything."

"But they picked those dates for a reason," Abby said.

Steve nodded. "I'm sure they did, but I look at the length of the count more than the actual dates. The full length of the Long Count is a total of five Great Cycles. The Maya believed in five world ages. The Long Count is just measuring one of those ages."

"The entire Count is only one age?"

"That's right," Steve said. "It's the fifth age. We live in the final one."

Abby felt a chill creep over her. She suddenly shivered, then smiled self-consciously. Steve just laughed. "It *is* kind of disconcerting, isn't it?"

"Well, yeah," she said. "That's not the type of thing you want to think about on a beautiful spring day."

"That's what we're here for, though," Dominic said. Abby looked up at him, still not used to his unconventionally handsome, unbearded face. He shrugged. "I know for some of you this is just a problem to be solved, something to play with. But I believe in the Long Count. It ends in December 2012, and I think something major is going to happen. I don't know if it's going to be the end of the world, but it's going to be something. We're here to find out what that is."

Abby nodded. "I don't have a problem with that," she said. "I just think we're all going to be hit with the thought of our own mortality quite a bit here, and that's going to take some getting used to."

"Yes it is," Dominic said, "but you can't let that bother you or we're not going to get anywhere. Time is a very fluid thing; it flows like liquid, seeming to pool sometimes in stagnant ponds; sometimes racing in splashing rushes. We all know we've got limited time on this planet – maybe we're the only ones who know exactly how much time we have left."

Steve smiled and shook his head. "That's funny coming from you, Dominic. As long as I've known you, you've never been willing to talk about death."

Dominic pushed back from the table and stood up. "No, I haven't," he said. "But I'm not certain that the end of the Long Count means death. The Maya could have been predicting almost anything, not necessarily the end of time. Let's face it, if something happened to our civilization now to wipe out our cultural memory, 2,000 years from now scholars would wonder how we came about the start date for our Christian calendar. Did we believe that life began at year zero? Did human beings land on Earth at that time? Why do we count up from there?

"Once the information is lost to time, any assigned meaning might be completely arbitrary. The Long Count could mean nothing. Or it could mean everything."

"Look at Stonehenge," Tina spoke up. "It's a 56-year calendar, as far as we can tell. But it's just repeating cycles; it's not mapping or predicting anything."

Dominic went to the window and looked out at the sprawling highlands, the yard rolling down to the pond and the forests beyond. He stared out across the grassy hillside to a place beyond the trees that only he could see. "It's there," he said quietly. "The story behind the Long Count is there. I've read the glyphs and the stories, and the whole history of the Maya is in them. If there's a combination that will unlock the Long Count, I think we'll find it here."

12.19.15.6.9

May 25, 2008 — "What exactly is it you do, Dominic?" Simon asked.

Dominic paused, a spoon full of cereal half raised towards his lips. "Well," he said, replacing it in the bowl untouched. "Currently, I work with archaeologists and other anthropologists to decipher exactly what the Maya were like, what they did and how and when they did it."

"Archaeologists do the actual digging and cataloguing," Simon replied. "What do *you* do?"

Dominic shrugged. "I take what they dig up and I interpret it. I see how it fits in with the history of the Maya and what other anthropologists have discovered. I verify and log the facts, connect them with our current information and record any corrections or new data, then build a story around the facts."

"So basically, you make shit up."

Dominic stood up, picking up his bowl. "No," he said simply. "I construct life from the remnants of history. I don't make things up. If you'll excuse me," he said, heading for the doorway. Before he could escape, however, Abby was there.

"Good morning, Dominic," she said with a smile.

"How you doing," he answered shortly.

"Great. I can't wait to get started today. Where are you going?" she asked, noticing the cereal bowl in his hand.

"Outside," he said. "I think I'll have breakfast in the courtyard."

"Good idea," she said. Noticing Simon, she smiled at him. "Hey, sweetheart. I wondered where you went so early."

"Just having a conversation with Ciriello," he said. "He was telling me exactly what it is a Mayan expert does."

"Excuse me," Dominic said again, moving around Abby and out the door.

Abby turned, watching his retreat. "What's with him?" she asked.

"He's full of bullshit, that's what's wrong with him," Simon said. Abby frowned.

"I think he's along for the ride," Simon explained. "He wants the rest of us to figure it out for him, and he wants to take the credit for it."

Abby went to the ice chest. "Do you really think so? I don't get that feeling from him. I think he's been working on this for a long time, and he's finally given in and asked for help."

"You defending him?"

"Of course not. I'm just ... what is it, Simon? What's wrong?"

He shook his head and stood up. "I just don't want to get taken advantage of, that's all. I want to stay one step ahead of this guy. If he thinks he's going to screw us, he'd better think again." He turned and headed up the stairs without another word.

Passing him on the way down was Dante. He greeted Simon, but got only a grunt in reply.

"He's in a pleasant mood in the mornings, isn't he?" Dante asked.

"I don't know what's been with him. Since we got here he's been crabby. Hopefully it's just the heat and the stress of trying to settle in here

46

and at the university on Monday. He should be in a better mood next weekend when he gets back."

"Man, I hope so," Dante said, reaching for the orange juice in the refrigerator. "I can't bear to think we're going to be pissy with each other all summer."

Abby smiled, then went out the door to the courtyard behind the house. The sky was gray and starting to cloud over, but the weather was warm, and it hadn't yet begun to rain. She found Dominic sitting on a large boulder, finishing his breakfast. He nodded as she approached, and she sat down on the rock beside him.

"I'm sorry about that," she said. "I don't know what's been with him lately."

"I don't know either, Abby, but it's going to have to stop. This isn't a competition. We're here to work together. I assembled this team with the idea that we were all an easy-going, albeit serious-minded, bunch of scientists. Simon was the only member I invited sight unseen. After I met you, I trusted your judgment."

Abby looked away, feeling her face flush.

"Hey," Dominic said, touching her elbow. "I don't mean that I hold you responsible for his behavior. I'm blaming myself more than anything. I'm not accusing you of misrepresenting him – you're his fiancée, of course you don't think ill of him. You had no way of knowing there might be some personality conflicts. No one is to blame for that. I'm sure it'll all work out."

Abby smiled, still looking down. "You've got a good heart, Dominic."

He shrugged. "I'm an optimist. Besides, I have my bad days, too. I'm just trying to build up enough good will with you now so you don't hold it against me when I get grouchy."

Abby laughed, feeling better as she stood up. She'd thought having Simon with her on this project would make her more comfortable, but she was already counting the hours until he left for the university. He tended to get short-tempered when he was stressed, so after he made it through his first week at school, she thought he should settle in and calm down.

Abby said goodbye to Dominic and headed back up to the house to see if Simon was ready to go to work with the others. He wasn't in the kitchen, or in their room, so after searching the house and courtyard and not finding him, Abby headed down to the lab.

The others were seated around the large room. Even Simon stood in a corner, flipping through a book on Mayan glyphs. "They were called the Lords of the Days," Dominic was saying. He saw Abby come in, and interrupted himself with a smile. "Hey, Abby."

She smiled back, glancing over at her fiancé, but Simon didn't even look up. Abby slid onto the bench next to Steve, across from Dante and Dominic. Tina was in the chair by the computer desk, trying to get reception on the wireless Internet.

"What are you guys talking about?" Abby asked.

"Mayan mystics were called 'Daykeepers'," Dominic answered. "The Long Count was used as a divining tool, like the I-Ching. Even today, the modern day Quiche Maya have priests and scribes called Daykeepers that use the Count to divine holy days, or 'good fortune' days for important events.

"This is where the history of the Count gets kind of muddled," he explained. "I want to study the pure count, the Long Count as a historical documentation of time, but it can't be separated from its mystic past, either. We can look at it like tarot cards, or astrology, and still study the history behind it. But I don't think that was the true nature of the Count."

"So you're going to interpret the data to your own whims," Simon said.

"Not at all," Dominic responded. "You just can't separate the historical count from the mystical side of it."

"How can you make sense of any of our hypotheses when you're not even clear on what the Count actually is?" Simon asked.

"*Everything they saw was clear to them*," Steve intoned, then smiled.

"What's that?" Tina glanced up. She'd stayed out of the conversation so far, but Steve's words had caught her attention.

Steve shook his head. "Just a line from the *Popul Vuh*."

"What the hell are you talking about?" Simon asked crossly.

Tina sat back in her chair, stretching and dropping her pen back onto the computer desk. "Tell us about the *Popul Vuh*, Steven."

"Come on, Tina, you know the story."

"Sure," she said. "But they don't." She nodded at the others seated around the room. "It's a dreary day, we can't get any reception, my hand and my brain are cramping, and I'd like to hear a story," she said.

"Okay then," he said, laying aside the notebook he'd been glancing through. "What is it exactly that you'd like them to know?"

"Tell us anything that has bearing on what the hell we're doing here," Simon said.

"All right," Steve said, "Let me tell you what it is, first of all.

"The *Popul Vuh* is the 'Council Book' of the ancient Maya. It was written as a history of the Mayan people, listing genealogies and myths, stories of heroes and tales of heavenly visitation. It's half history, half myth, I suppose. They used to study it when seeking the proper day for a ceremony, or political act, like Dominic said.

"The *Popul Vuh* is full of charts and pictures; it not only gave astronomical information and forecasts like the Venus cycle, it also told stories — long parables and fables; their creation myth. The *Popul Vuh* is kind of like the Mayan bible. It has somewhat mystical origins, though — no one knows who really wrote it.

"They say the first four humans put upon the Earth 'saw everything under the sky perfectly.' Apparently the gods weren't happy that the people could see the world as gods did, so they took that power from humans, leaving us with limited vision. Some say that phrase, 'they saw everything clearly,' meant just that: they could see everything in the world and in heaven, and everything that had happened in the past and would happen in the future. After the gods took this vision from them, the people went down from the highlands and found this book, which they called 'The Light That Came from Beside the Sea.' The Maya said that this council book gave them the ability to once again see everything. The book was a history of the things that had come before them, before even the dawn of Mayan civilization. It also told of things that were yet to come. The Maya were astronomers, priests, and diviners, and this was their reference book."

"Then why in the hell aren't we reading that?" Simon said.

"It's extremely complex, and would take a lifetime of study to understand it well," Dominic spoke up. "Besides, you don't need to – I already did. I've been studying Mayan life, myth, and culture all my life. If there's something you need to know about the Maya, I probably know it."

"So as long as nothing happens to you, I guess we're all taken care of," Simon said.

Dominic shrugged. "Guess so," he said. "If you all needed any more incentive to be nice to me, that should be it."

"Don't listen to him," Tina said. "He doesn't know anything Steve or I don't. Don't let him try to convince you he's the font of all knowledge here."

"Then you two are basically redundant," Simon said.

"Hey," Steve said uneasily. "Three heads are better than one, and all that."

"Yeah, lay off, man," Dante interjected.

Simon glanced around at the group, most of who were staring at him, perplexed.

"Hey, I'm just kidding," he finally said, holding up his hands in surrender. "Jesus, lighten up. Don't tell me I'm going to be stuck all summer with five people with no sense of humor. Damn."

Dominic looked at Simon for a long time, then turned his back on him again as he addressed the others. "The *Popul Vuh* has some interesting legends," he continued as if uninterrupted. "It describes the cataclysm that destroyed the world that came before this one."

"What cataclysm?" Dante asked.

"They say the world before this one ended in fire," Dominic said. "The description is wrapped up in myth, so is naturally vague and open to interpretation. There's no way of knowing what they meant. Volcano, a meteor, wildfires?"

"What does that mean, though, the world before this one?" Dante questioned.

This time, Steve answered. "The old Indian cultures of Mesoamerica believed in five worlds, or five ages. There's a famous Aztec sun stone that describes the five ages. The fifth age – our current one – is the 'Age of Movement.'"

"So how is the fifth age supposed to end?" Abby asked.

"Some legends say by earthquake."

"Guess that's my field," Dante said.

"That's what I'm hoping," Dominic said, returning to his seat on the bench. "If there's something geologically building up that we should know about, I hope you can find it."

"But how could they predict the exact day it was going to happen?" Simon asked, standing up. He tossed the book back onto the shelf. "Legend is fine; maybe they knew something about plate tectonics and pressure in the earth, something along those lines. But I'm sorry, you can't predict the exact day the world is going to end."

"Why not?" Dominic said mildly. "Don't forget, they were astrologers and diviners. Maybe they read some portent in the stars."

"Great, so now we've got the Mayan Psychic Friends Network? Come on. Let's stick to reality here."

"Well, that's part of the problem," Dominic said. "Just like most cultures, Mayan reality is completely intermeshed with their mythology and religion. Mayan myth described reality as undergirded by a system of threadlike links. Did they mean lava tubes? String theory? Something else, or nothing at all?"

Simon shook his head, crossing the room. He stopped in front of the computer desk. "Did you get any reception on that yet?"

"Not yet," Tina said. "With no land lines, Dominic said we'll get a few good hours every day, unless there's rain or really high humidity. I think today is a loss."

"Great," Simon said in disgust. He went to the window to look out. "So now what do we do?" He stared at the jungle beyond the clearing, thinking about Izapa on the other side. "Why are we even here?"

Simon asked. "A bunch of dusty old ruins aren't going to tell us what we need to know. Don't you think we need to look at the living count? You said people are still using it today, right?"

"They are, but it's corrupted," Dominic said. "It's like the *Popul Vuh* itself. It's been touched by Christianity. The *Popul Vuh* we use was written after the conquest; the authors of it say as much. They describe a previous book that has been lost or hidden. They declare that this 'Prior Word' has superiority over the word of God. They tried to recreate that book, but stated that they were re-writing it almost under duress, that they were writing, 'in Christendom, now.' An ancient race re-writing their bible amid the prostelazation of a conquering religion can't repeat it the same as the original. It's been altered, and the authors of the second book made sure that we knew it.

"The *Popul Vuh* we read is not the original *Popul Vuh*. And the Long Count in use today is not the real Count."

"So what are we working on, your word alone?" Simon snarled.

"Not at all," Dominic said, standing up. He went to the window beside Simon, who did not look happy: the smaller mathematics professor was no physical match for an on-site explorer who worked as much with his body and his hands as with his mind. If the move was intended to intimidate him, it worked, and Simon quickly moved away and sat on the edge of the lab table.

"You're welcome to any information you can come by," Dominic said. "The shelves over there are crowded with references: maps, journals, dictionaries, encyclopedias, histories, astronomical texts and mythologies. There's a computer with internet access, and a Sat-phone for you to call anyone in the world you want. I'm not keeping anything from you, but I'm not going to do your research for you, either. Ask me questions and I'll answer them honestly and as completely as I can. I'll fill in the blanks you have, just as I want you to do the same for gaps in my own knowledge. Feel free to debate me on anything I tell you. If you have better answers than I do, I'll listen. I'm here to find an answer, not teach you what I already know."

With that, he opened the door, walking out into the misty courtyard. As the door shut behind him, Simon stood up. "Great," he said. He looked around at the others. "Fucking great."

No one responded, and Simon walked over to the bookshelf. Without looking, he snatched a book off the stack and headed for the door. "He says we have internet, that's bullshit. He says we can ask him questions, then he walks out. So I guess we have to start working our way through the damn library. If you're looking for me, I'll be in my room." Book in hand, he walked out.

When the door closed behind him, Dante started laughing. "Nothing like a little ego-clashing," he said.

"How long is this going to go on?" Steve asked worriedly. "I've never seen Dominic so irritable before."

"He's never been antagonized like this before," Tina said, then stopped short. She put a hand over her mouth, turning to Abby. "Oh, Abby, I'm sorry," she said. "I don't mean anything bad against Simon. They're both acting like a couple of little boys."

Abby nodded and waved her off. "Don't worry about it," she said. "Simon is being difficult, but I think he'll settle in. He's just testing his limits, staking out his territory. I don't know — just being stupid."

The others laughed, and Steve turned to Abby with a smile. "We don't hold it against him," he said. "Believe it or not, we've worked with worse. Who was that guy in Belize, Tina? You remember him?"

"Yeah, that researcher from Bolivia," she laughed. As she and Steve proceeded to tell the story, Abby found herself relieved but tuning out. They might believe that Simon was just in a settling in phase, but she was starting to have her doubts. He saw Dominic as competition, and unless the other man backed down, Simon was going to make their time with him a living hell.

Just after dark, Simon headed for bed, although he'd barely left his room all day. He had to drive out to the university early the next morning. Part of his agreement with Dominic had been the use of one of the vehicles during the week, and Dominic had purchased the SUV for that purpose. It would leave the others with the pickup truck for any necessary trips away from the site.

Simon had originally planned to return to the lab on his off days, but after calculating the trip and the driving time involved, decided instead to find an apartment near the university. He had only two classes each day on Monday, Wednesday, and Friday; it was a light summer schedule, so he would have plenty of down time. He planned to make extensive use of the university library and computers, he told them, derisively claiming that he couldn't do any real work under the conditions Dominic had set up in the lab.

He had turned in early, and Abby waited for him to fall asleep before heading back outside. She sat now on the large boulder in the courtyard, watching the stars. The clouds had passed, leaving the sky clear and glittering with stars. Tina had questioned her earlier as to why Simon had even come along; after all, he wouldn't be with them most of the week, and didn't seem happy to be there. Abby had had no answer. She didn't want to explain to someone she'd just met that the only way Simon would allow her to come would be if he would be there, too.

"Mind some company?"

Dominic's voice, quiet and low, came disembodied out of the darkness. She turned to look for him and saw his shape outlined in shadow against the warm glow from the lab. "Don't mind at all," she answered.

He came over and sat on a smaller stone next to her. "Beautiful night."

She nodded, then realized he probably couldn't see the motion. The surrounding darkness was perfectly black, the stars brilliant pinpoints against the deep ebony background. Only the dim light coming from the lab up the hill washed out the sky around it.

"It's gorgeous," she said. "Although when I set up my telescope I'm going to have to either move farther out, near the pond, or ask everyone to shut the lights down early. Although to tell you the truth, I have no idea why I'm setting up my scope. What am I looking for?"

He shrugged. "I think you'd know that better than I. I know the night sky, but not the astronomical details. If there's a large-scale change, I might notice it. But if there's a pattern, I won't be aware of it. I want you to look at the same sky the Maya did, and I want you to find out what they were looking at."

She laughed. "You make it sound so easy."

"I know it won't be," he said quietly. "I just don't know what else to do. The Maya were astronomers. More than anyone else here, Abby, I think if someone is going to find the answer, it's going to be you."

"No pressure."

He grinned. "No pressure."

They sat in comfortable silence for awhile, watching the slow movement of the universe above them.

"What are there, about a trillion stars up there?"

"I'd say that's a pretty low estimate. Try maybe a trillion trillion."

Dominic exhaled audibly. "Damn," he said. "How many of those can we see?"

"With the naked eye? Roughly forty-five hundred."

"Well, that'll make your job a little easier," he said, and they both laughed.

"I hope the answer is in the stars," Abby said seriously. "I'd like to think the Maya were calculating some kind of cycle, like an orbit, or a comet. I think what you're doing is fascinating, Dominic, and in case I haven't done it yet, I want to thank you for letting me be part of it."

"Thanks for coming," he said. "I just hope this doesn't turn out to be a huge waste of all of our time."

"I'm not worried," she replied, looking back up at the sky. "If anything, I've had some beautiful views the last few days. That should make it all worth it."

"I hope you're right," he said. "I'll try not to let you down."

Abby smiled, then glanced over when she heard a rustling movement in the darkness as Dominic stood up. "I'll leave you to work then," he said, and after a quick good-night, he left her alone in the darkness.

Abby watched him leave, his silhouette blending in with the night, invisible until he was almost in front of the lab. She watched him open the door and disappear again into the building, the lights flicking out behind him.

With a smile, she turned her attention again to the night sky. Whatever the Maya had been watching, she hoped it was still there. And she prayed that it would make itself known to her.

12.19.15.6.11

May 27, 2008 — Dante was standing out by the edge of the courtyard, looking down over the small pond. In the darkness, it sparkled with starlight.

"Looks inviting," Abby said, wiping beads of perspiration off her forehead. She had been outside most of the day, enjoying the time spent with the rest of the team. Simon had left in the SUV the day before, just after dawn, and she hadn't heard from him since. Abby was a bit concerned; while she thought he was probably all right, she wished he would call, and she felt better just being around the others. Abby had followed Dante out to the hilltop above the water just for the company; but now that she was out there, she had to admit that the cool water looked wonderfully refreshing. Even after the sun had gone down, the air retained its humidity.

"Yes it does," he agreed. "It's kind of far down, though."

Abby nodded, looking down the hill at the water. The land sloped from the path down to the water's edge, at least a 12-foot drop. They could probably skid down it without falling, although the steepness of the slope would make it a challenge.

"Is it deep enough to dive?" she asked.

Dante shook his head. "Dominic says no. I guess out in the center it's maybe eight feet or so, but around most of the edges, where we'd probably land, it's only a couple feet deep. Not worth a broken neck."

"I'll jump in if you do," a bright voice suddenly called from behind them, and they turned in surprise to see Tina moving towards them through the darkness. Steve was at her side, recognizable only because his light colored hair shone in the starlight.

"I think you're on your own on that one," Abby said, "unless you can figure out how to get down there."

Tina stopped at the edge of the path, frowning down at the water. She looked around the hill and saw that thick brush covered most of it, but their only path down to the water was a bare steep hill of dirt and jutting rocks.

"Did someone call a meeting?" Another voice came from the darkness, and Dominic's shape loomed out of the shadows of the courtyard.

"Oops, forgot to invite you," Tina joked.

"We're trying to figure out how to get down to the cenote without killing ourselves," Dante said. "Any ideas?"

Dominic looked down at the pond. He visually measured the distance from the path they stood on to the water below, then glanced around. Without a word, he turned and disappeared into the darkness. A moment later, they hear a cracking sound.

"Wow, brute strength," Steve called jokingly. "You need some help?"

"Never," Dominic said back, and after the noise of more cracking and breaking, they heard him dragging something toward them.

Dante went to him, and they both reappeared moments later carrying a long, dead tree limb. Bare branches broke off as they hauled it toward the edge. They stopped and righted it, then lowered it carefully down the hill.

"Hold on, let's anchor it," Dominic said. He pulled his end over to a bush on the side of the path, hooking the broken branches through the thick, tangled base of the shrub. He gave it several strong tugs, and it looked like it would hold. The branch ladder now hung at a lopsided angle and stopped about three feet from the water's edge.

"You going to be first on that bad boy?" Dante asked.

"Sure," Dominic said. "I trust my work."

"I'll be back up at the house looking for a rope to haul you back up with," Tina joked.

"If we had rope we wouldn't be using this tree branch," Dominic said. He set a foot on the loose dirt of the hill. A few pebbles kicked down, but his footing was steady. Using the branch as a guide, he slid down the dirt slope, keeping his balance until he ran out of branch. He leapt the final few feet, landing at the water's edge, where a narrow rocky bank ran out into the water.

He turned around to receive their applause with upraised arms, and they all cheered. "Next," Steve said, grabbing the branch and swinging out onto the slope.

"Careful," Dominic called. "You can't see where you're putting your feet, and it's pretty loose ..." Before he could finish, Steve's foot slipped and he lost his balance. He grabbed the branch as he fell, hanging from it with his face pressed into the slope. Miraculously, the anchor held in the thick brush at the top of the hill. Dominic reached up and caught his friend's legs, helping him down to the rocky bank.

"Did I not just tell you to be careful?" he joked.

"Damn, you weren't kidding," Steve said.

"Watch out up there," Dominic called up to the others as Dante grabbed the branch. "If you guys are coming down, Dante, why don't you let the girls come down first? Then you can help them."

Dante nodded and stepped back, taking Tina's hand. She grabbed the branch ladder and used it as the guys had, sliding down the bank and holding the limb as a guide. She hit the bottom with ease, leaping the final few feet as Dominic had. "Good job," he said, helping her onto the rocky bank.

Abby was next, taking the branch nervously. She glanced down at the others below, thinking she had misjudged the height of the hill they were on. Dominic was the tallest of them all, and the top of his head should have only been five or six feet below her, but it seemed much farther away. She took a deep breath, set her foot on the dirt slope, and immediately slipped. She tightened her grip on the branch, scrambling for a foothold, and found one on one of the tree limb's outcropping branches. Using the long limb as a ladder, she scrambled down it quickly, jumping nimbly off the end to land with the others.

"Good girl," Dominic said. "That's what I originally had in mind with that branch, to use it as a ladder. It just didn't work out that well in practice."

"It'll probably make a better ladder going back up," she said, watching as Dante mimicked her on the ladder, descending quickly to end up beside them on the now crowded bank.

"Now what?" he asked, looking around at them. Without a word, Tina reached out and gave him a gentle shove. He backpedaled and hit the water with a splash.

"Hey!" he yelled, sputtering in the water. Grabbing Tina's ankle, he pulled her into the pond beside him. Dominic quickly stepped back up against the bank, hiding Abby behind him.

"You guys are nuts!" he called out over their splashing.

"No kidding," Steve said, reaching for the branch. "I'm not getting in that water."

56

"Chicken!" Tina called, and the three up on the bank made the obligatory clucking noises.

Steve grabbed the branch ladder, scrambling back up to the path, and Abby quickly turned to follow.

"Come on," Dante said. "The water's great!"

"The water's freezing!" Abby called back, wiping cold droplets off her bare arm. She quickly scaled the side of the slope, joining Steve up top.

"Come on up, Dominic," Steve yelled down. "Let those idiots play in the nasty water."

Dominic glanced up at him, shook his head, and with a grin, turned and cannon- balled into the pond. The huge splash even spattered Abby and Steve up on the path, and they turned away, sputtering.

"You're all crazy!" Steve shouted down at them, laughing.

"Come on in!" Dominic yelled up to him. "It's our own private lagoon."

"Our own private swamp is more like it," Steve said. "You guys going to make it back up the hill okay or do we need to sit here and lifeguard you?"

"Nah, we're good," Dominic said, waving him away. He ran a hand through his short dark hair, slicking it back against his skull. He was still grinning, laughing even as Dante approached from behind and dunked him.

"All right then," Steve said. "We're out of here."

He and Abby walked back up to the lab, and they could still hear the shouts and the laughter amid the splashing behind them. "Is that water clean?" she asked.

Steve nodded. "Dominic and I have stayed out here before, that's how he knew the spot. The pond is spring fed, and other than a mud bottom, it's pretty clear. There's no inlet from any other stream or anything, so there are no fish in it, just a lot of frogs and insects."

"Snakes?"

"Don't know," he said. "I've never seen any, but this *is* a jungle. There are bound to be snakes, and they have to drink too."

Abby shuddered. "Remind me not to go swimming at night."

Steve smiled. "Yeah, that's where I draw the line, too. During the day is one thing, but in the dark you don't know what the hell's swimming around in there with you."

They crossed the lab and went up to the house, parting ways in the kitchen, where Steve stopped to make a late night snack.

Abby headed up to her room, unused to the silence with Simon gone. She lay in her bed, dozing, listening to the crickets chirping outside her open window. A warm breeze came in and cut through the thick humidity, and every now and then she heard the flutter of wings against the eaves. She didn't want to think about whether they were birds or bats. The room and the bed felt very empty.

Abby didn't know how much later she was awakened by the sounds of laughter coming across the courtyard. Although her window was on the other side of the house, she could hear the three swimmers talking and laughing as they made their way back up to the house. A few minutes later, the back door opened, and she heard their whispered voices as they tried to quietly make their way up the stairs. Doors down the hall opened and closed, and as Abby drifted back into sleep, she was smiling.

12.19.15.6.12

May 28, 2008 — Abby was setting up her telescope for the first time; the humid, rainy weather seemed to have finally let up, and Tina and Dominic had come out to the courtyard to watch, and to keep her company. Tina had asked her what she knew about the size of the universe, and Abby was trying to answer.

"Space goes on for, as far as we can tell, forever. The distances are nearly impossible for us to even fathom. That's a lot of space to fill. There could be anything out there. And we don't even know what fraction of the universe we've been able to map. The observable universe is about twenty billion light years across, but we don't know how much of the *physical* universe that actually is. Have we seen half of it? A quarter of it? Less than one percent? We don't know. It could be infinite, and we're less than a speck.

"We know much of what's within our galaxy, even quite a bit of what's in our corner of the universe," Abby continued. "But we don't know everything. We don't even know how many dimensions there really are."

"What religion are you?" Dominic asked suddenly. Abby glanced down at him where he lay in the grass, sorting through the lenses for her telescope.

"I'm not," she said. "The more I look into the universe, the less I believe that there's any god out there who created it; especially not one who intervenes in our daily lives. I *used to* believe in a universal consciousness — we know that everything in the universe consists of energy, just vibrating at different speeds. We know that energy can't be created or destroyed; it just transfers from one form to another. So, I used to think we'd go on forever – our life energy would just transition into another form. I used to believe all this energy was interconnected, that everything was part of some grand universal consciousness and that everything together, on the Earth and in the universe, was God."

"That's not a unique concept," Dominic said. "It's a basis for several religions, actually."

"I'm not trying to be unique," she said, "I'm just telling you what I think. Or thought, anyway. What about you? What's your religious background?"

"I'm a roaming Catholic."

"Roaming?"

"Born and raised Roman Catholic, started roaming after that. Been doing it ever since."

"Do you think our religious points of view have any effect on how we look at this?" Tina asked, finally breaking her fixation on the sky and turning towards them.

"Of course," Dominic said. "It has an effect on everything we say or do. It's a frame of reference through which we see the world, through which we make judgments on the information we take in."

"And we have to take into consideration the religion of the Maya; it would have affected everything they did," Abby said.

"That's right," Dominic said. "And Tina, Steve and I have gone through every religious reference we could think of. The basics are simple," he explained. "The Maya were a polytheistic society. They believed that their line of kings was heaven sent, just like most monarchies – although Mayan kings were recorded as having ruled for thousands of years. That could be important, as far as their time references, or it could be of the same apologue as the Bible, where Moses is recorded to have lived more than 800 years.

"The Mayan religion did call for sacrifices to bless their harvests, but again, that's not much different than Christianity, Judaism, or Islam sacrificing lambs and calves and such to appease their gods."

"Except that they were human sacrifices," Tina pointed out.

"Well, again," Dominic said, "You can find evidence in the Bible of Abraham sacrificing his son, of Jephthah sacrificing his daughter in exchange for a victory in war."

"This is one reason why I don't subscribe to organized religion," Abby said. "I can't follow a religion where people think that sacrificing a living creature will make their deities happy enough to end a drought or bring them a better harvest. A loving god shouldn't need bribes or appeasement to do the right thing."

"People believe different things," Dominic said with a shrug. "What seems silly or puerile to some, another might find sacred and holy. There's no accounting for what causes faith, so you can't argue against it. All we can do is work with it."

"Or work around it," Abby said. She scowled as a cloud covered the moon. "It's just not going to work tonight. I can't get through the atmosphere."

"I'm ready to head on up, anyway," Tina said.

"Let me pack this up," Abby said, beginning to take down her scope. "It feels like it might rain, and I don't want this to get damaged."

Dominic unfolded himself from the ground, rising to help her store the lenses he'd been playing with. "I know you and Simon want to study this from a purely scientific viewpoint," he said, "but because the Maya were who they were, we can't. We have to take them as a whole to understand where they were coming from. Even if an event they recorded might be entirely scientific, or astronomical, they would have viewed it in a religious sense. We can't just read their parables and their myths; we have to interpret them to find out what really happened, and what they were really talking about."

"Like Ezekial and the UFO," Abby said.

"What?"

She was about to speak, but before she could get a word out, the skies opened up. Her words turned into a shriek as the cold rain fell, spattering them like drops of ice. Quickly, they gathered up the pieces of her telescope, laughing as they rushed to get back up to the lab and out of the rain.

When they had made it to shelter, all three were soaked. As Tina headed across the rocky space between the lab and the house, up to her room to dry off and change clothes, Abby and Dominic stayed behind to clean the water off her scope, chatting with Dante and Steve, and the rain continued to fall.

12.19.15.6.13

May 29, 2008 — "I think I've had about enough of this," Dominic said, leaning back and wiping his brow. He was bathed in sweat. The open windows of the lab did little to lessen the stifling heat.

"No kidding," Abby agreed. "You'd think as close as we are to the ocean, there'd be some kind of temperature moderation, you know?"

"Mountains block it," Dominic replied. "We're in a funny spot — not close enough to the water, not high enough in the mountains, and we're not in low enough of a valley. So we get the heat, we get the humidity, and once it gets on us, it just kind of stays."

"No wonder this area isn't populated," Abby joked. "Whoever sold you this land must've been laughing all the way to the bank."

He smiled. "You're probably right."

Abby gathered her long hair in one hand, lifting it off of her neck. "What do we do now? You going to break down and buy an air conditioner?"

"I don't know," Dominic admitted, standing up. "It's enough to run the refrigerator, lights, fans and the computer off that little generator. We can't do an air conditioner, too. I'm afraid even the fans running constantly might overload it. The computer can run off the battery backups for a few hours, and we have plenty of candles, but if we're without a fridge for the day it'll take to power that thing back up, in this heat, we're in some trouble."

Abby nodded. She wrapped her hair in a knot on top of her head, pinning it back with a clip. "Speaking of, how long do you think Dante and Steve will be out getting fuel?" she asked. "They said they'd bring back a couple bags of ice."

"Tina, too," Dominic added. "She wanted to grab some more fresh fruit and veggies from the market while they're in town, so she went with them."

"Well, no hurry, anyway," Abby said. "It'll probably be melted by the time they get here anyway, even in the cooler." She pushed her notebook away. "God, it's just too hot to do anything."

"I'll second that," Dominic said. He ran both hands through his damp curls. "I can't even think in here. I wonder if it's cooler out there on the mountain top."

Abby looked out the window at the hill rising in the distance. "You've got to be kidding me," she said. "You actually have the energy to go hiking?"

"Sure," he said. "The exercise is invigorating. Clears the head. You'll think a lot better after a stroll."

"I'll be unconscious after a stroll," she said, but couldn't help but smile.

"Come on," he said, "I'll grab a couple bottles of water, you get a towel and we'll be on our way."

A few minutes later they were crossing the courtyard towards the cenote, which they'd dubbed "the lagoon." Abby tugged uncomfortably on the baseball cap Dominic had brought her.

"Trust me," he said, "You'll appreciate that once the sun starts beating down on you."

"You sound like you've done this before."

He glanced down at her. "I've lived out in the middle of nowhere for a good part of my life," he said, then smiled. "Don't worry, you won't get lost."

"I'm more concerned about heatstroke," she muttered, but he only laughed.

They crossed over the path they'd worn above the lagoon. "What direction are we heading?"

"West," he said without hesitation. "Due west."

She glanced up at him. "Did you know that from the layout of the place, or ... ?"

He shrugged. "I have a general idea of which way is which; the ocean is to the west, Izapa is northwest of us. The rest of Mexico is east. Guatemala is southeast. That's about it. I just happened to notice the sun," he said.

Abby studied it, shielding her eyes with one hand. Even with her dark sunglasses, the sun burned bright as fire. "It's almost directly overhead," she observed.

"And you're an astronomer?" he teased. "Look where the sun is in location to us."

"Um ... above us?"

He laughed. "North, Abby. Below 23 ½ degrees latitude, the sun passes north of us. Above that, and it always passes to the south."

"Remind me not to play Trivial Pursuit with you anytime."

He smiled. "I'm full of 'em," he said. "You want to know how to start a fire with a pocket knife?"

He stopped when he realized Abby was no longer with him. Glancing back, he saw she had stopped, standing in the middle of the large clearing they'd entered, hands on her hips, staring out at the horizon line, above the trees.

"Beautiful, isn't it?" he said. To their west, the mountains rose high and lush; the forest surrounded them on all other sides, green and wild.

"Yes," she said. "It's perfect." She didn't lower her gaze from the skyline.

Dominic stepped up beside her, following her gaze. "What are you seeing?"

"The sky," she said. "It's huge."

Dominic looked up at the expanse of sky; the white clouds above them in the azure heavens seemed to roll on forever. Suddenly, he understood.

"If the ancient Maya could see this sky well enough to predict astrological events with the naked eye, just think of what you'll see out here with your telescope."

"It's incredible," she said. "I thought the view was amazing back up by the lab; I've never seen such perfect darkness. No city lights — hell, no lights at all. Even when I was studying for my Masters and took a road trip out to Montana, I've never seen a sky so huge."

"Then it's all yours," he said with sweeping grandiosity. "I hereby bequeath this clearing to you."

"Thanks a lot," she said. "You think you could install a swimming pool for me?"

"Sorry 'bout that," he replied. "But maybe I can find a cool spot up on this mountain."

"It's awful high," she said, gazing up at the volcano in the distance.

"The summit is about 13,200 feet above sea level," he said. "But lower than that, it's high enough to have some cool recesses and hollows."

They walked on in silence as she tried to keep up with his long strides, steadily ascending the hill. It wasn't as steep as she'd feared, but the hike was still an effort, and she was grateful for the water Dominic had brought.

"You done much exploring out here?" she asked. She was getting out of breath.

"Some," he said. "I usually camp closer to the ruins."

They came out on top of a short terrace, looking down over the trees. "How far away are we?" Abby asked uneasily.

Dominic smiled. "Don't worry," he said, "We've only come about a mile past your clearing. It just seems a lot further because we've been going uphill."

She glanced up at the sun, not yet at its zenith point. Abby hoped the air would indeed be cooler up the mountain. Most of its face was bare, but there were groves of trees dotting the hillside. "Can we try to stay in the shade?" she panted.

Dominic glanced back, concerned. "You doing all right?"

She nodded, breathless. "It's just so hot, I feel like I'm wilting."

He laughed. "Okay," he said. "I can't make any guarantees on what we're going to find in the woods, but it should be at least ten degrees cooler in the shade. And if I remember correctly, there's a trickle of a creek running down through one of those wooded areas. Not much, but we can at least cool our feet in it."

An hour later, they found the creek. It was more of a stream than a creek, rolling and tumbling down well-worn rocks with a cheery splash. "Oh, thank God," Abby said when they finally stumbled across it. Just the air off the cold mountain stream was refreshing.

Dominic laughed, passing in front of her to check out the water. It looked clear, and the only signs of animal life were small sections of crushed undergrowth where small animals had come out to drink. "Doesn't look like anything bigger than a fox lives around here," he observed. He found a large flat rock half-buried near the water's edge and brushed the grass and dirt off it, then turned and held out a hand to Abby, who took it, letting him help her up onto it. The cleared rock face was about five feet across, and it sloped down until the edge was almost touching the water.

They sat down side-by-side on the rock platform and peeled off their shoes and sweat-soaked socks. "I'm in heaven," Abby moaned, eyes half closed, as she slipped her aching feet under the cold water.

"Yipes!" Dominic cried, pulling his own foot back out as it touched the icy stream.

"You big baby," Abby teased, massaging the soles of her feet on the small pebbles on the bottom.

Dominic tried again, gradually sliding his feet under the cold water. He looked around him, watching small birds flit through the trees. They chirped and sang, a musical backdrop to the sunlight-dappled green foliage.

"It's beautiful up here," Abby commented.

"I've never been into the woods this far," Dominic said, looking upstream. The water ran quickly down the mountainside, disappearing into the darkness of the trees. "I bet this stream runs down and connects with Rio Suchiate. What do you say we walk up it?" he asked. "Keep our feet cool and keep us from getting lost."

"Good plan," she agreed, picking up her shoes and standing up. "The last thing we need is to be wandering around up here lost after dark."

"Nothing to worry about," Dominic said. "These trees aren't thick enough; all you have to do is walk in a straight line in any direction and you'd be out of them in about fifteen minutes. The view from the mountainside is spectacular. And, if it's too dark to see where you are when you get out there, you can always follow the stars."

They made their way upstream, stepping carefully across the smooth stones of the streambed. Abby slipped once on a moss-covered rock and almost went down; Dominic caught her just as she was about to sit down in the water. He pulled her up, laughing as she checked over her shoulder to see the seat of her khaki shorts soaking wet.

"Don't worry," Dominic said. "In this heat you'll be dry in about two minutes."

She was about to answer when she noticed something they had not seen as they passed it. "Check that out," she said, tugging on his arm.

He turned to see where she was pointing and noticed a dark shadow on the cliff face, buried in the darkness of the trees.

"Cool," he said, stepping up out of the water. "It looks like a cave, doesn't it?"

She nodded, following him up onto the grass. "Is it deep?"

He ducked into the trees, following the rock wall with one hand. The entrance wasn't high, and he had to duck in order to stick his head in. He looked into it for a moment, waiting for his eyes to adjust to the darkness, then went in. Abby waited outside, but it was only a moment later that Dominic came back out. "Not much to it," he observed. "It's about eight feet deep, maybe three feet wide for the first two feet and about five feet the rest of it. Come on in."

Tentatively, Abby followed behind him. "Is there room?" she asked to his back.

"It's not too bad," he said. While he had to bend over to fit inside the cave, the ceiling was several inches over Abby's head. There was room for them to stand side by side once they got past the narrow opening.

"No, it's not bad at all," Abby said. She crouched down, examining the back wall, and Dominic knelt beside her. He sat down, stretching out his legs, pleased to find that he fit comfortably. "I may have found my new thinking spot," he said.

"Until it gets dark and Mr. and Mrs. Jaguar come home," Abby joked.

"Nah, I don't think so," he said, touching the cave wall. "No scratches or other markings, no bones, no bedding, no animal smell. It doesn't look like a den, but I'm sure animals come in and out of here periodically. I don't think there's anything large enough to worry about."

"Well, if you're willing to make the hike, it's all yours," Abby said, standing up. Dominic pulled himself up beside her, bending over to avoid hitting his head.

"I think I am," he said. "It's only a couple miles from the lab. I can stroll out here in about an hour once I find a direct path. I'd say it's worth it, if I really need the peace and quiet."

"Will you be able to find it again?"

Dominic shrugged. They crawled out of the cave and headed back downstream, and Dominic looked around for landmarks. "I have a good memory for places," he said. "The stream starts rising more sharply out front, where you fell. The cliff comes right out into the jungle there. And let's see — those three trees are intertwined at the roots, right there on the left."

"Well, if I come out here I'd better follow you," Abby admitted, "because everything looks the same to me."

"Well, anytime you need a hiking buddy, let me know," Dominic said. "I feel a lot better already."

"Me too," Abby said, noticing for the first time how much she had cooled off. The shade of the trees, the cold mountain stream, and cool air inside the cave had comforted her, and she did feel more alive for the exercise. "Good idea, this hike. I think I'm ready to get some work done now."

"All right," Dominic said happily. "That's what I like to hear!"

They headed back down the mountain, and although the heat hit them again as they left the trees and entered the clearing, it somehow didn't feel quite as oppressive as before.

12.19.15.6.15

May 31, 2008 — "So what do you think, Abby?" Dante asked. Although night had fallen, the rain had left a haze over the sky. It ruined the night for stargazing, so Abby had joined the others in the lab.

"I'm inclined to agree with Dominic," she said. "From what I've seen of Izapa, and from what I know of Chichen Itza and other sites, the Maya were excellent astronomers, and used sky events to position their buildings, hold ceremonies, and foretell weather phenomenon. Any record of this length of time, in my opinion, would be measuring an astronomical event."

"But wouldn't it be boring if they were just predicting something like the return of a comet?" Tina asked.

"Not at all," Abby answered. "A 5,600 year cycling comet would be fantastic! It would tell us a lot about the universe and our solar system — and about the true astronomical abilities of ancient peoples. No matter what comes out of this, if the Maya did predict something — anything — I think it'll be a huge boon to science."

"Well, what about comets?" Dominic asked. "Could there really be one with such a long cycle?"

Abby weighed it. "Possible, but unlikely," she said. "It'd have one hell of a path. Comet Haley has the longest orbit we know of now, with a 76-year return, and there's no evidence that the Maya knew about it. I can't imagine that when the Long Count was created their civilization would have been around long enough to take notice of a repeating comet, keep written records, and predict its return. Certainly not for a 5,000-year cycle."

"A lot of ancient records and texts mention astronomical events that could be interpreted as comets," Steve commented.

"There *are* a few with extended orbits," Abby said. "Comet Ikeya-Zhang was discovered in 2002; there's reason to believe it could be the 'famed comet of 1532' that the Aztecs and Incas saw. It was so brilliant they saw it in the daytime."

"That one showed up around the same time the Spaniards did," Dominic added. "The natives took it as a portent of the gods."

"Five hundred years is a long time," Abby said. "But a 5,000 year cycle is a hell of a stretch. The comet would have an extremely irregular orbit, one that flies clear out beyond Pluto and then circles back. Its orbit would be highly elliptical; when it circled back close enough to Earth for us to see it, it would come very close to the sun. The heat would melt the ice of the comet, and there might not be enough of it left to make a return trip. In any case, it might not even have enough mass to stay attached to our sun."

"Plus, what would the significance be?" Dante asked. "Why build a whole calendar around the re-emergence of a comet?"

"Comets have always been seen as messages from the gods," Dominic explained. "When a strange light appeared in the sky thousands — even hundreds — of years ago, it was seen as a sign or an omen. It would have been recorded, if the ancient people had a system of recording. If not in writing, then certainly in their oral history."

"Heck, people still see comets as mysterious and meaningful," Tina reminded them. "Look at all the hoopla that surrounded Hale-Bopp in 1996; cults, a mass suicide. Even so-called 'normal' people thought there was something anomalous about it."

"Regardless," Dante said thoughtfully, "if it was a comet, then it was a natural event. There'd be records of it throughout history. Why wouldn't anyone have found it before now?"

"There aren't many records that extend as far back as the Long Count," Steve explained. "The Chinese, Egyptians, Greeks and Romans all had written histories – but only of events that happened to them. It's difficult to try to match events from one culture with something that may not have been visible from a different hemisphere."

"And there are no records whatsoever that extend back ten thousand years," Dominic said. "The comet would have had to have been noted back at the beginning of our recorded history. Maybe oral tradition would've mentioned it, but I have a hard time believing the connection would have been made five thousand years later. As Abby said, such a comet wouldn't have a lot of mass. There wouldn't be anything startling about it, nothing that would cause them to remember it and mark it for dozens of centuries. Not when brighter comets appeared more frequently."

Dante tipped back in his chair. "By your reasoning, Dominic, I'm hard pressed to believe that the Long Count could have recorded *anything* natural," he said.

"Maybe they weren't recording," Steve said. "Maybe they were making some type of long-term prediction. The Long Count could be a prediction, not a studied measurement."

"No one has any way of knowing what will happen five thousand years from now," Abby said. "We don't even know if human life will survive another five thousand years. It doesn't make sense."

"How do you know they weren't psychic?" Tina asked.

"Aside from the fact that never in the history of man has a psychic passed an unbiased double-blind test in controlled conditions — do you think a whole race of people could have been psychic?" Abby asked.

Dominic smiled. "Some cultures are or were very spiritual. Look at Native Americans."

"Sure, drug induced spiritual visions," Abby said. "If we were all sitting down here smoking peyote, we might have an answer by now."

The others laughed, but Dominic just shrugged. "The Mayan High Priests had a regular practice of drug use," he said. "Supposedly, these induced Shamanistic visions enabled the spiritual leaders to meet with otherworldly spirits, to travel to another plane."

"I refuse to even entertain that," Dante said. "If they took drugs, they weren't on another cosmic level anymore than LSD-tripping hippies were throughout the seventies. Drugs change the chemicals in your brain; they don't open doors to other dimensions or enable humans to see other planes of existence – they just alter our perception of what actually exists. I can't believe the Maya calculated all this to conjecture some chance occurrence, or to make a vague prediction like Nostradamus or Edgar Cayce. I think the calendar means something; it's a record of a specific length of time, start to finish, that was either recording something happening within that time, or building up to a specific event."

Dominic smiled. "Okay, so let's not consider the effects of any mind-expanding drugs as the sole basis of the Long Count. What else could be out there?"

Abby shook her head. "Anything destructive enough to annihilate the Earth this near in the future would be tracked already. And if it was going to just come out of nowhere and blow us away, then the ancient Maya couldn't have predicted it."

"What about supernovas?" Dominic asked.

Abby looked up. "Have you heard of HR 8210?" she asked. Dominic nodded, but the others looked blank.

"It's the closest white dwarf to our solar system," Abby explained, "and it's a huge one, with a greater mass than our Sun. If it goes supernova while it's this close to us, it'll wipe out all life on Earth — just vaporize us.

"The radiation and cosmic rays would destroy the ozone layer in minutes. Our whole ecosystem would be destroyed. The gamma-ray burst itself would be brief, but the cosmic rays would slam into us and bathe the planet in muons. Muons penetrate thousands of feet into the rock; even deep-sea creatures will die from the radiation."

"When the hell is that supposed to happen?" Simon asked in disbelief.

They glanced towards the doorway to see Simon standing there with folded arms. They had left him to sleep in, knowing how tired he was from his drive home the night before, and no one had noticed him come in.

"Sometime soon, they think," Abby said. She noticed the stricken expressions on the others' faces, and quickly corrected herself. "Soon, astronomically speaking, could mean anywhere from hundreds to millions of years from now. All we know now is that there's a white dwarf about 150 light years away, which is well inside what's deemed to be the safe zone for a supernova —160 to 200 light years away. If it goes up while it's within that range, we're done. If, with time, it passes into the safe zone first, we'll get some violent – even devastating – backlash, but it probably won't completely destroy our planetary system. The problem is, we don't know when its time is up."

"What are the odds of it?" Tina asked.

Abby shook her head. "Right now, there are no odds. It still needs to accumulate more mass. But it's not altogether unlikely — something similar has occurred in our neighborhood at least once before. Scorpius-Centaurus went supernova about two million years ago, causing a mass extinction of marine life."

Dante was nodding. "That's right," he concurred. "The geological record shows the supernova's fallout changed the Earth's mineral makeup, deposited some heavy isotopes into the geological layering."

"And that was twice as far away from us when it went up as HR 8210 is now," Abby continued. "But that's not the worst thing. The rate of mass global extinctions on Earth coincides with supernova explosions. Scientists are pretty sure they're caused by gamma rays from super-massive, collapsing stars, which are all over the place, sending out gamma ray bursts pretty consistently. Right now, the closest we know of is Eta Carinae — you can see it in the southern hemisphere; I'll point it out next time you're out by my scope. But it's facing away from us. Sooner or later, there'll be one we're in the path of, and when it hits, it'll hit with a lethal dose of radiation that will penetrate so deep into the oceans and rocks that you can consider life on Earth to be done for a long, long time.

"Anyway, the rate is every 100 million years or so that we get hit. We're due up again soon."

"Shit," Simon said. "I need a beer."

They watched as he turned in the doorway and left, heading back up to the kitchen.

Dominic smiled. "He doesn't much like to face the idea of his own mortality, does he?"

She laughed. "Not in the least. He still thinks he's invincible."

Dante shook his head. "What torture that would be for the rest of us."

12.19.15.7.1

June 6, 2008 — "Look, if I want to do it my way, just let me," Simon said.

"No one has a problem with you doing anything your way." Dominic answered. "I just don't want to waste time. The dates are correct. We need a mathematician to make sense of the numbers, not play around confirming things we already know."

"If you're so goddamn smart why don't you figure it out yourself?"

"Because you're confusing intelligence with frame of reference," Dominic answered calmly. "The most intelligent man on Earth can't work with something he doesn't have a background in. I can't work with something I've never seen before, and we don't have the time for me to go out and learn it. That's why I need you guys; you've spent your lives building up a frame of reference and knowledge about what we need to know."

"Then you'll get it when I've got a background that satisfies me. And not before."

When Dominic stood up, Simon drew back slightly, then looked relieved when Dominic turned and headed for the door. "I'm walking out to Izapa," he said. "Anyone want to come?"

"I'll go," Tina said, and Abby stood up with her. She gave Simon a guilty glance, but he waved her off.

"Go," he said. "Maybe you'll learn something. Just don't look at anything Ciriello already knows about — we can't waste precious time."

Dominic didn't reply, simply opened the door and walked out. Tina followed closely on his heels, with Abby right behind her. After a moment, Steve stood up and followed them out.

Simon sat back and laughed.

"Why must you be so disrespectful?" Dante said, his dark brows stitched together.

70

"Why must I?" Simon repeated. "I must, because I can. Look at this," he waved a hand over the room. "We're living on the trust fund of someone who has gathered us all to work on some crazy idea because he has no ability to do it himself, and he's kept us cut off from the world while we work our asses off for him. Who knows what he has planned for us when we're done?

"And besides that, how does he expect us to work in these conditions? We have one computer and internet access only when the weather is good. We're not even in touch with the real world."

"Well, that's what we have you for, isn't it?" Dante replied. "You're at a major university three to five days a week. And so far you're the least relevant person on this project. Can't you at least print off a web page for us?"

Simon colored, his fists clenching. "The least relevant? You son-of-a-bitch, I'm the one that'll solve this thing. You and Steve can go out there and talk to the goddamn natives for the next ten years, but I'll be front-page news by then. You wait and see — if I'm the only one who can get to the internet, why do I need to tell you what I find out? What's to stop me from keeping this whole fucking project to myself and then going public alone with the answer?"

"We're all on the same team, Simon," Dante said slowly. "We can't start keeping things from each other or we'll all be stuck out in this jungle until the end of time."

"I thought that was the idea," Simon said. He turned on his heel and stalked out of the room.

Abby heard a sound behind her as they entered the forest, and she glanced back to see Simon crossing the clearing. "Hey guys, wait up," she said to the others, and they stopped to let him catch up. As they waited, they saw Dante trailing behind him. Soon, they were a complete group again, and they passed through the perimeter of the woods, heading into the jungle.

"You sure you know where you're going, Ciriello?" Simon called, glancing nervously around him. They were only a few dozen yards into the trees, yet they could no longer see anything outside the jungle.

"Sure," Dominic replied without pausing. "Done this a hundred times."

Simon made a noise in his throat, but no one turned to look at him. Abby felt a little claustrophobic herself inside the thick forest surrounding them, but she trusted Dominic. He was far in the lead, chatting with Steve and Dante, pointing at some landmark only he could discern. Tina strayed behind them, enjoying the beauty of the rain forest, slowing to wait for Simon and Abby to catch up.

"I can't believe how easy it is to walk through here," Abby said, surprised.

"It's the canopy," Tina said. "It prevents a thick cover of undergrowth and keeps the base of the trees pretty clear."

"It's nice," Simon said, sounding unexpectedly mellow. "Have you spent a lot of time in the rain forests?"

"Yeah," Tina answered, "I've done a lot of research in Central America, working on overgrown Mayan sites." They fell into easy conversation, Simon and Abby attentive and interested as Tina regaled them with stories of hidden, ancient temples.

A short time later, they were standing in the ruins of Izapa.

"Look at this stela," Dominic said, pointing it out to them. There was a small tour group nearby, and Dominic spoke quietly so as not to draw their attention as he instructed his team. "Stelae are always read top to bottom, left to right, all the way down. The Mayan rulers were named after various creatures found in the local geography, with names like Jaguar Paw and Smoking Frog. These names were also used as day-names in the Long Count. This is yet another reason why scholars place the Count's beginning at Izapa: it's the only location where all the animals used as day-names are native.

"It's also the only site at the right latitude that dates back to the birth of the calendar," he continued. "Izapa is the only place in North America where the 260-day cycle can be measured by the sun's position. There are no Long Count dates found in Izapa, but this the birthplace of the Count – if not the calendar itself, of the knowledge that went into creating it."

They moved from stela to stela, with Dominic interpreting them as they made their way through the site. Tina and Steve had been there many times before with their friend, but they stayed mostly silent and let him speak. His knowledge was evident and his excitement contagious; the small tour group wandering through the site eventually attached themselves to the research group, listening to Dominic as he detailed the archaeological and anthropological significance of the site. He was obviously enjoying himself; not for the attention, but for the love of the subject.

They spent most of the day there, but as the dinner hour approached, the tour group left in their small bus, leaving Izapa to the scientists.

"Man, I thought they were going to ask for your autograph," Tina joked, nudging Dominic with her elbow.

"Screw the autograph, I was hoping they'd at least tip me," he responded.

"Does that happen often?" Dante asked.

Dominic shrugged. "You spend enough time at Mayan ruins and you run into tourists. Usually, everyone does their own thing. I usually know more than the guides, though, so they sometimes tag along with me."

Dante smiled. "I get hit up a lot when I'm working anyplace touristy," he said. "Most geological surveys are done far from civilization, but when tourists run into us and hear us talking, they think they've hit the jackpot."

"I don't mind," Dominic said. "I like that people are interested."

"This is warm and fuzzy and all, but it's going to get dark soon, and it's going to be pitch black under that jungle canopy. Don't you think we should be heading back soon?" Simon said.

"You afraid of the dark?" Dante asked with a bemused glance.

"No, I'm not," Simon retorted. He gave Dominic a diffident wave. "I'm just thinking of our leader here telling us about the indigenous animals. I'm personally not thrilled about knowing that the local wildlife consists of alligators, jaguars and other things that would rather eat me than run."

"Well, there aren't a whole lot of alligators walking around in the woods," Dominic answered, "but you're right; it is going to get dark before long. The jungle ceiling keeps out most of the moonlight, and none of us brought a flashlight. Let's head on back."

They stayed in a close group on the return leg, within a few feet of each other, and conversation was easier.

"Imagine that you're Mayan," Dominic was saying, "sitting around your temple, one hundred years before Christ. What could be in your cultural memory from three thousand years before, something so significant that would justify anchoring your calendar on it?"

"It would have to be catastrophic," Dante said.

"Why?" Steve asked, interested. "We based our frame of time reference on the birth of our purported savior. Some people on this planet might blame Christianity for everything from slavery, misogyny, racism, religious intolerance and homophobia to the deaths of millions of people during the inquisition, the Crusades, the Holocaust, you name it. But most people see the birth of Christ as the saving grace of humanity."

"That's true," Dominic said. "But we as a race don't have any definite cultural knowledge of anything specific that happened three thousand years ago. All we have to go by are broken historical records from civilizations we know virtually nothing about. I think we have to assume that the Maya did the same. They either had a legend of some distant catastrophic event, or they based their calendar on something significant that changed their world — the end of an era, or the birth of a savior."

"But we know the Mayan creation legend," Tina protested. "They believed in multiple gods and talking animals. There was no creator god. There was no prophet or savior."

"Well, there was Kulkulcan," Steve said.

"Who was that?" Dante asked.

"Both man and myth," Steve responded. "He lived about 2,000 years ago, and was said to have descended from Heaven. He was said to be able to heal the sick and resurrect the dead."

"You sure you have your religions right?" Abby asked with a smile.

Steve smiled in return. "Interesting, isn't it? Even aside from those things, Kulkulcan was an oddity. Think about the modern-day controversy surrounding Jesus. Christ was a Middle Eastern man, a Jew, yet since his story was first recorded, most cultures painted him as Caucasian. Kulkulcan had a similar issue — he was described as having white skin, a beard, and emerald green eyes. Definitely not a Mayan.

"Anyway," Steve continued, "one day Kulkulcan set off for the East … supposedly, walked right across the water. He promised he'd return again someday."

"Now I know you're confused," Dante said.

Steve laughed. "Well, neither Christ nor Kulkulcan has returned yet, as far as we know. Kulkulcan said he'd be back on the first day of the 52-year cycle. That would have been in 1519 AD. He didn't come back, but someone else did."

"Wait a minute," Tina interrupted. "I thought that legend was about Quetzlcoatl."

"In Aztec, Quetzlcoatl," Dominic said. "In Mayan, Kulkulcan. To the Inca, he was known as Viracocha. Same story, same man, if you believe their descriptions of him. Same time period. All the ancient Indian cultures put him in their histories at almost the exact same time, just about 2,000 years ago. He was a god come to Earth; he could walk on water and work miracles."

"He didn't happen to be a virgin birth, did he?" Simon asked.

"Not Kulkulcan," Dominic said. "Huitzilopochtli – Blue Hummingbird on the Left – did, though. He was the Aztec god of the sun, born of a virgin birth; his sisters and brothers were horrified that their mother was pregnant in such a mysterious way and tried to kill her, but Huitzilopochtli was born, and he killed his sister, then threw her head up to the heavens where it became the moon."

"Jesus God," Simon croaked, "where did these people come up with this stuff?"

"Doesn't matter," Dominic said. "It's an Aztec story, so it's not important to us or the Long Count. We're talking about Kulkulcan. They say that Kulkulcan – their Feathered Serpent god – descended to Earth by a rope ladder, climbing down from the sky to bring civilization to Mexico."

"Descended from where?" Simon asked. "The clouds? A spaceship?"

"The Maya say he descended from a hole in the sky," Dominic explained. "That's why when Cortez arrived, there was no struggle against him. Cortez was a white man who came from the east, at the precise time Kulkulcan had promised fifteen centuries earlier that he would return. The Maya naturally thought he was their god returning to Earth. But whereas Kulkulcan brought life, culture, and civilization, Cortez brought destruction and death. They thought he was a deity, but he was just another European explorer, spreading his own religion and culture and killing off the Central American civilizations."

"Killing off, my ass." Simon said drolly. "The Europeans brought civilization and Christianity to a backwards country."

Dominic shook his head. "At that time, the Central Americans were more advanced than the Europeans."

Simon was about to speak, but Abby, sensing another argument, quickly spoke up. "So if they weren't basing it on their religious beginnings, maybe they were using the actual beginning of their civilization, three thousand years earlier?"

"The oldest traceable sign of organized Mayan culture is a great deal younger than that," Dominic told her. "Izapa is one of the oldest sites; there's some evidence that it may have even been *pre*-Mayan. Some of the oldest relics from Izapa may be Olmec — a mysterious people who were around even before the Maya, Aztecs and Inca. Even so, the oldest date markers are from about 1500 BCE — not even close to the 3114 BCE start date of the Long Count."

"So if it was religious or personality-based, we're looking at what was probably a myth, a legend," Dante said.

"I think so," Dominic said. "It's the only way a story would stand the ravages of time to keep it alive through three thousand years. Our records that survive that length of time mostly reference politics and rulers, like Chinese emperors or Egyptian kings; or great legends, like Noah's flood." He stepped carefully over a large log, pausing on the other side to wait for the others to climb over it. Abby couldn't remember the log from their earlier trip through the forest on the way to Izapa, and she was amazed at how Dominic seemed to know his way; without a compass, map, or even a path through the brush, he strolled through the jungle like a man on a walking trail. It was only after everyone had safely made it over the obstacle that Dominic continued:

"You have to remember, they had no permanent way to keep records, at least not until the first glyphs, which are much younger than that. They did use paper and have written texts in later Mayan civilization, but those are long gone, and didn't exist at all back at the beginning of Mayan history. They probably went at least a thousand years without any permanent written record. Anything prior to that would have had to have been handed down by word of mouth."

It was much darker under the tree canopy, and they stepped carefully, keeping watch for unseen hazards. After a few minutes of walking in silence, Abby finally spoke up.

"Maybe this has nothing to do with a memory or story of an event. Maybe the beginning date wasn't as important as the end date. Perhaps they could calculate backwards," she suggested. "Today, we use our knowledge of astronomy, chemistry, and geology to calculate things that happened billions of years ago. If they were able to predict eclipses, the movements of constellations and the orbits of planets, then maybe they counted backwards an entire world age to anchor their framing of time."

"That's another idea," Dominic agreed with a smile. "And it has merit. Abby, I would love if you could look through some of my books back in the lab – if you can determine just how astronomically advanced they were, maybe we can establish their ability to adjust backwards to make predictions."

"Sounds good," she replied. "I just hope we can find something notable that they'd have calculated back to."

"Well, that's why we're here," Dominic said, "to see where the evidence leads us. Without evidence, the options are just about endless."

"So, let's try to narrow it down," Dante said. "Say it was a catastrophe. What could they have been talking about? What lines up with the autumn equinox of 3114 BCE?"

"That's the problem," Dominic sighed. "I've been through everything. Nothing fits."

"You've looked at the geological record?" Dante asked.

Dominic shrugged. "Not to know what I was looking at," he said. "Dante, you mentioned the deposition of isotopes from a past supernova – could you line up the start date with anything like that?"

"If there's something there, sure," Dante said. "Just because something wasn't recorded by an existing culture at that time doesn't mean it didn't happen; the Earth itself keeps a record. I'll start looking at geological histories, the earth record."

"Dominic has tried earthquakes, volcanic eruptions, all sorts of known occurrences," Tina said, "and he hasn't been able to place anything in that time frame."

"It doesn't have to necessarily have been a cataclysm for us, or anything that would have left a huge mark on our world today," Dante said. "The earth record can show us evidence of all sorts of things; chemical changes, for example, that might show the eruption of a volcano on the other side of the world, or the impact of an asteroid. We can date the evidence to put it within a certain time frame. For us, maybe it would mean nothing, but to an ancient people it could have been a significant event in their young history."

Abby was shaking her head. "The fall equinox is an astronomical reference. It starts on an equinox and ends on a solstice. They're astronomical dates. It wouldn't be a reference to anything geological."

"Maybe the start date is coincidental," Simon said, finally joining the conversation. "We can look at two views of the first Long Count date: One, that the Count starts on the fall equinox because of the astronomy; or two, that the date is arbitrary, and the event they were basing it on happened to fall coincidentally on that date. I would recommend that we avoid starting with either concept in mind, and just follow the evidence."

Dominic nodded, but Simon looked deep in thought. For the first time since Simon's arrival, Dominic thought he saw the intelligence behind the man's pompous façade.

"Agreed," he said. "I don't want any of us to try to guess at the answer, because then we'll just be trying to find facts that fit it. We can't discount something because it doesn't fit into what we want to believe."

Dante nodded in the darkness. "I'll look through the geological evidence and let you know what I come up with. Abby, if you look at the astronomical evidence and see if anything meaningful emerges, maybe we'll get lucky and converge on the same date."

"How can you look at astronomical history?" Tina asked. "It doesn't leave a physical marker, like an earthquake or something would."

"There's a lot we still see," Abby answered, "or can trace backwards. We can look at the microwave background radiation to calculate the age of the universe; we know what positions heavenly bodies are in, and can extrapolate their movements backwards. We know how gases and solids form, and from which elements, and can use scientific measurements to calculate from where – and when – specific types of matter formed, which elements were involved, and what pressures and temperatures were necessary.

"Granted," she said, "we're going to have a hard time finding evidence if it was something like a meteor shower or an asteroid; that'll come back to Dante's field of expertise. I've started considering the possibility of an asteroid. They return in comet-like orbits, and wouldn't have the melting problem that an icy body like a comet would. Asteroids are harder to find, though, and their orbits can change quite a bit over time, due to the planets' gravitational influence. The asteroid Hermes, for example, was last seen in 1937; then we lost it for 66 years before it was spotted again in 2003. It looks now like it's actually a pair of asteroids and not just one; either way, it travels on an elliptical orbit deep into the inner solar system. It's already passed within 378,000 miles of us — a hair's breadth in astronomical terms – but with its trajectory, it won't crash into the Earth for millions more years. And since it actually crosses Venus' orbit, odds are good it'll hit Venus before it would strike us."

"Even if it doesn't hit us, could one come back on a decreasing orbit, maybe to get closer and closer until just its proximity causes global devastation?" Tina asked.

"Its gravitational pull wouldn't be disastrous, although it could cause some problems with the tides – flooding, tsunamis, and so on, depending on its size," Abby responded. "But I don't think it'd fit with the Long Count's time frame."

"Even if the Maya backdated?" Dominic asked. "Say they observed a couple passages of it over a period of a couple hundred years. Maybe they calculated back to figure out when it had struck the Earth last — or came to its closest point— or possibly even when it was furthest away. There are many possibilities, none of which would require them to have been eyewitnesses to the event over millennia."

"But that's the problem," Abby argued, "this asteroid, or whatever it was, probably wouldn't have been visible with the naked eye. Unless it was the size of the one that killed the dinosaurs, a heavenly body so far away to take thousands of years of orbiting to get close enough to impact the Earth would've been too far away at that point for them to see. If it was closer than that, modern astronomers would've spotted it centuries ago, and if there was a pattern bringing it closer and closer to Earth, we certainly would've noticed. Don't forget, there are hundreds of thousands of eyes attuned to the heavens every night. Comets, asteroids, even moons of planets have been discovered by amateur astronomers with their backyard telescopes. The likelihood of such a thing being missed is slim. But back then, why would the Maya have noticed a recurring asteroid, even if they could see such a thing?"

"Anything that changed in the sky would've caught their attention," Steve said, "and in almost all ancient cultures, astronomical events would've been viewed in a religious light. The 'star' the three wise men saw has been theorized as a comet, or a bright convergence of planets." He thought for a moment, then added, "If there was such an event, it might be in the biblical record. Do you have the alignment of dates I can look at?"

"I have a computer program," Dominic said. "It can help you with the alignment dates, but you're on your own with the biblical references. I don't know a catechism from a cataclysm anymore."

Steve nodded, deep in thought. "There are a number of references I can think of right off," he said. "What year was it when Joshua made the sun and moon stand still?"

"You really think at some point the Earth literally stopped spinning?" Simon asked, batting away a heavy tree branch, then ducking as it snapped back towards him.

"Well, that's what the Bible says."

"The Bible says a lot of stupid things," Simon retorted. "It says that three thousand years ago, God created the Earth in six days and a talking snake got Adam and Eve thrown out of paradise. Don't tell me you're a literalist."

"Hey," Steve said, "I'm just trying to come up with some context for what we're talking about – something that might've been recorded. Is it possible?"

Abby shook her head. "If the Earth stopped for even a millisecond it'd have killed every living thing on the planet," she said. "The universe is in constant motion. Planets and other heavenly bodies can't just stop in their tracks. They're spinning for a reason: because there's nothing to stop them. Even if there was some outside influence, the drag to slow them down would be incredible, and would take millennia for them to come to a full stop. If they did eventually slow down and come to a halt, the consequences would be devastating."

"Such as?" Steve asked.

"If the Earth stopped moving in its orbit, it would fall into the sun in just under 65 days."

"Well, it didn't stop for 65 days; it just stopped for a few hours, right?" Tina said.

"Not possible," Abby responded. "If a heavenly body suddenly lurched to a stop, that'd be the end of it. Not only would it hurl every-thing off of it — don't forget, we're moving at 67,000 miles an hour —

but it wouldn't have any stimulus to start moving again. If it stops, it stays stopped."

"Not even the hand of God?"

Abby smiled. "We're trying to base this on science, aren't we? Verifiable facts? If we're going on faith, then we might as well stop right now. If you believe the Bible as fact, then no hypothesis would be out of the question. 'With God, all things are possible,' and all that."

"True," Steve added, "But the Bible says the sun and the moon stood still, not the Earth."

"Maybe that's why nothing is living on the moon," Tina suggested. "If it stopped moving, everything would have been flung into space."

Abby tried to suppress a smile. "In the book of Joshua, people still believed that the sun and the moon were placed in the firmament, which rotated around the Earth. We're not talking about a scientific concept here, but the mythology of a relatively primitive people who were trying to explain the world the best they could with what they had to work with at the time."

"Besides," Dominic added, "No other ancient texts make any mention of it. There were several civilizations going at that time, including the Chinese, who kept excellent written astronomical records, and they made no mention of anything out of the ordinary."

"Some people say everything that's recorded in the Bible is historically and literally accurate," Steve said.

"And most people don't," Abby answered. "People always pick and choose which stories out of the Bible they consider truth and those they consider allegory. Most people won't say everything in there is literal. It can't be; there are too many contractions. And word of God or not, mutually exclusive things can't both be true. Two different versions of the creation story; two different versions of Noah's ark; four different versions of the Resurrection — they can't all be true. You can't base scientific theory on cultural myths."

"But that's what we're doing," Dante said. "We're studying a culture to find out about something they wrote. It has to be done to give it context; a frame of reference, an insight into their way of thinking and living."

"Yes, but we're trying to study within the same culture," she said, concentrating on Dominic's back, barely visible ahead of her. The darkness was growing heavier, and she tried to stay as close on his heels as possible. "We shouldn't bring in stories from other cultures and try to make them match."

"But what if they correlate?" Steve said. "If several cultural myths support each other, it could be meaningful."

"Okay," Abby finally said, "Bring me a Bible and show me the passage you guys are talking about regarding the sun and moon standing still. Let me see what kind of reference it could possibly have to anything and we'll figure out a date."

"Sorry, guys, I don't have one," Dominic said. "Anyone else?"

The others shook their heads, indiscernible in the darkness. Still, from their silence their answer was clear.

"What, no one here has a Bible?" Simon said lightly. "What kind of scientists are you?"

"Well, that can be your first homework assignment," Dante said. "Bring us a Bible from the university library."

Simon looked up at him sharply, about to speak, then seemed to think better of it. "No problem," he said.

Dominic didn't notice; the others were behind him, and his thoughts were elsewhere. "What made you think of that, Steve? Why Joshua?"

"We were talking about a cataclysm," Steve said. "You and Tina and I have been studying the geography and archeology of this area for a long time, and we know the history of the volcano Tacana. There closest eruption around that time was about 14,000 BC. There were no floods, earthquakes, or anything else of significance that we think they'd anchor their timeline on. So what could be so catastrophic?"

"You weren't thinking of a local catastrophe, were you?" Dante asked. "You were thinking of a global cataclysm."

"Yes," he said. "After all, we think this was an event that'd been passed down through the ages. Every culture on the planet has stories like that, whether they had a written language or not. Most often, they're creation stories and flood myths. I thought maybe a tidal wave had hit or something. If this date was to be used as the beginning of a cycle, or an age, or their civilization, it had to be something major."

"But what could cause a global catastrophe that no one else on the planet noticed?" Tina asked. "Dominic, you've checked other references. There isn't a record of anything like that."

No one answered, and they finally came out of the woods and into the clearing Abby had claimed for her telescope. They headed across the field in a loose bunch, towards the darkened lab and house. At least out here the stars lit the path and they could see each other as more than shadows in the darkness. They trooped over the narrow land-bridge above the lagoon, quiet until they'd made it across. The path didn't seem hazardous by day, but at night it was impossible to see the edges, and too easy to imagine tumbling down the rocky slope to the pond below.

"I need to check something when we get back to the lab," Steve said when they'd reached the other side. "I remember one of these books

I was looking through when Dominic and I were packing up to move here had something in it about wooly mammoths."

"What about them?" Dante asked.

"They found bodies of wooly mammoths in Siberia, perfectly preserved, completely untouched by predators."

"Maybe they just keeled over and died," Simon said.

"They were flash-frozen," Steve said. "Some still had fresh green grass half-chewed in their mouths that they were eating when they died. Like something happened so suddenly, so immediate, that they died before they had a chance to swallow. There was undigested palm grass from tropical locales in their stomachs: the vegetation they were eating was plant life that was never found in those frozen climates."

"So you think, what? The poles suddenly reversed? Hot to cold, cold to hot, in a microsecond?" Dante asked.

"It would explain why the dinosaurs all seemed to die off at once," Tina suggested. "Abby said a sudden movement of the Earth would've killed all life on it."

"Then why are we here?" Simon asked. "Why is anything?"

"Some things always survive," Dante said. "The death of the dinosaurs was one of the most important changes on this planet – it enabled mammals to rise up as the dominant species. One possible explanation for the regular periods of mass extinction on this Earth is a pole shift."

"So now we have to figure out what killed the dinosaurs?" Abby asked.

"Or at least those wooly mammoths," Steve said. He smiled, barely visible in the starlight. No light came from the house or the lab; they had left in daylight, and had not left any lights burning.

"I'm going up to my room," Simon said as the lab came into view. "Let me know if you guys ever start talking about the numbers behind the count."

"We *have* talked about the numbers," Dominic said. "I gave them to you on the first day."

"You gave me a bunch of numbers with little reference. What do you want me to do with them?" Simon tried to maintain a calm, rational tone. "I have random numbers with no connection to anything. I know the numbers of the Count, the numbers of the days, but I don't know what you want from me. Take any number from the Count; any day, month, week or year. Take the full length of the Count; take any of these numbers. Should I just be trying to divide them in and out of one another? Should I look for similar references in nature or in history?

"I can do calculations forever, but they're not going to mean anything until we get some context. Taking the numbers from the Count means nothing. 20, 400, 144,000. What do you want me to do with them?"

"Jehovah's Witnesses believe that there are only 144,000 places in Heaven reserved for the faithful," Steve commented.

"Then why the hell are they still trying to convert me?" Dante asked.

Steve smiled. "I guess the others get a special place in the paradise on Earth, or something. But Heaven only has 144,000 berths."

"What does that have to do with anything?" Simon asked in frustration.

"Look, I'm just putting it out there," Steve said. "Simon, you have numbers, and we have knowledge of a lot of different disciplines. We're looking for connections. And the Long Count is as based in religious dogma as it is secular history. We can look for similar references in different cultures; as contradictory as different religions are, there may be some grain of truth in each of them."

"Comparative religion is your area, Steve," Tina said. "But as far as my knowledge goes, I don't think we're going to find much similarity between polytheistic Mayan society and monotheistic religions like Judaism or Islam."

"Religion is religion, worldwide," Steve said. "All cultures look for answers to the big questions, like what happens after death, and answers to smaller questions, like, what is that bright light in the sky? It's interesting that there are so many different explanations and beliefs, and that each group of faithful believes that his or her own is the one true religion – which is obviously impossible, since they're all mutually exclusive. Either Christ was the savior, or he wasn't. Either Islam is the one true faith and all infidels will perish in flame, or it isn't, and they won't. They can't all be true," Steve said. "But, if we can find certain features of each one that are immutable and exact, then maybe we can get to the starting point."

"Is that what you're doing here?" Simon asked. "Trying to establish the one true religion? *Christ.*"

Steve only smiled. "We're all here for our own reasons, aren't we, Simon? I simply find the Long Count interesting to my own research."

Before Simon could answer, Dominic interrupted again, trying to get them back on topic before a free-for-all began. "Steve, I agree: we need to establish a starting point," he said. "Simon, that's all we're trying to do right now; our methods and pathways of getting there might be different, but we're all trying to get to the same place."

"Please, you guys are talking about the damn dinosaurs. Hello, they died off a couple million years before the dates we're concerned with."

Dominic shrugged. "You have a point," he admitted.

"Damn straight I do," Simon said. "So, do you want to talk about the start date, or not? Can we talk about something other than Jehovah's Witnesses or anything else that has nothing to do with the Long Count?"

"We can't say that it doesn't," Steve said. "Many people believe that everything is interconnected."

"Since when is belief evidence?" Simon answered crossly. "Belief means bullshit to me. I want to talk solid facts. Numbers. Give me something I can work with. If the Long Count is a code, then I need to have some information I can apply if I'm going to break it."

"What about the Bible Code?" Steve asked.

"The *what?*" Simon turned to him with a look of confusion and irritation, visible even in the darkness.

"The Bible Code," Steve said, and there was a smile in his voice.

Dominic couldn't tell if he was kidding or not, but he thought it was time to put an end to the argument before it got out of hand. "It's a mathematical code worked out a few decades ago," he said, holding the lab door open to let the others pass. Once inside, he hit the light switch; the fluorescents flickered for a moment and then stayed on. "Supposedly, if you create a matrix of the words of the Bible, and pick out letters that are a set number apart, it forms words," he said. "Prophecies, predictions. Supposedly predicted the assassination of Yitzhak Rabin."

"That's complete bullshit," Simon said. "You can do that with any book, with any set of numbers. It's just chance and probability, and the fact that the alphabet only has a set number of letters. You're bound to come out with some words and phrases that seem more than coincidental. Especially if you're looking for the prediction after the fact; you find things that make sense according to what you already know."

"I have to agree with you," Dominic responded mildly. "The words found aren't generally real words; they're abbreviations, letters that *could* be words if you added a few vowels, or a consonant or two, and you know what you want them to say. It's basically open to the interpretation of whoever happens to be applying the code. All the 'predictions' *have* occurred after the fact, which makes them useless, and basically meaningless. Anyone can go back in history and pick out things that they consider prophetic, knowing what they know now.

"Besides, a critical researcher found the same phenomena in Moby Dick; actually post-predicted quite a few assassinations from it, if I remember correctly. People have played with other long tomes to prove the point — War and Peace was one of them, I think. You're right, Simon; it's just the product of chance."

"Than why even bring it up if everyone knows it's bullshit?"

"Not everyone," Steve spoke up again. "Believe it or not, the U.S. Pentagon actually used the Bible Code prior to Operation Iraqi Freedom in 2003. Apparently they thought that the outcome of the new Holy War in the Mid-East was set forth in the Bible."

"Oh, Christ," Simon said dismissively. "Our country is run by idiots. Big surprise. Now can we *please* talk about things that are based in fact? Please?"

Dominic smiled. "Since you asked so nicely," he said. "Anyone?"

"I'm kind of interested in something you mentioned before," Tina said, looking towards Dante. "You said something about a pole shift. What is that? What does it mean?"

"The poles usually align with the Earth's axis; they're created by the molten iron inside the Earth's core," Dante explained. "The core is well over four thousand miles across. The outer third or so is liquid, which swirls with the planet's rotation. This liquid iron magma rises and falls in waves, generating the magnetism of the poles."

"Why would they shift, then?"

"The molten core circulates. There's a lot of turbulence in there, so the magnetic field isn't steady, and the poles won't always be in the same place. Parts of the outer core will cool and sink, and the hotter liquid will rise. Sometimes we don't even have a dipole; we have poles all over the place. Sometimes the poles switch places altogether."

"How can you know that?" Tina asked, fascinated.

"We look at minerals," he said. "We measure the magnetism of ancient rocks. Geologists might just be looking at chemicals, rocks and dirt, but we're actually studying the Earth's history," he said with a smile. "From what we can tell, the last reversal was about 780,000 years ago."

"Was it sudden?" Steve asked. "That's why mammoths in Siberia were found with palm leaves in their stomachs?"

Dante smiled. "Sorry, Steve. It happened over a period of thousands of years. Your mammoths are a mystery."

"How do we know if it'll happen again?" Tina asked.

"Oh, it'll definitely happen again. In fact, satellite data shows there are some anomalies happening right now. They've been going on for quite awhile now – close to two hundred years. Canada's North Pole is moving steadily towards Russia. South Africa has a large magnetic patch pointing in the direction opposite the rest of the Earth's field."

"Will it cause a pole flip?"

"Eventually," Dante said. "The main magnetic field will fade away, and reappear later with the opposite polarity. If it keeps growing at the rate it is, our dipole will completely shift in a few thousand years."

"Why do we care about the Earth's magnetic field?" Simon said. "So the poles flip. We build new compasses. End of story."

"It's not that simple," Dante explained. "The magnetic field protects us from cosmic radiation. A reversal could damage satellites and the space station, as well as hurt our astronauts. It could also destroy the power grids, and affect the holes in the ozone layer, which would harm us and the planet."

"It also keeps our atmosphere from being ripped off by solar wind," Abby added. She'd been looking out the window, but now she turned back towards the group. "The Earth's magnetic field is vital to life on Earth. If you don't want the Earth looking like the moon, you want to maintain that atmosphere. Even if nothing so catastrophic happened, there'd still be some major problems — migratory animals would be thrown into confusion; birds, fish and land animals could suffer huge losses during these thousands of years of transition."

She turned to Dante. "We are talking about a shift in the Earth's magnetic axis, not the rotation axis?" she asked.

Dante smiled. "Good question," he said. "There are two kinds of pole shifts, and you just named them. Magnetic shifts are slow. Polar jerks, are just that — very rapid."

"Wait a minute," Tina said, shaking her head as if to clear it. "What's a polar jerk? What's a pole reversal? Why is that different than a magnetic shift?"

"That would be a geological shift where the Earth's crust slips around to the side, for whatever reason," he answered. "We know the outer crust, the tectonic plates, float on the Earth's inner crust; the idea is that a heavy density of population and building on one side could, theoretically, slide the tectonic plates. In an axial shift, everything would flip to its antipodal opposite — the point straight through the center of the Earth from your present location."

"Kind of like digging to China when you were a little kid?" Tina asked with a smile.

"Exactly," Dante responded. "If the points completely switched places like that, where we are now would end up in current location of the Indian Ocean. A major shift of mass by magma within the earth – within the mantle, or even between the mantle and the crust, forming a new volcano – could cause a shift of the rotation axis. Some scientists say that around 800 million years ago a surge or swelling of hot mantle in the Earth's interior shifted our rotation axis 90 degrees, completely tipping the planet over onto its side.

"Others say that couldn't physically happen; instead, the poles would shift slightly, moving in the direction of the rotation. The Earth's plates are too snugly fit together to slide around the globe like a skin. Still, if the mammoths were found chewing on palm leaves that could have never grown in Siberia, that would be explained by an axial pole shift, not a magnetic pole shift."

Dominic nodded. "So the North and South poles don't completely reverse their position; they'd actually end up somewhere around the equator, and all the tropical areas at the equator now would end up at the poles."

"Yes," Dante said, "which would pretty much destroy life as we know it."

"Then there's no geological record of it having occurred before?" Dominic said.

"Nothing that points towards this actually happening, all mammoths aside. It's just an idea, one that might be possible, with some vague evidence to support it."

"But *magnetic* pole shifts have happened before," Steve mused. "Several times."

"That's right," Dante said. "Lava flows and rock records from the ocean floor all show that the poles have shifted more than 180 degrees before. On several separate occasions."

"Is what you said about the Earth's core the only thing that can make it happen?" Tina asked.

When Dante paused, Abby answered: "We could also be knocked off our current axis by an impact from an asteroid or another planet," she said. "The magnetism of another planet is another theory pseudo-scientists always throw out there. It comes up every few years — even Nostradamus predicted a pole shift for 1969," she alleged. "Never happened. In 1999, supposedly Jupiter and the Sun were going to line up with Earth in such a way that their gravity would grab that of the Earth, yanking it around by about 90 degrees. Still never happened. There was to be another major alignment involving several planets in early 2003. Obviously, nothing came of that, either."

"What prevented it from happening?" Tina asked.

Abby looked out the window at the dark sky, tracking the planets that were visible among the stars. "The planets and the sun are just too far away. Think about their immense distances from us, and the proximity of the moon — just under 240,000 miles away." She shook her head. "Contrary to what astrologers insist, astronomical convergences have no significant effect on our planet. If anything came close enough for its gravity or magnetism to affect us as the moon does, it would wipe us out. Something so big would have so much gravity it'd destroy us, and something smaller would have to actually be within the moon's orbit — much, much closer to the Earth than the moon itself. Even the moon, the one celestial object that *does* affect the Earth, doesn't have a strong enough gravitational pull to do more than cause tides. It doesn't affect humans, and it doesn't mess with plate tectonics or the flow of lava inside the planet.

"Jupiter, on the other hand, is over 450 million miles on the *other* side of the moon. Any gravitational pull it has on the Earth is so slight as to be unnoticeable. The house up on the hill has more of a gravitational effect on us right now than Jupiter does. No alignment exerts any type of pull on the Earth — the distances in space are too great. For a planet, or even group of planets, to affect us, they must come very, very close — which is something that has evidentially never occurred.

"This goes for any number of planets that line up in conjunction; no quantity of planets in a row will increase the pull on the Earth, not over such immense distances. Astronomical alignments do not cause disruptions here on Earth, like earthquakes or volcanic eruptions or anything."

"So neither the gravity or magnetism another planet – or group of planets – can cause a pole shift, and a physical pole shift won't occur without a gigantic and sudden catastrophe of some sort ... but a magnetic pole shift does," Dominic summarized.

"Yes," Dante said. "Fairly often. The paleomagnetic records show major shifts every 26 million years or so; other reversals have occurred every 100,000 years."

"Well, I'll be staying up tonight worrying about that one," Simon said. "It has nothing to do with a five thousand year count, anyway."

"Well," Dante responded cautiously. "As I've said, the magnetic pole shifts typically don't happen in an instant – they're estimated to take place over a period of time; an age, if you will. A period of just about 5,000 years."

The group stared at each other in silence for a moment, then Simon interrupted with laughter.

"So this 'Fifth Age' of 5,000 years is actually measuring a pole shift?"

"Why not?" Dominic mused. "Would that be so bizarre? Don't forget, the Fifth Age is supposed to end with the destruction of the Earth by earthquakes."

"There *have* been some major earthquakes the last few years," Dante mused. "Although nothing collectively different than have occurred during any other period of recorded history."

"But we can't predict earthquakes, either," Tina pointed out.

"Not with specificity," Dante said, "But we've got some good models we can use now. For example, we know that California can expect — with about 99% certainty — a massive earthquake sometime within the next 30 years."

"Define massive," Simon said. "Is California finally going to fall into the Pacific?"

"No, nothing like that," Dante said. "More like a 6.7 quake or higher. There's a close to 50% chance that it'll be higher than 7.5. Deadly and destructive, but it's not going to change the face of the United States or anything."

"Well, anyway," Simon said, "we're talking about a magnetic reversal, not an axial pole shift. A magnetic reversal wouldn't cause an earthquake."

Abby moved from the window and went to the bench of the lab table, where she slid in beside Simon. He put his arm around her, and she leaned against her. It was early yet, but the long day in the hot sun and their long trek to and from Izapa had worn them out. Abby closed her eyes, but she was still listening to the others.

"Maybe we're in the end of that time," Steve suggested. "Dante, you said it would appear that the shift started about two hundred years ago ... but could it have been longer? Even many hundreds of years ago when the Vikings were exploring the world – if North was off by a degree or two, would that make so much difference? They were pretty much going by the constellations and their compasses. They were mapping out huge land masses, not tiny, precise coordinates."

"Sorry," Dante said. "We're pretty certain about the dates. Besides, didn't you say that the Fifth Age thing was Aztec?"

"It was actually Sumerian first," Steve confessed, "although I don't how much stock to put in Sumerian mythology. They had at least four different creation myths; four different explanations of man's origin."

"There's a definite repetition of the concept of five world ages among ancient peoples," Dominic said, sitting on the bench across from Simon and Abby. "It's surprisingly common. I think anytime we find a cohesive thread that connects in some way to the Count, we have to follow it." He fell silent, and his dark eyes were pensive.

Across the room, Tina rubbed her eyes and yawned; she leaned back against the wall, closing her eyes as she spoke. "So, what are you thinking, Dominic?"

"Just wondering," he said. "Abby, you mentioned that the only thing that could cause a sudden pole shift, literally pulling the planet off its axis, would be a rogue body, some cosmic anomaly coming within the Earth's gravitational range. The Maya would've seen something like that coming from a long way away, wouldn't they? It would be huge enough to cause changes in the planet's wobble, or changes in other planets' orbits if it were coming our way."

"Yes," she said, guessing where he was going. "But if it was big enough for the Maya to know it was coming 2,000 years ago, and predict the exact date it was going to be here, we'd have picked up on it by now. It's not like something that big is going to be hurtling at us so fast that we don't even see it coming, especially if it's due to strike in only five years."

"What if it isn't going to even come into our line of sight or realm of knowledge for another few years?" Steve suggested.

"No way," Abby said, closing her eyes again. "It'd have to be so big and so close that we'd have seen or measured it coming decades, if not centuries ago. We know about galaxies that will crash into ours, billions of years from now. We wouldn't miss a gigantic planet hurtling towards us."

"Enough with the pole shift already." Simon said, beginning to sound irritable. "What does it even matter?"

Abby, leaning against him, sat up straight again, still tired, but alert. "Pole shifts of the magnetic kind happen to all the planets," she said. "Mars has a regular cycle of the poles shifting."

"Is that what caused the cataclysm?" Steve asked. "Whatever it was that wiped out all life on Mars and made it a dead planet?"

"No one knows," Abby said. "Although magnetic pole shifts on Mars are normal, there is evidence of a major initial shift of its pole axis by as much as 50 degrees, or 3,000 kilometers on the surface, sometime within the past 2 or 3 billion years. While we don't know what caused it, the popular theory is that an asteroid or planetoid struck the planet, which would've wiped out any life or vegetation that might have been there and left it a bare rock."

"But life survived that here," Dominic said. "All sorts of life lived through the strike that killed the dinosaurs. That's why we still have birds, and crocodiles. And us."

"The difference is size," Abby said. "The impact that left the Chicxulub crater was created by something big enough to send enough dust into the atmosphere to block out the sunlight, killing off about 70% of Earth's vegetative and animal species, but not big enough to cause a pole shift."

Steve suddenly spoke up. "I remember reading something about a pole shift on Earth causing the ice age. Or maybe causing the *end* of the ice age?"

"Pole shifts are part of the planet's natural cycle," Dante said. "Scientists think that ice ages are caused by the arms of our spiral galaxy swirling through space."

Abby yawned again, then covered her mouth in embarrassment. "Sorry," she said.

Dante laughed. "Not to worry," he said. "I think we're all getting tired here."

"Why don't we call it a night, and pick this up again in the morning?" Dominic suggested.

"Fine by me," Tina said, pulling herself away from the wall. "I'm starting to get confused by all this anyway. I'll be more clear-headed after a good night's sleep."

"I'll walk you up," Steve said, standing up and holding an arm out to her, which she took.

"Anyone coming with us?" she asked, glancing back at the others seated around the lab.

"Not quite yet," Dante said. He paused, almost imperceptibly. "I want to look at something real quick, and then I'll be up."

"Well, I'm with you guys," Abby said. She pushed back from the bench, reaching out to Simon and helping pull him to his feet. He put his arm around her waist, turning towards the door.

"Let's get out of here," he said. "I think if I hear one more word about a pole shift tonight I'm going to lose it."

"No fair losing it," Steve said, holding the door open for Tina and waiting for Simon and Abby to catch up. "We're going to need all the help we can get with this. We can't afford to lose anyone."

Simon laughed, and the four headed out into the night, waving back at Dante and Dominic who remained sitting in the brightly lit lab.

After they had gone, their voices disappearing into the night, Dominic turned to the geologist. "Anything I can help you figure out, now that Simon is gone?" he asked.

Dante smiled. "Was it that obvious?"

He shrugged. "Just something I noticed."

"You're very observant," Dante said. "And you're right. I didn't want to say anything until I'd thought a little more about it. Simon seems very smart, and so far he's been congenial enough, but I just don't know – the way he acted when we first met him still makes me uncomfortable. Sometime he's friendly and pretty good-natured, but I feel like that's just a front, and when he's sarcastic and argumentative we're seeing him how he really is."

"I believe that Dr. Nieson is a very competitive man," Dominic said carefully. "I also think he believes he has to challenge us for us to respect him. Hopefully that will fade with time."

Dante nodded silently. He still appeared to be lost in thought.

"Well, whatever it is that you're considering – do you want to talk about it?" Dominic asked. "If you have an idea bouncing around in your head, maybe I can help you work it out."

Dante sat his chair forward again, all four feet on the floor. "When I said the core was filled with molten metal that magnetized the poles, I was right," he said. "But I wasn't complete."

"What did you leave out?" Dominic asked.

"Thousands of miles beneath us at the core of the Earth is a huge nuclear reactor."

"Pardon?"

Dante smiled. "Yep," he said. "It's the actual mechanism that generates the magnetic field. When you picture the Earth's core, picture a jawbreaker. But instead of a hard candy outer shell, the outer core consists of fluid iron. The inner core is the nuclear reactor, a solid ball of uranium about five miles wide."

Dominic nodded. "It makes sense," he agreed. "Uranium is the heaviest element, it would have collected at the center of the planet when the Earth was forming."

"Well, when enough uranium collects together, a nuclear reaction occurs." Dante said. "It's a fission reactor. We've found helium-3 isotopes in volcanic regions – an element that came from deep in the earth, and can be formed, to our knowledge, by no other method but nuclear fission."

Dominic was silent for a moment, then asked quietly, "Just about how much energy does a five-mile wide ball of uranium put out?"

"About four million megawatts."

Dominic whistled. "Damn," he said. "The average nuclear power plant only puts out about 1000 megawatts."

"Yeah," Dante said. "And all the nuclear plants on Earth combined put out less than 400,000 megawatts. This is more than ten times that amount."

Both men fell silent, and after a moment's pause, Dante spoke up again. "I didn't mention it earlier because it didn't seem like anything the Maya would've known about, and because I wanted to think about whether a fission reaction at the planetary core is something that we should worry about. There's no definite consensus on the probability of it blowing.

"With this … well, I don't believe the nuclear generator will destroy us; it needs to be weapons grade, or pure plutonium. Natural uranium, like that in the core, has too many impurities. I'm thinking out loud here," he apologized, "so forgive me if I'm not clear. But this is what I wanted to think about, without Simon's judgment or his input."

"Is there any evidence that it's acting up?"

Dante paused. "It's hard to say," he hedged. "Like I explained, the Earth's magnetic fields are growing in some areas, that's a fact. But that happens every now and then, maybe more often than we imagine.

Our nuclear reactor down there has been running for about four and a half billion years, and so far it's been safe. Geologists think the reactor is a breeder – it puts out more nuclear fuel than it takes in. That keeps it from setting off all the atoms in a chain reaction. No atom splitting, no explosion.

"But there's another concern: The magnetic fields move or switch because the iron outer core acts as a motor, fluctuating the output of the field. It's liquid. It's moving. The magnetic field is inherently unstable. It could eventually shut down completely if the reactor consumes enough energy."

"How does that work?"

"Without going into deep chemistry, suffice it to say that georeactors produce fission products of helium-3 to helium-4. As the reactor consumes energy, it depletes the uranium; the helium produced increases as the reactor ages. Our best evidence for what happens farther inside the Earth than we could ever drill are in lava flows from deep within the planet. Lava flows are showing increasingly higher and higher levels of helium."

"Not exactly reassuring, is it?"

Dante laughed. "Well, we don't have enough information for comparison," he said. "We need beryllium samples to really make meaningful estimates – so the time frame we're looking at for the reactor's shutdown could be anywhere from one hundred years to a billion or more. That's why I'm thinking it's not even anything to consider, Dominic. I was looking for a way to connect it to the Maya, but I don't think it fits. The ancient Maya were astronomers, not deep Earth explorers."

"That's true," Dominic admitted. "They couldn't have reached the core, or even gotten far below the crust. The volcano Tacana is right above Izapa, but they didn't have the chemistry to study lava or the makeup of rocks and dirt. And we still haven't traced any major event occurring at the beginning of the Long Count that would connect it with a pole switch."

"Exactly," Dante said, standing up. "So we won't worry about the nuclear reactor; it's not what we're looking for." He went to the door, giving Dominic a wave before stepping out into the night.

"Might not be, but it's sure not going to help me sleep any easier tonight," Dominic called after him.

He could hear Dante's laughter echoing back through the darkness as the geologist headed up to the house, and although Dominic smiled along with him, he couldn't bring himself to join in the laughter.

June 7, 2008 – After breakfast, the group met again down in the lab. Everyone seemed refreshed, but when they picked up their conversation where they had left off the night before, Simon was unable to hide his irritation.

"Dante, you said that pole shifts are a natural part of the Earth's cycle, right?" Tina had asked. Simon groaned. No one commented, and Tina looked at Dante expectantly.

He nodded, and she continued. "I was thinking about that this morning. We know that the Earth has many cycles, like seasons, for example. They're all based on the rotation of the planet, and the turning of the Earth on its axis. Is it possible for a pole shift to occur on a regular basis because of this motion?"

"It wouldn't bring about a magnetic shift on any predictable basis," Dante responded.

"What about that other kind?" Tina asked. "Axial slips, or whatever you called them. Couldn't they occur on a habitual basis because of the Earth's tilt, and spin? We know the planet wobbles – maybe it's working up to something, like a big shift."

"I don't think that's ever happened," Dante answered slowly. He saw Abby look up from the journal she'd been reading, and turned to her.

"It certainly doesn't occur on any regular basis," she said. "A pole shift isn't part of the precessional cycle. It's not like, at the end of the cycle, when the planet completes a full wobble, the Earth just flips over."

"But couldn't it happen?" Tina had asked. "Look at the Earth now. The greatest land mass is directly across from the greatest ocean mass. Wouldn't that make it overweighted on one side? Especially with all the people and buildings on it. Why couldn't that drag it over to one side, essentially flipping the poles?"

"Are you people done yet?" Simon's tone was bored, and when he had their attention, he stood up.

"Come on," he told them. "Use some common sense. The weight of the Earth's surface isn't going to flip the damn planet over. How the hell much do you think water weighs? Oceans of water almost seven miles deep are certainly heavy enough to counterbalance a land mass.

"Besides, we're on an almost purely liquid sphere spinning through space. The axis isn't going to just slide out of place. You could move the whole population of the Earth to one side of the planet and it won't just flip around. I know enough about plate tectonics to know that they're fairly limited in their movement."

He didn't look to Dante for confirmation, only continued his lecture. "We are where we are in space because of the pull of the sun and the moon, and of other planets. There's a slight precessional wobble because our axis is tilted, and that slowly aligns itself over a cycle of like, a million years …"

"Twenty-six thousand years," Abby corrected him. "A precessional cycle is around twenty-six thousand years."

Simon glared at her, and she looked away.

"Whatever," he said stiffly. "The point is, this whole discussion is ridiculous. The Earth isn't going to flip over on its poles. And if it did, there's no fucking way the ancient Mayans could have predicted it."

"Maya," Dominic said.

Simon turned his glare to Dominic, and his face flushed when the bigger man smiled.

"Call me back when you're ready for an intelligent discussion," Simon said shortly, heading for the door. "I'll be in my room dissecting the number system – a solid base of facts we can work with, not just bullshit speculation."

He stalked out of the room, slamming the door behind him, causing Abby to look away, mortified.

"Does he do that often?" Tina asked with compassion.

Abby stood up, turning away so they couldn't see her embarrassment.

"No, of course not," she said, going to the book shelves next to Steven. "It's just early, I suppose. He's achy from all the walking yesterday – Simon's idea of exercise is jogging on the treadmill at the gym, not cross-country hiking through the jungle and climbing ruined temples. Plus, he just doesn't have a lot of patience for speculation. We already discussed last night whether or not an axial shift had ever happened, and concluded that it probably wasn't possible. I guess he thought we were going over old ground … sorry, Tina."

Tina smiled. "No big deal – he didn't offend me any. When we were talking last night, my head – and my memory – weren't that clear. I wanted to go over it again by light of day. I guess he just didn't like us wasting our time on things he thinks we've already beaten to death," she offered. "Maybe he figured we should move on."

"No," Dominic said, "He just didn't like being corrected in front of everyone."

Abby felt her face flush, and was glad to have her back to them. "Don't worry about Simon," she said. "He just needs to spend some time alone and get involved with the numbers again. He just started a new job at a new university in a new country on Monday, and I think he was hoping to get a lot of work done this weekend."

"Well, this isn't going to get done in a weekend," Dominic said, standing up. "Or in a month of weekends, or maybe even a year. People have been studying the Long Count for decades and are no closer to an explanation than we are right now."

He went to the screen door that looked out onto the courtyard, then pushed it open and went out. The others watched him search the ground for a suitable rock, which he used to prop the door open before coming back in. A light morning breeze wafted in, slightly relieving the mugginess inside the lab.

"So explain again what precession is," he said to Abby.

She chose a book of star maps from the bookshelf, then returned to the table and sat down, opening the book on the table in front of her before answering him. "It's a natural event that the Earth uses to regulate itself," she said. "The Earth has a slight wobble as it rotates in its orbit. This wobble turns the Earth slowly and gradually; it's called Precession of the Equinoxes. The complete cycle for the Earth to right itself again by this slow wobble is called a precessional cycle. Each full precessional cycle is a period of roughly 26,000 years."

"Do you think the Maya could have known about precession?" Dominic asked.

Abby thought about it. "Possibly," she ventured. "They would have noticed the constellations above them moving slowly with each passing year. The sun might rise in, say, Pisces, for a period of time, but although the sun would be rising in the same place, the constellation would be gradually moving away from it. The western world declares its own world ages by this same observation; for example, right now we're in the age of Aquarius."

"Is it exactly 26,000 years?" Dominic persisted.

"Well, no, not exactly. It's a little less than that, but there's no precise number, because the wobble isn't exact, and may be a few years longer or shorter with each cycle. It's estimated to be between 25,000 and 26,000 years; I would place it somewhere between 25,600 and 25,800 years. Why do you ask?"

"The Maya believed in five World Ages. If a World Age was one Great Cycle, it was a period of 5,125 years. Five Great Cycles would be 25,626 years."

"Holy shit," Tina breathed. "They were measuring precession?"

"If they were, it still doesn't answer my question," Dominic said. "The Fifth World Age – the Great Cycle we're in now – is supposed to end in earthquake and cataclysm. So if they were counting the last World Age, my original question still stands: What happens when the Long Count ends?"

Many hours later, after darkness had fallen, Abby found herself alone at her telescope. The day had been long and hot, and the group had been unable to maintain a cohesive unit. Each researcher would wander up to their room for a nap, or go to the relative coolness of the tiled kitchen, set into the hillside, for a cold drink. By late afternoon they'd given up on trying to hold a group session and had devolved into individual study groups. Abby herself had gone upstairs to sleep, knowing that she'd be out at her scope all night. She had found Simon lost deep in his calculations.

"Are you okay?" she had asked.

"Why wouldn't I be?"

"You haven't come back downstairs all day. Do you want lunch or anything?"

"No, I don't want lunch. It's too damned hot to eat. I'm lying here with a huge fan on me, sweating to death. This is no way to work."

"It's cooler downstairs," Abby said. "The kitchen feels pretty good."

"I'm not going to sit in the kitchen with everyone popping in and out," Simon responded. "I have to have peace and quiet to work, you know that."

"Okay," Abby said. "Well, if you want or need anything, let me know. I'm going to lay down for awhile. I'd like to do some stargazing tonight, while it's clear."

"So I'm sleeping alone tonight?"

Abby sighed. She lay back on the bed and closed her eyes. "Simon, I have to go out and look at the sky. That's what I'm here for."

"Well, don't be out too late. This is my last night here."

Abby opened her eyes again, surprised. He didn't look at her.

"Aren't you staying tomorrow night?"

"Are you kidding me?" he asked. "I have to be in class early Monday morning. I'm not getting up at four in the morning just to drive there."

"I'm sorry, honey," Abby said, moving over and putting her arm around him. "I know this is rough on you."

"You're damn straight it is," he had answered, shaking her arm off. "I don't know when I'm going to get a break, between working all week and working all weekend. This had sure as hell better be worth it, Abby."

"I know," she said. "We're going to do our best, Simon."

"Screw 'our best,'" Simon said. "There had better be an answer at the end of this."

"There's no guarantee we're going to figure it out. We knew that coming in."

"Trust me," Simon had spoken grimly, "There *will* be a resolution at the end of this, if I have to come up with it myself. This is a hell of a lot more than I bargained for, and I'll tell you right now, I'm not happy about it."

Abby hadn't answered. There was no need to; she already knew that if Simon wasn't happy, then no one would be.

"Can we see a supernova with the naked eye?" Dominic asked.

Abby glanced around at him. She'd been peering intently through her scope; with the sky was startlingly crisp and clear tonight, she hadn't heard him approach.

"Sure can," she said, stepping back. She'd grown used to Dominic's non sequitors. He would ask his questions whenever the thought struck him, regardless of the current conversation or circumstances. Abby had already learned not to question it and instead just rolled with his train of thought. She looked up, then pointed towards Taurus, the bull constellation. "In 1054 AD, the Chinese recorded a 'Guest Star,' right up there," she indicated. "They called it a guest star because just showed up; it came and stayed for awhile, and then it was gone."

"It was a supernova?" Dominic asked.

She nodded. "We can't see it tonight – we're in the wrong season – but I'll show you sometime this fall, if we're still here. All that's left in that area is a debris cloud, the Crab Nebula, all that remains of the destroyed star."

"And that's the only one we know of?" Dominic asked. He sounded disappointed.

Abby smiled. "There have been a few since then, like Cassiopeia, where a supernova appeared in 1572. There was even one in the late 1980's, but it was so far away it would've appeared to us like a fourth magnitude star – very dim, and distant. Nothing to grab your attention unless you were looking for it."

"Or unless you knew the night sky well enough to notice a new star where there wasn't one before," Dominic said.

"Exactly. I would assume that the Maya knew it that well, but there isn't anything that fits into the timeframe of the Long Count. I mean, there *was* one – a huge one – right around the first millennium, but by then the Maya had already abandoned their cities and dispersed."

Dominic sighed. "I sure wish there was one around 3114 BCE."

Abby smiled. "There may have been," she said. "But it wouldn't have been close enough to leave evidence in the geological record. We have to go on eyewitness reports, and there are none. So, as far as we're concerned, there was no supernova."

"What if something happened, and no one recorded it?" Dominic asked.

"Yeah, a little independent confirmation would be nice," she agreed.

"Oh well," Dominic said. "It was just a thought. Back to the drawing board." He waved, then turned and headed back for the house. Abby watched him go, a look of bewildered amusement on her face. Dominic definitely had his own way of doing things; he wandered in and out of their groups, asking esoteric questions and collecting their answers, but never elaborating. She hoped that he was somehow putting it all together.

Shaking her head, Abby turned back to the scope, losing herself once again in the glittering night sky.

When she finally returned to the lab, Abby was surprised to find almost everyone else inside. She glanced at the clock on the wall and saw it was going on two a.m. Only Simon was nowhere to be found. Crossing the room, she joined Dante and Dominic, who were in the middle of an animated discussion.

"So now you're sure they knew about precession?" Dante was asking.

"I'm almost positive they did," Dominic answered. "If it was the largest astronomical time cycle they'd have known of, it'd make sense to calculate it as the entire period of existence – the totality of all the world ages."

"But how could they know enough to calculate precession?"

"They could've watched the constellations move out of view, and somehow they figured out it wasn't the sky moving, it was us." Dominic said. He looked to Abby for confirmation.

Abby smiled. "Come with me," she said, reaching out a hand. Surprised, Dante took it. She led him back across the room, releasing his hand when she stopped to hold the door for him. Dominic followed them out, giving Abby a smile as he brushed past her in the doorway.

Before she went out, she flicked off the lab lights. "Sorry, guys," she told the others, who had been left in the dark. "It's just for a minute."

"Good to know," Tina said, but there was humor in her voice.

Abby led Dante and Dominic across the courtyard, down the hill and across the path above the lagoon. They came out into the clearing she'd just left – the farthest from the house most of them had been so late at night. Without the fluorescents from the lab, there was no light but starlight, and the surrounding night was pitch black.

"Whoa," Dante said when he stepped into the clearing. He stared around at the darkness. The night around them was so dark it was almost palpable; the stars above them seemed so close they could almost reach up and touch them. It was as if brilliant, backlit diamonds floated in a pool of liquid night.

"Imagine this about two thousand years ago," Abby said. "No artificial lights of any kind; no factories, no pollution, no smog or haze. No city lights, no glare from anything. Nothing at night but pure, unadulterated darkness, and nothing but sky as far as the eye could see."

Dante's head was still craned back. "I see what you're saying," he murmured.

"Even out here, there's light pollution," Abby said. "There isn't an artificial light shining for at least six miles, but there's still enough light pouring off of every nation on Earth to pollute the atmosphere. The lights, the smog, cars, all of our manmade dust and smoke; they've all dimmed our view of the stars, washed them out. Even out here. We can't see the dimmest stars that would've been visible a thousand years ago. Yet, this is still the clearest sky you'll ever see."

She continued: "The Maya would know the map of the night sky as well as they'd know their own neighborhood. All they had to was look up every night. They'd notice the minute differences in the constellations; it was only a matter of time before they'd be able to predict exactly where Sagittarius would rise, and how the sky would change with each season. Precession would've been a way of life to them. Completely natural."

Dante didn't answer. His eyes were full of starlight.

"How could they not notice the shifting of the stars?" Abby continued. "They planted and harvested; lived and sacrificed; made war, traded and traveled by them."

"So what would they have noticed?" Dante finally asked. "The twelve constellations changing? How?"

"Actually, there are 24 constellations," Abby said. "We use twelve."

"The Maya used thirteen," Dominic said.

Abby glanced over at him, considering. "Well," she said, mentally filing the information for now. "Right now we see the sun rise every morning in a certain constellation. As time goes on, the sun rises in a different spot in the constellation. The sky is the same, the stars and constellations the same distances apart, but they're shifting to the east. After awhile, that constellational age is past; the sun is rising in the next one over."

"How long does a constellational age last?"

"About 2,160 years."

Both men were silent, then Dominic asked, "And you think they noticed the change over more than 2,000 years?"

"You said yourself they were expert astronomers," she teased. "They could've kept thorough records with which they could have compared current astronomical formations."

Neither man answered, and after a moment Dante looked over at her, then glanced up towards the lab. "I'll bet Tina's starting to freak out up there in the dark."

Abby smiled. "Ok," she told Dante. "I just figured it'd be easier for you to see for yourself what the Maya would have."

"Thanks," he said. He nodded at Dominic, then turned and headed back towards the lab in an easy jog. When he was gone, Dominic moved closer to Abby.

"It's been rare, but I've seen more perfect darkness than this," he said. "A couple times, it was even in Guatemala – some of the Mayan sites there are incredible."

"I'll bet," she said, smiling up at him. She noticed his intense gaze and suddenly felt a nervous chill. "Anyway, I just wanted to show Dante."

"Good idea," he said, turning towards the house. He put a hand on her elbow to guide her across the uneven courtyard, but she walked faster, just out of range. He didn't comment, simply walked a step behind her as they headed towards the lab.

"Do *you* think they understood precession?" he asked.

"Yes," Abby replied simply.

"What makes you think that they saw the constellations move and made the leap of logic that it was the Earth moving?

Wouldn't it make more sense for them to believe it was the sky that was moving? After all, they saw things move in the sky, some fast, like comets; some slow, like the planets. They couldn't feel themselves move, but they could witness the sky, alive, above them."

Abby didn't respond. Dominic looked at her as they entered the cool glow of the lights from the lab, and he could tell that she was considering it.

"I was thinking of something you showed me yourself," she said slowly. "Their pyramids. They were aligned with the sky. That doesn't necessarily demonstrate sophisticated astronomical knowledge, I know, but it's pretty impressive."

Dominic smiled. "What's *really* impressive is the fact that Mayan astronomers periodically reoriented the pyramids when precession caused them to go out of alignment."

Surprised, she looked up at him with a question in her eyes.

He shrugged. "I knew they were moving them to keep them in alignment. I didn't know how long a precessional cycle was."

"Well, I guess that confirms that they knew it was moving. But the sun appears to rise in a different constellation over the course of centuries. Individual people don't live for centuries. How could they have been aware of it?"

"I guess that's going to be something we have to figure out as we go along, isn't it?" Dominic smiled, holding the door open for her. "Let the fun begin."

12.19.15.7.9

June 14, 2008 – The team had spent most of the day in the lab together, and they were all getting irritable. Simon had filled both the chalkboard and the white dry erase board with numbers. He was arguing the correlation date, claiming it would make all work on companion numbers and fractals pointless unless he had the precise numbers to work with. "What's the point of their precision if we can't even figure out what date they were specifying?" Simon asked, annoyed.

"Because the correlation debate isn't the Maya's problem, it's ours," Dominic explained patiently.

"Come on, quit hedging," Simon said. "The fact is, no one can decide on the exact date it started. So no one knows the exact date it ends."

"Well, it's not like they're picking random dates," Dominic said, standing up. He went to the bookshelf. "There are three possible start dates: August 11, 12, or 13. That gives three possible end dates: December 21, 22, or 23."

"Why the confusion?" Dante asked.

"Most of the codices were destroyed in the Spanish conquest," Dominic explained. "A codex is a table of dates. A few still exist in European museums, but they're by no means complete. We basically had to find synchronizing events recorded on both Mayan and European calendars. It's the best we can do with what we have to work with."

"The correlation debate has been pretty much settled on the middle dates, mainly because of their astrological significance," Tina added.

"Unless they started it the day before or after for some significance only to them," Abby added. "It depends on how they count. When we count down to something like, say, Christmas, we don't actually include Christmas day. We count up to it."

"Regardless," Dominic said. "We have to look at a period of days, not just the precise day. I don't think that'll make our job any more difficult; it might even help us to narrow it down."

"That's ridiculous," Simon said. "Why would you even fudge around the date if you can use the formula we know they used, their counting method, and pinpoint it?"

"Because we *can't*," Dominic explained. He sounded like he was speaking to a child. "The correlation debate is just that: a debate. There are arguments in both directions; no one can settle on the exact date because there's a valid basis for each. We have to accept that this is as close as we can get, and work with it. If you think you can find the exact date using the same data scientists have been using for dozens of years, then fine, go to it. It'd be fantastic if you could make the sense of it that thousands of other people haven't been able to do.

"If you think you can find new information to go on, you're welcome to go do that too. But we'll have to release you, because you're going to have to do a lot of traveling, digging and research to uncover something new."

"I don't need to find something new. I have the formula, damn it. Someone else should go find the relevant archaeological information. I have the pattern, and I want someone to pinpoint the damn date so I can apply it."

"As much as the whole world would certainly love to revolve around you," Dominic said, "it just doesn't work that way. People have been studying this for a long time, and they can't resolve the correlation problem. So we have to deal with the information we have."

Simon looked away, his color rising. "Fine," he finally said. "When you want some answers, I'll be upstairs." He turned and stomped across the room. Pausing in the doorway, he looked back. "Abby, are you coming?"

"Um, I need to do some work here," she said, unable to meet his eye.

"I didn't hear anyone here ask you any questions," Simon said.

"No, but I need to ask them some," Abby said, her face coloring. "I need to talk to Dominic and Steve about the Mayan creation myths – they believe they were astronomy-based, so I need to know what I'm looking for ..."

"Fine," he said curtly. "Stay here. I'll be up in the room when you're done pissing around." Simon slammed the door open with both hands, walking through and letting it crash shut behind him.

Abby sat down quickly, not looking up at the others. She didn't notice Dominic watching her with an eyebrow raised, or the look that passed between him and the others.

"Okay," Steve said, finally breaking the silence. "What do you want to know about Mayan mythology?"

"Well," Abby faltered, "how about we start from the beginning?"

"The creation myth?" Steve said. "Okay. Before there was the Earth, there was nothing." He stood up and went to the bookshelf, thumbing through the titles. "We have a few books on mythology here if you want to look through them. The creation myth has a few variations, but this is the most basic:

"Several gods were sitting around in what they called the 'All-Night,' the complete darkness, with Hunab Ku, the Creator God. Also, the Maize God, the Moon Goddess, and Lizard House. They were arguing about who was the most powerful after Hunab Ku. The Creator God got tired of hearing them argue, so he spit into a jar and stirred it around, then poured it down through the darkness. The world grew up through the darkness: the trees, the oceans, the land, the animals. Hunab Ku called for his creations to worship him; but, being animals, they just made noise. Irritated, Hunab Ku told the other gods that whichever one of them created a creature that could worship them would be the second-most powerful, after him.

"So they took turns. Lizard House made a man out of dirt; Hunab Ku spit into it and brought it to life. It walked, and multiplied. But because it was made of mud, it couldn't think or speak, so Hunab Ku called for the Rain Gods to wash it away. The Maize God picked up a lump of the mud and saved it.

"Next was the Moon Goddess' turn. She twisted a tree into the shape of a man; Hunab Ku spit on it again, and the same thing happened. It walked around and multiplied, but still it couldn't speak or worship the gods. Hunab Ku destroyed them, while the Maize God picked up a twig and saved it.

"Hunab Ku was ready to destroy the world, but the Maize God stopped him. He spread the mud, then used the stick to make holes in it. He planted seeds of corn, and Hunab Ku spit on them. They rose up into human beings and thanked the gods for creating them. Hunab Ku was happy, and the Maize God went to sit at his side. The End."

Abby frowned. "That's kind of bizarre."

"No more or less than anyone else's creation stories," Steve said. "Even the Bible says man was created from the mud of the Earth. That's no stranger than one of the Mayan gods making humankind out of mud."

"I guess that's true," she said. "I guess I just thought Mayan myths were more astronomy based."

"They are in the way that Egyptian mythology is," Steve said. "They worshipped the Sun God, the Moon Goddess. They believed the constellations represented various animals and gods. They thought the movements of the heavens had some direct effect on their lives here on Earth."

"That much hasn't changed," Abby observed.

"No, it hasn't," Steve said. He took the book he'd removed from the shelf and carried it over to the table. "People have always believed in astrology; to the ancients, to people who didn't know any better, there had to be some correlation between the actions of people on Earth and movements in the skies above it. We're a self-centered species; anything that happens anywhere in the universe must be because of us or for our benefit, or have some effect on us."

He flipped the book open, and as he leafed through it, looking for a certain page, he continued. "This is the *Popul Vuh*. It's basically the book to go to for Mayan mythology. Read it from the beginning to figure out who the characters are and what they're all about, and it's fairly easy to understand that they're based on the stars and planets, and the movements of those bodies through the heavens."

"Can you give me an example?" Abby asked.

"Yes," Steve said, finding the page he'd been searching for. "Seven Macaw, for example, was the Big Dipper, or the North Star. The Maya didn't trust him – he was supposedly a leftover ruler from a previous world age – and one myth has The Hero Twins shooting him out of the sky. The Hero Twins were the sons of Hunab Ku. Pretty much every appearance of them in the stories references some type of astronomical event, and they're recorded on the stones of Izapa."

"Who were they?"

"Astronomically, I'm not sure," he said. "I think possibly Jupiter and Mars. But I couldn't trace them to any specific star or planet. They're very important to Mayan myth, though, because they brought about the resurrection of Hunab Ku.

"There's a long and involved back story, but eventually, Hunab Ku is killed and his head hung from a limb of a calabash tree along Xibalba Be, the road to the underworld. This is also called the Black Road, or the Dark Rift. It's both the road to the underworld and the birth canal of the universe."

"I'm not sure I follow," Abby said.

"The Maya said we were birthed from the galactic center," Dominic spoke up. "There's another Mayan myth that symbolizes our birth from the great mother's womb, from the cosmic birthplace. Everything came down the birth canal, or the Dark Rift."

"Where is this Dark Rift?"

"It's supposedly a dark streak in the Milky Way," Dominic said. "They speak of a 'crossroads,' four roads meeting at the galactic center. One is the Black Road; another, the White Road, is a visible streak of the

Milky Way, very compact with stars. There's also a Green Road and a Red Road, which are supposed to be the two ends of the ecliptic where it passes through and makes a crosshairs on the galactic center with the Black and White Roads."

"They knew where the center of the galaxy was?" Abby asked.

"Yes. The galactic center was the womb from which everything came."

"That's amazing," she said. "I can see the Maya recognizing the Dark Rift – it's easily visible with the naked eye; it's almost like a road right through the Milky Way. And it does point to the galactic center, almost like an arrow. But the ecliptic isn't a visible feature. For them to know where the center of the galaxy is – well, that's pretty amazing."

"You're talking about a rift in the Milky Way?" Tina asked. "How can you see the Milky Way? Isn't that the galaxy we're in?"

"Sure," Abby replied. "Just like we're in Mexico right now. If you look straight ahead, you still see Mexico, right?"

"Well, yeah," Tina said.

"It's the same thing. We're only getting one view of it, from our perspective here on planet Earth. Our solar system is on one arm of a spiral galaxy, so when we look out into space we see the rest of it, spilling out beyond us. It's a band of stars, real gauzy and indistinct. Like someone poured a glass of milk across the sky." Abby looked at Dominic again. "So they thought we were born from the Galactic Center, but they also called it the road to the underworld. Did they think we came from the underworld?"

"And why is it the underworld when it's over our heads?" Dante asked, half joking.

"The Maya believed that at night, the underworld rotated above us and became the night sky," Steve said.

"There's more symbolism there, too," Dominic added. "The Black Road was also looked at as a mouth. When you read the glyphs, you see that the mouths of certain creatures were seen as portals – like the sky portal the Mayan gods were supposedly birthed from. Gods were birthed from the mouths of jaguars, snakes, and toads. These were portals to the underworld, just like the Dark Rift."

"So they could come or go from the creation place?" Abby asked.

"Well, the Maya believed in rebirthing and reincarnation," Dominic said. "I suppose they could see the Black Road as kind of a two-way street."

"What about this crossroads?" Tina asked. "What did you call it? Where the red and green roads are?"

"The ecliptic," Abby answered. "It isn't a visible feature, but somehow the Maya were aware of it.".

"What exactly *is* it?"

"It's the path traveled by the sun. All the constellations lie along it, and the sun passes through all of them over a year's time. The planets and the moon also travel it."

"How would they know where it was?"

"Simple observation. It cuts across the Milky Way near Sagittarius, right through the highest star in Orion's belt. Intersects it, running in a straight line across the sky."

"Right at the center of the Milky Way."

"Exactly. The center of the galaxy."

12.19.15.8.0

June 25, 2008 – Abby heard voices down the hall. She groped for her watch on the night table, pressing the tiny light and peering blearily at the numbers. Four-oh-three.

She lay back on the pillow, staring up at the dark ceiling, trying to make sense of the words.

"I can't listen to his snoring anymore! I'll sleep out in the lab if I have to!" Dante's voice, angrier than she'd ever heard him.

"Sorry, man," Steve's voice was apologetic. "I need my eight hours. I can't function without it."

Tina's voice piped up, but Abby couldn't make out the words. Dante said something else, and then there was a pause. Not a pause, she corrected herself; Dominic was speaking, his voice quiet and low, nearly inaudible.

"Look, Dominic, I'm not getting a lot of sleep either! You come in and out of the room a dozen damn times a night! What the hell do you do, get up every hour and wander around the neighborhood?"

Dominic's voice came again, soft and muted. There was another cry of outrage from Tina and a burst of conversation, and finally Abby could stand it no longer. She stumbled out into the hall, where the other four were assembled.

"What's going on here?" Abby asked, running a hand over her mussed hair.

"Just some rooming differences," Dominic said quietly. He was leaning against the wall, wearing nothing but a loose pair of cotton pants, pale blue in the faded moonlight coming through the far window. His dark hair curled over his forehead, and Abby thought he looked like a tired little boy.

"Differences my ass," Dante said, crossing his arms. He stood by the window. His stance was angry, his voice ill-tempered.

"Look, hon, why don't you go back to bed," Tina said gently to Abby. "This doesn't concern you."

"I'm part of this team, aren't I?" Abby replied irritably. "And it's pretty hard to sleep with you people shouting three feet from my door."

Dominic smiled, looking down at his bare feet to hide it. He put a hand across his mouth, then looked up again. "She's right, guys. We all need to talk about this. There are six of us and three rooms. By all laws of mathematics, we should be able to figure this out somehow."

"Where's your man when we need him?" Dante asked Abby, and she shot him a dark look.

"Okay, look, people," Steve said, holding up both hands. "Let's not start snapping at Abby."

"Why not?" Tina asked. "She's the only one with her own room and a full bed, all to herself five nights a week. How does that work?"

"Do you want to climb in bed with me?" Abby responded, growing angrier.

"All right, enough already," Dominic said, stepping into the center of their circle. "Everyone to the kitchen. Now."

He turned and headed down the stairs, Abby close on his heels. The others followed, grumbling.

When they got to the kitchen, Dominic flipped on the lights. The bright glare of the fluorescent bulbs was startling after the dim moonlight hallway, and almost all of them put up an arm to shield their eyes. Dominic grabbed a chair and spun it around, straddling it backwards.

"Sit," he said, and no one argued. Each took a chair, silent and sullen as petulant children. Abby took a seat by the door, crossing her arms and legs uncomfortably. She felt suddenly naked, clad in only a pair of Simon's boxer shorts and a tank top. The air in the kitchen was cool, and she pulled her feet up from the chilly floor, tucking them underneath her.

"All right," Dominic said. "We have issues. We will settle these issues before the sun comes up, or none of us are fucking moving until we do."

The others sat more upright, taken aback by Dominic's humorless tone. He spun up out of the chair, going to the cabinet. He took down a glass, filled it from the tap, and still didn't speak until he'd taken a long drink. He set the glass on the counter and turned to them again. Abby was surprised by the stern set of his jaw; she realized he was trying to control his anger.

"Here are our faults, one and all," he said:

"Tina is a light sleeper. I've known that since I've known her." His voice betrayed no emotion. "She's up every time the house creaks, and more often than not she's freaking out about it. 'What was that noise?'" he asked, raising his voice mockingly. "'Is someone out there?'" Tina narrowed her eyes at him, but he ignored her.

"Steve snores like a son of a bitch. I've known that for a long time, too. He can shake books off the shelves if you let him get going.

"I come in and out all night, I admit it. I think a lot at night, and sometimes ideas come to me that I want to act on right then. I go down to the lab to try to work things out. I'll just get back up to the house and I think of something I hadn't thought of before, and go right back down to my work again. I might as well just stay down there; I can't sleep anyway with Tina across the room, waking me up half a dozen times a night to tell me she heard something."

"What about me?" Dante asked. "What's your complaint there, Dominic?"

"I've never shared a room with you," Dominic replied easily, reaching for his glass again. "And I haven't heard anyone else complain about you tonight, either. So relax."

Dante was about to speak, but stopped himself when he saw the water glass tremble as Dominic raised it to his lips.

"I don't need the full bed," Abby said tentatively. The others turned to her, and she smiled uncertainly. "Tina is right; Simon is gone most of the week and I have a room alone. Why don't I move into Tina's room, and Dominic can move in with Dante. Steve can have the big bed to himself. That way no one has to listen to him snore all night."

Steve smiled back, but Tina interrupted. "And what happens on the weekends? You think your fiancé will enjoy sharing a bed with Steve? Or do you go back on weekends, and Steve – what? Takes your spot? Or do we all have to switch back again every Friday evening when Simon comes home?"

"That's enough, Tina," Dominic said, setting his glass down on the counter. His voice was firm. "Abby and Simon stay. I'll share with Steve. I'm not there anyway, he can snore all he wants, and he sleeps soundly enough that he won't even hear me coming and going. You and Dante take the last room. Problem solved. I'm going to bed." He crossed the room, not looking at any of them as he passed through them, then through the doorway and up the stairs.

They sat looking at each other in silence, and a moment later, they heard the sound of drawers being jerked open, emptied, and slammed shut.

"Oh shit," Tina said quietly, "He's really pissed."

"Does he get that way often?" Abby asked.

"No," Tina said. "He's the most even tempered man I know. We really pissed him off though."

"Why?" Dante asked. "Jesus, all we did was switch rooms. What's the big deal? He doesn't like us questioning his organization?"

"He doesn't like pettiness," Steve said. "Dominic just deals with shit. He doesn't make a big deal out of things, he just changes them and goes on with his life. When people start petty bickering about bullshit like this, he gets irritated. And don't forget, for Dominic, this is his life's investment."

"He just wants us to work," Abby said suddenly. "He has the same work ethic as Simon, I recognize that in him. He doesn't sit well with people screwing around and wasting time. I mean, it's Dominic," she observed, "And he'll play around as much as the next person, but look at how intense he is. He thinks about this all day and all night. He's out there in the lab half a dozen times a night working on this while the rest of us are up here snoozing away. And now we come out fighting amongst ourselves like a bunch of little kids."

"Yeah," Tina admitted, "Dominic is dedicated, that's for sure. And he doesn't take bullshit lightly." She sighed, then stood up and stretched. "Come on, roomie," she said, punching Dante lightly on the shoulder. "Let's get up there before Dominic throws all my shit out the window."

"Isn't he moving his stuff?" Dante asked, standing up.

"Hell no," Steve laughed. "You hear him slamming stuff around up there? Ten to one we'll go up and find all Tina's stuff dumped in my room. If she's lucky. More likely, it'll be out in the hall."

Abby stood up, waiting for Steve as the other two went upstairs. "I'd never have thought that about him," she told him. "I mean, he doesn't seem like the vengeful type. Or even the foul-tempered sort, you know?"

"He's not," Steve said. "Dominic can be an asshole, but he's a likeable asshole. He just takes care of business. Tina wanted to move, so she's going to be the one to move. He wants to get some sleep, so he threw her stuff out in the hall, or into my room. Dominic's not petty or pissy," he explained, "He's just taking care of a problem. Tina knows it, she won't be pissed. She'll consider herself lucky for him doing the work for her."

Abby paused in the doorway. "You've known them both a long time, haven't you?"

Steve nodded. "Dominic for over ten years, Tina about five. Dominic knew her first, thought I'd get along with her. Set us up on a dig once, but she and I didn't hit it off as well as he thought we might." He grinned.

Abby couldn't help but smile back. "I'm a little surprised, though," she said. "I thought Dominic and Tina had – well, you know."

110

Steve shook his head. "Nah, not to my knowledge. I think there was a flirtation there when they first met, but the more he got to know her ... well, suffice it to say Tina is a little flighty. He brings her along on a lot of projects because she's a damn hard worker. But she's not the sharpest knife in the drawer." He smiled again at Abby's surprise. "You wouldn't know it because she works her ass off to make up for it. She does good, thorough work. She's one of the lucky few that can make up for a lack of intelligence by working twice as hard. I'm one of the other ones."

"What do you mean?" Abby asked. "You're smart, Steve."

"Not as smart as Dominic, though," Steve responded, and Abby heard no jealousy there, only admiration. "You hang around him enough, and you'll start to feel like me and Tina."

"You don't think I'm as smart as Dominic?" she asked with a smile.

"No one is as smart as Dominic," Steve said plainly. "Dominic is the most intelligent human being I've ever known. If it wasn't for this obsession of his, he'd be another Thomas Edison. Another Einstein. When we met back in college he had a lab in his garage. Not just an amateur chemistry lab, but a real lab: He was working with robotics, with communications – he has a couple patents, Abby, one of which was bought by a major technology company. After he got interested in anthropology, he published a couple books on the Maya." Steve paused, then grinned unselfconsciously. "Too bad he's no good with money; he could be a very wealthy man by now. But he lives simply, and all the money he's earned from his work either goes into the next project, or whatever his charity of the moment happens to be.

"I tell you, Abby, if he didn't get so bored so quickly, he could be next door neighbors with Bill Gates by now. But he's never stuck with anything for longer than a few years, just enough to find whatever answer he was searching for, and once he discovered it, built it, or took it apart and found the solution, he lost interest.

"The Long Count is the only thing he has never figured out, and it's driving him crazy."

Abby nodded thoughtfully. Steve surprised her with a laugh.

"You'd never know it, would you?" he asked, and she shook her head. "There are two kinds of geniuses, Abby. Simon and Dominic. Simon is brilliant, and he damn sure wants to make sure we all know it. He wants the world to know it.

"Dominic doesn't care. He knows it, and that's all that's important. What the rest of the world thinks doesn't matter."

He saw the look on her face and stopped. "Hey," he said. "That doesn't mean that Simon's a bad guy or anything. Most of the world is like

Simon. And that's not necessarily wrong. I mean, how would we have any technological advances or cures for diseases if people didn't want to show the world what they could do?"

Abby smiled. "Don't worry about it," she said, moving out of the doorway and up the stairs beside him. "Simon can be an ass, I know. But I still think the good outweighs the bad in him, so I can live with it."

"And hey," Steve said mildly, "He doesn't care if the world knows he's an ass, so that's something."

Laughing quietly, they ascended the stairs. All was quiet on the second floor, and after a quick goodnight, Abby headed back to the silence of her room. She was suddenly very tired.

12.19.15.8.10

July 5, 2008 – "Ugh, I can't stand this heat," Tina said, wiping her arm across her forehead.

"And just think," Dante said with a grin. "It's still early July."

"I'll be dead by August," she responded, running a hand through her short red hair. Her hand came away wet, and she looked at it and grimaced.

"There's always the lagoon," Dominic joked.

Tina stared at him. "Dominic, my dear, you are an absolute genius," she said.

"You're kidding, right?" Simon glanced over. "That pond has to be nasty by now. It hasn't rained in weeks; it's either dried puddles or stagnant."

"It's cool, and it's water," Tina said, pushing back her chair and standing up. "I'm going swimming."

Simon groaned, glancing over at Dominic, but Dominic was smiling. "You're going to let her go swim in that muck?" Simon asked.

Dominic shrugged. "I'm not her keeper," he said. "As long as she doesn't bring us back malaria or anything, I have no objections."

"I'm with Tina," Dante said, following her out the door.

"All right," Steve said, tossing his pen over his shoulder. "Guess we're going swimming."

From her corner by the computer, Abby looked up. "You think the water is really dirty?" she asked.

Steve shook his head. "It's probably okay," he said. "It comes from the same spring as our drinking water, and that hasn't dried up. It's clear, but man – from all the weeds and water lilies growing in there, I'll bet the bottom is pure mud."

"Cool mud squishing between my toes sounds pretty sweet right now," Abby confessed.

Dominic grinned. "Well, I aim to please," he said. "I picked out this spot particularly for that pond. I knew at some point this summer someone besides myself would want to stick their toes in the mud."

"Then let's go," she said, pushing back from the computer desk. Her shirt was stuck to her back with sweat, and she could almost feel the cool clear water splashing over her body.

"Sit down," Simon said.

Both Dominic and Abby turned to look at him. "Simon …" Abby began, but he cut her off.

"Let the others go splash around in that shit," he said coldly. "You promised to have those distances for me yesterday, and I still don't have them."

"The generator went down yesterday, Simon," Dominic said. "We were without power and lights all evening, and you know how early it gets dark here."

Simon turned his cool gaze on the larger man. "My fiancée doesn't need you to defend her," he said. He turned again to Abby. "There are no excuses. I've told you that. If the generator is down, then you work harder when it comes back up. I can't work until you do the preliminary for me. I've already wasted enough time waiting for you to do your damn job; what do you want me to do? Sit around and rot while you splash around in the water with the other children? Not a chance, Abby. No swimming for you."

Abby didn't respond; she just sat down again slowly, numbed. She pulled up the spreadsheet again, her ears burning with embarrassment, wishing for Dominic to go away, to head down to the lagoon with the others and leave her to her shame.

When she heard the bench scrape back, she felt a rush of relief. When she looked up, however, she saw to her dismay that it was Simon crossing to the screen door. He caught her eye and smiled sarcastically. "Well?" he said. "I can't work. Just because you haven't finished your work doesn't mean I should sit around. I'll be enjoying the cool water. You can sit here and sweat until you're done."

She felt the tears welling up in her eyes, and she didn't look up again from the computer screen even when she heard the screen door slam, then Simon whistling as he headed down the path.

"Abby?" Dominic's voice was quiet, soft. She didn't answer him.

"Abby, are you okay?" he asked again, and she heard the bench slide back on the tile floor.

"Leave me alone, Dominic. Please?"

"Abby, does he always treat you like that?" She heard the concern in his voice, but could only react in anger.

"No, Dominic, he doesn't," she said through tight lips, still unable to look away from the screen. "Do you really think I'd be marrying a man who treated me like that?"

He was silent, and she realized what she had said.

"Look," she said, turning to him. "Simon's had a long couple of weeks. He's having a hard time with the language, and he's not used to that. It makes him feel self-conscious, and he's ashamed to stand in front of a room full of students with his bad Spanish."

"Big deal, so he's human."

"To Simon it is a big deal," she stressed. "Simon has a lot of pride. He doesn't like it being challenged."

"So he takes it out on you."

"No," she shook her head. "He doesn't, Dominic. Really. I did promise to have those numbers for him yesterday. He's right – I had all week to do it, and I didn't. It's my fault for slacking all week and thinking I could finish it all yesterday. I'm holding up his work, and he only has two days to work on it with us."

Dominic was silent for a long moment. Finally, he asked: "How long have you been making excuses for him, Abby?"

She stared at the computer screen. "I don't need to explain myself to you, Dominic. We're just here to work for you, that's all."

"And I need to make sure my team isn't going to fall apart," he said. "If you two have issues, fine. I don't have to like Simon, and I don't have to protect you from him. But I'm going to try to do both. Because this is my project, and I need you both to work at it with everything you have. If he's stalking off in anger, and you're in here crying, my work isn't going to get done."

"I'm not in here crying, Dominic. Don't worry; your work will get done. Simon's work will get done. Now leave me alone and let me do mine."

She starting typing, fighting the tears that burned powerfully at the edge of her eyes. She tried to blink them away, but a teardrop finally rolled down her cheek. Wiping it away quickly, she glanced up to see if Dominic had noticed it.

The lab was empty. Turning around in her chair, Abby saw the back door swinging shut; Dominic had stepped out without her having heard him leave. She turned back to the computer, but could fight it no longer; Abby buried her face in her hands and let the tears come in raw, hoarse sobs.

She cried for a good long time, and when she was finished, she began to compile numbers again. She had to be finished by the time Simon returned from his swim.

Abby rubbed her eyes, peering through the telescope at M102, the dusty galaxy that was part of Draco, the ancient pole star. Precession had moved Ursa Minor into that position now, but Abby thought the old circumpolar constellation might hold some interest. The harder she looked, however, the more the stars swam in front of her. She'd had an exhausting day, between the work she'd done for Simon and the emotional toll it had taken on her, and she was ready to call it a night.

She pulled her face away from the telescopic sight, glancing around her in the darkness. It was hours before dawn, and the night was still dark enough to give her jitters when she looked at the hidden edge of the forest. The shadows reached out blackly into the clearing, but the sky was beginning to brighten, the stars fading into the graying background.. It was imperceptible to the untrained eye, but enough to disturb her viewing.

She stepped back from the telescope, gathering her shoulder pack with her thick spiral notebook sticking out the top. Guiltily, she reached past it for her flashlight; she'd done no note-taking that night, for the third night in a row.

Abby flicked on the flashlight, illuminating a swath in front of her. She was isolated out here, she knew, but she wasn't worried. They were alone in the highlands, at the foot of the volcano. There would be no strangers to bother them, and she knew was safe among the other scientists.

She decided to turn off the flashlight for the half mile walk back to the lab; the cloud cover that had interfered with her stargazing earlier was passing, leaving the moon bright enough to light her path.

Above the small pond they'd termed "the lagoon," Abby crossed the dirt ledge that Dominic had cleared of foliage for their usage, about four feet across and a dozen feet above the water. The land bridge dropped straight down to the pond on one side, while the other side sloped sharply down into a tangle of trees and underbrush. Her foot kicked a loose stone, and she watched it bounce down the steep grade to the water's edge, rolling to a stop before it hit the shiny surface of the water. "No swimming for you," she said softly, moving on. Through the trees she could see the lab, still a good quarter mile away, sitting on top of its hill. Between her and the lab was the clearing they'd called "the courtyard", an open field with large boulders. Dominic and Steve had rolled some of the larger rocks together to form a crude seating arrangement that vaguely resembled a table and chairs, where any one or more of the scientists could be found eating breakfast on any given morning.

She passed through the edge of the trees into the clearing. Under the moonlight, Abby could see a large dark shape atop one of the sitting stones. She crept cautiously closer. The sitter was leaning back on his arms, legs outstretched, and Abby thought for a moment that he was sleeping. Upon moving in closer, she recognized Dominic; his eyes were open and watching the sky. He looked serene and relaxed lying there, and Abby hated to interrupt his reverie. Still, she felt the need to speak to him.

"I hope your eyes are better than mine in this light."

He shifted his attention from his sky watching, eyes focusing on her in the darkness, and she thought for a moment that he actually might have been sleeping. Sleeping, or meditating.

"Hey, Abby," he greeted her. His voice was not drowsy; he sounded alert, just unbelievably calm. Abby moved closer.

"I was looking at the stars," he said. "The night just goes on forever out here."

"Yes," she agreed, stopping across from him. There was another large stone near his, and she lowered herself onto it. She slid her leather bag from her shoulder, letting it drop to the ground with a soft sigh.

Dominic was silent, watching the ancient stars twirling in the vastness of space, trillions of miles away. Finally, he continued: "The Maya believed the Earth went through cycles of creation and destruction," he said. "They divided history into five ages, each one building to its climax and then fading away. Everything comes to an end at some point; I think the Maya knew when that end was."

"That's cheerful," she said dryly.

Dominic laughed, turning his face to look at her. She glanced at him, and he was taken aback by her startling golden eyes, filled with starglow. "We've always thought we were living in the middle of time.," he said slowly, unable to look away from her. "Maybe we're actually living at the end of it."

Abby suddenly shuddered, even though the night was warm. She broke her gaze sharply, then rose ungracefully to her feet.

"I'm sorry," Dominic said, jumping off his rock. He stood tall above her in the moonlight, and she felt suddenly uneasy.

"I didn't mean to make you uncomfortable," he apologized.

"I know," she said, looking away. "It's just not a pleasant thought, I guess." She glanced back up at him, meeting his intense gaze. "Don't worry, Dominic, it's not like I can't handle it. I knew coming into it that we were studying what some people claim signifies the end of the world. But it seems a lot less ridiculous alone out here in the middle of nowhere. In the Maya's old stomping grounds."

"It is a powerful place," Dominic agreed, turning to survey the area. Off to their west, the volcano rose out of the forest, stark black against the surrounding darkness. The sky and the mountain blended together, stars sparkling around the mountaintop as if they were mere inches away instead of thousands of light-years. "At night it feels like a Mayan High Priest could walk out of those woods any second, looking for his next sacrifice."

"Thanks for the image," Abby said. Dominic laughed.

"Sorry again," he said. "Guess I'm not much for conversation at three a.m."

"Yeah," Abby agreed, "No offense, but I think I like this place — and you — a lot better during the day."

Dominic smiled and reached out to lay a hand on her shoulder, a small gesture that Abby found endearingly sweet. "Then let's go in, and continue this conversation in the daylight," he said.

She responded with a matching smile, and they headed back towards the house in comfortable silence.

12.19.15.8.17

July 12, 2008 — "So how did you and Simon meet?" Tina asked casually.

Abby glanced over at her, but the other woman didn't look up from her work.

"In college as an undergrad," Abby answered. "He was my advanced calculus professor. I thought he was a genius; the first instructor I ever had that absolutely fascinated me. All his students felt that way — his classes were captivating. Hard to believe math could be that way, but it was. And Simon was always more than happy to help me with my studies; he was really generous with his time and his knowledge. I thought he was just wonderful — kind, intelligent, fun to be with. I really fell for him. It wasn't long before I realized he was interested, too. But I had to wait until after I wasn't his student anymore before I called him."

"*You* asked *him* out?" Tina looked up with surprise.

"Kind of," Abby shrugged. "I was having trouble in a physics course I was taking; some of the math was really over my head. I figured, what the hell — I knew I wanted to see him again, and I thought maybe he'd want to see me too. So I asked him if he'd help me through some of the rougher passages.

"We met for coffee one day, and ended up spending a couple hours together, just talking. After that, we were seeing each other almost every day."

"How long have you been together?"

"Four years," Abby answered, pausing. "We had some bad spots, so there were a few months here and there when we were broken up. But we always got back together."

"What caused the breakups?" Tina asked.

Abby tensed. "That's kind of personal," she said.

"I'm sorry," Tina answered, laying down the textbook. "I know I don't know you that well, and it's none of my business. But I see the way he treats you, and it worries me."

"How do you think he treats me?" Abby asked stiffly.

"Like a possession. Like you belong to him, not because he loves you, but because he owns you. You see how he treats Dante, and Dominic. Steve he pretty much ignores, because he doesn't seem to see him as a threat. But the other two — he belittles them because he sees them as a threat to either himself or his control over you. He sees them as enemies."

Abby bristled. "Well, thanks for summarizing my entire relationship in your three months of observations."

"I'm not trying to interfere," Tina said, "I just think your fiancé has some serious insecurity issues, and I'm concerned. Not just for you, although I am worried about you. I'm also worried about the rest of us. If he keeps going nose to nose with every man here, I'm afraid it's going to get violent."

"If it does," Abby responded coolly, "It'll be because of Dante or Dominic. You don't know Simon, and you don't know me. And you definitely don't know *us*. He loves me and is scared of losing me. *He's* the one that's afraid; I have nothing to fear from him."

"What kind of relationship do you have that's based on fear?" Tina asked. "You're with him now, and you've promised to marry him, yet he still doesn't trust you enough to let you work closely with another man?"

Abby stood up. "I don't want to talk about this with you."

"You don't have to," Tina said as Abby heading for the door. "Just know that it's not just me that noticed. And that I'm not the only one concerned about Simon. Dante doesn't want to work with him anymore. Steven is afraid of him. Even Dominic has started having some doubts. We've been under enough stress. If this shit keeps up, someone is going to go. And if it's four against one on this, there isn't much of an argument."

Abby stopped in the doorway. "Don't I get a say in this?"

"Of course you do. You can side with him or against him. But if you decide to stay with him, then you can go with him. Because it'll still be four against two."

Her cheeks and ears burning, Abby walked out, letting the door slam behind her.

Abby knew Dominic would be outside; the night was warm and clear, and he'd been quiet and thoughtful all day. The others had gone to bed hours ago, and after she lay in bed beside Simon, staring at the wood ceiling of her room for an indeterminate amount of time, she finally climbed carefully out of bed. Barefoot, she headed down the stairs, two at a time, treading softly to keep from waking the others.

The lab was empty, so she crossed it and made her way out into the courtyard. The grass was soft and dewy under her feet. She paused for a moment, taking in the wide black sky, velvet dusted with diamonds.

She passed through the courtyard, surprised not to find him on his sitting stone. Abby continued on, negotiating the path across the lagoon, and had almost reached the clearing on the other side when she heard a soft, "Hey."

Abby looked down, searching for a moment before she located Dominic sitting in the grass on the bank. His shoes were off, and his feet were long and pale under the dark water. "Hey yourself," she called down, making her way carefully down the steep bank via the branch ladder. Dominic reached up a hand to her as she drew nearer, and she took it, trying to keep her footing on the uneven ground. She released his hand as she lowered herself to the ground next to him, pleased to find the thick grass warm on her legs.

"How're you doing?" she asked him amiably.

"Not bad," he answered. "Beautiful night for sitting."

"You're not worried about anything nibbling on your toes?"

"Nah," he smiled, flicking his toes under the water, making small splashes. "Nothing bigger than some frogs in there. The water feels good; you should try it."

Tentatively, Abby stretched out a toe, dipping it into the water. She laughed as it ran up over the top of her bare foot. "That's cold!"

Dominic shrugged. "You get used to it."

She dipped her toe again, shivering at the chill of the cool water against her skin. After a moment, she plunged her whole foot under.

"That's the way," Dominic smiled. "Dive right in there."

"Wow, I think my foot is already numb."

"I told you, you get used to it."

They both laughed, then sat in comfortable silence, watching the stars move slowly over head. The cool water did feel good on her feet, especially in the balmy night, with the grass underneath her still warm from the heat of the sun.

"Dominic," she started tentatively. "I was talking with Tina earlier. She mentioned that some people have been having a problem with Simon."

Dominic did not answer. Abby turned to see him biting his lip thoughtfully, and she felt her heart beat a little faster. "Was she right?" she asked. "Are you thinking about asking him to leave?"

"Well," Dominic answered slowly, "it hasn't come to that yet. I'd like to think it won't. But I'm only able to speak for myself. So far, he's no worse than anyone else I've ever worked with; but then again, I tend to be fairly easy going. So is Steve. He'd rather avoid Simon than talk to him, but he knows he has to work with him if we're to get anything done."

"He's a necessary evil?" Abby asked softly.

Dominic turned to her with a smile. Seeing her concern, he reached out and put his hand over hers. "Don't take it so hard," he said. "Personality conflicts are a part of life. I'm sure Simon doesn't like Steve anymore than Steve likes him; he probably considers Steve something he has to put up with to get any work done. It all evens out."

Abby nodded, still feeling the warmth of his hand even after he'd pulled it away. She leaned forward, sliding her hands under the cool water. "Tina seemed pretty antagonistic about it. And she said Dante didn't want to work with him anymore."

She heard a rustling sound and turned to see that Dominic had lain down in the grass, his feet still submerged like strange white fish in the lagoon. "Don't worry about Tina," he said, gazing up at the stars. "She can talk all she likes, but she doesn't have any control over what I do. She likes to be a part of everything that goes on, whether it's her business or not. She's only trying to help, in her own way; she probably thinks you can do something about Simon's behavior."

"And Dante?" Abby asked.

"Dante hasn't said anything to me about it," Dominic answered. "When he does, then we'll discuss it. If he goes directly to Simon, then they can hash it out themselves. I'm not anyone's father here; I assume we're all adults and can settle our own differences. Don't worry about anything anyone says unless it comes directly from me." He rolled his head towards her, eyes dark in the shadow of the hillside. "Lay down," he said with a smile. "The grass feels good, and you can see a perfect little section of sky through the branches."

Abby leaned back on her hands, tilting her head up to the stars. Thin gray clouds moved across her field of vision, occasionally obscuring the brilliant stars sparkling behind them. She felt herself growing drowsy, watching the universe twirl amid the gauzy clouds.

"Look at all that beauty," she said, gazing at the glittering night sky.

Dominic tilted his head at her. "Is that why you got involved with astronomy? For the beauty of it?"

Abby smiled. "Partially. I grew up in Oklahoma, where the sky is huge. I used to lie under the stars all night. I learned every constellation before I was ten. And I had to wonder — what else is there? What's past those? Why do they gather the way they do, and what are they made of?

How did they get there, will they be there forever? And what does it all mean?"

Dominic smiled. "A lot of questions for a ten year old."

"Well, I had a lot of time. I mean, it *was* Oklahoma."

He laughed. "I grew up in Chicago. Downtown. Couldn't see the sky for the skyline, for the city lights."

"So why Mayan history, of all things?"

He shrugged. "Seemed the most distant thing in the world from Illinois. Exotic, you know?"

She smiled. "I know. And it still is. I feel like I'm in another world, Dominic. Another time."

"Yeah," he said softly. "And I'd like to stay here forever."

She smiled, kicking her feet leisurely in the water, making small splashes in the huge night. "I can't help but wonder if you're wasting your time having me here," she said. "I mean, I understand that the Maya were astronomers. But on a cosmic scale, the time we're talking about is much too short to mean any significant changes."

Dominic nodded, sticking a toe into the mud. "It's a gamble, sure. I understand that on a cosmic scale, we're talking about millions and billions of years, and the Long Count only covers a few thousand of those. But there has to be something there. Everything the Maya did revolved around the sky: They claimed to have birthed from a space portal, and their gods descended to earth via snake chains. That's a metaphor for something, and I want to know what."

Abby was silent. She looked at her feet, pale and motionless under the water.

"What are you thinking about, Abby?"

"Wormholes."

He paused, considering. "Okay," he said. "Tell me about wormholes."

"You know what they are," she said.

"Of course I do," he said. "But I'd like to know what you're thinking about. Why wormholes?"

"Well," she said, "Couldn't they be a little like the 'snake chains' your Maya imagined? If the Mayan gods came from elsewhere in the universe, how would they do it? How could they cross such vast distances? Unless their gods had mastered the speed of light, and were physically able to withstand such speeds, the only way to fold space-time would be warp drive — to shoot through a wormhole."

"Which is …?"

"Well, our ideas of black holes have changed in recent years, since Stephen Hawking came out with the resolution that matter going into a black hole is distorted, but still there. But, in previous theory, a black hole is connected to a white hole, somewhere in another part of the universe. You know what a black hole is, right?"

He nodded. "A massive star eventually collapses, crushing the star's matter out of observable existence. Its gravitational force is so powerful it then continues to suck in anything around it, anything that ventures into its event horizon."

Abby nodded. "So, theoretically, anything it sucks into itself could pop out of a white hole somewhere else in the universe."

"Quasars?" Dominic suggested.

"Sort of," she said. "All observed quasars are far beyond our galaxy, but from studying them we've seen that energy pours from them in massive amounts. But the matter coming out of quasars seems to be gas and matter from the area around them. They suck in the surrounding material, which shoots out of it in either direction. There's no disappearance of the matter, or any inter-dimensional travel involved."

Abby was thoughtful for a moment, then smiled. "In one older theory of the Big Bang, our entire universe is just a different, previous universe that had collapsed into a black hole and we exploded into being out of a white hole."

Dominic lifted his feet out of the lagoon, watching the water drip off of them and hit the pond's surface in tiny eruptions. "So if we came into being from the death of a former universe, it's possible that our own universe might eventually stop expanding, begin contracting, and collapse into a black hole."

Abby saw where he was going. "You think this is the creation and destruction cycle the Maya believed in."

He shrugged. "Maybe. But the time scale is off. If we're talking about the current age of the universe, that's roughly 14 billion years. The Long Count is a period of just over five thousand years."

"So we can't mess with the time frame?" She teased. "Look at creationists. They say the Earth was created in seven days. Science demonstrated that the world was billions of years old. So what did the creationists do? Claimed that no one knows how long one of God's days is."

Dominic smiled. "Unfortunately, though, we know how long a Mayan day is. We know how many of their days are in a year — 365. Eighteen months of 20 days each, plus the five day uayeb tacked on at the end. There's no question as to how long a day is, and the Long Count measures 1,872,000 days."

Dominic put his toes back in the water. Feeling the cool water spill around them, he sighed deeply and slid his whole foot into the water. "God, that feels good," he said.

Abby smiled and dipped hers back in as well. "Yes it does. So, you would consider wormholes to be a valid supposition."

"Maybe," he said. "But I wanted to hear what you said about them. It can always be enlightening to get another point of view."

"Okay," she smiled, splashing her toes lightly. Her feet felt heavy, and she tried to clear her head. She felt as if she could doze off.

"Okay," Dominic said. "So the theory is that the black hole and the white hole are connected by the Einstein-Rosen Bridge, or wormhole. What are the odds that something like that could have happened on a smaller scale? Mini black holes allowing for travel through space, if not time."

Abby nodded. "There's only one problem with that: Singularity is unavoidable."

Dominic thought for a moment. "Explain," he said.

Abby lay back on the grass. Her feet still dangled in the water, and she splashed them softly. Out of the corner of her eye, she noticed Dominic lay down beside her again. She suddenly felt very tired.

"There's a lot to it," she said, "And to tell you the truth, my brain is a little muddled. Can we discuss singularity in the morning?"

"Sure," he said with a smile. "I always forget, most people don't do their best thinking after midnight."

Abby smiled sleepily. "I'm usually up all night, but I think this heat is sapping all my energy."

Dominic smiled back, but Abby's eyes were closed. He lay back and watched the sky, and they in silence for a long time. Finally, he spoke:

"It's like the whole world just fell away."

Abby heard his voice come from a million miles away.

"It's like we're floating in darkness."

All she could do was nod in agreement. She realized he probably hadn't seen it, but that didn't seem to matter. After a moment, she drifted away, sound asleep under the starry Mayan sky.

Dominic lay quiet and still beside her, not wanting to wake her. He propped himself up on one elbow, watching her breathe. A dark lock of hair, black against her moonlit skin, lay across her forehead, and he wanted to push it back. He glanced down and saw that her feet still dangled under water.

"Hey," he said, gently moving the lock of hair off her forehead. She stirred, and he was tempted to lean over and kiss her, waking her like Sleeping Beauty, or Snow White. She half-opened her eyes.

"What's up?" she asked sleepily.

"Time to head back up," he said.

She shook her head. "I'm comfy here."

He laughed. "Your feet are going to freeze."

She pulled them out of the water, curling them up underneath her on the bank.

"You're determined to sleep out here under the stars, are you?"

She nodded, and he smiled. "Okay," he said. "I give up. I'm going up to the lab, though ... I want to look up some things. The air is clear tonight; I should be able to get through on the wireless web."

"Okay," she muttered, and he knew she was half asleep again.

He patted her on the knee and stood up, glancing around. He knew she'd be all right out here; there was no one besides them for miles. Still, he felt a little guilty as he climbed back up to the path; what he really wanted to do was lay back down beside her, curl his body around hers, and drift off to sleep with Abby in his arms.

Instead, he headed back up to the lab to work.

Dominic had been working diligently for an hour or so, deeply involved in his work, and he didn't hear the door open. He was startled when an angry voice spoke directly behind him, "Where the hell is my fiancée?"

Dominic jerked, knocking his notebook onto the floor. "Jesus, Simon, do you have to sneak up on people?"

"I figured that since you were gone and Abby was gone, you were probably together."

"Do you see her around here?" Dominic asked irritably.

"No," Simon admitted. "So where the hell is she?"

Dominic shrugged. "She came through here a few hours ago. Probably headed down to her clearing to sky watch."

Simon looked as if he was going to say something else, but he just shook his head and crossed the lab, stepping out into the courtyard and letting the door slam shut behind him.

Dominic glanced at his watch and saw that it was almost four o'clock. He debated about going back up to the house for a couple hours of sleep, but decided to wait until Abby and Simon came back through. He wasn't entirely sure why he'd lied to Simon, but he thought for sure that Abby wouldn't dare tell him that she'd fallen asleep while lying with Dominic by the lagoon.

He didn't have to wait long, and he heard them coming before they reached the lab. As usual, Simon was berating his fiancée:

"You think it's safe out here? Who the hell knows what kind of animals are in those woods? Not to mention the natives around here."

"Simon, I'm out there almost every night, all week. There's no one around but us."

"Oh, so just because you've run out into the road a dozen times and not gotten run over you think it's a good idea to run out there again?"

"Simon, seriously; there's no one out here. The closest village is the one I worked in last summer, and they're kind and peaceful people …"

Dominic shook his head, listening to them approach across the courtyard. He'd be surprised if the others up at the house couldn't hear Simon's raised voice.

"Well, if anything happens to you you'd damn well better remember that I warned you. I'm just looking out for your best interests, Abby."

The screen door creaked open, and Dominic had to suppress a smile. The door itself was so flimsy and weak, they weren't any safer in the lab than sitting in the grass by the lagoon. Simon was a great believer in the safety of four walls, however, and Dominic didn't feel like starting up with him again.

"I can't believe you," Simon said, looking Abby up and down. Mud splatters from the wet bank dotted her clothing and bare skin, and her hair was wild and unkempt.

"It's just a little mud and water," she said.

"I know what it is," he said tersely. "You think we have high quality modern facilities here? You think you can afford to be muddy and sweaty?"

"Come on, Simon," Dominic spoke up. "A little mud and sweat is good for you."

Simon turned his cold glare to Dominic. "Good for you?" he echoed coolly.

"Good for the soul," Dominic replied with a smile.

Abby started to smile back, but a sharp look from Simon killed it on her lips.

"Screw the soul," Simon grouched. "You're not climbing into bed with me with mud on your feet. It's bad enough I have to sleep out here with no air conditioning; at least let me enjoy the clean sheets."

"Then why didn't you just leave me outside?" Abby mumbled, and both Dominic and Simon turned to her in surprise.

She plopped herself down on the bench, stretching forward to lay herself out on it. Her eyes were already closed again, and Dominic realized she probably wasn't even aware of what she had said.

Simon, sensing that he would get no argument from her tonight, simply turned on his heel and stalked back across the lab. "Fine, sleep here," he said. "And you'd better shower before breakfast; who the hell knows what kind of bacteria you picked up from that water out there."

With that, he left the lab, heading back towards the house. Dominic glanced back at Abby and saw that she was asleep again. With a smile, he turned off the computer, standing up to stretch. He turned and plucked his sweatshirt off the hook where he usually had it hung on the wall, folding it up as he crossed the lab.

"Lift," he said softly, and Abby stirred, mumbling something in her sleep. Dominic lifted her head gently with a hand under her chin, and slid the sweatshirt beneath it. She laid her head back down, breathing deeply, sound asleep. Dominic watched her for a moment, then turned and crossed the lab, flicking off the light as he left. When he got up to the house and climbed wearily into bed, he was still thinking of Abby, and he fell asleep with a smile on his lips.

12.19.15.8.18

July 13, 2008 — "Nothing in any religion or culture points to any historical, geological, or astronomical event of importance at that time," Steve was saying, frustrated.

"And yet, that's the start of the Long Count.," Dominic replied. "And 2012 is the end of it. Those two points are connected somehow. What could do that?"

"How about time travel?" Simon said. The others turned to look at him, and he laughed. "Wondered how many of you would fall for that," he said.

"Well," Dominic said, "why not?"

Simon laughed again, and this time, he wasn't the only one.

"Come on, Dominic, you can't be serious," Dante said.

"Why not?" Dominic repeated. "They weren't just mapping a period of time, they were charting two definite, distinct dates. One was thousands of years in their past; one was thousands of years in their future. They could have been mapping when someone – let's say, someone like Kulkulcan – first appeared. They say he came from the stars, descended from the heavens on a sky rope." He looked at Abby as he said this.
"Kulkulcan brought to them an advanced culture, and could perform what they thought were miracles. Maybe he said he was from the future, pointing to that date in 2012 from whence he came, so they charted the years and the centuries in between."

"Come on, Dominic, listen to yourself," Simon said. "I was joking. The whole concept is ridiculous."

"He's right, Dominic," Tina said. "Kulkulcan came around 2,000 years ago. The first date would have been meaningless."

Dominic sighed, sitting down. "You're probably right," he said.

126

"Of course she's right," Simon said. "Whatever happened to the whole, 'let's base this on facts' bullshit?"

Dominic shrugged. "I'm just trying to cover all bases, that's all."

"Well, let's not base it in the completely fantastic, okay?" Simon said.

Dominic nodded. "Time travel based on Kulkulcan is out."

Abby glanced up at him, and as Dominic turned away, she caught the beginning of a smile. Simon hadn't caught the qualification, but she had. Dominic was definitely a character, she thought, and she was beginning to think she might finally have him figured out. He might back down on the face of things, but he wouldn't let it go. She knew he'd be bringing up black holes with her again soon.

"Scientists say that if there's going to be any sort of time travel, the technology behind it is going to be based on the physics of wormholes."

Abby glanced up, unsurprised to see Dominic in the dark beside her. She hadn't heard him come across the field, but she'd been lost in her own thoughts.

"Are you seriously considering this as an option," she asked, smiling as he held out a bottle of water to her. She took it gratefully, thanking him before responding to his comment. She cracked open the cap, taking a drink of the cold water, then wiped the sweating plastic bottle across her forehead.

He shrugged. "I'm not completely discounting it," he said. "See, the problem we've had so far is that we keep thinking of things the Maya could have known in the past, and then we throw it out because we think there's no way they could have been that advanced 2,000 years ago."

"So you're thinking that this knowledge didn't come from an advanced ancient society — it came from one in the future."

"I think it's worth considering," he said. He took a couple steps away, hands on his hips, staring out at the moon. "Maybe the end date is actually the date this time traveler would have started out from. Kind of bringing things full circle."

"Do you really think we'll have time travel by 2012?" Abby asked.

He raised a hand, pointing toward the moon. "Fifty years ago landing a probe on the moon was an unobtainable goal. Today we're sending probes out beyond the edges of our own solar system, hurtling into deep space, into the reaches of the universe. "Technology is advancing at an exponential rate, Abby, and not just Hi-Def and TIVO. You know where we're going with nuclear technology and physics. We use the Hubble telescope to actually peer back into the universe, to look back in time. I think time travel — at least in some limited sense — could be within our grasp. The end date of 2012 is only four and a half years from now. Scientists have already teleported a beam of light. It won't be much longer before we figure out how to do it with matter."

"And you think that once we manage to move matter across space, we'll be able to transport it across time," she said. A statement, not a question.

He turned to her again, and his face in the starlight was serious. "What is time? When you look into dimensional physics, it's just another physical aspect of space to move through."

Abby took another long drink of water, then sat down on the grass near her telescope. Even the ground felt hot. "You're talking about time as a dimension," she said.

Dominic came over and sat in the grass beside her. He plucked a long blade of it and began to play with it distractedly as he talked. "Ours is a multidimensional universe, and time is the fourth dimension. We move through space by using our knowledge of the first three dimensions. To move through time, we just have to learn more about the fourth."

"But isn't time itself theoretical?" she asked. "We believe in a passage of time because we can't undo something once it's done. Time is made of individual moments, each one like a snapshot, lined up one after another. We just live moment by moment, until we run out."

"So doesn't that in itself prove that time exists? We eventually run out. Our cells deteriorate, our bodies age. We're not the same from moment to moment because time works its changes on us."

Abby considered. "We age because the world we live in has an effect on us. The constant, unending pull of gravity affects our cellular structure. As we stand here, we've got radio waves, microwaves, all sorts of radiation passing through our bodies. We haven't yet figured out how to prevent the effects of our universe on ourselves."

"You could argue, too, that time doesn't exist," Abby said. "We only witness change, so we have the illusion of time passing. Without change, everything would be stagnant, and what we perceive as time would stop."

"But we *do* witness change, so by very definition, time must be moving."

"Not necessarily," she argued. "If we live each moment, we do something in that moment. Actually, we never live in the present; if you really think about it, everything we ever experience has already passed. When we hear a sound, we don't hear it at the moment it occurs, but after the sound has been transmitted through the air to our ear, and the time after our brain processes and recognizes it. When we see something, we only see it after the image crosses the distance to get to our eyes and our brain observes and understands it. Everything we see, hear, touch, or taste — everything we ever perceive and experience is always just past. Still, we believe we're living in the present. But how long, exactly, is the present? A millisecond? Less than that? Even then, our psyches cause us to view these moments in a linear form, with a past, present, and future. Time itself, though, doesn't move."

"Plato called time a 'moving, unreal reflection of eternity,'" Dominic said.

"But what's moving?" Abby asked. "Time, or just us?"

"Jesus, Abby, now he's got you talking bullshit," a voice suddenly spoke from the darkness, and Abby felt her heart sink. She turned back towards the path to see Simon standing, arms folded, in the clearing. She tried to speak but her throat was suddenly too tight to make a sound.

"I mean, he's up there babbling like an idiot about time travel being a viable option, and we all laugh and agree that he's nuts, and then I find you out here talking about it with him like it's a perfectly natural road to be going down." He walked over to where they were sitting and stood above them.

"We're just talking theoretical physics," Dominic commented.

"Theoretical bullshit is more like it," Simon responded. "I thought we were here to find concrete answers."

"What's wrong with a little philosophical discussion?" Dominic asked. "It's late, we're tired, we're bullshitting. Where's the harm?"

"The harm is that I just got back here after being gone a whole week, and instead of spending the night with me, my fiancée is sitting out here with you talking bullshit." He looked down at Abby. "Are you finished yet, or am I sleeping alone tonight?"

Guiltily, she scrambled to her feet. "I'll come back with you," she said quickly. "It's too hot out here to do any work anyway."

"I'll talk to you in the morning," Dominic said easily, and when she glanced down at him, she saw he was amused.

"Ok," she said, taking Simon's hand. "Good night."

"Night," Dominic said with a little wave.

Simon didn't answer, and as Dominic watched them walk away and vanish into the trees, his smile disappeared.

12.19.15.9.5

July 20, 2008 — "So — you promised me that we'd talk about singularity." Dominic had broached the subject once again as they sat beside the lagoon, reveling in its coolness.

Abby smiled. "You have a good memory," she said. "That was a week ago. And I think I was half asleep when we talked about it; I barely remember the conversation. What do you want to know about it?"

"Is singularity an actual physical entity?"

"It's theorized, just like black holes are," Abby said. She dipped her toes in the water, relishing the chill. It was a relief to her hot skin, baking under the scorching sun. Adding to the enjoyment, Simon had gone into town that morning, so she wouldn't have to bear his displeasure — as long as she was cleaned up by the time he got back.

"Oh, it's real." She smiled, than added. "Ok, so it's still a concept. No one has ever seen one."

"It can't be observed?" Dominic questioned.

"Nope. The universe conceals them —an 'event horizon,' which prevents the singularity from interacting with the universe. If the singularity was naked it would destroy everything; the gravitational pull would be so overwhelming it would rip apart the fabric of time and space. That's what actually happens inside the black hole. So the event horizon cloaks them."

"And is this some great cosmic rule? All black holes are identical?"

"In that sense, yes. Singularity is unavoidable. Every black hole, no matter how large or small, or what matter it sucks into it, will have that singularity at its center."

"That's the nature of the beast," Dominic said with a smile. "Okay, so what exactly is it?"

"A black hole is a gravitational drain," Abby responded. She closed her eyes as she kicked her toes lightly in the water. "It won't go outside of itself to pull things in, but anything that ventures within its event horizon will get sucked in. Some scientists claim that transit-type wormholes can't exist because every black hole has a space-time singularity at its center where gravity and matter become infinite; where everything is so compacted it becomes a single point. It's where gravity crushes everything — matter, light, space — to an absolute infinite density. It completely destroys all laws of space and time; in fact, space and time no longer exist. This is why it's called the 'awful singularity.' There's no escaping it or avoiding it; therefore, there's no way to travel through a black hole, survive the singularity and come out the other side.

"A wormhole is only a theoretical solution to a mathematical problem. It can't exist. Anything traveling through would hit the singularity and be crushed into oblivion. More than oblivion; I don't even have the words for it, Dominic. This dreadful singularity is the antipathy of the universe; it's the opposite of everything as we know it. And you can't avoid it."

Dominic thought for a moment. "But we're talking about matter. Matter can't avoid the singularity."

"Well, of course we are. What else is there?"

"Photons," he suggested.

"Even light can't escape a black hole, Dominic." She paused a moment, tilting her head thoughtfully. "True, it has no mass. But even if it could pass through, the problem with using it for travel, or to send data, would be transferring matter to non-matter like photons. And once you manage to get matter out of its state, how do you get it back again? This is the secret to time travel — how do you return something to its physical state? How do you line everything up and get it working again, especially if working with living body systems?"

"In 2002, Australian scientists transported a beam of light," Dominic said. "They broke up a laser into three pieces, teleported it, and put it back together. Then, in 2004, scientists in the US and in Austria did it with atoms."

"They've replicated the characteristics of one atom and imprinted them upon a second in a different location," Abby gently corrected, "but to my knowledge, they're not much closer now than they were then to actually teleporting consciousness from one location to another. To the best of our current scientific exploration, consciousness and identity are based upon chemical and electrical impulses in our brain and the translation thereof. You can't separate those impulses and chemicals and send them through alone.

"The scientists and their atom or laser didn't do that. And even if they could —they aren't using a black hole to do it. Even a beam of light would hit the singularity and be crushed, Dominic, and the laws of physics would not apply. No wormholes. No space — or time — travel."

"Well, damn it, then. There goes the snake chain theory."

"Sorry," she said, and paused in splashing her feet. "But aside from bending space and taking a shortcut, there's no other way to cross such vast distances. Whether their gods were real or not, they didn't travel by wormhole."

Before he could answer, there were footsteps above them on the path. "Hey, hey, what's going on down here?" Tina called, and they turned to see her stumbling down the bank towards them. On her heels was Dante, and both were dressed for swimming.

"Are we interrupting anything?" he asked.

"Yes, you are," Dominic responded. "We were in the middle of a deep, intimate conversation regarding naked singularity."

"Jeez, you want us to leave you alone?" Tina asked, and Dominic laughed.

"That's quite all right," he said. "You guys are welcome to join in."

"The only thing I'm joining you in is the water," she answered. "You guys going swimming or just cooling your tootsies?"

"Just dipping my toes for now," Abby answered, "but if you guys happen to splash me, I'm not going to complain."

Tina laughed, ran down the rest of the slope, and launched herself into the water with a huge splash. The others ducked, but were instantly soaked.

Tina surfaced, laughing and sputtering. A second later, Dante was in the water beside her, and Dominic and Abby were splashed again.

"You asked for it," Dominic said, trying to protect Abby from the cold water.

"Well, since I'm already soaked …" she said, and suddenly pushed off from the bank. She hit the water with a huge splash, spraying the others.

"Oh my God that's cold!" she said, coming to the surface. "I think my heart just stopped!"

The others laughed, ducking as she shook the water out of her hair.

"Ok, I'm cooled off," Abby said, hugging herself and shivering. She reached out a hand for Dominic to pull her out of the water. He took it, but instead of pulling, he held it as he jumped in. The others shouted as the cold water splashed over them, and amid the splashing, the singularity was forgotten.

"So what *were* you guys talking about out there?" Dante asked later, after they'd arrived back at the lab, greatly cooled off. Simon and Steve were sitting on opposite ends of the room, reading.

Abby smiled. "Black holes. We were debating the possibility of wormholes."

"I thought you were talking about something naked," Tina said. Simon looked up from his work with a glare.

"Naked singularity," Abby said quickly. "We were discussing singularity."

Simon sat back again, and while Abby breathed a sigh of relief, Dominic just shook his head. He stood up and went to the window to look out across the courtyard.

"How did you get on that subject?" Dante asked with interest. "You guys have an idea?"

"Not really," Abby said. "We'd been talking about the Mayan creation myth. The Maya said their gods descended to earth via 'snake chains,' or 'sky ropes'. That sounded like wormholes to me."

"What's that?" Tina asked.

"In short, a theoretical two-way transit system."

"Really? How does it work?"

"It doesn't," Simon spoke up, sounding bored. "Black holes and wormholes are bullshit as a method of transportation. Even theoretically."

"Oh," Tina said, glancing over at him. "So black holes can't be used for time travel?"

"Or any other form of travel, for that matter," Abby admitted. "A black hole is a black hole — what goes in doesn't come out. Or if it does, it's incredibly distorted or destroyed."

"Which makes this whole discussion pointless," Simon stated flatly.

"Why is it that you think every conversation we have is pointless?" Dominic asked, turning to Simon, and Abby tensed at the irritation in his voice.

"Because it's not getting us anywhere," Simon retorted. "We keep going around in circles while you run your mouth, and we wind up right back where we started, no further ahead."

"I'd like to live in your world where you have these little formulas you can plug into each problem and come out with an answer."

"Look, Ciriello, I understand perfectly well that we can't just end up at an answer. But I'm sick of talking about shit that has nothing to do with anything."

"Then stay the hell out of it and let the rest of us talk."

Simon rose from his seat, face reddening. No one else moved, and after a moment, he lowered himself back onto his chair.

"Fine," he said. "Then talk."

The others looked at him, then slowly, deliberately, Dominic turned his back on Simon and continued to gaze across the landscape at the volcano beyond.

"Okay then," Dante said. "What could be done about avoiding the singularity?"

Abby shook her head. "Not a thing, to our present knowledge. Dominic and I talked earlier about sending photons instead of atoms, and I suppose a more advanced race could have solved that problem, but not an earlier race."

"Why not?" Dante offered. "The Earth is nearly five billion years old. It took us this long to start looking at the universe and traveling off of our own planet, but maybe we're slow learners. A hundred years ago we were staring into a void; today we're shooting probes and explorers into it, already planning ways to travel to distant stars.

"Another civilization might have kicked in before ours, and even a thousand years might be all it would take. Think of the scientific and technological advances we might have in the year 3000. There might be another race somewhere that has already passed that point."

"That's fine if you're talking about a current alien race, but you're not," Simon said, unable to keep silent. "You're talking about almost 2,000 years ago when this thing was created, not to mention three thousand years before that where they placed the start of the count. Even if some other race was thousands of years ahead of us, look at where we were then: somewhere between Neanderthals and the Dark Ages. If they were even two millennia ahead of us, they'd have been where we are right now, still far from figuring out interstellar travel. It was too far in the distant past for that kind of understanding of physics."

"You can't say that," Tina said. "Look at the Egyptians and the precision of the pyramids."

Simon scoffed. "So they had advanced mathematics. I don't see where they were doing any time traveling."

Dominic came back to the table and sat down beside Abby. "What more can you tell us about wormholes used for space travel?"

"Well," she said slowly, "I didn't get a chance to mention it before, but there *is* some speculation that wormholes could theoretically carry people."

Simon made a noise in his throat. "Please, honey. Wormholes are smaller than protons and electrons. They haven't figured out a way to make people that small yet." He then added sarcastically, "We can't disintegrate people and recreate them just yet, either."

Abby looked away, but before she did, Dominic caught her eye. "So how is it done?" he asked.

"Well," she said. "There's an energy field called ghost radiation. Ghost radiation is negative energy, so it cancels out positive energy. The problem with wormholes is that they collapse; any positive energy, like a human being, passing through it will add its positive energy to it, so it will collapse into a black hole. If we can add the right amount of negative energy to it, it'll keep the wormhole from collapsing. If we can add even more to it, we can widen it."

"That's awesome," Dante breathed. "I thought you were just a stargazer, Abby. What was your minor, particle physics?"

She glanced up and smiled. "I'm working on my PhD in astrophysics."

"And you have a long way to go," Simon spoke up, and the others turned to him in disbelief.

"Simon, she knows what she's talking about," Dominic said. "She's exactly what I was looking for when I set up this research group."

"To you, she's brilliant," Simon said. "To me, she's still a student. And she wasn't one of my best, either." While the others stared at him, Simon stood up and crossed the room to Abby. "You go ahead and spread your knowledge, sweetie," he said patronizingly, patting her on the shoulder. "I'll be upstairs packing. I have to leave early tomorrow morning, so I don't have time to waste on pointless theories. I'll see you in awhile." He kissed her lightly on top of the head and, without a word to the others, left the room.

Abby sat still for a moment, until Dominic broke the silence. "So wormholes *could* theoretically be used for travel."

"Well, sure," she said uncomfortably, glancing up at him. "But we're a long way from harnessing ghost radiation. And even if we could, there are so many issues that we shouldn't even touch it."

"What kind of issues?" Tina asked, leaning closer.

"Add too much negative energy and the wormhole explodes into a new universe. A little something we call the Big Bang."

"You're kidding me," Dante said.

Abby couldn't help but grin. "I kid you not. Unless we want to destroy the known universe, we shouldn't do anything but theorize about it, at least until we have a better grasp on it." She glanced over at Dominic, but unlike the others, he wasn't smiling. Instead, he looked thoughtful, his dark brows drawn together.

"What is it?" Steve asked, noticing his friend's intense look.

Dominic looked up at him, then shrugged. "Just thinking," he said. "But the dates don't line up."

"You were thinking that the Mayan creation ideology was true," Abby said.

"I considered it," Dominic admitted. "Their gods planned to travel via snake chains, or wormholes. What if they miscalculated and exploded their wormhole into a new universe, essentially creating the beginning, by accident?"

"That's fine in speculation," Abby said. "But those 'gods' would have had to create our universe first, which would have destroyed their old one. Kind of hard for them to come on through again a couple billion years afterwards and descend through another wormhole to explain to them what happened."

"Would it really have destroyed the former universe? Couldn't it have just created a new one?" Steve asked. "I mean, if their own universe would have still existed on the other side, they could've perfected the technology and then come through to check out their new wards at a later date."

"The universe as we know it is infinite," Abby said. "If we could travel at or above the speed of light to get to a point hundreds or thousands of light years away, and we messed with a wormhole over there, I suppose it could blow outward and create a new universe on the other side of the wormhole. Although, it's hard to define 'outward' when you're talking about infinite space.

"However, if it had no effect on our universe, it would be far enough away that we would still exist over here with no repercussions. It's so hard to even speculate on, though; like I said, the universe is so vast. There are billions of galaxies spread across it; there could be life and civilizations somewhere on, what is to us the 'other side' of it, so far advanced that it might be within their realm of ability to create new galaxies, or even a parallel universe.

"So it's possible," she concluded, "but not probable. At least not with our present grasp of physics; it just doesn't work. Our fabric of space-time wouldn't allow it."

"Okay, *our* fabric of space time wouldn't allow it. But what about something outside our dimension?" Dominic asked.

"String theory?" Abby asked. "Multiverses?"

Before Dominic could answer, the door opened again.

"Come to bed."

It wasn't a question or a plea; it was a command. Simon had returned.

"Simon, I'm not …"

"I said come to bed," he repeated, and without waiting for an answer, he turned and left, letting the door swing shut behind him.

Abby stood slowly.

"Oh, come on," Tina said with disgust. "You're not obeying him, are you?"

Abby felt her face redden. "He's leaving tomorrow," she said. "I've been out late every night since he's been here. I feel bad; he's gone all week, drives three hours to get back here, and I don't even make an effort to spend time with him."

"Hey, you don't have to justify yourself to us," Tina said. "If you really believe that you're going up there of your own free will, because you love and miss him, then don't waste time explaining yourself to us. Get to it."

Abby crossed to the door, but before she left, she paused, turning back to address Tina. "I don't expect you to understand," she said. "I know it looks like I just mindlessly do whatever Simon tells me to. But he and I have been through a lot together. I know him, and I understand him. Simon comes across as controlling and short-tempered, but he's only like that when he's tired and stressed."

136

"Abby," Tina said wearily, "You've been saying that since we met you. Simon's tired, Simon's stressed, Simon's whatever. Guess what: this is how he is. You can deny it, or try to convince yourself, but don't bother trying to convince us. We know better, Abby. Go to him if you must, or if you want to. But don't try to bullshit us about him."

Abby was startled, but she saw from Tina's expression that she wasn't angry, she was simply tired of excuses. Abby nodded, then turned and left the lab. As she crossed the small yard and headed up to the house, Tina's words echoed in her head. Abby put a hand to her cheek, feeling her face burning. Even in her own mind, her excuses had sounded lame, and she should have known that they wouldn't fly for long. It was time to either think of new ones, or face up to the reality that Tina was right.

Abby entered through the back door and went up the stairs. She would think about it later, she decided, pushing the confrontation to the back of her mind. Simon would be gone tomorrow. She'd think about it then.

12.19.15.9.12

July 27, 2008 — "Nostradamus predicted the end of the world in 2012," Steve said.

"Nostradamus predicted a lot of bullshit."

Dominic sighed, and Abby could tell he had had about enough from Simon. "Let him talk, will you?" he said.

Simon held his hands up before him, palms out, and went to the window. He turned his back to them, but not before Abby noticed his smirk.

"Go on, Steve," Dominic said.

Steve looked uncomfortable. "Well," he said, "It's just something I was looking into. Thought while you guys were covering the factual side of things, I'd look into the spiritual. Just thought there might be some kind of tie in."

"Did he give a reason for it?" Tina asked.

"I don't remember exactly," Steve confessed. "But it had to do with the end of a World War between the Muslim nations and the West."

"Oh, great," Tina said. "That makes me feel better."

"Come on," Simon said, unable to restrain himself any longer. He turned to them again. "We can't be basing our logic on the predictions of Nostradamus. The man made general statements about the time he was living in. People go in after the fact and try to make some of his bullshit fit with current facts. But you can't use them to predict the future; every time he's given an exact date, a year, he's been wrong."

"That's the trouble with making predictions," Dominic quipped, "anyone can predict; the problem is getting the predictions *right*."

"I agree, at least as far as using predictions or myths," Tina said. "We shouldn't even be looking at Nostradamus, parapsychology or mythology."

"I don't know," Steve said, "some myths have historical value. Look at Homer's Iliad; it's supposed to be pure mythology, yet it described the lost city of Troy with amazing accuracy. No one thought it really existed until the 1870s, when its ruins were located exactly where the Iliad said they'd be."

"That's true," Tina said. "But the Iliad was a poem, not a riddle or a prophecy. I just think it might be a waste of our time trying to find the answer to the Long Count there. No Nostradamus, no Edgar Cayce, no Bible. And no Iliad, for that matter."

"Or the *Popul Vuh*, then?" Dominic asked.

"You know what I mean," Tina said. "The *Popul Vuh* was created by the same people who created the Long Count. Whatever mythology is in there is relevant to the Count. But we're talking about mythologies of foreign countries and peoples — it can't be related."

"Maybe not," Dante said, "But it could be a good reference source. If we're looking at a certain date to find something, like an earthquake, for example, we might find a reference to it in a foreign text."

"But the predictions of Nostradamus?" Simon shook his head. "It's just stupid. He made convoluted, blanket statements about things that could possibly occur at some unspecified time in the future. There's no evidence of any of them occurring. It's bullshit."

Steve spoke up again. "Simon, you are right on one thing: Nostradamus based his predictions on events that had occurred or present situations happening at the time, in the 1700s. When he speaks of a World War between opposing factions, it doesn't mean it's necessarily between present factions today. He could have been thinking about warring nations back in his own time. We read them today and see similarities and say that that's what he meant.

"I think that mentality abounds when we're talking about the Long Count," Steve continued. "There are a lot of theories based on other cultural tie-ins. One researcher studied the I Ching, the ancient Chinese fortune telling book. He studied the text and decided that it formed a mathematical algorithm, something that could be altered to become a calendar. He believes his calendar follows the timeline of fortunes of people on Earth and lined it up into a chart; when it rises, life on Earth is good. When it falls, there are bad times — wars, famine, earthquakes, tragedies. In 2012, it dips off the chart."

"Does he believe that means the world ends?" Abby asked.

Steve shook his head. "He doesn't think the world is going to end in 2012. He thinks we're going to discover time travel."

Abby looked startled, but Steve continued without noticing.

"Apparently the theory is that once we have the ability to move around in time, we don't need a timeline anymore," Steve continued. "When the timeline disappears, I guess it could mean that either time ends, or our concept of the *nature* of time ends."

"We've been looking at black holes," Abby said slowly. "Where space and time are distorted beyond our current comprehension of reality. The Maya's mythology concerns the galactic center, and we know that there's a black hole at the center of our galaxy."

"We know there's a black hole at the center of our galaxy?" Steve echoed.

"Of course, although it's not a particularly large black hole — maybe 2.6 million times the mass of the sun. But there's a black hole at the center of every galaxy," Abby answered with a smile. "We're not sure yet what role they play in galaxy formation, but evidence indicates that they have everything to do with the size and shape of a galaxy, so it's possible that they're responsible for the existence of the galaxies themselves."

"I wasn't aware of that," Dante said, interested.

"We discovered it back when we were searching for the evidence of supermassive black holes," Abby explained. "We found one in Andromeda, right next door. At that time, it scared the hell out of us to know something so massive and potentially destructive was so close … until we started looking around, and noticed that all galaxies had them. Someone got the idea to turn around and look at our own galaxy, and there it was, dead center."

"So … is ours active?" Tina asked.

"When a galaxy is in a developmental or a destructive phase, black holes are active. We notice these because they're amazingly bright; we used to think this was the only type of black hole there was: a destructive one. We never noticed our own because it's hidden — lurking out there in the galactic center like a predator. It's been silent and quiet for a very long time. But there's been some evidence that it has begun to feed again."

"That can't be good," Dante mused.

"We don't think it is, but so far, it hasn't done much damage. The Chandra X-ray telescope measured a flare from where the edge of the black hole would be. Astronomers have recorded the light from stars as they disappear into it."

"Why would it become active again?" Dominic asked.

"It seems that black holes go through phases of inactivity that are determined by their former activity," Abby said. "For example, a black hole might be so powerful that it shoots all the matter around it out into space a million light years away. This matter will be trapped by the massive gravity of the black hole and end up in a permanent orbit around it. The black hole falls dormant because there's nothing close enough to its event horizon for it to pull in. Eventually, though, a star — or solar system, or constellation of stars and solar systems — wanders into its territory and gets pulled in."

"How far are we from our black hole?" Dante asked.

"About 24,000 light years."

"Twenty-four thousand years multiplied by almost 6 trillion miles — that would only take eternity to reach. Even *at* light speed," Dominic smiled, then looked thoughtful. "If the sky portal they've talked about really *is* some kind of opening, some kind of doorway that's going to re-open in 2012, it would be at the black hole at the galactic center."

"Well, it's one possibility we could look at. When you're talking about distances like these, though, second thoughts come to mind."

Dominic nodded. "If it opens a doorway, maybe it's not a doorway in space."

Abby understood. "You're saying it's a doorway in time."

"Maybe."

"Enough with this bullshit," Simon interrupted. "It's not a doorway in anything. It's a fucking black hole, and it's going to eat us someday. That's it." He stood up and went to the door, looking out into the courtyard. He didn't glance back before swinging open the screen door and heading out into the night. A low rumble came to them, like distant thunder, but the door slammed shut before they could see if clouds were gathering. The sound was not repeated, and after a moment, Tina turned to Abby.

"Is that true?" Tina asked worriedly.

"Of course not," she said.

"Andromeda will get us before that," Dominic added.

Abby glanced over at him, but he just shrugged and smiled. "Well, come on," he said. "Why are worrying about what's going to happen in billions of years? We're concerned with what's going to happen four years from now."

"What do you mean, Andromeda is going to get us?" Tina asked, looking from Dominic to Abby.

Abby sighed. "You're as bad as Simon," she scolded him, but Dominic only smiled.

140

"What he's saying is that Andromeda is falling towards us. Someday — and not for at least three billion years or so," she added quickly, seeing Tina's expression, "it's going to collide with us."

"What's it going to do, tear us apart?"

"Basically. Whether the physical galaxy hits us or not, the gravity of each will pull the two galaxies apart. Then the gases from all the stars will cause the dormant black holes at the center of both galaxies to kick into gear again, feeding off the gases and creating a supernova. Even if we're 'lucky' enough to get knocked out of the combined mess of the two destroyed galaxies and hurtled into deep space, where we'd die from the lack of sunlight, the radiation from the supernova will reach us and destroy our planet in a heartbeat anyway."

"Well, hell," Dante said. "That's a cheerful prognosis, isn't it?"

"I wouldn't worry too much about it," Dominic responded. "Not only will none of us be here, but with the way the world is going, the human race will have killed off the planet anyway, through either environmental damage or war."

"Well, you're in a cheerful damn mood tonight, aren't you?" Abby asked. When she turned to him, he saw she was getting irritated.

He shrugged. "Simon left, someone has to fill in for him," he said.

Abby sighed and stood up, then went to the window and looked out into the night. Behind her, Dominic stood up and went to the bookshelf while Steve excused himself, heading up to the kitchen for a snack. Tina and Dante went back to work on their own studies, and after a moment, the room fell into a comfortable silence again.

Abby peered through the screen, but she couldn't make out Simon in the darkness, even with the light falling from the lab. She had a feeling he hadn't gone far; as much as he complained about being left out of the loop, she couldn't imagine that he had strayed away, leaving them to debate without him. She gazed down the hill, across the courtyard and the trees that hid the lagoon below them, but nothing moved in the darkness.

Abby watched the motionless night for what felt like an hour, letting her mind wander, spreading out like so many strands of thought across the darkness. Suddenly, she spoke up.

"String theory," she said.

Dominic had found the book on Mayan stelae he'd been looking for and returned to the lab table. Now he looked up from the heavy tome to address Abby. "What about it?" he asked.

"Well, it's a way of working around the time travel problem. Instead of working in three dimensions with their space-time constraints, we're talking about ten or more dimensions."

"You want to fill the rest of us in on that?" Tina asked.

"The problem with quantum physics is that it doesn't explain large-scale phenomena," Abby explained. "We have two different explanations for life in this universe — small scale and large scale physics, and both are correct explanations of the universe we exist in, but there's no unifying theory. The two fields seem at odds with each other.

"There are three physical dimensions and one time dimension. These are the evidential dimensions of the universe: the three dimensional world we're all familiar with, plus the fourth dimension of time. String theory surmises that there are also six separate dimensions that we can't see or feel or touch; they're tightly coiled, and their vibration dictates the particle type, such as a photon, electron, even a gravitron.

"String theory is an explanation that comes closer to any other of being the Theory of Everything — a theory that ties in all the random, unexplainable details of physics and cosmology. Or so we thought," she said. Abby paused, and across the room, Dominic picked up where she'd left off.

"String theory didn't provide a proper description for quarks, for fermions," he said. "So string theory begat superstring theory. Problem there was that there were five different superstring theories, all equally viable. These were then combined into M-Theory, which is, thus far, the most complete explanation we have for the physical laws of the universe. We're still testing the theory."

"Fascinating," Tina said, "But what does this have to do with time travel?"

"Time is a dimension," Abby explained patiently. "If we look at it as a dimension alone, then time travel can't occur. We can't turn the arrow of time. But if we look at time under M-Theory, which allows for not four, and not even ten, but actually eleven dimensions, we have a better idea of how these strings may be manipulated to accomplish such a thing. It all starts with agreeing on the existence of time," Abby continued, "and determining through classical mechanics where you are, where you're looking and which one you're using."

"Which what you're using?" Steve asked. "There's more than one kind of time?"

"At least two," Abby smiled. "It's all relative."

"Special and general." Dominic's voice came muffled from across the room. His head was down again as he studied the copied stela with a magnifying glass.

"That's right," Abby replied. "Special relativity describes objects that are moving very, very fast. General relativity concerns the universe, and motion near massive objects: planets, stars, black holes, galaxies. Time passes differently from different points of view. It slows down near large objects like black holes. In fact, some theorize that data flow at the center of a black hole as it heads toward the singularity is slowed down to near motionlessness. Time is very, very fluid."

"They said we were birthed from the galactic center," Dominic explained to the others, setting down the magnifying glass as he addressed them. "We now know that at the galactic center is a black hole. Maybe they couldn't physically travel through it, but they could use it to send a message through time."

"It's a possibility," Abby admitted. "I mean, we've sent messages of our own out there into deep space; the voyager message, the Arecibo message. We carved messages into the side of spaceships and beamed them out via radio waves because that was the extent of our technology at the time. Who's to say an advanced astronomical civilization didn't have an advanced way of sending their own messages? They didn't have to show up here physically, or shoot anything physical through the black hole. Perhaps all they had to send was a data stream. Just like we can send data through a cell phone or wireless internet, a technological civilization that's hundreds or even thousands of years ahead of ours could have figured out how to send a message through space — and time. Maybe when the doorway opens in 2012 we'll receive some archaic message from another civilization."

"From our creator civilization."

Abby looked at Dominic, who had his chin in his hand, gazing at her in a friendly challenge. Before she could respond, however, Tina let out a heavy sigh.

"I can't follow this," she admitted. "If they had to send a message back in time to us now, how could they have been part of our past? Or responsible for our development? And then be sending a message into what is actually our future? It's just too confusing," she said, shaking her head.

Dante put an arm around her. "Don't stress yourself out over it," he said. "I prefer to leave the physics of time travel up to those two." He nodded towards Abby and Dominic. "I'm here to explain the physical Earth to them; you're here because of your knowledge of Mayan archaeology. We'll leave the complications up to them."

"Sounds good to me," Tina said, standing up. "I think, on that note, I'm ready to call it a night."

Dante rose with her, and with a wave and a goodnight, they headed back up to the house.

"Looks like it's you and me again," Dominic said.

"Lucky us," Abby replied, returning his smile. She returned to the table and sat down across from him. They regarded one another for a moment before Abby asked, "So, how is this going to work? We just use

Steve and Tina and Dante when we need their area of expertise, but they don't actually take part in the discussion?"

"They're welcome to join in anytime they want. I'm not keeping anyone from anything."

The screen door opened behind them and Simon came in. Spotting Dominic and Abby alone in the lab, he looked around suspiciously. Abby could have sworn that for a moment, she saw the doorframe shift slightly as the lab floor beneath her seemed to tremble. She pressed both feet to the floor and blinked hard, and the world settled.

Dominic rose from the table, his voice suddenly tired. "I'm going to bed," he said. "Good night, Abby. Simon."

Simon grunted a response, and Abby raised a hand. Dominic gave her a smile and left, heading back up towards the house.

Simon slid onto the bench next to Abby. "You two seem to be getting cozier and cozier, don't you?"

"What?" She turned him in surprise. "Where did *that* come from?"

"It just seems like every time I come home, you're alone with our goddamn host. I leave the room for twenty minutes and there you are, just the two of you. How do you get rid of the others?"

"For crying out loud, Simon, what the hell are you talking about? We didn't chase them out any more than we made you leave. You got up and walked out. So did the others, for various reasons. It's no conspiracy, Simon."

He stood up suddenly, grabbing her by the upper arm. "Don't talk to me like that, Abby. I don't know what the hell is going on here, but I don't like it."

"Maybe you'd know what was going on if you'd quit walking out," she retorted, then ducked as Simon raised his hand.

"Hey, where's … *whoa.*"

They both turned to see Steve framed in the doorway, a sandwich in one hand and a soft drink can in the other. He was staring at Simon, eyes wide.

Simon lowered his hand, but didn't release his grip on Abby's arm. "We're just going to bed," he said. He headed for the door, pulling her with him. Abby caught Steve's troubled eye as they passed. Neither of them spoke.

Steve turned and watched them go, waiting until they'd disappeared into the house before heading back across the courtyard. He hadn't seen Dominic pass while he was in the kitchen, so he knew he must be out wandering somewhere. Steve set his drink on a rock outside the door, then laid his sandwich on top of it. He'd suddenly lost his appetite.

12.19.15.9.13

July 28, 2008 — "God, I hate numbers," Dante muttered.

"So what? They're not your responsibility," Simon said shortly.

Dante looked up at him, eyebrows knit together in irritation. "There's no need to be a jackass, Simon."

"Then don't insult my work."

"Oh, for God's sake, I'm not insulting your work. You are not the master of all things numerical. Everything anyone says and does is not a personal attack on you. Quit being so damned sensitive."

Simon laid down his pencil. "You want to tell me how I should be, do you?"

"Guys, come on," Tina said nervously. "Cut it out."

"Don't tell us what to do," Simon said without dropping his eyes from Dante's.

"Don't talk to her like that," Dante responded.

"Stop it," Abby said. She looked over to where Dante and Simon sat across from each other at the lab table. Tina was sitting in front of the computer, and Abby had been standing by the bookshelf, glancing through some of the physics texts Dominic had supplied her with.

"Please," she said. "Simon, Dante didn't mean anything personal. I asked him to look up some geological facts for me regarding this area of the country; he's just trying to work out some terrestrial distances. It's not about you."

"Stay out of this, Abby," Simon said shortly. "I'm tired of you sticking up for them."

"And I'm tired of you."

Startled, the others turned to the doorway where Dominic stood, having appeared silently and unnoticed. He strode into the room and went to the bench, stopping next to Dante. He leaned over the table, his face mere inches from Simon's. "I've had enough of it. I don't give a flying fuck what you think or do, but it's time that you started showing some respect for your fellow researchers. We're not here to listen to you. I don't care if you like us or not, but you're damn well going to stop treating people with such disdain. Do you understand me?"

Simon stood up, and Dominic rose with him. They stared across the table at each other, and as Simon looked up at the other man – who towered over him by an easy six inches and outweighed him by at least forty pounds – he seemed to realize his disadvantage.

"Whatever," he said, turning away. He grabbed his notebook and pencil from the tabletop, but before he could move away, Dominic's hand shot out, grabbing Simon firmly by the upper arm.

"Hey," he whimpered, trying to pull away. Dominic's grip tightened, his long fingers easily wrapping around the smaller man's bicep.

"Not 'whatever,'" he said. "You don't dismiss me, and you don't disregard what I'm saying. We're all equals here, professionals in our own fields. Having a PhD in advanced mathematics doesn't make you any more intelligent than a man with a PhD in geology, or even a man with no PhD at all. We all know what the hell we're doing here, and no one appreciates being dismissed by you out of whatever ego trip you happen to be on."

"Fine," Simon responded. "Let go of me, will you?"

Dominic paused, his eyes locked on Simon's, and his grip tightened for just an instant before he let go. He saw the pain in the other man's eyes before he released him.

"Get out of here," Dominic said.

Simon didn't respond; he just turned and headed out the back door, moving quickly, as if he was afraid Dominic would reach out and latch onto him again. As he moved across the courtyard, he rubbed his sore upper arm. It would bruise deeply.

Just as quickly and quietly as he had come in, Dominic turned and left the room, going out the other door, back towards the house. The door swung shut, leaving the others gaping in disbelief.

"What the hell was that all about?" Dante asked, stunned.

"I don't know," Tina said slowly. "I've never seen him that angry in my life. I don't know that I've ever seen him lose his temper before."

"I guess I should thank him," Dante said. "Simon and I were about to come to blows."

"I almost thought *they* were going to," Tina said. "I think Dominic was hoping they would."

"Damn," Dante said, shaking his head. He lowered his head over his book again. "Mornings sure are never dull around here."

As he and Tina returned to their work, Abby remained shocked and still, standing motionless next to the bookcase. She knew Dominic must have found out about Simon's rage the night before. She hadn't known that he had a violent side, but coming out of nowhere as it did, it had scared her more than any of Simon's outbursts ever had. She slowly pulled a book from the shelf without looking at it, then lowered herself onto the bench next to Dante. She thought she might spend the day as close as she could to the others; she didn't want to be alone with either Simon or Dominic for a very long while.

August 1, 2008 — The nights had been nearly as hot as the daytime almost all summer, but this evening was warm and comfortable, and Abby decided to go stargazing. The others came with her, looking for a reason to be outside on such a beautiful evening.

"The moon is at perigee right now—when its orbit is closest to Earth," Abby said, as the group headed into her clearing. "It'll give us a good chance to look at the maria."

"The seas," Dominic said.

"That's right."

The two continued across the field, side by side. Impatient, Simon had walked ahead. He had never been much for stargazing, and didn't seem to like the attention Abby was getting for it. Tina and Dante hung back, chatting and laughing amiably. Steve strolled along behind them.

"They act like they're on a field trip," Abby commented.

Dominic laughed. "Tina and Dante can have fun doing pretty much anything. Steve's not a night person, though," he said, glancing back at his friend. "As long as I've known him, he's been in bed by eleven. This is a whole new world to him. But I wouldn't count on him staying with us long — I give him a half an hour, max, before he's either sleeping on the ground over there or heading back up to the house."

"Then I guess I'd better set up fast."

Sure enough, Steve excused himself and headed back up for the house only twenty minutes after Abby had the moon in full view of her scope. She had pointed out the maria first, explaining their geological makeup and how they were seas not of water, but of basaltic lava.

"Lakes of lava?" Tina asked, intrigued.

"Not liquid," Abby explained. "Somewhere between three and almost four million years ago this iron-rich lava erupted to the surface and filled the impact craters that were already there; the oldest are the irregularly shaped ones, like Mare Foecunditatis — the Sea of Fertility. The more recent ones are more circular, less damaged, like Crisium, the Sea of Crisis, or Serenitatis, the Sea of Serenity."

"I thought it was tranquility?" Tina said.

"That's a different one," Abby explained, adjusting the focus to find the lower sea. "Tranquilitatis is the site of an Apollo landing."

She pointed out all five visible seas. "We can't see the others, like the Sea of Rains, or the Sea of Clouds. They're only visible when the moon is waxing, and it's waning right now."

"Did the Maya know about the seas of the moon?" Dante asked. He was standing a little distance away, studying the moon with the naked eye instead of the telescope.

"Not what they were," Dominic said. "Just like western people saw a man in the moon, and various others throughout the world have their own myths, the Maya did too. When they looked at the dark seas, they saw a leaping rabbit. The Mayan moon goddess was often portrayed as holding a rabbit."

"Did they have a lot of moon mythology?" Abby asked, adjusting the focus on her telescope as tightly as she could.

"It was mentioned some," Dominic replied, "But remember, the Maya were sun astronomers. There are various Mayan myths regarding the moon, though – one is that the sun and moon fell in love and ran away together. The moon's grandfather was so angry that he had her murdered and dismembered; dragonflies found her body and stashed it into thirteen stumps. The sun, who'd been looking for her for thirteen days, finally found it and brought her back to life."

"They were slightly obsessed with the number 13, weren't they?" Dante said.

"Thirteen baktuns," Dominic agreed. "The end of the Long Count."

"There are many cycles of 13 in the Count," Simon said, speaking for the first time since they'd assembled in the clearing. "You all just focus on the big one, the main cycle. But the Count breaks down into many revolutions, and just as there are thirteen baktuns, there are thirteen katuns."

"One of these nights, look through the bookshelf in the lab," Dominic said. "I brought copies of pages from the *Books of Chilam Balam*. The thirteen katun dates are extremely important in Mayan astrology. Each describes the history of the previous cycle and a prediction for the next."

"What does the one say that ends in 2012?" Abby asked, curious.

"It's the time of Judgment," Dominic said, thinking carefully. "There will be plagues and famine. Governments will collapse, nations will perish. It will basically be the end times."

"Oh, fucking great," Simon said, laughing quietly.

"Well, that's not really outrageous," Dominic said. "Twelve of the thirteen katun prophecies were negative. Only one was of peace and harmony."

"Hopefully that comes after the 2012 cycle?"

"Sorry," Dominic answered, "The last of those cycles began in — let's see — I think 1914."

"Just before the first world war? Great predicting skills, those Maya," Simon scoffed.

"What do you mean 'the last of those cycles?'" Dante asked, ignoring him.

"The cycles repeat," Dominic explained. "The Maya believed that history repeated itself. So the thirteen katun prophecies repeated every twenty years."

"So this judgment time has come and gone before," Simon said. "Obviously, we've lived through it already, probably several times."

"When was the last time?" Abby asked.

"I'm can't remember the exact date," Dominic admitted, "but I have it all in my notes from previous research. I'll look it up when we get back up to the lab."

They gazed at the stars a little while longer, discussing various formations and different aspects of the moon. Dante and Tina had moved away, putting as much distance as possible between themselves and Simon while still remaining in the group. Simon didn't seem to be paying much attention to the others, however; he was lost in his own world, standing with folded arms, staring at the sky.

Dominic and Abby sat in the grass at the foot of her telescope.

"I think it's interesting that the Maya didn't do much with the moon," she said. "Most ancient cultures inscribed moon cycles on their tablets and literature, even in the walls of caves. It was the one cycle of nature they could easily recognize and always count on. It seems like the Maya were a little more hit and miss, with a focus on Ursa Major, Orion and the sun."

"The sun is the giver of life," Dominic said, "so a lot of cultures focused on it. Look at the 'Eye of Ra' symbol — it, or something extremely similar to it, has been found in a lot of different cultures. Some people think that it means some connection between ancient races, a common cultural link. But it's just a solar event that people around the globe experienced."

"What is it?" Abby asked, curious.

"It depicts a solar eclipse," he answered. "The corona of the sun around the moon might, for an ancient culture that saw gods in the constellations, look like the eye of God watching them."

Abby nodded. "Intriguing," she said. "If the Maya were interested in sun cycles, the Long Count might revolve around that. That is, if it wasn't just one of the many things they were recording through their mythology."

"Well, it wasn't like they were aimless in their science," Dominic said. "They had two main concerns: Charting time, and finding the center of the universe."

"Seems like two fairly unrelated goals," Abby commented. "You don't think they are, though, do you?"

"When they leave us with something like the Long Count and we know it was only one of their obsessions," Dominic responded. "What are the odds that it has nothing to do with their second one?"

"Obsessed with time," Abby mused.

"Somehow, time and the galactic center have to be connected," Dominic said.

"Everything is connected with time, Dominic. We use angular measures to calculate distances in the sky based on a 360-degree circle, with each degree divided into 60 arc minutes, which are divided then into 60 arc seconds. We put the 'arc' in front to differentiate distance from time, but it's the same deal. If two stars are 2 degrees apart, they're 120 arc minutes or 7200 arc seconds apart."

"So how does that figure into space?"

Abby was about to answer, then looked to Simon. Although he stood a few yards away, she knew he was listening.

"Simon, can you help with the geometry?" she asked.

He kept his back to them, but motioned with his hands as he explained.

"You're viewing the sky as a circle, the celestial sphere," he said. "If you want to figure out the surface area of that sphere, it would be four times pi times the radius $^{\wedge}2$. The radius is 360 degrees, so the surface area of the sky would be ..." he paused for a minute, closing his eyes and calculating.

"Forty-one thousand, two-hundred fifty-three," Dominic said immediately. Simon opened his eyes, turning to Dominic in surprise. He looked as if he was calculating again, then appeared to give up.

"Whatever," he said.

Dominic nodded. "So what is that in comparison?" he asked. "Forty-one thousand square degrees doesn't sound that big when we're talking about something billions to trillions of light years across."

"Well, the moon is about half a degree across," Abby said. "What does that make it?"

"It'd have an area of 0.2 square degrees," Dominic said without hesitation.

"Okay," Abby said. "So that helps us calculate distances in space. But it's not going to help us much with time."

They fell silent again, thinking. Tina and Dante wandered back over and sat in the grass beside them. Simon stayed where he was, a short distance away, his back to the rest of the group.

"360 degrees is the perfect degree of a circle," Dominic finally said.

"Yes."

"It would also be the degree of a perfectly round Earth. Or, one that may be rounding out over time?"

"Well, yes, but no planet is perfectly round. The moon isn't even round; it has a massive bulge on the dark side. It's had that bulge for about 4.6 billion years, and it's not trying to straighten itself out."

"What makes it bulge?" Tina asked.

"We don't know," Abby admitted. "It's not a gravitational bulge; otherwise, it'd be on the bright side, where the Earth's gravity would be pulling it, making it bulge out towards us."

"Hmmm," Dominic said. "Does it look like something could have exploded out that way?"

"Like what, an atom bomb?" Simon asked sarcastically.

"I was thinking more of a geological explosion," Dominic said. "Something like plate tectonics. That's what pushed the Earth's crust up into mountain ranges; maybe something similar could have happened on the moon."

"Don't look at me," Dante said. "I'm an Earth geologist, not an astro-geologist. I don't know much about the formation of any other planet but this one."

"The moon isn't a planet," Simon said under his breath, but the others ignored him.

"We're still unsure about how the moon was even created," Abby said. "The moon rocks we collected indicate that the moon is older than the Earth. The going theory has it that the moon traveled here from an older part of the solar system, then was captured by the Earth's gravity. If it was formed elsewhere, the gravity of another planet or star could have formed the bulge. The problem with that is that there would have to be a slowing mechanism, which there wasn't. Also, the orbit would be a lot more elliptical than it is; our moon's orbit is circular."

"I thought the moon was just chunk of the Earth," Tina said. "Some catastrophic collision with the Earth knocked the moon off into space, where it couldn't escape our gravity."

"That's another theory," Abby said. "The moon rocks our astronauts returned to Earth are made up of the same elements you'd have found in the early stages of the Earth's formation. They consist of the same material, but again, they're much older than the Earth. All goes to show, the moon is a mystery. We still don't know all that much about it."

"The moon has nothing to do with the Long Count," Simon said. "All we're doing out here is wasting our time. I'm going back up to the house."

"I'll join you," Dominic said, surprising the others. He stood up and brushed the dirt and grass from the seat of his pants. "I want to verify the Ahau dates."

"The what?" Dante asked, standing up. He held out his hands to Tina and Abby, pulling them up.

"The Ahau dates. The katun beginnings we were talking about earlier."

They all headed back up towards the lab, bunched together in their small groups, Simon again in the lead.

When they'd reached the lab, Tina and Dante excused themselves, returning to the house. Abby considered following them, but was wary of leaving Simon and Dominic alone. She felt silly, but still, she sat down. If her presence kept them civil, it would be worth staying.

Dominic went to the bookshelf, pulling down several notebooks. He brought them over, tossing them onto the table and climbing onto the bench beside Abby. He pushed one volume in front of her and kept the other. Abby flipped hers open, scanning the pages, even though she had no idea what she was looking for.

Simon sat down across from them, then pulled the notebook from Abby's hands. She didn't comment, and Dominic was too busy searching through his own book to notice. As he flipped through the pages, he explained:

"The short count is 256 years, a cycle of 13 katuns – the 20ths of the Long Count. The Maya believed that at the end of each 13 katun cycle, it starts over. The katun names fall on the end date of the previous cycle. Here we go," he said, finding a list of dates. He read over it for a moment, then sat back. He put a hand over his mouth.

"What is it?" Abby asked.

"I was wrong."

Simon's head jerked up sharply. "About what?" he asked.

Dominic shook his head. He took his hand from his mouth and pointed at a date on the page. "I was thinking of 13 Ahau," he said. "I guess I had the thirteen in my head. But 13 Ahau isn't the beginning cycle of the end date; that would be 2 Ahau."

"Two?" Simon asked. "Don't they go in order?"

"No, they're numbered oddly," Dominic said. "Each katun prophecy is numbered two Ahau less than the one before it." He shook his head again, staving off their questions. "Don't ask," he said. "It's complicated. They range from 13 Ahau, in odd numbers, down to 1 Ahau, then from 12 Ahau in even numbers to 2. Anyway — 2 Ahau isn't catastrophic."

"Well, what does it say?" Simon asked impatiently.

"Not much. 'For half, there'll be prosperity and fortune. It's a time of union, and a time of disintegration, of the end of the time of God.'"

Simon laughed. "They did cover all bases, didn't they? Some will eat, some will starve; some will do well, some will do poorly," he mocked. "Today's astrologers haven't come that far from them, but they at least wait a day or two before contradicting themselves."

He pushed back from the table and stood up. "I should've known better than to take any interest in prophecy," he tossed the notebook back onto the table and announced, "I'm going to bed."

Dominic nodded dismissively, bending over his book again.

"What does that mean, 'the end of the time of God'?" Abby asked.

Dominic looked up at her, but Simon, standing in the doorway tapping his foot, interrupted.

"Abby?" Simon said.

"Good night, Dominic," she said, standing up. He barely acknowledged her, giving her a simple nod.

She followed Simon out, turning back momentarily at the door. Dominic was lost in his book, hunched over the table, reading intently. Abby turned and trailed behind Simon, back up to the house and to bed.

12.19.15.9.18

August 2, 2008 — Dominic and Dante were poring over a geological relief map. "I'm sorry," Dante said. "Other than the volcanoes Tacana and Tajumulco, neither of which was active during the Mayan era, there's nothing geological in this area that would have regularly affected their lives."

"How about earthquakes?" Dominic asked. "This area is part of the ring of fire."

"Sure it is," Dante said. "And I can research earthquake history in this area, but there's no way to predict earthquakes. Maybe they'd noticed some kind of regular pattern to them and thought they knew when another one — maybe the Big One — was coming. But I don't believe that's it — scientists have been looking for centuries for ways to predict earthquakes. With all the studies that have been done on the subject, and with all the records we have, we'd have found a pattern."

Dominic sighed, sitting down. He smoothed out the map. "Well," he said. "This is still a great topographical map of Izapa. Very detailed. I'd like to head out there sometime this week with it and compare it with the site."

"Count me in," Tina said.

"Me too," Steve said. "We could use another trip out there, anyway. I wouldn't mind sleeping over on site. Hell, maybe even for a few days. We really need to spend some time at the birthplace of the Count. Somehow, maybe we can see what they saw; get a feel for what they were thinking. Maybe something will strike us."

"And maybe pigs will fly," Simon muttered.

Tina and Dante exchanged a weary look.

Abby quickly spoke up. "I think it'll be good for me, at least, to spend a night or two there. We're certainly close enough to it so I'm getting the same sky, but I'd like to see the exact view they had. I'd like to see what horizons they had, what they could see through the mountains. I know the tree line won't be the same, but still, the basic views will be helpful."

"Great," Dominic said. "Then we'll take a field trip out sometime this week. Simon, you want to come?"

"Hell no," Simon said. "This is as roughing it as I want to get."

Dominic nodded, as if he'd expected no different. "Then we'll wait until after you've left for the week."

"How considerate of you," Simon said sarcastically.

Dominic shrugged. "Actually, I was just counting sleeping bags. If we wait until you're gone, we don't have to come up with an extra."

Simon was silent, but his face was beginning to redden. Again, Abby jumped in to defuse him. "Do you think we'll have a lot to carry?" she asked Dominic. "I would really like to take my scope. I'd like to find several places at the site to set it up, to compare views. The way they set up their shrines and temples might be to site different astrological events. They could have set up the stelae to mark the passage of different planets as they moved across the sky."

"Do you think they could have been following orbits?" Dominic asked.

"Come on, they didn't even know the Earth revolved around the sun until Galileo discovered it, over a thousand years later," Simon said derisively. "How could they know about orbits?"

"Simon, you're thinking in terms of European history," Steve argued. "We're talking about Mayan history. When Europe was in the Dark Ages, burning books and holding inquisitions on anyone that questioned their specific religion as the only explanation, the Maya had built pyramids aligned with heavenly bodies, observatories to study them, and created the first calendars. Who knew what they were thinking? How can we know what they knew?"

"Come on," Simon said disgustedly. "Quit trying to bestow all these mystical qualities on them, damn it. They didn't hold the secret to the universe. If they did, they wouldn't have been massacred and annihilated."

"Having knowledge doesn't necessarily make them invincible, or even powerful. If a stronger force attacked them, they'd be killed just the same," Steve said.

"Enough, both of you," Dominic said. "The Maya were killed by European diseases, not weapons. Smallpox and diphtheria did them in. The Maya were astronomers, not physicians. They didn't have the antibodies, and they didn't have the cures. Game over. Case closed."

"No, it's not case closed," Simon said. He stood up, looking down at the others who were cast loosely around the room. "You guys are acting like the Maya were some kind of metaphysical beings that knew the past and future of the universe. They weren't. They were just people like any others; the only difference is that they lived a long time ago. They knew the same things anyone else did two thousand years ago — absolutely nothing."

"Well, they weren't exactly a cave dwelling society banging clams open on rocks, Simon," Dominic said. "Look at their art. Look at the pyramids. We tend to think of two thousand years ago as the biblical era. We think of people living in mud huts, wearing robes and riding mules. We don't think of the Inca city on top of Machuu Pichu, or the observatory at Chichen Itza. These weren't stone-age people, Simon. They were advanced far beyond any European or Middle Eastern society at the time in art, astronomy, architecture. They could have known far, far more than we do now."

"And they could have not known shit. Look, they based their calendar on astronomy. They probably calculated backwards the way we do now to figure out where a constellation would've been a couple thousand years ago. For whatever reason, they based their calendar on it and blocked out a chunk of time, maybe until one of their formations came back around. And that's it. No mystery, no predictions. Just basic astronomical calculations."

"Well hell, I guess we can all go home now," Dominic replied in disgust. He threw up his hands and stood up, then headed for the door. "Thanks for your brilliant observations, Simon. I don't know what the hell the rest of us were thinking." He held the door open.

"No need to be sarcastic," Simon said. "You don't have to throw a fit and leave."

"I'm not," Dominic said. He didn't move. Simon stared at him for a moment, and as the realization dawned on him, his jaw tightened.

"Well, I'm sure as hell not leaving."

"Guys," Steve said, standing up nervously. "Can you cut it out? This isn't helping anyone."

"Stay out of this," Dominic said quietly.

"Dominic," Steve said again, as the others stayed dead silent.

"Steve, stay out of it," Dominic repeated, not taking his eyes off of Simon.

"So what do you want me to do?" Simon asked petulantly. "You want me to get out? Fine. I will. Abby and I are both out of here. The rest of you can screw around these woods until the ball drops. I'm not helping you."

"*You're not helping us now!*" Dominic roared, and Abby could practically feel the others take a step back. Never before had they heard him raise his voice, and it was obvious now that he was not messing around. Even Simon was taken aback.

"Okay," he said quietly, and suddenly sat down. "You're right. That wasn't helping."

He and Dominic stared at each other across the room for a long, silent moment. Without a word, Dominic nodded, then turned and walked out.

"Holy shit," Dante breathed.

Steve followed after him.

"Where are they going?" Dante asked.

"Dominic will go be pissed off somewhere, Steve will sit and bullshit with him, and after awhile, they'll be back," Tina said. "Just leave them alone."

Dante looked over at her. "You wanna go grab a beer?"

She laughed, standing up. "You're on," she said.

The two left, tossing a quick smile to Abby, but she was still in shock. She glanced over at Simon, and saw he looked as stunned as she was. Without a word, he got up and went out into the courtyard. Her heart skipped a beat, afraid he was going after Dominic, but she watched as he simply went out and sat down on a boulder. He had been silenced, finally, as Dominic had reached the end of his patience, and he apparently didn't know how to take it.

Sighing, she turned back to the work in front of her. Tina had seemed unconcerned, matter-of-fact that this would all blow over, and Abby believed her. Still, she thought she'd stay up late and stargaze tonight. It seemed like all of them could use a little time away from each other.

Her private time was not to be allowed, however. She'd been deeply intent on searching the deep sky with her scope when she heard Dominic's voice behind her.

"Mind some company?"

Abby sighed, straightening up. "Do I have a choice?"

Dominic was unruffled. "Sure," he said. "I can always keep going. I was on my way to the cave when I saw you here. Thought I'd stop and say hi, but if you don't feel like talking, I understand."

"What did you want to talk about?"

Dominic shrugged. "Whatever. The moon. The sky. The moon. The stars. The moon."

Abby had to smile. "Anything in particular about the moon?"

"I've been curious," Dominic said, approaching her. "The Maya went by a 13 day cycle of the moon."

"Thirteen days is the observational cycle," Abby said. "From new to full, it's actually 14.5 days. But the Maya didn't have a scope like mine to discern the waxing and waning. They were going by what they could see with the naked eye, and the visual phase is 13 days."

Dominic nodded, leaning over her telescope. "You mind?" he asked.

"Knock yourself out," she answered. She watched Dominic peer through the eyepiece, his tall frame awkwardly bent over the low scope. She smiled. "Let me raise that for you."

"No, that's okay," he said, straightening and turning to her. "You're the astronomer. Adjust it how it's best for you. I'll leave you to it."

"Well, now that you've interrupted me, you may as well stay."

For once, Dominic looked uncomfortable. "I'm sorry, Abby. Was I interrupting? I didn't mean to intrude."

She waved him off. "I'm just glad to see you back to normal again."

He laughed. "I didn't know I had a mode that could be considered 'normal.'"

"Well — as opposed to angry and freaking out, I guess."

"Yeah," he said quietly. "Sorry about that."

"Trust me, it's not a problem. You owed Simon that. He's blown up at the rest of us a dozen times already. You have far more patience than I could have in such a situation."

"Not at all," he said, stepping back so she could readjust the scope. "You've put up with him for several years now. I don't know if I'll make it a few more months without killing him."

Abby laughed and raised the scope.

"So," Dominic said. "What are you looking for?"

"Anything that catches my eye," she said. "I've given up on having a game plan. I've examined everything that they could have seen with the naked eye. I'm studying specific planets, stars and other objects;

I'm trying to figure out if they were noticing patterns. Basically, I'm just watching the sky and waiting for something to hit me."

"As long as it's not a meteorite or anything," he joked.

Abby smiled and stepped back from the telescope. She looked up at the evocative night sky, at the brilliant, glittering stars above them.

"Whatever it was, it had to be something powerful or compelling," she said. "I can't imagine they would have styled the Long Count after the monotonous patterns and repetitions of the cycle of the moon, or the planets."

"I'm a little disappointed that we haven't hit on anything yet," Dominic said, "but I have faith. Somehow, it'll come together."

"Do you have any ideas at all?" Abby asked.

"Nothing to base anything on," he said. "Just a feeling. Or, maybe just what I want it to be."

"What is it?" she asked, curious. She turned to him in the darkness, but could not make out his expression.

"I don't know what they designed it around," Dominic said, "but I think that for the Maya, it really was the end of an age, and the start of a new beginning. I see it like a yin-yang symbol; an energy transference, a slow change from one extreme to another. Like the slowly changing face of the moon."

"What extreme are we at?"

"So many. I think we're at the culmination of modern technology. We're at the saturation point of the Earth. We've overpopulated it, polluted it, poisoned it and depleted it. If we're allowed to continue, we'll destroy the planet. It has to protect itself. It has to switch over and recover, and our technology and growth must begin a steady decline."

"Some say this has happened many times, that there were many advanced civilizations before us."

"It's possible. Everything in the universe goes in cycles; civilization and culture could go the same way. We look at history over the period of about two to three thousand years, and to us it looks like a steady climb from the Stone Age to the space age. But there is technology from history that we still don't understand. There's some evidence of advanced civilizations that are astronomically old, ancient beyond comprehension. Sunken cities that were above ground long before the end of the last ice age ten thousand years ago."

"So you think there really have been four previous ages? That we're living in the fifth and final age?"

"That's what I want to find out."

12.19.15.10.0

August 4, 2008 — Along with the relief map, Dante had found a geological survey of the area, which he brought with him on their overnighter. Steve had supplied a book with an old Mayan map of the area, and they used it now, traipsing through the Izapan site, maps in hand.

"Guys, look: we're talking about dimensions here," Dominic said. "What direction is north?"

Dante checked his compass, then turned and pointed.

"Wrong," Dominic said. "North is up."

Abby turned to him with a surprised smile. "They worked in 3D?"

"At least three dimensions," Dominic said. "When Mayan maps indicate north, they meant the realm of the sky. The sky was as much a part of their world as the ground below them."

"It seems like they knew a lot more about the sky than the Earth, actually," Dante commented. "I've read through the stelae translations you gave me, and there's nothing of any geological significance there. Either there were no earthquakes or anything during this period, or they didn't bother to record it."

"And actually, I can't say they knew a lot about space, either," Abby added. "They recognized planets and stars, but all they did was make up stories about them. There's no advanced astrological knowledge other than their simple observations."

"Jeez, you guys are rough," Dominic said amiably. "You two ganging up on me?"

"Yeah," Dante said, "we thought we'd lure you out here and abandon you, then hurry back and escape. Simon's actually back at the lab packing up the truck."

This brought a round of laughter from all of them, including Abby. "That'll be the day," she said. "If he's packing up the truck, we'll all get back in time to find a note left from him saying, 'So long, suckers.'"

"Yeah, his loyalty to us isn't exactly overwhelming," Tina commented. She looked around. "What do you think? Should we set up our tents by the edge of the woods? I know there aren't any park rangers or anything around here, but I still don't think we can set up right in the middle of the site."

"I think the jungle will be fine," Dominic said. "Just keep your sleeping bags zipped tight. There are a lot of snakes and spiders out there."

"Oh God," Abby shuddered. "I forgot about that part."

"Don't worry about it," Steve said. "They won't bother you. You're too big for food for them. Except for the boas, that is."

She gave him a withering look, and Dominic laughed. He slid an arm around her shoulders. "I'll sit at the foot of your sleeping bag and scare them all off," he said. "Don't worry; Steve and Tina and I have camped out near here almost half a dozen times, and we've all survived so far."

"Although there's a first time for everything," Tina joked.

"You know, maybe I don't need to study the star positions out here," Abby said. "I think the lab is close enough."

They laughed, then went about finding a place to set up camp. There were no tourists that day, so the team spread out their sleeping bags and left their backpacks near the site.

Abby sat down to make herself a sandwich from the supplies they had packed while Steve went to gather firewood. Tina and Dante took off towards the ballcourt, and Dominic sat down beside her. "Dinner?" she offered. He smiled and shook his head, lying down in the grass.

"You're going to just take it easy, huh?" she asked.

He laughed. "Yeah, I could use a break."

"So while the others set up the tent and gather firewood and I make our dinner, you're going to lay there?"

"That's the general plan." He propped himself up on one arm to watch her. "You seem very relaxed out here yourself," he said.

She shrugged. "No Simon hanging over my shoulder."

"How are the two of you doing?" Dominic asked softly.

Abby shrugged, putting the two sides of her sandwich together. "We're okay," she said evasively.

Dominic sat up, scooting next to her. "Abby," he said, "I need to know. He hasn't been as rough with you in front of us anymore because he knows I won't stand for it. But how is he in private?"

She sighed. "Dominic, I know you mean well. But I'm not comfortable talking about Simon."

He put a gentle hand on her arm. "Okay," he said, his eyes solemn. "But if you ever want to talk to me, I'm here, Abby. I'm your friend, and I care about you. Please don't ever feel that you can't come to me if you need to."

"All right, Dominic. Thanks."

He looked troubled, but he smiled. He kissed her lightly on top of the head, then jumped to his feet. "I think I'll go help Tina and Dante with the fire," he said.

"You do that," Abby answered. "I'll have sandwich plates made up when you guys get back."

160

He waved back over his shoulder, heading off into the woods. Abby watched him go, wishing she could call him back. She couldn't talk to him about Simon — it wasn't that she didn't want to; it was that she was too ashamed.

It was past midnight, and although the others had turned in not long after dark, Abby knew that she wasn't the only one still awake. Standing on the flat top of the pyramid, sketching her view of the sky by the red beam of her flashlight, she paused, looking outwards, down towards the jungle's edge. All seemed peaceful and quiet at the campsite. She turned and saw a shape down below her, moving across the main courtyard below the temple. Abby smiled and turned back to her drawing. It had to be Dominic, up roaming again at night. The last she had seen him, he was explaining the significance of Stela 5, which showed the World Tree, to Dante. That had been hours ago.

She finished her sketch and noted the time and direction. Ideally, she would have loved to have a recorder to videotape the sky in each direction from dusk until dawn. She wanted to record from each spot at Izapa, from the stelae to the ballcourt. If they had set up the site astronomically, then she wanted to note the views from each location. She would have liked time-lapse recordings of the movements in the sky, but the lab wasn't set up for high-tech equipment. She would have to make do with her drawings. As long as she knew what was visible from each point, she thought, she would be able to calculate the movements, and map which constellations and planets would be visible during each season.

She was about halfway through with her sketch of the east when she heard light steps on the stone stairs below her. Abby didn't turn around. "Hey, Dominic," she said.

"Hey Abby."

"You just out prowling, or are you thinking about something?" she asked.

Dominic laughed. "I'm always thinking about something. I don't know how to stop."

"Must be exhausting."

He stopped beside her, and she could see his dimly lit shape in the glow of her flashlight. He shrugged. "It's the only way I know how to be," he said.

Abby smiled at him, then returned to her sketch. She had a long way until daylight, and wanted to get as much of the sky mapped as she could.

"We may have to cut this trip a little short," he said. "Steve has the radio on over there. It's supposed to rain tomorrow night and keep up for at least a couple of days. Tonight may be it as far as stargazing goes."

"Damn," she said. "Well, hell. How artistic are you?"

"Not very," he admitted. "But if you're sketching the sky, I can draw circles and dots. That's all the stars look like to me anyway. Although you're going to have to help me label them."

She laughed and tore a page from her sketch pad. Handing him a pen from her bag, she pulled out a hardcover book. "Here, you better put the paper on top of this to draw," she said. "The stone is too rough."

"Cool," he said. "Which direction do you still need?"

"Just the south," she answered. "If you don't mind doing that for me, I'll finish up the eastern view. Then we can move on to the next monument."

"My pleasure," he said, moving across the top of the pyramid. He flicked on his flashlight to draw, and it was then that she realized he'd been moving around in the dark below without one.

"You must know this place pretty well," she commented.

His voice came back to her across the temple. "Like the back of my hand," he said.

They worked in silence for a while, and just as Abby was finishing up, she sensed Dominic at her side again. She turned to look up at him. "Done already?" she asked in surprise.

"It's much easier when you don't know what you're drawing, and you're not worried about labeling anything," he said.

Abby laughed. "Well, I guess I'd better double check your work," she said. Dominic bent to scoop up her backpack, and they headed back across the temple top to compare his map with the view. Abby sat down and began to label the main stars and planets he had drawn.

"I hope this helps," Dominic said.

"Me too," she agreed. "I think it will. This is how the Maya viewed the world. They were definitely watching something, tracking patterns. Whatever's going on out there they noticed it."

"They were a fascinating people," Dominic said. "I could live here at Izapa and look at these ruins forever."

"You care more for the dead than the living." It was a question.

Dominic smiled. "That might be true."

Abby glanced up, but his eyes were unreadable in the darkness. "You ready to move on?" she asked.

"Ready when you are."

"All right, then, let's go," she said, gathering her paper and book. They descended the stairs together, ready to move on to map the darkness.

They left Izapa late the next morning as the sky began to cloud over. Halfway back through the woods, the rain began to fall. They were lucky that the jungle canopy protected them from the light drizzle, but they stepped up the pace just the same; it hadn't been a drizzle the radio had been predicting, but a rainstorm.

"Did you get your drawings done?" Tina called back. She and Dante were leading the pack with Abby and Steve close behind. Dominic was lost in thought as he trailed along behind them.

"Most of them," Abby said. "It was getting too light for me to finish the last few. I'm okay with that, though; they weren't major monuments, Dominic says, and they look like they were aligned with the other stelae, so I'm probably not going to miss anything."

"That's good," Tina responded. She focused her attention on the jungle ahead, stepping over a fallen tree.

The birds whistled and chirped in the branches overhead, and the warm rain drizzled down on them. Every now and then the foliage at their feet rustled as some small animal darted across their path. Chatting easily with Steve as she followed Tina and Dante through the rainforest, Abby couldn't remove the smile from her face. She thought that she'd never been happier.

12.19.15.10.1

August 5, 2008 — Abby stepped outside, relishing the breeze that gently moved through the courtyard. She'd been sitting in the hot lab for over an hour, compiling numbers for Simon. He'd asked for distances of the various planets to Earth, for some reason, as well as their respective velocities. The lab was unbearably humid, however, and she could hardly think.

"Hey there," she said as she crossed the lawn, spotting Dominic lying in the grass. He had a thick volume open in front of him.

"Hey yourself," he said amiably. "Need a break?"

"Yeah, actually I do," she confessed, sitting down on a rock beside him. "All the fans are doing in there is moving the hot air around."

"Yeah, I'm sorry about that," he said. "Air conditioning was too much of an overload on the generator."

"Oh, I didn't mean to complain," she said, embarrassed. "I just meant ..."

He waved her off. "I know you didn't," he said. "You don't complain, you just deal with everything, don't you?"

She didn't know what to say. Dominic saw her discomfort and shrugged. "Nothing wrong with that," he said. "You're a lot easier to get along with than a lot of people I've worked with. They complain about everything, no matter how good they have it. Makes you wonder how some people function in life."

They sat in silence for awhile, enjoying the cool breeze.

"Where did everyone else go?" Abby finally asked.

"I'm not sure," he said. "Steve was out here with me for awhile, and he said the heat was making him sleepy so he went inside. He's probably up in his room taking a nap."

"What about Dante and Tina? I haven't seen them all morning."

"Actually, I haven't either," Dominic said. "They don't come out a lot on weekends."

Abby was quiet for a moment. "You think they're avoiding Simon?"

He shrugged again, but didn't answer.

Abby stood up. "Is he really that offensive?" she asked quietly.

Dominic sighed and rolled over onto his back to look at her. "Abby, he's your fiancé. You've known him a long time, and I'm sure you know him in ways that the rest of us have never seen. All we see is the way he acts around us, which is condescending, arrogant and dismissive. That's fine; that comes with the territory. I've met a lot of pompous scientists in my life, and even more arrogant pseudo-scientists. But if they act that way, they need to back it up. So far, Simon hasn't. And I think that's what puts the others off."

"What about you?"

Dominic got to his feet. "It doesn't much matter to me one way or the other. I'm like you, Abby: I can put up with a lot if it gets me what I want." He dusted the loose grass and dirt off his legs, then leaned over and picked up his book. "I'm heading down to the lagoon to stick my feet in the water," he said. "Care to join me?"

"No, I can't," she said. "I promised …" She trailed off. "Well, I have some work to do in the lab. I'll talk to you later."

Dominic nodded, then turned and headed across the courtyard, whistling. Abby sat down slowly on her rock. She knew Simon could be difficult, but still; for Dante and Tina to hide out in their room to avoid him came as a surprise to her.

Abby watched Dominic head down towards the lagoon, smiling as he crossed the courtyard. She liked the way he walked. Dominic was a big man, tall and broad shouldered, but he moved with grace. He was also soft-spoken and gentle natured, quiet and attentive. So very different from Simon.

She shook her head. Dominic had disappeared into the trees.

"Did you compile the distances for me?"

Simon's voice, sharp and impatient, came from the lab.

"I'm still working on it, Simon. Hold on." She opened the screen door, allowing herself one last long look into the trees where Dominic had disappeared. "Okay," she said. "I'm coming."

12.19.15.10.12

August 16, 2008 — "Goddamn lights," Simon muttered, lighting the hurricane lamp on the lab table with a long match. He shook it out and tossed it onto the table.

"Sorry," Dominic said. He was sitting across the table from Simon. "I don't like running the generator during lightning storms."

"Well, it's damned inconvenient," Simon retorted, yanking his book into the glow of the lamp.

Dominic sat back in his chair, considering the other man.

"What?" Simon finally asked, pushing his book away. He looked nervous.

Dominic smiled. He and the blond man were virtually alone in the lab; the others were still up at the house, not daring to brave the phenomenal storm. Only Dante had come down to join them, and he was across the room, his nose buried deep in a book. Outside, lightning flashed, and Dominic saw the expression on Simon's face in stark clarity: The mathematician knew he was not among friends.

"What are you reading?" Dominic asked amiably.

Taken off guard, Simon glanced down at the book. "Finite Probability," he said. "Just refreshing some math. Permutations, combinatorics and recurrence relations."

Dominic nodded. "That's good," he said. "I appreciate all of us being at the top of our game on this."

"Yeah?" Simon asked, looking at Dominic warily. "So tell me, Ciriello, what are you doing? From what I've seen, this calendar is all about numbers; it seems like I'm going to be doing all the work."

Dominic smiled, looking down at the burnt match on the table. He picked up the matchstick and turned it over, laying it across the back of his hand and walking it along his long fingers.

"The fact that this calendar was created by the ancient Maya, and I'm considered somewhat of an expert in that field, I'd like to think I have some place here."

"The ancient Maya can't tell us anything now. This is about figuring out an answer to something based on good, clean numbers."

"Numbers are fine, but they can't answer everything. We have a mystery here; we need to look at the culture, the people, the language it was created in."

"Math is the universal language," Simon said. "Why get sidetracked with the rest of it when we can look at the math they used? The numbers are always the same. The rules never change."

"That's great," Dominic said, "But it doesn't tell us what to apply them to. Nothing exists in a vacuum."

"You don't know shit about math."

"I don't need to."

They both fell silent for awhile, then Dominic spoke up again. "I'm going to have to differ with you, Simon. You can't judge something outside its context. Math can give you an answer, but what if you're not asking the right question?"

"Look, math is concise. It's exact. You study myths and legends; fine, good for you. All you have is the opinions of people who looked at these glyphs as to what they actually mean. There's nothing exact about it."

"They're not opinions, Simon. Certainly you don't need me to explain archaeology to you, do I?" Dominic sighed. "Come on; you're teaching an advanced calculus course right now, right? Look at what you're doing with it; you're not testing the theorems for yourself, you're not creating your own. You're just taking for granted that what someone else said is right."

"Someone else has already done the proofs and the theorems. Why should I do it again? It's been proven correct. It's redundant."

"You're a different person than the one who came up with the theorem," Dominic said. "You have a different way of looking at things than he does. Maybe you'd get the same results he did — if you were looking for the same answer."

"Big deal," Simon answered. "You and I are two different people. So we both do a calculus problem. If you know what the hell you're doing, we get the same results. No matter how different we are or how different our way of looking at things is, we still get the same results."

"Guys, enough already," Dante suddenly spoke up from across the room. He tossed his book onto the desk top, then pulled himself lazily out of his chair. "You two can sit there and argue as long as you want, and you're never going to get anywhere. You want to put an end to a dispute, you have to deal with facts, not just your opinions. You're supposed to be scientists, I thought you knew that."

"What exactly are you suggesting?" Dominic asked, settling back into his seat, the tip of the burnt match he'd been toying with resting gently against his lips.

"Give me that," Dante said as he came over to the table.

Dominic pulled the match away, looking at it quizzically, then handed it over to Dante.

Dante took it from him, then picked up the box of matches and dumped several more onto the table before him.

Counting out six, he pushed them across the table to Simon. He poured six more onto the table and pushed them to Dominic, who picked them up.

"Okay," Dante said, "Make four triangles out of these six matches."

Simon frowned. "I'm not in the mood for parlor games," he said.

"Come on," Dominic urged. "You're a mathematician. You should be able to do this."

Reluctantly, Simon picked up the matches. "Do you know how this works?" he asked Dominic. He began lining up the matches, forming one triangle after another.

"Not a clue," Dominic responded, lining up his own matches. He too formed one triangle after another, but was unable to form four complete triangles using the six matches.

"What's the trick?" Simon asked after failing for the dozenth time. "You have to make each one touch the edge of the other, right?"

"It's not a trick," Dante answered, leaning on the table to watch them. "For all I know, there could be a dozen different ways to do this. I know of one. What I'm trying to see is your way of thinking."

Dominic smiled. "Clever," he observed. He lined up his matches again, studying them. Across the table, Simon glanced over at Dominic's matches to see if he was having more success.

"This is stupid," he grouched, forming another triangle. "It's a parlor trick, pure and simple."

"Not at all," Dominic said, putting three matches together in an equilateral triangle. "It's a logic test. It's a matter of looking at things a little differently. Good thinking, Dante," he added. "I couldn't have come up with a better idea myself."

"I guess that's a compliment," Dante said, but there was a smile in his voice. He watched them both carefully. Simon was growing frustrated, forming shape after shape, counting them with his fingers. No matter what the configuration, he could come up with no more than three triangles.

Dominic, on the other hand, had a single triangle formed with three matches and was studying them with his chin in his hand. Dante imagined he could almost see the wheels turning in his head.

Outside, lightning flashed again. "Damn it," Simon cursed, sweeping his matches off the table. "This is bullshit. So you're proving that you know the answer to something you already learned. Big deal. Show me the answer to it and I'll know it too. It'll prove nothing."

"Shhhh," Dante said, silencing him. He was watching Dominic.

Simon sat back, crossing his arms over his chest. "So you're trying to prove what, that Ciriello there is smarter than I am?"

"Not at all," Dante said. "You were arguing about whether he needed to be involved in this project. He was defending himself by saying that sometimes you needed different views to get an answer. I'm trying to see which one of you was right."

"And I didn't think you were listening," Dominic murmured. He picked up a match, standing it up inside one corner formed by the triangle. He held it there, and with his other hand picked up the other two matches and stood them in the opposite corners. Balancing them carefully for a moment, he propped them up against each other, then slowly drew his hands away. "One on the bottom, and one, two, three triangles on top," he said. Dominic glanced up at Dante and smiled. "I was using straight, linear thinking. It took me a minute to realize I had to think up, as well."

Dante applauded lightly. Outside, a clap of thunder echoed him. "You got it," he said.

"Bullshit," Simon said, his face reddening in the candle light. "You didn't tell us we could do it in 3-D."

"Do you need someone to tell you everything?" Dominic asked. "How the hell do you go through life if you need someone to lead you every step of the way? When are you going to learn to think for yourself, and how are you going to help us until you do?"

Without a word, Simon stood up and slapped Dominic's matchstick tower off the table. "Fuck you," he said.

They watched him stalk across the room and slam the door open. The wild rainy wind blew the door back against him, but Simon forced it open and stormed out into the night.

Dominic and Dante looked at each other and started laughing. After a moment, Dominic pushed the bench back and began to pick up the matches.

12.19.15.10.19

August 23, 2008 — "Are you guys going to be up late?" Abby asked the others seated around the lab.

"No telling," Steve replied. "I'll be here at least another hour or two. I'm searching for some references in *The Descent of Ishtar into the Underworld.*"

Dominic glanced up. "That's a Sumerian text," he commented.

Steve nodded. "It was just something I was thinking about — made a connection that I want to check out."

"Well," Abby said. "I'm going to head out to the clearing and sky watch for awhile. I was just wondering how late you'll have the lights on in here."

"I can read this up in my room," Steve said. "The dim lights up there won't reach all the way out to your clearing."

"Thanks," she said. "I appreciate that. But I'm not trying to run anyone out; you can all stay in here and work as late as you want or need to. I'll just wait until after it's perfectly dark to use the scope."

"Do you really think you're going to find an answer out there?" Dante asked.

"I hope so," Abby said. "There's not a doubt in my mind that it's astronomical with its beginning on the fall equinox and ending on the winter solstice."

"That doesn't sound right to me," Tina said. "For the ancient Maya, the winter solstice wasn't the end, it was the beginning. It is for us, too — all western cultures celebrate their New Year right near the winter solstice."

"Actually," Dominic said, "The Maya didn't celebrate their New Year at the end of the year like we did. For them, the cycle started over around February every year. More like the Chinese New Year than the American one."

"Sometimes I think I'm better off not knowing these things," Abby said. "That way I'm just looking at my own data, not trying to create connections to things I already know about."

"Why don't we keep you blind, then?" Dominic suggested. "Field some data and turn it in to me periodically. I'll try to interpret it according to Mayan psychology."

"Why the hell do you get to be the one to interpret it?" Simon asked in an accusatory tone.

"What exactly are you going to do with it?" Dominic asked, his voice tired.

"I could work with it, too," Simon said. "Astronomy is about distances; physics is about numbers. You were so enthralled with your damn time travel discussion; how do you think you're going to find out if it's possible or not without a mathematician?"

"Fine," Dominic said, waving a hand dismissively. "Abby, do what you want. If you don't want to be involved in the discussion, if you think it'll bias your thinking, then just don't stick around when we talk about it. You can turn in your notes and we'll share them among the group. That sound good?"

She nodded, but her expression was uncertain. "I'm heading out now," she said. "I'll see you guys in the morning."

"Don't stay out too late," Simon warned. "I'd like to spend *some* time with you on these weekends. What the hell do you think I come back for?"

Embarrassed, Abby nodded, then slipped out the back door.

There was an awkward silence, then Tina turned to Dominic again. "So how do we know when we're done?" she asked. "We keep thinking and putting things together — how will we know when to stop? I mean, we're just hypothesizing, right? How long do we work on our hypothesis?"

Dominic glanced over at her with a smile. "Until we get it right," he said.

"Oh Christ," Simon said, rolling his eyes. "You people are unbelievable."

"Well excuse us," Tina said, turning back to her book. "I suppose we'll just wait until you tell us we're done."

Dominic laughed, but stopped abruptly when the other man stood up.

"You just don't get it, do you?" Simon asked. "You act like this is some kind of game. Well, it's not. You wanted scientists, Dominic, and you got one. *One.* If you count Abby out there staring at the moon, I guess you have two. So if you want scientific theory, you come to me. If you want to keep screwing around and chasing your own screwed up imaginations around this jungle, well … then I guess you're doing well enough on your own."

Dominic stared at him. "You are so unbelievably full of yourself," he said in wonder. "You must think the rest of us can't even find our way down to the lab without your help."

"I've wondered about it," Simon said. He glanced around the room. Both Dominic and Tina were staring at him. "Look," he said. "I'm just saying."

"That's the problem," Dominic said. "You're always just saying. Do the rest of us a favor and quit saying until you have something to say."

Simon stared at him in disbelief. Dominic glared back, and as he began to stand up, Tina jumped to her feet.

She bolted out of the room, heading for the house.

"Come on, man," Simon said, raising his fists. "I've been waiting for this."

Dominic leaned back against the lab table. "I'm not going to fight you, Simon. I don't have any reason to fight you."

"Well, I have reason to fight you," Simon responded. "I'm sick of your little barbs, your smarting off to me. You walk around here like some kind of fucking genius, like you're so much better than the rest of us."

"So you're going to what? Beat the shit out of me? And that's going to help how?"

"For one thing, it'll make me feel better. And maybe it'll show you who's in charge around here."

"Jesus, Simon, is that what this is about? No one is in charge. This is teamwork. It's a group project. If you want to feel like you're in charge, fine, so be it. You're in charge."

"Godammit, that's what I'm talking about," Simon said, furious. "Quit patronizing me."

"I'm not," Dominic said wearily. "I just don't understand you. I thought we were all working on this for the same reason — because we want to know the answer. Why are *you* here, Simon?"

Simon paused, and as the silence drew out, Dominic got up. Simon took a step back, raising his fists again, but Dominic walked by him. He pushed the screen door open and reached outside. When he pulled his hand back in, he held two beers by their necks.

Crossing the room again, he tossed one to Simon. "I'm not an animal," he said. "I understand words. Use them."

Simon caught the beer, watching Dominic as he lowered himself to the bench. "Personally," Dominic said, twisting the top off his bottle. "I'd rather sit here and have a beer with you and talk about our problems than have the two of us try to kick the shit out of each other. So tell me — what do you want? Do you want the fame? The glory? You want to publish the results? That's fine. It's yours. You can have it."

Simon opened his beer, watching Dominic warily. "You mean it?" he asked.

"I mean it," Dominic said, raising his bottle in a toast. He lowered it and took a long drink before he continued. "I told you before, I just want the answer. I want to know what it all means. I don't care who gets the information or what they do with it afterwards. We're coming at this from different lines of thought, Simon. All I want is your help."

Simon looked at him carefully. "How do I know I can trust you?" he asked.

Dominic opened his mouth, but before he could answer the door burst open. Dante rushed into the room with Tina close on his heels. They pulled up short when they saw the two men on opposite sides of the room, each holding a beer.

"Oh thank God," Tina said. "I thought you two would've killed each other by now."

Dominic shrugged. "I think we came to an agreement," he said, taking another draw off his beer.

"That so?" Dante asked, looking to Simon.

"Guess so," he answered.

The four looked at each other, uncomfortable in their silence.

"Fine then," Dominic said. "I'm going out to finish my beer," he said. He got up and headed outside.

Simon looked after him, then turned and crossed to the other side of the room. "I'll be in my room," he said. Tina and Dante stepped apart, and Simon slipped out between them. As the door swung shut, the two looked across at each other in stunned silence.

"One of these days," Dante said, pulling the door open for Tina to exit. "We're either going to find one or both of them dead."

12.19.15.11.6

August 30, 2008 — Abby couldn't believe how clearly the Black Road had come into view; the Milky Way parted in a perfect, gauzy path, showing the dark rift stark and black against the fuzzy whiteness of the galaxy's arm. She ran up the path, crossing the narrow bridge above the lagoon, hoping she could get the others and get back before the feature disappeared behind the clouds that were rolling in from the ocean.

Without warning, the rocks gave way and she slipped, her ankle rolling outwards with a sudden sharp pain. She cried out, scrambling for purchase, but the loose pebbles of the path wouldn't hold and she tumbled down towards the lagoon, wincing as she felt the sharp stones cut her skin. She reached out, trying to claw a hold on the bare dirt wall, but only managed to scrape her arms on the rocky outcroppings.

Quickly, Abby braced her feet and pushed off the wall, then rolled herself into a ball as best she could, her head tucked into her chest. A moment later, she plunged into the cool water of the lagoon.

Scrabbling against the wet rocks, she kicked and splashed until she was able to pull herself up onto the bank. Abby rolled over and lay staring up at the moon, panting heavily. She did a quick mental body check and decided nothing was broken. Her skin stung from the many tiny cuts she'd received in the fall, and she knew she'd be bruised and aching in the morning. Still, she thought, looking up at the path high above her, she had been lucky. Had she struck her head on one of the larger rocks on the way down, or on one of those surrounding the shallow edges of the lagoon, she could have been knocked unconscious and drowned.

Abby didn't know how long she'd been lying there when she heard feet above her on the path. She craned her neck to look up, grimacing at the pain, and saw a shape in shadow against the moonlight.

"Abby? Is that you?"

It was Dominic's voice calling down, and Abby smiled in relief. She'd have been humiliated to have Simon find her this way, and knew he'd have nothing but a lecture for her.

"Hey," she called back weakly.

His feet scrambled on the path as she heard him sliding down the side, and in a moment he was beside her.

"Your descent was a lot more graceful than mine was," she said with a smile.

"Are you okay?" he asked, kneeling beside her. "What happened?"

"I'm okay," she said, grimacing again as she tried to sit up. Dominic's warm hands were immediately on her back and stomach, supporting her as she pulled herself upright. "I don't know what happened. I was running, and I guess my foot slipped. Next thing I knew I was in the lagoon."

"I heard the splash," Dominic said. "I was sitting out in the courtyard, just trying to make some sense of everything, and I heard something pretty big fall into the water. I knew it wasn't just a rock, so I figured I'd better get out here and see what it was."

"Just me," she said, pulling her feet underneath her and trying to stand. "Thanks for the compliment."

Dominic stood with her, keeping his hands on her as she tried to rise. As soon as she put her weight on her feet, her right ankle buckled.

"Whoa," Dominic said, grabbing her before she fell. "Are you all right?"

Abby sighed, relaxing back into his arms. "My ankle," she said. "I think I twisted it."

"Okay," he said. "No problem." Sliding his arms under her back and rear, he scooped her up into his arms.

"Whoa," she echoed him, surprised to find herself so far off the ground. Dominic adjusted his hold on her, switching her to a fireman's carry as he reached for the branch ladder.

"We have to get this fixed," he said, climbing back up towards the path. He found the footholds easily; digging into the hill and holding onto the branch with one hand, Dominic stayed almost completely upright as they rose. "The part that went out from under you wasn't shored up underneath," he explained. "I'll bet a lot of the path is like that. Next heavy rain, it'll wash right away."

"And next time I might not be so lucky," she said, wrapping one arm around his neck. "I got a sprained ankle and a ride home. Couldn't have planned it better."

He grinned and held her a little tighter as they crossed the fallen portion. "Well, next time you plan something like this, give me a call ahead of time," he said. "I'll meet you here."

She laughed, comfortable in Dominic's arms until the light of the lab came into sight.

"Is Simon in the lab?" she asked carefully.

"He was when I left," Dominic answered. "That was maybe an hour ago."

"Maybe I can try to walk now," she said, struggling to get down.

"Hey," Dominic stopped. "What's wrong?"

"Nothing," she shook her head, but kept trying to slide out of his arms. He bent his knees to lower her to the ground, but still didn't completely release her.

"Abby, what is it?" he asked. "Are you afraid of what Simon will think?"

"It's more complicated than that," she said, testing her weight on the injured ankle while balancing against Dominic's shoulder. "I don't want to explain it all, Dominic."

"Abby," he took her hand gently. "You're a brilliant woman. You should have the brains not to stay with a man you're afraid of."

"I'm not afraid of him," she said, pulling away. "I just don't want to upset him. He won't like it if he sees you carrying me up to the house, and I don't want to explain to him about how I fell on the path. He'll think I'm careless, and he'll be right. I was in a big rush to get back to the house, and I wasn't watching where I was going. I'm kicking myself for doing it; I don't need Simon doing it for me, too."

"Abby, it was an accident. Don't be so hard on yourself."

She shook her head again, then ran both hands through her wet hair. "Dominic, please. I'll tell Simon, I have to. I mean, I'm wet and cut and bruised. I'd just rather go in there and do it alone. I don't want him going after you."

Dominic stared at her incredulously.

Abby paused, then, in a rush, confided: "When you and I met the first time, Simon and I were having some problems. Problems with trust, and infidelity. I forgave him and took him back. Now, I trust him entirely, but he doesn't trust me. He knows that when I get angry about something, I usually let it simmer, and I never take it out directly on him, or with him. He's afraid that I'll take it out in another way."

"He's afraid that you'll cheat on him to get him back for what he did," Dominic said.

Abby nodded without looking at him. "I'm sorry, Dominic. I didn't want to bring our problems to you, but I guess they came along with us. If you and I come in together and I'm all messed up, then give

174

him a story about falling on the path, he's going to think we're making it up. Let me go in and talk to him. He can say whatever he wants about it. You said there was a slide on the path; I can show it to him in the morning."

"So what do you want me to do, sit out here for an hour and wait for you to hash it out with the boyfriend?" Dominic's voice didn't rise, but Abby could tell he was angry.

"Dominic," she started, but he held up a hand.

"I'm going in," he said shortly. "It's late, I'm tired, and I'm not sitting out here while you and Mr. Wonderful argue about what happened. For God's sake, Abby, it was an accident. I don't even want to know what line of thinking either of you are going through to make it a bigger deal than that. So I'm going to bed.

"You can sit out here until you think you've given it sufficient time since I came in, and then you can crawl up to the lab. Or you can go back out and lay by the water if you want, and maybe Simon will go out there sometime before morning and find you. Goodnight, Abby."

"You don't understand," she said, but Dominic had already turned his back on her. He retreated to the lab, his back stiff.

She watched him go, waiting until he reached the lab door; then she sunk to the ground in pain, tears coming to her eyes. She held her ankle, which she could already feel swelling. She swiped an arm across her eyes, wiping away the wetness, then buried her face in her arm, sobbing quietly.

A moment later, there was a hand on her shoulder. She looked up quickly to see Dominic kneeling beside her, concern in his eyes. She hadn't even heard him come back.

"It's okay," he said quietly. "There's no one in the lab. I guess everyone went to bed. You can probably even get cleaned up before you go to bed; he'll never even notice. If you're cut or bruised or limping in the morning, you can tell him the path gave way under you. We need to go fix that anyway so no one else falls. Your head will be much clearer in the morning, okay?"

She nodded silently, biting her lip. Dominic pushed a lock of wet hair off her forehead, then slid his arms around her.

"I'm sorry," he said, his breath warm in her ear. She shivered, and he held her closer.

"If you have any problems with Simon, you let me know," he said softly. "It's your life, and I won't interfere in it. I won't do anything to make him mad at you. If you ever need anything, or just want to talk, you can come to me." His lips brushed her ear and she shivered again, then pulled away.

"Thank you, Dominic," she said, her voice rough, and he smiled.

"Come on," he said, standing up and holding out a hand. She took it gratefully and let him pull her to her feet, his hand on the small of her back for balance. He kept his arm around her waist and helped her across the field towards the lab. Her ankle hurt, but the pain wasn't as bad. She hoped the swelling would go down by morning.

Dominic held the door as she limped into the lab, empty but for the two of them.

"I'm going to stay here awhile," Dominic said quietly. "I need to think about some things, and I can't do it with Steve snoring in the bed next door. Will you be okay going up to the house?"

Abby nodded. "I think so," she said. "I'm going to go take a hot shower, I think, and clean up some. I'll see you in the morning, then."

"Good night," he said, releasing her hand. He watched her for a moment, and she stared back, noticing not for the first time how deep and expressive his eyes were. Impulsively, she leaned forward and kissed his cheek.

"Thank you, Dominic," she said. "For everything."

He smiled, but didn't answer as she turned and left the room. After a moment, he reached up and touched his cheek, still tingling where her lips had touched.

For the first time since he'd planned this project, he was truly worried.

12.19.15.11.7

August 31, 2008 — Abby found Dominic by the lagoon the next day. He was on his knees on the side of the hill, shoring up the path.

"Good morning," she called down to him.

"Hey there," he said, looking up with a smile. "How do you feel today?"

"Pretty good," she said, squatting down, watching him over the edge. She cradled her coffee mug in both hands. "My ankle is sore, but it's not as bad as I thought it'd be. I can walk on it, at least. I'm kind of scratched up, but I'll live."

"How'd Simon react?"

"Barely," she smiled. "He was asleep when I went to bed last night, so he didn't see me until this morning. He asked what the scratches were from, and I told him. He –," she paused for a second, rubbing a scratch along one cheek. "Well, he complained some about you. More about the spot you picked out, the lousy job you did building this place. You know." She looked away, embarrassed, but Dominic just laughed.

"I figured," he said. "But don't worry about it, I'm patching up the trail. Steve promised to come out after breakfast and help me put some kind of rail up. Nothing elaborate, you know, just something so you can tell when you're close to the edge."

"Okay," she said. "Do you need help?"

He shook his head. "I'm okay. Steve should be out soon."

"Can I at least bring you a cup of coffee or anything?"

"Thanks, I'm good," he said, continuing to dig into the loose bank and fill in the section she'd knocked out of the path.

"Okay, then," she said, standing up. "I'll head on back."

"Mm-hmm," he murmured, not looking up from his work. She watched him for a moment, then turned to go back to the house. She looked back over her shoulder several times, but Dominic, deeply involved in his work, never looked up.

12.19.15.11.8

September 1, 2008 — The rain beat down hard on the tin roof, pattering past the open windows in a steady pattern.

"Look, guys, I'm just saying. I don't think we can afford to ask him to leave."

"Jesus, Dominic, what is it with you?" Tina asked. "Absolutely no one here can stand him. He's rude and downright offensive. *I* find him absolutely intolerable, and he doesn't say two words to me."

"I know," Dominic said. He stood up and began to pace. "It's just that if we ask him to go, we have to make sure we want him to. If we give an ultimatum, we can't back down. Because if he insists on staying, life will really be unbearable. You think he's bad now, just wait until he finds out we want him gone. He'll stay just to prove himself. And to tell you the truth, I don't trust him."

"I'm not afraid of him," Dante said. "I'd love for him to try something."

"It's not that," Dominic said, waving a hand dismissively. "Any of us here could take him. What I'm afraid of is that he'll sabotage the project. Or take what he has now and go work with it on his own, or with another research team. We've put too much into this to lose it to a personality conflict.

"Frankly, guys, and I hate to say it, but Simon is the only one making real progress — he's been working through prime numbers, looking for patterns; working out every combination of inner cycles in the Count and giving them to me to match up with known events; he's dividing the other calendars and cycle harmonics into it ... look, just because he's not likable doesn't mean he's wrong. He may be an asshole, but he's dedicated and a hard worker, and every weekend he comes back here with an armload of work he'd been doing. Which is more than I can say for any of us."

"Well, it's not for lack of trying," Steve spoke up.

"I know that," Dominic said, glancing over at his friend. "We've all been working our asses off, but we haven't found any common thread yet. Simon seems to have found something, and I don't think he's told us all of it. He gets a look in his eye like he's hiding something, and I don't trust him."

"You think he's going to run off with it?" Dante asked. "Hell, if he's going to go anyway, let's get rid of him now and save ourselves the irritation."

Dominic shook his head. "I'd rather have him right here under our noses where we can keep a better eye on him."

"But he's not," Tina protested. "Other than those few weeks when he didn't have any classes this summer, most of the time he's holed up in that apartment at the university, and who knows what he's keeping there, away from us?"

"I have an idea," Dominic said. "I know more than he thinks I do."

"So, you're keeping stuff from us too?" Dante asked.

Dominic turned around, catching Dante's black eyes with his own. "That's not what I meant. I'm just saying, I'm not as stupid as Simon thinks I am. I'd prefer not to change his opinion. Let him think I'm just some lumbering dolt, and that he holds all the cards. It doesn't bother me any, so it shouldn't bother you."

"But we have to live with him too," Tina said.

"You said yourself he's not here most of the week," Dominic pointed out. "You only see him Friday night through Sunday. I'd think if I'm willing to make the sacrifice, the rest of you can, too."

"Why are you defending him, Dominic?" Dante asked.

"Because we need him," Steve said slowly, before Dominic could speak. "Like him or not, we need him. He's the only one of us with regular remote access. He has the internet, the university library, access to books at other universities, regular telephone and long distance service — every resource the rest of us need to do any real research. If we get rid of him, we lose that. Unless we find a way to wire this place up, two hundred miles from nowhere, or one of us makes that trek into the city every week.

"I can't afford either option," Dominic added. "I've spent almost every cent I had left on this place. Any more major problems will break me."

Tina sat down heavily. "Fine," she said. "He stays. Dominic, this is your project, and I respect that. But I can only take so much of it. I will not let him talk to you the way he does."

178

"Yes, Tina, you will," he replied. "You guys know that Simon is foul-mouthed, mean-tempered and potentially violent, but you may not have noticed something else: he's unstable."

Dominic went to the window and pushed the thin curtain aside, watching the rain come down. "I'm not so worried for any of us," he said, "Because if he lashes out, it won't be us that will bear the brunt of it. It'll be Abby."

The others were silent for a long moment, and finally Tina spoke up. "She's a sweet girl," she said slowly. "And I like her, don't get me wrong. But isn't it up to her to get away from him? Do we all have to walk on eggshells around him, because she can't walk away from him herself?"

Dominic didn't answer, just watched the rain fall, and for a moment, Tina thought he was angry. Finally, though, he spoke, and his voice was calm.

"Abby has the same problem we do right now," he said. "She's entangled in this deeply, and if she tries to disengage herself from him, his whole world is going to come down. He blames her for bringing him down here, for making him have to make that drive every week, for having to live out here in the middle of nowhere. He blames her for all of it, and reminds her of it nearly every day. If she tries to toss him aside, I can't even imagine what he's going to do."

"We'll protect her," Dante said.

Dominic shook his head. "Her best protection is with us, right here. If we ask him to leave, he'll take her with him. She's not strong enough right now to turn him down."

"Well, thank you for deciding my life for me," a voice broke in, and they all turned to see Abby in the doorway, yellow raincoat dripping water onto the lab floor. She had pulled her hood down, exposing damp hair sticking out wildly in all directions, but now she yanked it back up again. "And not one of you has any idea how strong I am," she said stiffly. "Not a single damn one of you."

She turned and stepped back out into the rain, the door slamming shut behind her.

Several hours later, the others had gone back up to the house, leaving Dominic alone in the lab when Abby came back in. Her hair and clothing were still dripping wet, and she stopped in the doorway to remove her raincoat.

"Don't worry about it," Dominic said without looking up. "It rained in here anyway; just watch out for the puddles."

She came across the room slowly, sliding off the yellow rain slicker. It dripped as she carried it, but he was right; the windblown rain had come through the screens onto the lab's tile floor. Abby stopped at the long table, then slid onto the bench next to him. She dropped the wet raincoat onto the floor beside her.

Dominic looked up as she sat down. Abby's eyes were red from crying, and her wet hair hung around her face in sodden strands. He smiled, then reached out and pushed a section of it back from her face.

"Don't worry," he said. "We're not going to throw you guys out."

Her face wrinkled up, and he knew she was going to start crying again. "Hey," he said quietly, putting a hand on her shoulder. "It's okay. Please don't be upset. It's not personal, Abby. Everyone here likes you. I'm sorry if what I said before offended you. There's been a lot of tension here, and we all just had to talk it out."

"Couldn't you have at least invited us to the meeting if you were going to discuss our future?" she asked, and he saw her muted anger returning.

He shrugged. "We certainly couldn't bring Simon in talk about it; we'd never had gotten a word in. It wasn't about arguing, it was about seeing if we could resign ourselves to dealing with an obvious difference in personalities. We're all professionals here. We can deal with it. It's the project that's important, not any individual one of us."

Abby didn't answer, just looked at his hand, which still rested on her shoulder. He removed it.

"I can't figure out if you're trying to protect me, or you're looking down on me," she said.

"Abby —," he started.

Abby held up a hand, then continued as if she hadn't been interrupted. "You say that Simon will turn on me if you guys gang up on him, and you're right. But when you say that I'm weak, that I can't stand up to him, and that you have to protect me from him — well, Dominic, you're wrong. I've been with Simon for a very long time, and I can handle him. Don't think for a minute that I'm with him for any other reason than that I want to be."

"All right," Dominic said quietly. "I apologize, Abby. We are looking out for you. I don't doubt that you can handle yourself, but I don't want to do anything that's going to make matters worse for you, either. You have to agree, Simon has a very difficult personality. We're all working together here, but he always wants to 'one up' us. I don't imagine that he's going to get any better, so the rest of us are going to have to deal with it. I don't want to lose either of you. I don't want to build a new team now. This is the group we started out with, and I'd like all of us to see it through to the end."

Abby nodded, looking away. After a moment, she cleared her throat. "I'm sorry about the trouble Simon has caused," she said. "He's very strong willed and opinionated, I've learned that. The problem is that he doesn't understand why everyone doesn't see how right he is. He gets impatient. He also knows that he only has about a year to do this, and he hates wasting time."

"Do you always make excuses for him?"

Abby stopped. "No," she said. "I'm just trying to explain the way he is."

"It doesn't matter," Dominic said. "Understanding why he acts like an ass isn't going to make anyone here like him any better. He's chosen to project himself in a certain way, and that's how we've received him. We put up with him because we have to, and we'll put up with him as long as we can. But I think you need to know, Abby, that we won't put up with it forever. If you can control him, please do it. Because I can keep these guys on my side for awhile, but they're only human. There's only so much abuse they're willing to take before someone blows.

"Personally, I think maybe a good throw-down would be for the best – we need to clear the air around here if we're going to get anything done. But right now isn't the time for it. I'll try to keep the peace as long as I can, but if things come to a head, I'm not going to stop it. This is my project, but I'm not a babysitter. I can only take so much responsibility for all this. Everyone here is on his and her own."

Abby nodded. "I've been with Simon for a long time, and I just accept his idiosyncrasies as a part of him," she said. "But I can't expect everyone to. I'll do what I can, Dominic."

He smiled. "That's all any of us can do. And Abby?"

She looked up at him wordlessly.

"I'd never look down on you. Never."

She tried to smile, but couldn't. Instead, she just nodded, standing up. "Good night, Dominic."

"Good night, Abby."

12.19.15.11.11

September 4, 2008 — "I've heard you have some kind of problem with me."   "What?" Dominic asked. He was momentarily disoriented. He'd been lost in his notes, sitting on a boulder in the courtyard. It was twilight, and he strained to make out his own handwriting in the growing dark.

"Abby told me that there's some — dissention — among the group, caused by personality conflicts." Simon stood with his hands on his hips, and his voice was stiff. "She asked me to try a little harder to get along with everyone. Why am I supposed to try, but no one else is?"

Dominic sighed and closed his journal, holding his finger between the pages to keep his place. "Everyone needs to try to get along better, Simon. We have work to do, and it doesn't do any one of us a bit of good if there's constant arguing. The rest of the group is willing to work on it if you are."

"What the hell do I need to work on?"

"Where to begin?" Dominic said under his breath. Louder, he said, "For one thing, it would help you stopped antagonizing everyone. And stopped taking everything we say or suggest so personally."

"I'm just trying to guide the discussion away from off-the-wall ideas," Simon responded, and he sounded almost hurt.

"I know you are," Dominic said. With the brightly lit lab to Simon's back, Dominic couldn't make out his expression. "Look, Simon, I'm not blaming you for anything. I'd like it if you wouldn't blame the rest of us, either. I'll tell you the same thing I told the others — we have some personality differences here, and every one of us is going to have to work on getting along. It won't help if we're always at each other's throats, or mocking the other one's ideas. If you don't like the direction the discussion is going, either try to let it go — you never know where it will end up, or what ideas will come out of it — or just leave us for awhile. Some things need to be talked out."

"But, time travel? Come on — some of these things are a total waste of time. One of these days I'm going to walk in and find you guys in earnest discussion about the Loch Ness Monster or Bigfoot or something."

"Well, if we're talking about it, maybe there's a reason for it," Dominic answered. "Maybe we're just having a chat. Just because we converse about something doesn't mean that's the path we're following to the end of the Long Count."

"But I'm only here for two days a week. I'd like to be in on interesting, scientific, professional discussions. Talking about the existential nature of time makes me think I'd be spending my six hours of driving back and forth better by staying at school and working during that time."

"I'm sorry that you feel that way," Dominic said. "We *do* need you, Simon."

"Pains you to admit it, doesn't it?"

Dominic sighed. "See, that's what I'm talking about. Here we are having a nice civil conversation, and you go and get all confrontational with me. What's the point of that?"

"What do you and my fiancée do while I'm gone all week?"

"*What?*" Dominic was so startled by the sudden switch of topics he thought he must have misheard him. "What do I *what?*"

"You heard me," Simon said. "What the hell do you do with Abby all week?"

182

"The same thing I do with the other three members of our team," Dominic said. "We discuss our relevant fields and try to apply them to the numbers and dates of the Count. We each do our independent research and take notes, then get together and compare them and talk through our ideas."

"It seems to me like you pay way too much attention to Abby."

"I pay no more attention to her than I do the others," Dominic said, but it had a false ring, even to his own ears.

"Bullshit," Simon said. "Every time I come home you're with her. You go out and sit with her in that damn field in the middle of the night. She comes down and joins you in the lab while I'm sleeping. I know Abby too damn well to think she's up to something. You, though, I don't trust."

"Come on, Simon," Dominic said. "Of course I'm out there with her; she's pointing out the things to me that the Maya would have seen. I'm trying to help her make some sense of them, and trying to match them up in my own head. We're all part of a team, Simon; we're all working towards one goal. We need to agree to all try to get along so we can solve this thing. That's all that's important to me."

"It'd better be," Simon said, his voice gruff. "And I'll try to not rile up the others, but you need to make sure that's all you're working on together."

"What are you, her handler?"

"I'm her fiancé, damn it, and that's something you'd better not forget."

"Look, Simon, I don't know what your problem is. I don't care about you, and I don't care about Abby. I'm here for one thing; my love is for the Long Count of Days. All I want from either of you is to help me with that."

"Fine. I won't mess with your love if you don't mess with mine."

"Deal."

Dominic watched as Simon turned and walked away. He had made the promise easily, but he thought he was going to have a very hard time keeping it.

Part II: The Dark Rift

"If we knew what it was we were doing, it would not be called research, would it?"

— Albert Einstein

"It is the mark of an educated mind to be able to entertain a thought without accepting it."
— Aristotle

"If you shut your door to all errors, truth will be shut out."

— Rabindranath Tagore

12.19.15.11.14

September 7, 2008 — After a week or so of cooler weather, the oppressive heat returned, making an early fall comeback; and while the others stayed in their rooms with floor fans blowing, Dominic and Abby retreated to their mountain hideaway. They sat outside the cave, in the thick grass of the forest where the sunlight filtered through the heavy tree cover and hit them in bright streams. The babbling of the nearby brook was a pleasant backdrop, and Abby was relaxed. She leaned against the stone wall, rolling her head lazily towards Dominic.

"I've been trying to placate Simon, but I'm not having much effect. No one still likes him much, do they?" Abby asked.

Dominic smiled, running his fingers through the grass. He shook his head. "Afraid not. Tina's given up even speaking to him. Dante still tries to bait him every now and then, but even he's tired of his games. Steve calls him Simon Magus."

"Who's that?"

"Some guy from the Bible who thought he was God."

Abby laughed. "That sounds about right."

Dominic turned to her, mildly surprised. "A few months ago you would have been offended by that," he said.

She shrugged. "I'm used to an extremely closed relationship with Simon," she confessed. "It's always been basically him and me — and whichever colleagues he felt the need to impress. He'd bring them by the house, or take me to a faculty party to introduce me around. Other than in class, it's the only time I ever really see him interact with other people, and of course, he's on his best behavior then. You wouldn't even recognize him, Dominic — he's witty, charming and self-deprecating. Everyone loves him."

Abby sighed and continued, "He has a terrible relationship with his own family, and so doesn't understand why I'd want a close one with mine. My family didn't like him much anyway, so things would be tense when he came along, or they came to visit. After awhile, it became easier to just stay home with him on the holidays than argue about going to see my parents, or putting up with him being sullen and moody the whole time we were there. A couple times I went home alone, and he didn't speak to me for a week when I got back, accusing me of choosing them over him, telling me that they didn't like him and I should support him and stand up for him, not run off to mommy and daddy.

"Same thing happened with friends. He'd tell me why they were no good for me — especially if they didn't like him for any reason. I'd end up defending him, and after awhile, they'd mostly drift away. Couldn't stand to be around him, I guess. I took that to mean that they weren't good friends; they would rather abandon me than put up with my boyfriend for a few hours at a time. I only had one really close friend left, and she would tell me that she stuck by me because she wanted me to know that there *were* other people out there that cared about me, and that Simon didn't have to be my whole life."

"She sounds like a smart woman," Dominic said.

Abby nodded. "She is," she said. "In fact, most of my friends were. They just couldn't put up with Simon's abuse after awhile, and got tired my not being able to see them without him coming along, and of my defending him, or making excuses for him."

"So why did *you*, then? Put up with his abuse?"

Abby was silent. After a moment, Dominic glanced over at her, concerned, but she was simply tracing meaningless designs in the dirt. She saw his movement and looked up, meeting his eyes. He smiled; even a month ago, she wouldn't have been able to look at him directly while talking about Simon.

"I never considered it abuse," she said slowly. "Even now, I have a hard time calling it that. Simon loves me; I have no doubt about that. I never have, even when —well, even when we had problems. All relationships have problems; ours have been nothing out of the ordinary, nothing that a million couples haven't dealt with at some time in their lives. And he'd never been violent to me. Even when he was restrictive it seemed normal; I thought he was just jealous, and protective. I didn't realize how much he was alienating me until I left him last summer, and discovered that I really had nowhere to go."

Now it was Dominic who was silent, and Abby glanced up at him. "Hey," she said. "You don't want to hear this."

"Actually, I do," he said, meeting her light brown eyes with his dark ones. Even in the bright sunlight his eyes were soft and sensitive, and Abby found she couldn't look away. Dominic reached out and took her hand.

"I care about you a lot, Abby," he said. "I don't want to see you hurt. No one here is judging you, and we're really not even judging Simon. We've tried to get along with him and he's rejected us every time. And I'm sorry to say it, but we're not here to psychoanalyze him or try to fix him.

We need him to work, and as long as he's capable of doing that, we'll put up with him. It doesn't mean that we have to like him. But if I ever hear of him hurting you …" His voice trailed off. He squeezed her hand, then released it.

"I'm going to head on further up the stream," he said. "I'm curious to see where it goes."

"You hoping to find some lost Mayan ruins?" Abby teased, getting to her feet. She was momentarily hurt at how quickly he'd dropped her hand, but didn't let it show.

"You never know," he said. "There could be anything hidden by the jungle. They found new ruins just a few years ago — well, new *old* ruins. A huge city, completely overgrown, and they only located it by the shape of the growth as seen from the air. Even Palenque, where they've been digging for decades, still has over a thousand ruins still covered by jungle growth. Personally, though, I'd be happy just to find a waterfall."

"I could live with that," Abby said.

"Come on, then," he said, starting back towards the stream. Abby half-hoped he'd take her hand again to help her across the slippery stones into the water, but he walked ahead, not looking back.

Abby hurried to catch up.

12.19.15.12.1

September 14, 2008 – Abby was concerned when Dominic wasn't at breakfast, but Tina seemed unfazed.

"Dominic has always been a loner," she explained. "I'm kind of surprised he's with us as much as he is. Sure, he disappears a lot, and he stays up by himself after the rest of us have gone to bed, but in all the years I've known him, of all the trips we've been on together, this is the most I've ever seen him hang around a group. I think it has something to do with you, Abby."

Abby looked uncomfortable. "I don't know," she said carefully. "He's usually with you guys when I come in."

Tina laughed. "Oh, don't act like you don't know it. Dominic will never show it outwardly, and I doubt that he'll ever admit it, but he cares for you — a lot. I think it's sweet."

"Well, don't let Simon hear you say it," Abby warned. "The last thing I need is him getting jealous. He has a temper, you know."

Tina laughed. "No offense, Abby, but the thought of Simon standing up to Dominic would be a hell of a sight. I've only ever seen Dominic in a fight once — have him tell you about it sometime. He avoided it for weeks until this guy finally cornered him. And he took him out in about 10 seconds. It was great. And that guy was a hell of a lot closer to Dominic's size than Simon is.

"Don't let Dominic's calmness fool you. One of these days he's going to have enough, and then Simon had better hope to hell he can run fast. And I for one won't be sorry to see it."

Abby didn't know how to respond, but she didn't have to; Dante came down to join them for breakfast, pleasant and good natured, and Tina's comment fell away, untouched.

But to Abby, it wasn't forgotten.

Simon also didn't join them at breakfast, or even lunch that day; Abby apologized to the others, explaining that he was deeply involved in some work and was staying up in their room to finish it. None of the others were overly dismayed at the loss of his company.

Dominic, missing since he'd disappeared the afternoon before, rejoined them after lunch without a word of explanation.

It wasn't until after dinner that Simon finally came down to the lab, and his presence once again cast a pall upon the group. They'd been comparing notes from their individual studies and hashing out potential similarities; but when Simon entered the lab, their conversations slackened, eventually dwindling into silence. They each went back to their reading, until the quiet grew uncomfortable. It was Simon himself who finally broke it.

"Look," he said. "If you want to make any progress on your damn Long Count, why don't we start with some solid facts, like the numbers?"

"All right," Dominic said amiably. "Tell us something about the numbers. What do you have?"

"Well," he said. "How complicated can you take?"

"Oh for God's sake," Dante said, "we're not idiots. Everyone here works in a field that calls for mathematical ability. Quit assuming we're morons and just explain yourself. If you lose us on something, we'll stop you."

"Fine then," Simon said, walking stiffly to the board. He picked up a marker and began writing numbers on the board to illustrate his point.

"Okay," he said, "You know the Maya had the concept of zero — one of only two world cultures that did at that time, by the way; I have to give them credit for that — and that Mayan mathematics was a base twenty system. Now, you'd think that, being based on twenty, they'd go in multiples like we do — you know, ten, 100, 1,000. When you write out the Long Count notation, like 13.0.0.0.0, you might think each position would be filled with a multiple of 20. But it doesn't go from 20 to 400, as 20 times 20 would; instead, the next set starts with 360. In other words, they multiply 20 by 18 in the third position; after that, they work with multiples of 20s again. Doesn't make any damn sense."

"Well, there's a slight problem with that," Dominic said. "The Maya used symbols for numbers — a 'one' is a dot; it most likely came from a stone or nut or something when they were counting, as they didn't have paper or writing implements. For each multiple of five, they used a bar – most likely a stick, or a line drawn in the dirt. For zero, they used a shell. This was still a relatively primitive society; they had to use what they had," he said. "When you read the glyphs – the inscriptions on the ruins – they have symbols representing the numbers."

He went to the board and stood by Simon, picking up a piece of chalk from the tray and drawing a few symbols on the board. "This is seven," he said, drawing a line with two dots over it. He moved slightly to his right. "And this would be seventeen." The second drawing consisted of three lines, with two dots over top of the third line.

"You might think they would go through the whole number set like that, but they don't — it'd take up too much space. Twenty-seven is actually three dots and one line, drawn like this:"

$$\cdot$$
$$\cdot \ \cdot$$
$$\underline{}$$

"Now, what the hell is that?" Simon asked. "How do you tell the difference between that and the number eight?"

"It's all in the layout," Dominic said. "This would be eight:"

$$\cdot \ \cdot \ \cdot$$
$$\underline{}$$

"So the twenty is just a dot above the seven."

"Exactly," Dominic said. "Now, there are certain numbers that have their own symbols, like the number 20. The next number that has one is 400."

"Not 360?"

"Not 360," Dominic agreed. "Even though their numbering in the Long Count multiplies out by 360 in the third position, their numbering symbols are consistent with their base 20 system."

"All right," Simon said. "So even if they dated it correctly, that doesn't help explain why the count is off."

"But it's not off," Dominic said. "The Count is consistent with itself, and with the other calendars."

"That other calendar you told us about, the Tzolkien, is 260 days," Simon said. "That's 13 months of 20 days, right?"

"Yes," Dominic said. "With each month named after a Mayan god. The Tzolkien was the ritual calendar."

"So why do they have a third calendar, the Haab, which is 18 months of 20 days?"

Dominic shrugged. "The Haab was a calculation of a different *type* of time period; the 18 months were named after events, usually of a religious, but sometimes an agricultural nature. It was the common calendar, the civilian calendar. And don't forget they added five days to the end of it, so it was actually 365 days."

"So if the Tzolkien was 13 months of 20 days, based on the 'gods,' and the Haab was 18 months of 20 days – plus five – based on agricultural events, what was the Long Count?" Simon asked. "It's actually 93,600 months of 20 days. So what the hell are they counting?"

"That's what you're supposed to be finding out for us," Dante said.

Simon gave him a dark look. He did a quick multiplication on the dry erase board. "I've tried my best to make some connection," he said. "If the ritual calendar was 260 days, and the Haab was 365 days, then they would meet up every 18,980 days. That'd be every 52 Haab years and 73 Tzolkien years. Was there something special, mythologically or religiously, that occurred on those dates?"

Dominic shook his head. "Nothing that repeated. Anything that fell on those dates was coincidental, it seems. They did celebrate the Venus count, though."

"Holy Christ, what's *that*?" Simon said in frustration. "Another calendar?"

"Kind of," Dominic said. "Venus has cycles like the moon, and the Maya kept track of it. They had it calculated to 584 days."

"So that would be …" Simon turned to the board, scrawling quickly as he divided the Venus count into the civil and ritual calendars. "I guess only the Haab fits into it, doesn't it?" he said. "Every two 52-year cycles, Venus would have gone through 65 cycles. That would mean a conjunction of the calendars every … 104 years. Was there anything recorded then?"

"The Venus round was really important to the Maya," Tina spoke up. "It was a big part of their ritual cycles. So when it met up with either of the calendars, it was probably a cause for celebration."

"See what you can find out," Simon instructed, and Dominic raised an eyebrow. Surprisingly, though, Tina just nodded.

"I'll do what I can," she said.

"Cool," Simon replied absently, studying his numbers. "I'd bet money that the answer is somewhere in these numbers." He turned to the others, his eyes gleaming. "I'll start marking the important calendar dates, and you be ready to match them up. We'll break this bastard yet."

"All right then," Tina said, turning back to the computer screen. "Give me some time, and I'll give you something to work with."

Simon turned back to the board and began to scribble again as the others returned to their reading. Dominic sat back and watched for a long while. For the first time, the entire group was working together, consulting each other and their notes when they had a question, not arguing or snapping at one another. It seemed that when Simon was working, he could be almost civil, possessing a competent, take-charge personality that was for once not offensive. The others must have seen the change in Simon too, or were just excited to have something to work on. Dominic didn't care how it had happened, but he certainly hoped the peace would hold for awhile.

It didn't.

Not two hours later, Dominic heard their voices from across the courtyard. He had strolled out to Abby's clearing, but it was not yet full dark, and the stars were barely visible in the dusky evening sky. With Abby nowhere to be found, he turned and headed back.

Hands in his pockets, whistling, he'd been halfway across the courtyard when he heard angry yelling from the lab. "Shit," he said under his breath. He quickened his pace, but when he reached the back door, he paused.

"Look, you silly son of a bitch," Simon was storming. "*I'm* the mathematician here. If it was up to you, you'd probably start using the fucking Bible Code on this shit. I've had enough of this, all right? Enough already. Leave the numbers to me and stay the hell out of it!"

Dominic turned and headed back across the courtyard. He'd had enough, too. For once, the others were on their own.

12.19.15.12.3

September 16, 2008 — "I realized I'm looking for the wrong thing, Dominic."

"How's that?"

"I'm looking through a telescope," Abby replied from the ground beside it. Next to her, Dominic sat fiddling with the lenses, fascinated as always with all things technical. "I'm looking for small scale movements, things the Maya never could have seen."

Dominic understood. "You need to view the sky the way they did, without instruments."

"That's right," she said. "And I need a better viewpoint."

"Your clearing won't do?"

She shook her head. "The forest is right in the horizon line. I want to look from somewhere flat, where nothing interferes with the horizon. I need to see where earth meets sky."

"I think that happens pretty much everywhere," he said, and even in the dim light she could see his smile. She punched him gently in the arm, and he caught her hand.

"I know what you mean," he said, sliding an arm around her in a brief hug. "You need an unobstructed view. No problem. Hike about four miles to the other side of these trees and you're in the clear. Nothing but a highland plain for miles and miles."

"Really?" she asked, turning to him. He nodded.

"Four miles," she echoed, biting her lip. "That's going to be a hell of a trek every night."

"You could set up camp out there, if you want," he suggested. "Steve and I brought our camping gear. A compass, tents, sleeping bags; whatever you need."

"I don't know," she said, troubled. "I'm not quite at ease with camping in the middle of nowhere, four miles from the rest of you. Four rough miles, through a tropical rainforest."

"I've done it a dozen times," Dominic said. "There isn't much that can bother you out there. Snakes, some spiders, not much else. You'd be all right."

She stared at him wordlessly, and he laughed. "Oh come on," Dominic said. "What are a couple of bugs, in the big scheme of things?"

"Snakes are not bugs," she said. "Unless we're taking the whole team out on a field trip, I guess the clearing will have to do."

"Take Tina with you," he said. "She's an old pro at this. I don't think she's afraid of anything that creeps or crawls."

"Didn't you say she wakes up a million times a night when she hears a noise?"

He shrugged. "She's always done that. But I think it's people she's afraid of." He paused. "Tina had some rough experiences in her life. It still haunts her."

"I'm sorry," Abby said. "I didn't mean anything by that."

"I know," Dominic said, tossing her a smile before rising to his feet. "You have a good heart, Abby. I don't think you're capable of saying anything mean about anyone." He held out a hand, and she took it, letting him pull her to her feet.

194

"Let's talk about it in the morning," he said. "See what the others think."

As they walked up towards the house, he gently teased, "Never met an astronomer who was afraid of the dark before."

She laughed, and after they had passed through the lab and crossed the inner courtyard to the house, after Abby was cozy in bed upstairs under the cool sheets, she could still hear his gentle laughter echoing softly in her head.

12.19.15.12.7

September 20, 2008 — Abby finished her shower and changed into warm clothes. Even this far south, the nights were beginning to cool, and she was expecting to be out until dawn. She headed downstairs to the lab, and was surprised to find the group intact.

"Hey, Abby," Dominic greeted her. "You're out early."

Simon looked at him sharply, but addressed Abby instead. "It's only midnight," he said. "How late do you usually stay up?"

She shrugged, sitting down. It was obvious her fiancé was ready to pick a fight. "I'm up when the stars are, Simon. You know that."

He regarded her for a moment, then relaxed. "So you're heading out to have another look. Are you onto anything?"

"I'm still compiling data," she said. "Trying to make some sense of it, see if anything stands out."

"Well, how long do you think it's going to take you to come up with something?"

"We're not on a schedule here, Simon," Dominic broke in. "She'll take as long as it takes."

Simon glared at him. "Just because you have nothing else to do, don't think the rest of us don't have a life to get back to," he said. "I don't want to be stuck in this shithole any longer than I have to."

"No one has chained you here," Dominic answered coolly.

Simon stood up suddenly, pushing off from the table. The solid table didn't budge, and he only succeeded in throwing himself off balance. He righted himself and stepped back, arms folded defiantly over his chest. He was about to speak again when Dominic stood up.

Simon took another step back, but Dominic just said, "I'm going outside. Abby, do you mind if I use your scope?"

"You're always welcome to it," she said.

Dominic nodded. "Good night," he said, addressing the room in general. He turned and went out. Barely a moment passed before Tina and Dante also stood up.

"We'll be upstairs," Tina said. "See you in the morning."

"Fine," Simon said, sitting down again. "Steve? You want to go too?"

Steve stared at him. "What's with you, Simon? We're all working together here. Why are you so damned confrontational?"

"I'm trying to keep you honest."

"Well, thank you," Steve said. "But last time I checked, my moral and ethical standards were well intact."

With that, he left, following Tina and Dante up to the house.

Simon turned to Abby. "And where are you going?"

She sighed, lowering her head into her hands. "Nowhere, Simon."

"Then come to bed," he said. "It looks like another wasted night here. No one's even around to work with. Might as well do something to make it worth my coming back here."

Abby fought to hold her tongue, feeling a shiver of revulsion. "In a minute, Simon. I need to put some things away here."

"Well, hurry the hell up," he said. "I'm fucking tired. I worked all week, then drove all the way out here. The least you can do is act excited to see me."

"I'll be up in a minute."

"Don't keep me waiting long," he said. With that, he turned and left, letting the door slam behind him. Abby put her head down on the table and closed her eyes.

Dominic stared down at his hands, floating pale, ghostlike, in the darkness. He hadn't made it beyond the courtyard. "What are you doing here?" he asked without looking up.

Abby paused. "I don't know," she said honestly.

She saw his slight smile in the darkness as he turned to her. "Well, have a seat then," he said.

She moved onto the rock next to him, but didn't say a word.

They sat in silence for a long while, and when they spoke, they began at the same time.

"Dominic, I just ..."

"Abby, I'm ..."

Both stopped, then Dominic laughed softly. "Go ahead," he said.

"I just want to say I'm sorry," she said. "I know Simon will never say it, so I will."

"You already make excuses for him. Now you're apologizing for him, too?"

"No," she said. "I'm apologizing for me. I haven't been able to do a thing to change his behavior; I haven't been able to get him to stop being so mocking, so selfish and so goddamn arrogant. I've tried, and every time he speaks to you the way he does, I just cringe ..."

Dominic suddenly turned to her, placing a hand on the back of her neck. He stroked her hair gently with his thumb. "You don't have to apologize for that," he said. "Simon is who he is, and nothing you or I or anyone says will change him. Don't ever think you can, Abby. It's just going to give you a lifetime of heartache."

"It already has," she said, and her voice broke. She turned away so he couldn't see her tears.

"Abby," he said, and suddenly his arms were around her, and he pulled her close against his chest. She sobbed wretchedly, embarrassed for herself, but unable to control it.

Dominic didn't say a word; he just held her, stroking her hair and letting her cry. When her tears finally abated, he released her. She sat back, wiping her cheeks with the backs of her hands, avoiding his eyes.

"How was that?" he asked. "Cathartic?"

He surprised a laugh out of her. "Kind of," she admitted. "I've needed to do that for a long time. I thought I was just weary when I came out here, and now I feel more —awake, I guess. More alive. A lot lighter."

"Good," he said. "You feel light enough to go for a walk?"

She glanced at his earnest face. "Sure," she said. "I'm not in any hurry to get back to my room, that's for sure."

He smiled, standing up and reaching for her hand. She let him pull her up off the rock, and they turned towards the lagoon.

They walked along in silence for awhile, and Abby smiled when Dominic began to whistle.

"Doesn't anything bother you, Dominic?" she asked.

He shrugged. "Sometimes. Then I think, is this something I can change or not? If not, then I don't worry about it. If I can change it, then I think, should I? And if not, then I don't worry about it."

"So what happens if you can, and you should?"

"I've managed to avoid that so far in my life," he answered with a smile.

Abby smiled. "Sounds like a good way to go."

"Sure it is," he said. "You just sit back and relax and let life flow around you, without even making a ripple."

"Don't you want to make a ripple? Leave your mark?"

He shrugged again. "For how long?" he asked. "Life moves around us like a current. How long do you think my little ripple will remain?"

"So don't make a ripple," she said. "Make a big splash."

"That's what I plan on," he said, gesturing widely with his hands. "I plan to be a tidal wave."

She smiled, but it faded quickly. "I think I'd be happy right now with just a sea of calm," she said.

Dominic nodded. They had crossed the lagoon and passed into the clearing, and he stopped, gazing up at the hazy night sky. "Then you need to ask yourself: Is this something I can change? And if I can — should I?"

She was silent, contemplating the stars. A shadow passed over the moon, and she suddenly felt very cold. As if sensing her sudden chill, Dominic moved behind her, placing his warm hands on her shoulders. He bent over to put his lips against her ear.

"You don't have to answer that, Abby. At least not to me. I already know the answer. When you find it, it'll be on your own, when you're ready for it."

He stepped back, then strolled off up the field. Abby watched him go, and the loneliness welled up inside her once more. Being with Dominic was natural, relaxing and comfortable. The thought of going back up to face Simon's ranting was almost unbearable. Still, though, she knew the answer: Dominic needed them both on the project. Neither was replaceable at this stage, and besides, she didn't want to leave. The last time she was in Mexico, all she'd wanted was to go back to her life with Simon. This time, the thought of going back to Boston alone with him horrified her.

If she broke up with him and remained in Mexico, there was no guarantee that he'd go, staying just to make her life — and the rest of theirs — sheer torture. And at this point, she didn't know if it was possible for the others to make him leave. He was worse than he'd ever been. This was a time, Abby thought, to not make ripples.

"Dominic, I'm heading back up to the house," she called. Across the clearing, he lifted a hand to acknowledge her, but didn't turn around. She watched his back for a moment, following his dark outline as it faded away into the night.

With a sigh, she turned and headed back towards the lagoon, back towards the courtyard, the lab and the house. Back to where Simon waited, growing angrier by the minute. It was going to be a long night.

12.19.15.12.9

September 22, 2008 — Abby wasn't surprised to find Dominic at the kitchen table, even though it was barely dawn. She'd heard him go to bed a few hours earlier, but knew he'd be up again with the sun. When he slept, she had no idea.

She grabbed a clean glass from the counter, then sat down across from him, reaching for the orange juice. "I'm not trying to put myself out of a job here, but I kind of think we may be looking in the wrong place."

"What do you mean?" Dominic asked.

Abby took a sip of juice. "I mean that we've been looking up this whole time. Trying to figure out what the Maya saw in the stars."

"And you don't think we should be?"

Abby shook her head. "I don't know," she said. "But I'm starting to have my doubts. I mean, sure, they were astronomers. But they lived here on Earth."

"But all their temples are built to the skies; their architecture and customs and culture were built around stargazing. Their myths mirror the constellations. It only makes sense that they were mapping the skies, charting the stars."

"But it makes just as much sense that they were timing something that was going to happen to the Earth. Maybe something that came from the stars, but maybe not something that occurred there. Whatever is going to happen in 2012 is going to affect mankind, or else I can't imagine they'd have taken the time and effort to schedule it for us. If it's an invitation or a warning, it's because something is going to happen to us. Down here. On Earth."

Dominic was thoughtful, stroking his chin. "So do you think we should work backwards, then?" he suggested. "That we should figure out what type of catastrophe could befall us and then see how it figures into the Mayan time schedule?"

"Why not? I know it's not the scientific way of doing things, but we're running out of options here. We don't seem to be getting to the end point by starting at the beginning. We're worrying at these numbers and trying to see where and how they lead; why don't we come up with some ideas and see if the numbers fit?"

"I don't know," he answered. "I've never been much of a fan of tweaking facts like that — I think you can get almost anything to fit if you work at it long and hard enough. Science is studying the facts and coming up with the best explanation for them. I don't want to go about this by choosing our answer and then trying to find facts to support it."

"But we already have our facts," she insisted. "As long as we stick to the integrity of the Long Count. No playing around with the dates and times and assuming they could have different meanings. If the Bible says a day is a day, than it's a day. We're not going to say it's two and half billion years."

"So if we say a tun is twenty days, than it stays twenty days."

"Exactly," she agreed. "No fooling around with the numbers or dates. If we hit on an exact match, then we're in. Otherwise, we keep looking."

"And we'll still keep looking the long way," Dominic said.

"Of course," she said. "Maybe if we work at it from both ends, we'll meet somewhere in between at the right conclusion."

"Well, I won't stop you," Dominic said, standing up again. "At least, it shouldn't put us a lot farther behind than we already are. So — you want to work on natural disasters or you want me to?"

"Let me look into it," she said. "As an astronomer, I can think of more catastrophic events that can hit our planet than most people have ever dreamed of. Maybe we'll get lucky and one of them will fit."

Dominic laughed shortly. "'Luck' is an interesting choice of words," he said.

Abby smiled. "Well, I'm an interesting person."

Dominic was standing in the doorway, his back to her, but he looked over his shoulder at her with a small smile. "Yes," he agreed. "You are."

He gave a small wave and headed up the stairs into the darkness. Abby remained at the kitchen table, still smiling.

12.19.15.13.12

October 15, 2008 — Abby spent most of the day hanging out with Dante and Steve, and when the two men headed back to the lab around mid-afternoon, she joined them.

Simon was scribbling some numbers on the blackboard when they came in; the others spread out along the lab table benches, and Abby sat down at the computer desk. She half-listened to the others, in the middle of a discussion about the Golden Mean, mostly tuning out of the conversation until it fell away. She looked up and caught Dominic's eye as he was addressing the group: "We've gone through the numbers forward and backward. We've matched the Long Count dates with known historical events throughout the world. We've studied Mayan archeology, anthropology, and architecture. We've studied the lay of the land, the topography, and the geologic history of the area. We've studied their mythology and matched it with constellations and astronomical events. So where else *can* we go?" he continued. "Is it possible there's something else out there? Something in our galactic neighborhood or solar system that we've managed to miss, or just never noticed?"

"Well, there's always Nibiru."

"What's that?" Tina asked.

Abby smiled. "A joke," she said. "I'm just messing with you. Nibiru is a theoretical tenth planet that orbits out beyond Jupiter. Actually, the ancient Sumerians considered it to be the twelfth planet, since they considered the sun and moon to be planets, too. The first recorded sighting of it was by the Sumerians as it passed through the solar system in 160 AD."

"I've heard of it," Dominic said. "There was a big to-do about it a few years ago; a surprisingly large contingent of people thought it was supposed to smack into us in 2003, and the government was keeping it from us. The planet never appeared, but that didn't stop the conspiracy addicts. They just figured that they miscalculated and it'd show up again later."

"Is there any evidence for it?" Tina asked with curiosity.

"No astronomical evidence," Abby said

"There's a 6,500 year old Sumerian tablet that shows their observations of our solar system," Steve said. "There are a couple freaky things about it; but what I think is the weirdest is that they had the sizes and the order down pretty much exact."

"What's so odd about that?" Tina asked.

Dominic spoke up before Steve had a chance to answer. "Until the late 1700s, we didn't know there *were* any planets beyond Saturn. We discovered Uranus in 1781, Neptune — when? Sometime in the 1800s?"

"1846," Abby answered. "Then Pluto in 1930. So the fact that they had a diagram of the nine planets of the solar system – still including Pluto, of course – in the right order with their sizes in correct proportion to one another; plus the sun and the moon, was pretty unbelievable."

"But there weren't nine," Dominic said. "There were ten."

Steve nodded. "That's true. The Sumerian tablet shows a tenth planet, smaller than Saturn, bigger than Neptune, orbiting between Mars and Jupiter."

"Nibiru means 'Planet of the Crossing,'" Dominic said. "The ancient description of Nibiru's orbit has it crossing right through the asteroid belt."

Abby was thoughtful. "Was the asteroid belt on the Sumerian tablet, too?"

Dominic smiled. "You're thinking that the asteroid belt could be the remains of Nibiru."

Abby smiled. "Obviously, it would have happened a heck of a lot further back than Sumerian times, but it's interesting. If a planet passed through there on a regular orbit, it could've eventually struck another celestial body, and the asteroid belt could be the remnant of that planet, or the one it hit."

"Or Tiamat," Dante said. When the others turned their attention his way, he continued, "Some claim the Earth was part of a watery world called Tiamat. Something hit us a long time ago, carving out a huge chunk and sending us spiraling into our present orbit, like a billiard ball. If you look at the Earth's geography without water in the oceans, you'll see that it's very lopsided — there's a massive chunk taken out, a big pit we call the Pacific Basin."

"So the asteroid belt would actually be the remaining chunks of the Earth," Tina said.

"Or the remains of whatever tore into us," Dante responded. "It could have been a comet, a moon, a large asteroid or meteor that came along and smacked into Tiamat. Or two planets collided. A theory is that Mars was actually a moon of that planet, and that's why they say our moon is too large to be a naturally captured satellite; it was a moon of the other planet that was thrown out with us in the collision."

"That's so cool," Tina said, and Abby laughed.

"It would be cool if it meant anything," she said. "But it doesn't. There's nothing between Mars and Jupiter but the asteroid belt, and there's no evidence that the asteroids were ever a planet. There are certainly a lot of hypotheses regarding it, but none of them have held any water. The asteroid belt was never the tenth planet."

"And even if it was, it's gone now."

"Well ... not exactly," Abby said.

"What do you mean?"

"There's another school of thought regarding Nibiru, among people who take such things seriously. One that doesn't involve its destruction."

Dante was shaking his head. "It can't still be out there," he said. "We'd have definitely found it by now."

"The story is that Nibiru is on a 3,600 year orbit around the sun," Abby said, "which is why no one in recent history has ever seen it. Nibiru is supposed to swing far out beyond Pluto, so it would return into our system of planets every three and a half millennium. But Pluto is only in a 248 year orbit; Nibiru would have an unbelievably bizarre orbit, almost fifteen times further away from the sun than Pluto is."

Abby could see from Dominic's face that he was quickly calculating, and she stopped him. "It doesn't work," she said gently. "We're looking for 5,100 years, not 3,600. Something was recorded in 160 BC, which believers claim was Nibiru. Counting back to its previous arrival would put it at 3,760 BC, which is meaningless to the Long Count."

"Interesting," Steve said. Abby glanced over at him, and he smiled. "The year 3,760 BC is the start of the Jewish calendar."

"So the Jewish people knew about Nibiru?" Tina asked.

Abby shook her head. "You're missing the point, Tina. The start date is incorrect for the Mayan calendar. If they were counting the next time Nibiru would return to our solar system, they were wrong."

"So is that possible? Could they have made a mistake?" Tina asked.

Dominic sighed. "Doubtful. The Long Count is too exact, too precise. Whatever they were counting, they knew what it was. They wouldn't have miscalculated."

"What makes you so sure?" Simon said. "All they had to do is be off by a year, and by the time it cycled through 13 baktuns, they'd have been off by hundreds of years."

Steve spoke up. "It still doesn't work. Besides, there's a story behind Nibiru. According to the ancient myths, the inhabitants of that planet came to Earth and started civilization here. If the Maya were actually counting down towards the next time they'd be in our neighborhood, they'd have had to have been here the first time about 1500 BC. We know for a fact that civilization, even advanced civilization, was around long before that; we have beautiful works of art and literature that are thousands of years older than that."

"And besides that," Abby said, "we have recorded accounts from that time period, and no one else mentioned that a new planet had suddenly shown up. And with such a wide orbit, there wouldn't be enough warmth or sunlight for anything to survive on it. Nibiru isn't about science, it's about science fiction."

"I thought they found a planet out beyond Pluto?" Tina questioned.

"They've found a lot of things out there," Abby said. "None of them planets, though."

"What about Qu — what the hell was the name of it?" Dominic asked.

"Quaoar," Abby smiled. "Actually, they renamed it a few years later; it became Huya, named after the Venezuelan rain god. It was hard to define. It's a billion miles out beyond Pluto — not exactly a close neighbor, but still part of our solar system. You can find it with a powerful scope, northwest of Scorpio. There was a lot of excitement when they first discovered it, but now we just consider it another Kuiper Belt object."

"What's the difference?" Tina asked.

"The Kuiper Belt is out beyond Pluto's orbit, surrounding our solar system," Abby said. "As you move out away from the Kuiper Belt, you head out into deep space, out into the universe. The Kuiper Belt is filled with icy objects; it's where comets come from. Most of these objects are asteroid sized, but astronomers have believed for a long time that there were much larger objects out there. In 2002 they found Huya."

"So what is it?" Tina asked. "Is it a planet?"

"When Huya was discovered, scientists knew of about five hundred other large Kuiper objects. Huya is only about fifty percent larger than the largest of them. It's just not massive enough to be a planet. And it never gets close enough to the sun to warm it up. Basically, it's a giant frozen rock. Defining it in terms astronomers use today, Huya is not a planet. I wouldn't expect to find any new planets in our solar system. There could be some out even beyond Huya — there is some evidence of something very massive moving around out there; possibly a Brown Dwarf. But the data isn't there yet. Since Huya, they've found some more out there about the same size; large Kuiper objects, but no planets."

"A Brown Dwarf?" Tina asked. "Could that be Niburu?"

Abby shook her head. "Brown Dwarfs are a type of burned out star. Life, as far as we know it, has never evolved on a star. Besides, it's still only theoretical, based partly on the thought that our sun, like most other stars we've found so far, may have originally been part of a dual system.

"But let's face it; Huya is frozen and lifeless. With an orbit close to three hundred years long, it'd never be able to maintain enough heat to even develop life, let alone sustain it. Especially not advanced, intelligent life forms. Nibiru, with a theoretical 3,600 year orbit, would be so far from the sun that even bacterial life could never develop on it. Nibiru is a bust."

"Of course it is." Simon sounded irritated. He sat down on a bench, across the table from Dominic. "Even if Nibiru actually existed, and the Maya noticed it as a celestial object, they'd have no way of knowing that when it passed out of our sky, it wouldn't come back for nearly 4,000 years."

"Unless they had contact with the Nibiruans," Dominic said with a straight face.

"Damn it," Simon said, "The 'Nibiruans' don't exist."

"So," Abby said, "the Maya would have to be an absolutely ancient race to know their own orbit, to recognize the patterns in the sky that only repeat every 3,600 years, and to have recorded them for future generations."

"Mayan civilization is old, but we'd have to assume that they were prehistoric," Steve concurred. "It would've taken them thousands of years to even observe the orbital movements."

"Maybe they had better instruments than we think," Tina said. "Maybe they weren't that old, they just had incredible astronomical technology."

"If they did, where would it have come from?" Simon protested. "And where did it go? The Spanish never found anything like that when they moved into this area."

"Maybe they just didn't recognize it. That whole European Dark Age thing, remember?" Tina argued. "They didn't have the imagination for such things. They destroyed a lot of native artifacts and codexes when they got here, to better convert the 'savages'. While advanced cultures appear to have popped up simultaneously all over the planet around the time of the Incas, ancient Greeks, and Chinese, over the next millennia or so there was a major decline in technology, astronomy, science, even philosophy in their cultures. The Europeans were advancing, while the rest of the world was declining. But since the history we learn is European history, we act like civilization was on a steady climb from the caves up to the International Space Station. We didn't kick it into gear with architecture, astronomy, or science until about the mid-1500s; by then, the Maya were long gone, an ancient age already past."

"Since we don't have the instruments, we can't assume they existed," Simon argued.

"We can't assume that they didn't, either," Tina said, "There's a lot of buried history. The most interesting archeological information we get is from the Middle East. If we could get into some of these places and have free movement to dig and research, I think we'd have some absolutely stunning finds.

"Mesopotamia is the oldest civilization on Earth. Sumeria, Babylon — they gave us the first writing, the first mathematics, astronomy, irrigation, grain cultivation, pottery, metal working, livestock domestication, plumbing, architecture, literature. They gave us the Code of Hammarabi, a set of laws that way predates the Bible; they had surgeons, they had medical books thousands of years before Christ — I think that if we could get freedom to excavate there, it's possible that the whole of world history as we know it could be challenged. But we can't. And we lost so much irreplaceable history when Iraq was looted after the fall of Saddam Hussein. Not just the artifacts stolen from the museums, but the destruction of ancient ruins and the looting of digs without recording what was found where and with which other items. We'll never know the stories that were once there, that took place thousands of years ago."

Steve was nodding. "It's tragic, what's going on in the Middle East. Not just for the people there — that's horrible enough, living day to day with oppression and terrorism, the chance that you or your family could be killed for absolutely no reason but intolerance and hatred — but for civilization as a whole. I mean, the tiny Israel-Palestine area is the holy land of three major world religions. Why? Why were the origins of

Judaism, Christianity, and Islam there? What happened there in ancient times that that little patch of land would be considered sacred ground? That area is the cradle of civilization, where the human race first began to keep their society, or at least their recorded history. And we could lose every remaining sign of it because of war and looting, and because we can't get to those sites."

"And don't forget," Dominic added. "The Sumerians appear in history as a fully advanced pyramid-building civilization. Their Ziggurats in the Middle East were as great of pyramids as the Mayan or Aztec ones. They had a complex written language and advanced astronomical and mathematical skills."

Simon was shaking his head again. "It's ridiculous," he said. "People don't just forget those kinds of things. They don't reach a technological peak and then just stop, regress. How could someone be brilliant enough to build the pyramids, then forget everything and have to start all over?"

"Good question," Dominic responded. "But you're missing the point: Someone *did* build the pyramids. They exist. They're sitting right there on the Giza plateau not far from the Sphinx, the tallest things for miles, rising up out of the sands like the masterworks that they are. And we still don't know exactly how they did it. We've tried to reproduce them through the methods that were available to them at the time, and all efforts have failed. We've managed to move some of the mid-sized stones they used, but never the heaviest. And if you can't move the heaviest with those methods, they couldn't have used them. Yet someone created the pyramids."

"There's always an explanation," Simon argued, "We just haven't found it yet. Just because we don't know the answer doesn't mean it occurred by supernatural or superhuman means."

"Okay then," Dominic said, running a hand through his hair. "Is there any reason to go further with this? The idea of previous advanced civilizations, is fascinating, but none of these have any bearing on the Long Count, except to suggest that the Maya could have been more advanced then we think. Unfortunately, it's all speculation. Unless anyone has anything else?"

"Well, there's another story I remember," Tina said. "It's really stupid, but I remember hearing something about how the ice age was ended deliberately by an advanced technological civilization."

"What'd they do?" Dante asked, smiling at her. "Melt the ice cap?"

"Actually, yes," Tina said. "They knew that to improve our climate and make continents habitable, they'd have to sacrifice some coastal areas."

"You're talking about aliens, then?" Steve asked.

"Maybe," Tina said. "I don't know. I'm certainly not saying that I believe *that*, but I do think there may have been an advanced civilization with a much higher degree of technology than we've been raised to believe. It's one of the reasons I went into archaeology — I wanted to find out for myself. Just because all we find are clay pots and stone pyramids doesn't mean they weren't building from wood and metal, too. I mean, what would our own civilization look like ten thousand years from now, after a great catastrophe?"

"I wouldn't think we'd lose everything.," Dante said. "Wood and fabric would rot, but metal would still be intact. Any kind of machinery would still be recognizable – maybe not what it was used for, but as machined parts put together for a purpose."

"What about after a nuclear war?" Dominic asked.

Dante looked over at Dominic. "Hard to say," he said. "From what we've seen at Hiroshima, everything would be either pulverized or frozen in time. Stone would be vitrified. After many thousands of years, though, who knows?"

"What does vitrified mean?" Abby asked.

"Generally, it's stone that's made into glass, or becomes glass-like, because of extreme heat. Like that from a nuclear explosion," Dante explained. "Very high temperatures fuse the stone."

"Dominic, Tina and I were discussing something similar a few years ago in France," Steve mused. "There was an archeological site where the stone had been vitrified. At the time, we were talking about a nuclear war, but I can't remember the context."

"We were talking about desert glass," Dominic said. "Silica fusion."

"What the hell are you talking about now?" Simon asked.

"Atomic weapons were first tested in White Sands, New Mexico," Dominic explained patiently. "One of the effects of the atom bomb was the desert sand: the nuclear reaction fused the sand into smooth green glass. To our knowledge, an atomic reaction is the only method to fuse sand in that way."

"What about lightning?" Abby asked.

Dominic shook his head. "Lightning has been known to fuse the desert into glass, but not in a smooth sheet. Lightning creates a signature branching pattern, like tubular tree roots."

"What did you find, Dominic?" Abby asked.

"Reports of sheets of green glass, in ancient deserts around the world. Most written accounts are from the 1800s and early 1900s, before we'd even discovered nuclear energy. There's recorded evidence of these glass sheets having been around for thousands of years."

"What about a meteor strike?" Abby suggested. "That would put out enough heat to fuse the sand, and over a large area."

Dominic nodded. "It would," he said, "but something that big would also leave an impact crater, wouldn't it? There've been a few, but in the majority of sites, the glass is found with no impact craters and no other anomalies."

"So you're saying there was an ancient nuclear war?" Abby asked, barely able to hide her skepticism. "Or a nuclear explosions? Several, in fact, if vitrification and desert glass is found worldwide."

Dominic shook his head. "I don't know," he admitted. "And I don't know what bearing this could have on the Long Count. I just don't want to completely discount the possibility that an ancient culture might have been much different than we believe."

"I can buy *some* advances," Steve said cautiously, "Some old cultures were amazing; the Chinese, the Romans. The ancient Greeks were brilliant writers, mathematicians, philosophers. But they were also alchemists — they believed they could turn lead into gold. They weren't chemists or physicists. A nuclear war is a bit of a stretch for me to believe, Dominic."

"Well, if there was any kind of nuclear war, it would predate the ancient Greeks," Dominic said. "It'd have even been before the Olmecs. Any knowledge of it the Maya would've come by wouldn't have come from their own time; it would've been passed down to them."

He smiled. "Anyway, I'm just throwing it out there. I've read some interesting interpretations of ancient structures. The Egyptian pyramids, for example, are one hell of a huge undertaking just to bury the dead. A pyramid is the strongest architectural structure, and some fringe architects have hypothesized that such massive, three-sided structures with underground and interior tunnels might have been built for another reason: To withstand a nuclear blast."

"And the pharaohs died in them?" Tina asked, wrinkling her forehead.

"Maybe the pharaohs came along later and used them for their tombs," Steve offered. "Or maybe they found bodies in them and thought that's what they were intended for, and that such a monumental structure should be fit for the tomb of a king.

"After all, we've found skeletons in other ancient structures that we believed were tombs. Newgrange, for instance, in Ireland; we've found the remains of women and children huddled together, ducking and covering in the entryways and tunnels. Would someone actually bury their dead in such a way, or is this what we'd find if we dug up a bomb shelter after the war?"

Simon stood up and went to the end of the lab table, looking down the length of it at the others. "So, we've found sheets of green glass in the desert. Maybe it wasn't a huge meteor, maybe it was a bunch of smaller ones that wouldn't leave a huge crater. Or maybe a big one skipped off the sand, leaving a shallow crater that would be filled back in again. Whatever the case — what makes you go from that to hypothesizing an unbelievable nuclear war for which there is zero evidence? Why must you jump to such outrageous conclusions from so little information?"

"Because I'm not talking about a few small anomalies," Dominic explained. "I'm talking about a sheet of green glass in Africa, silica fusion unbroken from horizon to horizon. Identical to New Mexico after nuclear testing."

"If it's such a big deal, why haven't I ever heard of it?"

"Because you never listen to anyone?" Dante said. Simon turned and glared at him, but Dominic broke in.

"You've never heard of Libyan Desert Glass? Or tektites? Glass that's 98 per cent silica – absolutely pure. They've found it used in nomadic weapons; knives, jewelry, and more, from thousands of years ago."

Dominic continued. "The most interesting thing about it to me is the concentration. Take Saudi Arabia, for example; there's a ring of desert glass that's thirteen miles across. The inside of the ring is completely clear — like whatever was inside the circle exploded outward."

Abby smiled kindly. "Remember Tunguska?" she asked.

Dominic glanced over at her. "You think a meteor exploded just above the surface?"

"It's more probable than an ancient nuclear war," Abby said pointedly. "It'd have scattered its energy in the same kind of pattern, just like the explosion in Siberia. Tunguska was so phenomenally powerful — a force of ten to twenty megatons, more than 500 to 1000 times the force of Hiroshima — that it destroyed everything for hundreds of miles around the site of the explosion, blew all the trees and everything outward. It downed trees out from the epicenter for thirty miles. Yet it didn't leave a crater, because it exploded before it hit the ground — estimates are that it exploded about five and a half miles up. And it was still powerful enough to cause a seismograph to register it a thousand miles away."

Dominic smiled. "Ok," he said, "we have historical evidence for such a thing. It could have caused the desert glass. But what about the vitrified rock? Atomic reactions are one of the few things that will fuse rock. Yet, in Scotland, there are more than fifty ancient forts, over 3,000 years old, where the stones have been literally melted and fused together."

"Volcanoes," Dante said. When the others glanced at him, he smiled. "Volcanoes will fuse stone. Although as far as I know, there aren't any volcanoes in Scotland."

"How high of a temperature does it take to melt stone?" Abby asked.

"As high as two thousand degrees," Dante said. "You can do it if you can put it somewhere concentrated and keep an incredibly hot fuel source on it. But I'm guessing your forts weren't created this way?"

Dominic shook his head. "These are massive forts; in their day, they covered over 120 acres. They were huge for the time they were created — fortifications on an Egyptian scale. I've studied European history, but I'll be damned if I can figure out who the Scots were defending themselves against that they had to build structures of that size. They wouldn't have even had the troops to man a fort like that.

"And Scotland's not the only place," he continued. "Vitrified ruins have been found throughout the Middle East. There's even an ancient, vitrified megalithic Hittite city in Turkey, from thousands of years before Christ."

"So you're suggesting there was a world-wide nuclear war that did all this," Simon said, arms folded, expressionless.

"Maybe." Dominic's face was equally unreadable, and Abby couldn't tell if he was serious. "Maybe it wasn't one major war; maybe there were several smaller ones."

"Dominic, we know that even one single nuclear exchange between India and Pakistan would forever alter this planet," Dante said. "Life might not survive. And if it did, it would survive in a world greatly changed. I can't believe a series of nuclear wars could've occurred without leaving a lot more physical evidence than a few vitrified buildings."

"There wasn't exactly a lot around back then for it to leave a mark on," Tina reminded him. "And half a dozen countries have tested nuclear weapons by now, and it hasn't destroyed the planet yet."

Dominic continued. "There's much written history of ancient warfare; the problem is that we pick and choose, fairly arbitrarily, which we consider truth and which we consider mythical. The Bible describes talking animals and the dead coming to life, and some consider it to be God's honest truth. Yet stories of flying crafts, which we know exist today, are discounted as fanciful tales.

"No one doubts the historical accuracy of Alexander the Great's conquests, yet they leave out two specific UFO events in the historical record: In Asia in 329 A.D., his troops reported seeing silver shields in the sky, swooping down upon the soldiers and breaking up the fight. In 336, near Venice, the flying shields came back, shooting some type of beam at a city wall and destroying it, allowing Alexander's troops to easily conquer the city. Soldiers on both sides gave the same reports. Yet, we read such a story, say, 'that's impossible,' and throw it out.

"We decide what we'll believe is accurate, ignoring what doesn't fit with our concept of reality, or of history as we know it. Yet, it's all over, in historical reports throughout the world. Ancient Indian texts and poems describe wars fought with airships and advanced weapons. They describe, in detail, what could be taken to be plasma guns, or laser beams, and we call it myth."

"Plasma guns?" Simon asked in disbelief. "Come *on* already."

"There are such things," Dominic said. "Plasma guns emit a stream of electrified gas up to almost 11,000 degrees. That'd vitrify stone, wouldn't it?"

"This is stupid." Simon said, slamming a fist onto the table top. He turned to Steve. "Why don't you put an end to this idiocy? You're the biblical scholar here. Don't you religious people think the world is only a couple thousand years old anyway?"

Steve smiled. "Different people believe different things," he said. "Personally, I'm fascinated that the Bible often speaks of the ancients, and of the stories passed down by those before them." He stood up, going to the bookshelf. He located the black leather-bound book Simon had brought back to the lab at Steve's request and plucked it off the shelf, taking it back to the bench. He sat down, flipping the book open, leafing through the pages until he found what he wanted. "Look at the Book of Job," he said. "It's supposedly the oldest known book in existence. It's about 5,000 years old, yet it speaks of the ancients. Look at Psalms; again, about 4,000 years old. Yet Psalms mentions, 'the years of ancient times.' What would someone 4,000 years ago consider ancient? And isn't that in itself good evidence for a previous civilization advanced enough to pass down stories of their culture?"

"No, it's not," Simon retorted. "If they had no way of recording time, ancient could be 100 years before. They wouldn't know the difference."

Steve was nonplussed. "Some people believe the biblical stories of God and angels actually describe aliens. The word Nephilim, for example, doesn't mean 'giants,' the way it's been commonly interpreted. In the original Hebrew, it means, 'those who came down.' And remember when Moses led the Israelite slaves to the promised land? They were guided through the desert by a pillar of smoke during the day, and a pillar of fire by night. Exodus, 14.21."

"A pillar of smoke?" Simon scoffed. "That doesn't sound like a spaceship to me."

"It sounds like what people might see from Earth — the exhaust, visible by day as smoke, by night as fire. And what about when Moses carried the stone tablets down from Mount Sinai?" Steve continued. "Exodus again. It says the mountain was covered in smoke, and when Moses came down, his hair had turned white, and his skin glowed."

"You're talking about radiation exposure," Dante said.

Steve nodded. Simon looked disgusted.

"Abby," Dominic said, "A while back you mentioned something about Ezekial and a UFO. What were you talking about?"

She looked confused for a moment. "I don't remember," she said. "Either you have a good memory, or mine is going."

He smiled. "It was just something you mentioned in passing but never elaborated on. What did you mean by it?"

"There's a story in the Bible where Ezekial sees a big cloud of smoke and fire come out of the sky," she said. "The way he describes it is really bizarre; totally different than the usual talk of angels. He calls the creatures that came down 'cherubim.'"

"Ezekial," Steve said. He began to search for the specific passage. "He describes amber cherubim coming to Earth in a great cloud, coming out of a whirlwind of smoke and fire. He describes the cherubim as having hands under wings on four sides, joined together, with the wings sticking out straight and unturning. It also says they had four faces."

"That's some pretty fucked up aliens, even by today's standards," Simon observed.

"Maybe the cherubim weren't the aliens," Dominic said. "Ezekial could have been describing the spaceship."

The others turned to him, and he shrugged. "Think about it. You have a primitive culture who knew very little about metal and absolutely nothing about technology. They didn't have words for machines and engines and spaceships. This wasn't India, where historical records include these descriptions. Here's a guy living in a desert, in a house of brick and mud trying to describe a modern day spaceship. How would he know it wasn't alive? Look at the words he uses to describe it.

"He says there were hands underneath their wings — that could be some kind of struts, or even the type of grasping, picking tools we use on our moon probes and Martian landers. He says the wings stuck out, unmoving; look at the stationary wings of the space shuttle.

"He says it has four faces. Could be windshields, or portholes. Maybe he even saw the astronauts peering out through these windows. He says the creature was amber, which could be the color of whatever type of metal or finishing process was used on the spaceship."

"Ezekial goes on to explain how the cherubim moved," Steve said. "He says they had lamps like burning coals of fire, going up and down, and that a bright fire went out like lightning."

"That's an easy one," Dominic said. "Running lights and the fire of rocket fuel as it lifted off."

Steve nodded. "They wouldn't have had those kinds of words or descriptions back then. Ezekial would have had to use words like 'burning coals,' and 'lightning.'

"He does go on to describe the wheels, though. That would have been something he recognized." He'd located the passage, and began to read:

"Ezekial 1:20: '*Withersoever the Spirit was to go, they went, thither was their Spirit to go; and the wheels were lifted up over against them: For the Spirit of the living creatures was in the wheels.*'"

He went on to Ezekial 1:21: "'*When those went, these went; and when those stood, these stood; and when those were lifted up from the earth, the wheels were lifted up over against them: For the Spirit of the living creatures was in the wheels.*'"

"So what the hell does *that* mean?" Simon asked.

"Didn't you ever do riddles when you were a kid?" Tina asked.

"Simon was never a kid," Dante joked, and Simon glowered at him again.

"I'd say it's actually a pretty good description, coming from someone who had no idea what he was looking at," Dominic said. "He says that when the wheels turned, the whole thing turned. Where the wheels went, that's where the ship moved. He wouldn't have known or understood that someone inside the ship was steering and moving the wheels, he just observed the wheels turning and assumed that's where the spirit dwelled; that the wheels were the living creatures making the decision and controlling the beast."

"And it sounds like the wheels drew up against the ship when it lifted off," Dante said.

Steve held up the Bible and continued reading. "Ezekial 1:24: '*And when they went, I heard the noise of their wings, like the noise of great waters, as the voice of the Almighty, the voice of speech, as the noise of an host: when they stood, they let down their wings.*'"

"Beautiful," Dominic said. "The ship lands — or stands up, ready to take off —and the wings come down."

"And the sound is the noise of the engines," Tina added.

Steve looked at her with a smile. "They had to describe it with natural words," he said. "They use, 'the noise of the waters,' because that's the only sound they had for comparison with for such a roar."

"And the voice of the Almighty," Dominic said. "It must have been an incredible noise, something so great and loud he'd never have heard anything like it in his life; it was so powerful and loud it could only be the voice of God."

"Why the hell are we interpreting the Bible?" Simon said irritably. "I thought we agreed that it was all myth, and nothing to do with the Long Count."

"Some of it has been historically documented. We've found lost cities, records of kings," Steve said. "The problem for scientists trying to interpret it is that it runs its view of every event through a God filter. For example, if this is an actual event Ezekial was recording, what could it have been? Ezekial didn't know. He called it cherubim, an angel of God. He didn't have any other frame of reference to describe something that came down from the sky and landed in front of him spitting fire and smoke.

"He gives the exact date it occurred: In the thirtieth year, in the fourth month, on the fifth day. He said the heavens opened, and down it came. We have no way of tracing it back to find out exactly what it is that Ezekial saw. We know that he told us it was cherubim. But if such a thing happened to us in this age of technology instead of the Stone Age, what would we call it? A UFO."

"That's jumping to one hell of a conclusion," Simon said.

"Maybe," Steve responded. "But many Biblical scholars are confused by that passage. It doesn't make a lot of sense, and stands out by itself as something distinctly odd, unlike anything else in the Bible. It's surprising that it made it through all the edits and revisions; look at Noah's grandfather, Enoch."

"Enoch? I've never heard of him."

"That's because it was cut. The Book of Enoch was part of the original compilation of writings that went into the Bible — it's dated about 200 BC. It was edited out by Ecumenical Christians because it was so controversial. I guess no matter how the early evangelistic Christians tried to make sense of it, it was just too bizarre, so they cut it. They said it was blasphemous."

"What the hell did it say?"

"It's very similar to many other Old Testament books; it tells the same stories, repeats the same history. But Enoch speaks a lot about angels. He describes them coming to Earth and bringing an advanced technology, and being taken up to the heavens with them. He describes being able to see things that no man has ever seen, and described the glories of Heaven. His astronomical descriptions are pretty accurate, surprisingly so —this, more than anything, is why they took it out of the Bible. It didn't jibe with the current belief that the Earth was the center of the universe and everything else revolved around it; it was heresy. And he didn't just mention things in passing, he wrote pages about the orbits of the sun, moon, and planets."

"Where did the angels take him?" Tina asked.

214

"He describes flying over the seas and mountains of the Earth, and then up into space. I can't remember exactly what he described; he says he was shown the wonders of Heaven, and I believe he met with more angels. He could have been taken to another planet, or a mother ship. He mentions some kind of grand device he saw, but just like Ezekial's text, it's described in such odd terms that you can't make much sense of it. I'd imagine the editors of the Bible were confused by it, and since it went against the grain of the church's teachings, they just cut it."

"You really believe this shit, don't you?" Simon asked.

"It's not a matter of belief or disbelief," Steve said. "The Book of Enoch exists. The words he wrote exist. Go find a copy of the Dead Sea Scrolls, you can read them yourself. It's not up to me to interpret what they say; you can do that on your own if you're so inclined. Fact is, Enoch wrote about being taken to the heavens by angels, and he gave a fairly astronomically accurate description of what he saw. Whether that means that he was taken into space by a UFO, or that he was an early Galileo and truly believed in planetary orbits, so much so that he disguised it in the form of a story and tried to pass it off as prophecy, shown to him by angels, I don't know."

"If so, it didn't work," Dante said.

"Fighting church doctrine usually doesn't," Dominic said.

Steve looked thoughtful. "There are other Biblical anomalies," he said. "The original versions of the Bible talked about *gods*, not *a* God. We all know the Bible went through who knows how many revisions and rewrites and copies and edits before it became the King James version that we use today. You can still find references to gods in it, though. They're rare, but if you look carefully you can find them. Genesis describes the sons of the gods mating with the daughters of men, for example. It also says that after the deluge Noah went to live with gods. Gods, not God."

"Figures," Simon scoffed. "Mayan gods, Hindu gods, Christian gods, aliens, they're all the damn same. Figments of the imagination of a people that have to create invisible friends to explain their world. You all can't accept that human beings might have had the brains to develop math and create the pyramids on their own; it had to be alien intelligence that gave it to us.

"Man has launched himself into space and landed on the surface of another heavenly body, then returned safely. He's completely obliterated several devastating lethal diseases, and built machines that let us fly in the sky and breathe under water. The mind of man is an incredible thing. I don't doubt for a moment that all of our creations came from that great mind. And so did our gods. Mankind has an imagination that can create grand architecture and micro-chips, that can understand how to harness the power of the atom. We can also create gods. And aliens."

"I don't disagree with you," Dominic said. "We're not trying to prove the existence of God, or gods, or even aliens. We're not trying to prove that the Maya were right. But no matter how ridiculous some of these options may sound to you, we can't rule them out just because they sound silly to us; there are similarities between cultures.

The Maya believed in many gods – some who lived in the sky, who they say descended to bring them culture. They made blood sacrifices to them nearly one hundred days out of the year. We may be horrified and appalled by that, but that's the way they were. We can't discount a hypothesis because we ourselves don't like it. Not if we think it'll lead to the way the Maya thought."

"So we need to think like a Mayan," Simon said, and even though he was being facetious, there was a trace of humor in his voice.

"Exactly," Dante said. "Just please do us a favor, Simon — no human sacrifices."

Simon didn't answer, but Dominic wasn't listening anyway. He stood up and went to the chalkboard, the head of the room, like a professor addressing his class, or a preacher his congregation. "I think it's entirely plausible that our ancestors had far more scientific and astronomical knowledge than we give them credit for," he said. "Think about it; how much sense does it make that something like the pyramids were actually built at the beginning of man's ascent? At the start of human civilization? Isn't it far more rational to think that they were created somewhere in the middle to the end of an advanced civilization? From there, we only declined, losing the scientific knowledge that our ancestors seemed to have owned, falling into the trap of myth and the worship of gods, looking for supernatural answers instead of scientific ones. Might not a meeting with such supernatural beings have spurred this change?

"There is evidence that ancient man did possess much of the same knowledge that we have today. And who knows, maybe they *were* more advanced than we are now. For whatever reason, civilization fell, and we started over. It's not too far of a stretch to believe it could happen again — all it takes is one mad dictator, or one nuclear accident, and the entire world could go up again in flames. There would probably be survivors, but they might be at the most remote areas of the Earth, in the Amazon, or on small islands in primitive societies where the fallout might not reach. By the time they advanced enough to build boats and explore, crossing the vast oceans, it could be thousands of years in the future, and time and the Earth's geology would have recycled the world we once knew.

"By the time these primitive survivors advanced to the level we are now, it could be another few thousand years. By then, their archaeologists might be discovering some of our artifacts, and their anthropologists would be piecing together what they know of our society, our ancient, primitive society. They might find a flight manual — like the text in which writers in ancient India described pilot training — and consider it a work of fiction. They may marvel at our creativity, but probably not at our genius. Because, after all, doesn't civilization only advance? Who ever heard of a cultural decline? Other than, of course, the decline of the brilliant philosophers of ancient Greece and Rome into the Dark Ages and the Inquisition."

"We can't assume that what we know is what has always been true. When man is confused or ignorant about something, he makes up stories to explain it. These stories become myths; legends to be passed down and recycled. Look at the Epic of Gilgamesh; it predates Genesis by several hundred years, yet it describes the Noachian flood in pretty exact detail. We know that Gilgamesh came first — so was the Genesis flood a re-telling of an even more ancient tale? Are the close similarities just coincidence?

"The fact is," Dominic went on, "much of what we know — or believe — to be true is based upon legends passed down for hundreds, if not thousands, of years. We choose which of these to give credence to, depending on how history treats the authors, or upon our religion. Much of Judaism and Christianity is based on the Zoroastrian faith, one of the first monotheistic faiths — the doctrine of one God, the concepts of heaven and hell; even the Messiah, the final judgment, the three kings who appeared at Christ's birth — all based on the religion of the prophet Zarathushtra. But since most of these texts were destroyed by Alexander the Great, and because Persia turned Islamic, we don't study these ancient texts anymore. Instead, you follow the religion you were born into, or you choose to believe. If you're a Christian, you give more credence to the Bible than you do to the *Popul Vuh*. If you're Muslim, you treat the Koran with respect while you throw out the *Tao Te Ching*. All are ancient texts, all might have as much — or as little — truth and historical accuracy as any of the others. Yet the society we're raised in, or choose to live in and relate to, dictates in which of these we will place our beliefs. This is our frame of reference, and our view of history.

"I, for one, am willing to admit that what I know of history may be wrong."

Abby rubbed her eyes. "Dominic, I don't disagree with you. But I'm getting too tired to think about it clearly. I think I'm going to go to bed."

"Not yet," Simon informed her. "If we're going to bullshit about ancient nuclear wars and shit, and somehow convince ourselves that the Maya were more advanced than we are, then you should be a part of it."

"Simon ..."

"Don't whine," he told her. "Just sit back and listen."

A dark look crossed Dominic's face, but Simon continued: "So, how the hell long is all that going to take?"

"Might take us to the end of time."

"Funny," Simon answered, sounding irritated once again. "How about we try to simplify all the hypotheses and not even consider the bullshit ones? Anything that has to do with dead mammoths and ancient nuclear wars can go straight out the window."

Across the room, Dominic had finally had enough. "We'll discuss what we need to," he said shortly. "You can like it or not, Simon, I really don't give a damn. We're not here to listen to you and your bitching. If you don't like it, go back up to your room. Otherwise, you can sit here and listen to us talk."

Simon stared at him incredulously. Dominic ignored him and went to the bookshelf. He searched the titles and quickly found what he was looking for, a book with detailed maps of the various Mayan sites. "Here," he said, tossing it to Simon, who lunged forward to catch it awkwardly. "I've been considering the layout of each site. I've considered the map of the Mayan world in general. We know from other ancient civilizations that there's mathematical perfection in the layout of the temples, in the creation of the monuments. If there's anything similar with the Mayan world, I want to know about it. I want to know angles, distances, relationships. You're the only one of us that might recognize a pattern, or have a grasp of the mathematics involved in their orientation. Please help us out and study these, see what you can find."

Simon looked uncertain, but Dominic moved back to his place at the table without further comment. The blond man began to leaf through the book, examining the maps. With Simon distracted, the others picked up their notes again.

"Abby," Dominic said, "Go to bed. We'll catch you up in the morning."

"Are you sure?" she asked warily.

"Positive," he responded. He looked at Simon, but the other man didn't look up from the book he'd been given.

"All right," Abby said, rising from the table. "I'll see you all tomorrow, then."

"Good night, Abby," the others said. Simon remained silent.

Dominic waited until she'd left the room, the door swinging quietly shut behind her. "Okay," he said, "So where were we?"

October 27, 2008 — Abby came down for breakfast to find Tina, Steve and Dante already cleaning and drying their dishes.

"You have a good sleep?" Tina asked.

"Yeah, actually I did," Abby said. "It felt great to sleep in."

"You missed Simon. He left early this morning."

Abby didn't respond. Simon hadn't even woken her to say good-bye, and now he'd be gone for a week. Mildly surprised to find that she really didn't care, Abby grabbed an apple from the basket of fruit on the counter. "Where's Dominic?"

"I haven't seen him yet," Tina responded. "He was up later than the rest of us last night; for all I know, he's probably still out in the lab."

Abby actually found him out behind the lab, having a cup of hot tea and looking out over the lagoon. He nodded to her in greeting as she came to join him, seating herself on the rock opposite him.

Dominic said: "It was Rivarol who said, 'When one is right a day before the common run of people, one is taken to have had no common sense for a day.'"

Abby laughed. "I get the feeling you've been taken to have no common sense on more than one occasion."

Dominic smiled. "I've been called crazy a time or two – but I'm usually right."

"Usually?"

He shrugged. "I've been known to wander off the beaten track, but I always find my way back."

"Do you usually know when you're wandering down the wrong path?"

"Usually. Sometimes I'll catch myself in a major lapse of reason. I question my every result and how I got there. If I can't back it up, I throw it out. And if I don't find my own mistake, someone else will. They have before, when I've been blinded by my attachment to an idea. I can admit when I don't have the evidence, and I can admit when I'm wrong."

Abby smiled wryly. "Unlike someone we know."

"Well …" Dominic started, then trailed off.

"It's ok," she said. "I used to believe that Simon was never wrong. Now I think only he believes it."

"Actually, I don't think he does," Dominic said. "I think he knows as well as the rest of us that he's full of it, but he's not willing to admit it. He started off on the wrong foot with us, and now he's been playing the game so long it's impossible for him to back down. But he knows he's fallible. I think that's why he stays away so much, and takes off in a huff every time we question him too deeply. Simon can't back it up, so he avoids it."

Abby looked uncomfortable, and Dominic smiled. "Hey, it's fine by me," he said. "He can stay away as long as he likes. Maybe he really does think he's never wrong. Either way, as long as he's working hard, I'm happy with him."

She smiled. "That makes one of us."

Dominic raised an eyebrow, but Abby stood up, brushing off her pants. "Come on," she said, offering him a hand. He took it and she helped him to his feet. "Back to work."

Dante kicked back, leaning his chair against the wall. He crossed his legs, feet propped up on the computer desk. "What are the odds all this is a fraud?"

"Like, whoever 'discovered' the calendar actually made it up?" Tina asked with a smile.

"Sure, why not?" Dante said. "Just some bizarre little mystery for us to waste our time on, like the Piltdown man, or William Niven's tablets 'found' here in Mexico that supposedly proved the existence of Atlantis."

"Uh-uh, sorry," Tina said. "The calendar is tied together from archaeological records all throughout Mesoamerica. The Long Count is for real."

"That's what I was afraid of," he sighed.

The door opened and Dominic came in, his arm around Abby companionably. "Hey, what's going on here?" he asked, seeing Dante's feet up on the desk. "This looks a lot like slacking to me."

"What's with me?" Dante asked, feigning offense. "What the heck are *you* doing?"

Dominic looked at Abby, who quickly slipped out from under his arm. "Just sharing a joke," she said, crossing the room.

"So, remind us again what's so important about the winter solstice?" Tina asked, ignoring Abby's quick escape.

"It's the day of least sunlight; it marks the beginning of increasing daylight," Abby responded, sitting next to Steve at the lab table. "It's seen as a new beginning. The resetting of their calendar on the winter solstice is more than just coincidence. It's the start of a new Great Cycle."

"So they're resetting it? Not ending it?" Dante asked.

"Well ... it *is* ending, isn't it? Instead of just flipping over, like it does at the end of every series of tuns and katuns and whatever else, it would reset again to zero, wouldn't it? It's the end of the fifth age, the fifth world. They don't mention anything about the beginning of a sixth."

Dominic shook his head. "None of the South American Indians did. For some reason, five ages was a common count; the Incas, Maya, and Aztecs all had their own legends about it. In Aztec myth, monsters from the sky descend to Earth to devour mankind at the end of the fifth sun."

Dante laughed. "Is that something we should be looking into?"

"It's no worse than the other alternatives," Abby said with a smile. "When you think about our sun engulfing the Earth, or an asteroid destroying all life on our planet, or galaxies colliding and pinballing us into the far reaches of space — being consumed by monsters is the least of our worries."

"That's still pretty worrisome, though," Tina said. "When you couple it with the Mayan end date, and stories of gods descending from the sky — is something going to come down?" Suddenly she laughed. "Thank God Simon's not here. I can't even imagine what he'd say about that."

"Oh, I almost forgot," Dominic said, reaching into the bookshelf. He pulled out a small digital recorder. "Say hi to Simon."

"What the hell is that?" Dante asked, pulling his feet from the desk and standing up. "He's spying on us now?"

"He dropped it off this morning," Dominic said. "Told me he didn't trust us to faithfully record our discussions for him."

"That paranoid son of a ..."

"Watch it," Dominic warned, "this thing is voice sensitive — it comes on when we start talking."

"Give me that damn thing," Dante growled. "I'm throwing it in the lagoon."

The others laughed. "Don't tell me we've got to carry that with us everywhere," Steve said.

Dominic shrugged, returning the recorder to the shelf. "I don't mind. We don't have anything to hide from him. And this way he can't complain that we're not reporting everything to him that we talk about. Look at the bright side: this thing can't talk back."

Amid their laughter, Dominic returned to the lab table, where he sat next to Abby. She avoided his eyes when he turned to her; he might not feel that he had anything to hide from Simon, but Abby thought she did.

12.19.15.14.14

November 6, 2008 — "The most UFO sightings occur when Venus is at its brightest. Literally, hundreds and hundreds of them pour in." Abby and Dominic sat on the westernmost side of her clearing, her telescope far across the field, momentarily abandoned. The autumn sky was crisp and clear, and with the naked eye, it seemed that they could see for a million miles. Abby knew they literally could, when they looked up; the stars were hundreds, even thousands and millions of light-years away.

"Most people will insist they can tell the difference between a planet and a UFO," Dominic answered with a smile.

"They can insist they can *logically*, but in reality, how? If they see it in the night sky and can't identify it, to them it literally is an Unidentified Flying Object, whether it seems to be suspended in space or moving. Both our atmosphere and our eyes create peculiar effects: the curtain of our atmosphere makes even stars and planets seem to waver, or move. Even through the telescope, you see the different color refractions as the star's light travels down to us. Our atmosphere changes the spectrum of color we get from different heavenly bodies; some seem to change color, to flicker and sparkle.

"Our eyes do the same thing; they create what's known as the autokinetic effect," she continued. "The muscles around the human eye are constantly moving, though we don't feel it or notice it; but even things that are utterly still can seem to jitter and jog. We see movement that isn't there. It's not difficult to be mistaken – even Jimmy Carter mistook Venus for a UFO while he was Governor of Georgia. It happens to the best of us."

"Even you?"

She smiled. "When I was a little kid, riding in the car at night, I used to look out and think the moon was following us. Eventually I figured out about perspective, and applied it to other heavenly bodies. People in cars often claim that a UFO was chasing them, when it's only Venus and their eyes playing tricks on them. Just because it appears to move when you do doesn't mean it's actually moving. Trees do the same thing. It's a matter of perspective, part of our physiology; you feel like you're sitting still, so it must be everything else that's moving."

"Hmm. Unidentified Flying Trees," Dominic mused.

Abby laughed and gave him a gentle elbow to the ribs. "You wouldn't think that was so funny if you heard some of the stupid things people have reported — blimps, satellites, the space station, and of course, the good old fashioned weather balloon."

"I believe it," Dominic said. "I run with a fairly interesting crowd. You think the things the average person sees in the sky and misinterprets are bizarre, you should hear what people theorize about ancient artifacts."

Abby leaned back on her hands, looking up at the vast glittering sky. "So, should we go get Simon's tape recorder?"

Dominic smiled and put his arm around her. "I don't think he has to know everything, does he?"

Abby felt her breathing come a little faster and hoped that he couldn't hear her heart beating.

They sat in silence for awhile, Dominic's warm hand on her back. She shivered.

"You cold?" he asked.

"A little. Not too bad."

"You want to go in?"

"No," she said. "I'm okay. It's probably only about 60 out. It just feels cold, compared to those hot humid temperatures we endured all summer."

"It probably won't get much colder than mid-fifties all winter," Dominic said. "But after what we're used to, it's going to feel like it's in the thirties."

Abby didn't answer, and they watched the sky a little longer.

"Peso for your thoughts," Dominic finally said.

Abby shrugged. "Just thinking about the seasons changing, I guess. Cyclical, like the Long Count. A lot of beginnings and endings."

"The Maya believed very much in cycles," Dominic commented. "They believed in rebirth — that we lived after we died, and that we were dead before we lived. Death was a doorway — and so was life."

"Is that why they also believed in sacrifice?"

"Yes. Death was nothing to fear – it was what fed life, in an endless cycle …"

"Endless?"

"Sure." Dominic paused. "Wait, I see what you're saying; if they believed the cycle was endless, why would the Long Count end?"

"Exactly."

"Maybe it doesn't end, then," Dominic said. "We know the end of one cycle is the beginning of the next — the seasons flow into one another, and the world ages do, too. Wish I knew why there was no sixth age, though." He laughed softly, pulling his arm away. He stood up, then reached a hand down to help Abby to her feet. "It's a never-ending cycle, isn't it? A catch-22."

"We do seem to be going in circles," she admitted. She paused to stretch, then watched him turn back towards the house.

"I think I'm going up to my room and do a little research," Dominic said. "We keep running into these philosophical blocks. You're right; the Maya didn't believe in endings. And here we are, trying to figure out the meaning to the end. Looks like if we're going to find the answer to the Long Count, we'd better be able to answer some of these other questions first."

Abby nodded silently. She was tired, and didn't feel like heading back up to see Simon. In fact, she planned to stay up at her telescope most of the weekend in the hopes of avoiding him. She said good night to Dominic and watched him stride off up the hill towards the house.

Still, she thought, the next time anyone offered to buy her thoughts, she wasn't selling.

Steve looked up uneasily as Simon came in. They were alone in the lab, and it was late.

"Where is everybody?" Simon asked. He was carrying a six pack of beer he had brought in from outside. Since the temperature dropped, they had started leaving some of their refrigerated goods on the steps outside the lab overnight to preserve energy.

"I don't know," Steve said, looking down at his notebook. "I haven't seen Dante or Tina since dinner, and Dominic left about an hour ago."

"So where's Abby?"

Steve didn't look up. "I haven't seen her for awhile, either. I thought she was out at her scope."

"Great, so I'm losing track of my own damn fiancée," Simon said, throwing himself into a chair. "I'm only here two days a week, how hard is it for her to stick around me for two damn days?"

"I don't know," Steve said, obviously uncomfortable.

"Yeah, I know you don't know," Simon said, switching on the computer. "So what do you know, Steve? What do you guys talk about when I'm not here?"

"Pretty much the same thing we talk about when you are. When we come up with anything that might be valid, we always bounce it off you when you get back."

"Always?" Simon asked, looking back at Steve over his shoulder.

"Yeah, sure," Steve said. "We always keep plenty of notes of our meetings, and you always go through them. You have your recordings."

"There aren't any notebooks I've never seen? No conversations you guys fail to record?"

Steve looked up at him. "Not to my knowledge, Simon. We leave everything out for each of us to flip through and compare notes. I can't imagine why anyone would hide anything from you."

"You can't, can you?"

Steve suddenly closed his notebook and stood up. "Look, Simon, I don't know where this is going, but I don't like it. No one is keeping anything from you. We're not hiding anything, and no one here is out to get you, no matter what you might think."

Simon stopped cold. "No matter what I might think?" he repeated. He swiveled around in his chair. "What the hell does that mean?"

Steve paused. "You know what, Simon? It's late and I'm not making any sense. I'm leaving."

"Come on," Simon said. He pulled out a beer and tossed it to Steve, who caught it reflexively. "Have a drink with me."

"Simon, I really don't want to."

"Just finish a beer and yap with me a while. I never get a chance to talk to anyone around here. It seems like you all either avoid me or ignore me. Dante and Dominic are the only two I can get a rise out of, and all they do is argue with me. Why can't we just talk?"

Steve sat down again slowly. He twisted the cap off his beer. "What do you want to talk about?" he asked warily.

"Whatever," Simon said. "Tell me, do you think we're getting anywhere?"

Steve shrugged. "Not sure," he admitted. "Some of the others think we're getting off on a pointless tangent, talking about aliens and ancient astronauts. We've got a lock on the galactic center — we know the Maya considered it their birthplace, and recorded it over and over in their glyphs, so there's a good possibility it has something to do with the Count — but we don't know how it fits in. Somehow, Mayan mythology and astronomy have to come together to predict some occurrence on the end date."

"I want to know if it's supposed to be the end of the world," Simon said.

"The end of the world," Steve said, shaking his head. " 'Of that day and hour, knoweth no man.' Jesus said that. No one is supposed to know when he'll return, or when the world will end."

"When Jesus will return?" Simon asked. "What do you think, it's the fucking Apocalypse?"

"Could be," Steve replied. "Apocalypse literally means 'unveiling.'"

"So what would it be unveiling if it's the end? In the Christian sense the Apocalypse is the unveiling of Christ on Earth, right? When he suddenly appears?"

"To start with," Steve responded. "Then, it's the end of life as we know it, after Christ returns and takes all the holy people up to Heaven. The rest of the world is left to wait for Armageddon."

"So for the holy rollers, the Apocalypse is the end of life on Earth," Simon said.

"Well, if you've been saved. Those left behind can still save themselves in the thousand years that Christ reigns on Earth."

"So even the Apocalypse is meaningless, as far as saying it's the true end of the world. Is there really an end in any philosophy or religion that you know of? What about this sense of five ages? Each world ends, right?"

"Well, yes," Steve said. "But there were five ages. The end of each age is the beginning of the next." He drained his beer. "You have to understand endings the way the Maya saw them. They had a practice called 'end-naming' — they didn't see the end of a cycle as a definite *end*; they saw it as the beginning of a new phase. It was like ... like a pregnancy, I guess. We count nine months, and the end of the pregnancy is a birth."

Simon looked at him, then at the empty bottle Steve was holding. He reached for another beer and tossed it to him. Steve tipped it to him in thanks and cracked it open. "Some say the Tzolkien, the 260 day calendar, is a count of the gestational period of a human being. The concept of birth and rebirth was very important to the Maya."

"So you think the end of the Long Count signifies a new beginning," Simon stated flatly. "It's not the end of the world, but the end of the waiting period."

Steve nodded. "It's possible."

"Well, what brings it on, then? Did they just pick a period of time for each world age? Or is there some event that's going to usher in their new age?"

"Personally, I think it's some kind of astronomical alignment with the dark rift. It's considered the birth canal of the great mother, and the Maya believed in reincarnation and rebirth. It seems to me that the Count, with its repeating cycles, symbolizes the cycle of life, of birth and death and rebirth. When there's a certain alignment, to the Maya it could've symbolized the birth of the next world age."

"What's the alignment?"

Steve shrugged. "That I don't know," he said. "I'd imagine that Abby can find it for us, though. She's been out there charting patterns for months now. I've found a great program for the computer I was going to order and surprise her with — it'll run the star cycles back for thousands of years, finding the precise alignment with the dark rift on that date. If she can work with that, and match up Dominic's mythology with it, I think we'll have the answer and be back home by Christmas."

Simon took a long drink of his beer. "So you think it's that simple?"

"Yeah, I do. You always laugh at me because I reference everything to religion, but religion is the basis for most cultural myths, from the primitive to the civilized. They construct their cities around their temples and places of worship; they write laws and create societal mores

226

based on their religion. It imbues every part of life, and I think it was even truer in ancient times than it is today. Every aspect of Mayan life was based on either astronomy, religion, or both. So it makes perfect sense to me that no matter how advanced they may have been, the Long Count was still based on religion."

"Have you told any of the others about this? Tina? Dominic?"

Steve shook his head. "I was waiting to talk to Abby first. She's been getting frustrated with her star charts; she can't find any relevant constellations or alignments they might have given significance to. I was going to tell her to start looking at the galactic center. She's reading too much into the physics of space; she's trying to find relevance in black holes and apply it to the Long Count. I think she needs to back off a step and just look with her eyes, not with her mind. The Maya would have seen something pass into the dark rift and would have counted on that to usher in the next world age."

"But we're living in the final age."

"Meaningless," Steve said. "The Maya didn't know how many world ages there were, and there's no evidence for anything that would make us think there are only five ages to be lived. In fact, the entire designation of a world age is arbitrary. The Earth is billions of years old, and mankind has only begun making his mark on it in the last ten thousand years or so. The Earth is ageless – at least until man or an asteroid or something destroys it. I don't think fate decides that, or that God has a plan to let us live for so long before decimating the planet. Life could go on forever, until the sun burns out. We're just looking at one culture's myths."

"But their mythology said we're living in the final world age," Simon repeated.

"And how is that different than all the doomsayers we have running around now?" Steve asked. He finished his second beer, and Simon silently tossed him another one.

"Ever since the beginning of recorded time, man has thought he was living in the end times. The Bible predicted Armageddon within the writers' generation, but we're still waiting for it. There have been cults in every decade of this century, from Jonestown to Waco to Heaven's Gate, each with their own charismatic leader predicting the world is going to end and only his followers will be saved. People thought the world would end in the year 2000; they thought the same thing in the year 1000.

"It's a natural aspect of our character to consider ourselves living in the end times," Steve continued. "We always think that we're at the peak of humanity. After all, who can imagine what the world might be like in 4000 AD? To us today, that's as difficult to picture as it would have been for the Maya to imagine us now, 2000 years ago."

"So their mythology is just mythology."

"I believe so," Steve said. "As much as we might want to make more of it, we can't. They say the simplest solution is usually the correct one, and that's what I think is going on here. You were right — we try to give them these mystical qualities, make it seem like they were an advanced race with lost knowledge, and the Long Count is the key to unlocking it. But it's not. It was a calendar, just like the Haab, just like the Tzolkien. End of story."

"Dominic will be disappointed."

Steve smiled. "Not Dominic. He'll laugh at himself for getting so sidetracked, but he won't be disappointed. I've seen him obsess about lots of things before, and they always end the same way: He figures them out, and goes on with his life."

"But he didn't figure this one out. You did."

Steve shrugged. "No matter. Dominic doesn't much care one way or the other. That's why he brought us all here. He won't be at all irritated or jealous of whichever one of us figures it out. After all, there's not much money to be made here. I'll be more than happy to let Dominic write this up and publish it, if I'm right. All it'll do is be published in a few peer-reviewed scientific and archeological journals. He might write a book, but mainstream society won't exactly make it a best seller – there's a small niche market for this type of thing. Other scientists will debate it, and maybe they'll agree, or maybe they'll shoot us out of the sky on it. But that'll be it. No fortune and glory to be made off an astrological alignment."

"You don't think the common media would pick this up?"

Steve shrugged. "Maybe as a blurb sometime in 2012. It'll hit the weekly news magazines as a timely interest story, but that's it. The date will come and go; people will flock to ancient Mayan sites to watch the alignment, just as they go to the Pyramid of the Sun every year to watch the snake make its way down the steps. It'll be good for tourism that year, anyway."

Simon finished his beer and set the bottle down. "Then I guess we're done here."

"Soon, anyway," Steve said. "If I can get Dominic to pay for that software I found — it's not cheap, but I'm sure he won't argue — Abby can probably figure it out in no time. You might be back in Boston in time for spring semester."

Simon pushed his chair back. "Come out and show me," he said.

Steve looked up at him, bleary eyed. It was late, and the three beers he'd drunk in such a short period of time had hit him harder than he'd expected. "Show you what, Simon?"

"The dark rift," he said. "The Black Road. Whatever the hell you people call it. I want to see it."

"Can't you have Abby show you?" Steve asked.

Simon stood up. "I don't know where she is," he said. "Come on. It's a clear night, I don't know when I'll get the chance to see it again. It'll only take a minute, right?"

Steve sighed and stood up. "All right," he said. He went to the door, debated about grabbing his jacket, then shook his head. The night was chilly, but it would only take a moment to head out to the clearing, away from the lights, and point out the dark rift. He figured he could last outside — even with Simon — for just a minute.

"Dominic?"

He turned around. Abby was in the doorway, leaning lightly against the frame. She wore just a tank top and sweat pants, and on her face was a nervous smile.

"Hi Abby," he said, rising from the bed.

"It's okay," she said quickly, coming into his room. "You don't have to get up."

"No, I'd better," he said. "You don't want Simon coming in and seeing us sitting on my bed together. Come on, let's get out of here."

Abby paused for a moment, and Dominic stopped. "Is that okay?" he asked. "Do you want to stay here?"

Abby shrugged. "I don't know," she said, sitting on the edge of the bed. She wrapped her arms around herself, shivering a bit in the chilly room. The window was open, and a cool breeze came in.

Dominic went to her side, sitting down gently on the bed beside her. He put his hands on her bare shoulders, rubbing them lightly. She shivered.

"Now you know we're going to get our asses kicked," Dominic joked, and Abby smiled weakly.

"Maybe we *had* better go somewhere else," she said.

"Okay," Dominic said, standing up. He took her hand and helped her to her feet. "It's chilly out though, you'd better grab a jacket."

Abby nodded, but Dominic could see that she was distracted. He grabbed a sweatshirt off the nightstand and laid it over her shoulders. He lifted her hair, feeling it flow through his hand like silk.

Abby pulled the sweatshirt around her neck and shoulders, then turned and smiled up at him. He released her hair, smoothing it down across her back, then steered her out of the room.

"Come on," he said in a low voice.

They crept down the hallway, slipping out the front door. Silently, they moved around the side of the house, heading towards the small shed that housed the generator.

As soon as they had crept around back of it and were out of view and earshot of the house, Abby began to laugh. It tinkled, airy and silvery as moonlight, and Dominic was struck by it. In all the time they'd been here, there had been little laughter, especially not from Abby.

"What is it?" he asked, raising a quizzical eyebrow.

"It's nothing," she explained. "But we're creeping around here and sneaking out like ... well, you know."

She felt herself blushing, and was happy for the darkness.

"Seriously, though, Dominic – I'm worried."

"About what?" he asked, stopping.

Abby was silent, and after a moment, he took her hand and lowered himself to the ground, leading her down with him. They sat on the chilly ground at the edge of the woods, side by side, and again, Abby shivered.

"Here," Dominic said quietly, pulling the sweatshirt from her shoulders. He unzipped it, then held it out as she slid her arms inside it.

"Thanks," she said with a small smile he could barely see in the moonlight.

"Now," he said, settling onto the ground again. "What's going on?"

Abby looked at her hands, folded tightly in her lap. "Simon is ... well, he's different," she said. "I've known him for years, you know, and he's always been ambitious. He's always been controlling, and possessive, and he'd do pretty much anything to get to the top.

"Lately, though ... I mean, it was happening before we came down here; I'd told you when we first met that he and I were having problems. I didn't tell you why, though."

Dominic didn't say a word, but reached out and took one of her trembling hands. Abby did not pull away; instead, she wrapped her cold fingers around his and continued. "I caught him in bed with someone else. I couldn't believe it. It was like everything we'd had meant absolutely nothing. I felt like our whole relationship was a big joke. I had to take some time off, to decide whether I could forgive him or not, whether I wanted to try to work out our relationship or not. That was when I met you.

"When I got back to Boston he and I had a lot of heart to hearts, and I finally took him back. I thought at the time that his infidelity had to do with his own insecurity. But now I see that it was just part of his power trip — his desire to get whatever he wants, regardless of who or what tries to stop him. He thinks he can get anything he wants.

230

"When I got back, he was heartbreakingly apologetic – but he was also possessive to the point of scaring me. I thought it was because he was having some problems at work – he never let me in on what it was, but I got the feeling his department was unhappy with him for some reason. Student complaints or something.

"Simon's never been good at handling things when they start falling apart; I was always there to keep things together for him. At that point, though, I was so busy with school I didn't have time to really deal with it. I think he needed to keep me so that he didn't feel like a total failure – he would have still kept one thing, you know? So everything important to him wasn't gone. He needed stability, so I went along with it. To keep him stable."

Dominic nodded, but still didn't speak.

"Anyway, you've only known him since we've been here, but you've seen how he is. Arrogant. Bossy. Mean. He wants to be in charge of everything, and God help whoever gets in his way. It's a relief when he goes away to work all week, and I've started to dread when he comes back."

"Me too," Dominic said under his breath, and Abby turned to him.

"Nothing," he said, rubbing her hand with his. "Go on."

Abby looked down again. "That's about it," she said. "I guess I just wanted to let you know that something's different. He's never been good with other people, but even now, he's not himself, and it's getting worse. He doesn't see this as your project, your place. He wants to be in control. He wants to take over, and I don't know what we can do."

"Maybe we don't have to do anything," he said quietly.

"What do you mean?"

Dominic shrugged. "It's my project," he said. "No matter what he thinks, it'll always be mine. If he wants to take it over, he'll work harder. He'll put more into it. I don't care what he thinks. He can think this is his project if he wants. He can take the credit for it. I don't want fame and fortune; I just want the answer."

Abby squeezed his hand. "You're an incredible man, you know that?"

Dominic smiled. "No, but as long as you think so, I'm happy."

They stayed out a while longer, sitting side-by-side and talking. When they finally stood to head back, they found they were still holding hands.

They didn't let go until they were in direct sightline of the house.

Abby slipped into the dark room, trying not to make any noise when she saw Simon's shape under the sheets. She had just pulled her end of the blanket back when she looked at her arm and realized she was still wearing Dominic's sweatshirt. Quickly, she stripped it off, retreating to the doorway. She cracked the door open, reached out, and flung the sweatshirt down the hall. She figured she would explain to Dominic in the morning.

Abby closed the door and crossed back to the bed; Simon had not moved, and his breathing was smooth and even. She slid under the covers beside him and lay on her back, waiting for him to ask where she had been. He never moved, however, and after a moment, she relaxed.

It was a long time, however, before she was able to fall asleep.

12.19.15.14.15

November 7, 2008 — "Where's Steve?" Dominic asked, glancing around the lab. "I never heard him come in last night, and he wasn't in the room when I got up."

"I haven't seen him yet, and I've been here most of the morning," Abby said.

Dante swiveled around on the bench. "Tina and I just got here about twenty minutes ago," he told Dominic. "We didn't see him anywhere, though. Kitchen and bathroom were both empty."

Dominic frowned. He walked across the lab to the screen door, pulling aside the sheer curtain to peer into the courtyard. After a moment, he turned around again. Simon, sitting with his back to everyone, caught Dominic's eye.

"Hey Simon, you see Steve yet today?"

Simon didn't move, just kept his eyes trained on the papers in front of him. "Not since last night," he said.

"About what time?" Dominic asked, coming around the table to face him.

"I don't know," Simon looked up, his blue eyes dark. "We were in here late. I found out something I thought might be really important. I told him about it, and he got all excited — wanted to have a couple of beers to celebrate. I declined, told him I wanted to work on it a little longer. He said he was done for the night and if I didn't want to come along, he'd go out and celebrate on his own. He went outside, and that was the last I saw of him."

"And you don't know what time it was," Dominic stated.

Simon sat up a little straighter in his chair, but before he could answer, Dante spoke up. "Abby, what time did Simon come to bed, do you know?"

232

Before it sounded too accusatory, Tina quickly added, "You know, so we might guess about what time Steve went out."

"Why does time matter?" Simon asked in irritation. "He was here last night, now he's not. He's probably outside sleeping it off somewhere. I was in here for at least another hour before I went to bed; if he was out drinking for at least an hour by himself, he was probably out late and got shitfaced."

Abby glanced at Dominic, but he never looked her way; instead, he crossed the room and went out into the courtyard. After a silent moment, Tina was on her feet, going after him. Dante was behind her, with Abby on his heels. After a long moment, Simon pushed himself up from the bench and followed.

Abby strolled across the courtyard alone; Dominic had gone ahead, calling Steve's name. Dante and Tina had followed, and before the two disappeared down the hill and into the trees above the lagoon, Abby was amused to see that they were holding hands. Her amusement changed to dismay, however, when Tina came tearing back up from between the trees only moments later.

"Oh my God, call an ambulance!" she screamed. "Call the police!" Her face was pure white, her eyes wide with shock.

Abby didn't hesitate or ask any questions; she simply turned and raced back towards the lab. She didn't know what she was calling to report, but by the look on Tina's face, she knew there was no time to lose.

Tina turned and ran back down to the path above the lagoon, stopping by Dante's side and taking his hand again. "Jesus, now what do we do?" she said, breathless.

"We call the police is what we do," Dante said, eyes wide and horrified.

"What do the police have to do with anything?" Simon asked, coming up behind them. He saw Steve's body lying in the mud at the water's edge and stopped. "Holy shit," he said.

Dominic had slid down the slope to check on Steve, to see if he could help him, to verify that he was really dead. The unnatural stillness of Steve's body gave the others no doubt, but Dominic had to make sure.

"Well, really," Simon insisted, coming closer. "What do the police have to do with it? It was an accident, right?"

All eyes turned to him.

"What the fuck?" he asked. "I'm just saying. How the hell else would he wind up dead? I mean, he *is* dead, right?"

"Yes, Simon," Dante said coldly. "Steve is dead. And we're calling the police because I'd imagine that even in the far fucking reaches of the Mexican jungle they perform some kind of inquest when you find someone dead."

Simon snorted. "Bullshit," he said. "If he'd died on the streets in Mexico City you could've stepped right over him. Five guys'd have gone through his pocket before you realized he was dead."

"Steve is dead," Tina said tearfully. "We can't leave him out here, and we can't ship him back to the United States without an explanation. His family will need to know, and they'll want to know what happened, exactly. We can't just tell them we think he got drunk and drowned."

Abby came jogging down the path, breathless. She still held the cellular phone in her hand.

"So tell them that since Steve was so hung up on God, maybe he wanted to go meet him," Simon said.

"Fuck off, Simon," Dante said.

Dominic finally stood up from his friend's body. "Steve came from a wealthy family," he said quietly. "If they need to, they'll spend every dime they have to find out what happened to him here."

"Oh, just fucking great," Simon threw up his hands. "We'll have coroners, police, media, every fucking asshole in Mexico with nothing better to do crawling all over here. Screw this; I'm going back to the university. Call me when all the bullshit's over with."

"As stunning as your compassion is," Dante said in a hard voice, "I don't think the police will like it if any of us leave."

"I'm not leaving the goddamn country," Simon answered. "If they want me, they'll know where to find me." With that, he turned and stalked back towards the lab.

After a moment of stunned silence, Tina finally spoke. "Jesus, girl, what the hell does he have over you?"

Abby didn't speak, only turned away and wiped the tears from her reddening cheeks.

"Doesn't matter," Dominic said shortly. "Steve is dead. Dante, can you or Tina go up to the house and wait for the police? We can't move the body, but I don't want to leave Steve here alone. It's the least I can do for him."

"I'll stay with you," Abby said, sniffling.

"No," he said, and it came out harsher than he intended. "No," he repeated more softly. "Steve and I go back a long way. He was the closest friend I ever had. Just leave me alone with him, okay? Leave us be."

Abby nodded, then turned and followed Tina and Dante back toward the house. She only looked back once, but by then Dominic was out of view, mostly hidden behind the underbrush surrounding the lagoon. She could see his shoulders heaving, and knew that he was crying.

12.19.15.14.16

November 8, 2008 — "How can you just go back to work, Simon? Steve is dead."

"I know he's dead. I saw him laying there. What do you want me to do, take time off work to think about it? There's nothing I can do. It's not going to help any to sit around and cry about it." He strolled over to the sink, swearing when the faucet would only spit. "What the fuck is wrong with the pipes now? Fucking well run dry?"

"Jesus, Simon," Dante said with disgust. "You're the most heartless son-of-a-bitch I've ever run across in my life."

"What's your problem? We're still on the right side of the grass."

Dante shook his head, but before he could answer, there were footsteps on the stairs. He glanced over just as Dominic came into the room. They gave each other a nod, but Dominic hadn't even made it to the refrigerator before Simon went off on him.

"You know the pump is screwed up? I can't even get any damn water out of the faucet today."

Dominic swung open the refrigerator door. "So fix it."

"Me? It's not my fucking pump."

"You use it, don't you?" He located the orange juice and took it out, then shut the door.

"Yeah, but I'm not responsible for the upkeep on this rathole. Shit breaks, and I'm supposed to fix it?"

"Then don't fix it. If you're not going to fix it, then it won't work. Then you can't use it. Why is that my problem?" He pulled a glass down from the cupboard and filled it.

"Oh, so you don't give a shit if the place falls apart, yet you still expect us to work for you?"

"I don't give a rat's ass what you do or where you do it. I just don't want to hear about it." He headed back towards the kitchen door.

"Well, screw you, then, Ciriello! I'm going back to the university where there's plumbing that works!"

Dominic lifted a hand in acknowledgement but didn't turn around.

"You can all stay back here with your dead buddy for all I care. You can … "

Simon didn't have a chance to finish his thought; Dominic whirled around, letting the half-drunk glass of orange juice fly. It struck the wall mere inches from Simon's head, shattering against the tile. Simon let out a shriek and ducked as slivers of glass exploded in all directions. He rose up again, sputtering, just in time to see the door swinging shut again.

"He's fucking crazy!" Simon shouted.

"You're an asshole," Dante said, standing up from the table. He followed Dominic outside, leaving Simon alone with the mess.

12.19.15.14.17`

November 9, 2008 — "They'll be flying his body back to Oakland for the funeral," Dominic said quietly.

"Are you going?" Tina asked.

Dominic shook his head. "I'll say good-bye to him here." He glanced up at the others, gathered around the kitchen table. "The rest of you can go if you want. No hurry to get back to work here."

Tina walked over and hugged him from behind, resting her chin on his shoulder. "I'm sorry," she whispered in his ear. "I know how much you loved him."

Dominic nodded silently, but Abby saw the tears shining in his eyes. He closed them, squeezed Tina's hands quickly, and pushed away from the table.

Tina released him, then watched him go. When he'd disappeared up the stairs, she turned back to the others. "I'm flying home with the body," she said. "I know Steve's family, and I'm going to the funeral. If anyone else wants to come with me, I'll get all our tickets together."

"I will," Dante said, and Abby caught the tender look between them. She felt a pang of jealousy, knowing that even if Simon had not gone back to the university, he wouldn't have been in the kitchen to comfort her. If he'd have been in the kitchen with them at all, he'd have had something insensitive to say. With a sigh, she headed towards the stairs.

"I'm sorry," she said to Tina as she passed. "I liked Steve a lot, and I'll miss him. But I don't know his family. I knew him here. I'll say good-bye to him here, too."

Tina nodded without comment, and Abby knew she hadn't expected any different. Her face burning, Abby ducked her head and ran up the stairs. Never before in her life had she felt so chained to Simon; it seemed that every opinion anyone formed about her here was based on him.

In their room, she flopped on the bed, feeling entirely selfish as she began to cry. Her tears were not all for Steve, she knew. Some of them were for her.

236

November 10, 2008 — Dominic was sitting on one of the large rocks in the courtyard, staring down through the trees to the lagoon.

"Dominic?"

He turned to see Abby, standing alone, bathed in moonlight.

"Are you all right?" she asked.

He shrugged. "Just thinking."

"About Steven?" she asked, coming closer.

"About death."

She paused. "Do you want to be alone?"

"No. Please, come over."

She sat down beside him, trying to catch his expression in the moonlight, but his face was hidden in shadow.

"Is Simon coming home tonight?" he asked quietly.

Abby shook her head, then realized he wasn't looking at her. "No," she said.

"Good."

They sat in silence for awhile, and after a long time, Dominic spoke again.

"What do you think happens?" he asked.

Abby was confused for a minute, thinking he was asking what she thought had happened to Steve; after a moment, however, she remembered what he'd been thinking about.

"I think we continue," she said. "Death is a natural part of life. I think it's just a stage. Think about it," she said, looking up at the star-scattered sky. "We're part of the universe. We're made up of the same stuff as the universe — the same elements, the same minerals. We're a part of everything."

"So you believe we just … go on?"

Abby nodded. "I think the part of us that's 'us' does. Our bodies fade back into the earth we came from, but the rest of us goes on. Call it soul, call it spirit; personality, whatever you want. Whatever it is that gave life to that body doesn't end when the body does."

"So if you think we go somewhere else when our lives are over … do you think we were somewhere before we were born?"

"I think we'd have to have been," she said. "I'm not saying I know where — I don't believe in Heaven and Hell; I don't think we're out there floating among the stars; and I don't think we're waiting in some cosmic nursery, either. But I do think there's some natural progression, and this is only part of it. All energy came into being at the big bang, and you know that energy can neither be created nor destroyed — so the energy that makes us move and think had to come from somewhere, and has to transfer to another form when we die."

Dominic thought for a moment. "Why don't we remember it, then?" he asked quietly. "If we came from somewhere else, and we stay awhile, and then we move on ... if we don't remember where we were before — what if we don't remember who we are now, when we move on to the next stage, Abby?" he turned to her with eyes red from crying. "What if we're still alive, somehow, wherever we go, but we forget this life? Steve, my parents — what if they really have moved on, and I'll never see them again, or I won't recognize them if I do?"

"Oh Dominic," Abby said, reaching for his hand. He lifted it away, wiping the tears from his eyes. They sat for a moment in silence.

"Plato thought a lot about death," Dominic said suddenly. "Several of his dialogues were about the fate of the soul after death — *Phaedo, Gorgias, The Republic.* He believed that there were higher realms beyond this world; other planes and dimensions of reality."

"Did he describe these realms?" Abby asked.

"In detail," Dominic answered. "He was surprisingly accurate, when compared to accounts of present-day Near-Death Experiences. The soul leaving the body, heading down to meet with dead relatives, guardian spirits who welcome it and transport it to the other realm, the life review where everything you've ever done flashes before your eyes."

"And then what?"

"Plato believed that the body was a prison of the soul. Death was a release." He paused for a moment, then continued thoughtfully. "He said that birth was like going to sleep; we forget everything we knew in the other realm, all the truths we were aware of. We go from a state of great awareness to one of muddled consciousness, of forgetfulness. Death is awakening, and remembering."

"That's hopeful," Abby said.

Dominic nodded. "He said that time is irrelevant in that realm. Time doesn't factor in at all; the other realm is eternal."

"And what do you believe?" she asked quietly. "What do you think happens after death?"

He shook his head. "I've tried to never think about it," he said. "Death is a bogeyman. I've always been superstitious about it — if you start thinking about it, it'll notice. I never wanted it to notice me. I never wanted it to find me. I always believed that if I never thought about it, it would pass on by."

"But it didn't, Dominic. It found your parents. It's touched your life."

"But it never touched *me*," he said petulantly. After a moment, he sighed, and when he spoke again he was subdued. "I was only three when my parents died. They were killed in an accident; a private plane crash. They left me, an only child, all their money in a trust fund. I would get a third when I turned eighteen, a third at twenty-one, and a third at twenty-five." He looked up at her from lowered brows. "I'm down to the last third. I blew everything when I was eighteen because I knew I'd be getting more at twenty-one. Did the same thing at twenty-one, but at twenty-five I at least made some investments. Now, that's all I have — money all tied up in stocks and bonds. I spent the rest of the inheritance on my education, travel, my excursions down here, and on this place. I never gave much thought to where the money came from, because I never really knew my parents. I had little memory of them, and what I did was so vague, so far away, it was like a story someone told me.

"So if I see them again — will I know them? Will they know me? And if they're able to see back into this world ... are they ashamed of me?"

"Oh Dominic, no," Abby cried, and when she reached out for him this time, he let her. She held him close, and he buried his face into the dark silkiness of her hair.

"Of course they're not ashamed of you, Dominic. You're their son. Even if they don't approve of your decisions, they'll always approve of you."

He squeezed her tightly, then released her. Dominic sat back again and looked up at the sky. After a long moment, he spoke again. "So you think they're out there, somewhere?"

Abby looked up at the twinkling stars. "Yes," she said definitively. "Maybe among the stars. Maybe in the solar wind. We're part of the universe, Dominic. We're just moving through it in a different way right now."

"And Steve?"

Abby glanced down from the black sky, meeting his eyes. "And Steve," she repeated. "He's out there, and if he can see this, he's probably laughing at us right now. We're here wondering where he is, missing him, feeling so broken up about the life he's missing, and he's moved on."

"I wonder if he misses us?" Dominic asked. "If he can see us, does he miss us?"

"I don't know," Abby replied honestly.

"I wonder if anyone tries to make contact?" Dominic said, looking up towards the sky again. "If they're part of the wind, or, hell, even living out the rest of their existence in heaven — why can't they cross over again? We can't see them or feel them or hear them. Why would they be able to see us?"

"I don't know," Abby answered again, and suddenly shivered.

"Hey," Dominic said, putting his arm around her. "Let's go back in. This is no night to sit around and think of death."

"Is there any night for that?" she asked, glancing up at him.

Dominic didn't answer. They walked back up to the house in silence, and he didn't take his arm from her waist until they reached the lab.

"One day we'll know," he said suddenly. She turned to him questioningly.

"One day we'll all know. Where we go, if there is somewhere to go. If not — then, I guess we *won't* know. Everything will end, and we'll just disappear."

Abby frowned, and Dominic put a hand to her cheek. "Hey," he said. "It's okay. Steve is wherever he is. But we're here. I don't know what to believe about death; I've always looked at the evidence, and the evidence shows that no one has ever communicated from the other side, and no one has ever come back, so there isn't anything out there. Death truly is the end of us. But I know what I want to be true, Abby, and I do hope to see him again someday, and I hope he can see us. Whatever is waiting for us, it's out there, somewhere. And someday we'll find out.

"In the meantime, I'm going to keep chasing the Long Count, and hopefully I'll find out what it means before it forces itself upon us. Maybe it will be the end of everything. But death — well, I think I'll just leave that one alone again. It'll come to me someday on its own. If I don't go looking for it, well, maybe it won't come looking for me."

He smiled at her sadly, then opened the door and went into the lab. Abby followed, still frowning.

Hours later, she awoke to the sound of muffled crying. Her heart tore at the sound, knowing that Dominic was lying alone in his room, crying for his friend. She sighed, rolling over to stare outside. The chilly air seeped in through the window she had cracked open, and she stood up and went to it, pulling it closed. Abby paused to stare out into the darkness, lost in thought. After a moment, though, her reverie was broken by the painful sound of harsh sobs coming from down the hall. They were cut off, muffled, as if Dominic had smothered his tears with a pillow. Abby hesitated only a moment, then headed down the hall to his room.

"Dominic?"

"Go away, Abby." His voice was muffled, his face buried in his pillow. His back was to her.

She didn't answer; just crossed the room and sat down on the edge of his bed. Abby laid a hand on his back, feeling him tremble beneath her palm. Without saying a word, she lay down beside him, wrapping her arms around him from behind. They lay that way, not speaking, until Dominic's sobbing finally quieted.

He rolled over, still in her arms. Abby reached up and stroked his hair. The thick, dark curls were damp. "Are you okay?" she asked quietly.

He nodded, pulling her close against his chest. "Thank you."

Abby gave him a squeeze. "How many times have you held me while I cried?"

She was surprised to hear him laugh quietly, and she drew back to look into his tear-streaked face.

"I'm here anytime you want or need me, Dominic. I can never be as close to you as Steve was, but I am your friend. And your well-being means the world to me."

Dominic kissed her lightly on top of the head. "Thanks, Abby," he said softly. "Now that I don't have Steve to watch over me anymore, I need someone to take his place. Maybe it's time I settled down."

"With me?" she asked jokingly.

"I'd like to give it a try. Anytime you're ready."

Abby was uneasy. She couldn't tell if he was serious. "I don't think I can do that, Dominic."

"I know," he said. "But I mean it. Any time you're ready. This year, next year, ten years from now. Any time you're ready."

She smiled, reaching out a hand to his cheek. He closed his dark eyes, taking her hand and kissing the soft palm. "Slowly," she said. "You know I'm in no situation right now to make any decision about my future. I'm barely making it day by day with Simon."

"I know," Dominic said. "I'm not going anywhere, Abby. Not for awhile, anyway. But when I do, I'd like you to come with me."

She didn't answer, and he squeezed her hand lightly. "No pressure," he said. "Like I said — whenever you're ready."

"What if I never am?"

"Then I'm going to have a long wait," he said, but there was no humor in his voice.

She squeezed his hand in return, and Dominic pulled her close again. They lay that way for a long time, until Dominic's breathing grew deep and steady, and she knew he was asleep. As Abby relaxed in his arms, curling up against his chest, was thankful that the others were gone. She laid beside him, listening to him breathe, thinking of the many long years she'd spent lying awake in bed beside Simon, wondering what he was thinking, wondering if he was angry with her, wondering if he still loved her. Never before, however, had she doubted that she loved him. Not until now.

12.19.15.14.19

November 11, 2008 — "I never knew your skin could actually hurt from crying," Dominic said as they were leaving the house after breakfast. He seemed a little better this morning. "Did you know that? That the skin of your face could actually be worn raw and painful from so many tears?"

"Yes," she said simply.

Dominic was lost in his own thoughts and did not answer as he opened the door and went out. Abby stayed back, watching him slowly cross the courtyard to the sitting stones, where he seated himself with his back to her. He sat still, with his hands in his lap, staring out across the trees to the clearing and the lagoon below. Abby watched him for a moment, then pushed open the door and went to him.

She stopped behind him, then without hesitation, leaned over and wrapped her arms around him. He didn't react, simply lifted a hand to take hers. They stayed that way for a long time, without speaking. Abby closed her eyes, feeling a tear slip out and roll down her cheek. She didn't bother trying to wipe it away.

"I fixed the path, Abby. He never should have slipped."

"What?"

"The path." Dominic released her hand, turning to face her. "After that night you fell into the lagoon and sprained your ankle, remember? I went out the next day and shored up the path. I built it up, and Steve and I moved those large boulders to the edges. He couldn't have fallen off the path without climbing over them."

"Maybe he stumbled and tripped over one?"

Dominic shook his head. "I don't know. Steve was never a big drinker. He's the one that helped me when — well, I used to drink a lot, when I was younger. Way more than I should have. Hell, more than anyone should have." He noticed her look of surprise and managed a small smile. "I never went completely on the wagon, but I'm not an alcoholic. I'll have a beer or two with you guys, but you notice I never get drunk. Steve was the same way — he always stayed sober to keep an eye on me. Steve helped me to focus, to quit pissing away my time, and my life. He was a great guy," he said, and she heard his voice break.

Abby knelt down beside him and took his hand again. "I know he was," she said. "You don't think he was drunk?"

He shook his head again. "I don't know, Abby. Maybe he was. Maybe he was tired. It was awful late for him to be up. I don't know what he was doing out there by himself so late at night anyway."

"Won't the toxicology tests show if he'd been drinking or not?"

Dominic nodded. "I talked to the police again this morning. They've closed the case and ruled it an accident. There was alcohol in his blood, but he wasn't legally drunk. It was enough for him to have been impaired, though. Especially on an unlit path in the dark of night."

"So he fell, hit his head on a rock, and drowned?"

"They said there was very little water in his lungs. He must've barely been breathing when he hit the water. It was a head injury from the fall that killed him."

"My God," Abby breathed. She closed her eyes, trying to picture Steve's earnest, open face. All she could see was his crumpled body sprawled on the muddy shore of the lagoon, face half underwater.

"And why was he out there?" Dominic continued. "It was a cold night, remember? He wouldn't have gone out to stargaze, and there's no way he was going swimming."

"Simon was down in the lab, remember?" Abby said. "You and I had to sneak around the front of the house because we knew he was down there. Maybe Steve was avoiding him."

Dominic nodded. "Simon said Steve wanted to go for a walk and he wanted to stay and work. Maybe what he really meant is that Steve didn't want to stay there in the lab with him and took off."

Abby didn't answer. She was glad Dominic was looking down at his hands, and couldn't see her face. She felt cold all over, a deep fear settling in the pit of her stomach. She tried to push from her mind a thought that was gnawing at the edges of her sanity. Simon's behavior had been worse than usual lately, but he wasn't psychotic. He couldn't have killed Steve. She shook her head, trying to dispel the thought. She couldn't even consider it. If she did — and he had — then how could she ever be alone with him again? And how could she protect the others?

"I think I want to be alone for awhile," Dominic said, finally glancing up at her. If he had noticed her expression, he didn't let on. Abby knew Dominic had to have already considered it, and she didn't want to know what he was thinking. Nodding mutely, she released his hand and stood up. Dominic looked away again, gazing silently across the courtyard to the trees and lagoon below. It would be a long time before they sat at the water's edge again.

Abby backed away, then turned and headed back towards the lab. She was grateful once again that she and Dominic were the only two there; she didn't know if she could face any of the others right now. She couldn't even face herself.

November 14, 2008 — Abby didn't see much of Dominic over the next week, even though they had the place to themselves. He left early in the morning, and she sometimes didn't hear him come in until late into the night. Abby looked all over for him, but after she couldn't find him the first few days, she let him be. He obviously needed to be alone, and he was still coming back to eat and catch a few hours of sleep, so she assumed he was doing all right.

It wasn't until the night before Dante and Tina were to come back that she had a chance to talk to him. Abby had spent several hours at her telescope, and her eyes were beginning to blur. She was just capping her scope when she heard Dominic's voice behind her.

"Hey Abby," he said softly.

Startled, she turned and saw him in the shadows. "Hey, Dominic," she said. "How are you?"

He shrugged. "How's the viewing?" he asked, approaching her.

"Pretty good," she said. "There's hardly any moon. It's a beautiful dark. My eyes are getting tired, though, so I'm packing it in."

"Would you mind leaving it out?" he asked. "I'd like to take a look myself, if that's okay with you."

"Of course," she said. She removed the cap and opened the lens box again. "Do you need any help?"

"I think I can figure it out," he said, stopping beside her. He looked up at the dark sky above them.

"Do you want me to leave?"

He looked down at her and smiled. "Of course not," he said. "I never want you to leave." Dominic bent down to look through the eyepiece, waiting for his vision to adjust.

Abby watched him fiddle with the scope for a moment, then asked, "How have you been, Dominic?"

He didn't look up. "I'm okay," he said. "Been doing a lot of thinking."

"Haven't seen much of you lately."

"I've been wandering," he said, adjusting the viewfinder. "Been up on the mountain."

Abby paused, about to mention how Biblical that sounded, but she knew it would just remind him of Steve. Dominic continued: "I went out to Izapa. Spent a night there."

"Did it help?"

Dominic straightened up, squinting at the stars. "Helped clear my head," he said. "I think I've made some peace."

Abby watched his back, about to speak, but he went on:

"Life is so fragile. It makes me want to believe there *has* to be something else out there. There has to be more after this. I mean, you can get killed so easily. One minute you're a happy little kid playing in the street, the next minute you chase your ball in front of a car and you're gone. Or you eat a piece of bad fish, or slip in the shower and fracture your skull. Is that it? Is that all you get?

"It can't be. There has to be more. You can't waste your only shot in all of eternity on an accident, on being distracted or clumsy or stupid or in the wrong place at the wrong time. There has to be more."

Abby nodded, even though he still had his back to her and couldn't see her. It didn't seem to matter anyway, as Dominic kept talking. "I've never believed in an afterlife. It seems like such an invention, a human rationalization to make sense of things, a hope that this isn't all there is. It doesn't make sense from any scientific point of view. And there's no rationale for it, no justification. It demeans our precious time and existence upon this Earth, in the brief time we have here. Instead of cherishing and celebrating every moment, we keep looking forward to what's going to happen afterwards. Instead of taking care of each other and doing everything we can to help other human beings, we say that God will help them, or that their suffering is their own fault. But still – I *want* it to be true."

"That's the basis for religious belief," Abby said, stepping up beside him. "We feel too alone, even here on this Earth with billions of other human beings. Somehow we can't justify our existence without some greater purpose, without some higher being controlling everything. We want to feel safe, like everything is under control, no matter how horribly unfair things are, or how screwed up they get. We have to believe there's a purpose, a divine plan, a sense of cosmic fairness, or we'll go crazy from the hopelessness. We want reassurance that everything will be all right."

Dominic glanced down at her, then slid an arm around her shoulders. "I know," he said. "And I understand that. I know that I'm probably fooling myself. But it doesn't change the *want*."

Abby put her arm around his waist, and laid her head against his shoulder. "You're human," she said. "We all are. We do what we have to in order to get through this life. You're no different than millions of others on this planet."

"That's reassuring," he said, and she looked up, hearing the humor in his voice. He looked down at her with a slight smile. "I've needed a lot of things at different times in my life," he said. "This is the first time I've ever felt I needed religion."

"Nothing wrong with that," she said. "And who knows, you may even be right."

He laughed. "Maybe. Although I'm sure that this too will eventually pass. But right now it feels good. Comforting."

Abby nodded. "I think it's an extremely vague possibility, but there's so much about the universe we don't know. There may be multiple dimensions; it's possible that some part of us might continue to exist in another one. It would require the existence of a soul, of course — but if there is one, there's a chance that it won't die when our bodies do."

Dominic laid his head on top of hers. "Sometimes I think, having known Steve, how can anyone doubt there's such a thing as a soul?"

Abby smiled, but before she could respond, Dominic answered himself. "Sometimes I wish I hadn't spent so much time studying biochemistry," he said. "I know that the chemical reactions in our brains and the reactions of our nervous system and all of our sensory organs can explain everything from thought to speech to emotion to creativity. I don't doubt that — but it can be so depressing."

Abby laughed, startling them both. He pulled away to look at her, and she reached for his hands. "Not at all," she said. "I think it just makes us appreciate what we have right now even more. Even if we're nothing but an electro-chemical biological creature and not an immortal soul, we're no less human. We can still think and play and create, and have an incredible capacity for love. When we start thinking we'll be here —or somewhere — forever, we don't appreciate our time on this Earth as we should, being grateful for every day we wake up alive. We don't take as good of care of each other as we should. We're horrendous caretakers of our planet. We're evil and cruel to each other; more inclined to want to change people, or punish them for not being just like us, than to care for each other, or relieve the suffering of millions. Religion proffers that suffering is good, so we assume that people starving or in pain will get repaid for it someday, or that they did something to deserve it. It absolves us of our responsibility to our fellow man. We need to appreciate every moment we have — because you never know when it's all going to end."

Dominic squeezed her hands. "For such a depressing topic, you sure make it sound hopeful."

Abby shrugged. "I love this world," she said simply. "I'm happy here. I don't want to base all my hopes on the chance of an afterlife. I want to live this one."

Dominic was silent for a minute, they leaned over and kissed her quickly on the lips. "Me too," he said, stepping back. They stared at each other for a long moment, and Abby felt herself flush.

"Come on," Dominic said, sliding an arm around her waist. "Let's head back up. I've been out in the woods all day and I'm starving."

"A shower wouldn't hurt you, either," Abby said jokingly, and Dominic laughed. They headed back up to the house in much better spirits, and Abby was relieved to think that he may be over the worst part of his grief. Although she knew they would be hit with reminders of Steve every day and it would be a long time before it got much easier, she was glad to see that Dominic was thinking clearly again. She had been scared that he might have some kind of breakdown, and when he'd disappeared, she'd feared the worst.

Dominic was back now, though, walking back towards the house with his arm around her, talking amiably and cheerfully. Abby was chatting back, but her mind wasn't completely with them. She was still thinking about that kiss.

12.19.15.15.5

November 17, 2008 — Around eleven o'clock, Abby headed downstairs. The door to Tina and Dante's room was closed, but Dominic's was wide open, and the light was out. She crossed the empty kitchen to get a bottle of water out of the fridge; she expected to be out with her telescope most of the night.

Surprised to find the lab dark when she went outside, she flicked on her flashlight to light her way. Without any light coming from the lab or the house, it was pitch black. Abby cut through the lab into the courtyard, the thin beam of her flashlight illuminating her path.

When she came out from under the trees above the lagoon, she turned off the light, knowing her way out to her telescope by feel. Clouds covered the moon, making her frown; she was worried that the haze was going to linger again tonight, making stargazing near impossible.

Lost as she was in her own thoughts, she was startled to walk up on a dark figure hunched over her scope. She let out a small cry of surprise, and the figure stood up and turned around.

"Dominic, you scared the hell out of me," Abby said. "I didn't expect anyone to be out here. I didn't know what you were."

"Sorry about that," he said, coming forward to meet her. His smile faded when he saw her face. "You look like you saw a ghost."

"No ghosts. Just you."

Abby shifted her backpack off her shoulder and dropped it on the ground. She knelt next to it and unzipped it, taking out her notebooks. She gave the jungle behind them an uneasy glance. "Good thing there's no such thing as ghosts."

Dominic crouched beside her, watching her flip through the pages, looking for her last entry. "So they say," he commented. "Have you ever wondered why ghosts wear clothes?"

"I've never really thought about it," she answered, amused.

"As a physicist, you've never thought about that?" Dominic asked. "People that describe ghost encounters always describe what the spirit was wearing. They're assuming that not only their souls, but their clothes survived."

"You're also assuming that their clothes died."

Dominic laughed. "I guess you're right."

Abby smiled, joining him beside the scope. "Out here sometimes it's hard to tell what's real and what's just a figment of our imaginations." She put the red filter back on her flashlight, dimming the glow so it wouldn't interfere with the light she collected from the stars.

"Yeah, fact and fiction intertwine in the Mayan jungle." He watched her readjust the height of the eyepiece on her telescope. "I hope you don't mind me using your scope," he said. "I was sitting in the lab thinking, and I wanted to check something out. You'd already gone up to your room, so I thought you'd gone to bed; I hated to wake you up to ask you."

"No problem," she said. "You know how to use it; you're welcome to it anytime. What was it you were looking at?"

"Just looking for the black road."

"Yeah? Did you find it?"

"No. I don't know what I'm looking for."

"Well, you don't need the scope for it," she said, stepping away from it. She surveyed the sky. "There's too much haze tonight. But one of these days it'll come into view and I'll show you. The black road is exactly that – a black road, a dark rift. It'll look like a tear in the fabric of the Milky Way."

"And the Maya could easily see it?"

"Of course. Today's children are the first in history who have never seen our galaxy. The light pollution floods the night sky, washing out the stars. In Mayan time, the Milky Way was a hazy band circling the Earth. I'm sure they didn't know what it really was, though; it was only when the telescope was first used in the early 1600s that we realized it was made up of billions of stars."

"So they'd have seen the band of it with the dark rift in the center … how would they have known that it pointed to the center of the galaxy?"

"That I can't answer," Abby confessed. "It's one of the things I want to research more — how did we know the direction of the galaxy before modern times?"

"Maybe through mathematics?"

"That's what I would think, too. I haven't figured it out yet."

Dominic put his arm around her shoulders, then, spontaneously, leaned over and kissed her on top of the head. "I have complete faith in you," he said. "If anyone can figure it out, you will."

"Well, thanks," she said, slightly embarrassed, "but I'm not working in a vacuum here. I guess I'm going to need as much of your help as I can get on exactly what the Maya knew."

"My pleasure," he answered. "Although I don't imagine our working closely together will make Simon very happy."

Abby made a dismissive wave. "What he doesn't know ..." she said.

Dominic laughed. "Somehow, though, he always seems to find out, doesn't he?"

They strolled slowly towards the edge of the clearing, his arm still around her. Dominic looked up at the sky, at the haze of stars overhead.

"So when we look out at our galaxy, what is it exactly that we're seeing?"

"The Milky Way has four spiral arms: Centaurus, Sagittarius, Orion, and Perseus. Our solar system is in the third arm — the Orion arm. When we're looking out at the universe, we're seeing the Sagittarius arm — the next innermost arm of the galaxy."

"We see our galaxy from the inside."

"Somewhat," Abby said. "We're closer to the outer edge, looking towards the center. I'd say we're more on the outside, looking in."

"If someone were at the center, looking out at us, what would they see?"

Abby frowned thoughtfully. "It would depend on their exact location and the direction they were looking. And don't forget, the galaxy revolves. Just like the Earth turns, so does the Milky Way. The sky is always changing, no matter where you are in the universe. But it always comes back around."

Dominic put both hands on his hips and stared at the dark sky. "How long is a revolution of the Milky Way?"

"I don't know," Abby said slowly.

He gave her a quick smile. "You know where I'm going with this, don't you?"

"I assume you're thinking that if someone was waiting at the center of the galaxy for a certain feature to come back into view, maybe to give them a straight shot to another location, they would have calculated how long it would take for that pathway to line up again."

"You always seem to read my mind, Abby."

She smiled. "I'll make a note and look into it, Dominic, but it seems unlikely. In fact, it'll probably be more of that circular reasoning we've talked about. Don't forget about the distances involved."

"Which are …?"

"Well, like I said, the Milky Way consists of billions of stars. We know the size of the system around our own star, which is apparently pretty average in the universe. Imagine that multiplied billions of times, plus the hundreds to thousands of light years of empty space in between each solar system. That's pretty damn far for someone to be traveling from the galactic center just to get to our tiny little planet. There'd be no point in even calculating the time, Dominic, because they'd have to start out far before the original point of calculation. They'd have to start at a certain point, calculate when the alignment would be right, and then time travel back a couple hundred thousand years — minimum — to start traveling to us. It's impossible."

"And that would be from anywhere?" he asked.

"Basically, yes, even if they were coming from the star next door — where we know conditions are wrong for extra-solar life, by the way. It's just impossible for any visitors from within our own galaxy to calculate an arrival time and then meet that window, unless they were calculating an arrival a couple hundred thousand — or a couple million — years into the future."

"What about from somewhere else?"

Abby shook her head. "It just gets worse. Look at the nearest galaxy to us: Andromeda is 2,300,000 light years away. You know that a light year – the distance light travels in one Earth year – is six trillion miles. So, even if we could travel at the speed of light — which we not only don't have the technology to build a craft that can do that, but human beings would be torn apart because of our physiology – it would still take us two million, three hundred thousand years to reach it. But since we can't physically travel at the speed of light, we'd be moving a hell of a lot slower. That's two million, three hundred-thousand multiplied by six trillion miles. *Those* are the distances we're talking about."

"So much for the extraterrestrial visitor angle, I guess."

"Yep. Back to the drawing board."

"You can go back inside to the drawing board," Dominic said. "I'd rather stay out here in the starlight. Even if it is hazy and bad for viewing."

"Mind some company?"

"Not if it's yours," he answered, putting his arm around her again.

Abby was amazed again at how relaxed and comfortable she felt with him. "Let me get my notebook then," she said. "If we're going to talk about Mayan astronomy, I'd better take some notes."

"Do we have to talk about Mayan astronomy?"

Abby stopped. Dominic put his other hand on her waist, turning her to face him. "We never just talk, Abby. It's always about work. Or worse, about Simon."

"Ok," she said. "What else do you want to talk about?"

Dominic didn't answer; instead, he leaned over and kissed her. She resisted for only a moment, then melted into his arms. They kissed for a long time, alone under the moonlight, and when they finally broke away, Abby stayed in his arms.

"Well now," she said breathlessly.

He laughed softly. "Beats Mayan astronomy any day."

"Dominic ..."

He kissed her again lightly. "I know," he said. "And it's okay. I guess I shouldn't have done that. But I've wanted to for so long now I don't think I could've held it any longer."

"I don't know where to go from here."

"How about back up to the house?"

He saw her expression, and gave her a quick, apologetic hug. "Not for that," he said. "But just to go to bed. It's getting late, and Simon will be home again tomorrow night. I know you'll be up all weekend, so why don't we head up and call it a night? I don't want to stress you out any more than you need to be."

"It's just more than I can deal with right now, Dominic. You know the situation."

"I know it very well," he said. "That's why I think we'd better call it a night."

Abby stood on her tiptoes, kissing him quickly before stepping away. He reached out and took her hand, and they went back up to the house. Abby's heart was beating rapidly, and her palm inside Dominic's hand was sweating. As long as she'd been waiting for this turn of events, she couldn't help but think it was a huge mistake. Simon would be home tomorrow, and just like she'd had to for the past few months, she would have to pretend she was still in love with him. But to make matters worse, she had a new dimension of dishonesty: She would have to hide that she was in love with someone else.

12.19.15.15.11

November 23, 2008 — Abby and Simon came down to the lab after breakfast to find the group in a more positive mood than they'd been in quite awhile. Simon went to the bookshelf to peruse the titles for what must have been the thousandth time, while Abby sat at the bench next to Tina. "What's going on?" she asked.

Tina smiled. "We're thinking about getting out of here for a little while. You know, just a day trip to some of the local ruins. You up for it?"

"Definitely," Abby said. Across the room, Simon grunted noncommittally.

"Where did you have in mind?" Abby asked, ignoring him.

Dominic was thoughtful. "There's always Teotihuacan, although it's probably too far away. You'd love the Pyramid of the Moon, Abby."

"What the hell is Teotihuacan?" Simon asked, impatient.

"It means Place of the Gods," Dominic said. "We don't know what it was called when it was populated. The local people named it long after the city was abandoned."

"Place of the Gods," Dante mused. "The natives must've been awed by it."

"As well they should have been," Dominic said. "Teotihuacan *is* awesome. In 450 BCE, when the biggest cities in Europe were made up of a couple hundred people, Teotihuacan had a population of a quarter of a million."

"So what happened to them all?" Abby asked.

Dominic shrugged. "Same thing that happened to the rest of the Maya. They abandoned the city sometime around 600 AD."

"And now you want to go stomp around in their ruins to find out why?" Simon asked.

"I'm not trying to find out," Dominic said.

"Then what's the point of this field trip?"

Dominic shrugged. "Just a change of pace," he said. "Why don't we head for Tikal? It's closer, with the largest pyramids in Central America. We've been having so much discussion as to just how advanced the Maya really were — I think this will clarify some things."

"Great, another trip out into the jungle — to where this time, Guatemala? Why don't we take a run somewhere civilized?"

"You don't have to go," Dominic said calmly.

"Yeah, right," Simon sneered. "Like I'm going to sit around here while you guys traipse all over the place. You're not leaving me out of anything."

12.19.15.15.17

November 29, 2008 — Tikal was amazing.

"You still believe these people were from the Stone Age?" Dante asked, waving a hand towards the site. Simon ignored him.

"My God, it's absolutely beautiful," Abby said, staring out at the city. The massive temples stood like quiet sentinels, whitewashed gray stone rising from the green jungle like sacred mountains.

"Can you imagine what this would have looked like when it was new?" Dominic asked. "Painted in vibrant colors, brilliant stone shining under the sun. Breathtaking."

"It's incredible," Abby agreed. "Every time I see another Mayan structure, I'm even more amazed by them."

"They *were* amazing," Dominic agreed. "Tikal was so advanced so early. It was a metropolis when most cities in Europe were villages, small market towns. London didn't have more than a thousand people when Tikal was at its peak."

"So what happened to it?"

Dominic sighed. "The Maya abandoned their cities and spread out across the land. There's been some indication in recent years that they destroyed the environment around the cities, much like we're doing today."

"Like what?" Abby asked. "Mayan global warming?"

Tina spoke up. "Some of the cities weren't built near any accessible water; others were found by what were thought to be seasonal bogs. There was always a question about how so many people lived there when the water wasn't there year round. But lately, they're thinking that it was the population itself that created both the lack of water and the seasonal nature of the bogs — they drained too much of it, they used it too much, and half the year, there was no water."

"There was also a prolonged drought during the last few years of the Mayan empire," Dante said. He saw Dominic's surprise and smiled. "I checked some of the weather patterns that we knew of during Mayan time. All indications are that there was an environmental reason for them to abandon their cities. An extreme and prolonged drought, as evidenced by the geological record, would send them out across the land in search of water and fertile land."

Dominic nodded. "Makes sense, I suppose," he said. "Once they were spread out, creating their own small villages that might have prospered, they'd have been less likely to return to the cities to live under the rule of the priests. And if the land around the cities wasn't conducive to crops, they wouldn't have been able to survive there even if they'd wanted to return."

"So much for the great Mayan mystery," Simon said.

Dominic shrugged. "Some claim that warring between the different cities became constant, and either they annihilated each other or ran each other out of the cities. Others blame an unknown epidemic, or even peasant revolt. Or, like Dante suggests, the cities could no longer sustain such large populations. Nothing mysterious or supernatural about it; the only mystery to the Mayan exodus was that we didn't know exactly which it was."

"Like it matters," Simon said dismissively. He turned away and looked over the site. The pyramids and other structures rose like tombstones in the gray November chill. "I'm going for a walk," he said. "Come on, Abby."

She glanced apologetically at the others, then followed after Simon as he headed into the abandoned city.

Hours later, Abby came up beside Dominic where he stood by the ball court, hands on his hips, staring at the stones. He glanced down at her with a smile. "Where'd you lose Simon?"

"He got bored," she said. "Decided to go sit down somewhere. I wanted to look around more. And I wanted to look for you — if I'm going to visit an archaeological site, I'd like to see it with an archaeologist."

"Then you should find Tina," he said. "She's the archaeologist. I do a little digging, but officially I'm an anthropologist; I'm more interested in the story behind the artifacts than the artifacts themselves."

"Then you're exactly who I want to talk to," Abby answered, and he smiled down at her.

"Okay, so do you want the full tour, or did you have something specific in mind?"

"The flow of the calendar is from past to future," she said. "They followed the sun, which flows from east to west. They followed precession, so the flow would be from south to north. What is it we should be looking for?"

"We want to start with the direction of their observatories," he said. "Here, and in every Mayan site. We follow the layout to see what they were watching."

"Okay," she said, running a hand through her hair, mentally calculating the hundreds of Mayan sites spread across Central America. The wind was picking up a little, rifling through the grass at their feet. It wasn't cold yet, but there was a definite chill in the air.

"Come on," he said. "Let's head back before it gets dark." He reached out a hand, but Abby didn't take it. She gave him an apologetic look, and as they crossed the courtyard, she glanced around for Simon, then saw him in the distance, leaning against one of the Southern Acropolis pillars.

"Where is everyone?" she asked Dominic as Simon spotted them and stood up. He didn't come forward to meet them, but waited for their approach.

"Well, there's one," Dominic said noncommittally. They met up with Simon, who joined them as they walked around the site, finally finding Tina and Dante with a small group of men.

"Dominic, Abby, I want you to meet Felipe, John, and Mike. They're grad students studying Mesoamerican Indian cultures."

"Great to meet you," Dominic said, extending a hand. "Your first time down here?"

"I've traveled throughout the Yucatan and most the Guatemalan sites before," a thin, bearded man said. "But these two are on their virgin trip. I figured we'd hit all the major stops."

"Yeah," one of the others said, "Michael's been our tour guide so far, through Chichen Itza and Uxmul. This has been incredible."

"Where are you guys staying?" Dominic asked.

"We're set up not far from here," Mike answered. "We've got a little campground off site; it's not the Four Seasons, but we've got a campfire and some warm beer. Want to join us?"

"We've been hanging out with these guys for the last hour or so," Tina explained. "They're fascinated with what we're up to."

"You told them what we're doing?" Simon asked incredulously.

"For god's sake, it's not a state secret, Simon," Dante retorted. "Dominic, how many other people are working on this right now?"

"Impossible to say," he responded. "Individual researchers, probably dozens, at least. Amateurs, probably thousands."

"So what do you think, we need more?" Simon snapped.

"Hey, man, settle down," Mike said, holding up both hands, palms out. "We're archeology and language students. I don't even understand the Long Count, let alone think I can tell you what it means."

Simon crossed his arms, glaring.

"Well, Dante and I are going to go back and have a beer with them," Tina said staunchly.

"Then enjoy your walk back to Izapa," Simon said.

Dominic glanced at him curiously. Purposefully, he reached into his hip pocket for the car keys, pulling them out and dangling them before him. "What kind of beer?"

It was warm sitting around the crackling fire, and the tepid beer tasted good in the cold. Abby felt drowsy, and couldn't remember the last time she'd felt so comfortable. The trio from Maryland were friendly and fun; John had an acoustic guitar he played quite well, a pleasant background to their chatter. Dominic was in his element, spinning tales of the ancient Maya and their Count, a bottle of tequila in one hand. He'd made a quick run into town for some food for them to cook over the fire, grabbing a bottle of the local brand of firewater while he was there.

Tina and Dante were chatting happily with the three newcomers, but Abby just sat back, eyes closed, listening. Simon sat off a ways by himself, drinking warm Corona and glowering.

"We just came from Dos Pilas."

"That's about seventy miles south of here, right?" Dominic asked.

Mike nodded. "It was founded as a military outpost of Tikal. The ruler of Tikal placed his brother on the throne of Dos Pilas when the kid was only about four years old."

"The kid who then turned on Tikal," Felipe added.

"Not by choice," Dominic said. "They were peaceful and worked together for almost twenty years. Then Calakmul, which is in Mexico — about sixty miles north of here — which was an enemy of Tikal, conquered Dos Pilas."

"If Calakmul was conquering from the north, why would Tikal set up a military base to the south?" Dante asked.

"Dos Pilas was placed down at the border of the Mayan lowlands. They controlled trade coming through there — jade, goods from the Caribbean, all valuables that came in between the highlands and lowlands. It was an important stronghold, which is why Calakmul attacked it."

"What a mess," Abby said, eyes still closed.

Dominic nodded. "The king of Dos Pilas was forced to fight against his brother, and ended up killing him and other members of the royal family."

"That's horrible."

"It *is* horrible," Dominic agreed. "The description, carved in glyphs in the stone steps at Dos Pilas, is very graphic. It says that the skulls of the leaders of Tikal were piled up in pools of blood."

"Tell me again why the hell we're studying these people?" Abby asked.

"Oh come on, you don't find this fascinating?" Mike joked gently.

"I can do without the violence and bloodshed," she responded.

"It wasn't done for the love of violence, though; the king of Dos Pilas was just a puppet, forced into the confrontation by the puppet master of Calakmul."

"I wouldn't say he was an unwilling participant, though," Mike said. "The final glyphs on the staircase show the king of Dos Pilas doing a victory dance."

"Maybe the king didn't commission the glyphs. You have to remember that his city had been conquered by an invading enemy, and he essentially had to do what they ordered. Lots of kings of the different cities were owned by other kingdoms." Dominic explained. "What's interesting is that according to the inscriptions, the attack was based on astrology — they timed it to coincide with the movements of Venus. Apparently that's when the alignment was right for victory."

"Guess it worked," Abby said.

They all laughed. Michael reached for another beer, tossing one to Abby.

"I guess so," he said. "I can't see the good in any of these people. They were in constant conflict, all warring among themselves. After awhile, Tikal became strong again and ended up routing Calakmul. I'm not even going to start guessing who the bad guys were."

"Maybe there really weren't any," Dominic said. "Sometimes there's no black or white, no evil conqueror attacking a peaceful race. Sometimes everyone's to blame. Or no one. The Maya weren't fighting for love of fighting; their wars had a purpose. They were trying to create a single empire. The problem seemed to be who was going to rule it. This kept them constantly fragmented into small kingdoms run by warlords, constantly at war with each other, and caused the eventual collapse of their civilization."

"You're saying the Mayan world fell apart because of fighting?" Tina asked.

Mike shrugged. "It could be. The inscriptions at Dos Pilas are from three hundred years or so before the Maya abandoned their cities. At some point, they left these beautiful fortresses and city states and went to live in the villages we find them in today. Why would they leave their palaces to go live in shacks, unless they were run out of the cities or in fear for their lives?"

"You can only sacrifice so many humans before the humans run like hell," Felipe said. "Maybe the common people finally rebelled against the priests, and the priests and rulers fled. The common folk couldn't run the cities, so they ended up going back to farming and letting the cities fall to ruin."

Mike shook his head. "I don't think so. I think for them to have completely abandoned their cities and let the jungle reclaim them, even through today, it had to be something catastrophic. It'd be like us leaving our cities and moving out to the suburbs, letting downtown New York and LA just fall into disrepair and grow back into the landscape. Why would they leave the cities?

"It is sad, though, that so much brilliance was lost to the ravages of war. Their architecture alone could teach us so much."

Abby opened her eyes, gazing out at the pyramid in the distance. It rose tall and ghostly in the darkness. "It is impressive," she said, "but I can't say the design is the most effective. I'd be scared to death to climb those stairs; they're practically vertical."

"Well, that's what I'm talking about," Mike said. "The architecture isn't just about efficiency — it's about design. Acoustical engineering."

Abby's expression was questioning, and Mike laughed. "Have you taken her to Chichen Itza?" he asked Dominic.

Dominic shook his head. "We've just spent our time in this area. I know what you're talking about, though. The acoustics of the temple of Kulkulcan are built into the design, just like the snake climbing down the Temple of the Sun."

"What acoustics?" Abby asked.

"The quetzal bird had sacred meaning to the ancient Maya," Michael explained. "The bird's tail feathers were more valuable than even jade, or gold. The quetzals had a special part in their sacred ceremonies. And when you stand at the base of the staircase at the temple of Kulkulcan and clap your hands, the pyramid echoes in the cry of the quetzal bird."

"Really?"

"Really. It's built into the dimensions of the stairway — the steps at the bottom are high, but with a short width. The higher steps are easier to climb, shaped more like a traditional riser. The lower steps make the 'chirr' sound, the upper steps the 'roop.' It's an amazing feat of architectural engineering, used for religious purposes. During ceremonies the priests would have the sixty thousand or so attendees clap their hands together, and the sound coming out of the pyramid would be deafening – like Kulkulcan himself was answering them."

"Teotihuacan does the same thing," Dominic explained. "You can get a chirped echo from the main pyramid. If you move around the base you can get a range of pitches, up and down half an octave, but all the same sound."

Abby smiled, raising her beer. "Then I change my position on the Maya," she said. "Even with the violence and war. If they can incorporate beauty and brilliance into their engineering, then they weren't completely horrible."

"I guess that's the best we can ask for," Dominic said. "Cheers."

The others laughed, raising their drinks in a toast. "Cheers!"

Abby was dozing, half asleep under the starlight, when she heard Dominic's voice beside her.

"Hey, Abby, what are the directions into our galaxy?"

"Hmmm," she said sleepily, trying to get her thoughts together. "Sagittarius points the way into it. Gemini, or Orion, points the way out." She sat up slowly, looking around her. Most of the others were sleeping; Dante and Tina had moved off by themselves, and Simon was gone. She glanced around for him and saw him sacked out under a tree. His head rested on his chest, and though she couldn't see his face in the darkness, she thought he was probably asleep.

"What time is it?" she asked Dominic.

"Around one," he said quietly. He was crouched beside her, hands dangling between his knees. He didn't glance at his watch, and she looked at him curiously.

"Michael and I have been up yapping," he said. "Everyone else checked out early."

Abby rose to her feet, joints cracking. She groaned and stretched her arms above her head.

"I think I'll stretch my legs a little," she said.

"Want company?"

She shook her head. "I'm not going far," she said. "I'll just stroll over towards the monuments."

"Okay," he said. "Yell — loudly — if you need us."

She smiled, putting a hand on his shoulder, then headed past him. The stars above were clear and bright, but with no moon, the night was very dark. She stopped at the edge of the clearing, hands on the small of her back as she stretched, watching the sky. The Milky Way sprawled out above her, and she tilted her face up to it, closing her eyes, letting the cool night and the quiet wash over her.

She stayed that way for a while, feeling herself swaying slightly, and realized that she wasn't as sober as she'd thought. She headed back to the warmth of the fire, hugging herself tightly. The stars shone brightly in the cold, but right now, the glow of the fire was the greater draw.

"So what's with her?" Mike asked.

Dominic turned to see where he was indicating. In the bright flames of the fire, Abby crouched, warming her palms; glowing embers danced around her, and she looked like an Indian goddess.

"Forget it," Dominic said, surprised to find his words beginning to slur, "She's with the asshole."

"Oh, you are kidding me," the other man said.

"Swear it on my Patron," Dominic said, raising his bottle of generic tequila, and the two men toasted with a laugh.

Dominic tossed back another burn of the fiery golden liquid, then turned to watch Abby. She'd risen from the fireside and strolled a little ways away. Lifting a hand to shield her eyes from the fire's glow, she scanned the sky for the icy beacons of the stars.

Dominic rose to his feet, stumbling a bit, but a hand from Michael steadied him. "I'm okay, man," Dominic muttered, waving an unsteady hand in his direction, then tottered off in Abby's direction.

She turned his way when she heard him coming; he was hard to miss, as big as he was, weaving and tripping among the stones. He held up the bottle when he knew she had seen him, but she only smiled and turned away.

"What's up?" he asked when he was by her side.

"Up there?" she asked, waving a hand across the pallet of the night sky.

"For starters," Dominic said.

"Come here," she said, taking his arm. "Away from the smoke of the fire. I want to show you something."

Abby gripped him by the wrist to lead him away from the group; after a moment, his hand slipped into hers.

They moved a good distance away from the fire, and Dominic was about to ask her what would happen if Simon came looking for her, then realized he didn't care.

"Stop here," Abby's voice came softly from his side. "Tell me what you see, Dominic."

He looked up, scanning first the dark countryside, which was nothing but shadows. Ruined temples rose against the skyline like eerie ghosts, long-dead remains of another lifetime.

His blurry eyes focused upon one tall stele, smoky gray against the blacker backdrop of sky.

"Look up," Abby whispered.

Dominic's eyes followed the inky sky, the stars shining out like crystals, diamonds upon velvet. The sky itself was black as pitch; no man-made lights cast themselves against the darkness, and the sky above them, surrounding them, was truly ancient. The swirling stars were billions of years old; trillions, eons, ageless, eternal. Dominic was breathless, leaning back, staring upward; the sky felt both enveloping, suffocating, surrounding him and smothering him like a vast blanket, yet eternal, spinning away out of reach to distances so vast they were unimaginable. The universe felt so near he could touch it, yet so far away he could not get his mind around the far reaches of it; could not grasp even the thought of its vastness.

He stumbled backwards, then fell down, pulling Abby with him. She had not yet let go of his hand.

"Dominic, are you all right?"

He rolled onto his back, staring at the sky above them. "'Sky above us, earth below'," he quoted.

"And us caught in between," she finished. She lay on her side next to him, and put a hand on his face. He rolled his head to focus on her.

"I'm okay," he said. "Just a little overwhelmed."

"And a little drunk," she said, taking the almost-empty tequila bottle from his slack fingers. She set it beside them, then snuggled next to Dominic in the grass. "I thought you didn't get drunk," she commented.

"Tonight I'm making an exception," he said. "I guess I do need to find someone else to watch over me." They lay in silence for awhile before Dominic spoke again.

Drowsily, he said, "Did you know that the Maya thought the Otherworld — you know, the underworld — was below us? Just like me, when I was raised Catholic, to think there was a fiery pit below us, and if I was bad I was going there, to burn in hell forever."

He gazed up at the black sky, dotted with its brilliant gems of stars. "That's what they thought during the day, anyway. The Maya, that is, not Catholics.

"At night, they thought the Earth and the Otherworld traded places — that at night, the Otherworld rotated above them, and that's what they saw burning in the night sky."

Abby nodded. "That's what I wanted to show you, Dominic. Look up, at Orion. See him, with his three-starred belt?"

Dominic nodded, tracking the constellations until he focused on the Archer. He rose slightly to see it better, and his head drooped back. Before it struck the ground, Abby's hand was under it, catching his head in her palm.

"Oops," he said, and she slid her arm around his shoulders.

"Are you going to pass out on me?" she asked. "Because you're way too damn heavy for me to drag back to camp. If you pass out, I'm leaving you here for the jaguars."

"Jaguar-paw and Jaguar-frog," he said solemnly, and Abby rolled her eyes.

"Dominic, are you going to remember any of this in the morning?" she asked.

He smiled and rolled towards her. "Of course I will. Best night of my life. How could I forget it?" he lifted slightly to take her hand, kissing its palm lightly.

Abby pulled it away, laughing. "Damn it, Dominic, that's not what I'm talking about."

"So what are you talking about?" he asked, his voice more clear. He lay down besides her, sliding his arm around her shoulders again, and at once she realized that he wasn't nearly as drunk as she'd thought him to be.

"I'm talking about the Black Road," she said.

This time, Dominic did sit up straight. Abby rose with him, and she picked up his hand and aimed it, pointing towards the visible stream of the Milky Way, streaming out like a river alongside Orion.

"That's it?" he asked excitedly. "That's the Black Road?"

"Right in the center of the Milky Way," she said. "It's kind of like standing on an island in a wide stream — you have a permanent view of the same part of the river, forever, until you get off the island. We can see the same view of the Milky Way that the Maya had.

"See there, where there's a dark rift in the middle of it? It looks like someone took a piece of white gauze and tore a shred of it, right near the middle. That's it. That's what the Maya called the Black Road."

"The great cleft," Dominic mused. "The Great Mother's birth canal, they called it. Such an interesting reference — was something birthed from the galactic center?"

Abby smiled. "They had so many names for it. The dark rift, the great cleft, Xibalba be."

"The Road to the Underworld," Dominic said, his eyes luminous.

They sat back and stared at the pathway between the stars, the physical reality behind so much mythology. Abby watched Dominic through the darkness as he gazed at the foggy band of stars. She turned again to the blackness of the great rift in the galaxy, and it did indeed appear like a road; a black road leading to — or from — the center of the galaxy.

She suddenly shivered.

"Hey, come on," Dominic said, turning to her. He helped her up, and she was unsteady on her feet. She held tight against him for a moment, embracing his warmth, before stepping away.

"Come on now, I'm the one supposed to be the drunk around here," he teased gently, putting an arm around her. He lead her slowly back to camp, all the while gazing up at the black sky, silver galaxy, and ebony cleft ripping through the Milky Way, mapping out the road to eternity.

As they drew closer to the camp, the smoke from the fire began to fog their view, and the tall monuments blocked the sky. Dominic's arm slid from Abby's shoulder to her waist, which he gave a slight squeeze before releasing her. He took her hand, and stopped.

"What is it?" she whispered, as they were just outside the camp, hidden by a tumble of ruins.

"I just wanted to say thank you," Dominic said. "Thank you for clearing my head, for inspiring me again, and for showing me the road."

"My pleasure," she said with a slight smile, and he couldn't stop himself: Dominic bent and kissed her gently, briefly, on that sweet smile; it lasted only a moment, and was gone.

He released her hand and headed back to the group, but Abby stood frozen where she was, the warmth of his lips still felt. There was a flutter inside her, in her stomach, or her heart, and as she raised a hand gently to touch her lips to feel the slight smile that still lay there, she couldn't help but feel a quiver of fear. If she didn't put a stop to this right now, she knew there was going to be serious trouble.

12.19.15.16.0

December 2, 2008 — While the night was clear and perfect for stargazing, it had become too cold to sit out in the open clearing, and Abby and Dominic headed back towards the lab. They crossed the field, silent and bathed in starlight. As they reached the land bridge over the lagoon, they heard voices below them. Dominic looked down to see Dante and Tina by the water's edge.

"Hey down there!" he called.

"Hey yourself," Tina called up amiably.

"Mind if we join you?" Dominic asked to Abby's surprise; Dominic had avoided the lagoon since Steve died.

"Come on down," Dante said. "Careful, though; you don't want to fall in the water tonight."

"I'll bet," Dominic said. He reached out a hand to Abby, who took it; he helped her to the strong branch, which she quickly descended. A moment later, Dominic joined her on the bank.

Dante and Tina moved over to make room for the two newcomers, and Tina looked up at them with a welcoming smile. Abby couldn't help but notice how close together they were sitting. "I hope we're not interrupting anything," she said.

"Not at all," Tina said. "What can we do for you?"

"I've been thinking about your nuclear reactor," Dominic said, sitting down on a large boulder. He motioned for Abby to join him so she didn't have to sit in the cold mud. "I've been thinking about it in relation to ancient nuclear war."

"You think if there was radiation or vitrification from atom-splitting, it wasn't from a manmade catastrophe, but a natural reaction," Dante suggested.

Dominic nodded. "Something like the Oklo reactor."

Dante thought about it. "It's possible," he said, considering. "Although the Oklo reaction would have been about two billion years ago. The desert glass might have survived for thousands of millions of years, but the ruins in Scotland sure weren't around then."

"Can you back up a minute?" Abby asked. "What is the Oklo reactor?"

"It's actually several natural reactors, or at least the remains of them, found in the Oklo uranium deposit in Gabon, Africa," Dante responded. "Billions of years ago, when the Earth was still forming, uranium was much more common than it is today. There are different kinds of uranium, and without getting into the spectrometry, suffice it to say that there were places on Earth where the uranium was unstable enough to cause a reaction. They found the remains of several reactions at Oklo, with the nuclear waste still largely intact after all these years. Just goes to show that shit stays around forever."

"If there were reactions in Africa, there could have been reactions elsewhere," Dominic mused.

"Sure," Dante said. "There could have been. We still don't have the complete history of the Earth. Most of the geological record is pretty straightforward, but periodically, we find things we don't expect. The Oklo reactors have been there since long before the dawn of man, but we only just discovered them in 1972."

"If one occurred within the time of man on Earth, it could explain a lot of the anomalies we discussed — the vitrified ruins, hell, even the destruction of Sodom and Gomorrah; when the city was blasted off the face of the Earth, Lot and his family were told to run to the mountains to escape the devastation and not look back — Lot's wife trailed behind and was consumed. Had they found her body after the nuclear reaction, a 'pillar of salt' might have been a pretty good description of it, just like the bodies found in Hiroshima that had been reduced to ash, but still held their shape."

"Anyway," Dominic said, "it gives us an alternate explanation for any evidence that might point to an ancient nuclear war."

"That's kind of disappointing," Tina said. "The thought of a lost civilization, a mysterious ancient history of the world where man had nuclear weapons and flying machines, then destroyed civilization and lost it all to the dust of time is absolutely fascinating. Exciting. A natural nuclear reaction is dull."

"Maybe for you," Dante smiled, "but you're not a geologist."

Tina laughed. "Sorry," she said. "It is intriguing in its own right. But it's no Atlantis."

Dominic stood up. "I guess that answers my questions, then," he said. "Thanks, Dante. I think I knew the answer already, but I had to talk it out."

"Glad to be of service," Dante said. Tina gave them a wave, and Abby stood up.

"See you guys later," Dominic said, and he and Abby made their way back up the hillside. They crossed the bridge into the courtyard, and finally, Dominic spoke.

"Maybe Tina's right," he said. "Maybe science does take the romance out of life."

"Not at all," Abby responded. "We live in a fascinating world; I don't understand the need to invent supernatural realms or make up stories to make it exciting. The world is full of romance; all science does is help us understand it."

"So even though you know a star is nothing but a blazing ball of various gases, it's still romantic to you?"

"It's no less beautiful," she said with a smile.

Dominic slid his arm around her. "Come on in," he said. "It's cold out here."

Abby leaned against him, enjoying his warmth. It *was* getting cold. The hot summer and cool autumn were officially over now; with Steve's death, winter had come, and they still had a long way to go.

12.19.15.16.8

December 10, 2008 — "Christmas shopping?"

"Sure," Tina said, "why not? I think it'll be worth it just to get out of here for awhile."

The two women sat across the table from each other, sipping their coffee. Dante was taking a shower, and Dominic was nowhere to be found. It'd rained fairly hard the night before, but Abby had not heard him come in, and she had not seen him yet that morning. Abby felt a twinge of concern, but Tina seemed unruffled.

"It's not a bad idea," Abby said. "I hadn't even thought about it until now. It doesn't quite feel like the Christmas season."

"That's the point," Tina said. "We need to get this place spruced up a little. Maybe some holiday cheer will take some of the gloom out of the air. Besides, this is getting depressing; all we're doing is sitting around here trying to think up all the possible ways the world will end."

"Well, I'm all for it," Abby said. "Do you want to take the guys along with us?"

"We might as well ask them," Tina said. "Dante doesn't seem to mind not being anywhere near civilization — as a geologist, he's used to spending most of his time out in the middle of nowhere. And Dominic is a loner anyway. But still, I think they're starting to go a little stir crazy. It'd be good for them to get out among people again. Especially Dominic. He's going to feel Steve's loss a lot more around the holidays. Can't hurt to ask him."

"I agree — if you can find him. I haven't seen him since before dinner last night."

"He's around. Dominic always turns up. I'll go get Dante; it'd be good if we could head out right after breakfast."

True to her word, Tina had Dante in the SUV around seven o'clock. Dominic still hadn't turned up, however; when they were unable to find him after fifteen minutes of calling and searching, Tina sat down at the kitchen table to write him a note. "I'll just let him know we went into town," she said. "We should be back by dark."

"Wait a minute," Abby said.

Tina paused. "What is it?"

"Hold on, I'll be right back." She went up the stairs, ducking into her room. She had brought her telescope inside last night when the rain had started to fall, and she picked it up now, taking it to the bedroom window. Quickly, she set it up, searching the clearing, then the mountainside, and finally focusing on the base of the mountain. She fine-tuned it, pulling in a shape moving through the trees. "I've got him!" she called.

She heard footsteps on the stairs behind her, and after a moment, Tina came into the room. "You see him?"

Abby stepped aside, motioning to her scope. Tina came over and had a look. "Where the hell was he all night? Up on the mountain?"

"Probably got caught in the rainstorm," Abby said. "Found someplace to hide out, I guess." Abby didn't mention the cave; for some reason, she thought Dominic might want to keep that private.

"I'll tell Dante to hold up, then."

"Okay," Abby said. "I'll go out and meet Dominic halfway, see if he wants to come with us or not."

"If he does, he's going to need to hurry up and shower and change," Tina said. "It's a long drive into town and back, unless we want to spend a night there."

"I'll tell him," Abby said. She and Tina headed downstairs, heading off in opposite directions when they reached the kitchen as Tina went out the front door to talk to Dante and Abby headed out the back door to meet Dominic at the base of the mountain.

Dominic was surprised to see Abby coming across the clearing towards him. He raised a hand in greeting, which she returned. She paused in the center of the field, waiting for him to reach her.

"Hey, Abby. Did you miss me?"

She laughed. "Well, I actually was worried. You never came home last night —not that that's so unusual for you, but with the weather and all ..."

He smiled. "Thanks for your concern. I was okay, though — I headed up the mountainside to look down into Izapa from above. I ended up getting caught in the storm, and by the time I made it back around to this side of the mountain, I was exhausted. I decided to hole up in our cave until the storm passed, but I ended up falling asleep."

They crossed the field slowly, and Abby could tell he was still tired. "How do you feel now?"she asked.

He shrugged. "Damp. Tired. A little grubby. But a shower and a hot breakfast, and I should be fine."

"How do you feel about strolling around Tapachula for a couple hours?"

He turned to her with a questioning smile. "You guys are going into town?"

"Tina thought a little Christmas shopping would be fun."

"Damn, I forgot all about Christmas," Dominic said. "What day is it, anyway?"

"Wednesday," Abby said. "December tenth."

"Well, hell, I guess we'd better get into town, then."

Abby smiled in surprise. "Are you sure you're up for it? You just hiked, what, about ten miles of rough jungle since yesterday? And slept in a cramped rock cave in a rainstorm?"

"It was more like fifteen miles," Dominic said. "I had to go around the other side of the mountain to see Izapa, then climb fairly high to see over the jungle."

"Maybe you'd better stay home and rest."

He laughed. "I'll be fine. I'll take a nap in the car on the way."

"How about if I run ahead and start breakfast for you? It should be done by the time you're done in the shower."

"Are you guys in that much of a hurry to get going, or are you just being sweet?"

"If Tina asks, it's because we're in a hurry," she said. She gave him a smile, then hurried off.

Dominic shook his head, smiling slightly, as he strolled along behind. His muscles ached from the walk, cramped from the night spent on the hard stone floor of the cave and wet from his hike through the cold rain. The sun on him was warm, however, and as he watched Abby jog across the land bridge above the lagoon, he stepped a little more quickly.

"Eggs and pancakes?" Dominic asked, coming into the kitchen. His hair, still wet from the shower, clung around his head in damp dark curls.

"I'm jealous," Dante said. "All Tina made for me was a glass of orange juice and a pre-packaged muffin."

"And coffee," Tina protested, and they laughed.

"Regardless, I wish I was still hungry," he said.

"I'll buy you lunch when we get into town," Tina said.

Dominic sat down at the table next to Abby. "Thank you," he said.

"My pleasure. You want coffee?"

"Tea would be great."

As Abby got up to boil a pot of water, Tina spoke up. "Do you think we should call Simon? Let him know we'll be in town?"

Abby thought about it, balancing her own desire to enjoy a day without Simon against how he'd react if he knew they came into town and didn't tell him. "Well, he's in class most of the morning — this is finals week. I think he's done around one o'clock, then he has another class in the evening. Maybe he can join us for a late lunch."

"You want to give him a call?"

"Yeah, why don't I?" Abby said. "I can leave a message at his office, anyway. Dominic, the water's still heating on the stove; here's your cup and tea bag."

"Thanks," he said. He waited until she'd left the room before turning to Tina with an arched eyebrow.

"Hey, 'tis the season," she said. "I'm feeling particularly filled with the holiday spirit this morning."

"You must be," Dante said. "Now I'm glad I wasn't eating; I'd have choked when you just suggested inviting Simon out with us."

"Well, really, what are the odds that he's going to come along?" she said. "He'll probably deride us for celebrating a religious event, then explain the holiday's pagan origins to us."

The others laughed, and while Dominic finished his breakfast, they waited for Abby to get back.

Tapachula was busy, the streets bustling with vendors and shoppers. Businessmen and students mingled with local merchants and farmers who'd come into town to sell their wares in the open-air market.

"What do you want to do, stick together or split up so we can get gifts for each other?" Dante asked.

"Why don't we stay together for now?" Tina said. "Maybe do some running around, find our way around town, and then split up for awhile? We can meet at some appointed time somewhere for lunch."

"I think we should at least stay in pairs," Dominic said. "I've been mugged a couple times here, and had it attempted on several more occasions. It's not safe for any of us on our own."

"You were mugged?" Abby asked. She sized him up, unable to imagine him at anyone's mercy.

Dominic shrugged. "Had my pocket picked my first time here, when I was a lot more naive. Held up at gunpoint once, at knifepoint another. Size and weight stops making much difference when there's a gun in your ribs."

"Damn," Tina said. "I forgot about that. I've only been here together with you and Steve before. Okay … well, maybe we can stick together for now, then separate later. Dante and I will go out for an hour or so, then meet up with you two. Then we'll switch; I'll head out with Dominic, Abby can go with Dante. That should cover everyone enough to get a surprise gift for all of us."

"Sounds good," Dominic said. "At least we don't have to worry about hiding Simon's from him."

"Yeah," Tina said, "too bad he couldn't join us."

Abby shrugged. "He said he had end-of-semester meetings with some of his students and wouldn't be able to cancel them. That's okay, I guess. I'll see him Friday, anyway."

Abby couldn't remember the last time she'd had so much fun. She and Dominic wandered the shops together, laughing and relaxed, enjoying the afternoon. Abby picked out a pair of silver earrings for Tina and a heavy silver bracelet for Dante — he'd complained that the minerals in the lagoon had ruined the one he had. She found a great hemp shirt she knew Dominic would love; he was on the other side of the shop when Abby found it, and she was able to get the merchant to hold it for her. When she and Dominic split up, she would return with Dante to buy it. So far, the only person she was having trouble finding a gift for was Simon.

Across town, Dante and Tina were doing just as well; for the first time since Steve's death, they were relaxed. They were lost in their own world, just enjoying the day, and totally weren't expecting it when they came upon Simon.

"Holy crap, is that who I think it is?" Tina asked, grabbing Dante by an arm and pulling him to a stop. They peeked around the corner of the building, trying to get a better look. Simon was sitting at a table outside a small café, leaning across the table with a smile, deep in conversation with the woman across from him. Her back was to them, so Dante and Tina couldn't see her face, but Simon's was completely clear.

"What the hell?" Dante said.

"That son of a bitch," Tina said. "I don't believe it."

"Well, wait," Dante said. "They're not holding hands or anything. Maybe she's just a colleague."

"Please. Look at the expression on his face. It doesn't matter if she's just a colleague, he's sure as hell not looking at her like she is."

"So let's go over there and say hi," Dante said. "See what he says."

Before Tina could answer, Simon pushed his chair back and stood up. The woman across the table did the same, and as they both walked out to the street, Simon put his arm around her. They strolled away, their backs to Tina and Dante.

"Shit," Tina said. "Should we go after them?"

"No," Dante said. "We can't run down the street and confront him."

"Well, damn," she answered. "Then what are we going to do?" She watched as Simon and the woman turned the corner.

"I don't guess we have to do anything, do we?" Dante said. "I mean, what did we see? Simon having lunch with some woman."

"Oh come on, he had his arm around her."

"And that's any different than the way you've seen Dominic act with Abby?"

Tina fell silent.

"Look," Dante said, "you know I can't stand that man. I'd be more than happy to come up with a reason to get rid of him. But what we're talking about here is between him and Abby. And that's not up to us to get involved with."

She sighed and took his hand. "I know," she said, "but he's such a shit, I can't stand it. I'll never look at him the same way again."

"Can you really look at him with any more contempt than you do now?" Dante asked, eliciting a smile from her. "Come on," he said, "it's just about time to hook up with the others. We'd better get back."

They turned and headed back, their good mood somewhat dulled by what they'd just seen. Tina knew Dante was right; they hadn't really observed much, and Abby was guilty of the same behavior they'd seen in Simon. Still, though, she thought when she got Dominic alone, she would bring it up to him. If anyone would want to protect Abby and confront Simon, it would be Dominic.

After they'd finished their lunch at a teeming sidewalk café, Tina stood on the corner and watched Dante and Abby disappear into the colorful crowd, waiting until they were out of sight before she turned to Dominic. "Dominic — Dante and I saw Simon at a café back there."

"Really?" he said. "I thought he told Abby he'd be in conferences or something all day."

"He did. That's why I'm concerned. He was with another woman."

Dominic didn't answer. He put a hand on Tina's arm and guided her off the busy sidewalk, leading her across the street to an open-air market. He started searching through the blankets, and after some time he finally spoke again.

"Did you see anything that would conclusively point to his being up to something, or was he just having lunch with her?"

"They were having lunch, but the way he was looking at her ..."

Dominic held up a hand. "Did you see anything, Tina? Kissing, holding hands, anything?"

"He put his arm around her when they walked away."

Dominic pulled out a length of beautiful fabric, woven with thick yarn in different shades of blues and browns. "Do you think Abby would like this? I'm looking for a blanket or something for her to sit on when she's out by her scope."

"It's nice," Tina said, distracted. "Dominic, are you listening to me?"

He sighed and laid the blanket back down on the table. "I am, Tina. But do you really see Abby confronting Simon over something like that?"

"I don't know," she answered. "She pretty much puts up with whatever stupid shit he pulls, but I can't see her just accepting him screwing around on her."

"But we don't know that he is."

"Trust me, he is. If not now, he's sure as hell trying. I saw him, Dominic. I know you've never looked at me as one, but I am a woman, Dominic, and I recognized Simon's expression. He's not just interested in friendship with that woman, for sure. Let's face it, he could come home a lot more often than he does. Sometimes he doesn't even come back until Saturday now, and then leaves Sunday afternoon. And when he *is* home, Abby doesn't even come in from her telescope until way after Simon has gone to bed — and I've never once heard him complain about it."

"Or her," he commented. "And really, Tina, is it any of your business?" he asked bluntly.

"I don't care," she said. "If it was me, I'd sure as hell want to know if my fiancé was out lunching with some other woman — while making excuses that he couldn't see me."

"You're not Abby," he repeated. "Is her relationship any of your business?"

"Well …"

"Well nothing, Tina. You know it's not. I don't know what Simon's up to, and I don't know how Abby feels about it. From the way she's acted lately, she seems to welcome any alienation of his affection. But either way, it's none of your business, and it's none of mine. I'm not going to get involved in someone else's relationship."

"I think you already are, Dominic."

He turned to look at her. "I'm not interfering, Tina." Even to his own ears, though, his words sounded hollow.

"You can't say that you're not influencing her feelings."

He shook his head. "I don't know what she's doing or thinking, Tina. I only know how I feel. If she comes to me, then I'll be here. But I'm not pressuring her, and I'm not going to start accusing Simon of sleeping around. Personally, I wouldn't put it past him; but if something's going on, it's between the two of them. She'll find out eventually — she's not stupid."

"You just don't want him to leave," Tina responded. "This project of yours is more important than Abby's feelings."

"Nothing is more important to me than Abby's feelings," Dominic said, his jaw tightening. "But damn it, Tina, this is not my issue. Simon is unbearable as it is; I'm not about to start flinging unfounded accusations at him."

"So why don't we just casually mention it to Abby; you know, 'Hey, I saw Simon having lunch in town.' She can ask him about it herself."

Dominic turned away, picking up the blue and brown blanket again. "You do what you want, Tina. You know I've never been good with relationships. I'm of the opinion that we should stay out of it — it's only going to cause trouble, and we already have a rift in our group. This will just widen it."

"Well, it's sure as hell not going to heal itself," Tina said. "What it comes down to is, do we want to ignore it and let Simon do whatever the hell he wants to do, letting naïve little Abby sit there thinking all is right with the world? Or do we want to give her a heads up?"

"Abby's not as naïve as she comes across," Dominic said. "She knows what Simon's about. And she understands that her relationship isn't perfect, but she's dealing with it as she sees fit."

"Then I think she should have all the information," Tina said. "Just like anything else we do, Dominic, if we're going to make a decision, we need to have all the information in front of us. I'm not going to tell her what to do about it, but I think she should know. I have too much respect for my fellow woman to see her get blindsided by this."

"Fine," Dominic said, folding the blanket over his arm. "I'm buying this."

Tina stopped, watching him take the fabric to the shop keeper, making friendly conversation in fluent Spanish as he paid for the blanket. She had never understood Dominic, but now, even less than ever. Regardless, she thought; for once she would do what her heart, not Dominic, told her.

They hid their packages from each other on the drive back, joking about some of the purchases they had considered. An hour or so into the trip, Tina finally leaned forward between the front seats.

"Hey Abby, when Dante and I were together, I could have sworn we saw Simon."

"Did you?" Abby asked, turning to look at her. She tried to keep her voice light, but her heart was already pounding. "What was he doing?"

"Having lunch," Tina said. "I couldn't see who he was with; just the back of her head. They were across the street, so I couldn't be completely sure it was him, but it sure looked like him. He was wearing that tailored leather coat of his."

Abby turned to the window again, a lump rising in her throat, feeling a hideous sense of déjà vu from a year before. "I'll have to remember to ask him about it this weekend," she said. "He said he had student conferences all day; he was probably just taking a break for lunch."

"Yeah, it could have been with one of his students," Tina said. "I never went to lunch with one of my professors before, but hey, this is Mexico. Who knows how they do things down here."

Dante put a hand on Tina's shoulder, and she sat back. Up front, Dominic continued to drive in silence while Abby stared unseeingly out the window. Her good mood had fled like a bird; all she wanted now was to be back in her room, alone, where she could hide under the covers and think about things. Or not think about them. Either way, the information was unwanted and unexpected, and she thought of the gift sitting in the bag between her feet. She'd spent most of the day trying to find the perfect Christmas present for Simon, knowing how hard he was to please. She'd finally settled for a pewter picture frame, hand-made and beautifully detailed. She'd planned to have one of the other researchers take her picture sometime before the holiday, something to present him with that he could keep in his office at the university.

Abby put a hand to her forehead, closing her eyes. A moment later, she felt a gentle weight on her knee; she turned to look and saw Dominic's hand. He gave her a smile, and her knee a slight squeeze. She tried to return his smile but couldn't; before she turned away, however, she caught his look at Tina in the rearview mirror. His eyebrows knit together and the corners of his mouth turned down; in the back seat, Tina turned away.

"Hey, can you turn up the radio?" Dante suddenly asked, breaking the silence. "I'd love to hear some Mexican Christmas music."

Abby felt the weight of Dominic's hand lift from her knee as he tuned the radio, searching to find a station. She was grateful for his distraction, and as she stared at the fields rushing by outside her window, she lost herself in thought. It was always something with Simon — even when he wasn't with them, he managed to ruin everything.

12.19.15.16.16

December 18, 2009 — "I called his department at the university and pretended I was a student," Tina said carefully. "I told them he'd given me his home number but I'd lost it. I guess universities down here aren't quite as concerned about the safety and privacy of their professors as we are in the United States. Or they're used to Simon handing out his home number to women."

"So what happened?" Dante asked.

Tina sighed. "I called it and some woman answered. I was kind of taken aback. I told her I'd been trying to reach the apartments where Simon told Abby he was staying."

"And?"

"And she said I'd reached the home of Dr. Casteneda. I said thanks and hung up. I went back to the university website where I'd gotten the number of the math department, and I found her name. She's one of his colleagues at the university."

"So you think what? That he's living with one of his colleagues?"

"Why not? He was fumbling around for an apartment for weeks until he came back one day all pleased with himself and said he had found a place and moved in. Why would it be so hard for him to find an apartment? I looked up the place he said he was living, too — it's huge, and has a ton of openings. A university professor couldn't get an approval to move right in?"

"How would he get a colleague to let her live with him in only a few weeks, though?"

"I don't know," Tina said. "He does have a certain — well, charm. He's not unattractive. I don't know, maybe he told her he needed someplace to stay while he looked for a place, and he ended up staying there for good. Or he really was living in the apartments for awhile, and then moved in with her. Or is just over at her place so much he gives that out as his home number."

"You don't think it's possible that the secretary in the math department just mixed up their numbers?" Dante asked gently.

Tina paused. "You think I'm jumping to conclusions?"

"Maybe," he said with a smile, then leaned over and kissed her. "You have been known to make some leaps of logic."

She smiled. "I guess I didn't think about that. She could have screwed up the numbers, although I don't see Nieson and Casteneda next to each other in any phone book I've ever seen."

"So maybe the directory screwed up the numbers."

"Maybe."

"Why don't we test it?" a voice came from the doorway. They turned in surprise and saw Dominic.

"I didn't know you were there," Dante said, sitting back.

"Sorry," Dominic said, coming into the lab. "I didn't mean to eavesdrop." He sat on the edge of the table. "I just caught on to what you were discussing. If you think the university reversed the numbers for Simon and whoever this other person is, there's one way to find out."

"Call and ask for Casteneda's number," Dante said.

"Exactly."

Ten minutes later, they had their answer, but they were no closer to understanding than before.

"So what does it prove?" Tina asked.

"Not necessarily anything," Dominic said. "The only evidence we have is that the university is giving us the same phone number for two different professors. What that's evidence of, we don't know. It could be evidence that Simon is living with this woman or it could just mean the university directory is messed up. We don't know."

"Should we ask him?" Tina asked.

Dante laughed. "Yeah, you go right ahead," he said. "I'd love to hear how you phrase that. And his answer."

"I'm not afraid of Simon," she responded.

"It's not a matter of being afraid of him," Dominic said. "It's a matter of respect. You know you have no business checking up on him, Tina. If he is two-timing Abby, I'll be the first to be furious about it, but it's none of my business, either. I don't like him, and I don't like the way he treats her. But it's not my place to get involved in their relationship. Yours, either."

"Even as her friend?" Tina asked. "Come on, you guys are close. I know you care about her. You don't think it's your duty as a friend to let her know if something's going on that she doesn't know about?"

"If I knew for sure, yes. If I had evidence that he was cheating on her, I suppose I'd point her towards it. But it's not my business, even as a friend, to confront him with accusations, especially when the only evidence I have was gained through ill-gotten means; I mean, you're checking up on him at work — how do you think he's going to react when you tell him that?"

"So you think we should just let it go? Let him go on being an ass to her?"

"You know what happened when you told her you saw him in town with someone else; all it did was upset her. She's been stressed out ever since, and I don't think she even mentioned it to him."

"Well, that's her prerogative," Tina said. "But I think she should at least have the option."

"Let me handle it," Dominic said. "I'm a little more even-tempered than you are. I can confront him without him knowing he's being confronted. And I can get more answers. If there's anything going on, I'll find out about it."

"And you'll tell us?" Tina asked.

"Do you really need to know?"

Tina paused. "Well, no. But ..."

"But nothing," Dominic said. "Let's keep on track here and not let personal relationships get in the way. If it's not your business, don't try to make it so. That goes for all of us."

Tina and Dante exchanged a look. "No problem," Dante said. "Everyone minds their own business, and we'll all be happy."

"Not necessarily happy," Dominic said, "just indifferent. We need to be getting the job done – whatever else goes on around it isn't important as long as it doesn't affect the work. I don't want to see anybody here unhappy, but I don't want to have to be involved in the day-to-day interactions between you all, either."

"So you'll handle it."

"I'll handle it. Now ... back to work. Or whatever it is you were doing." He turned away, heading to the bookshelf, and Tina glanced at

Dante and rolled her eyes. She'd seen Dominic start to smile, though, before he'd turned away.

"Back to work," she said softly, and Dante grinned. They opened up the book they'd been sharing between them, and the lab once again fell into silence.

12.19.15.17.3.

December 25, 2008 — Christmas went quickly, at least. Everyone was happy with their gifts, and while Simon seemed somewhat miffed that no one had mentioned exchanging presents with him, he was pleasantly surprised by their gifts. He even had the decency to look embarrassed for not having anything prepared.

That in itself was present enough for everyone.

12.19.15.17.9

December 31, 2008 — They rang in the New Year with abandon; the group started drinking somewhere in the neighborhood of eight o'clock, and by midnight they were well on the other side of drunk. Even Simon was relaxed; several shots of tequila followed by a few beer chasers had mellowed him out. Sitting around the kitchen table, playing poker, they counted down the year.

"It's almost 2009!" Tina called out. Abby glanced at her watch and saw there was less than a minute until midnight. Tina scrambled around the table, and as Dante pushed his chair back, she plopped down in his lap. Dominic, standing at the counter, began a final countdown. The others quickly joined in.

"Ten-nine-eight-seven," they chanted in unison. Dominic rattled a spoon handle inside his empty beer bottle, and Dante stomped his feet.

"Three-two-one — Happy New Year!" They all shouted. Tina gave Dante a wet smooch, and Abby leaned over to give Simon a kiss. Dominic turned away, cracking open a new bottle of tequila.

"Happy twenty oh nine!" Tina said.

"Right back at ya," Dominic said, raising the tequila in a salute. He took a long draw straight from the bottle.

"Hey man, maybe the rest of us wanted some of that," Simon said.

Dominic shrugged. "I'm not diseased," he said. "You're welcome to it. Or, there's another bottle out by the lab."

"Shit, I'm not walking all the way down there," Simon said.

"I'll get it," Abby said. She stood up, swaying a bit.

"Don't worry about it, Abby," Dominic said. "I'll go get it."

"You go, and we'll never see you again," Simon said. "Let Abby go get it."

Dominic stared at him in disbelief, then shook his head. "I'll escort you," he said to Abby. He pulled the door open, casting another look of disdain back at Simon, then followed her out.

"Come on," Simon said, grabbing the loose cards. He began to shuffle the deck. "You guys in?"

"We're in," Tina said. "Although I'm running out of cash pretty quick."

"I've got you covered," Dante said, planting a kiss on her forehead. "Shouldn't we wait for Abby and Dom, though?"

"Fuck 'em," Simon said, dealing out the hands. "He's won more than enough tonight. Give the rest of us a chance."

Giggling, Abby grabbed Dominic's arm to keep from falling.

"Watch it," he cautioned, "Simon sees this, he'll come after both of us."

"Screw him," she said, sliding her hand down to his. Surprised, he took her hand.

"Now you're really going to get us in trouble."

"He's too lazy to stand up and look out," she said as they neared the lab. "Besides, we're almost in shadow now."

"That we are," he said, pushing open the door. He turned and took her other hand, pulling her into the dark lab.

"Whoa," she said, stumbling over the doorstep. Dominic reached deftly around her waist and picked her up, lifting her over the stoop. When he set her down again, she leaned back against the wall. The room was spinning.

Dominic leaned against her, and before she knew it they were kissing again, drunkenly and passionately, in the darkness. After a few minutes, Abby finally pushed him away. She broke loose from his embrace and stumbled away, sitting down heavily on the bench. Her legs suddenly felt too weak to support her.

"Damn," she said, putting her hands on her trembling knees.

He came over and sat beside her, putting an arm around her shoulders.

"Dominic, don't," she said. "It's not that I don't want you to, believe me. It's just that …"

"I know," he said. He kissed her again, lightly, then stood up. "Let me go grab the bottle, I'll be right back," he said.

Abby could only nod silently. As soon as she heard the screen door swing shut, she let out an explosive breath. She tried to compose

278

herself the best she could, smoothing down her hair and straightening her clothes. A moment later, the door opened again as Dominic returned.

"You ready?" he asked, holding out a hand. She took it and let him pull her to her feet.

"How long have we been gone?" she asked as they headed back across the stone path towards the house.

"Not too long," he assured her. "I'll just tell him I couldn't find the bottle. It *is* pitch black out here, after all."

They reached the back door, and as soon as Dominic pulled it open, they heard sobbing. Quickly, Abby entered the kitchen, just in time to see Tina running up the stairs.

"You're an asshole, Simon," Dante was saying. He stood by the table, both hands balled into tight fists, but he didn't take a step towards the blond man, who still sat at the table, smirking.

Dante looked up as Dominic came in. He looked about to speak, but instead shook his head. With one hand, he pushed his chair up against the table so hard that an empty beer bottle tipped over, falling off the edge and shattering on the floor. He turned and stormed off up the stairs without a word.

"What the hell did you say to her?" Dominic asked.

"Not a thing," Simon said. He reached out a hand, and after a moment, Dominic tossed the tequila bottle to him.

"Watch it," Simon growled, ducking. He managed to get a hand up to catch the bottle before it cracked him in the head. He set it on the table in front of him.

"What did you say to Tina?" Dominic repeated.

"*Noth*ing," Simon said. "She got all upset, talking about Steve. She's drunk and emotional and started crying."

"And you had nothing to do with it."

"Of course not. She's upset that her buddy couldn't be here for the New Year, that's all."

"Then why is Dante calling you an asshole?"

"Because he blames me for everything. Just like the rest of you do." Simon stood up, surprisingly steady on his feet. "I'm going for a walk," he said, snatching the tequila bottle off the table. "Abby, are you coming?"

"I don't think so," she said. "I want to go see how Tina's doing."

"She's fine," he waved dismissively. "Dante will kiss it and make it all better."

"I'm not up for a walk," she said, crossing her arms over her chest. She was unsteady on her feet, but managed to hold her ground.

"You were fine to stroll out to the lab a minute ago," he said. When Abby didn't answer, Simon said: "Fine. Whatever. Happy fucking

New Year." He went out, letting the door slam behind him, rattling against its frame.

"Jesus," Abby said, leaning against the wall. She looked across at Dominic, who also had his arms folded across his chest. He was leaning back against the counter, staring down at his feet, crossed at the ankles. She went to him and put her arms around him. After a moment, he hugged her in return.

"Happy New Year anyway," she said, and he smiled. Kissing her on top of the head, he gave her a quick squeeze.

"I think I'm going to call it a night," he said. "Care to join me?"

Abby raised her eyes slowly to his, but his expression was unreadable. She shook her head. "Better not," she said, although her heart had begun to pound again.

"You sure?" he asked lightly. "Simon might be gone for awhile."

"I'm sure," she said, entirely unsure.

"Okay," he said. He leaned down and kissed her again, briefly. "Good night, Abby."

"Good night, Dominic," she said. She stayed where she was, listening to his slow footsteps on the stairs. She waited a good five minutes after he'd gone, holding herself steady against the counter, letting her breathing return to normal, before she finally headed up to bed.

It took all the willpower she had to stop at her own room; her feet wanted to carry her down to the room at the end of the hall. Once in her own bed, though, she'd barely lifted her feet off the floor before she fell over the edge into sleep.

12.19.15.17.14

January 5, 2009 — "Come on, guys," Simon said. Although argumentative as usual, he wasn't aggressively so. The trouble on New Year's Eve hadn't been brought up again, and Simon seemed to be making some concessions. Abby attributed it to the fact that he still had a week left before he had to return to the university; the others were just grateful for the reprieve.

"You're making predictions after the result is already known," he continued. "All you're doing is making the data fit your hypothesis."

"No," Dante said. "we're not *creating* facts to fit a pre-existing hypothesis; we're trying to write the hypothesis around the facts."

"Then we need to narrow it down," Simon said. "It's going on a year now, and we're still all over the board on this. We need to get a working hypothesis to start testing."

"That's what we're working on," Dominic said.

"For all the talking you people do, I'd have thought you'd have something by now. Damn, Abby, you sit out there and stare at the sky just about every night. Haven't you figured anything out yet?"

"Nothing that researchers before me haven't already come up with," she replied. "There are various conjunctions that would have been important to the Maya; the only problem is that none of them will occur in 2012."

"There has to be something," Simon insisted. He stood up and went to the bookshelf. Pulling down a book of star maps, he tossed it to Abby, who caught it in surprise. "Check the constellations again," he ordered. "There has to be something."

"We already have, Simon," Dominic said. His tone was steady, but stern; he wanted to stop Simon before he went off on another dictatorial rant.

"Well, you're obviously missing something. Have you checked back through the different Mayan ages? Have you looked for recurring patterns?"

"Yes," Dominic replied. "We looked for correlations between myths, archaeology, and astronomy. I've looked at a lot of alignments for the pyramids and structures, but I don't think have any bearing on it, like the Orion-Sphinx connection."

"The what?" Simon turned to Dominic, his forehead wrinkled.

"Some Egyptologists saw the similarities between the Giza pyramids and the stars on Orion's belt," Dominic explained. "They hypothesized that the position of the pyramids along the banks of the Nile were a reproduction of the stars of Orion's belt, positioned alongside the river of the Milky Way. Egyptian mythology told of a 'Golden Age,' a 'First Time.' It was part of the Egyptian creation myth. These researchers calculated back in time to find when the stars would have lined up exactly as the pyramids, to 10,500 BC. This was the same time, it turns out, when the Sun would have been in Leo — thus tying in the position and location of the Sphinx."

"Don't tell me you're going to try to prove the Sphinx is more than 12,000 years old," Simon said.

"I'm not trying to prove anything," Dominic answered. "I'm just telling you the story. The researchers in question weren't trying to prove the age of the Sphinx, either; they figured it was actually created when history says it was, as a monument to the First Time."

"Well, if they could count back to find Leo and date the Egyptian version of Genesis, we should be able to do the same thing with the Long Count and the *Popul Vuh*," Abby said.

"If there *is* such a connection," Dominic said. "There's not necessarily an astronomical connection to the Long Count that we could see in the form of a constellation or conjunction. After all, the Egyptologists were wrong."

"What? I thought you just said they dated it back to 10,500 BC."

"They did. Then independent researchers checked the numbers and found that the angles weren't a perfect match between the stars and the pyramids. The actual date they should have been looking at was 12,000 BC — and even then, it's not an exact match. Pushing the years back cancelled out the Leo/Sphinx connection. Besides — just because we see the constellation as Leo doesn't mean the Egyptians did. Constellation names are arbitrary between cultures."

"Well, that's what I'm talking about," Simon said. "Let's get *some*thing out there. Those Egyptologists were famous for their idea for a little while, at least. It'd be nice to at least have something to work with and put up for review."

"Well, what do you have to contribute?" Dante asked. His tone was light, but Simon turned to him with a glare.

"I'm working on several problems," he responded icily. "It's just hard to look at numbers with no context."

"I thought that's what mathematicians did," Dante answered.

Simon glared at him, but Dante just smiled.

Deciding to put a stop to the Simon-baiting for now, Dominic said: "Let me give you some context, then," he said. "Certain numbers to the Maya were considered magic, or at least meaningful: The number of the Earth is seven. The number of the heavens is nine, and the underworld is thirteen. See if you can work those into any of the cycles."

"Don't you think you waited long enough to give me this information?" Simon retorted. "Didn't you think it was pretty goddamn important?"

Tina stood up, drawing their attention before the fighting could get under way. "We do need to start putting things together," she said. "So far, all we've managed to do is exclude possibilities. We could exclude a thousand ideas and never be a step closer to knowing the real one. If we find something that sounds plausible and we can't disprove it, then we'll put it to the test on December 21st three years from now."

"We have to wait until the end of the freaking Count to test it?" Simon said. "How are we supposed to publish our findings if we can't prove our theory before hand?"

"Aside from the fact that a 'proven theory' is an oxymoron, I don't see how we're going to," Dominic said. "Sure, we can try to disprove it through testing; if we can't do it, then the odds are good that we're at least in the ballpark. But no matter what we come up with, the final test will be December 21, 2012. Whether we're right or wrong, there'll be no getting around it on December twenty-second."

"Then find us some shit to test," Simon said.

"I don't understand how you test something like this," Tina said. "We can't reproduce what actually happened."

"It doesn't have to be reproducible," Abby explained to her. "It's called predicting 'in principle.' All the prediction has to do is follow logically from the theory. You don't have to actually test or prove your theory, like, say, the eventual heat death of the universe. There's no way to test that until it happens. You just have to make predictions that explain the evidence, don't break any rules of physics or anything, and don't invoke the supernatural as an explanation. It doesn't mean that your theory is correct; just that your predictions based on it are."

"What's the point of that?"

Dominic shrugged. "It makes sense in a lot of fields, specifically physics. It's not within the bounds of possibility to test some theories, like Abby said, so scientists make predictions based on those theories. If the predictions are logical, and the results of the predictions come true, it gives the theory validity. Look at the theory of gravity; we can't prove it, as such, but we theorize as to how it would work, and so far, our predictions have always come through. From dropping objects off buildings to using gravity to slingshot spacecraft around other planets, gravity always follows the expected behavior."

Tina shook her head. "I don't know much about making predictions or finding facts that are falsifiable; just give me something to work with. That's all I'm asking for."

"We will," Dante assured her. "We just need somewhere to start from. So … anyone? Any ideas?"

Abby stood up. "Not a clue," she said. "I'm going for a walk. I want to clear my head and see if anything will come into it."

"Where are you going?" Dominic asked.

She shrugged. "Up the mountain, I guess. You said you've walked around to the other side and looked down on Izapa. Maybe I'll do that; I could use a good long hike."

"I'll go with you," he said, standing up. "We can talk about Mayan mythology a little more — you've been good at assigning astronomical notations to some of their stories."

"I'll come too," Tina said. "We might as well all try to put this together."

"Well, count me out," Dante said. He stretched out, putting a foot up on the bench across from him. "I'll have dinner waiting for you guys when you get back."

"We might be gone quite a while," Dominic said. "It'll probably be late tonight by the time we get back."

"Then you'd better pack a lunch," Dante said. "And a flashlight."

"I'll go make up a picnic for us," Tina said, turning to go back up to the house.

"What the hell is this, freaking family fun time?" Simon asked in irritation. "I'm sure as hell not climbing a mountain and hiking around in the woods after dark."

"You don't have to," Abby said. "I just wanted to go out by myself and try to straighten some things out in my head. Although anyone that wants to come along is welcome," she added quickly.

"You said we need to come up with a working hypothesis, and I agree," Dominic told Simon. "We've discussed every angle we could think of. We've been working for nine months now and can't come up with a starting point. Maybe a little physical exertion and a look at the Mayan countryside around the birthplace of the Count will help us out. At least it'll get some of us tossing ideas back and forth again, applying them as we can. You should think about joining us."

"Fuck that," Simon said. "I'm on vacation."

Before Dominic could respond, Dante stood up. "I am too," he said with a smile. "I don't think you guys need a geologist along for the mythology talk, do you?"

"Maybe," Abby said. "What if we see some geological feature that we need you to explain?"

"Take a picture of it," Dante answered. "I'm gonna go take a nap."

"Great," Simon said. "I guess I'll just sit here alone, then. I'm so glad I'm here for this."

"We invited you along," Dominic reminded him. "It's your choice to come be part of the group or to sit here on your own."

"Look," Simon said, irritated, "I work all week, then drive for hours to come back here every weekend. This is the first break I've had, and I'd like to sit around and relax for once. Is that too much to ask?"

"Not at all," Dominic said. "But don't blame us when you don't want to come along. It's your choice. No one is forcing you to come with us, and no one will complain if you don't."

"I'll bet you won't," Simon said. He looked over at Dante. "So it's just you and me today. You sure you haven't changed your mind about going with them?"

"And miss out on some quality time with you, Simon? Never."

Dominic had to turn away so they didn't see his smile. Dante would be fine, he knew. He didn't expect the two scientists to get any work done together while the others were gone, but it wouldn't hurt them to be left alone with each other, either.

"All right," Dominic said, clapping his hands together. "Let's get some supplies and get this show on the road."

Several hours later, they were high enough on the mountainside to begin traveling around to the side that would overlook Izapa. The three were already sweating, and the water bottles they'd brought along were half empty.

"I sure hope you know where you're going," Tina said.

Dominic shrugged. "I've been up here a couple times," he said. "I have a compass, and I've been marking the trees. We won't get lost."

"I hope not," she said. "I'm not too cool with spending the night up in these woods."

"Not to worry," he said. "Your trusty guide is in the lead."

They moved on through the thick underbrush; even on the mountainside, the jungle was overgrown and the going was relatively slow.

"You okay back there?" Dominic called.

Abby, bringing up the rear, simply nodded. She was moving slowly, not because she was tired or out of breath, but because she was watching the environment around them carefully. They were deep in the midst of the trees, and couldn't see anything out in any direction around them. From the condition of the jungle, she didn't think anyone had been through here since the ancient Maya, and very possibly, not even then.

"Is this the same way you came before?" she asked.

"It's the same general direction," he said. "I've passed some of my previous marks from my last trip up —I'm using a different symbol now on the trees so I don't get them confused and end up wandering around in circles — but it's not the exact same path. Last time I was up here it took me too long to get to a good viewing spot; I'm trying to cut the angle now so we get there quicker."

Abby nodded, looking around. "I don't see how in the world you can tell where you're going."

"I have a good sense of direction," he said. "And I'm an experienced hiker. Don't worry. We'll come out on the other side of these trees in about twenty minutes. There'll be a fairly sharp drop. If we follow it around the side, though, we'll come out on a pretty good-sized cliff. It's bare dirt and rocks; not the most comfortable spot for sitting, but there's a great view down over Izapa. There'll still be some tree cover — we're not directly above the site, so we're looking across and down, and the jungle is in between us. But you can see some of the highest monuments sticking out above the trees. It'll be good enough to see the general map of it."

They continued on in silence for awhile, following Dominic as he marked out trees and rocks, keeping moving in a straight line.

"You think Dante and Simon are okay back at the lab?" Tina finally asked.

"Dante can handle himself," Dominic said. "I wouldn't worry about him."

Towards evening, Dante returned to the lab to try to do some work. He was pleased to find it empty, but only moments later, he heard footsteps on the walk outside. Simon came in carrying a six pack of beer he had picked up from the back steps. Dante was reading his notebook, comparing his notes against a mythology book Dominic had given him. He didn't look up.

"So how long do you think they'll be gone?" Simon asked, sitting down heavily in the chair across from the computer.

"I don't know," Dante said, uninterested.

"Yeah, I know you don't *know*," Simon said, switching on the computer. "So what do you know, Dante? What do you guys talk about when I'm not here?"

Dante set down his book. "You know damn well what we talk about, Simon. You record all our conversations. You have access to all our notes."

"All of them?" Simon asked. He waited impatiently for the computer to boot up, uncapping a beer and tossing the cap across the desktop.

"Yes, Simon," Dante said. "I know you're paranoid as hell, but you have everything available to you that we've ever discussed. Everything work related, that is."

Simon was taken aback, but recovered quickly. "There aren't any notebooks I've never seen? Any discussions you've failed to record?"

Dante stared across the lab at him. "What the hell would the point of that be, Simon? You think we're going to sit here and pretend that we can't figure it out, then go running off without you? Trust me, no one wants you here anyway, except maybe Abby, and I can't even vouch for that. If we didn't need your help, you'd be gone already. So give me one reason it'd make sense to keep you out of the loop, when we'd be thrilled to just throw your ass out."

Simon paused, setting down his beer. "So you all hate me, huh?"

"Pretty much."

Simon looked stunned, then suddenly laughed. "Come on," he said, pulling another beer from the six-pack and tossing it to Dante, who caught it deftly. "Have a drink with me."

Dante cracked it open and took a long draw. "That's not the last of the beer, is it?" he asked.

Simon shook his head. "There's a whole case out there," he said. "I figured you could sit and drink it with me."

"I have work to do."

"Oh, come on. Just have a couple of beers and yap with me a while. Everyone always leaves when I show up."

"No," Dante said, "you're the one who always storms out. You're the one who refuses to sit and have a respectable conversation. You're the one who starts a fight every time we try to have any kind of discussion."

"Well, you have to admit, you guys don't seem particularly thrilled when I do hang around."

"Like I said, that's because we hate you," Dante said. He took another long drink. "Besides, we've always been honest and forthcoming with you. No one has ever avoided any topic of conversation, no matter how ridiculous it is."

"Well, do you think we're getting anywhere?"

"No," Dante replied. "No matter what we try, all we come back to is pseudoscientific bullshit. I'm starting to think there is no real answer to the Long Count. The Maya believed in cycles, that's all. Every calendar they had involved cycles; when one cycle ended, another would begin. The end of the Long Count isn't the real end; it's just the end of the current cycle."

"So you don't think the end of it is the end of the world," Simon said.

"Of course not," Dante said. "There's no reason the Maya would have been able to predict the end of the world. The closest they could have come would have been to calculate the arrival of some recurring event, and we have yet to find what that event was. So — anything else falls into the realm of prediction and prophecy. In the realm of science, that doesn't count for shit."

"Amen, brother," Simon said, tipping his beer towards Dante. He took a long swallow, finishing it off. "You need another?" he asked, pulling another bottle from the pack.

"Hit me," Dante said, reaching up to catch the bottle Simon tossed his way.

"So basically, there's no fame or fortune to be had off the interpretation of this shit?"

"There never was, Simon. Why do you think Dominic has always been so open and free with our work?"

"But if we figured out what it meant …"

"We'd publish the results," Dante interrupted. "If it was just a repetition of a non-lethal astronomical event, the scientific community would find it interesting. We could probably make a couple bucks on the lecture circuit, maybe hurry up and publish a book before the end of 2012. There'd be some publicity, but interest would pass soon enough.

It'd just be another footnote in the history books, the last chapter on the Long Count in the Mayan texts."

"But not if it was a *life-threatening* event," Simon said, thoughtfully tapping the mouth of his bottle against his teeth. "If it was something catastrophic, they couldn't book us fast enough. People would be falling all over themselves, competing to get us on their shows. The money would come rolling in. The book deals, the lecture circuit ... I'd be addressing sold out houses every night, all over the world."

"And if pigs had wings, I suppose they'd fly," Dante replied. "Keep dreaming, Simon. Fact is, we haven't found shit. At this point, all our research points to one thing: nothing."

"Maybe we haven't looked hard enough," Simon argued. "Maybe we're looking in the wrong place."

"That very well may be true," Dante conceded. "But even if we haven't found exactly what it means, we've pretty much eliminated the possibility that it's going to be catastrophic. The end of the Count is three years away. Any geological event that had been building for well over five thousand years would be reaching its culmination now; we have no signs of anything coming. There are some events — potentially cataclysmic events — that we know of, like the Yellowstone Caldera in Wyoming. It erupts about every twenty thousand years, and it's close to fifty thousand years overdue. It's a supervolcano, and if it were to go off, it would bury pretty much the entire western half of the U.S. in ash – not to mention fill the entire Earth's atmosphere with poisonous gasses.

"But the Maya would have no way of knowing about that, and besides, it doesn't fit into the timescale of the Long Count. Although," Dante said thoughtfully, "Dominic says the Great Cycle — the Long Count itself — is only one Mayan creation cycle. They actually count all the way back to the Big Bang."

"Oh, fucking come on," Simon said. "Before the Earth even existed?"

Dante shrugged. "They've been measuring time for a long time, Simon. Maybe they counted back to the beginning of it. And as far as we know, to the end." He considered for a moment, then picked up again where he had left off. "We know that earthquakes occur without warning, but if there was one coming that the Maya knew about, they'd have to have an awareness of plate tectonics like we don't even have today. We've never been able to predict an earthquake. As for any other type of catastrophic event that'd be coming, there should be signs. There are no signs. Unless you count flooding or destruction of the atmosphere and climate from global warming, but the Maya couldn't have possibly known about that.

"And as far as death coming from above, it looks like that's a bust, too. Any type of comet, asteroid, or whatever coming at us to wipe out life on Earth would be visible in the sky by now. There's a lot of activity up there, but as far as the death-planet approaching, the sky looks pretty empty."

"What about that stupid Nibu — whatever you called it."

"Nibiru," Dante responded. "That's what I'm talking about. If a big-ass planet was re-entering our solar system, not only would the thousands of professional astronomers worldwide studying the universe have found it long ago, but by now every kid with a backyard telescope would see it. Hell, you could probably see it with the naked eye. Abby said that by the end of this year, it'd be the brightest object in the sky besides the sun and the moon. Brighter than Venus."

"How about the alien bullshit Dominic was babbling about? That whole ancient advanced civilization thing?"

Dante shook his head. "First of all, the 'evidence' there is for that is scant, and when tested, usually found to be incorrect. Second, we don't have the resources to investigate it," he said. "We have a couple archaeologists and an anthropologist, and we could study it pretty in depth. But not from here. They'd have to do some serious traveling, study a lot of things firsthand, and compile resources from museums and universities around the world. I don't think Dominic and Tina are interested in doing that. Hell, I don't think there's any group of professional researchers in the world prepared to do that – not based on the lousy evidence that would even support such a hypothesis."

"Yeah?" Simon asked. He shook his bottle, but it was empty. He reached for another, then tossed the last beer to Dante. "At least it's a hell of a lot more interesting than just back-dating the pyramids to reach some kind of astronomical alignment. And alien visitation is pretty hard to disprove."

"Not hard to disprove – impossible," Dante said. "Don't forget that you can't prove a negative. Can we prove that the ancient Indians could fly? Sure, if we find an ancient flying machine. Can we prove that they couldn't fly? No. We can spend the rest of our lives searching for that flying machine and never find it, and thereby assume, through the lack of evidence and common sense, that they didn't have any advanced technology and could not fly. But we can't *prove* that they couldn't. Hell, remember the WMD fiasco from the Iraq war a few years ago? No matter how long we went without finding any, we still couldn't *prove* they didn't exist. To prove that Saddam Hussein had a weapons of mass destruction program, we only had to find one. One bomb, one vial of anthrax, that's all it would take. But to disprove it? There's no amount of evidence that could do that. Hussein's scientists and ministers denied it; we found no evidence for it. Yet, there's no way to disprove it — after all, there was always the chance that the WMDs existed; we just hadn't found them yet."

Simon didn't answer. He stood up and went to the door, pushing open the screen and reaching out. When he came back in, he was carrying the case of beer.

"You *are* planning on drinking all of that, aren't you?" Dante asked.

"Maybe. I only have a week left before I'm back into the same old grind of teaching and traveling, testing and grading. Fuck it. I'm relaxing while I can."

"Congratulations," Dante said. He set his bottle down, then flipped his notebook open again.

Simon took a long drink. "All that bullshit we talked about earlier — the nuclear war, the solidified buildings, whatever you called them —."

"Vitrified."

"Yeah, vitrified. Did someone write all that down?"

"Tina always keeps notes from our discussions. I haven't looked at that one in particular, but I'm sure she did."

Simon got up again and went over to the bookshelf. He picked up the large stack of notebooks they had filled with their meeting notes.

Dante glanced up at him, curious, but he didn't ask. Simon returned to his seat at the computer and began leafing through the notebooks, trying to find the right dates.

Dante began comparing his notes against the mythology book again, and the lab fell back into silence. Periodically, he glanced up, watching Simon as he read the notebooks, studying each one seriously. Dante didn't understand Simon's sudden interest in what he had always considered pointless bullshit, but he was grateful at least for the silence.

"Hey guys, I don't want to be up here all night."

"The viewing is going to be fantastic, though," Abby said. She glanced at the other woman, but paused when she saw how nervous Tina was. "Okay," she said reluctantly. "I guess we'll head back."

"Why don't you stay?" Tina asked.

"I don't know if I could make my way back down in the dark." Abby said.

Dominic was thoughtful. "Maybe I could walk Tina most of the way down the mountain — at least get her out of the woods and back on the pathway down. Then I could come back for you."

"You'd be walking for hours, though. You don't have to do that, Dominic; we've already been stomping through these woods all day."

He shrugged. "I don't mind. What else do I have to do?"

"I don't want you hurting yourself," Abby said. "You'll be so tired. Why don't you walk Tina back tonight? I can sleep out here. You can come get me in the morning."

"You know what I'd get from Simon for that? He'd kill me when he found out I left you up here alone."

"You guys go ahead," Abby said. "I'll deal with Simon."

"Yeah, tomorrow," Tina said. "We'll have to put up with him tonight."

"I trust you guys are capable of handling him," Abby said. "Neither of you have ever balked before at standing up to him."

Tina looked surprised. "No, neither of us have a problem with it. But do you?"

"I've lived with Simon and his attitude for going on five years now. Don't worry about me."

"Okay," Tina said. "If you think you'll be all right ..."

"I'll be fine," Abby answered. She crossed over to the edge of the outcrop they were standing near, looking out over the valley below. It was growing dusk, and she could just see the lights of the house and lab, dim specks on the landscape far below. She tossed a smile back at Dominic. "Just don't forget to come get me in the morning. I can probably find my way, but I'd rather not take any chances. If I get lost, you'll never find me."

"Then don't move from here," Dominic said. He slipped out of his overshirt, the one Abby had bought for him for Christmas, and handed it to her. "It shouldn't be too cold tonight — maybe mid-fifties or so — but you never know. I wish we all had sat phones or walkie-talkies or something."

Abby took the warm hemp shirt with thanks. "I'll be okay, Dominic. I'm going to be up most of the night anyway, stargazing. I'll be alert to anything out here. Don't worry about me."

"Well, just don't fall off that cliff," Tina said, nodding towards the edge.

They said their good-byes, and Tina and Dominic finally left.

"You think she'll be okay?" Tina asked when they were out of earshot.

"Of course," Dominic said. "There's no one around, and no dangerous animals that she doesn't know to watch out for. She should be fine. But I'm not going to leave her alone."

"You're going back up there?"

He nodded. "You were right. Simon wouldn't let me hear the end of it if anything happened to her. He acts like she's not bright enough or mature enough to make her own decisions about what to do and where to do it, and he's managed to convince her of it, too. She's just recently started becoming more independent from him, and I'm more than happy to encourage it. I trust her to do all right by herself, but still — I'd feel more secure about it if were with her. And I really don't want to listen to Simon's ranting all night."

"What do you think he'll do when he finds out you're up there spending the night with her?" Tina asked.

"Oh come on," Dominic said. "He leaves me alone with her four to five nights a week. If anything were going to happen between us, there's been plenty of opportunity for it."

"And *has* anything happened?" Tina asked lightly.

Dominic shrugged. "Doesn't matter. Not as long as she's still attached to him."

Tina shook her head. "I'll never understand that," she said. "What would cause an otherwise intelligent woman to be so dependant, so enslaved to anyone? Especially to such a piece of work like Simon."

"People are complicated," Dominic said simply.

They headed back towards the house, picking their way along carefully, following the notches Dominic had previously made in the trees, illuminated by his flashlight. When they reached the clear spot on the mountainside leading back down to the valley, they stopped.

"Are you going to be okay from here?" he asked.

Tina shone her light down the hill. "I think so," she said. "It's just straight down, right? It'll take me into that small grove of trees and then out into Abby's clearing?"

"That's right," he responded. "It should take you about an hour to get down from here, then it's just a straight shot back to the lab."

"Okay," she said, a bit hesitantly. "I guess I have to explain it to Simon, then."

"Just tell him you lost us," he said. "He'll probably be overjoyed to think I'm lost somewhere up on the mountainside."

Tina laughed. "You'd never hear the end of it. Neither would Abby," she added more seriously. "I'd prefer not to even open that one up to him."

"Agreed," Dominic said. "Anyway, it's already late. He's usually in bed by midnight. Maybe if you walk slowly enough, you'll miss him."

She laughed again. "Screw that; I'm starving. He can bitch at me while I eat dinner."

Dominic gave her a quick hug. "Be careful," he said. "It's a pretty easy walk down, but still — there are some loose rocks and a few slick spots. Not to mention the snakes, bats, and whatever else you might run across. Just keep your light moving and your eyes open."

"Great," she said. "I could've done without the reminder about the wild things."

"You'll be fine," he reassured her. "Just be careful."

"Not a problem," she answered, and with a wave, headed off down the mountain.

Dominic watched her for a moment, making sure she was on the right path, and then turned back the way from which they had come. A second later, he had disappeared into the darkness.

It was a good two hours before he came out onto the rocky outcropping where Abby sat, her back to him, watching the sky. Dominic had moved almost silently through the woods, and when she heard his footsteps on the rocks behind her, she jumped.

"Sorry," he said softly, lowering himself beside her. "I didn't mean to startle you."

"I thought you weren't coming back until morning."

He shrugged. "A few hours either way didn't seem to make much difference."

"It's nice to have you," she said, "but I'm a little worried about what Simon's going to think." She paused, and he could hear her nervousness when she spoke again. "Maybe we should go on and head back."

"It's too dark now," Dominic said. "It'll be a three hour walk in the daylight; it would take at least twice that long to do it tonight."

"I'm just concerned about what Simon is going to think," she repeated.

"I'll deal with him."

She sighed. "At some point, Dominic, I suppose I should."

"That's up to you," he said.

"Dominic ..."

He glanced over at her, her features barely visible in the darkness.

"Well ... aren't you concerned about the direction things are going?"

"With what? The Long Count? Us?"

"Everything."

"Why worry about things you can't control? I mean, everything is just going to happen anyway."

"Dominic, be serious."

"I am. Of course I care about the future, Abby. There are things I want, but you can't force them. Things have to happen in their own time. You can't make things happen before their time."

"But don't you think it's important to prepare for them?"

"Sure, if that's what you're doing. Are you? Or are you just dwelling on things and feeling hopeless? There's a big difference between thinking through a problem and creating a plan of action, and just fretting about it."

"I do worry too much, don't I?"

He smiled and put an arm around her shoulders. "You worry because you're you, Abby. If that's what it takes you to make the decisions you need to, then go for it. I personally don't think it's healthy, but it's not me. I'm not going to tell you what to do, and I'm sure as hell not going to tell you how to think."

"That's refreshing."

"Abby … if you want me to leave so you don't have to answer to Simon tomorrow, I will."

"No," she said. "Please stay. You're right — things will happen in their own time. I've been fighting them. I guess it's time to let things start to run their course."

He kissed her lightly on top of the head. "Then forget about Simon for tonight. Tell me what we're looking at here."

Abby slid away from him a bit, leaning over to unzip her backpack. She pulled out a few star maps, bound in spiral-bound books. "Okay," she said, opening one. "We're going to search the constellations as they appear over Izapa. I've got charts of the same view going back about a thousand years. I haven't been able to get my hands on anything older than that. Either I'll have to order some through some of my connections, or it'll have to wait until we leave here. But hopefully these patterns will start making sense after awhile; maybe something will strike you. I'll show you the stars, you tell me the mythology behind them."

"All right," Dominic said, holding out a map at arm's length. Abby shone her flashlight on it.

"Flip it," she said. "Astronomical maps are south-up orientated."

He did so, then glanced over top of it at the view above them.

"I still don't know what I'm looking at."

Abby pointed out the various constellations and the major points.

"Most of these aren't of any great importance in Mayan myth," Dominic commented. "The stars had some symbolism, but most important were the planets, and the sun and the moon."

"What can you tell me about them that would relate to the Long Count?" Abby asked.

Dominic sat back, propping himself up on his arms. "Let me see," he said. "Well, you know the Count is based on the moon. To the Maya, the moon was a goddess, Ix Chel. She was supposed to be a protector of women in childbirth, and she carried a jug of water that she could pour onto the earth to cause rainstorms and floods."

"Floods ... that's interesting," Abby noted.

Dominic shrugged. "That wasn't her sole purpose," he said. "There was another rain god, Xib Chac, or Chac Mool. He was a benevolent god, and had many sacrifices made to him year round."

"Human, I assume?"

Dominic smiled. "Unfortunately. Slaves and children, mostly."

"That's so awful," Abby said.

"That was life in the Mayan world," he said. "The priests would sacrifice a victim while a Chilam — a visionary — would receive prophecies from the gods, which the priests would then interpret."

"Too bad none of them ever advised that they should stop killing children."

Dominic rubbed her back. "You asked about the moon, not about the ceremonies," he said. "The phases of the moon influenced life on Earth, and human actions. Kind of like modern astrology, or lunatics that think their emotions and psychological impulses are affected by whatever stage the moon happens to be at."

"What else?" Abby asked. She searched the sky. "You mentioned the planets."

"Yes," Dominic said. "Venus was the most important. The Maya knew the Venus cycle down almost to the precise day. They had it calculated at 584 days."

"It's actually 583.92 days," Abby said.

Dominic nodded, then remembered that she couldn't see him behind her. "That's right," he said. "They knew the synodic cycle; they knew Venus' correlation with the movements of the sun. It was so important that they built the openings of their buildings — doorways, windows, whatever — along the sightline of Venus. We haven't had a chance to go to Uxmal, but I'd like to take you there. Every building on that site is aligned to the same direction."

"Why the fascination with Venus?" Abby asked. "Is it because it's the brightest object in the sky other than the sun and moon? Because it's the morning star?"

"And because it represented Kulkulcan."

"Really?" she said, turning to him in surprise.

"Really."

She turned back to the sky, comparing it against her chart. "So the Maya thought Kulkulcan would return, just like Venus?"

"Perhaps so. But instead of every 584 days, every 5,126 years?"

Abby mused silently for a bit. She sat back, settling down beside him. "So the planets, sun and moon were gods. But I want to hear stories. What can you tell me about the constellations?"

Dominic put his arm around her. "You want stories, I've got stories," he said. "Sit back, relax, and let me tell them."

Tina was surprised to hear voices as she came across the clearing; the night was cool, and earlier in the day, neither Dante nor Simon had seemed interested in leaving the lab. It was now close to midnight, and she could hear the two men talking as they stood on the path above the lagoon, staring down at the moonlit water. She slowed down, trying not to make any sound as she made her way through the high grass, straining to hear them. Their voices carried on the light breeze that had kicked up.

"So why'd you bring me out here?" Dante was asking.

"You guys seem to spend a lot of time out here. I want to see what the attraction is."

"The attraction is one hundred degree heat, cool water, and Tina and Abby in their bathing suits. Standing out here with you on a cool night just doesn't have the same effect."

Before Simon could respond, Dante raised his head. "Did you hear something?" He turned around and spotted the beam from Tina's flashlight skimming across the edge of the path.

"Hey," he called, heading towards the light. "It's about time you guys got back!"

"Actually, I'm on my own," she said, coming out of the clearing and onto the path. "Abby wanted to stay up on the mountainside and watch the constellations over Izapa."

"And Ciriello?" Simon asked. His tone was unreadable.

"He stayed to watch out for her. He mentioned a discussion you'd had with him over the summer about leaving Abby out in the woods alone."

"That son of ..." He stopped. "Fine," he said. "I'm going to bed."

Tina stopped beside Dante, and they watched as Simon went back up towards the lab and the house. When he was out of earshot, Tina took Dante's hand.

"What were you guys doing out here?" she asked.

"Honestly, I don't know," he answered. Slowly, they began making their way back up towards the lab. "We were sitting in the lab bullshitting, and he said he wanted to show me something out by the lagoon. Said it was something he and Steve were discussing the night Steve died.'

"You're kidding me," Tina said.

"I kid you not. I asked him if he had been out by the lagoon with Steve that night, but he wouldn't answer. I don't know, Tina. He's got me a little freaked out. I'm starting to think he might have had something to do with it."

"You don't think he pushed him? Or hit him in the head with something and rolled him down there?"

"I don't know. But being alone with him in the lab tonight really introduced me to the real Simon. I mean, he's definitely the asshole we know and despise, but there's something underneath it. Something unbalanced, I think."

"What does he want?" Tina asked. She lowered her voice as they crossed the courtyard. "Credit?"

"More than that. He wants it all. Credit for doing it, fame from promoting it, and whatever fortune he can rake in from it. And God help anyone that gets in his way."

Tina didn't answer for a moment. They stopped outside the lab, and Dante glanced in to make sure it was empty. Simon had gone up to the house.

"I'm really surprised he didn't have a bigger reaction to Dominic and Abby spending the night up on the mountain," she finally said.

"Yeah, I don't know what's up with him. He's either too distracted by what he and I were talking about earlier, or he's keeping it under control pretty well. I can't imagine that if he's boiling over with rage, he's going to share it with us."

"Maybe he figures hey, he's screwing around, so she might as well, too."

"No, I can't see that coming from Simon. Whatever he does is justified, but Abby has to put up with it, and follow his rules. He's sure as hell not going to give her release to run around on him."

"What exactly do you think *is* going on up on the mountain?"

"I don't know," Dante said, suddenly scooping her into his arms, "but why don't we go to bed and talk about it?"

"Talk?"

"Whatever," he said. Tina pulled open the door and they went in, crossing the empty lab and heading back up towards the house.

12.19.16.1.1

February 1, 2009 — Abby and Dominic were quiet, studying in silence. Simon had left about twenty minutes earlier, having griped about the chill air and headed back up to the house for a hot shower. They were enjoying the relaxed atmosphere without him, but knew it wouldn't last long. Abby knew that if she didn't follow him up to the house within the hour, he'd either come back down to the lab and throw a fit, or sit up at the house and pout all night, then give her hell when she did come up.

Abby got up and went to the window, staring silently at the darkness outside. After a few long moments, Dominic noticed and looked up.

"Everything okay?" he asked.

"Have you ever used a gun?"

"Me?" Dominic said in surprise. "Hell no. I wouldn't even know what to do with one. I'd probably shoot myself in the ass with it or something."

Abby smiled, but it was a worried one.

"What's wrong?" Dominic asked, his brow furrowed with concern. "Why are you asking?"

"Simon has one."

Dominic stopped. "He what?"

She came back to the table and sat down beside him. "I saw it in his suitcase when he came back the other night. I thought I'd help him unpack, you know. I reached for the shirt he had lying on top and he grabbed my wrist, told me to stay out of his things. I guess I kind of jumped back, and the suitcase shifted on the bed. I saw just the butt of it sticking out from under his clothes.

"I didn't say anything, just pretended I hadn't seen it. I was afraid to draw attention to it. He obviously doesn't want me to know he has it."

What do you think he's going to do with it?"

Abby shook her head, her dark hair flopping across her face. Dominic reached out and pushed a lock of it across her forehead, his touch lingering for a moment as he tucked the stray hair behind her ear.

"I don't have any idea," she said, her skin tingling where his fingers had been. "I hope he hasn't noticed ... well ... *us*. He *is* getting awful possessive of this project. But I can't imagine he's going to hurt anyone."

Dominic frowned. "He hasn't been as argumentative lately, but he has seemed more rushed. More insistent."

"Exactly," Abby nodded. "So while I don't think he'd kill us all and run off with the answer, if we find it — I don't know what he's planning."

"Well," Dominic said, "I'm uneasy as hell about someone bringing a gun in here. I'll keep an eye on him. I don't want him to know I know about it — it's already been an 'us against Simon' thing, and I don't want to make him even more paranoid. I don't want him to think he has any reason to use it."

Abby nodded. "I agree. I keep thinking — I don't know, maybe it's just a power thing. He's always needed something to make him feel important: His professorship and his tenure, his published articles, me ..." Her voice trailed off.

Dominic gave her a sidelong glance, then smiled. He put a hand on her knee.

"Just watch yourself," he said. "You're the only ally he thinks he has here, and I think he knows he's losing you. You don't jump and run to his every beck and call anymore. You spend more and more time with the three of us, and now you're usually with me, even when he comes back for the weekend. You laugh easier, you smile more, and that scared expression, that *'what is he going to jump on me for next?'* look is gone from your eyes. For the most part."

He shrugged. "Anyway," he said. "All I'm saying is, be careful. Simon thinks you're all he has, and if he starts thinking he lost you, he could be unpredictable."

"He *is* unpredictable," Abby said.

"Yeah," Dominic agreed, "and now he has a gun."

12.19.16.2.0

February 20, 2009 — "The numbers really are fascinating," Dominic said, sitting on the edge of the lab table. "The Maya, or the Olmecs before them, calculated the solar year the closest it's ever been calculated, at least until modern times. We know now that it's actually 365.2422 days; the Maya had it calculated out to 365.2420 days. Pretty damn good, for what they had to work with."

"Wait a minute," Simon said, "what do you mean, 'the Olmecs before them'?"

"There's a remote – and I mean very, very remote – possibility that the calendars may not have been created by the Maya after all."

"*What?*"

Dominic stood up and went to the windows. He stood with his back to them as he explained. "Long before the Maya, there was a mysterious culture called the Olmecs. No one knows much about them. Some theorize that they were actually some of the missing tribes of China that managed to cross the pacific to land in North America. The few relics we have from their culture give some evidence toward it, from their writing to the Chinese pyramids.

"The pottery and artwork are also extremely similar between the Shang culture of China and the Olmecs. And since the Shang dynasty ended around 1600 BCE, and the Olmec culture began around 1500 BCE, it's interesting to contemplate. The ocean currents were exactly right at that time to have brought unpowered boats from China right to the Western coast of Mexico.

"We don't know much about them, but the Olmec culture is a fascinating one. They were the first to develop a sacred Almanac, with 260 days. But, there are a lot of shadows around the Olmecs; like we said, we don't know who they were, where they came from, or where they went. The few relics we have are over 3,500 years old.

"As far as we know, the Olmecs just happened to inhabit some of the same areas where the Maya later built their cities. That it was they who created the calendars and not the Maya is only speculation; there's no supporting evidence, archaeological evidence shows that it was the Maya."

"But we could be basing all our research on a flawed foundation," Simon argued.

Dominic sighed. "The fact is," he said, "We don't know shit. We don't know intentions of the creators of the Long Count. We don't know what they were thinking or planning. Basically, the only thing we have to go on is the Count itself. Anything else is guesswork, but we assume the Maya created the Long Count because they used Long Count dating throughout their recorded history."

"Again with false logic," Simon said. "If it was something that had been created and used by their ancestors, they might still use it."

Tina interrupted. "There's no evidence that the Olmecs were related to the Maya."

"There's no evidence of goddamn *any*thing," Simon argued. "Everything we've done so far is speculation; when I ask for some hard evidence, it all falls to shit."

"Well, for God's sake, Simon, talk about a cold case," Dante said, "We're researching something that's thousands of years old. Most of the evidence we're looking for has been destroyed, lost long ago to time and weather and war and grave robbers."

"Or maybe it never existed at all."

Dominic sat down heavily on the bench. "So what are you saying, Simon? What do you want us to do? Manufacture evidence? You know what we have to work with. We work with it or we don't. It's there or it's not."

"Well, it's sure not a hell of a lot to go on."

"You knew that coming in."

"No, I didn't. I assumed you people knew what the hell you were doing. I heard you had a group of researchers put together; I thought this was well-researched, well-thought out, and well-planned."

"And whose fault is that?" Dominic asked. "You claim to be so big on research, but you didn't do any yourself?"

"Look, I trusted Abby. She brought this to my attention; I assumed she did the necessary background checking on it."

Dominic stood up suddenly, looming large and menacing over the smaller man sitting across from him. "Don't even blame this on Abby," he said.

Simon stood up too, and this time he didn't back down.

"And don't you defend her," Simon said. "She got me into this bullshit, so I'll damn well blame her for it."

"Nothing is ever your fault, is it, Simon?" Dominic started around the table towards him.

"Dominic, don't," Abby said, sitting tensely on her seat across the room. Her hands were clenched together so tightly they were shaking.

He glanced towards her, and Simon danced back away from him.

"Come on, Ciriello," he said. "You've got my fiancée on your side now. You want to talk about that?"

"Simon –"

"Shut up, Abby," he snapped. "You got me into this shit, and now you're siding with him. I'll deal with you next."

"The hell you will," Dominic said.

"God damn it, enough all ready. That's enough out of both of you," Tina said suddenly. "This is ridiculous. You two want to beat each other's asses? Fine. Take it outside and knock yourselves out. Or knock each other out. But enough petty bullshit. Simon, you're being an asshole. Dominic, you're being an idiot. Both of you — you're acting like a couple teenage boys. I've had enough with the ego-clashing already; if you're going to fight it out, then do it already, but then can we please get back to work?"

Dominic paused, then stopped, running both hands through his thick dark hair. "Okay," he said. "All right. Tina, you're right. I'm sorry. Fighting isn't getting us anywhere. I'm going outside to cool off a little bit."

"Yeah, you would do that. Run away…"

"Shut the fuck up, would you?" Dante said suddenly. His tone had an edge of finality to it.

"Fine, then," Simon said. "Abby, come upstairs with me. If anyone wants to continue this, you know where to find me. And you just might get more than you bargained for. I think I've had about enough of dealing with this shit."

"Is that a threat?" Dante asked. He and Simon locked eyes, and when Simon turned away first, it was with a smirk.

"Come on, Abby. Get upstairs. The others might defend you, but you know damn well this is your fault."

"Abby, don't go," Dominic said.

She gave him a guilty look, still wringing her hands. "It's okay," she said, standing up.

"Come on," Simon said, heading towards the door. He didn't look back to make sure she was following, but he knew she was, her head bowed. She didn't glance up at the others as she left.

"FUCK," Dominic said suddenly, turning and hitting the wall hard, open-handed. The whole lab shook.

"Shit, man. Watch your hand," Dante commented.

"My hand is fine. This is bullshit."

Tina went to his side, putting a hand on his back. "Why don't you ask him to leave?" she asked. "He hasn't done much for us anyway. I don't see why we need him."

"Galileo said, 'The Book of Nature is written in mathematical symbols,'" Dominic said.

"Great, so let him decipher nature for us. He hasn't done shit with the Long Count."

Dominic smiled in spite of himself. He turned and gave her a quick hug. "I'm going for a walk," he said. "If I don't head in the other direction, I'm going to go up to the house and strangle him."

"And you want us to do what, talk you out of it?" Dante asked.

Dominic flashed him a grin, patted Tina on the shoulder, and moved out past them, going out the screen door to the yard.

"Jesus," Dante said. "Are you starting to think this is more trouble than it's worth?"

Tina went and sat beside him. "It *is* getting a little rough."

"How much longer do you want to do this?"

She sighed. "I don't know. When Steve and I came here, we planned to be in it for the long haul. Here we are now, nearly a year later, and we haven't gotten one bit closer to the answer than we were when we showed up. We've already lost Steve, and I don't like the direction things are going with Simon and Dominic, with Abby stuck in the middle. I get a real uneasy feeling that something serious is going to happen, and I don't want to be around for it. Dominic is my friend and I love him, but I can't sit by and watch this."

Dante put his arm around her. "I'm with you on that," he said. "And frankly, I don't see us making any more progress on the Count, either. I have a lot of hobbies, but beating my head against the wall isn't one of them. Every day, this seems more and more like a waste of time."

"Then let's make better use of our time," Tina suggested with a wink. "Simon and Abby are probably fighting up at the house, and Dominic's gone God knows where ... looks like we have the lab to ourselves."

"That we do," Dante smiled. He gave her a kiss. "That we do."

12.19.16.2.1

February 21, 2009 — "The Long Count isn't really a calendar, is it?"
Abby asked. The rain was falling outside, and they were spread
throughout the lab, each working on their various projects.

"What do you mean?" Dominic asked, looking up. Abby was
standing by the cork board next to the bookshelf, examining some of the
printouts Dominic had hung of Mayan glyphs.

"It's more of a timescale," she said, pulling one down and
studying it. "Mayan inscriptions give dates, right? Dates of wars, of kings
rising to and falling from power, ground-breaking for cities?"

Dominic nodded. "Ceremonies, the end of a major event, even
an accusation against a ruler — the glyphs mark everything that was
important to the Maya, everything they wanted to be noted for posterity."

"So all these events — they're all recorded in Long Count
notation. It was simply a way of keeping time."

"Then why does it end?" Dominic asked with a smile.

Abby smiled back. "It always takes us back to that, doesn't it?"

From his seat at the computer desk, Simon laid down his book
and leaned back, watching them. He didn't say anything as Dominic stood
up and went to Abby's side. He took the picture from her hand and
pointed to one of the carvings.

"The Mouth of the Jaguar represents the entrance to the
Underworld," he said. "It's the portal between the realms of the living and
the dead."

"Hmm." Abby studied the picture. "What was their belief about
death?"

"Remember the legend about the Hero Twins? They were
supposed to have visited the Underworld and freed the souls who were
trapped there. In a sense, they killed Death, and the Underworld was no
longer a place to be feared."

Abby took the picture back and tacked it to the bulletin board
again.

"I'll never figure these out," she said. "They're worse than
hieroglyphics; at least with those I can make a distinction between the
different pictures. These all look the same to me."

"You just have to know how to read them," Dominic explained.
"Tina, how long did it take you to figure these out?"

"Forever," she laughed. "The subtleties in them are amazing. For
the longest time I thought all the curlicues were just for effect; I didn't
realize just how integral they are to the design, how they change and
enforce the meanings."

"We still can't read them precisely," Dominic said. "By we, I don't just mean Tina and me; I mean Mayan researchers in general. Most Mayan texts were burned in the 1500s by a Spanish Bishop, Diego de Lauda, after Spain conquered Mexico. Without a codex to go on, researchers have spent decades trying to interpret the glyphs. They're astoundingly complex — each one has at least three or four different symbols — and the meanings can be either symbolic or literal. Some are detailed histories of Mayan wars and ceremonies; others are mythological, like the Jaguar's mouth."

Abby was examining some of the others. "You picked some weird ones to print out," she said. She pointed at one. "What's this?"

"You were talking about the Long Count being a timescale," he said. "Some of the time-keeping glyphs have places as well as dates, to show not just when, but where the event occurred."

Dominic went to the board. He quickly sketched a larger, rough facsimile of the relevant glyph. "Mayan creation events specifically mention a hole in the sky. The place-glyph of zero-time is actually translated as a black hole. The Mayan creation event, or birth event, occurred at the black hole."

"It looks like a chair," Dante commented.

"It's a throne," Dominic explained.

"So what the hell does the black hole represent?" Simon asked. "Why would they be putting a black hole in their carvings?"

"The black hole is the portal to the Otherworld," Dominic said. "The galactic center is the astronomical birthplace of the Maya."

"So zero-time is a place?" Abby asked. She sat down on the edge of the lab table. "Okay, Dominic, so what is this about? Time, or space?"

"Both, I think," he replied. He turned to the board again, finishing up the glyph.

"I think it revolves around the Galactic Center," Dominic said, indicating the glyph on the board. "Zero Time is the black hole at the center of the universe."

Abby shook her head. "I don't know what it could mean, though, Dominic. We've determined that there are no related alignments scheduled to occur on that date — or even that year. The universe is random and chaotic, sure; an asteroid could blast through there, or a comet; but the Maya couldn't have predicted random events. The universe is also extremely steady and methodical, and nothing that we know of is going to occur near the Galactic Center in 2012."

"Those are the key words," Dominic smiled. "*Nothing that we know of.*' Don't forget — the center is located not just in space, but in time."

"What does that mean?" Simon asked. He folded his arms, leaning back against the wall. He regarded the others. "You said earlier that this was about both space *and* time. What do you mean?"

"I think they're coordinates," Dominic said. "We live in three dimensions, plus one."

"Time," Abby stated. She smiled. "You think they were giving us directions."

"Think about this," Dominic said. He stood up and began to pace, gesturing as he spoke. "The Mayan god-man Kulkulcan descended from the sky via a snake chain. I'm going to venture to say the Maya described wormholes this way — after all, why would they call them wormholes? That's a modern description and a modern term. If Kulkulcan was trying to explain the concept to the ancient Maya, maybe his best way to communicate it was to point out the similarity to the local jungle snakes.

"At the time he came through, the alignment was right for him to travel through the Galactic Center; whatever had to fall into place to complete the right timing, did, opening the portal and allowing this method of travel."

"What's the point of designing a system of transit that's good only once every several thousand years?" Simon asked.

"Time doesn't matter when traveling through wormholes. Look at the length of time the Maya assigned to the lives of their gods. I mean, they were hundreds, even thousands of years old. Other cultures did the same; if Steve were here, he would easily cite examples from the Bible of people who lived for nearly a thousand years; Methusalah was 969 years old; Noah, 950. Even Adam supposedly lived for 930 years *after* he ate the forbidden fruit. If someone was traveling from another part of the galaxy, it wouldn't mean that time would be on the same scale on this end."

"How does that work?" Tina asked.

"It's a little hard to explain," Abby admitted. "It's called the twin paradox. It has to do with relativity, and the different kinds of time."

"Am I going to be sorry I asked?"

Abby smiled. "I'll try to keep it short and simple," she said. "Einstein theorized general relativity. It's the theory of gravitation, and describes motion near massive objects; stars, planets, black holes.

"Special relativity, on the other hand," she continued, "describes things when they're moving very fast. This is where the twin paradox comes in. Say you have two identical twins; one is a homebody, the other an interstellar explorer. So one twin stays on Earth and ages normally, while the other twin travels to a distant star and back. Because the twin that's traveling is moving at light speed, time is much different for him. At the speed he's going, he can reach a distant star and return in what to him is, let's say, only a matter of months. Meanwhile, back on Earth, decades, if not centuries, have passed. The twin that stayed at home is limited to the laws of Earth-time and is long gone. Meanwhile, the twin speeding through outer space has hardly aged at all. So, if a visitor to here were to come and go, to us, they'd barely appear to be aging; but here on Earth, hundreds of years would pass between sightings. When a future generation saw the same visitor their ancestors wrote about, they could only assume that the visitor was hundreds of years old."

"That's amazing," Tina said.

"It's one of the physical laws of the universe," Abby said. "And it *is* something that we consider when we debate about the future of human explorers. At some point, when we prepare to send astronauts into the farther reaches of our solar system, or out of it, we're going to have to accept that the explorers we send out – even if they can go out and come back from a distant location within a few months or years – will never see their families again. That's a hell of a burden to put on a person."

"No shit," Dante said. "Doesn't give me much hope for us expanding the human race outside of our own solar system."

Dominic shrugged. He'd stopped his pacing and leaned against the windows. "There've always been brave souls, willing to go out and explore the unknown. I don't think there'll ever be a lack of them. There will always be people with the drive for knowledge and the passion for adventure. And there are always people that crave immortality."

"I guess they would be considered immortal, wouldn't they?" Dante said thoughtfully. "If we somehow knew how to send someone out through the Galactic Center, and they could come back five thousand years later — well, we certainly would think they were immortal, wouldn't we? And over that time period, life on Earth would probably be so greatly changed, who knows what he might find when he gets back? If man would even still be here. Or the Earth, for that matter. It's a scary thought."

Dominic turned to watch the rain fall. "I remember when I was studying theoretical physics a long time ago, they were talking about a similar situation and the moral and cultural consequences of it. There was another aspect of it, but I don't recall right now what it was. Something about immortality, about traveling to another universe and living forever. I wish I could remember it; I seem to think it would be relevant."

"I think I know what you're talking about," Abby said. "It has to do with the destruction of the universe, if I remember correctly. Theoretically, no life is eternal. The only option for continued survival is hibernation. You'd have to get past the physical aging, of course; the theory is that you could inject your mind into a type of eternal hibernation, maybe like into a computer .Then, you create a baby universe and let it grow; when it's ready, you wake up and project your consciousness into it. But an entire race can't go into hibernation without an alarm clock — how will they know when to wake up?"

"So they send an envoy," Dante suggested. "Maybe through some kind of lineage, someone who's job would always be to keep checking, to see if we were ready yet to sustain life."

"That is extremely fucked up," Simon said. "I can go with a theory of coordinates; it's stupid, but possible. If we ourselves could open a stargate of some sort and travel through a wormhole, and if we found a primitive civilization on the other end, I don't think we'd hang around there for thousands of years. We might let the explorer dig around for a little while; but after all, time passing there would be real time for him. He'd age, too, just as the inhabitants of that planet or place would age. But he could stick around, do some scientific experiments, maybe bring some advanced culture or science to them, and then head back. While we sat around here for a couple months or years, checking out the data, debating about what we should do, how to approach and deal with these people, thousands of years would be passing for them. We might decide to go back through and visit them again a couple weeks later, but when we'd get there, we might find their entire civilization had changed. Maybe the industrial age had come and gone, and they were in the nuclear age now, the space age. Maybe they were ready and able to come through looking for us."

"It's interesting to consider," Dominic agreed. "After all, the Maya were birthed from the Galactic Center, so they say. Their gods descended from the sky and brought them civilization and culture. One of their gods, Kulkulcan, then left, promising that he'd return again. And the Maya created the Long Count, counting down, cycling through not just years and centuries, but thousands of years. What were they counting towards if not a specific alignment, something that also had to go through its cycles, where everything had to fall into perfect place?"

"It does make some kind of sense," Abby said. "After all, we have to time our probes perfectly with the movements of the planets. If we want to launch a probe to Mars, we have to wait until the heavenly bodies are in perfect position in their orbits to align correctly so we can plan out trajectory and telemetry to make our mission successful. It's the difference between a successful landing and skipping our explorer off the surface of the Martian atmosphere, or veering off into outer space."

"So obviously, waiting for the proper alignment to send a probe through the fabric of space itself would take very careful, very precise timing," Dominic remarked.

"Exactly."

"So how do we open the doorway?"

Abby smiled. "I don't think it's up to us."

"Maybe we need a human sacrifice," Simon commented dryly. "They were killing people left and right out here, weren't they? For everything from thanking their gods for the harvest to praying for more rain. I'd assume that for something like this they'd want to massacre half their village."

"I don't think they had any real successful results with that technique," Dante said. "You'll note they're not ruling anything anymore."

Dominic didn't appear to be listening; he turned suddenly from the windows to address them. "Where do you think they'd have come from?" he asked.

"They could come from anywhere," Abby said, "from one of the stars next door, or the other side of the known universe."

"Interstellar travelers would have had to come from absolutely tens of light years away, don't you think? We've observed so much about our part of the universe, I would think we'd have seen a rip in the fabric of time and space, wouldn't we?"

"Is that what it would involve?" Tina asked.

"Well, it'd be a hell of a thing," Abby said. "We can theorize that it's possible to bend space, but we're not certain exactly how it would be done. We would be talking about quantum mechanics as well as cosmology. We're still not sure how they interrelate, but we're a long way from putting it into any practical experiments."

"Sorry," Tina said, "but I still don't get it. Is it nuclear? What do you mean by quantum mechanics?"

"We live in a multiverse," Abby explained. She considered going to the board to diagram her points, but decided it would complicate matters even more. "We use the term 'universe' to describe reality as we know it, but there are really innumerable universes within it. Dark matter, for example, or photons. They react to our physical reality, but we can't see them, we take no notice of them, and they have their own little thing going on. It's like they're part of a separate, smaller universe all their own. Different parts of our universe coexist with the larger universe we know. When we talk about physically folding the fabric of space like you would fold over a piece of paper, we have to take all of these into consideration; we would need to understand everything and how it interrelates. It would require almost infinite knowledge of the universe. To not do so could trigger a chain reaction, like a nuclear reaction, that could destroy the universe and everything in it."

"Jesus Christ," Simon said. He laughed.

Dominic looked at him curiously, but only addressed Abby.

"Maybe the Maya knew this," he said. "Maybe they saw the world differently. After all, the Popul Vuh says they 'saw everything perfectly.'"

"You think they could have known about a multiplicity of universes?" Dante said. "Sorry, I've been following you guys so far on this, but I can't accept that they were that advanced. I don't think that unlocking the secret of Mayan time is going to involve multiverses."

"Why not?" Dominic asked. "We're talking about the visitor Kulkulcan as a physical being, a traveler from a distant part of the universe. But what if what we're really talking about are transdimesional beings? String theory holds that the universe is made of many more than three dimensions; in fact, it suggests ten to twelve. There could be more, and our travelers may not be interstellar, but interdimensional. Maybe the end of the Long Count will be the end of time and space."

Abby smiled. "We're not discussing a Theory of Everything, are we?"

Dominic sat down again on the bench across from her. "Frankly," he admitted, "I don't know what the hell I'm talking about."

The others laughed, and Dante stood up and stretched. "It's getting a little too deep for my liking," he said. "I'm all for an advanced Mayan civilization and all, but no more so than what I've seen with my own eyes. I've seen stone temples, and yes, they've been aligned to the stars with dramatic accuracy, but I haven't seen anything yet to suggest they were anything greater than equal to the Egyptians. Both used pyramid tombs and possible star alignments, which in itself is interesting, but doesn't make me think they were visited by aliens. Yeah, they were certainly astronomically advanced, but that doesn't mean that the Maya got their knowledge from some surveyor from another world."

"That is true," Dominic said. "We're not only reading between the lines here, we're making things up as we go. But that's why we have to apply scientific method to our ideas, not just run off with wild theories."

"I was thinking," Tina spoke up hesitantly, "you say that we can see certain brilliant events in the sky, like supernovas exploding, right?"

"Yes," Abby said. "When the last nearby supernova went off, it would have been a brilliant light, even during the daytime, brighter than a full moon."

"Then don't you think that a split in the space-time continuum, or whatever the hell you guys are talking about here, would have been visible from Earth? If the Mayan gods came through the Galactic Center, and it made a huge burst of, I don't know, light and matter, wouldn't another culture on Earth like the Chinese have noted it and recorded it? I mean, even cave drawings show some knowledge of astronomical cycles, marking off the moon cycles, and timing eclipses. Certainly someone, somewhere would have made note of someone coming through the black hole."

"They did," Dominic said. "The Maya."

Abby smiled at him, then turned to Tina. "Well, for one thing, we're assuming that there would have been a huge burst of light or matter, or a temporal change. We have no idea what we could expect from an entry via wormhole. But even if it did, it wouldn't have occurred right then. Say we see a supernova exploding this year. If that supernova is 100,000 light years away from us, the actual event took place 100,000 years ago; the light from it is just now reaching us."

"So we never see anything in space precisely as it happens."

"Other than our own man-made events, like the orbiting space-station, things like that. We can look at a distant object in space three million light years away; but if you want to see the way it looks right now, you'll have to wait another 3 million years. If there was some type of explosion at the Galactic Center five thousand years ago, and the Galactic Center is 26,000 light years away, we can't expect to view the light from it for another 21,000 years."

"So how the hell does that help us?" Simon asked. "We're constantly going to be running behind; by the time we'd get visual evidence, the human race will be long gone. It's moot."

"That's where physics comes in. Based on the way something appears, the distance at which we're viewing it, and our knowledge of the laws of the universe, we can tell a lot of things about it. For example, we talked about relativity before; we've never actually traveled at the speed of light, but we can make prediction as to what would happen if special relativity were true. The predictions turned out correctly, exactly as we expected them to – observers record different time than the object that's moving. We therefore hold special relativity to be true."

Dante shook his head. "Let me know when you guys come back down to Earth," he said. "That's my field, and it's all I'm going to pretend to know anything about. I think I'll go make lunch."

"I'm with you," Tina said, rising from the bench. "Leave the science to the scientists. When you guys want to talk about Mayan archaeology again, I'll rejoin you."

Dominic smiled. "Actually, I think we could all use a break." He stood up. "So, what's for lunch?"

12.19.16.2.7

February 27, 2009 — Simon's good mood seemed to last, and when he rejoined the group the following Friday, he was ready to share his week's work. "I've been playing with what they call the Mayan 'supernumber'," Simon said.

"What's that?" Abby asked.

"And who calls it that?" added Dante.

"I found it online," Simon admitted, then quickly backpedaled. "Well, I first found it as a common divisor, and when I looked online to see if anyone else had discovered it yet, I found that it was called the Mayan supernumber."

Frowning at the look that passed between the others, Simon continued: "It's a number that works with all the counts," he explained. "The number 1366560 is evenly divisible by every important Mayan cycle: The Haab, 365 days. The Tzolkien, 260 days. The Tun, 360 days. The Calendar Round, 18,980 days. The Venus Round, 37,960 days. The Venus cycle, the Mars cycle, the Mercury cycle. All divisible into the supernumber."

"Does it mean anything, though?" Dante asked. "I mean, the supernumber was created to fit into the counts, and the counts fit into it. But the supernumber wasn't part of Mayan mathematics."

"The Maya didn't have mathematics," Simon answered crossly. "If they did, they wouldn't have used such huge ridiculous numbers to count with."

"Simon —" Dominic began.

Simon interrupted him with a wave of his hand. "I know, I know," he said. "They had zero, they had a system based on twenty, they had this, they had that. Big fucking deal. They didn't have advanced mathematics."

"I'm not going to argue math with you," Dominic said. "Just tell us what you found."

"Well, like I said — the supernumber is divisible into all of the calendars. It's also divisible into the cycles of all the planets they were aware of and studied in depth. Take the Venus cycle, for instance; the Haab is a measure of the Venus cycle."

"What was their interest in the Venus cycle?" Dante asked.

"Good question," Dominic said. "Why are we so fascinated with the phases of the moon? Despite popular belief, the moon really *doesn't* have any effect on our moods or behavior. So why did our ancestors — even back in the caveman days — mark its phases?"

"I suppose it was our way of trying to figure out the world around us," Abby proposed. "The moon went through observable changes every 28 days; yet it always came back to full. They could use it as a timekeeper and could accurately predict its phases. They probably also recognized the effect of the moon on the tides."

"So why the Venus cycle?" Dante asked again.

"I would think the ability of the ancient Maya to observe the similar changes in Venus is a great tribute to their astronomical advancement. We have to assume they were making these observations with the naked eye. That's amazing."

"Venus was a major deity to the Maya," Dominic added. "Just like almost all ancient races, the Maya believed the celestial bodies were gods. And Venus was one of the most important; look at Uxmal — the Palace of the Governor has over 350 Venus glyphs, and is aligned with a rare Venus rising that takes place every eight years."

"Why Venus?" Dante asked.

"Venus is the morning star," Abby said. "It's also the brightest light in the sky, beside the moon and the sun."

"Maybe there was some other significance," Simon said. "After all, it spins backwards. And didn't it form differently from all the other planets? Like, upside down?"

Tentatively, Abby responded. "Sorry, but it didn't. The friction between the planet's core and mantle, combined with the sun's gravity pulling on Venus' dense atmosphere – and the heating of that atmosphere – show that the planet could have ended up in the position it's in now from virtually any starting position."

"Is that so?" Simon said. "Well, it doesn't mean that it *wasn't* formed upside down," he insisted.

"Quite true," Dante said. "I've also read in scientific journals that the planet's thick atmosphere could have changed the rotation, too. Seems that the atmosphere is always lagging behind the actual planet itself as it rotates; that could slow down the planet enough to actually reverse its spin."

"Well, big fucking deal. So there's more than one option. Congratulate yourself on a single partial victory," Simon said, crossing his arms over his chest.

"Partial victory?" Dante laughed. "Come on, it's been years since science has believed Venus formed upside down. Try to keep up."

"You bitch when I want to check on something, like the start and end dates, and now you bitch because I didn't thoroughly research an offhand remark about Venus," Simon spat.

"You want to check on something that's been checked and re-checked, tested, and confirmed," Dominic said. "It's common knowledge now, as reasonable to use as any of your mathematical theorems. You don't need to check the dates. Yet, you throw an anecdote out to us without having checked on the story behind it to see if it really happened or not."

"An anecdote eventually becomes common knowledge," Simon argued.

"No," Dominic responded. "It becomes an urban legend."

Simon stood up. "Fine," he said, "remind me not to say fucking anything to you anymore without checking it out first." He went out, letting the door slam against its frame behind him.

Dominic tossed Abby a quick smile. "Well, it'll either keep him quiet or busy. I'm good either way."

She shook her head. "You two are hopeless, you know that? It used to be Simon that would try to push all your buttons, try to goad you on. Now it's you that delights in messing with him. Boys."

"You have to have some fun somehow," Dominic said. He stood up. "I think I'll wander around aimlessly outside for awhile. Care to join me?"

Abby laughed. "Go on," she said. "I want to look at the supernumber. There may be a distance or a time period or something that it correlates to."

"Good luck," Dominic said with a smile and a wave as he too left the lab, leaving Abby alone with her books.

"Anything?"

Abby looked up to see Dominic framed in the doorway. She glanced at her watch, surprised to find her eyes so blurry. She hadn't realized that several hours had passed. She shook her head in frustration. "I just can't make anything match up."

"What have you found?"

"Well, looks like Simon's full of bullshit, as usual. I gave up on him and went off again on my own. I've been checking out the solstices and equinoxes. Since that's what they started and ended the Count on, I thought they had to have some important meaning. But none of them seem to. I tried to match up the equinoxes with the different World Ages, but nothing. I tried to match them up with important dates or eras in other cultures; for example, in 4,400 B.C., the fall equinox sun aligned with the Milky Way. In Mayan history, this brought in the Golden Age. Then precession caused it to move out of alignment. I thought maybe they were predicting when it might come around again, to bring in the second Golden Age."

"But that's too long ago. The alignment would have already occurred again —when, in the late 90's?"

Abby nodded. "They're all like that. Nothing works. Precession brings one of the seasonal quarters into alignment with the Milky Way once every 6,450 years. But that's too long, even for the Long Count."

"So there's nothing on December 21, 2012?"

"Well," Abby said hesitantly. "There is one interesting occurrence. The winter solstice sun will be very close to the ecliptic — the sun's orbit — and the equator of the Milky Way."

"The Sacred Tree?" Dominic asked.

"That's right," she said. "It's not exact, though. Which is too bad, because it might have been the answer?"

Dominic went to the cork board, searching quickly through the photographs of the different Mayan glyphs. He located the one he was looking for, pulling it off the board. He carried it over to Abby and set it in front of her, then slid onto the bench beside her. "Here," he said, reaching around her and pointing at it. His breath was warm on her neck, and Abby tried to focus on the picture.

"This is Izapan Stela 11," he explained.

"I recognize it," Abby said. "What is it?"

"It shows Great Father in the dark rift. It's the image of the conjunction you just described."

"That's amazing," Abby said. "It was obviously important to them, wasn't it?"

"Very much so. It's the symbol of rebirth."

"Then it *is* possible that that's what they were counting to. It's a slow convergence that would take thousands of years to move into alignment."

"But you said it's not exact."

"No," she said, "it isn't. It's outside a perfect alignment by several degrees, so their timing is off. Is it possible they could have miscalculated? I mean, they were working with huge periods of time."

"No, I don't think so," Dominic said. "They knew their astronomy too well. Is there anything that could have altered it?"

"Altered what, time?" Abby asked. "Not at all. Not time, not the movements of the universe. What they'd have actually been counting would have been the orbit of the sun, in conjunction with precession and the path of the Earth. The Milky Way hasn't moved; the ecliptic hasn't moved. And as far as we know, precession hasn't slowed down in the last five thousand years, either."

"I didn't think so, anyway," Dominic said. "The conjunction didn't occur on the beginning date, did it?"

"No," Abby answered with a smile. "I checked."

"So there's nothing to tie it together." With a quick movement, Dominic swept the photograph off the table. "So much for that."

Abby laughed, and Dominic shrugged. "I'm not worried, though – I have faith in you, Abby. If there is an alignment, or conjunction, or anything astronomical, I trust that you'll find it."

"Glad one of us has confidence in me," she said.

314

They heard footsteps on the walk outside, and Dominic quickly slid away. The door opened and Simon peered in. "Are you coming to bed, or what?"

"In a minute," Abby said. "Let me put my things away."

"I've got them," Dominic said, scooping up her notes. "If you don't mind, I'd like to look through them a bit, anyway."

They traded smiles, and Abby stood up from the bench, surprised at how cramped and tired she felt.

"Come on, then," Simon snapped impatiently. "I have a long drive tomorrow. I'd like to get to bed."

Abby held her tongue, and when she and Simon had left, Dominic flipped open her notebooks. He read for awhile, then reached down and picked up the photograph of Stela 11. He studied it for a long time before re-pinning it to the bulletin board.

12.19.16.2.8

February 28, 2009 — "I can't believe you're even contemplating this," Dominic said, bemused. "What's gotten into you?"

Simon shrugged. "I just figured I'd give your method a try. Humor me."

"All right," Dominic said. "I'll play along. So, tell us what you're thinking."

"Well, why can't it be an opening?" Simon asked. "A portal."

"From where?" Abby's voice was tired.

"From another portal," Simon responded, no trace of irritation in his voice. "Dominic, you said the ancient Maya believed that their gods came to this Earth from somewhere else, dropping down to land from 'snake chains'".

"Straight out of the *Popul Vuh*," Dominic said. "We've talked about this before, Simon. Had us thinking about black holes."

"That's right," Abby added, "and we determined that they had no bearing on the Long Count."

"Simon," Dominic said slowly, "you've been here for most of this. We've argued about it already and you pretty much called us a bunch of morons for even considering it. So what's made you change your mind?"

Simon shrugged, coming over to join them at the table. Across the room, Dante looked up warily, but didn't comment.

"Just looking at some numbers," Simon said lightly. "And I'm starting to see some connections. Just started thinking about what you were saying earlier — that the Mayan gods descended to Earth from their snake chains in the sky. What do you think they meant by that?"

Abby was disconcerted by Simon's conversational tone, but Dominic didn't let it throw him. "They could have meant anything," he answered, his tone just as light. "After all, these are the same people that claimed man was created from corn by a bunch of gods in a fight. You can't put a lot of stock in their mythology."

Simon stood up again, shaking his head. "No," he said, "this is different. It's phrased differently; it's not the same as their creation myths. They speak of their old gods coming down from the sky and bringing culture and civilization to the primitive people. The tale of Kulkulcan is very unique when compared to the mythologies of the Hero Twins and Jaguar-frog and Seven Macaw and the World Tree and the other crap they came up with to describe the world. They were talking about a real person."

"I see you've been doing your reading," Dominic commented.

"Well, you brought this damn library down here for a reason, didn't you?"

"That I did."

"So, theoretical physicists have come up with ways time travel could be executed; several time machines have been designed already."

"You *have* been doing some research," Abby said, surprised. "But Simon, none of these designs are possible right now. They involve impossibilities – shaping a cosmic string into a rectangle and collapsing it; creating a wormhole with conductive plates miles wide with one pair shot off at light speed while another ages normally on Earth, creating negative energy in the space between them. Theoretically, the designs work, but there's no way to prove it because we can't build them. The Thorne plates would create a wormhole less than the width of an atom; and how in the world would you locate a cosmic string? Taking into consideration that string theory isn't just theoretical, of course."

"We can't do it *now*," Simon said. "But science is growing by leaps and bounds, exponentially, in fact. It used to take us years to create simple inventions; now, we have thousands of high-tech devices coming out every year. A hundred, a thousand, a hundred thousand years from now, who knows?"

"But Simon, the portal you're suggesting would either be smaller than an atom, or it'd have to be half the size of the Milky Way. It's just preposterous," Abby exclaimed.

Realizing what she just said, Abby bit her tongue, but Simon appeared not to notice. Instead, Dante spoke up. "So what are you saying, Simon? That Kulkulcan was an alien?"

Simon turned his cold gaze on Dante. "You don't have to be a smartass," he said. "You haven't seen the numbers that I have. You don't even know what I'm talking about it, so why don't you stay the hell out of it?"

"Why don't you tell us what you're talking about, so we're all on the same page?" Dominic asked.

Simon shook his head. "I'm not ready yet," he said. "I haven't finished my calculations. When I do, I'll let you know."

Dante stood up. "For God's sake, Simon, I just don't get you. You bitch that we don't understand because we don't have the same information that you do, but you won't share it with us, either."

"I don't want anyone skewing the information," Simon responded. "You people just keep working on what you're doing, and I'll do what I'm doing, and if we're on the right track, maybe we'll meet somewhere in the middle."

Dante shook his head. "We're all over the place with our ideas, Simon. The other three and I have been working closely together and we're still not on the same track."

"Then don't involve me in your incompetence," Simon said, going to the bookshelf. He pulled out a thick volume and tucked it under one arm. "I'd think you'd be acting more like scientists now, now that your religious freak is out of the picture."

The silence that fell over the lab was almost audible. Slowly, Dominic turned to Simon. "What did you just say?"

"You heard me," Simon said, quickly heading for the door. "I was damn sick of hearing him bringing up religious shit every time we tried to deal with fact. Maybe your hypotheses will be a little more grounded from now on."

Before any of the others could respond, Simon was out the front door and heading back towards the house. In an instant, Dominic was on his feet and heading after him.

"Dominic, don't," Abby pleaded, racing around the table to block the door. "Please don't go after him. He's just trying to get you stirred up. Let me go talk to him. Please."

He didn't respond, but when he felt Dante and Tina's hands on his shoulder and back from behind, he finally stopped.

"She's right, Dominic," Dante said. "Trust me, I want to kick his ass for him too, but we can't do it. He's just trying to get a rise out of you. Little Simon is pissed because we dismissed his stupid theory and chastised him for not sharing with the rest of us. All he can do is verbally attack, and the one tender area he has with you is Steve. Don't give him the satisfaction of letting him know he got you."

"Come on," Tina said gently. "Let him go. If you don't respond, he'll sit up there wondering if he got any kind of reaction from you. Don't play his game, Dominic. Let him sit up there and be a shit by himself."

Dominic lowered his head, finally letting out a deep sigh. Without answering any of them, he turned around and headed for the back door of the lab. He pulled open the screen door, crossing out into the dark courtyard, down towards the lagoon.

"Shit," Abby said, running a hand through her dark hair. "I'm more and more ashamed of that man every day."

Dante and Tina looked at her mutely, and Abby nodded. "I'll go up and let him have it," she said.

"It'll just make him proud," Tina said. "He may not know if he got to Dominic or not, but he'll at least get to take pride that he offended you."

"At least he'll know it's not acceptable," Abby said.

"He should know that already," Dante said. He turned and went out, following Dominic across the courtyard.

"He's right, you know," Tina said. "Simon knows what he's saying, and he doesn't give a damn. If you think you can make any kind of a difference with him, you're even more naive than I thought." She too turned and left the lab, heading towards the lagoon with the others.

Abby slumped against the door, wondering what she could possibly say to any of them that would make any difference. Unable to think of anything, she turned and pulled open the door, walking slowly up the path back to the house.

12.19.16.2.9

March 1, 2009 — Dominic was trying to remain patient, but he was finding Simon's hypocrisy increasingly intolerable.

"Look," he said, "we've ruled out time travel, not just because it's currently impossible, but because there's no evidence that's what the Maya were referring to."

"The Long Count is all about time," Simon said. "We obviously can't find any connection to worldly events, so I'd say it could very well be about the nature or the physics of time."

"As far as we know, the Maya *had* no theoretical physics," Abby spoke up, ignoring Simon's scowl. "They believed in astrology, not astronomy, as such. They knew what they would see in the sky every night, but they didn't seem to make any effort to figure out what they were looking at; they just made up stories about constellations and used them as predictors.

"They didn't know what the stars were made of; they didn't know that the bright spots of light they saw up there were actually other planets. They most likely didn't even know that the *Earth* was a planet. For all our talk of precession, we don't even know if they knew the Earth was round, and they had no evidence whatsoever that we were suspended in the fabric of space. The Maya saw the stars and made up stories about them; myths to explain the history of their people, even the story of the Earth. They weren't scientists, Simon, and they didn't theorize about the universe."

"So they just did what, took drugs and sacrificed each other?" he responded impatiently.

"Pretty much," Dominic said, standing up. Simon took his cue that the discussion was over, but still, he wouldn't give up.

"So what if I find evidence that that *is* what they were talking about? That there are such things as wormholes, and that there's another civilization out there that knows how to use them?"

Dominic laughed out loud. "Then you'd win a Nobel and change everything we know about history, physics, astronomy, biology – everything. If you could actually prove wormholes, *and* extra-terrestrial intelligence, *and* time travel, you'd be a hell of a lot more than the next Einstein, Simon – you'd be closer to God."

Simon stood up, giving the others a quick nod. "Then I'll bring you the proof," he said, strolling across the room. A moment later, he was gone.

Tina glanced up at Dominic. "Does he really think he has evidence for that?" she wondered aloud.

Dominic just laughed. "No," he said, "he just already thinks he's God."

12.19.16.3.9

March 21, 2009 — The wind struck the side of the house with a violent blow. The entire structure shook, and the windows rattled in their panes. An instant later, the windows blew out.

"Dominic, what the fuck kind of research did you do before you chose this spot?" Simon shouted, jumping from the bed. He had barely crossed the room when the shaking of the floor drove him to his knees. Downstairs, something rattled and crashed. A moment later, the air was filled with the rending sound of boards being torn asunder, then collapsing.

"Oh shit," Abby said, holding the covers tightly around her chin. "There goes the lab."

In the hall, she could hear people running, and shouting. Their words weren't audible above the sound of the storm, but she could hear the panic in their voices. Quickly, she jumped out of bed and headed for the door.

Simon was already past her, racing down the hall with the others. As Abby moved through the doorway, she heard another horrendous crash, and this time, cries of pain. "Dominic!" Tina's voice shouted, but her next words were drowned out by a crack of thunder.

A flash of lighting followed, and Simon's voice was clearly heard: "What the fuck did you build this shithole out of, balsa wood?"

More voices joined in, shouting and angry, but Abby couldn't hear what they were saying. The rain was pouring through the roof in front of her in a torrent, blocking her view of the others, who were stranded down at the end of the hall. Moments later, a figure cut through the waterfall, ignoring the torrential downpour as if it was no more than a light spring rain.

"Dominic?" Abby asked. He started to reach out for her hand, but Simon was suddenly behind her. Dominic shot him a dark look, then moved past her and down the stairs without answering.

"Come on," Simon said, stalking by her and grabbing her arm roughly. "Leave these jackasses the fuck alone. They can drown out there for all I care."

"Simon," she pleaded, trying to pry her arm free, but he dragged her down the hall.

"You heard me," he stated. "Fuck all of them. This whole place is falling down around us and all I care about is living 'til morning. Then we're out of here."

"Where are we going to go?" she asked.

"We'll sleep in the damn SUV," he said, pulling her down the stairs with him. Behind them, there was a huge crack as the roof gave way, and the others were right on their heels.

"We'd all better sleep in the SUV," Dante said, "As long as it doesn't float away."

"We're going to either drown or get hit by lightning," Tina said. "Right now, I'm more worried about the flooding."

"I'll get us to higher ground," Dominic said. He was already heading out the front door, keys in hand. "The ground will be solid enough if I drive around by the road — I can get us partially up the mountain, where there's a rocky plateau. It's near a good stand of trees, so we won't be the lightning rod, but nothing can crash down on us, either."

"Then get us the hell up there," Simon said sharply. "I'm sure as hell not going to drown down here."

Dante and Dominic exchanged a look, then turned away as they started, unbelievably, to smile. Amidst the wreckage and the storm, the thought of losing Simon in the disaster still brought a momentary guilty pleasure. In a moment, however, Dominic had the keys to the SUV in hand, and they were all racing through the rainstorm to the protection of the vehicle.

12.19.16.3.10

March 22, 2009 — "Christ, what a fucking disaster."

Simon stared at the wreckage from the doorway of the lab. It was as if a tornado had blown in through the doorway, taken a turn around the room, then blasted back out through the far wall. The whole structure was severely leaning, as if a giant hand had tried to push it towards the lagoon.

"Oh no," Dominic said from behind him, spotting the damage. "Oh no, oh no." He pushed past the smaller man, shoving him against the doorframe without thinking as he squeezed by him into what was left of the lab.

"Watch it," Simon snarled, righting himself and rubbing his shoulder.
Dominic paid no attention to him; he stood in the middle of the wreckage, his hands thrown out in front of him as if trying to raise the dead.

"Oh my God, Dominic," Abby said, pushing past Simon into the room. He reached for her, but she had already slipped by him, going to Dominic's side.

"Oh Dominic, I'm so sorry," she said.

Dominic said nothing; he just gazed around the room at the mess the storm had left in its wake.

The only object left standing was the lab table, thickly covered with debris. The roof had collapsed, raining into the room in a thousand pieces. Scraps of wood were scattered from one end of the room to the other; one large beam had crashed onto the computer desk, knocking the laptop onto the floor behind the desk.

The far wall had fallen over, the chalkboard crashing into the courtyard and cracking down the middle. The sunlight hit the wet, broken surface and reflected back at them, glowing like a mirror amidst the broken branches and rubble that surrounded it.

Only the frame of the screen door still stood; the door itself had been torn from its hinges by the force of the storm.

"It'll be okay," Dominic said suddenly. "It'll be all right. It's just a room. It can be rebuilt."

"Are you fucking nuts?" Simon said. He was crouching on the floor behind the desk. The computer had indeed been swept to the floor and shattered and the whole apparatus lay in a pool of water. Simon snatched it from the floor, dangling it by the cord.

"It can be rebuilt," Dominic said, barely glancing at the ruined computer. "I can get another computer. I can reinstall the program. We saved everything to CD. It's nothing. It will barely set us back."

"You're nuts," Simon said, dropping the broken computer in disgust. "Those precious CDs are strewn from one end of the jungle to the other."

"Then we'd better start picking them up," Abby said. She stepped through the broken door frame into the courtyard, where most of the lab had been blown outside. Inside, Simon and Dominic continued to argue, and after a moment, she could hear another voice added to the mix. Dante, loud and angry. Abby couldn't help but smile; in a minute, she knew, no matter how upset he was about the disaster, Dante would be siding with Dominic against Simon.

"Do you think he knows what he's doing?" Tina asked in a whisper. She and Abby sat on the stones in the courtyard, surveying the wreck of the lab. A comprehensive examination of the grounds had shown the storm to be both more *and* less damaging than they'd previously thought. The house seemed to be in fine condition, except for the roof, which had several spots that would need repaired, including one section that would need rebuilt. The lab, however, was completely destroyed.

"I don't know," Abby answered, brow wrinkled in thought. "I trust him — I really do. But this is unbelievable, Tina. I can't even imagine what it's going to take to rebuild the lab. Almost everyone here wants to give up.."

"Do you want to go?"

Again, Abby frowned. After a long moment, she admitted, "I don't know. When I think about it, I think I've spent way too long in the jungle, chasing shadows, and I want to go back to my old life. Yet, when I think about that — what do I really have to go back to?"

"Simon will never leave, will he?"

"No," Abby answered immediately. "No, Simon will never leave."

"Then he's as crazy as Dominic is," Tina said. "Those two are like a couple of mad dogs fighting over the same bone. They won't let the other one win, but they'll never let it go. And they won't let anyone else near it."

March 23, 2009 — Dominic stood in the doorway, watching as Tina packed her suitcases. He wore an expression of disbelief.

"What? You can't leave. You can't quit now."

"The hell I can't, Dominic. Dante and I both are getting the hell out of here"

"Please," he said. "You can't."

"What's this 'can't' shit, Dominic? We're out of here, and you can't stop us."

"It's not over. We can rebuild the lab."

"Dante said this was more than a storm," Tina said. "He swears he woke up with the ground moving. Lightning didn't knock down the lab – an earthquake did."

"Tina, please. You've always stuck by me before," he pleaded.

"The lab is gone, Dominic. It's been torn apart. And an earthquake this close to the volcano is a bad sign. Dante wanted to look up more data on Tacana, but … well, the computer is gone. Even without a full eruption, a plume of ash and steam coming out of that thing would destroy anything here you rebuilt and take us along with it.

"Besides, Simon has been making everyone else miserable. You two have been at each other's throats like rabid wolves. We haven't gotten any farther than we were before we even came down here. And Steve is dead. I've abandoned everything for almost a year now and it hasn't gotten us anywhere. I want to get back to my life, Dominic. There's been nothing but misery and heartache since we've started. I want to put all this behind me. How can you stay here?"

Dominic was silent, staring at his hands. "Because this *is* my life."

Tina shook her head, then continued to pack her suitcase. "That's fine, then, Dominic, but it's not good enough for me. I want out. Dante wants out. We're leaving."

March 24, 2009 — Dominic sat alone on the bench, hands dangling limply between his knees.

"Are they gone?" Abby asked.

"Yeah," he answered. "My friend has run off with the geologist."

"And then there were three," Abby intoned.

Dominic couldn't manufacture a smile. "Two, if you want to be honest about it," he said. "Simon the mathematician is more like a magician — or an apparition. He appears when he feels like it, then disappears for days or weeks at a time. You and I have to wait until he decides to grace us with his presence again. The end of the world will be here before we three come to a consensus on anything."

Abby thought for a moment. "Can't you bring someone else in? Just so we have someone here every day to work on it?"

"Even if I manage to find someone, if I bring them in now, by the time I catch them up with everything I've lost another few months," Dominic said. "Do you know what Simon said when I told him Dante and Tina left?"

She shook her head.

"He said, 'Good. The fewer we have on the project, the more room in the spotlight.' This, after he was so adamant about getting out of here himself. I knew he was a son of a bitch, but damn. He'd be happy if every one of us would drop dead and leave him with the credit for whatever we come up with. You included."

Abby sighed. "I never should have brought him with me. Everything would've been so much better if I had just come alone and left Simon where he was."

"It's too late now," Dominic said. "As much as we wish he had never come, the thing is, we need him. And he needs us. He can do the math, but he doesn't know jack about finding the references he needs to work with."

"Yeah, and we don't know jack about what to do with the numbers we get when we get them. So I guess we're stuck."

"In league with the devil," Dominic agreed.

"Yeah," Abby said. "I won't argue with you about that. We've spent a year in hell."

Dominic sighed. "Has it really been so miserable? Have you been that unhappy here?"

Abby looked up in surprise. "Not at all. We've had great times — swimming in the lagoon, our hikes up the mountain. Trips to Izapa, Tikal, even Tapachula. And you." She looked away again quickly. "I've loved it down here, Dominic. The only bad spots have been Steve's death, of course — and Simon."

"Yeah," he responded. "And we had some good times with Steve before he died. I wish he'd never come, since this trip was the cause of his death. But on the other hand, I'm glad that I got to spend so much time with him. I'm glad he was here — he loved this place. I think he was happy."

"I'm glad I got to know him."

Dominic smiled and put his arm around her. "Steve liked you a lot, Abby. He thought you were a good person. But like the rest of us, he could never understand what kept you with Simon."

Abby sighed. "I guess it's like you and the Long Count, Dominic. You're tied to it. You can't figure it out, and maybe you'll never get what you want out of it, but you can't let it go, either."

"If it was hurting me, I'd let it go."

"Would you?" Abby asked, looking up into his dark eyes. She motioned around at the lab. "You've sunk almost all your money into this place, and now it's gone. You've lost your best friend to it. You just lost a second friend to it, along with your other researcher. What else do you need, Dominic? Does the roof have to fall on your head next time?"

He surprised her with his laughter. "What the hell is wrong with us?" he asked. "Are we masochists?"

"I don't think so," she replied. "I just think sometimes that neither of us is as smart as we like to think we are."

Dominic tilted his head thoughtfully. "You may be right."

Abby reached out and put a hand on his knee. "Maybe it's time we both wised up."

He put his hand over hers, giving it a squeeze. "I can't be a hypocrite," he said. "I want you to run from Simon – far, and fast. I'll help. I want to be rid of him in any way we can be. But I don't think I can give up the Long Count."

Abby nodded. "I didn't expect any different," she said, withdrawing her hand. "We're both locked in, Dominic. It doesn't look like any of us are going anywhere." She stood up, and Dominic followed.

"Then I guess we'd better see about getting the lab rebuilt," he said. "I'll head into town today and round up a construction crew. If the supplies are available, I think we can be up and running again inside of two weeks."

Abby walked back to the house with him, not necessarily disappointed. She knew in her heart that he wouldn't give up the Count; he was as obsessed with it as Simon was with fame and notoriety. As much as that concerned her, she was also secretly pleased that they were staying. Seeing Dominic every day was the only thing that she had to look forward to anymore. The thought of heading back to Boston with Simon felt like a death sentence.

12.19.16.5.8

May 1, 2009 — "Hey Dominic! Come look at this!"

"What is it?"

"Just come quick. It's high noon."

Dominic squinted up at the sun high above them, then looked at her questioningly.

"It's the Zenith passage," Abby said. "When you and I first met, you told me about the May Zenith passage and mentioned a crossroads. I thought you were talking about the Southern Cross. But it's at the wrong place in the sky."

Dominic shielded his eyes, peering up at the sun. "Where's it supposed to be?"

"Over farther," she answered, gesturing. "The point isn't where it's *supposed* to be; the point is, it's not there."

"It means something," Abby said. "I don't believe the Maya were wrong; they didn't design anything by accident, right?"

Dominic was thoughtful. "May first is the zenith passage over Izapa. But over Chichen Itza it's May twentieth. That's the date the snake climbs down the pyramid of Kulkulcan."

"Chichen Itza is farther to the north. The date changes according to your latitude."

"Will the location of the passage itself change?"

"No ... the definition of the zenith passage is the sun crossing directly overhead, at its highest point, its zenith. Although the conjunction of the constellation will depend on the age of the Earth."

Dominic paced a little ways away. "The solar zenith is very important to Mayan cosmology. They had a ceremony, the New Fire Ceremony, that ushered in the new age; it was a renewing, a rebirth, of the Earth. I can't remember the conjunction, though."

"I'll look it up," Abby said, making a note in her book. She glanced up at him. "You want lunch?"

"I'd love it," he said. "Our last meal before Simon comes home tonight."

"We might be able to slip dinner in there, too," she said. "He's been leaving there later and later."

"Then let's celebrate," Dominic answered, putting an arm around her shoulder as they walked back. "I'll break out the canned ham."

Abby laughed. "I guess it beats tuna again."

"What do you think the odds are of Simon bringing us home a good take-out meal one of these days?"

"Slightly worse than alien visitation on December 21, 2012."

Their laughter carrying across the field, they headed back up to the house.

"I found the passage I was looking for," Dominic said. It was not yet dark, and he and Abby were sitting in the lab, which was little more than four walls. The lab table had been set up again, but the chalkboard, bookshelves and computer table hadn't been replaced. "The New Fire

Ceremony celebrated the conjunction of the sun with Pleiades. They held a ceremony at midnight to celebrate the Earth's renewal."

"The zenith repeats twice, though. Once in May, once in August."

"May was the Pleiades conjunction, when the Earth was renewed. The August conjunction was a holy date; it was considered the day of the year when time began."

"Was that based on the Long Count? Or was the Long Count based on it?"

"The chicken or the egg," Dominic said with a smile.

"But does it have anything to do with the Long Count?"

"I'm not sure," he admitted. "You know the Maya built their monuments in alignment with the solar zenith. Monuments in the north had the same alignment, only on different dates. In Teotihuacan it's May 17. In Chichen Itza, May 20."

Abby wandered away a bit, thinking. She put her hands on the ledge of a windowless frame, but she looked down, not out across the courtyard. Across the room, Dominic watched her, not speaking, giving her time to think. They sat in silence for awhile.

Finally, Abby turned around again. "Which are the more recent Mayan cities?" she asked.

Dominic considered. "Well, we know Izapa is one of – if not *the* oldest. Then, they move north — Palenque, Teotihuacan, Chichen Itza."

"As they moved north, they continued to build their monuments to align with the solar zenith," Abby said.

"That's right."

"With precession, they would have kept the dates similar by moving north."

Dominic sat back and smiled. "Abby, you may have a future as an archaeo-astronomer yet."

She laughed. "Maybe I do," she said. "The more time I spend wandering around the old sites, the more interested I am in the ancient astronomers. It's interesting to take the knowledge we have now and apply it, to see what they knew."

Dominic stood up. "Praise be, I've converted you," he said. "Does this mean I can look forward to working with you again in the future?"

"Maybe," Abby answered with a smile. "You find another tropical paradise to send us to, and I'll certainly consider joining you."

"Paradise?"

Startled, Abby and Dominic both turned towards the door; neither had heard Simon come in.

"Fucking paradise? It's a shack at the edge of a stinking jungle. We're standing in the frame of a building. There's a muddy pit at the bottom of a dangerous hill. What the hell are you thinking, Abby?"

"I'm thinking I've been having more fun here in the last year than I have in the last five," Abby said bluntly.

Simon stared at her; he opened his mouth to speak, then turned and strode out without saying a word, slamming the door behind him.

"Oh shit," Abby said, sitting down hard on the window ledge. She was shaking.

Dominic crossed to her quickly, taking her in his arms. "It's okay," he said.

"I shouldn't have said what I did," Abby answered.

Dominic smiled. "He'll get over it. It'll give him something to think about, anyway."

"That's what I'm worried about."

Dominic stepped back, holding her at arm's length. "Abby — I'm not trying to tell you what to do. You know better than that. But at some point, you're going to have to face Simon."

"I know," she said. "I've just been avoiding confrontation with him for so long, I can't imagine standing up to him now. I keep hoping that maybe he'll just go away."

"Yeah, so do I," Dominic said. "I'll back you up if you want or need it, Abby, but until you ask, you're on your own. I'm not going to come between you."

"You already have."

They stared at each other for a moment, and then Abby melted into his arms again. Dominic kissed her gently on the top of her head.

"If you want me to step away, Abby, all you have to do is say the word."

"Of course I don't. I mean, I want to keep the distance we've kept so far, out of necessity. I can't get involved with you, Dominic. Not here, not now. But physical distance doesn't seem to make much difference with you. Every time I'm with you, I'm with you. No matter how much space is between us."

"Abby, I'm more than ready to send Simon away if that's what you want."

"I don't know if you can."

"I've stood up to him before, and I'll do it again. I'm not afraid of him, Abby."

"I know, Dominic. But now he has a gun."

"Do you think we're in danger?"

"I don't know. But that's what I want to avoid. I need to go to him, Dominic."

"And apologize again?"

"Whatever it takes."

She walked away, unable to meet his eyes. At the door, she finally turned back. "I'm caught in the middle of everything. Balancing between keeping Simon here to help your work, and staying far enough away from him to avoid him. Trying not to set him off, trying to keep him placated."

"Abby, I'll drop everything and take you away from here right now."

"I know," she said, turning away again. "But I can't ask you to do that. You asked me here in good faith that I would help you and your team find the answer to the Long Count. I brought Simon along. Now everything has fallen apart, and everyone is gone except me — and Simon. The least I can do is keep him in line and fulfill my part of the agreement."

"You're not responsible for Simon."

"Aren't I?" she asked. Without another backward glance, she went out, shutting the door gently behind her.

12.19.16.7.11

June 11, 2009 — Abby was drying her hair with a towel as she came out into the courtyard. A long day of working on the lab had left her dirty and exhausted. She felt cleaner after her shower, but not much cooler. It was only June, but the tropical heat had already fallen upon the lush valley.

She stripped off the towel and threw it over her shoulders. It was damp, but still didn't cool her off much. Even in a tank top and shorts she felt smothered.

"Hey, Dominic," she said, spotting him sitting on one of the rocks near the edge of the courtyard. He was drinking a chilled bottle of water; he must have gone down and snagged it out of the pond where they kept their drinks cool. He'd stayed working on the lab until almost dark, and now sat back, either inspecting or admiring his work.

"It looks good," she said, sitting down next to him on the rock.

"It's coming along," he conceded, looking over their work. They'd been working steadily for almost two weeks, and the new lab was almost done. "It's smaller than before, no bookshelves, not as many windows. But it'll be fine. We just need a place to keep all our notes and books so everyone can go through them, a place away from the house to sit up late and talk without keeping anyone else up. The more I think about it, though, the more I wonder what the point even is." He glanced down at her. "It's just us and Simon now anyway, and I haven't seen him for a week. Is he going to be teaching summer school until August again this year?"

"I hope so," she replied. "He hasn't said much to me about it, but I assume so. He'll do just about anything to stay away from here."

"Just as well," Dominic said. "I like it better with just the two of us anyway."

Abby smiled, but didn't answer. She reached out and took his hand, and they sat in silence, watching the light from the setting sun glinting off the roof of the lab. After awhile, she spoke again, breaking the comfortable silence. "I've been thinking, Dominic. The years between the Long Count —3114 BC to 2012 AD — are basically the peak of human civilization. At least so far."

"You think it's all downhill from here?" he asked with a smile.

"Maybe."

Dominic rubbed his chin, thoughtful. "We can't imagine technology more advanced than what we have now," he said. "But even as a simple example – when it was first discovered, people couldn't imagine more advanced technology than being able to record sound and picture on film. Then they were amazed at the technology of the VHS recorder, when it was first invented. Now we're onto DVDs, thinking that it can't get more advanced than this. The Blu-ray technology came along. Yet, it won't be long before that's outdated. There's no culmination to technology; we're always moving ahead, beyond what we ever thought was possible.

"I think it all goes back to the whole apocalypse mentality. It's a powerful draw for people, thinking that you're a part of the end times. Of all the past ages and eons of the Earth, here you are, living at the end of time. It's an ego thing: It's so much more interesting to think you've been chosen to witness the apocalypse than to think the world might end sometime around, say, 9000 AD, and nothing we say or do today as individuals is going to mean anything 7,000 years from now. No one will even know we were here. It's disheartening. We may not want the world to end, but if it's going to, then by God, we want to be a part of it."

"It's about mortality, then," Abby suggested.

Dominic shrugged. "We all know that we're going to die, but it doesn't seem real to us. If it did, there'd be a lot fewer smokers and drunk drivers out there. We don't have any real sense of our own mortality; that someday — hell, any day, maybe even today — it's going to be over for us. We simply won't exist anymore. And when we do, the world will go on without us. Yet we'll never see another sunrise, never feel the grass under our feet, never sing in the shower again or hug our loved ones or taste our favorite food. We'll be done. And yet the world will spin on.

"I think that gives us some sense that if we don't exist, then the world won't, either. We can't imagine the world without us; therefore, it ends when we do. Maybe that's why every generation seems to think they're living at the end of time. Thousands of years ago, people were predicting the same thing. Thousands of years from now, they probably still will be."

Abby was quiet. "It is kind of depressing," she admitted. "I'd much rather be a part of something bigger than me, than to think that when I'm gone the world will go on as usual, and no one will ever know I was here."

"So you'd rather take the rest of the world with you?" he teased.

Abby smiled, watching the sun sink below the roof of the lab. "Not particularly, no," she said. "But when I go out, I wouldn't mind something spectacular.

12.19.16.8.14

July 4, 2009 — Abby leaned against the lab table, her bare midriff touching the cool surface. "God, that feels good," she murmured, running an icy glass over her sweaty forehead. Her dark hair stuck to her head in damp ringlets; she'd pulled it up but the wetness still soaked through. The daytime heat had been unbearable, and hadn't dropped off the slightest bit since the sun went down.

Dominic glanced over at her, taking in her low-slung, baggy cotton shorts, darkened at the waistband with a moon of sweat. Her tank top rode up at her waist, showing the small of her back and her lean, flat stomach. A drop of perspiration beaded between her shoulder blades, then ran down, staining the dusky gray shirt a shade darker where it soaked into the thin fabric.

"Wish we could've splurged on another fan," he said.

She looked over at him with a slight smile, catching his dark eyes. His gaze was intense, and her smile wavered. Her breathing was already labored in the stifling heat, and as her tawny eyes locked upon his dark ones, her breath faltered.

The air in the room was completely still, the thin curtains unmoved by any breeze. As they stared at each other across the empty room, their hearts beat faster. Both were barely breathing.

Abby brushed a damp lock of hair away from her forehead. The air felt like a heavy liquid as she moved through it slowly, the tile refreshingly cool on her bare feet.

Dominic leaned back on the bench, his eyes never leaving hers, as she paused in front of him. Slowly, papers still clutched in one hand, she lowered herself down onto one of his outstretched legs. He touched her leg gently, apprehensively, his long fingers playing lightly on the taut skin of her thigh, then spreading out as he gripped her leg tightly.

She reached out to cradle his face in one hand, running her soft palm along the curve of his jaw. He tilted his head slightly, laying his cheek in her hand, his eyes closing.

"I love your face," she said.

Dominic reached up and took her hand, turning it over gently, and kissed her palm. Her breath caught in her throat and she closed her eyes, gripping his fingers tightly with her own. He reached up with his other hand, his fingertips barely brushing a damp curl of hair off her smooth forehead. Suddenly, he stood up, lifting her with him, pressing her back against the cool stone table.

"Dominic," she murmured, eyes still closed, reaching up to put her hands upon his broad shoulders.

His hands moved to her waist, resting on her narrow hips, and he lowered his face to her neck, nuzzling his lips into her damp hair. He breathed in the musky smell of her, and his hands tightened around her waist as he brushed her neck with his lips.

With a low moan, Abby wrapped her slender fingers around the back of his neck, lifting her face towards his.

He was lowering his lips toward hers when the door slammed open.

"What the fuck is this?"

The bench screeched back as Dominic pulled away, tripping over it and stumbling. He caught himself and turned to face Simon in the doorway. Before either of them could stammer out a word, however, Simon crossed the floor in just a few strides; Dominic had barely turned to fully face him before the first punch struck him on the cheekbone. He grunted and staggered backwards, tripping again over the overturned bench, going down this time, sprawling onto his back with his arms underneath him to break his fall.

"Stop it!" Abby cried out, rushing to Simon's side and grabbing his raised arm. He shook her off and bore down on Dominic, who was crawling on his back away from him.

"You son-of-a-bitch," Simon said, grabbing him by the collar of his t-shirt, easily lifting the larger man off the floor. They scuffled briefly before Simon threw Dominic up against the thin door; the large man's body broke through the screen and he fell backwards onto the lawn.

"Stop it, Simon!" Abby cried out, reaching for his arm again. "Leave him alone."

Again, he shook her off, but his fury seemed to be dissipating as quickly as it had come. He paused in the doorway, watching Dominic struggle to his feet.

Dominic danced away, backing away from the door. "You're fucking crazy!" he shouted.

Laughing, Simon threw himself against the shattered door, framing himself in the torn screen. "Damn straight I'm crazy, you bastard. I'm fucking crazy. You touch my fiancée again and you'll find out just how crazy I am."

Simon turned, his bloody fist dangling by his side, his other hand gripping the broken doorframe.

"Leave him alone, Simon. Don't hurt him."

"He was touching you. He's lucky I didn't kill him."

Abby backed away, trembling. She glanced past him into the darkness, but there was no sign of Dominic. Nothing moved in the black Mexican night.

"I'll talk to him," she said, turning her nervous attention back to him. "He's not a threat to you, Simon. He won't come near me again if I tell him not to."

"Fuck that," he answered, turning to peer through the doorway into the darkness. "I don't even want him thinking about you."

"Simon," she said, lowering her voice, searching again over his shoulder for any sign of Dominic. "It'll be okay. Dominic is harmless. You know we need him. I need to work with him directly. We can't do this on our own. Trust me, I'll talk to him. It'll be all right."

His shoulders froze, and he turned slowly to face her. Standing up straight, he looked down for a long moment at his bloody fist.

"You do that," he said. "You talk to him. Because if I have to do it, he won't be speaking to anyone again. I'll bust every tooth in his lying mouth." He paused, then looked up at her slowly. "And if I ever find out you let him touch you again, then that goes for you too."

Abby moved slowly out the broken door, trying not to let its hinges squeak. Simon had stormed out of the rebuilt lab moments earlier, threatening her to make Dominic "fix the door he broke," before the next morning. She'd promised to do so, but wanted to clean up her scattered papers first — the thick humidity foretold the coming of a heavy rain, and if the rain came through the broken screen, her work would be ruined. When he had left, she tossed her pages aside and squeezed out, holding the broken door and letting it close gently, careful not to let it hit the frame. The air outside was cooler than in the lab, and a slight breeze had kicked up. It wasn't much, but she could feel rain in the air.

Silently, she crossed the lawn, glancing back to make sure Simon hadn't returned to the lab. All was silent.

A few minutes later, she found him: His dark shape was hunched over, and his face was buried in his hands. He was seated on the large rock near the lagoon, blending in with the darkness. Only the moonlight glinting off the water gave her enough light to silhouette him against the backdrop of the night.

"Dominic," she whispered. He didn't answer.

Abby lowered herself to the ground in front of him. "Dominic," she said, reaching up to take his hand. "I'm so sorry."

"Is this the way it's going to be?" he asked, lowering his hands to his lap. He did not pull away from her, but he would not look at her. "We have to live in fear of Simon, all the time? When we're working, when we're not working, when … well, whenever. Always. We're always running from Simon."

Abby didn't respond as she knelt in front of him. She put one hand on his knee, reaching up with the other to examine his face. He winced and pulled away.

"I'm so sorry you're hurt," she said, sliding her hand around to cradle the back of his head. "I'm sorry I can't help."

Abby moved closer, sliding her hand from his knee to his waist. Gently, she kissed his neck.

Dominic made a low sound in his throat, reaching up to take her face in his hands. "Don't," he said, turning her face so he could look into her eyes. "We can't do this."

Abby closed her eyes, tilting her forehead down to touch his. "I know," she said. "But I want to." She kissed his cheek lightly.

"And what are we to do about Simon?" he asked, his voice rumbling. His eyes were closed, and she kissed them. "What about your fiancé?"

"I don't care," she said. "We'll deal with him. He doesn't own me, or you. If we need another mathematician, we'll find one." She nuzzled his neck lightly, rising up slightly to kiss him in front of his ear.

"We might never finish the project," he murmured, kissing her neck, then her cheek. "Everything might fall apart." Lightly, he kissed her lips. Gently, at first then harder. She dug her hands tightly into his damp hair, pulling him to her as she kissed him deeply. After a while, breathlessly, they parted. Abby laid her forehead against his chest.

"Then it falls apart," she said quietly. "If everything falls apart, and we don't find out what the Long Count meant, then what?"

Dominic was silent. "Then everything I wanted ends right here," he said.

Abby sat up straight. "Everything?"

He turned away, his dark eyes hidden. "You know what this means to me. All the years the Long Count has been studied, no one has ever discovered what it meant. I want to do that."

"And what if you don't?" Abby asked, crossing her arms over her chest. "Will the Long Count still end? Will you figure out what it means then?"

Dominic shook his head, standing up. "I don't want to wait until it happens," he said. "What if it's a warning? What if we sat here for five thousand years and never read it?"

Abby stood also, but didn't respond. Dominic paused, putting his hands on her waist.

"I care about you a lot, Abby. You know I do. But as long as you're not willing to end it with Simon, I can't do a damn thing about it. I didn't stay and fight tonight because I would have seriously hurt him. But I won't run from him again, and I won't sneak around. If you want me, I'll be here. But not as long as he is."

He released her, then strode past her, back to the house.

12.19.16.8.15

July 5, 2009 — Abby wiped the sweat off her forehead. She had finally reached the small cave after more than an hour of hiking, and now all she wanted to do was lay down in the cool stream. She slid her backpack with the telescope in it off of her shoulders, setting it in the grass outside the cave. She planned to head higher up the mountain, to see what kind of view she could get across the top of the jungle, but for now, she needed a rest.

She didn't realize she had fallen asleep until the sound of water splashing woke her. She sat up inside the cave, shielding her eyes with one hand. The bright sunlight glinted off the ripples in the stream, blinding her. A pair of long, blue-jeaned legs came into view, attached to a pair of dark brown hiking boots as the figure stepped out of the stream and onto the bank. As he ducked down to look into the cave, Abby was met by Dominic's open, concerned face.

"Hi Abby."

She just nodded, unsure of what to say.

"Can I come in?"

"I don't think there's room in here for both of us," she answered.

"Then can you come out?"

Abby looked at him warily, but his face showed nothing but concern. She scrambled out of the cave, getting to her feet when she reached the grassy forest floor. He took her arm to steady her.

Abby reached up to run a hand through her damp her, realizing she must be a mess. She had lain in the stream to cool off, wetting her hair and her clothing before crawling into the cave to rest. She had no idea how long she'd been asleep, but her cotton tank top and khaki shorts were almost completely dry.

Dominic took her hand and led her a few steps away from the mouth of the cave. He sat down in the grass, urging her down with him. They sat across from each other, and he took her other hand, holding them both in his lap. He looked at their clasped hands for a moment before finally raising his dark eyes to meet hers.

"I'm sorry about last night," he said.

"Why does it seem like we spend so much time apologizing to each other?"

He laughed. "I wish I knew. But I really mean it, Abby," he said. "I'm sorry. I went off on you because I was so angry with myself."

"About what?" she asked.

"I didn't stand up for you," he said. "I didn't stand up for myself. I was afraid if I fought back, I'd kill him. Today, I feel like an ass, running from Simon. I don't want to run from him anymore, Abby. I can take him any time, and I'm damn well ready to. I'm tired of hiding."

"Hiding?"

"The way I feel about you."

"Dominic …"

She raised her eyes to meet his, and suddenly, she was in his arms. She raised her face to his and he kissed her. After a long, breathless moment, she pulled away.

"We can't do this, Dominic."

He sat back, his hands still clasped behind her back. "Okay, then. We'll just talk." He paused, then shook his head. "I don't know if I can. It's getting hard to find words to describe the way I feel, Abby."

Abby laid her head on his chest. "I know, Dominic. I'm having the same problem. So let's try to talk about something else."

"As long as I don't have to let go of you."

She laughed. "I can't vouch for my willpower."

He smiled and kissed her gently on the forehead. "Well, what can we discuss that'll take our mind off of this?"

"Probably not much," she admitted. "Especially with us. We actually find theoretical physics interesting. Maybe we should talk about baseball."

Dominic laughed. "I haven't followed the season much from down here. How about time?"

"Okay," she said. "We never did get a chance to finish our discussion the other night."

"Good," he responded. "Time."

336

They stared at each other, and after a long moment, he leaned down and kissed her again. Abby did not resist, and in a moment's time she was in his lap, her arms around his neck, kissing him back.

After what seemed like an eternity, he finally pulled away. He brushed her damp hair away from her face.

"So, do you think there's such a thing as time?" he asked, kissing her throat.

"Hm?" she murmured breathlessly, her eyes closed.

"Time," Dominic repeated, burying his face in her hair. "We only witness change, so we have an illusion of time passing. Without change, all would be stagnant, and what we perceive as time would stop."

Abby didn't answer, couldn't answer as she held him to her. She kissed him long and deep, then pulled away and kissed his forehead.

"I wish time would stop," she murmured.

Dominic smiled, running a hand down her lean torso. "Time is made of individual moments," he said. "Like this one. Each one, like a snapshot, frozen. Lined up, one after another. We live, moment by moment, until we run out."

She kissed him again, holding him tightly. "Then if we can have one moment, forever, I want this one."

"Not me," he said, then laughed at her startled expression. "I want the next twenty minutes or so." Holding onto the hem of her tank top, he pulled it up over her head. She raised her arms so he could pull it off.

"Only twenty minutes?" she whispered.

"If that," he joked. "You don't know how long I've been waiting for this."

"Well, I sure hope it was worth the wait."

He kissed her again, and they moved down onto the grass. "You already were."

"I'm in love with you, Abby. I shouldn't be, but here it is. I've tried to hide it, I've tried to stop it. But I can't."

"Dominic ..."

"It's okay," he said. "You don't have to answer me. I'm just telling you. I love you."

"I love you too," Abby said. "But I don't know what to do about it."

"We don't have to do anything." He stroked her bare back lightly.

"We can't keep sneaking around behind Simon's back."

"Do you want to stop seeing each other?"

"No. Of course not."

"Then we can either address him and tell him what's happened, or we can keep things as they are. Personally, I'd rather tell him. I'm not proud to be sleeping with another man's fiancée."

"I wish you'd stop calling me that. I know have to end it with him, Dominic, but I'm not ready yet. I know it's the chicken way out. I'm sorry for that, and I hate myself for it. But Simon is so unpredictable — I don't know what he'll do. It would put an end to this project, that's for sure."

I'm willing to defer to you on this, Abby," Dominic said quietly. "I'm not afraid of Simon. I know that you are, and I hate it. For the time being, I know your safety and security is more important than how I feel. But I can't promise you how long I can keep the status quo."

"I know," she said. She rolled over and kissed him. "And I appreciate it, Dominic. Right now I'd rather just keep things as they are."

"Okay." He kissed her on the nose. "Your wish is my command."

She smiled and snuggled closer against him, shutting her eyes against the bright sunlight. They had several days alone together before Simon came home again, and she planned to enjoy every moment of them.

12.19.16.9.8

July 18, 2009 — "Where have you been?" Simon asked.

"At my telescope," Abby said, honestly surprised. She had told him several hours ago that she would be out in her clearing; he could have come out at any time and found her. Instead, when she came in just past midnight, she found him, sitting in the lab, alone. All the lights were out.

"What are you doing in here?" she asked, looking around, unable to see much in the shadows. The moon outside had been bright, making for lousy viewing, but it did little to illuminate the dim lab. Simon didn't seem to have any papers or books in front of him, and he sat still, unmoving. "Why are you sitting here in the dark?"

"You always say that you need complete darkness for looking at the sky, right?"

"Well, yeah, but ... don't you have a lamp? A flashlight, candle, anything?"

"No, I don't. Your boyfriend didn't think to provide any."

Abby ignored the comment. "Simon, there are candles in the kitchen, and several flashlights, with batteries. Besides that, our room is on the opposite side of the house from my clearing — you could sit up in the room and read ... or whatever it is you're doing out here."

"Are you telling me what to do now? Where I should be?" he asked, but immediately continued on, not giving her a chance to respond.

338

"Besides, it's hotter than fuck up there. I'm not sweltering up in that little fucking box."

Abby shook her head. "Whatever. I'm going to bed, Simon."

He stood up, and even though he was across the room from her, and not that much taller or stronger than she was, the movement was menacing. Abby sidled around the lab table, then stopped. She wasn't sure if she should head back outside, or up to the house. Her mind raced, trying to think of where Dominic might be.

"I'm coming with you," Simon said.

"Fine," Abby said, trying to keep her voice steady. She waited where she was, but Simon didn't move. They stood for a long moment in silence, neither moving, and Abby felt the sweat running down her back. Dominic hadn't passed through the clearing in the last few hours; in fact, she hadn't seen him since dinner. She thought he might be upstairs at the house, but was afraid that he had gone on a stroll, either up to the mountain, or through the woods towards Izapa.

Across the room, Simon laughed softly. "Screw it," he finally said, sitting back down. "Go to bed, Abby."

"You aren't coming?"

"No. I have work to do."

"Here in the dark?"

Simon's voice was distracted. "Don't worry about what I'm doing. You'll find out soon enough."

Abby waited for a moment, but it seemed as if Simon was finished speaking. "All right then," she said, heading for the door. She paused in the doorway, but Simon still sat silently, his back to her, his head slightly down. Frowning, Abby pushed the door open and headed up to the house.

She was on her way up the stairs, wondering if she should lock the bedroom door, and wondering if Simon was capable of breaking it down, when Dominic appeared on the second floor landing.

"Oh, thank god," Abby said, quickly taking the last few steps and collapsing into Dominic's embrace. "I didn't know where you were. I was afraid I was alone here with Simon."

"Not a chance," Dominic answered in his low, soothing voice. "I wouldn't go too far, sweets. I'm just trying to stay out of his way."

"What the hell is he doing?" Abby asked, stepping back out of his arms. "I found him down in the lab, sitting in the dark, not doing anything."

"I don't know," Dominic confessed. "He's been down there for a couple of hours now. He had a flashlight, and was reading, it looked like. I think he's trying to stay away from me, too."

"Do you just think he doesn't want us to know what he's up to, or is something more … I don't know …"

"Sinister?" Dominic supplied with a smile in his voice. "I don't know, Abby. He *has* been scary and weird lately, but honestly, not much more so than usual. I think we're just feeling guilty and paranoid, that's all."

She stepped up and kissed him lightly. "I hope that's all it is," she said. "Because if Simon's planning something, Dominic, I don't want any part of it."

"That makes two of us," he replied. "So — I guess we'd better not push our luck. Why don't you go to bed? I'm going to sit in the kitchen and look over some of our notes. I'll keep an eye on him. Don't worry, sweets, I'll never be far away."

"That's good to know," she said, closing her eyes as he kissed her again.

"I love you," he said.

"I love you too, Dominic," Abby answered. She watched as he took the stairs in twos, heading down to the kitchen. The light came on down below, and she heard the scratch of a chair on the linoleum, then a light thump as he sat down.

Abby went into the room she still shared with Simon on the weekends, kicking off her sandals as she headed for bed. She wanted to believe that Simon was simply being his usual standoffish, arrogant, domineering self, and really, she had no reason to think otherwise, she told herself. But then again, there was the gun. And Simon, sitting silent, hiding in the darkness like a cancer, alone.

Waiting.

12.19.16.9.14

July 24, 2009 — They stood together in the clearing, the bright sunlight flashing around them, shining off the bare, tanned skin of Abby's shoulders. Holding both of her hands, Dominic said: "We'll finish this soon. And then we're out of here, together. Simon can stay or go or do whatever he wants. But the day we put this thing together, you and I are packed up and gone."

Abby thought for a moment. "How are we going to conclude the project, Dominic? Are we going to write it up for submission? Or just say, 'Ok, this is what we think,' and call it a day?"

"I don't know," he admitted. "I think once we start getting close to the answer, we'll know. All I want is the answer. If you and I can get there without Simon, then we'll take off and leave him. He can do what he wants with the information he has. You and I will finish up on our own."

Abby frowned. "Simon is a smart man, Dominic. He may come across as impulsive and quick-tempered, but I've seen how he reacts when he thinks he's been wronged. If he gets wind that we're up to something, he won't burst out with it and call us on it. He'll bide his time and keep it to himself, until he gets a chance to take us by surprise."

Dominic sighed, stroking her long hair, hot and silky under the Mexican sun. "He doesn't know," he promised. "I don't think he suspects anything, Abby. He's pretty far gone now — way off in his own little world. I don't think he'd notice anything if we did it right in front of him."

Abby smiled, but it was uneasy. "Don't count him out yet, Dominic. He might not be paying attention to us in any obvious way, but I'm sure he's watching. He'll play the waiting game. He sees much more than he'll ever let on."

"I know," he said. "But I'm not afraid of him, Abby. If I thought either of us were in danger, I'd get us out of here. But I think there's still work to be done. I think Simon can still be a help to us."

"I hope you're just being goodhearted and not naïve. Well, at least it keeps us here, together. I don't know what will happen when it comes time to leave."

Dominic sat back, his dark eyes serious. "That's going to be your decision, Abby. You can go wherever you want. I'm hoping you won't go back to Boston."

She sighed. "I'm sure I won't. But it's the only home I've known for the past nine years. I don't know what else to do. I need to try to make up with my family, but I don't know that I'm ready to go home to them yet."

"There's always Chicago," he said lightly.

She smiled. "I know. I do want to be with you, Dominic. You know I love you. But I don't know that I'm ready yet — I don't know that I want to go straight from living with Simon to living with you."

Dominic shrugged. "You don't have to move in with me," he said. "You can be on your own, get your own place. It'd just be much more pleasant if I can see you whenever we want, instead of having to drive across a couple states to be near each other."

"What are you going to do back in Chicago?" Abby asked. "Why can't you move somewhere else?"

"I could," he said. "But at least in Chicago, I have a job waiting for me. I've worked in the research department at the University of Chicago for many years, and one of my colleagues told me I have a teaching position in her department any time I want it. I've always planned on taking it, once I was ready to finally settle down."

Abby laughed. "From university professor to university professor. I sure know how to pick 'em."

Dominic kissed her. "I'd like to think that's the only thing Simon and I have in common."

"Without a doubt," she said. "We need to get back. Simon's going to wonder where we are."

"Let him wonder," he said, but he released her. She stood on tiptoe and gave him another quick kiss, then stepped away.

They headed back up towards the house, careful to keep some distance between them in case Simon was watching their approach from the lab. Again, Dominic was tempted to take Abby's hand, to let Simon see them, and to finally allow the confrontation. He knew that Abby wasn't ready for it, yet, however, and he resigned himself to following her silently back up to the house.

12.19.16.9.15

July 25, 2009 — Simon came into the lab to find Dominic and Abby sitting across the table from each other, deep in conversation. Without a word, he slid onto the bench next to Abby, slipping an arm around her waist.

"Hi Simon," she said, not looking up from the notes in front of her.

"Hi, Simon?" he repeated mockingly. "The new semester is starting next week, you only have me here for a few more days, and all you can say is 'Hi, Simon'?"

Abby sighed. "What do you want me to say, Simon? I've seen you all day every day for the last month, since your summer classes ended. You coming in here isn't exactly a surprise to me."

Simon paused, but only for a moment. "You're getting a little too smart-assed for your own good, sweetheart." His tone was cold.

"Lay off, Simon," Dominic said. "Abby's life doesn't revolve around where you are and what you're doing — she's not waiting breathlessly for the next time you appear."

"Why don't you stay the fuck out of it?" Simon said.

"Because I'm tired of sitting here listening to your low-self esteem issues. You sat down, Abby said hi. Why is this even an issue?"

Simon stood up suddenly. "You can't wait for me to leave next week again, can you? You just want this place and Abby all to yourself again."

"That's not all I want," Dominic said. "I want peace and quiet. I want to know I can get some work done without your wandering stupidity crashing in to interrupt and annoy me. I can't get you away from me fast enough."

"Fuck you, Ciriello," Simon said, pushing the lab table. It barely budged, but Abby jumped, startled. "You'd better watch who you're messing with, you hear me? I don't give a shit if you're bigger than me. You don't want to turn your back on me."

"I don't plan to," Dominic said. There was no threat in his voice, only the same calm, matter-of-fact tone that Simon found so infuriating. Unable to come up with a good retort, he simply stormed out, slamming the door behind him. The flimsy, light-weight screen door landed gently in the frame, taking even that satisfaction away from him.

Dominic turned around and glanced out the window to see Simon taking out his anger on a small rock, which he gave a mighty kick, immediately followed by him swearing and hopping around on one foot.

Dominic turned away quickly, trying to smother his laughter, and he glanced up to see Abby doing the same. When they both had control of themselves again, their eyes met, and Dominic reached out and took her hand.

"He's out of control," he said.

"That he is," she said. "I think it'd be in our best interests to not push his buttons anymore."

"I don't plan to," Dominic repeated, but this time, with a smile. "Simon might be a jackass, but I'm not stupid. I don't intend to let him see me laughing at him, and I don't plan to egg him on. I was never one to throw stones at beehives, or tease the neighbor's dog."

He barely had the words out when they heard the door open again. Quickly, Dominic moved his hand, reaching for the notebook in front of them. He need not have rushed, however; Simon didn't look at either of them. They sat and watched as he limped across the room, grabbing the door and swinging it open, heading back up towards the house. He didn't say a word, and Dominic and Abby had decided it would be wise to not comment.

They waited until he was gone, almost up at the back door of the house, before Abby said, "I hope he broke his damn foot."

Dominic laughed. "I don't," he said. "He'd probably play invalid and make you wait on him hand and foot for the next six weeks. And we'd never get rid of him."

"You do have a point."

"Come on," Dominic said, standing up. He held out his hand, and she took it, rising from the bench.

"Let's get the hell out of here for awhile," he said, "across the field, up the mountain, anywhere. Simon is being foul and pissy today, and I can live without that."

"I agree," Abby responded. "How about we head out to Izapa? You can read the stelae to me. I want to finish my matrix of the sky-map of Izapa and Mayan mythology."

"Sounds good to me," Dominic said. "Let's get the hell out of here."

12.19.16.11.4

August 23, 2009 — Simon looked impatient, waiting for Dominic to sit down.

"All right, Simon, tell us what you have."

"The Long Count *was* the original Olmec calendar," Simon said. He saw Dominic's look of surprise and nodded. "What the hell do you think I did all week at the university?" he asked. "I had plenty of time between classes, and I did some research. I looked into what you had said earlier about the Maya not being the native culture of Central America; that there was someone here first."

"The Olmecs."

"That's right. And no one knows who they were or where they came from. The only relics they left were mysterious markers like those huge stone African heads."

"African heads?" Abby echoed, mystified.

Dominic shrugged. "Not like the Easter Island heads, but similar in size. These statues were absolutely massive. Big round heads, with hair and facial features like black Africans. Absolutely beautiful, intricately detailed work. If it's a sign of the civilization that pre-dated the Maya, then history has a lot of explaining to do."

Simon looked perturbed that Dominic had stolen some of his spotlight, but he quickly continued as if uninterrupted. "So either there were black Africans in central America 1,500 years ago, or the civilizations around here had done some traveling overseas, both of which are supposed to be impossible according to history. That's not my point. My point is that the Long Count begins in the time of the Olmecs. Mayan civilization didn't come for hundreds of years more; their golden age wasn't until 600 AD."

"That's true," Dominic said patiently. "But that doesn't mean the Olmecs created the Long Count. I mean, it's a valid hypothesis, one that other researchers have posited before you. But there's no conclusive evidence of it."

"Yeah?" Simon challenged. "I can't prove it, either. But I know what the beginning date means. And *that* I can prove."

Dominic was careful not to let his expression change. "So what is it?" he asked. He folded his arms and leaned against the lab table, watching Simon with a mistrustful eye.

"The start date is the date of Quetzlcoatl's arrival."

Abby and Dominic exchanged a look, which Simon caught. "I told you I could prove it," he said.

"Go for it, then," Dominic said, sitting down. "This should be interesting."

"All right, I will." Simon sounded like a spoiled child. He stalked over to the white board, picking up a marker and starting to write. His body blocked the board for a moment, but after he had to bend over slightly to write on the lower board, Abby could see that he was making a long list, and she began to smile. Simon turned around and caught her look. "Ok," he said. "You want to tell him what these numbers are or do you want me to?"

"They're the distances I compiled for you awhile ago," she said. "I'm interested in seeing what you did with them."

"Then I'll tell you," he said. "But first, you tell me." He pointed again at the board: "What are these?"

"Numbers," Dominic said, and now it was his turn to sound impatient.

"That's right," Simon answered. "And what do you use numbers for? Counting. Time. Distance."

He turned to them again. "You talk about the Great Year, the precessional cycle, being 25,920 years. Damn close to the Maya's five ages of 5,126 years each, right?"

"Right," Dominic said. "But we've already gone over that."

"I'm just telling you how I came to this," Simon said. "What the hell do you think a calendar measures but astronomical distance? It's measuring the movements of the sun and Earth. All calendars do." He pointed to the first number he'd carefully printed on the board. "This is the speed of light: 186,000 miles per second. You said this was a calendar based on sun cycles, but it's not the sun they were concerned with, it's the light. The speed and distance of light are evenly divisible into the numbers of the Long Count."

"So they were measuring light years?"

"Very possibly," Simon said. "We've been all caught up in concept of the Long Count as a measure of time. But they could have been calculating distance. You and Abby were raving a while back about the distance to the galactic center. My hypothesis is this: The Long Count actually is a set of coordinates — time and location. And when those points come together, a doorway will open near the center of the galaxy. The time it will happen is on that date, and the Long Count is giving us the distance to the doorway. Or the distance from which our visitors are traveling. Maybe even some point, or coordinate, where they're originating from."

"Would the Maya have been able to measure light years, though?" Abby asked.

"Obviously, whoever came to visit them the first time gave them the counting system. How else would they know the distance between the planets, or between star systems, unless someone who'd traveled those distances told them? And it wouldn't have been the Maya they'd told it to, it'd have been the Olmecs. They're the ones who were around at the beginning date."

Dominic shook his head. "It's too messy, too complicated to work with. Visitors from another planet would have a far more advanced mathematics, a much quicker system than this long, involved multiplication of numbers. Hell, you've said as much yourself."

"And you've said, how do we know how advanced they were? Maybe they were able to calculate distances in time and space and calculate light years to get here, but they hadn't learned to annotate yet."

"That makes no logical sense," Abby insisted. "To work with such complex mathematics, they would have to have had a less ungainly system. They could never have traveled great distances using such an awkward method. They couldn't have calculated anything."

"But the Maya did," Dominic said. He stood up, crossing to the board to study the numbers up close. "How many dimensions are we working with here? Time, space, distance, velocity? What were they measuring? Distance? Was this a map, not a calendar?"

Simon beamed. "Very possibly. I know I laughed at you before when you were talking about UFOs, but I think now you have to consider an advanced intelligence that might have been giving us directions. I'm tempted to think they were giving directions into our galaxy — look at that Sumerian tablet you were talking about, where they embossed the planets of our solar system. They knew where we were, where to find us."

"Where are they pointing us?"

"To some destination in the stars."

Dominic examined the numbers thoughtfully, then returned to the bench and sat down, leaning back against the lab table, crossing his long legs at the ankle. He folded his arms across his chest. "Just one small argument, Simon: Why would the Maya — or the Olmecs, if you will — be using the American system of measurement? Why not the metric system? Or the Imperial system? Your numbers work just fine in miles, but when you transcribe them to kilometers they won't stand up.

Whatever their system of measurement – call it 'Mayan Standard Time,' or whatever you will – the numbers don't match up unless you assume they were using the same system as you are. That's more than doubtful; it's improbable. Even today, Mexico uses the metric system.

"It just doesn't work, Simon. I'm sorry, but it's coincidence. Forcing the numbers to bend to your criteria isn't going to work. All you're doing is data-searching and pattern seeking."

Simon looked stunned, then furious. "Well, screw you, then," he said, dropping the chalk back into the tray. "I *know* what this is. It's a map of the stars. I'm finding numerical solutions, one by one — it's like a bunch of tumblers falling into place, a combination we only need the right numbers to unlock. Time, distance, and space — if we can get all of them right, and lock them into place at the right moment, we could unlock the secret of the universe! And what will happen when the final tumbler falls?"

"I'd very much like to know," Dominic admitted, "but I also know you can't force the numbers to fit your hypothesis."

"Look, Ciriello, I know this is right. The numbers will work. I just need to play with them enough."

"Then prove it," Dominic said. "This is interesting, and I'd like to see you go farther with it."

"Why the hell is it up to me to prove it? I'm right. What else am I suppose to come up with that'll make you happy?"

"The burden of proof lies on you, Simon. Scientifically, theologically, mathematically, whatever; if you come up with a theory, it's up to you to prove it. It's not the responsibility of the rest of the world to prove you wrong. You made the claim; back it up. Science is different than mathematics, Simon — we don't prove things, we support them with evidence. You can say whatever you want, but you need to back it up."

"I am," Simon stormed. "Look, the numbers work. It's not just light speed; it's the speed of our own planet, and the length of our orbit. All the numbers are evenly divisible into the Long Count. How could they know this? How could they possibly have figured out how fast the Earth moves? How would they know the velocities of planets and their distances from Earth, and from the sun? The distances to the nearest star system? How could they measure the distances the Earth travels through space?"

"How did *we* do it?" Abby countered. "Observation, and measurement. We've calculated distances we've never traveled."

"Cultures more ancient than the Maya figured out the Earth was round long before anyone ever traveled around it," Dominic spoke up. "Erathosthenes calculated a nearly exact diameter for it, measuring the lengths of the shadows of two different sticks at two different latitudes, using the difference in the lengths and the difference in the distance between them to calculate."

"You of all people should know, Simon," Abby said. "You don't need to actually travel when you have math."

Simon shot her a hard look, but for once, she didn't avert her eyes. "There's a big difference between calculating the size and shape of the Earth, and calculating its speed," he said.

Dominic rose to his feet again. "So what are you saying, Simon? That the Maya were really aliens that traveled across the universe to get here?"

"You don't have to be sarcastic about it."

"Well, what else could it be?" Dominic threw his arms wide, coming around the table. "How else could they make these computations without modern instruments? How else could they calculate such distances?"

"Good questions," Simon said. "What's your explanation?"

"My explanation is that your hypothesis is wrong. You're forcing the data. I'm all for looking at whatever evidence we have before us. But your numbers are wrong."

"Bullshit. My numbers are right. Maybe not exactly; maybe the system of measurement needs adjusted— but I know I'm onto something here. You just wait until I get it worked out. This will be the most important discovery known to mankind."

Dominic shook his head. "Just leave my name off of it."

"Don't worry about that — you think I'd let you in on this?"

"I'd be eternally grateful to you if you didn't," he said.

"You just wait. You'll be begging me to recognize you when I'm on all the talk shows, telling the greatest story ever told."

"I'd be willing to bet money against that, but do what you have to do, Simon. Work on your numbers. Let the rest of us know when you've got them working."

"Hell no. Why should I let either of you in on it? Here you are mocking me now, but as soon as you realize I'm right, you'll be clamoring over each other to steal my theory."

"Jesus, you're insane," Dominic said. "You think either of us would embarrass ourselves by putting forth such drivel?"

"Your boy Steve would've shit himself over this," Simon said. "He'd have been all over this."

"Don't desecrate the memory of the dead," Dominic said, his smile fading. "Steve had way too much sense for this bullshit."

"Yeah, that's why his main argument for anything was 'that's what the Bible says.'"

"Drop it, Simon," Abby said. "You can't push that button anymore."

"Can't I?" he asked quietly. Abby turned to Dominic, but the larger man had turned away, bracing himself against the screen door as he stared out into the darkness. All humor and expression had gone out of his face. Without a word, he stepped back to swing open the screen door, then went out into the night.

"Why are you so hateful?" Abby asked, standing up.

"You're too damn sensitive," Simon said, shaking his head.

She didn't respond, just opened the door and followed Dominic out into the darkness.

"Great, why don't you go out into the fucking courtyard and talk about what an asshole I am," Simon said, raising his voice as the other two moved further away from the lab. "Meanwhile, I'll be in here being the only one working!" He finished with a shout.

There was no response from the darkness, and with a sound of disgust, he turned back to the board to begin double-checking his numbers.

12.19.16.11.9

August 28, 2009 — "Where the hell have you been?" Simon asked. He was standing by the window in their bedroom, illuminated by the moonlight. His back was to her, but she could see his arms folded across his chest. Even in the sweltering heat, he was wearing a heavy shirt.

"I've been down in the lab."

"Bullshit. I checked there. I've fucking been home since six o'clock. It's almost two a.m. I've looked all over this damn place for you. Where have you been?"

"I told you," she insisted. She was exhausted, having just returned from the lab after a long trek around the base of the mountain. "Dominic and I went for a walk up the mountain earlier today. We took lunch, and went around the side to look down into Izapa. We ended up being up there late, and just got back an hour or so ago. We've been down in the lab ever since."

"I don't believe you."

Abby slipped off her shirt and reached into a drawer for another, sliding it on. She knew she needed a shower, but right now was too tired to care. "I'm telling you the truth. Go ask Dominic if you don't believe me."

"Right, like he doesn't have the same story prepared that you do."

"We were just walking and working, Simon. That's all. We were looking for landmarks, for geographical features around Izapa to see if there was any placement or anything that might be meaningful."

"Bullshit. You've had a year to look at that place."

"I give up, Simon. You're not going to listen to me anyway, so I'm going to bed."

"You fucking whore."

"That's what whores do, don't they, Simon?" Abby answered wearily. "They fuck. Now why don't you grow the hell up? I'm tired of your language, I'm tired of your jealousy, and I'm damn tired of your paranoia. But most of all, I'm just tired. Now leave me alone and let me go to bed."

Simon was floored.

"You did not just speak to me like that."

"You heard me. Look, Simon, I've been up all night and I'm too tired to argue with you. Believe what you want to, I just don't have the energy to fight about it."

He came across the room, grabbing her arm. Abby struggled briefly. "Damn it, Simon. What is it? What's the problem here?"

"The problem is that you don't even speak to me anymore. You're with Ciriello all the time. You don't even notice whether I'm here or not."

"Trust me, I notice," she said, twisting out of his grasp. She pulled back the sheets and climbed into bed. "And it's not exactly like you come looking for me. I don't know when you get here, and you don't even tell me half the time before you leave. And you never call to tell me whether you're coming back or not. It's a crapshoot as to whether you'll show up or not on any given weekend."

"You try driving several hours to get back here at the end of a long work week," he stormed. "What's the fucking point? I'm so damn tired when I get here that I can't even do anything except rest until I have to turn around and drive right back again."

"Or maybe you just have something more interesting back in the city to keep you there."

He froze. "And what is that supposed to mean?" he asked icily.

She rolled over, turning away from him and pulling the covers up to her chin. "You tell me, Simon. I call the number you gave me and no one ever answers. Every now and then I get your office voice mail. You won't even give your own fiancée your home number?"

"I don't have a phone there," he said quickly. "Why pay to hook one up when I have one in the office I use all the time?"

She sighed. "Drop it, Simon. I don't give a damn anymore. Let me sleep."

He stared at her, speechless, watching the covers rise and fall with her breathing. He was thrown by her sudden fearlessness, and while part of him was tempted to drag her from the bed and have it out with her for daring to stand up to him, he was also afraid of where this might be going. And he knew that Dominic was only a few yards down the hall and he didn't think the larger man would sit and listen to Simon berating Abby for very long.

"I need a drink," he said, mostly to himself. He flicked off the light and left the room, heading down to the kitchen. He was shocked to find that he was shaking.

Once he had poured himself a drink and was standing at the doorway, looking out into the darkness of the courtyard, he reached around to the small of his back, feeling the handgun he now always carried. The night-vision monocular was hidden upstairs, and he considered bringing it down. He'd been practicing with it, learning to sight through it while aiming with the other hand, but he could still use some practice. The silencer was upstairs, too, though, and he knew that rummaging around to locate both, and then taking the chance of getting caught with them, were more than he wanted right now. He thought Ciriello might still have some information he needed, and until then, he thought his target practice was better kept secret. He was counting on the element of surprise, hoping to catch the larger man somewhere remote – preferably on the mountain, or in the jungle, where weather and predators would take care of any evidence.

As for what to do about Abby, he still hadn't decided yet. He took another belt of his drink, weighing whether he'd get more enjoyment out of forcing her back to Boston with him, or leaving her in Mexico to rot, and the more he thought about it, the wider his smile became. Whatever his decision, he finally concluded, he could live with it.

12.19.16.12.3

September 11, 2009 — They sat watching the starlight on the water, Abby resting comfortably between Dominic's legs, leaning back against him. "Simon was off in his numbers."

"What do you mean?"

"I double-checked them. He's basing most of this on the importance of the Venus cycle to the Maya; the problem is, the Venus cycle isn't divisible into the supernumber."

"Sure it is. 584 days."

"That's the problem — the Venus cycle isn't 584 days — it's 583.92 days. I know the rounding seems small, but it really makes a difference when divided into the Count."

"Did the Maya know that?"

"Of course they did. They were astronomically and mathematically precise. They had the Earth's solar year measured to 365.2420 days; they were only off by .0002 days, which is almost meaningless. They knew what a sidereal year was. They were exact. They wouldn't have fudged the Venus cycle to fit their numbers. Only Simon would do that."

Dominic laughed. "I knew it was all bullshit, but he did have me curious when he claimed that the different planetary cycles fit the Long Count."

Abby shook her head, and she sounded almost disappointed. "Whether they do or not, they don't seem to have any bearing on the end of the Count. It's not the answer we've been looking for."

Dominic kissed the top of her head, hugging his arms tighter around her. She settled back against him again. "I'm not worried about it," he said. "When we came out here, I thought the Long Count was the most important thing in the world to me. I've come a long way since then."

She looked down at their linked hands. "I think when Steve died, it put all of our priorities into the proper order."

"Yes," he said, looking out at the rippling water, black in the moonlight. "I think I realized that life is short enough as it is. I don't need to worry about when the world is going to end — I just want to make sure that I live while I'm here."

Abby tilted her head and kissed him, catching him on the chin. He smiled.

"So — regarding Simon's bullshit," she said, turning back to the water again. "Do you think he'll try to go forward with it?"

"I don't know," Dominic answered honestly. "He's so proud of his degrees and his public persona, I can't believe he'd go that far. Not once he gets back to U.S., anyway. He has too much to lose."

"You may be right. Besides, do you really think anyone would believe him?"

"Some would. There are a lot of people out there who wouldn't question it — any idea, if it's interesting enough, has merit to them. Screw evidence, screw possibility; people don't want to hear why the laws of physics disallow something, they just want a good story. And a lot of people want to believe."

"But this is pretty far out."

"Sure it is. It sounds like H.P. Lovecraft. His alien gods gave the gift of civilization to Earth's backwards people. The only difference is that Lovecraft made a point of reminding people his work was fiction, and told them not to take it seriously. But like I said, people don't question.

Simon's idiocy is no more far out than Heaven's Gate or the Raelians. People will believe anything; all they have to do is *want* it to be true ."

"Hah — that'd be Simon's dream job; starting his own cult."

"Why not? He's a smart man. There's a lot of money to be had in it, and he knows that. Hell, L. Ron Hubbard, a science fiction writer, who said that if you really want to make a lot of money, start your own religion. And he did; Scientology is one of the wealthiest religions on Earth."

"I don't think Simon would take it that far."

"He'll take it as far as he can. You know that. He could start off selling books. He'll do lecture tours. He'll put up a website and sell videotapes and transcripts of his lectures, and probably ask for donations and investors in his research. He wouldn't be the first to do it, and he sure as hell won't be the last."

"I feel like we should stop him," Abby said, troubled.

"Should we? Where's the harm in it? He's not selling a cure for cancer, or a pyramid scheme. If people want to spend their hard earned money on bullshit, is it up to us to stop them?"

"I understand that, Dominic, but still … I feel like we'd be knowingly aiding and abetting a criminal. I mean, we *know* his numbers are wrong. We know he's selling a load of bull. I want to put out a warning."

"There's a huge audience out there for this kind of crap, but it's not like they're going to make much difference in the big scheme of things. Their numbers aren't great enough to matter. So a few hundred, even a few thousand nuts dig bomb shelters and hide out with their shotguns and toilet paper on the night of December twentieth. They'll come out again on the twenty-second, and life will go on."

Abby sighed. "I suppose you're right. I just keep thinking about Heaven's Gate. They all committed suicide because of the comet Hale-Bop. Who knows what people will do if they think the entire *world* is going to end?"

Dominic put his arm around her and pulled her tight. "If it looks like it's going to come to that, we'll out him," he said. "There won't be any mass suicides or homicides on my watch, Abby."

She smiled and held him close. "I hope you're right, Dominic. I have enough faith in humankind that Simon will sell a few books to the random curiosity-seeker, and that'll be the end of him. He'll be like every other amateur loon on the internet hawking his own brand of UFO history."

"Exactly," Dominic said. "Meanwhile, you and I are *out* of here."

12.19.16.12.4

September 12, 2009 — "So, you're going to promote your distance theory."

"Damn straight I am. Because I'm right."

"Simon, you're *not* right. This is pseudoscience of the worst sort. You *know* you're wrong, yet you're hiding facts that disprove your theory and selecting your data to fit it."

"So what's it to you? Do you want to be part of it?"

"Good god, no. I don't want anything to do with your bullshit theories. I don't want my name mentioned with yours."

"You don't think it'll come up? When I publish my theory and people start investigating, you don't think they'll come to you? You need to support me on this."

Dominic laughed derisively. "You're insane. You know I'd never support this."

"Then I'll make you look like a fool in the scientific journals. Trust me, I can be convincing, Ciriello. Either you take my side, or you take the blame for it. You can be the hero, or you can be the goat."

"I'm not going to be anything, Simon. Leave me out of it. You can put forth any bullshit theory you want, but it won't stand alone. In pseudoscientific circles you can all sit around and kiss each other's ass over your theories as much as you want, without any actual fact-checking. But once you put it out into the real world, independent scientists are going to go through your numbers, and they're going to call you on it."

"We'll see about that."

"It's not a threat, Simon. It's a warning. Most pseudoscientific claims can't be disproved. Now, we both know that they're not worth anything if they can't be falsified — it does no good to put out a claim that you can neither prove nor disprove. You're not even that lucky. You *can* be disproved. Easily."

"Again," Simon said, "we'll see about that. I just need to do a little more work on it. You think you speak for everyone, but you have no idea what the public thinks."

Dominic sighed. "That's the sad thing. I do. I'd like to think I speak for the scientific community, at least, even though I know it doesn't much matter to the world at large what science disproves. The public believes more and more in magical thinking; psychics, spoon benders, people who talk to the dead. You can prove cold reading, magicians, and fraud, but people will believe what they want to believe. And sadly enough, they'll probably believe you."

"Not if you have anything to do with it, though, right, Ciriello?"

Dominic shook his head. "I'm done with you. You can run out into the world with your flawed theory and see who buys it. Sooner or later, someone will bring you down, and I'll love seeing it. But it won't be me — I just want to be shut of you. Don't worry, Simon. I won't tell anyone that you're a fraud."

Simon waved a hand dismissively. "I'm not worried about you, Ciriello."

"You don't have a problem with us just up and leaving." It was a statement, not a question.

"I'm beyond the point of giving a shit what either of you do."

"When you came down here, it was only to make sure Abby couldn't get away from you. What have you found that means more to you than that?"

"None of your business, Ciriello. You win. Take her. I don't want her. I don't want to hear anything from either of you ever again."

"Fine by me," Dominic said. Relieved as he was that Simon was putting up no argument, he was unnerved. Simon should never have acquiesced so easily.

"What are you up to, Simon?"

"Nothing. You guys always accuse *me* of being paranoid; what's gotten into *you*?"

Dominic shook his head, then turned and walked a couple steps away. He paused to stare out the window into the night, hands on his hips. "What are you hiding, Simon?"

"God damn it, I'm not hiding anything." His voice was finally beginning to rise. "Just take your bi ..." He cut off suddenly.

Dominic turned around slowly. "Take my what?"

Simon shook his head quickly, backing away. "Abby. Just get the hell out. Leave me here with the lab."

"You hate it here."

"But I want to keep working on the Long Count. I need to be here where I can measure, where I can count."

"Then set up a tent by Izapa like all the other researchers. I didn't just pay for this place, I built it with my own two hands. I'm not turning it over to you."

"What if I refuse to leave?"

Dominic's look was the only answer he needed.

"Fine. Just because you're bigger than me. Big fucking deal. Fine. Settle things with violence. I knew you weren't the brain you pretended to be; you're just like any other big dumbass, wanting settle things physically because you don't have the brains to talk about it. Fine. I'll leave. I'll pack my shit up and be gone by morning."

"Make sure that you are," Dominic said. He stood his ground.

The two men stared at each other for a long moment, and finally, Simon laughed. "You think you're kicking me out, that this is insulting me in some way. But I don't give a shit. We weren't getting anywhere here anyway. It was a total waste of fucking time. So it's time to go. Hell, it's past time to go."

"I love the way your opinion changes every time you lose another point."

"I haven't lost anything, Ciriello. You haven't gotten anything over on me. I don't need to stay here; I'll probably do better back in Boston, in my beautiful home with my huge salary. I wasn't meant to live in this shithole, so it's a good thing we're all finally leaving." Simon smirked, then turned and left the lab.

Dominic watched him go, still uneasy about his reaction. He'd expected anger, maybe even a physical confrontation. But Simon had taken it all in stride. Whatever was going on with him, Dominic didn't trust it. Still, he figured he'd give Simon time to get his things together before he trailed after him, so it was a good twenty minutes later before he headed out the door and back up towards the house.

"Dominic!" Abby hissed.

Dominic paused, coming up the walk. He peered into the darkness beside the house until he saw movement.

"Abby, what are you doing, hiding in the shadows?"

"Being a wuss," she whispered, pulling him into the dark shadow of the house. "I didn't know where to go. Simon stormed into the house and ran up the stairs – a few seconds later I heard him throwing stuff around up in the bedroom. I don't know what he's doing, but I didn't want to be in the house when he came back down. I didn't know what he might say to me, and I didn't want to be alone with him. But then again, I didn't want to stray too far away, either, and leave you alone with him. I don't know where the gun is. It wasn't in the room."

Dominic reached out and took her hand. "Come on," he said. "We're getting out of here for awhile."

They moved swiftly down the hill, skirting the lab and crossing the courtyard in a near jog. Far behind them, the door to the house slammed open, and Abby felt a surge of panic. "Where are we going?" She whispered.

Dominic shook his head, hurrying her along. They crossed the bridge above the lagoon and headed into the clearing, and she understood. The keys to both vehicles were still hanging from their pegs up in the kitchen. Simon might come looking for them on foot along the path they'd worn through the jungle between the house and Izapa, or by car out to the old ruins themselves.

There was one place, however, that Simon didn't know about, and had never been. From the cave up on the mountain, they'd be able to watch the house below and see when one of the two vehicles out front had gone. Simon would never climb the mountain to look for them, and with the sheer size of it, the odds of him ever finding their cave would be slim to none.

"What if he doesn't leave, though?" Abby asked. "We can't wait him out forever."

"I have a feeling we have more patience than he does," Dominic said, but before he could continue, they heard the loud, splintering crash of glass shattering. Both Dominic and Abby stumbled, trying to look back towards the house as they ran, but they could see nothing in the distant darkness. The sound was repeated, several times more, as more glass was pulverized.

"That had to be the car windows," Dominic mused. "It's the only glass we have out here."

"Why would he do that?" Abby asked, starting to pant from fear and exertion. Still, neither of them slowed down.

"Taking out his frustrations since he can't find us, maybe?" Dominic suggested. "Or else he wants to render one of the vehicles inoperable so we can't get away. He probably grabbed the keys to the other one."

"We can still drive with a seat full of broken window glass," Abby said.

"He probably shot out the tires, too," Dominic said. "Or slashed them. We just can't hear that from here."

"Why can we hear breaking glass, but not gunshots?"

Dominic shook his head. "I don't know. Even at this distance, maybe he doesn't want anyone to hear gunshots. There could always be tourists at Izapa, or someone that could overhear and point it out to the police if we end up shot, or missing."

"My God," Abby said breathlessly. "He probably *could* get away with killing us, couldn't he? Neither of us have families looking for us. He could bury us somewhere and we'd never be found. Or if anyone ever asked, he could say we ran him off and he has no idea what became of us."

"Well, let's not give him that chance," Dominic said, quickening his pace.

Abby squeezed his hand a little tighter, and they rushed silently into the darkness.

12.19.16.12.5

September 13, 2009 — "Abby. Abby, wake up."

"Hmmm? What is it, Dominic?"

"Wake up. The house is on fire."

"What?" She jerked awake, almost striking her head on the cave roof above her. She crawled out, scrambling to her feet beside Dominic. On the valley floor far below them, the hillside was in flames. The orange and yellow columns licked the darkness, illuminating the house and lab as they began to collapse in on themselves, consumed by the fire.

"That son of a bitch," Abby said. Dominic reached out blindly, putting an arm around her shoulders, not turning away from the destruction below.

"I'm so sorry, Dominic," Abby said. Her voice was full of tears. He pulled her against his chest, holding her against him, but still, he didn't turn away from the flames.

Suddenly, a huge explosion rocked the hillside, and Abby jumped with a small shriek.

"The propane tank," Dominic explained emotionlessly, holding her against his chest again. "The next one you hear is going to be the truck."

"Oh shit, Dominic. I can't believe this."

"Believe it, Abby."

She pulled away from him and turned around, watching the fire rage on the hillside below. Dominic put his arms around her waist, supporting her against him. Her legs felt weak as she watched the house and lab burn.

"Better cover your ears," Dominic said. Abby looked to see the flames beginning to overtake the pickup truck parked out front of the house. The SUV was gone.

Abby turned her head, and a moment later, the sound of another explosion roared across the valley. She listened to the fire burn, roaring and crackling, the sound carrying easily in the high, clear air. "So how do we get out of here?" she finally asked.

Dominic shrugged. "If the fire doesn't draw anyone's attention, then we walk to Izapa in the morning and wait for a tour bus. We'll have the driver call the fire department, or whoever they can get out here to put this out before the whole jungle goes up in flames. If all else fails, we'll walk a little farther out to the village you worked in a couple years back. They might remember you, and someone will have a phone, or some transportation."

Abby nodded. "It's summer; there may even be another charity group out there."

"It's cloudy anyway," Dominic said, "it'll probably rain in a few hours and help put this out before it spreads too far. We'll be fine. So, the only question I have for you now is: How do you feel about Chicago?"

Part III: Xibalba Be

"The hardest thing of all is to find a black cat in a dark room — especially if there is no cat."

— Confucius

"Man prefers to believe what he prefers to be true."

— Francis Bacon

"What the caterpillar calls the end, the rest of the world calls a butterfly."

— Lao Tzu

12.19.18.10.16

August 5, 2011 — "I first became involved with the Long Count in 2008," Simon said. The lights were hot on his face, and he could feel perspiration beginning to dampen his hair at the temples. He resisted the urge to reach up and wipe it away, praying they would break for a commercial soon.

"A student of mine introduced me to a group of researchers who had an interest in the Count. I met with them and we compared notes, which gave me a better background of Mayan history and mythology for me to work the numbers. Once I really started looking, I started to notice the patterns. I spent over a year teaching advanced mathematics in southern Mexico, and I drove out to Izapa, the birthplace of the Count, every weekend. It was a lot of work, but by the end of 2009, I had my theory well established."

"Your book, *Countdown to the End of Time*, will be coming out in a few months," Anne Norton, the popular morning host of the Boston news program, commented. "What can we expect to learn about what will happen in 2012?"

"Well, the theory is complex, but I've tried to explain it as simply as possible. I was afraid that if I got into the numbers too much, it might put people off. So I stuck to the basic story, with the belief that most intelligent people would recognize my credentials and understand that I had done the science to back it up.

"You see," Simon continued, "the Mayan civilization was started by a mysterious stranger named Kulkulcan. Kulkulcan and his brethren brought civilization to all the indigenous peoples of Central America — the Maya, the Inca, and the Aztecs. The culture-bearers were called different names by the different tribes, but it was the same race of people that helped all the Indians. This group educated the people, taught them how to cultivate crops and domesticate animals. Their civilizations rose to their glory days, and Kulkulcan and the other visitors left, just as mysteriously as they had appeared. He and the others promised that they would return some day."

Norton was nodding, but Simon saw her eyes dart to her producer. He knew he had to hurry.

"I have worked the numbers of the Count and determined that the Maya were counting down to the return of Kulkulcan. The date of his return will be December 21, 2012."

"What can we expect when he returns?"

"You'll have to read my book," Simon said, then tempered her look of disappointment with a disarming smile. She smiled back, and he leaned forward a little. "I would love to be able to tell you all about it, but I know we don't have much time."

"You're right," she said, and turned to the camera. "We're speaking with Boston University's Dr. Simon Thomas Nieson, about his startling theory of the Long Count. We also have live via satellite a visiting lecturer of astronomy at Harvard University, Dr. Mao Lin. Dr. Mao, tell us why you disagree with Dr. Nieson's theory."

"The Maya were astronomers," the scientist said, looking down disdainfully from her screen. "They could calculate astronomical alignments, conjunctions, and eclipses hundreds of years into the future. They were very capable mathematicians when it came to working with the movements of the stars and planets, but that's as far as their mathematics went. They were incapable of measuring the distances between heavenly bodies, or their velocity, or their orbits.

"The end of the Long Count signifies an alignment or conjunction," Dr. Mao stated flatly. "To think that it's counting down to anything significant — the end of the world, the return of Christ — or Kulkulcan — is simply not possible."

"That's why you'll have to read my book," Simon replied, trying not to wince as a bead of cold sweat trickled down his neck. "I explain precisely which astronomical alignment the Maya were waiting for, and why this alignment — which only occurs once every five thousand years — will usher in the return of the bringers of Mayan civilization."

"Dr. Nieson, is there any mention of this in the Mayan records?" the host asked.

"There's plenty of talk of Kulkulcan," Simon responded. "He's the most important figure in Mayan history."

"That's simply not true," Dr. Mao interrupted. "He's part of their legends, but he's certainly no more important than any of their leaders, or anyone else in their myths. And there's no mention whatsoever of visitors coming from another star system."

"You're not an expert on the Maya," Simon snapped.

Before he could continue, she answered: "Neither are you. But I know enough to know that the Maya recorded practically everything, and yet there's no mention of this."

"With all due respect, I have much more experience with Mayan mythology than you, Lin," Simon replied, "And just because there's no specific glyph saying that on December 21, 2012, Kulkulcan will return, it doesn't mean that it isn't true. The Maya may not have had reason to specifically point it out, because they didn't know that they wouldn't be there. When the end of the Count rolled around and Kulkulcan returned, they fully expected to be there to welcome him. Besides," he added, "such a glyph might very well exist, but it could have been destroyed, or we just haven't found it yet."

Before the astronomer could reply, the program's theme music started up, and the host interrupted: "Dr. Nieson, Dr. Mao; thank you both for joining us this morning. When we come back, we'll have Blair Lewis with us live from Jerusalem with an update on growing tensions. We'll be right back."

The host smiled brightly into the camera until the red "On Air" light winked out. She quickly thanked Dr. Mao once more before the satellite link was disconnected, then turned again to Simon. "So, I'll have to wait until December to hear your complete theory?"

Simon gave her an easy smile, as smooth as ever. "Not necessarily," he said to the pretty blonde host. "I'd love to give you a private interview. Imagine the benefits of having the exclusive on it. The book won't be out for several more months, and you can be the first to know the details. You have no idea how world-changing this event will be," he said.

"Well, I'm not sure ..." she began, her smile faltering.

"Trust me," he said, reaching out to touch her hand lightly. "Let me take you to dinner and we'll discuss it. I can give you a preview of the book."

"That would be great," she said, brightening again as she gazed into his blue eyes . "I'd like that."

"Me too," he said, but as he set about making plans to get together with her, his mind wasn't on the lovely young newscaster.

He was thinking of an hour long TV special, all about him.

12.19.19.0.14

January 10, 2012 — "I can't believe this."

"What is it, honey?" Abby asked. She took a step back and looked through the kitchen pass-through. Dominic was sitting at the dining room table, half dressed for work; he was finishing his cup of tea and reading the paper.

"Damn it, he *knows* his numbers are wrong. I can't believe this."

"What's going on?"

"Simon is promoting his theory." Dominic shook his head, half in disbelief, half irritation. "He knows damn well it's based on faulty logic and that his data is flawed. But he's going ahead with it anyway."

"Sure, when has Simon ever let a little thing like a fact get in his way?"

"But surely he realizes someone will catch it," Dominic mused, almost to himself. "He couldn't take the embarrassment of being caught in a blatant mistake and have his theory debunked in the public eye."

"He is, though? He's going ahead with it?" Abby turned off the burner on the stove, then went out to the dining room. She looked over Dominic's shoulder to read the small article in the Chicago Tribune. The headline read, "Boston Mathematician Predicts World's End."

"Maybe we should say something," Abby said. "Point out his error to the press."

"Do you want to? Do you want him to know where you are?"

Abby sighed, sitting down next to him. "No, I don't."

Dominic put an arm around her shoulders. "I wouldn't worry much about it," he said. "It's a pretty glaring error. And a very small article. He might have national attention right now, but it'll be brief, I'm sure. The only reason anyone is paying attention to him is because of his credentials. If just any yahoo off the street had proposed something this idiotic, it would never make it to print."

"What if it doesn't go away, though?" Abby asked, worried.

Dominic shrugged. "Let him enjoy the attention while he can. Let him build himself up. Someone will catch him at it, and when they do, he'll look like a complete fool."

Abby kissed him gently on the cheek. "I'm surprised at you," she said. "After everything he put us through, I'd expect you to be more vindictive."

"I'm just letting him have what he always wanted —fame and celebrity," Dominic said with a shrug. "He told us pretty much every day that that's all he wanted out of life. Let him enjoy it while it lasts."

"And the bigger they are, the harder they fall," Abby quoted.

He laughed. "I'm not going to say that that's what he gets, but he knows what he's doing. Simon might be a lot of things – combative, selfish, insecure – but he isn't self-deluded. He knows damn well that he's putting this out there based on bad data, yet he's marching it out there and backing it up like he really believes it."

"By now, he probably does," she said. "He's probably got himself convinced that he's right, and that the differences don't matter."

"Well, then someone will prove him wrong," Dominic said. "He's not our problem anymore."

Abby stood up, then kissed him on top of his head. His hair was still wet from the shower. "You're going to be late," she cautioned.

He shrugged, but laid down the paper. "My students are used to me not showing up on time," he said.

"Well, they're paying to hear you talk, so go talk to them."

He stood up, taking her in his arms. "You trying to get rid of me?" he asked.

"Never," she laughed. "I just don't want you getting fired."

"Fire me? They love me," he said, stepping out of her embrace. She followed him to the bedroom, where he took his shirt off the hanger and slid it on. "This is only my third semester teaching, and my Mayan studies class was the most requested in the Anthropology department."

"Congratulations," she said, leaning against the doorframe. Dominic heard the smile in her voice and glanced up from buttoning his shirt.

"You're not impressed, are you?" he asked with a smile. "Just because you're working with NASA."

Abby laughed. "I'm working on a NASA project," she corrected, "And only thanks to you." Her voice turned more serious as she continued. "If it weren't for you introducing me around at the last campus fundraiser, I might still be unemployed. I didn't know the science department was working on a joint venture with NASA – and I can't believe they hired me to help with the project."

"Your qualifications speak for themselves," Dominic said. He had looped a tie around his neck, but after fumbling with it for a few moments, gave up. Abby stepped forward and tied it for him, then kissed him lightly.

"We're quite a team," Dominic said. "Without me, you wouldn't have such an awesome job. And without you, I couldn't leave the house."

Abby laughed, swatting him on the rear as he passed her, grabbing his suit jacket off the hanger. "How you managed to dress yourself before I came along, I'll never know."

"Well, you saw what I looked like when you found me," he said. He slid on the dark jacket, examining himself in the mirror.

"You're beautiful," Abby said, "Now come on and give me a ride to work."

"My pleasure," he said. "And if you can get away at noon, I'll take you to lunch, too."

"I'll make the effort," she said. He put an arm around her waist and flicked off the light, and they headed out into the gray Chicago morning.

Abby and Dominic sat on a bench on the quad, watching the students pass. It was warm for a January day; there was no wind, with temperatures in the low fifties and the sun shining, and they were able to enjoy their lunch outside for the first time since the previous semester. They shared a drink, eating sandwiches they'd picked up at the commissary. While they talked about their mornings so far, Dominic could tell that Abby was distracted.

"What is it?" he asked. "Are you still upset about Simon being in the paper?"

She nodded. "It's disturbing, Dominic. He's proposing a theory he knows is false. And he's apparently foregoing the peer-review. I can't imagine what he's up to."

"I know exactly what he's up to," Dominic said. "He wants fame and fortune; that's all he *ever* wanted. We couldn't find the answer to the Long Count, so he just went with what he had. He knew it wouldn't stand up to a panel of scientists, so he bypassed them and went straight to the press. I checked the internet between classes; he's put up a website, advertising an upcoming book. He's also started doing radio interviews." He glanced over at Abby. "Now here he is in the Chicago newspaper. I'm sure his ridiculous theory was carried in several papers nationwide; the byline was Associated Press."

Abby shook her head. "I just don't get it. He has so much pride. It seems like this would be so destructive for him; it can't help but come crashing down when someone points out the flaws."

"Maybe it's subconscious," Dominic suggested. "You know, he's trampled so many people to get to the top, maybe he's just looking for someone to knock him down."

"I can't believe that," Abby said. "Not about Simon, anyway."

"We all do things that are subconscious, Abby, including me. I've wondered sometimes if I'd have fallen in love with you if it wasn't for the ego clashing with Simon." He glanced at her quickly. "I'm sure I would have; I know I would have. But somewhere inside me, I think there was a desire to take something of his, to be to you what he could never be, to hurt him somehow in a way he never expected."

"But Dominic, you never acted like anything he did ever bothered you; only when he'd bring up Steve did you get upset. But it seemed like anytime he tried to push you, he never got to you."

"No, not enough to make me act out," he agreed. "But inside, it got to me. And I think maybe you were something he had that I wanted. And knowing what it would do to him — well, maybe that made me want you even more."

Abby paused thoughtfully. "Well," she said, "does that change anything? Now that we're alone, and he's not here for competition, what's the point of having me?"

"Because I can't live without you," Dominic said simply. He smiled down at her. "At least I don't want to."

"Then you won't, as long as I have anything to do with it," Abby said. She gathered up their trash. "You ready to head back?"

"Sure am," he said, standing up. He reached down a hand to help her up from the bench. "Back to work."

12.19.19.2.4

February 9, 2012 — The Boston Globe reporter lay down her pen. She let the recorder continue to run, but she herself was starting to run out of patience. The interview had gone on for nearly an hour already, and Simon had been speaking for most of it. Unable to slip in a question, Sara Ontiveros finally sat back and let him continue until he began to wind down.

"Therefore," Simon concluded, "They believed the world would be re-created in 2012."

"Then the end of the Long Count isn't really the end of time," the reporter stated.

Simon paused, but only briefly. He corrected himself quickly and responded with a dazzling smile: "My theory can only go so far as to specify what's going to happen on December twenty-first. That is, the sky-portal will open and our visitors will come through. I believe the Maya saw this visitation as the end of the current age; these were the same culture-bearers who brought in the Fifth Age, after all. Therefore, their return would signify the end of that age, and the beginning of the next one. I believe this is the true nature of the Count: that *the end of the time of waiting* has arrived. What happens next, nobody knows."

"Dr. Nieson," Ontiveros said, "there are a lot of people out there who will dismiss this without even a cursory glance. After all, there's no evidence whatsoever to back you up."

"There can't *be* any evidence," Simon said. He didn't allow his smile to slip, but he spoke a little more forcefully. "I'm interpreting data that's thousands of years old. There's very little to base any calculations on. The correlations that I found match up with the distances from various objects in the galaxy and various speeds of certain planets and stars to create a star-map.

"My interpretations of Mayan history and mythology lead me to believe that Kulkulcan was a real man," Simon continued. "But he wasn't a man from anywhere on Earth; he was a visitor from an advanced civilization that brought culture to the uncivilized tribes of Central America. The Maya began keeping their count as a calendar, using dates that started at the arrival of Kulkulcan, like we in the West use Christ's birth as a start date. Only, we in the West don't have anything to count down to. The Maya did."

"What do you have to say to the skeptics who won't take your theory seriously?"

"Prove me wrong."

"The only way to do so is to wait for the end of the Count, isn't it?" the reporter asked.

Simon smiled. "I'd like to believe the intelligent and perceptive members of our society will understand my theory and make preparations. It would be almost sinful for the time — and the visitors — to arrive, and we hadn't made any plans to greet them. After over five thousand years to prepare, we'll have done nothing."

"What do you feel we should do?" Ontiveros asked.

"Prepare," Simon said simply. "We should have a contingent of politicians and other civil leaders — scientists, theologians, and such — waiting to greet them. We need to show them how far we've come, and let them know that we understand their message to us. As well as letting them know how intelligent of a species we are, we need to have leaders there who are intelligent enough to understand *them*. Thousands of years ago, they were advanced enough to be able to travel across the universe. Who knows how far ahead of us they are now? We might not even be able to communicate with them. We need to prepare a group to greet them and isolate them from the community at large."

"Why would you keep them isolated?"

Simon smiled, at ease again. "For their own protection, of course. A lot of people might consider them dangerous. There could be assassination attempts. And, just in case they bring us a little something more than culture, we can protect ourselves from them."

Ontiveros leaned in a little closer, an amused smile playing on her lips. "You think they might plan to take over the Earth?"

"They might have had something more in mind when they began to cultivate the Maya. They taught us to build and to advance. Maybe now, we're ripe for the picking."

In spite of herself, the reporter suddenly looked uncomfortable. Simon's smile grew wider, and he winked at her conspiratorially.

"I wouldn't worry," he said, "unless we don't get the word out there, and prepare a coalition to meet them. Then, the fate of the world will rest on those who chose to do nothing."

February 17, 2012 — "Simon's finally lost it, sweetness," Dominic said. "He's completely turned his back on science. He's gone over to the dark side."

Abby came around to sit on the arm of his chair. He slid an arm around her and they watched the weekly evening news program together in silence. After a few moments, Abby suggested: "They were giving him more attention. In the time since we went our separate ways, he's probably run this by anyone that would listen to him. I'm sure mainstream science was laughing at him. Pseudoscience was encouraging him. Simon went into this with one purpose only: He wanted the attention. In the rational world, he was a joke. But to the world of irrational thinking, he was a hero. He didn't care which side he got the attention from, as long as he got it. So the dark side is where he ended up, because that's where the love was. And the money."

"Man," Dominic shook his head. "I could almost feel sorry for him. What the hell happened to him, that he'd abandon his whole career and everything he stood up for his entire life just for the adoration of a bunch of lunatics?"

Abby smiled and kissed the top of his head. "It doesn't matter," she said. "Simon is an adult. He's made his choice. I'd rather stay out of it."

On the TV, Simon was speaking authoritatively. "*All* of our ancient leaders were of the alien race," he said. "All monarchies across the world stayed in power because the common people believed their leaders had either been ordained by God, or were actual deities themselves."

Across from him, the interviewer, James Pontier, was nodding, hand on his chin.

"That's why there were such efforts to maintain the bloodline," Simon continued. "Look at ancient Egypt. The kings and queens were extremely inbred, with most of the royal marriages occurring between brother and sister. They had to make sure at all costs that the leadership would not be tainted by human blood. That's why it was a matriarchal lineage, too; they knew that at least the mother was of the right race – there was no way to prove who the father was, but there'd be no doubt about the mother. They couldn't take a chance on any marriage or reproduction where they couldn't trace the bloodline completely on at least one side.

"The group of visitors that would have arrived on this planet would have been very, very small," he explained. "They couldn't mix with human kind, and there weren't enough of them to produce a large population when they had to intermarry among the group. The only option was a single family line, which eventually ended up with brother marrying sister, and their children marrying each other."

"It's no wonder the royal lineage died out," Pontier commented.

"Exactly," Simon concurred. "They created the pyramids at the peak of their civilization, when the last of their rulers were dying. They entombed them within these massive structures for protection and mummified them so they could possibly be cloned, or even reanimated, when their race returned to Earth in the future."

"Do you believe, as Edgar Cayce, the sleeping prophet, claims, that there is a hidden Hall of Records somewhere in the area of the pyramids?" Pontier asked.

"Of course," Simon said smoothly. "This is a highly advanced race that came to Earth and brought technology that was literally millennia ahead of its time. When they realized that they weren't able to survive here, spreading their kind throughout the planet, they would have sealed up their records and hidden them. Mankind at that time wasn't able to understand the advanced technology that they brought, and they would've either misused the information, or destroyed or lost it. So the visitors would have hidden it until their people came back, or until man had evolved enough to understand it. I believe that the message to where the Hall of Records is hidden is encoded in the structure and the layout of the pyramids. We still don't understand it, for all of our work, but the aliens will translate it immediately upon their return."

"If the ancient alien rulers created some kind of code that has to be broken, why couldn't we figure it out? We've been studying the pyramids for thousands of years. What if the aliens that come back can't figure it out, either, after all the time that has passed?"

"Look at Yucca Mountain, which we're designing as a nuclear waste burial site," Simon responded. "As it will be a lethal threat for hundreds of thousands of years, we're trying to devise a warning system so that mankind, if it still exists, will know to stay away from it eighty, ninety, one hundred thousand years from now. It's very difficult, because we don't know how far humans will have evolved by then; what kind of changes we'll have undergone culturally, or even psychologically or physically. We might not speak even remotely the same languages, or understand any of the same symbols.

"Yet, if we could jump ahead in time from today to that point eighty thousand years from now — with only mere moments; days or weeks at the most — having passed by for us, we would certainly understand our own signs, and be able to read our warning. The alien race that's returning to us next year will have no trouble doing the same with the messages their ancestors left behind, because for them, only a short time has passed while centuries have gone by here on Earth."

"For God's sake, turn that off," Abby said.

Dominic smiled. "Come on, you don't find this hilarious?"

She shook her head. "I find it insulting. Embarrassing. I still can't understand how this insanity has gone mainstream. It's all about ratings now, isn't it? No mainstream media used to take this kind of thing seriously, yet here he is on national television, on every talk show that can book him, and they're taking him completely in stride. No one is questioning him on his work anymore; no one is trying to disprove him. They just listen to what he says like it's totally rational."

"And you don't find that funny?"

"I don't," she said. "It scares me. I mean, listen to what he just said. He has so many fallacies of thinking it just floors me. He's said so many things that have been long disproved, and the evidence is freely available in the public record. Yet no one is questioning it."

"Anyone with even the most basic knowledge of history and physics wouldn't even consider taking him seriously," Dominic said. He flicked off the TV and tossed the remote aside, then turned to Abby, taking her hand. "Most of the news media is humoring him because he's good for ratings, just like some of the more controversial talk show hosts, or the people that put forth the 'moon hoax' idiocy.

"When his book falls off the best seller list and people stop paying attention to him, he'll drop out of sight, just like anyone else that makes major, provable predictions. As soon as the crisis point has passed and nothing happens, we never hear from these people again. They maintain a certain amount of followers by saying they miscalculated by a year or so. The story will keep changing, and people will keep following them because they *want* to believe. When people have no critical thinking skills, then there's no point in trying to convince them otherwise. And, they're following willingly. It's no big deal, Abby – Simon will get his time in the limelight, just like he's always wanted. He'll entertain some gullible people along the way, and when nothing happens on December twenty-first, he'll fade into the annals of history like every other madman who predicted the apocalypse, or the second coming of Christ. We don't even remember most of their names."

Abby stood up, and Dominic stood with her. He hugged her close, and she spoke against his chest:

"I know he's not embarrassed for himself; he loves the attention," she said. "I just hope no one ever finds out I was associated with him for so long. Or that he's a product of your research team."

Dominic laughed. "I don't think you have to worry about that," he said. "The last thing he wants is to give anyone else credit for his 'brilliant' discovery. I'm a little surprised he hasn't trashed the rest of us yet, but I'm okay with it either way. If he tells the world that we were worthless and ridiculed his genius, it'll just get us off the hook. If he never mentions us at all, that's even better."

Abby stepped back and looked up at his sweet face. "I love you so much, Dominic," she said. "I'm so grateful that you saved me. If it weren't for your patience and tolerance, I might have still been chained to Simon, smiling for the cameras and acting like I agreed with every word out of his mouth."

"Instead, you have the opportunity to debunk him if you want," Dominic said. "You're in a position to do it, if you have the inclination."

Abby nodded. "I know," she said. "I just don't know that I want to take him on again. It's stupid, Dominic — after all this time, I'm still intimidated by him. I've been waiting all this time for someone to step up and put him in his place, but no one has challenged him. It's like you said, he's just dismissed by mainstream scientists. No one is going to bother rehashing things that have been long disproved, so no one has exposed him. I want someone to do it — I just don't know that I want it to be me. You know how he is; he'll change history and make me look foolish. I just don't want the hassle."

Dominic kissed her. "Then stop worrying about it," he said. "You don't need to challenge him. If the world wants to believe him without questioning him, then they'll follow him right up to the end. These things always resolve themselves, Abby. Don't let it get to you. By New Year's Day 2013, Simon will either be a joke, or forgotten — the two things he dreads most. And no one will be any worse for the wear except those who believed him, and maybe they'll chalk it up as a learning experience. If people don't know enough to investigate something before following it without hesitation, then they'll have to suffer the consequences of finding that out later. If they actually learn from their mistake, then they'll know better the next time. And the next time some idiot comes on TV telling them something unbelievable, they might not just blindly accept it."

"You're so easygoing," Abby said. "I'm a ball of stress over here; I'm going to probably die of ulcers. You're going to live forever."

Dominic smiled and kissed her again, lingering this time. "Only if I can live forever with you."

"You will if I have anything to do with it," she said, and without another glance back at the silent television, they left the room, hand in hand, Simon all but forgotten.

374

12.19.19.3.6

March 2, 2012 — "It's perfect," Simon said, stopping in the front room of the office. He looked around, already visualizing a receptionist's desk in the corner. His own personal office would be in the rear, and there was a large meeting area where he could gather the press. It was all about appearances, he knew, and he needed a professional image. He would have no trouble gathering enough wide-eyed groupies to volunteer for him, manning phones, answering mail, and sending out his literature, books, and videos.

Simon turned to the real estate agent with a smile. "I'll take it."

12.19.19.5.12

April 17, 2012 — "It's a little like Carl Sagan's *Contact*, except that we were contacted a long, long time ago. We're only just now making sense of it."

"Let me get this straight," Tom Shepherd, the host of the primetime news magazine said. "You're claiming that there's a super-advanced civilization somewhere on the other side of the universe that is many millennia ahead of us technologically, and has figured out how to travel through wormholes. This civilization came to earth thousands of years ago and brought culture to the native tribes of Central America. The Maya devised a calendar to count down to the next time the stars and planets would be in the proper alignment that would allow some type of portal to open and permit the culture-bearers to return. Is that about right?"

"That's pretty close," Simon said, sounding magnanimous. "There's certainly much more to it than that, but you've managed to summarize quite well."

"Dr. Nieson, you've shown us the way that numbers from the Long Count move in rotating cycles and work with various astronomical distances, planetary orbits, and even planetary speeds, which you claim create a sort of three-dimensional map to the galactic center. How could the ancient Maya have known these speeds and distances?"

"I asked myself the same question, Tom. That's how I began considering the possibility that these numbers had to have come from an advanced race, not a primitive one. I was extremely skeptical, of course. I'm a scientist; a mathematician. I thought the entire concept was ridiculous — certainly the Maya couldn't have been that advanced; after all, they had no electricity, no alphabet, no plumbing. Any civilization able to calculate the distances between the stars would have had to come through certain cultural and technological milestones to get there, so I knew that couldn't be the explanation. I checked and double-checked my numbers; I knew I wasn't wrong. The only other option seemed to be that the information had been given to them."

"So it came from aliens from outer space?"

Simon smiled, but he felt his face beginning to flush. He was grateful for the heavy makeup that had been applied before the filming. "Of course, it sounds silly when you say it like that. When you use the word 'alien,' we automatically think of gray humanoids with the large black eyes. But that's a description that has only come about within the past twenty, twenty-five years. Prior to the *Close Encounters* movie, aliens were usually depicted as human. In the 1950's, when the first modern reports of alien encounters came about, aliens were described as beautiful human beings, almost angelic; bathed in a glorious light. They came to warn us about nuclear war and environmental damage, and were usually referred to as our 'space brothers.'"

"But if these 'space brothers' were seen in the 1950s, it would contradict your theory, wouldn't it? We wouldn't be waiting until 2012 for them to return."

Simon reached forward and picked up his water glass, trying frantically to recover. By the time he'd taken a sip and returned his glass to the table, he had.

"The space visitors that came to the ancient Maya were very possibly the first to make the discovery of this space portal, or at least the first to use it to come to Earth. There's evidence that they visited several parts of the Earth — places like the Mid-East, where they appeared to Enoch and his grandson, Elijah. They were thousands of years ahead of us, technologically. Someday, we'll have the same technology they will, and the same abilities. But that doesn't mean that they and we are the only two out there. There are billions of planets in our galaxy alone that have the potential for life; there must be millions of stages of development in between those of our visitors and us."

"You're saying that aliens from yet *another* planet discovered the way to zap across the galaxy via wormhole? And they're the ones who visited us in the 1950's?"

"Why not?" Simon responded, cool again. "Look at what happened when the United States discovered atomic energy in the thirties; before long, the Russians had nukes, starting the Cold War. It only took sixty years or so for India, Pakistan, and North Korea to have the technology."

"That's not the point," Shepard said. "Here's what I'm having difficulty with: We have no evidence whatsoever that even the most primitive life has ever evolved anywhere else in the entire universe besides here on planet Earth. You're suggesting that not only did it evolve elsewhere, but intelligent life has evolved and developed into beings that can defy the laws of physics to visit us here on Earth — on a repeat basis, it would appear. Now you're saying that not only did it do so in one incidence, but it's happening all over the place? That's a claim that requires some pretty extraordinary evidence, Dr. Nieson."

Simon managed a smile. "I concur. It's just evidence that's hard to come by, given the situation. I'm sure you'll agree."

Tom Shepherd didn't return the smile. "I believe without evidence, your theory is only that: a theory."

"Let me point out to you that a theory is the absolute top of scientific research, Tom," Simon replied. "It isn't a guess, or a partial concept that will later be filled out. A theory is the endpoint of all the research; it's the unifying answer that ties together all of the evidence. I don't mean to say that it's the end of the study — a theory will change to include new evidence if it's found — but it's certainly not just some random thought I'm putting out here. My theory is complete."

"I understand that," Shepherd responded. "I suppose I should clarify: I'm using the layman's definition of theory. Not the scientific sense of the word, as an explanation we can take for granted, like the theories of relativity, gravity, or evolution; but instead, just a theory, a hypothesis; an unsubstantiated guess at an explanation, like saying that crop circles are caused by energy vortexes from the Earth and not the hoaxers who claim — with a great deal of video evidence — that they've created every single one of them.

"You're a scientist, Dr. Nieson. Certainly you've heard the maxim that extraordinary claims require extraordinary evidence?"

Simon did not respond. Shepherd hadn't really expected him to, and he simply continued on: "I can make the claim that if I walk through that door, I'll find myself out in the hallway. This is not an extraordinary claim. I have the historical evidence that I've walked through that door a thousand times before; therefore, I can reasonably expect to know where it will lead me. To prove the claim, all I have to do is walk over there and go through it. Not much was claimed, so not much evidence is required. In fact, you can probably just take my word for it.

"But what you're claiming defies the laws of physics; it contradicts all evidence we have for everything we've ever known. For your hypothesis to be true, the theories that we've used to locate stars and planets, to break the speed of sound, to put spacecraft into orbit, would all have to be wrong. An extraordinary claim such as that requires extraordinary evidence. That means your numbers won't do, doctor.

"The scientific community requires physical evidence for your theory to be seriously considered. An actual alien. An alien spaceship, or at least a piece of it; something that can be proven to be material not of this Earth, an isotope from a star other than our own. Some element or chemical from another solar system. Some type of actual physical evidence that can be tested, can be studied and proven beyond any semblance of a doubt to be alien material. Until some alien abductee manages to get some alien skin under their fingernails, or scrape a piece of metal off the side of the ship, maybe steal an anal probe, I'm afraid your theory is useless, Dr. Nieson."

"I'm not talking about alien abductions," Simon said coolly. "The alien greys could certainly be yet another race that has discovered how to transport from another place or dimension, but I am not prepared to make that claim. I leave it up to the so-called abductees to prove their own claim. My sole concern is the Mayan Long Count, and what is going to happen when the Long Count ends."

"What *will* happen, Dr. Nieson, when the Long Count ends? When the portal opens and the visitors come?"

"That remains to be seen," Simon answered, and this time his smile was genuine, for he knew the interview was over. "It's my hope that the world population heeds this warning and prepares for their coming. This is my message to the world: I can tell you when they'll be here. What happens after that is up to you."

12.19.19.7.5

May 20, 2012—"Sir, with all due respect, I can't believe that you're considering this seriously."

"You don't think the prospect of alien visitors to our planet is something we should be serious about?" General Addison was expressionless, as usual. Lieutenant Marquez couldn't read his thoughts, so he continued cautiously:

"Of course I do. But there's no evidence that this guy's theory is anything more than bullshit, General. What's the difference between him and every other wacko on the planet that insists they're channeling beings from another planet, or were flown to Altair 4 on a spaceship with the Spiders from Mars?"

"He's a well-respected professor with two PhDs in advanced mathematics," Addison said. "This isn't just some random yahoo putting out his ideas on the internet." His lieutenant nodded. He knew the general always did meticulous research; however, Marquez also knew he was hard to read, his face as smooth and placid as a lake on a clear summer day, feeling out his lieutenant to get his opinion and reaction.

Knowing he would get no visual response from the general, Marquez paid careful attention as Addison explained: "I've read through his previous essays; he's written for several esteemed science journals and publications. A few years ago he had an original approach to using

378

Euclidian geometry for calculating distances; they debated about it for quite awhile — in fact, I think it's still under discussion. If this guy thinks something is going to happen, then I'm going to listen."

"What do you want to do, then?" Marquez asked.

"Have the NSA look into this guy. I want to know his background; I want to see where and how he came up with his theory. And I'd like a serious survey of whether or not it has any merit. If so, I think we should begin organizing a response."

"With all due respect, General — I've also read his book. I've looked up a lot of stuff on this Great Cycle, and I'm sorry — I just don't think there's anything to it. I can't see why the Pentagon should be so interested in the last day of this end cycle. So some Mayan wheel flips to 13.0.0.0.0 ... what does that have to do with the real world?"

"I'm more interested in what happens when it flips to 0.0.0.0.1," Addison responded.

Marquez watched the general for a moment. As usual, the Addison's face was unreadable.

"Sir, you do realize you'll be making a decision on whether or not to deal with an alien threat?"

"Lieutenant, this has nothing to do with any decision of mine," the general answered, his expressionless gray eyes locked on Marquez's.

"I'll get right on it," Marquez answered. He turned and left the room, trying to not let his discomfort show.

12.19.19.7.6

May 21, 2012 — Abby had just finished setting the table when she heard the apartment door open. She smiled; even after all this time, her heart still beat a little faster when Dominic came home.

"Hey sweets," he said, coming into the dining room. He laid his jacket across the back of a chair, then gave her a kiss.

"Whatcha got there?" she asked him, noticing the new paperback under his arm.

He tossed it onto the table. "Just a little something I picked up at the campus bookstore."

Abby reached out for it, turning it so the title was right-side up. *Countdown to the End of Time,* it read. She was momentarily puzzled, but then she saw the byline: Simon Thomas Nieson.

"Oh no," she said, dismayed. "He published this stupidity?"

"And got it out in record time," Dominic mused, going into the kitchen to check on dinner. "They must've worked double-time to get that out while he was still riding the publicity wave."

"I can't believe you bought it," Abby said, picking it up. She turned it over to read the back cover.

"Well, I can't imagine the royalties from a single book sale are going to make or break him," Dominic said from the other room. "Besides, I got a discount." Abby could hear the smile in his voice, and could imagine his shrug as he continued: "Besides, I'm intrigued to see how he managed to fill an entire book with his unsubstantiated bullshit."

"If there's one thing Simon can do well, it's bullshit," Abby reminded him. She flipped open the small book, skimming the chapter headings. Dominic returned to the dining room; stopping behind her, he slid his arms around her waist and put his head on her shoulder.

"Listen to this," Abby said, holding the book so they could both see it. "'It makes sense that they'd position the start of their new age right around the new year,'" she read.

Dominic laughed. "He never learned a damn thing, did he? The Maya started their new year on February 26."

"Well, we both know he was never much on research."

"Or on paying attention to any information that refuted his theory."

As Dominic went to the bedroom to change clothes, Abby glanced through the book, unsurprised to find that Simon had copied most of their ideas — the ideas he had previously dismissed in disgust. Shutting it quickly, she tossed the book onto the table.

"He's useless," she said.

Dominic's laughter came from the other room. "I couldn't agree more," he said.

"Are you going to read it?"

"Of course. I'm teaching courses on Mayan anthropology, sweets. Simon is big news in the world, as silly as it is. My students are already asking about him. I'd like to be familiar with his exact claims," Dominic said, returning to the dining room. He finished pulling a sweater over his head, then stopped beside Abby's chair.

"Can't we just ignore him?" Abby asked. "Why dignify him with a response?"

"Because your average person on the street doesn't know much about physics, astronomy or archaeology, honey. Even my students, who are mostly history, archaeology or anthropology majors, don't know much about this exact area. It's not common knowledge, and there are going to be questions. I'd rather address them and help them figure out for themselves, using logic and critical thinking. If I just stand there and tell them why Simon is wrong, it's no different than Simon telling them why he's right. Then it simply comes down to making a decision about which one of us to believe. Simon has the book, the media attention, the name recognition, and the charm and charisma to maybe win them over to his side. I'm just a lowly college professor. I don't want to get into a popularity contest with him; I want to familiarize my students with his claims, and then let them dissect them. If they can't figure out why he's wrong, I'll guide them. But I want them to use this as a learning experience.

"After all," he continued, "If you just attack fallacies and poor logic instead of teaching critical thinking, you might stop a few frauds, but more will spring up in their place. I think my students will figure him out — when someone has to lie about something to convince others that it's true, you can expose the lies. The more people who can think critically, the fewer will fall to those selling false information."

"Teach a man to fish, right?" Abby said, then shook her head, smiling.

Dominic kissed her forehead, then stood up. He reached for her hand and pulled her to her feet.

"Enough about Simon," he said, placing his hands on her waist and kissing her. "I'm hungry, and I want to hear about your day. Leave Simon to me and my students — if it's up to me, there won't be a student at the University of Chicago that believes him."

12.19.19.7.19

June 3, 2012 — "Our history with astronomy is amazing," Simon stated. The cable talk show host, Alan Wilson – as well as his audience, most likely – listened intently. "After all, it was only in 1543 that Copernicus theorized that the sun was center of solar system. It took us just over two hundred years from that momentous revelation until we sent our own message out into space: the Arecibo message that gives directions to our planet and a description of ourselves — a message that has now passed beyond the limits of our own solar system, out into the far reaches of space.

"In two hundred years, we've gone from thinking we were the center of the universe to discovering more than three hundred extra-solar planets — planets revolving around a sun other than our own. We've walked the surface of a heavenly body other than Earth. Who knows where we'll be in another two hundred years? Colonizing Mars? Beyond that? Traveling to a distant star, perhaps, or even to another dimension? It's only a matter of time."

"The Big Bang was roughly 14 billion years ago," Wilson said agreeably. "Another race could be literally light years ahead of us."

"I concur entirely," Simon said. "The human race has been civilized for only a few thousand years. Imagine if those few thousand years had been purely scientific and technological ascension. Had we not engaged in the whole horror of the Inquisition and the pointless massacres of the Crusades, had we not wasted over a thousand years lost to religious mumbo-jumbo, we might be there right now, too."

The host frowned. "I wouldn't consider our religious heritage an entire waste of time."

"Of course it was," Simon retorted. "We spent the Dark Ages in decline. Lost were the great philosophers, the high civilizations of ancient Greece and Rome. Instead, we wallowed in self-loathing, convinced that God or Satan would torture our immortal souls just for being alive. The Middle Ages were focused on nothing but religion, and that time period produced absolutely nothing."

"Many of our greatest works of art came from the Middle Ages," Wilson said. He glanced offstage to his producer, looking for a bit of help.

Simon shook his head derisively. "Art. Please. You'll note that it's all religious iconery. So much for the Biblical law about not creating idols.

"Besides," he continued, "How far as a society has art pushed us? Look at what science has brought to us: Medicine, surgery, technology; surface, air and space travel. There is no part of our lives today that isn't touched by technology, from the moment your alarm clock goes off in the morning until you turn off the lights at night. You can safely have bacon and eggs for breakfast that were brought in from another state – or even another country – and when the cholesterol clogs your arteries, you can take drugs to fix it, or travel to the other side of the world for surgery. This is the legacy of science – agriculture, heart transplants, travel. Our lives are not only easier and longer, but far more enjoyable.

"What has religion wrought but torture, oppression, intolerance, and murder? Look at the Middle East before religion — four thousand years ago, the Sumerians and Babylonians were great metal workers and beautiful artisans. Today, the people there are stagnant, oppressed; they produce nothing — except oil — and the lives of the people are intolerable. They're not moving forward; hell, they're not even moving backwards. They're not moving at all. Imagine the mid-East without religion: No suicide bombers, no terrorism. Women – half the countries' populations – would be able to take jobs and be educated. Men would be turning their attention to betterment of the world, not the destruction of it."

"Well then," the host replied with obvious discomfort, "Let's take a short commercial break, and we'll pick up our discussion of space travel when we return."

Both men watched the "ON AIR" light wink out, and the host turned to Simon with a dark look. "When we come back, we're only talking about space travel and alien culture, all right? No more talk of religion."

Simon was surprised. "I'm not saying anything that isn't true," he said.

"In your opinion," Wilson said. "Personally, I think religion has brought us wonderful things. Peace, love, generosity ..."

Simon laughed. "Peace? Are you serious? Where on this Earth has religion ever brought peace? What war has ever ended *because* of religion? Practically every war on the planet has been wrought due to religion! The thirty years war was about religion. The Holocaust was about religion. The war on terror is about religion. Religion has been used to justify hatred, intolerance, slavery, even murder. Every religion on Earth has some group they oppress, whether it's women, homosexuals, or other religions."

"Stop," the host said, becoming visibly angered. "I'm not going to waste my time on my show debating religion with an atheist."

"And generosity?" Simon said, incredulous. "Global agriculture has advanced enough that we could easily feed the entire planet, but we can't get food to those who need it most because of politics. And in much of the world, politics is steeped in religion."

"Two minutes," the producer said, interrupting them.

"Say what you will," Wilson sniffed. "I will not debate your lack of morality."

"*My* lack of morality?" Simon said, laughing again. "Please. You only do things because you expect a reward in heaven, or fear punishment in hell. That's only about selfishness; it has nothing to do with morality. Morality is doing something because it's right, or refraining from doing something because it's wrong. What you're talking about is like raising a child with no internal sense of right or wrong — teaching them only to do things because you'll reward them for it, or not to do it because they know you'll punish them for it. What would happen to that kid when you sent it out into the world? Do you think it would be a good, moral person? Or someone that only does something when they get something out of it – or get away with it – or refrains from doing something because they think they'll get into trouble for it? It might keep them out of jail, but does it mean they're moral? Show me someone that unselfishly gives of themselves, someone that takes care of other humans and tries to do no harm because they have a true empathy for the human condition, and I'll tell you that it has nothing to do with whether you worship some type of supernatural being.

"And when have you seen an evangelist with any sort of morals?" Simon continued, his voice slightly rising. "Taking the last few bucks from sick old people who can't even afford food, so he can add another mansion, or car, or swimming pool to his collection. Grabbing all that tax-free cash while taking away their real hope: Going to a doctor for their ailments, and not depending on some charlatan to heal them in the name of *God*. These people call themselves the religious right, but they're the ones who are morally wrong."

"And who decides right and wrong?" the host argued, seething. "Without God, there'd be no right or wrong."

"One minute," came from the producer.

"Without God, you wouldn't know what was right, and what was wrong?" Simon asked. "Really, you're saying that God is the only thing keeping you from murdering me right now, or from going out and raping or beating someone? The only thing keeping you from robbing a store and killing the employees is the fact that the Bible says 'Thou shalt not kill' and 'Thou shalt not steal'?"

"Of course not," Wilson replied scornfully. "But it's imbedded in us from childhood that killing and stealing are wrong. It's in God's commandments. That's God's morality."

"No, that's *human* morality. We don't kill or steal because it's an affront to humanity. You don't hurt other people. You don't take things from them, especially not their lives. Life is the most valuable thing anyone has, because you only get one of them. Really, who better than an atheist can better understand the value of life? There is no second chance. You treat someone like shit in this lifetime? Guess what? You don't get to make it up later. You don't get to apologize for it, or an eternity to discuss it. You'll never have a happy reunion up in heaven where you can all dance around in the clouds and sing kumbahyah and forgive each other. So you'd damn well treat people well now, and make any apologies you have to before it's all over, because once you're gone, you're gone. You kill someone, and it doesn't matter what their personal religious beliefs were — they're still dead and gone, forever and ever, amen."

"Thirty seconds."

"We'll be back on the air in half a minute, and we're not going to discuss this," the host responded. "We're going to pick up where we left off before you went off on this tangent. Ok?"

"It's your show," Simon said. "You ask the questions."

"Fine," Wilson replied shortly. "I'm warning you now, though, stay off of religion. You have no business discussing it."

"I have every business discussing it. Religion, or the lack thereof, isn't solely the possession of those who think they're unerringly holy and right. I can say whatever the fuck I want about it; I'm not living in fear of some imaginary friend or fiend who's going to punish me for questioning if it's even there or not."

"Fifteen seconds."

"Whatever. Drop it. If you have any kind of morality, you'll understand that you're offending half of the country with that blasphemy."

"Fuck your blasphemy. You're offending half the country with your second century ignorance. Besides, I never claimed to have any morality."

"Excuse me?" the host said. "Two minutes ago you were back there claiming to be more moral than the staunchest Christian."

"Not I," Simon declared, a smile creeping back onto his lips. "Atheists, agnostics or humanists in general treat humans with kindness because they have an internal moral compass that prevents them from hurting others — because they respect life and freedom; because they value life for life, not because your god instructs them what to think and who to hate and how to feel. But I never claimed to be a humanist. And I have no such affinity for my fellow man."

"You're a sociopath."

"Five seconds."

Simon smiled, but didn't respond.

"Three ... two ... one. You're on the air."

"Thanks for coming back with us," the host turned to the camera with a wide smile. "I'm Alan Wilson, and our guest today is scientist and mathematician, Dr. Simon Thomas Nieson ..."

12.19.19.8.0

June 4, 2012 — A small blurb went up on the website of the news channel that had hosted Alan Wilson's interview of the day before, raising the question of Simon's religious faith — or lack thereof. It wasn't much – more of an editorial than a news item, and for most people, it was simply a side-note of little interest. Most of Simon's comments had been off-air, off the record; only Alan Wilson and a few tech people running the cameras and sound had heard them. Simon had become too big; he had too much of a following from spiritual groups worldwide for anyone to take much notice of an article questioning his religious convictions.

For most of the world, Simon's spirituality was beyond question; since he'd never publicly announced his personal religion, they simply assigned to him whatever religious leanings they wanted him to have. He fit well into any of them: The ancient Maya had been a mystical people, and their astrology, calendar, and predictions reeked of prophecy. Simon's book had tied in the coming of the visitors with many religious events of the Middle East, and explained them using a great deal of Eastern philosophy. He was a man who was outside of religion, yet bigger than religion; Simon had incorporated elements of most of the Earth's major faiths into his story, ensuring support from all cultures, all religions, all people.

Adding to the mostly-ignored commentary on the web, however, Alan Wilson began to talk. He was a man of deep spirituality, and his interview with Simon the day before had left him deeply unsettled. He had gone to bed that night questioning his own behavior — the interview had played live on national television, and perhaps it would have been in his best interests to let Simon reveal his opinions instead of just promote his theory. Wilson thought if the majority of the country knew this man they had begun to worship as a genius, perhaps even a prophet, thought so little of their beliefs, maybe they would begin to look at what he had to say a little more carefully.

Wilson lay awake for a long time, debating with himself. On one hand, he believed in UFOs and the actual possibility that what Dr. Nieson was promoting could be right. On the other hand, the mathematician showed nothing but disdain for the very people to whom he was selling his theory. Could he be trusted to not take advantage of them? More important, could he be trusted at all?

The next day, Alan Wilson called his reverend and good friend to discuss his troubled mind. The confession and resulting conversation confirmed that he should do what he'd already planned: Start spreading the word. His friend, Reverend Owen Doone had been shocked and horrified by the mathematician's godless statements. Maybe the rest of the country would buy Simon's story without hesitation, he had said; but then again, in his opinion, most of the rest of the country were godless heathens, and the next generation was going to hell anyway. Reverend Doone had wanted an immediate appearance on Wilson's show to expose Simon's statements; Alan Wilson had to explain to him that since Simon's comments had taken place off the air, and there was no transcript or recording of them, he couldn't allow the reverend to go on air and attack him. What was important to Wilson was among his friends, colleagues, and fellow church members, people saw the mathematician for what he really was: A tool of Satan, spreading the word of evil, drawing in the masses so that when the sky-portal opened, they would be weak, accepting, unquestioning, and at his mercy. He had to take care of those he loved first, making sure that they knew what Simon was all about.

The rest of the world would have to come later.

June 5, 2012 — "Here's a headline for you, sweets: *THE FINAL COUNTDOWN.* Pretty good, until you read the article. Three pages of scare tactics and advertisements for Simon's theory."

"The media is just accepting Simon's word that 2012 is the end of the world now, aren't they?" Abby asked.

"Well, the world has to end sometime, right?" Dominic said.

Abby laughed, glancing over at him; Dominic was sitting on the couch with a weekly news magazine in his lap. "Sure," she said, "If you look at it that way. The death of the sun will be in about five billion years."

Dominic smiled. "So maybe he's only off by four billion, nine hundred million, nine hundred thousand, and some-odd years."

She shook her head. "For Simon, that's probably accurate enough."

They both laughed, and Abby felt her spirits lift. Maybe Simon's folly wasn't as devastating as she had feared.

NASA's Goddard Space Flight Center in Greenbelt, Maryland was divided, although not evenly. Although over eighty percent of the staff realized that Simon's calculations were incorrect, it was the minority that won out. Oliver Hines, the lead scientist on the project came from the smaller group.

"Let's face it," he stated in a press conference, "it won't hurt to study the galactic center a bit more. We know there's an inoperative black hole at the center of the galaxy, and we know the ancient Maya were aware of it – they deemed it to be a place of death. Black holes *do* destroy, but we believe they also create: the outpouring of matter from a quasar, for example, is the star-stuff of the surrounding galaxy being forced out of a black hole. Galactic core bursts radiate many times more energy than all the stars of that galaxy. Such eruptions, although infrequent, are devastating — they can be equivalent to the energy of a supernova — or a billion supernovas. We've witnessed it in other galaxies; even our own Earth has suffered the effects of a galactic core outburst.

"Our galactic core experienced a cosmic ray event that lasted for several thousand years, finishing up near the end of the last ice age, over 14,000 years ago. This caused one of the most intense extinctions in our planets history."

There was a murmur from the crowd of reporters, and Hines quickly raised a hand. "Please," he said, "it's no reason for panic. There is no evidence that this type of event is starting up again. We believe such explosions occur every 13,000 to 26,000 years, and while we're certainly in the range for another event, there have been no signs of such activity. We have, however, decided to turn our telescopes to the galactic center in order to more fully investigate it, and look for any possible signs that might indicate such an eruption."

He held up a hand again to halt the next volley of questions. "Please," he said, "I will not be taking any questions or comments today. The purpose of this press conference is simply informative. NASA wants to advise that they are looking into the scientific evidence behind Dr. Nieson's theory, which has run rampant through the media and garnered more attention than the evidence currently supports. We will release our findings to the public as they come in; for now, however, rest assured that there is no sign of a core explosion. Or, for that matter, aliens."

Hines left the stage amid the audience's laughter, and he was relieved to have escaped questioning. The fact was, he would have had to confess if asked, galactic ray volleys moved at the speed of light — and there was no way to anticipate one, and no way of observing one until it hit.

12.19.19.8.15

June 19, 2012 — "Don't you think it rather odd that they'd look just like us?"

"Not at all," Simon replied. "Evolution has proven that ours is the most efficient biological structure; after all, humans are the dominant life form on this planet."

"But only because of our brains, not because of our physical structure," the interviewer, Diane Foster, said. She leaned forward slightly, towards Simon. "Physically, we're practically defenseless. Compare us to any animal — a lion, tiger, or bear, for example. Throw any human into a room with any of them and there's little doubt who'd come out on top."

"We developed our brains so we wouldn't have to use our strength. We don't need claws, or sharp teeth. We can make tools and weapons."

"Ok," she responded, "So let's assume that an upright, two legged, two armed creature would be the best evolutionary form to protect our brains against the elements and predators of Earth. But what about another planet? We know nothing about what other kinds of life forms might be found there, what type of environment they're in. What about the chemical makeup of this as-yet unknown planet? We don't know how long their day might be, or what kinds of moons they would have, what kind of tidal pull might influence their bodies. We don't know what types of elements another world might have. We are made of zinc, iron, copper, and water — the elements found on Earth and in the stardust of our solar system. We know that life can develop in extreme environments; temperatures extraordinarily hot or cold; in streams of acid or geysers of steam. What if another world has astoundingly high temperatures, an atmosphere of methane, and pools of liquid nitrogen? The odds that the life on that would look just like us, and breathe oxygen, seem impossibly high."

Simon only smiled. "Astrobiologists feel that intelligent life might need certain specific conditions to develop. A planet with a lot of water, a certain distance from the sun, with one moon, in an orbit of a certain length of time. If that's true, then we could expect the same type of life to develop."

"Even that isn't necessarily true, Dr. Nieson," replied Foster. "We know that there have been mass extinctions on this planet every few hundred thousand to few million years. If it wasn't for the chance impact of an asteroid, the dinosaurs might still be ruling the Earth. Without the loss of the dinosaurs, mammals never could have risen as the dominant life form on the planet. With each mass extinction, another evolutionary branch is cut off, and a different one grows stronger. Throughout the Earth's history, these massive extinctions have occurred because of cosmic accidents. Had even one event not occurred, our evolution could have taken an entirely different path. We can't possibly expect that this exact same series of accidents would have occurred anyplace else in the universe."

"Maybe it didn't have to," Simon argued. "Man may have developed last up to this point in our history, but that doesn't mean the same order of events happened elsewhere in the universe. Maybe that's why they're thousands, or even millions of years ahead of us."

Foster paused and Simon pressed on. "You know that my theory includes the concept that the gods of the past were actually advanced alien visitors that came to Earth and awed the native people with their knowledge and technological abilities. It fits in with ancient mythology and Biblical teaching. Zeus and the other Greek and Roman gods could travel by air or through space; even the Ten Commandments acknowledge that there are other gods — God implies as much when he commands the people not to worship any of the others ahead of him. Humans were said to have bred with these gods. Why else are the gods of the past always described as appearing like men? And that man was created in their image?"

"Have you ever seen Shiva, Dr. Nieson?" the interviewer asked. "Vishnu? Ra? If the aliens look anything like an eight armed goddess with a head like an elephant, then I don't think I want to meet them when they come back through."

Simon was nonplussed. "We have to accept that they'll look like we do," he said, ignoring her last statements. "After all, no matter how the ancient people stressed that Kulkulcan and Quetzelcoatl were gods who descended from the heavens, there was also never any doubt that they looked like men. We just have to accept their word for that, as recorded in their history."

"You think your theory is more likely to be true than that these human men simply told people they were gods?"

Simon crossed his arms over his chest. "These 'men' brought civilization to savages," he said.

"Like Europeans claim they brought it to Native Americans?" Foster asked.

"We know that Columbus left Italy and came to America," Simon argued. "We know that the Spaniards came to Mexico and conquered the natives there. No one knows where Kulkulcan or Quetzelcoatl came from."

"Would Kulkulcan have told the Maya he was a god, or did they just assume he was?" Foster asked.

"I don't think that the gods *had* to tell them who they were. Folks in Jerusalem knew who Jesus was, didn't they?"

"You consider the gospel of Jesus Christ equivalent to the arrival of Kulkulcan?"

"It's a simple comparison," he said. "All these ancient races predicted that their saviors would return. We're just waiting for one of them."

"Dr. Nieson, we're talking about a very ancient people, a race of people from thousands of years ago. They were very superstitious, with little to no knowledge of even the most basic of sciences. Everything to them was supernatural; all their leaders were ordained by God. Don't you think it's just possible they claimed that certain people such as Quetzelcoatl or Kulkulcan were gods, just as those in Europe and Russia around that time were claiming that their own kings and royal families were chosen by God?"

"I've explained that in detail in my book. If you've read my complete theory, you'll see that those items are connected. You're looking at it from the view that they were all wrong. I'm taking the view that all of them were right.

"Look," Simon continued, "when you go back through and read ancient texts with the idea that the gods were actually living beings, maybe humans, maybe aliens, suddenly all sorts of things that never made sense before start to become clearer. For example, I always used to wonder why the Biblical God always demanded burnt offerings. What would an incorporeal, all-powerful deity possibly want with a cooked lamb, or a fatted calf? There'd be no use for it. But a man, or group of physical, biological beings living up on a mountain would sure need one. They'd need one often enough to command the people to bring them one every week."

Diane Foster smiled. "When you have a preconceived notion, Dr. Nieson, you can make anything fit your hypothesis."

"At some point, Diane, the coincidences become too many to explain away as bias. There is simply too much support for my theory. There is too much that went on in Biblical times that they couldn't have done without assistance from above. Until now, we've always attributed that assistance to God."

"What occurred in Biblical times that we would need advanced knowledge to accomplish?" the interviewer asked in surprise. "Dr. Nieson, you're speaking of people who lived in mud houses, who had no weapons but slings, swords, and sticks. Their transportation — oxen and carts — kept the majority of the population from traveling more than twenty miles from home over the course of their lifetimes. There was nothing technological, no inventions that changed their lives. People subsisted from day to day, and if they reached the grand age of thirty, they were considered old. What exactly did these wise aliens bring to them?"

"I'm not talking about the Middle East," Simon said, "Look at ancient Egypt. Look at Greece and Rome. These were civilizations with abilities far beyond their peers."

"Do you believe that the ancients had knowledge that man today doesn't have?"

"Of course I do. There are many examples of ancient wisdom — look at Plato's writings on everything from philosophy to surgery, thousands of years old. Look at acupuncture, still in use today."

"But even after thousands of years, we still can't come up with evidence that acupuncture works — or, at least not like its practitioners claim it does, or for the reasons they base it on. Plato's philosophy was interesting, sure; but his medical knowledge, his physiology, is useless. The ancients used leeches and bloodletting as a cure for disease, believed all disease was caused either by spirits or by an imbalance of five humors, or liquids, in the body. They believed that schizophrenics were possessed by the devil and that women who enjoyed sex were suffering from a form of psychosis. *Ancient* doesn't mean *wise*. Or even accurate.

"Besides, Dr. Nieson, what you're talking about is accepting your ideas on nothing but your word. We can't make any proposals or predictions based solely on faith. Is there any actual evidence to support your theory?"

"There's theoretical evidence," Simon replied. "It's all Newton had, all Einstein had. Yet no one denies gravity, and we've recently managed to prove relativity through a series of related experiments and observations. On December 21, 2012, I expect to prove my theory beyond any denial. The evidence will be there. All we have to do is wait."

12.19.19.9.0

June 24, 2012 — "Honey, can you come out here for a minute?" Dominic called.

Abby hesitated at the bedroom door. She had just come home from work and was changing clothes when the doorbell rang. Dominic went to answer it and had been engaged in conversation with whoever was at the door for the last several minutes. Abby tried to listen in, but couldn't hear their low voices from the bedroom. At Dominic's call, she headed out into the living room.

"Sweetheart, these are Lieutenants Burns and Marquez," he said, motioning towards the two military men standing in the foyer. "They've come to talk to us about Simon."

"Oh," Abby said shortly, surprised. She motioned them towards the sofa, where they seated themselves awkwardly beside each other. Abby sat in the chair across from them, and Dominic sat on the arm of it.

"Can I get you anything?" he offered.

"No, thank you," Burns said. "We won't take up much of your time. We just need to ask you a few questions about Dr. Nieson."

"What do you need to know?" Dominic asked.

"Is it true that the two of you worked with Dr. Nieson on his Long Count project?"

"*His* project?" Abby said sharply. "It was Dominic's project. Dominic originated it, funded it, and organized it. He invited me to join him, and I asked Simon to come along. It was never Simon's project."

"I see," Burns said. He appeared momentarily surprised, but let it pass. "How long did the three of you work together?"

"Just over a year," Dominic said. "About sixteen months. If you've found us, though, I'm sure you've found Dante and Tina, too. So you know there were actually six of us on the project."

"Yes," Burns said. "It's our understanding that one of your researchers passed away during the project? A fatal accident, the way I understand it. Can you tell us about that?"

Dominic looked down at his hands when he spoke. "Steve. He was my best friend; we'd been working together for a dozen years or so. One morning we couldn't find him, and when we went to look for him, I found his body by a small pond we used to swim in. He had a bad head wound, and he was face-down in the water. The Mexican police concluded that it had been a bizarre accident: he fell, struck his head and was rendered unconscious, then drowned."

"I see," Burns said. Abby was curious that neither man was writing anything down. She wondered if they were recording the interview, and if so, why they hadn't mentioned it. She was under the impression that an interview subject had to give permission before being recorded.

"Tell us about your work in Mexico," Marquez said, speaking for the first time. He was a stocky Hispanic man, older than his partner, and from his demeanor, Marquez was the one in charge.

Dominic shrugged. "There actually isn't much to tell. We discussed a lot of ideas, and threw all of them out. We finally concluded that there was no answer we could find."

"Did Dr. Nieson bring up his theory at that time?"

"It wasn't *his* theory," Abby broke in again, visibly irritated. "He concocted it from a dozen different things we'd discussed before and dismissed, not only because there was no evidence for them, but because the ideas themselves were absolutely ridiculous. Before we broke up the team, Simon told Dominic he was going to sell these ideas as his 'theory.' At that point, we didn't care. We just wanted to be done with him."

"Why was that?"

"Simon and I were engaged before we went down there. Our relationship fell apart, and I ended up leaving with Dominic," she explained matter-of-factly. "For obvious reasons, there was a lot of tension between the three of us."

"And Simon had become dangerous," Dominic said. The others looked up at him, and he shrugged. "He purchased a gun and began carrying it with him. He'd always been verbally abusive to the rest of us, and there'd been one physical confrontation. I believe he began to get paranoid and defensive. I no longer felt safe around him."

"Have you given any more attention to the problem of the Long Count?" Marquez asked. Although his voice remained serious, he sounded curious.

"No," Dominic responded. "I had more than enough of it in the time we were in Mexico. I came to the conclusion that if there had been something we were able to find, we would have found it in the time we had, with the team we had. I'm still interested in the Count, don't get me wrong. I read up on new evidence as it comes out, and I follow the publication of other researchers who are still working on it — but I haven't put any more effort into trying to find the answer."

Lieutenant Marquez stood, and his partner rose to his feet also. Dominic got up and walked them to the door.

"Thank you both for your time," Marquez said, shaking each of their hands. "We'll be in touch if there's anything else we need."

After the two uniformed men left, Dominic closed the door and locked it behind them.

"What the hell was that about?" Abby asked.

"I'm not sure," he said. "I guess they're investigating Simon."

"I wonder what the hell he's done this time?"

"No idea," Dominic said, "But if he's got the United States Army after him, he's certainly up to something."

12.19.19.10.2

July 16, 2012 — "We should keep them isolated, certainly," Simon said. He was slightly nervous – this was his first prime-time special, and he'd heard the viewership was going to be huge. Still, he kept his voice cool and confident, buoyed by his teaching experience and more than half a year of giving interviews to the press.

"We have no idea what kind of organisms they might be," he continued. "Biological creatures like us could carry disease — disease that we have no cure for, no vaccine, and no antibodies against.

"Look at what happened to the Central American Indians," he said. "When the Europeans came, they brought pathogens with them that the Maya had no immunity to. Masses of Mayan Indians were killed by such things as measles and the flu. They died from smallpox, rubella, typhus, and chicken pox. Contagion could come with our interstellar visitors, as well."

"Dr. Nieson, I know you're only speculating, but can you tell us what you think they might want?" The host – a fan of Simon's book – was enthralled. "When the Europeans came to the New World, they were exploring, looking for new lands. Eventually, their exploration brought them new worlds to conquer."

"I don't think that's such an extreme consideration," Simon responded. "After all, why does anyone explore? We want to find new places and new things. From our experience on Earth, however, every time we've found new people, we've conquered them. In some areas, we've simply spread our culture or our religion, conquering societies in a spiritual way. We go in and find a civilization that's different than we are, and we immediately say that they're wrong. All their culture myths are wrong — we consider them quaint and exotic, of course, but wrong — and they need to be saved. We have to bring the heathens around. If our visitors are anything like us, can we expect any less from them?"

The host, Mike Trudy, frowned. "Once a society becomes highly technologically advanced, they also seem to adopt some concept of democracy. There are some holdovers, of course — China, for one — but for the most part, they aren't trying to conquer their neighbors. There's respect for the boundaries of others. Do we have any hope that our visitors would have the same respect for any new societies they might find themselves in?"

"Well, I'm no sociologist," Simon said self-deprecatingly, but humility sounded hollow even to his own ears. He continued quickly, "but I would think, from their previous visit, that they come in peace. After all, the natives loved Kulkulcan. They worshipped him as a god."

"Well, he apparently descended from a hole in the sky. In Mayan times, that would automatically qualify one for godhood, I'd think. And you have to admit, the visitors did influence Mayan society. Mythology says that they brought culture to the Maya. Sounds an awful lot to me like they were beginning to conquer those Mayan tribes."

"It brings an interesting question to mind," Simon said, smoothly transitioning to agree with the host. "How much of what we think is our culture is actually that of our visitors? It happens all the time. Explorers will visit a tribe, and inadvertently introduce their own culture to the natives. When they leave, other explorers will return a few generations later and find that the tribe has adopted certain scientific facts, religious stories, or culture myths into their own mythology. The interesting thing is that when questioned, the natives believe that that is the way their stories always were."

"If that's the case, then the aliens must not be too different from us."

"That's true," Simon said, "Although you have to understand that they were visiting us two thousand years ago. Just as our own culture has undergone major changes in that time, the visitors could be completely different by now. They could have changed from a peaceful race to a warring one; from culture-bringers to conquerors."

Trudy paused. "In a previous interview, I remember you brought up the Twin Paradox, the fact that time passes very slowly for those remaining in one place, while it barely moves at all for those traveling. If that's the case, and only a few days, weeks, or months have passed since the visitors last trip to see us, then we're not talking about a period of two thousand years."

"Of course," Simon agreed quickly. "This is why I'm not concerned. I do believe the visitors have the same intentions that we do as interplanetary explorers — we want to learn. We want to share the knowledge we have, and to learn everything we can from everything we find."

"His story changes day by day, doesn't it?" Abby said.

"Of course," Dominic smiled. "He has to keep responding to critics. And he can't bear to have someone point out something that he hasn't thought of yet. So he has to keep expanding his theory, trying to incorporate everything, even if it completely contradicts something he just said the day before. Or ten seconds earlier."

"It amazes me that no one has called him on it."

"Well, you know what they say, sweetheart," he responded, putting his arm around her. "Give him enough rope, and he'll hang himself."

"I sure hope so," she said. "As long as I've known him, he never got tangled up in his own lies."

"He's never been on a national stage before, either, with every statement he makes going on the record. It'll be easy enough to start pulling his statements and calling him on his contradictions. Don't worry, sweets. He'll get caught."

"I hope so," Abby replied, her brow still wrinkled with worry. "He seems to come out of everything squeaky clean, no matter how much shit he throws out there. Just once, I'd like to see him found out."

"That makes two of us," he said. "Give it time, sweets."

"We're starting to run out of time."

Dominic kissed her on the cheek and stood up, releasing her. "I've got to get going," he said. "I don't like having to leave for night classes, but my students await."

"All right then," she responded, distracted. Dominic glanced back at her with concern, but her eyes were still focused on the television screen.

"It'll be all right, Abby," he reassured her, but she did not seem to be listening. Simon had a close-up on-screen, blond and blue-eyed and charming, and he was smiling widely as the host agreed with him on his final statement. He looked up into the camera, a gleam in his eye, and to Abby, it seemed as if he was staring right through her. Their eyes met, and she could almost swear that he was seeing her.

Suddenly the screen went dark, and she jumped. Guiltily, she glanced over her shoulder to see Dominic standing above her with the remote.

"It's bullshit, Abby," he said simply. "Let it go."

He dropped the remote onto the couch next to her and headed for the door. Abby turned back to the blackened screen, still shaken. It *was* bullshit, she knew. But the sight of Simon's piercing blue eyes staring steadily into hers, with that self-absorbed arrogant smirk on his lips, had chilled her.

"Let it go," she murmured, shaking her head. She stood up and crossed the room to say good-bye to Dominic.

12.19.19.10.7

July 21, 2012 — "Dr. Simon Nieson?"

"Yes," Simon said, pausing. His secretary was at lunch, and Simon didn't recognize the voice on the other end of the line.

"Dr. Nieson, I'm Lieutenant Marquez, U.S. Army."

Simon lowered himself slowly into his chair. "What can I do for you, Lieutenant?" His mind was racing as he tried to figure out if he'd actually broken any U.S. laws.

"A group of high-ranking officials would like to meet with you in person, Dr. Nieson. We're interested in finding out more about this theory of yours."

"I'm not sure I understand," Simon responded. "I've published a book explaining it in detail ..."

"Dr. Nieson, if I may," Marquez interrupted, "We've all read your book, and we have transcripts of all your radio and television interviews, as well as the presentation you gave before the Paranormal Society last month. That's why we're interested in discussing this with you in detail."

Simon didn't answer for a moment, and Marquez thought he might have lost him.

"Dr. Nieson?"

"I'm here," Simon said. "All right. When and where did you want to meet?"

As Marquez gave him details, Simon felt his forehead and wasn't surprised to find it damp with sweat. He wasn't sure why the military wanted to talk to him, but he didn't think it could possibly be good.

12.19.19.10.11

July 25, 2012 — "All cultural myths speak of an earthly paradise that would someday return," Simon said, pleased to be starring in his second prime time news magazine special in two weeks. *Thank god for media competition*, he thought to himself.

"So you believe that the return of the visitors will usher in a period of peace and prosperity, another Golden Age?"

"Very much so," Simon said. "The Maya were looking forward to this for hundreds of years. They couldn't wait for the visitors to return."

"This claim of yours has created some unease in the religious community. Some say that you're predicting the return of Christ, which will usher in Armageddon."

Simon smiled. "Perhaps I am," he said. "The story of Quetzalcoatl – who I believe is the Aztecs' name for Kulkulcan – is very similar to the story of Christ. The Aztec man-god was a healer and a miracle worker, and he disappeared by walking on water, out towards the east, claiming that he would return again someday."

"You think he walked to the east to become known as Jesus Christ?"

"I think it's possible," Simon said. "After all, nowhere in the Bible does it describe the life of Christ. We have the birth story – which was actually written a century after the crucifixion – and the events that lead up to his death; there's nothing in between. We know nothing of his childhood, of his formative years, of his young adulthood. We have no idea how he spent his twenties, or any of his life up until the age of thirty-three. The tale of his birth is so unbelievable, so mythological – it sounds very much like a romantic story created after the fact to befit the birth of a god, albeit a humble one. It probably *is* a created story – there's no historical evidence of Herod ever calling for the massacre of children. It's entirely possible that Christ showed up in the Middle East as an adult, trying to get the people to be kinder and more loving to each other, where he was crucified for his efforts. It was easy for the Maya and the Aztecs to accept a man who claimed to be a god; for the Jews, it was blasphemy."

"Actually, it was the Romans that crucified Christ."

Simon waved a hand dismissively. "The Maya wouldn't have known that this particular figure wouldn't come back. They only knew that he left, promising to return."

"So if Christ was an alien visitor and we killed him, what are the odds that his people would send another envoy?"

"Well, that depends," Simon answered smoothly. "Perhaps they're able to monitor us from where they are. If so, they'll know that their envoy is now worshipped as a god by nearly a third of people on Earth. Certainly they'd see no problem with sending someone through again."

"My god," Abby said, flicking off the television set and watching it fade to black. "He can switch sides faster than anyone I've ever seen."

"He's hedging his bets," Dominic answered, not looking up from the papers he was grading. "Either way now, he wins. If someone actually shows up, he's right. But if – I mean, *when* – no one does, he can claim that it's because Quetzelcoatl was actually Jesus Christ, and after we killed him the visitors decided not to come back. It's win-win."

"For him," Abby mused. "Everything he's doing is a huge loss for the rest of us."

398

12.19.19.10.13

July 27, 2012 — The general stood at the head of the table. He was a large man, even overweight; but his hair was neatly trimmed, and his uniform was immaculate. Simon was nervous, and although he tried not to let it show, he had an eerie feeling that the general knew it; the general knew everything.

Simon reached for his water glass, but when he noticed that his hand was shaking he lowered it back to the table top. He glanced around to see if any of the military men and women assembled had noticed, but no one was paying attention to him. Their eyes were on the Secretary of Defense seated near the end of the long oval table, watching him attentively as he spoke.

"The Maya were a blood race," the Secretary was saying. "As I understand it, they had bloodletting sacrifices to their gods on more than one hundred holy days per year. They cut out the hearts of their living sacrificial victims; they drew thorn-studded rope through their tongues in exchange for rain, for a good harvest, for a mild winter. They were a warring race that fought among their various city-states, massacring brother against brother."

"Superstition," Simon responded, his voice surprisingly steady. "That's what religion gets you. People murdering each other to appease their personal gods."

"We're not here to discuss religion with you, Dr. Nieson," said the general. "We just want to know if this is something we should consider a threat."

Simon cleared his throat, then sat up a little straighter. He tried not to let his nerves show — or his relief. "We can't know exactly what to expect," he said. "I'm afraid that I'm only a mathematician, not a Mayan scholar. But in my research, as I worked on my theory of the Count, I studied their culture in depth. You're right; they were a blood race. But I don't think Kulkulcan asked for human sacrifice; that might have been the Maya's own doing, in the hopes that he would smile upon them, and bring them luck. Maybe even call him to return early," he added, warming to his subject. "Throughout the world, religions have always made sacrifices to their gods. Even in the Bible, men sacrificed everything from lambs to calves to their firstborn sons. I think it's more man's interpretation of what we think a god would want, rather than a god asking us to kill someone, or burn an animal in his honor. After all, what would an all-powerful, all-knowing, benevolent god want with a dead, cooked cow?"

"Perhaps we should call in a specialist in Mayan studies," General Addison said. "This isn't something to play around with; we're talking about organizing a military response to an unknown threat. We need to learn more about the area and the people. We would be placing our soldiers on the ground in a foreign country, and if something did happen, the United States would want control of the situation.

"We're not just talking about military affairs, but international diplomacy," he continued. "If the Maya were a warmongering people who practiced human sacrifice, we should know what our military would be facing. We need to find out exactly what it is we're dealing with here. Someone more versed in the Long Count could be highly beneficial, from an intelligence standpoint."

"No!" Simon said sharply, half rising out of his seat. All eyes were on him again, and he sat back, smoothing his tie and adjusting his lapel. "I'm sorry," he said, "I just feel strongly that a Mayan specialist can't possibly do us any good. We're not concerned with the ancient Maya; they weren't the ones that came down from the sky portal. They were just mindless saps. When the visitors came, they were kind and helpful, right? Look at the literature. The Inca said three brothers came through a series of portals and brought them culture. The Aztecs said Quetzlcoatl came and brought them civilization; the Maya said the same thing about Kulkulcan. This wasn't an evil group of visitors intent on conquering us; if they were, they could have done it easily back then, when man was still crawling out of the forest."

The general was silent, pacing slowly across the front of the room. He pulled thoughtfully at his lower lip. After a few moments, he turned back to the table.

"Let's assume that your hypothesis is correct. You said in your book that the Maya were a warring race," he said. "They were constantly battling each other for control of the region. Maybe your visitors didn't bring with them the type of weaponry they needed to overtake them. By bringing art and culture and civilization, they were helping to bring peace to the region. They'd probably figure that by the time they returned again, bringing their army with them this time, our people would be like sheep. They could overtake us without a struggle."

"If they had the technology to cross galaxies to get to us, certainly they'd have the advanced technology to destroy a people that hadn't even heard of gunpowder yet." Simon responded.

"But they wouldn't have brought it with them," General Addison empathized. "When we went on an exploratory mission to the moon, we didn't load up with armaments. Sure, we were almost 100% positive the moon was dead, with no atmosphere and no water to support life, but we didn't know for certain. When we finally send a team to Mars, we won't take weaponry with us. We're sure the planet is lifeless, but we can't know for sure until we get there that there's nothing hiding in the mountains, canyons, or soil that's going to attack us. In ancient Mayan times, there was nothing to show that there was life here. From where they were, maybe the visitors could've seen our water and some of the CO_2 put off from the plant life here, but there were no satellites around our planet, no radio signals beaming into space. There were no large buildings and no emissions from factories or automobiles. Even if they were unsure of what kind of animals might live here, I can't imagine a few visitors bringing anything more than a few guns with them. They wouldn't be able to conquer an entire planet of people with just a few guns. No," Addison said. He began to pace behind the table again, rubbing his chin thoughtfully. Simon watched him with interest, but the general's face was impassive. The Defense Secretary, on the other hand, seemed just as fascinated as Simon.

"They would have come on a science mission, and brought just enough equipment for testing, probably some recording and specimen gathering equipment so they could report back," Addison said. "They'd have made their reconnaissance and tried to neutralize their opponent as much as possible without an actual strike. If they'd have known they wouldn't return for several thousand more years, they'd have left us with the tools to destroy our resistance, to make us as pacifistic as possible. How else, but to claim they'd come from God — easy enough to back up, with their advanced technology that'd have wowed these jungle and desert dwelling natives — and teach peace, love, and harmony. Love thy neighbor, lay down thy sword. All to prepare us for the slaughter and enslavement when they returned."

He turned around. "You say that they'll return on December 21, 2012."

"That's right."

"And you're sure that when this portal opens, the visitors will go to this ... Izapa, is it?"

"That's right," Simon said. "They were counting down until the visitors returned to them ..."

"Fine," Addison said with a dismissive wave of his hand. "I want to be there."

"General?" Lieutenant Marquez asked with hesitation.

"Not me," the general replied crossly. "I want *us* to be there. The U.S. Army. I want a U.S. military presence to be there. If these 'visitors' are coming through looking for a fight, I'm sure as hell not going to let them come out and find a bunch of sight-seers and Mexican farmers waiting for them. They're going to get more than they can handle."

12.19.19.10.18
August 1, 2012 — "Abby, you're really taking this too personally."

"I'm not, Dominic." She was near tears. In the years they'd been together, it was their first real fight, and Abby couldn't stand it. She also couldn't bear for him to not understand. "It's not personal at all. I just can't keep listening to this. Simon has finally achieved the fame and notoriety he's always wanted, but I don't care about that. I just can't stand to see him deceiving the world like he is."

"It's a willing deception, Abby. Practically every human being in this country is capable of doing the research for themselves. There's nothing that's stopping anyone with internet access or a library card from checking out his facts on their own. It's not a matter of understanding advanced mathematics or Mayan mythology; all you have to do is know how to read – and apply logic."

"Dominic, you know science education in this country has gone downhill. And if people see someone on all the news shows — especially a Ph.D. like Simon — they'll figure that he knows what he's talking about."

"So he's taking advantage of ignorance and blind acceptance. When this huge hoax is revealed, maybe the public will learn to take these pseudoscientific 'breakthroughs' with a grain of salt next time.

"I don't agree with anything Simon's doing, or anything he's ever done," Dominic continued. "But I can't say that he's altogether evil for doing what he's doing now. They say you can't take advantage of someone without their permission; if the public is willing to lie down for him and not do any fact-checking themselves, then let him run right over them."

"And you don't think anyone should stop him."

"Abby, we aren't the only two people in the world with the ability to speak out against him. Tina and Dante know just as well as we do that he's full of shit. But they've taken the same route that so many other scientists have taken when faced with such asininity in the past: they've ignored it. It's not worth their time to address."

"And so the world remains ignorant."

Dominic looked at her stern expression and her arms folded tightly across her chest. "A few months ago you wanted nothing to do with outing him," he said softly.

"I was being selfish," she responded. "I thought the way you did — if people were falling for his crazy ideas, then it was their own fault. But the more I see him and hear him, the more convincing he is. He's starting to really buy into his own story. It's hard to believe, but I'd forgotten how appealing he could be — he comes across as competent, intelligent – hell, even sexy. People are buying what he's selling because he's a damn good salesman, Dominic. I can't blame the world for not double-checking him when the media promotes him with little question and there's barely a peep from the scientific community. I don't want to stand by anymore, honey. Not when he could cause so much damage, and we could do something about it."

Dominic looked into her earnest face for a long moment, and finally said: "'All it takes for evil to prosper is for good men to do nothing.'"

Abby didn't answer, just waited for him to work it out in his mind. Finally, he sighed. "All right," he said. "What do you want to do?"

12.19.19.11.0

August 3, 2012 — "It's blasphemy," said the reverend. "To claim that Jesus Christ, our savior, the son of God, was an alien being from another planet? It's ludicrous. God is not laughing."

"Dr. Nieson isn't the first to suggest such a thing," the host commented.

"No, but he is the most vocal," the reverend said, crossing his arms before him. "He's spreading his sacrilege, mocking the Lord with arrogance, as if this sinful, prideful foolishness was nothing more than a discussion of the latest novel in a book club. It's shocking. You here in the mainstream media treat the subject so lightly, giving him all the airtime he wants, helping to spread this filth."

"Reverend," the host interrupted, "Before you start blaming me for the downfall of western society, please keep in mind that we're giving *you* airtime right now. If you want to refute Dr. Nieson's opinion — and that is what it is, after all; without any supporting evidence, it is simply an opinion — then you have a national forum to do so now."

"Yes, you're right," the reverend responded, admonished. "You must understand my passion on the subject, however. Here we have a scientist denying the existence of God. Nothing unusual. But to claim that Jesus Christ was an alien is ridiculous — and blasphemous."

"Do you think anyone really takes him seriously, though, Reverend? Polls show that most people in the United States still believe in a god of some type, whether they're Christian, Jewish, or Muslim. Certainly people of faith are going to discount his story as pure fabrication."

"I would hope so," Reverend Doone said, "but these days, people are falling farther and farther from their faith. They may claim to believe in God, but do they go to church every week? Do they read their holy books? Do they know and follow the tenets of their faiths? Or are they apathetic, even hypocritical?

"I believe that in this day and age, people are more interested in the next movie coming out, or the next episode of their favorite sitcom, or their jobs or hobbies or vacations. God takes a back seat," he continued. "They don't insist that their children follow the path of the righteous, and these children are easily swayed by tales of magic, or aliens. People have 'better' things to do on Sundays than attend church. And half of those who do attend are faithless, only going along with spouses or parents. You have these Wiccans and Taoists who believe that God is in nature, or the Earth, or trees or what have you; they're only a step away from accepting Christ as an alien.

"Maybe the good, church-going adults among us will hold fast to their faith, but those who are apathetic, who raise easily influenced children of no particular beliefs —will they listen to his garbage? I believe they will."

"Reverend, if aliens really do come through a portal on the twenty-first of December, and they do look and act very much like us, and they claim to have been here two thousand years ago — will you change your mind?"

"Of course not," the reverend snapped. "I believe in the words of our Lord. The Bible is one hundred percent Truth. Every word in it is divinely inspired, and there is not one place in the Good Book that mentions aliens, or outer space. This man is a farce, and he's only leading the gullible and the faithless astray. They'll all wake up on December twenty-second and realize they've been made fools of. And as always, the church will welcome them back, and forgive. But I don't know if God will. They should save themselves now, and turn back from their sinful, unbelieving ways, or they're going to burn in the Pit forever."

"So you don't believe that anything is going to happen on the twenty-first?"

"No," the reverend replied staunchly. "The Lord knows everything that has ever happened, and everything that will happen. The Book mentions revelation and the end times, but it doesn't mention a portal opening in outer space and bringing in strangers from another galaxy." He paused. "But if they *do* come," he amended, "we shouldn't trust them. Satan appears in many forms. The Prince of Darkness is a master of disguise. The world needs to be on alert."

"So they're not coming, but if they are, we should watch out for them."

"Exactly," the reverend responded, crossing his arms over his chest triumphantly. "But they won't come. Mark my words: Nothing is going to happen on December twenty-first. Absolutely nothing."

August 7, 2012 — "Do you know how mathematically sophisticated they were?" Simon continued. "They understood the concept of zero. Up until that time in history, the only others who did were the Babylonians and Hindus. They were one of the few peoples in the world who could measure time so precisely."

He sat back, looking smug. The British commentator studied Simon for a long moment before he spoke.

"So you're saying that they mathematically calculated the end of the world."

"No," Simon said. "I'm saying that their mathematical advancements were incredibly rare."

"But your theory is based on the concept that they mathematically calculated the end, right?"

Simon sounded impatient. "That's self-evident. My point is that they didn't come up with something like that on their own – not when most people all over the world were struggling with the concept of keeping a roof over their heads when it rained. It came from somewhere else."

"Why don't you believe human beings were smart enough to come up with mathematical constructs themselves? After all, we've devised theories of advanced physics on our own; we've invented computers and a world-wide internet. We've sent manmade spacecraft outside our solar system, still sending back data to us. Why do you have so little faith in the mathematical competence and intelligence of man?"

"Why do you think we did all that without any outside help?" Simon countered. "The U.S. space program was useless until Roswell. Once we began to reverse-engineer the alien technology, we were able to break the bounds of the Earth."

The commentator smiled wryly. "You're promoting an idea that cannot be disproved," he observed. "If I could give you names and contact numbers for every scientist that worked on the first spacecraft, and you could interview them, and they gave you detailed descriptions of the physics involved and how they came about their design, all you'd have to do is say they were lying. Or that they didn't know that the actual physics they were using came from the aliens interviewed at Roswell. There's no way to disprove your case because all you have to do is insist that everyone is lying, or that we don't know the actual history of the world and its hidden secrets."

"Well, that could be true for anything, couldn't it?" Simon said with a slight smile.

"Certainly," the interviewer replied. "That's exactly my point. There have been many hoaxes throughout history: the discovery of Noah's Ark on Mount Ararat, crop circles, the alien autopsy, the Planet X fiasco of 2003 — why should we believe *you*?"

"Honestly, it means nothing to me whether you believe me or not," Simon answered. "The truth will come out on the winter solstice of 2012. You can believe want you want to before that, but afterwards, there'll be no doubts."

Simon turned to the camera with a broad smile. "And if you want to find out more about the end of the world in our time, the end of the Mayan Long Count, please buy my book …."

12.19.19.11.7

August 10, 2012 — "I can't believe it," Abby said. "Not a single publication is interested in our side of it?"

"Not once they realize we're refuting his story," Dominic answered. "They're all excited when I tell them that we were part of the research team near Izapa, but once I tell them that I want to give them the real story — and they find out it has nothing to do with ancient aliens or the end of the world — they lose interest."

"I don't understand that," Abby said.

"Of course you do, sweets; you know the reasoning. Why ruin a good story with facts?"

Abby shook her head. "I thought they'd want to sell magazines and newspapers! This would be a great public interest story."

"Sure it would," Dominic said. "It'd be a one-time boost in ratings. Then, when the public realized we were right and his story was bullshit, it'd be the end of Simon — which would mean the end of a popular story that will carry the media through to the end of 2012, with a monstrous climatic ending. No matter if anything happens — or nothing happens — they're guaranteed the biggest story of the year. Simon is a money-maker. We're just a blurb." He smiled and gave her a quick hug. "It's not all bad news, honey. *Science* magazine, *Scientific American*, *New Scientist*, and *Discover* magazine have already run stories against Simon's theory, but a couple of them have offered to do a Q&A with us, if we want. I'm more than willing to do it, even though they're not going to reach the mainstream public."

"Me too," Abby agreed. "Anything we can get out there, let's do."

"Well, I also have the option of doing a satellite appearance for a show on the BBC," Dominic said. "Most of the show is in support of Simon's theory; I'd be the lone skeptic on it."

"Sounds like an ambush," Abby said.

He smiled. "Could be. It's one of those shows that claim to be balanced, and then they'll have ten believers and one skeptic or scientist. The scientist will have about 30 seconds to try to refute the last hour of programming. Still, I think I should do it."

"Do you think you'll make a difference?" Abby asked.

Dominic shrugged. "Maybe. Like you said, it'll at least get our side out there. Maybe people will think that we're jealous, like Simon's been telling them. Maybe they won't believe a word I say. But someone might. And if one person does, then it's worth my time."

Abby was thoughtful. "And it might open up a few more venues, once people hear what you have to say."

"It might," Dominic admitted. "Simon started small and picked up publicity; I suppose we could do the same thing."

They were both silent for awhile, and then Abby spoke again. "What about other countries overseas? Europe, Australia?"

Dominic kissed her on the forehead. "Sweets, they already know. I've done a lot of work trying to find people that would listen to me. I've seen skeptic sites in Australia, Sweden, all over, that have demonstrated that Simon's calculations are wrong, and his theory is ridiculous. They aren't much interested either; they know it only takes one fact to destroy an entire theory, and they have handfuls of facts. Why keep beating the same dead horse?

"A lot of sites overseas have debunked him," Dominic continued, "but you know how few Americans pay attention to the European press, or to pretty much anything that doesn't involve the U.S. Hell, we never even know or care what goes on in Canada or Mexico, and they're right next door. Let's face it, honey – this is going to play out how it's going to, no matter what else we do."

"So you think we should give up?"

Dominic shrugged. "We can keep fighting and see who will listen. Maybe we'll get a few converts, or at least get our story out there. But people are going to believe what they want to anyway, sweetheart. They always do."

12.19.19.11.9

August 12, 2012 — "We're here on Channel 4 with Dominic Ciriello, an anthropology professor at the University of Chicago in the United States. He's jumped the pond to join us today and discuss the Long Count. First of all, Dominic, thank you for joining us."

"Pleasure to be here."

"Now, you have some insight into the sensation that's captured the world's attention and imagination: Dr. Simon Nieson's theory of alien invasion at the end of the Long Count." The host, Lauren Michaels, flipped her short blonde hair back and leaned a little closer to Dominic. "What can you tell about your experiences with Dr. Nieson?"

"Well, I first want to address your use of the word 'theory,'" Dominic said. "In science, a theory is an explanation of facts. Scientists compile facts and look for an explanation which will explain them without breaking the laws of physics or invoking the supernatural. A theory is developed to explain the facts in a coherent manner. Over time, as more evidence is discovered, it will either add support to the theory or oppose it. Its proponents will have to rework the theory to incorporate the new evidence, or dispose of the theory altogether. Good scientific theory is useful; the theories of relativity and gravity are used for designing everything from buildings and transportation to space travel. The theory of evolution is used for virology, for creating new medicines. We can use scientific theory for prediction, like geologists predicting where to find oil.

"Simon has not composed a scientific theory. He took information and facts and built a scenario that would incorporate them, but does not properly explain them in any scientific way. He could have easily come up with the explanation that invisible purple jaguars from the jungles of Guatemala provided the Maya with the numbers of the Long Count, and the Count is winding down to the birth of the King of Invisible Purple Jaguars. There's equally as much evidence for that scenario as there is for Simon's story about aliens hopping through wormholes on the winter solstice."

"There is some backup for it, though, isn't there?" Michaels asked. "We know that there's a black hole at the center of our galaxy; we know that Kulkulcan existed, and that he brought culture to the Maya ... "

Dominic held up a finger, and she paused. "Actually," he said, "there's no proof that Kulkulcan existed. The Maya documented him, but they also documented the Hero Twins and many other clearly mythical characters. The Maya claim that Kulkulcan brought them culture, but they also claim that man was created from corn. We must be very careful about what we consider 'evidence.'"

"That's fair," the host acknowledged. "But if Simon's story is just that — a story — he has incorporated many facts into it, and it's difficult to flat out disregard."

"We believe that alien visitation is possible because we believe aliens are plausible, even though there is zero physical evidence for their existence," Dominic said. "There's also zero physical evidence for invisible purple jaguars, but people — most people, anyway — are less likely to jump to believe in them. Yet, the Maya documented jaguars extensively in their writings; mythical figures, as well as leaders, were named after them. Why isn't this as likely a scenario as the idea of time warps?"

Michaels smiled. "Dr. Nieson has wrapped his story in physics and mathematics. Most people feel like he knows what he's talking about, but that they're just not intelligent enough to understand it completely. Meanwhile, you're talking about invisible, imaginary creatures. It's science versus magic."

"Pseudo-science," Dominic corrected. "Just because something is wrapped in scientific language doesn't mean it's correct. You have to look at the big picture around it. Simon, for example, has been dismissed by reputable scientists. He hasn't published his work in peer-reviewed journals for other mathematicians and scientists to study his methodology and examine his research. Instead, he went straight to the media, and received such an outpouring of support from the public that anyone who opposes him now seems unimaginative, stick-in-the-mud, jealous."

"Like yourself."

Dominic smiled and leaned back, crossing his long legs. "Myself more than others," he said. "I worked directly with Simon for nearly two years; I imagine that my speaking out against him now sounds like me being a sore loser."

"A little," she said.

"The Long Count itself is a fact; there are things we know about it, and things about which we can only speculate. For example, the Long Count is supposed to be time elapsed from creation, calibrated at Izapa. We know the numbers of the Count and the dates of the Count, but little else. We want to come up with a theory to explain the facts, but right now, we don't have enough facts to do so. Science compiles facts and comes up with a theory – then sets about trying to prove it wrong. Simon has never tried to prove his story wrong, or he would've easily succeeded long ago — like many others have already done. Simon had an idea, then tried to find evidence to back up his claim. When he couldn't find any, he went ahead with it anyway, because for the most part, it's impossible to prove him wrong.

"The problem is that Simon is picking the data that supports his ideas, and dismissing that which doesn't. In science, that simply can't be done. A fact doesn't cease to exist, or cease to oppose your theory, just because you leave it out. Ignoring research is ridiculous, and dangerous."

"What are the chances that the end of the Mayan calendar is actually predicting the end of the world?"

"I can't give you odds," Dominic said. "I can tell you that the intention of the Long Count does not seem to be the end of creation;

Pacal of Palenque — an old Mayan king — predicted that the world would end in the year 4772. I'd say the odds of the world ending on December 21 are pretty much the same as any other day of the year — probably even less than times we're at war.

"Simon has it in his head that this major event will occur when the calendar ends," Dominic continued, "yet there's no evidence whatsoever that anything extraordinary will occur in 2012."

"But the calendar *does* end, Dominic."

"But the calendar isn't *time*. It's a representation of time. If you tear up a picture of a clock, the clock isn't destroyed, and time doesn't end. The calendar is not time itself. Otherwise, time would end at the end of every calendar year. Even several times a year, if you consider all the different systems of time measurement on this planet."

"So you claim that not only is Simon's theory wrong, but that nothing at all will happen at the end of the Long Count."

"That's pretty much it," Dominic said. "I can't say for sure that it won't. My team – of which Simon was a part – researched everything from geology to astronomy, and there doesn't appear to be any event expected to occur at the end of the Count. But that doesn't mean I know everything, or that I haven't missed anything. But I believe I can say without hesitation that aliens will not come out of the galactic center and appear here on Earth on December 21, 2012."

"You heard it here, ladies and gentlemen. The world will not end at the end of the year. My thanks to today's guest, Dominic Ciriello. Tomorrow we'll hear from the other side of the coin, Dean Morse, the president of Dr. Nieson's 'Final Days' group."

12.19.19.11.10

August 13, 2012 — "Hey honey, did you know Simon was the Antichrist?"

"It's crossed my mind," Abby called back from the bathroom.

"I'm serious! Come in here! They're calling him Satan!"

"What?" Abby came into the bedroom, toweling off her hair.

"Yeah, check this out," Dominic said, sliding an arm around her waist and pulling her onto the bed. "This is nuts—I mean, I can't believe they have this guy on CNN."

"Shhhhh," she said, leaning against his chest.

On the television was a popular Christian evangelist and head of one of the west coast's megachurches. He had been in the news over the past year for preaching against Simon and his theory, and against the idea of the Mayan Long Count in general, claiming that it was a tool of pagans and that a Christian society should reject even the concept of it.

Much to his dismay, however, the issue had refused to go away; the Long Count had become a popular topic among students, researchers, and theologians together. Without the backing he'd been looking for, the Reverend Owen Doone had returned to his original plan of attack.

"Look at the numerology!" he cried. "Simon Thomas Nieson. Each word of his name has six letters: 666.

"Each word of his name has two syllables: 2+2+2=6.

"Even his initials give away his name! S-T-N. He has come to us with word of the Apocalypse, with news that the world will end and the dead will walk the earth! Satan has spoken, and Satan has brought the end of the world upon us!"

Disturbed, Abby reached for the remote, hitting the mute button.

"Look at that, sweetheart. You could have been the bride of Satan," Dominic joked.

Abby frowned uneasily. "How long has that been going on?" she asked.

Dominic shrugged. "I was watching it while you were in the shower," he said. Noticing her expression, he pulled her closer. "Honey, you knew there'd be religious overtones to this. You knew it couldn't be avoided. And look at it this way," he said with a smile. "You and I just narrowly missed being the Antichrist. Thank God we let Simon run with this — he can get all the religious nuts after him and take the rap for it."

Abby put her hand on his waist and looked around him at the television. They both turned to the screen and Dominic turned the sound back on so they could listen.

"It's all right there, not just in the Bible, but in this man's own words! He has claimed that the 'man' that will be coming back to us, to finish conquering the world, was called Quetzalcoatl in his day. Mythology says that after Quetzalcoatl left, he returned to the sky as the Morning Star."

"Venus?" Peter Yang asked.

"No, not Venus! Have you read the Bible, Peter?"

"No I haven't," the newsman replied, not a bit perturbed. "But I have studied a little astronomy. Venus *is* the Morning Star."

Reverend Doone ignored him. "The Bible gives Satan many names, but one might sound familiar even to you: *Lucifer* is the Morning Star."

"So you belief that when the portal opens up, it will be Lucifer who comes through?"

"Yes!" the minister shouted. "It's all there, laid out before us, in the Bible! The story of Revelation details Satan's return. Not only is it spelled out for us, right there in words anyone can read and understand, but we have used the Bible Code!"

"You've found Dr. Nieson's theory hidden in the pages of the Bible?" Yang asked, his tone a bit incredulous.

"Not just in the Bible! We've run this man's book through the Bible Code as well. We have found, at minimal distance, without possibility of chance, the following phrases: Simon, Satan, the End, Hell has Come … And these are only examples, Peter. These are repeated throughout, with the same themes of Satan and punishment and death."

"But Owen, the theme of the dissertation is the End of the World. I mean, the entire paper is about the apocalypse. Certainly you don't have to go to much length to find an apocalyptic theme."

"It's beyond what he's saying, Peter. It may be on purpose; maybe he's mocking us with his words, telling us one thing while he's hiding the meaning of another."

"But why would he hide what he's really trying to say, if he has a true meaning? Isn't that what he really wants us to know?"

"No!" the Reverend roared, practically rising out of his seat. "The devil will not show the true face of Evil until it's too late! He will hide his grinning skull behind scientific words and flowery phrases. While the world waits in breathless anticipation for something glorious to happen, he'll be plotting our demise, laughing as we fall right into his trap!"

"Turn the channel, honey," Abby said uneasily. "This is creeping me out."

Dominic picked up the remote, hitting the power button. He tossed it over his shoulder. "I can think of better things to watch," he said, tugging at Abby's towel.

"Is that right?" she murmured, trailing her damp hair across his lips. As he rolled her onto the bed, she tried to put the evangelist out of her mind, but the image wouldn't fade. Fire and brimstone, she thought, closing her eyes.

12.19.19.11.11

August 14, 2012 — "I'm curious about some of your detractors," General Addison said.

"Who, that Ciriello guy? Come on," Simon scoffed. The general sat across the table, his index fingers steepled in front of him. His heavy face was without expression; his tone detached, and Simon felt his forehead already breaking out in a sweat. Although several guards were stationed outside, he and Addison were alone in the general's quarters.

"Dominic was the name of the first inquisitor in the Holy Inquisition, did you know that?" Simon asked. He started to smile at his own cleverness, but Addison's face remained impassive.

"He was one of the researchers on my team," Simon sighed. "He ran off with my fiancée. Let's face it, the guy never liked me; from the start, he was jealous, competitive. Now that I'm getting press for my discovery, he just can't stand it. I wouldn't trust anything he has to say. Hardly anyone is listening to him, anyway."

"I'm listening," Addison said. His voice was as smooth and even as his expression.

"As well you should; I'm sure you didn't rise to the rank you did by being a stupid man, General. I'm sure you listen to everything and weigh it carefully. But you'll have to trust me on this one: Ciriello is lying, or mistaken."

"And what about the rest of them? The scientists, the skeptics, the religious front?"

"Everyone has their own agenda," Simon said. "If I'm saying something that devastates years of scientific theory, of religious belief, of course they don't want it out there. Everyone is out to protect their own little piece of the pie, you know? If I come out with something that will destroy the faith of their followers, what are they going to do, encourage me? Look at the Mormon Church — they bought every document that ever came out that dared to expose their founder as a con man who made up the whole story about the angel and the tablets and Jesus appearing in North America. They locked them up in a vault that no one could ever see, that only the head of the church could access. People in power don't want the truth, General — they want to maintain their power."

Addison rubbed his cheek, but his impassive steel gray eyes didn't leave Simon's bright blue ones. "I won't completely disagree with you," he said. "My job is to protect power. But I also want the truth. I've listened to your detractors, and I have to say, some of them make a hell of a lot more sense than you do. Quite frankly, Dr. Nieson, I don't like you. But I don't have to," he continued, ignoring Simon's startled expression. "My job isn't to make friends; it's not even to decide whether or not to involve the U.S. military in this. All I'm to do is report the validity of the remotest plausibility of your claim. I'm under direction, too, and those in command have decided that if what you say poses even the slightest threat; if there's even a faint possibility that something is going to happen on the twenty-first of December, then they want a U.S. presence there."

The general stood up, hulking over the mathematician. Quickly, Simon scrambled to his feet.

"Go on, get out of here," Addison said, sounding suddenly tired.

Simon nodded, moving quickly. Even after he was out the door and moving down the hall, he could almost swear he still felt the general's hard grey eyes boring into his back.

12.19.19.11.18

August 21, 2012 — For the third week in a row, Simon found himself fighting through a crowd of protesters just to get to his office. In the beginning, when he'd first made his address public, the loiterers outside the door had been autograph hunters and enlightenment seekers; in the past few weeks, however, he'd drawn mostly protesters and cynics. Just making it to the door from his Porsche, which he'd left in the parking space out front, was an ordeal.

"Oh, get out of my way," Simon said crossly. He elbowed his way through the crowd, careful to keep his temper in check in case there were any cameras around. A tall woman in a long white robe grabbed hold of his arm as he passed, her fingers clenching his forearm tightly.

"Hey," he said, "Let go." He felt a brief moment of panic as he clawed at her hand, unable to dislodge her tight grip; he grabbed one of her fingers and bent it backwards, hard. The woman cried out in pain and released him, dropping back as he quickened his step.

"Move it," he muttered under his breath, pushing through the crowd. He kept his eyes on the door far ahead, trying to ignore the protest posters waving above the crowd. "Sinner!" someone cried.

"Bite me," Simon answered. Another face loomed up in front of him, a woman waving a Bible. Simon pushed her aside, hard this time. The woman's face registered her shock, then she shouted: "God shall send them strong delusion, that they should believe a lie: That they all might be damned!" The Bible passage spewed forth like a jet of poison, her condemnation dripping with venom.

"Move it, damn it," Simon said. "I don't go to your church and scream outside your door. Now leave me *alone*." He lowered his shoulder and plowed through the crowd. He had almost made it to the door when a black-clad figure blocked his path. Simon scowled when he saw the white collar.

"Please move, Father," he said. "I have nothing to explain to you, and I'm not answering questions."

"Perhaps I should offer to pay you," the priest responded. "You seem to speak to anyone with a camera or a paycheck."

Simon stopped. "Excuse me?" he said.

"These good, God-fearing people simply want to engage you in discussion. You've stopped taking calls on religion when you do your television and radio appearances. This seems to be the only way to get you to listen."

"Listen to what?" Simon asked. He turned around and waved a hand over the crowd. "This insanity?"

As if on cue, a man near him called out, "Turn away, Satan! Renounce your demons now!"

Simon waved dismissively and turned his attention back to the priest. "What the hell does that even mean?" he asked. "I'm the devil because I don't embrace your religion?"

"You've announced, rather proudly, that you're an atheist. If you're not with God, then you're against Him."

Simon scoffed. "If you're going to profess to be an expert on theology, you'd better learn to define your terms. An atheist is a *non*-theist. "A" means "not," not "against." It means I don't acknowledge any god. That means I don't acknowledge Jehovah, Zeus, Satan, or Kulkulcan. I can't worship Satan, Father – I don't even believe in him."

"Your non-belief is a tool of the devil," the priest replied. "Just like the science you use to attack the truth of God."

"Jesus Christ," Simon swore, and smiled inwardly when the priest flinched. "Science isn't an attack on god. It has nothing to do with any god, for or against. All it does is try to organize actual facts into explanatory theories. Attack the theories all you want, but that doesn't change the facts."

"Your reliance on scientific matters is turning public perception away from God. If we lose our spirituality, we lose everything. Science *is* the enemy of God; look at your science classrooms, where no other alternative is permitted but evolution. You're up there speaking of your theories as if they *are* fact, and it's going to create a generation of soul-less criminals who believe they're no more spiritual than a monkey."

"You know, it amazes me," Simon fumed. He took a step closer to the priest, cornering him against the door. "People like you who live in houses with electricity and running water, who watch TV and listen to the radio and use computers and drive cars and ride in airplanes ... I'm sure you're the first one to rush a family member, a sick child, to the doctor for antibiotics when he's sick; you don't hesitate to trust science, technology, and medicine when it benefits you to do so, yet you seem to think the same sciences that brings ease and comfort to your everyday life are somehow wrong when it comes to this."

"Medicine and evolution are two entirely different things."

"That's ignorant," Simon snapped. His voice was rising, and the chanters nearby fell silent, listening. "If you believe that biology, genetics, and other sciences have nothing to do with evolution, then you'd better go start drinking unpasteurized milk and praying over the sick instead of

sending them into surgery — well, hell, you probably do that anyway."
Simon was almost shouting now, and the priest glanced from side to side,
as if searching for an escape, or a savior.

"Do away with vaccines," Simon yelled, "I hope all the children
of your parish end up with Rubella, Scarlet Fever, and Polio. You say you
want to 'engage me in a discussion,' but all you people do is scream insults
and Bible verses. None of that means shit to me. I think you're just
jealous — religion has always held a monopoly on the end-times, haven't
they? The final judgment is all about punishing sinners and rewarding the
holy, isn't it? If it turns out that the end of the world has nothing to do
with your god, you can't handle it, can you? You'd rather shut me up.
Well, you can quit trying, because I'm not about to shut up. Religion has
been raking in money and maintaining power off the fear of millions for
thousands of years, and I'm going to get my share of it. Now leave me
alone before I have the police throw you all in jail." He pushed past the
priest and stormed into his office, slamming the door behind him. He
locked it quickly, his fingers shaking, slipping on the slick doorknob.
When he'd succeeded in slamming shut the deadbolt, he turned around,
then leaned back against it, breathing out heavily. With the back of his
head resting against the door, he could still hear the chants from outside.

"Fuck it. That's it," he said, straightening up, then heading into
the inner office. Stalking past his secretary's desk, he thrust out the folder
he was carrying, and she took it gingerly. He continued past her down the
hall to his office. "Lock all the doors and windows, and keep the press
out. I'm not taking any calls."

He stormed into his office and slammed the door so hard that it
rattled in the frame. Going around his desk, Simon swept the papers off
the top of it in his rage, then sat down heavily in his leather chair. He
dropped his elbows onto the desktop, then buried his head in his hands.
He hadn't wanted anyone to see how shaken he was. He was done with
the crowds, with the press.

Simon rubbed his temples, feeling the throbbing at the back of
his skull beginning to pound. He couldn't quit with public performances;
his speaking fee was too high to give up. Still, he was starting to worry –
as the end grew closer, the public grew restless, and the crazies seemed to
be flocking to him.

The religious right had startled him with their substantial
presence. He hadn't expected such vehemence from people who
considered themselves so moral, so emotionally close to God, but he
knew now what he was up against. He could either try to appease them,
or continue to fight. Fighting would bring him more publicity, he knew.
But there were a lot of them, most of the country, he knew … and where

there were people, there was cash. Somehow, there had to be money to be made.

Simon sat upright again, a small smile starting in the corners of his lips. He reached across the desk for his pen and notebook. He had some thinking to do.

12.19.19.12.6

August 29, 2012 — Walking past the student center on his way to his first class of the day, Dominic spotted a large poster in the front windows. He stopped dead in his tracks, not even noticing when the student walking closely behind him ran into him. The crowd of students parted around him, some with curious glances in his direction as they passed. They were used to the eccentric professor, though, so most paid him no attention. Dominic was oblivious.

His trance suddenly broke and he fumbled in his satchel for his phone. Dialing up the familiar number, he jammed the phone up to his ear, still reading the poster over and over.

"Abby?" he said. "You're not going to believe this …"

"Do you want to go?" Dominic asked. He had met Abby at her favorite restaurant after work, and they now sat across a candlelit table, holding hands. He massaged the back of her hand with his thumb. He could tell she was upset.

"I don't think I can," she said. "I just can't face him again."

Dominic nodded. "I understand," he said. "But I think I'm going to have to."

"Why?"

He shrugged. "My students know about Simon," he said. "They know something about our history. Some of them are sympathetic to his ideas; they haven't learned enough yet to differentiate between good, factual archaeology and the conclusions to which Simon has jumped based on erroneous information and poor interpretation of the real discoveries. I want them to listen to him, to hear him out. I want them to ask questions. I want them to come to me looking for validation of what they've heard, and I want them to look for the errors in his conclusions. I want them to think about what he says, to weigh his words against the evidence, and to find out why he's wrong. It'll be one of the best lessons they'll get in their university education, and they're getting it for free. I can't pass up an opportunity like this. It could train a complete set of new archaeologists, anthropologists, and historians to think critically, and give them an important guide for the interpretation of data."

Abby sighed and squeezed his hand. She tried to smile. "I love how you can completely embrace Simon's lunacy. Here I am, shell-shocked by the thought that he's going to be right here in our own backyard spouting his nonsense, and you're running out there to meet him head on."

"The only way to bring magical thinking out of the darkness it loves is to shine the light of inquiry on it. If we blindly believe whatever anyone tells us, we're lost. We'll be back in the dark ages in no time. Ever since the turn of the millennium there's been an increasing interest in magical thinking: psychics, cold-readers, 'alternative' medicine, new-age thinking, aromatherapy, palmistry, astrology, iridology … next thing you know, we'll be having witch hunts and inquisitions again. Religion has shown a growing trend towards extremism; from radical Muslims to fundamentalist Christians, there's been crusading from all religions against all others. We need to step back. The only remedy for paranormal, supernatural, and magical thinking is the clear light of rationality. Ideas like Simon's that are completely baseless will shrivel up like some blind cave creature when the bright light of scientific inquiry hits them. If we can't kill these ideas, we can at least chase them back underground where they flourish."

"I agree," Abby said. "I agree completely, Dominic, and I'm so grateful that you're able to do this. But I just can't go. Just thinking about being in the auditorium while he's up there speaking is making me shake."

"Abby, you put up with his control and his abuse for years. I'd never expect you to subject yourself to that again. If you can't face him, I respect that. I just want you to understand why I want to go."

"I love you, Dominic," Abby said. "I appreciate that you can do what you're doing. And I want to hear all about it when you get back."

He smiled. "You certainly will," he said.

12.19.19.13.0

September 12, 2012 — Simon strode out onto the stage after his introduction, relishing the applause from the packed auditorium. "Thank you," he said modestly, smiling under the bright stage lights. The applause died down, and he began to speak:

"Four years ago, I set out for Izapa, Mexico with one question burning in my mind: What did the Long Count mean?

"For those of you still unfamiliar with it, the Long Count was a Mayan counting form, long thought to be a calendar or a dating system. It *was* a system of dating, of recording events. There was never any doubt about that, nor was there any doubt that the Count was winding down, counting down to some event that would only occur after a long period of five millennia. The only doubt was what that event *is*."

Simon didn't take long to warm to his subject, and Dominic noticed how well he played the audience. Simon was indeed handsome, and could be charming when he made the effort; he was certainly making it now, and Dominic was amused to see most of the females in the audience around him gazing at Simon with rapt attention. Onstage, Simon would flash them a smile, or turn his crystal blue eyes on them and hold their gaze for a long moment. It was a look like that that would've charmed Ted Bundy's victims, Dominic thought. It didn't matter what kind of claptrap Simon was spouting; he was good-looking, funny, and attentive to his audience, and he had captivated them.

Dominic settled back in his seat, arms crossed over his chest, trying to follow Simon's line of discourse. It seemed to be a hodge-podge blend of almost every theory the mathematician had mocked back in Mexico. He had managed to tie most of it together with a thin strand of a theory, heavily veiled in math so esoteric and beyond the ken of most of his target audience that it was easy to see why they would simply accept him as the expert, and take for granted that he had done the proper research. They might not have known what he was talking about, but they automatically assumed that he did. He spun out a mystery story, enchanting his audience with his vivid descriptions of the bright stars over the dark ruins of Izapa; he invented various native characters to give the story depth, and to make himself the explorer, the Great White Hunter, the Indiana Jones on a quest for the truth. He wove in pseudo-archaeology and pseudo-history from around the globe, stories of lost civilizations and ancient astronauts. He told of the five ages of the Aztecs, building suspense before declaring solemnly that we were now living in the final age. His story entranced, enthralled and delighted, building up to the excitement of when he finally broke the code and realized the hidden truth about the Maya which mainstream archaeology chose to ignore. He dipped into astrophysics and dove into mathematics, and his calculations ran unopposed.

Simon spoke for the good part of an hour, cool and easy even up under the hot spotlight. He would pause to pour himself a glass of ice water, a movement perfectly practiced and measured to come after a particularly poignant statement, giving the audience time to ponder it before he would speak again. All his mannerisms and speech were carefully honed to show himself to his best advantage, charismatic and intellectual, yet down-to-Earth, with an easy smile and a quick wit. Dominic could see Simon captivating class after class of young students, appealing to them with his charm and fascinating them with his knowledge and expertise. How easy it would've been for Abby to have fallen for him so many years ago, Dominic thought. At least, until she saw through him for what he really was.

It was nearly an hour after Simon had first stepped onto the stage that he finally began to show signs of winding up his act. He had described how he had come to the final conclusion, and now began to summarize:

"There are many alternate fields of archaeology that refuse to follow the mainstream interpretations published in the history books. These alternate views may sound outlandish when you look at them alone, as alternate explanations, but when you tie them together they present a consistent history that is much, much different than the established historians would like you to believe. In fact, these alternate histories fill in the gaps and answer many ancient questions much better than any of the mainstream explanations can.

"There is evidence that human beings as we know them today did not evolve independently like biologists insist. Instead, visitors from a much more highly advanced civilization than ours genetically engineered us from the existing Neanderthal or other pre-homo sapiens that existed on the planet at that time. This was done around 450,000 years ago.

"It's quite possible that the Biblical story of Genesis is true, in a way: Adam was created, but perhaps not by a supernatural being at all, but by a creator in a lab. It truly was intelligent design; we were genetically designed by a race that wanted us to be more like them; truly, as they say, created in their image. Generation after generation we were developed, honed, and perfected. Soon we were recording our own history, on paintings in caves, carved on stone tablets, inscribed upon scrolls and hidden away.

"This is not *my* theory, mind you; it's a theory that was proposed decades ago and laughed at by mainstream scientists. When you tie it in with my theory, though, it certainly becomes less laughable and actually very possible. The visitors returned at the time of Kulkulcan, Quetzalcoatl, and Jesus. Had they come before that? Perhaps established a base on Earth and lived here for a long time, in what many ancient historians like Plato termed 'The Golden Age'? We know for a fact that there was world-wide flooding at the end of the last Ice Age, around 10,000 years ago. Every culture on Earth has legends and tribal memories of a former advanced civilization which was destroyed by a great flood.

"Is it only coincidence that our earliest artifacts are dated back to this time, 10,000 years ago? We've found nothing from earlier, yet it seems as if global civilization began out of nowhere all at the same time. Were all traces of the former society, this Atlantean or Utopian perfection, destroyed forever by the flood; and are all the stoneware, tools, pottery, and art dating to the years after the last ice age the remnants of the survivors, those who had to start again from nothing?

"The timing fits, ladies and gentlemen. It's possible that these stories of ancient cultures are true; however, it's also possible that man really *was* dropped onto Earth about 10,000 years ago, fully formed as we are today. We ourselves could be the descendants of the visitors that first came to settle this planet, after the ice age ended and left the planet habitable. If you count backwards with the Long Count, you'll find that it fits.

"The Long Count *is* a record, my friends. And it is a calendar. It's counting the most important event to ever take place on this planet, an event that involves the entire human race and everything we stand for. It shocks us out of the long-standing concepts we hold, everything we believe about ourselves. The Long Count is timing the return of our ancestors and our spiritual and cultural guides. And this time — they're coming to stay."

Simon paused for a moment to let that sink in, then dipped his head humbly and said, "Thank you."

Most of the attendees burst into applause; some stood, whooping and whistling, clapping loudly as if they were at a rock concert, or a political rally. Dominic smiled to see that many were still sitting, not applauding, but simply shaking their heads.

When the applause died out and the hall fell silent again, Simon raised both hands, palm out, to shoulder level. "I'll try to answer any questions you might have now," he said. "I'm afraid I'll have to keep it short; I have a plane to catch. But I'd like to help you to understand as best I can, and will clarify anything you need help with."

Dozens of hands shot up, some people standing up and waving theirs to try to get Simon's attention.

"You there," he said, pointing to a male student in the center of the auditorium. He'd stepped out a bit into the aisle to make himself more visible.

"I'm puzzled," the young man said. "I'm a student of archaeology here at the University, and I've been on a few digs. One thing I've learned in my experience is that no matter where man goes, he leaves traces of his existence. The basis of archaeology is finding things that people have left behind — in effect, their trash. Their refuse. Garbage. Things they've used, lost, or thrown away.

"Rare is a find of gold or treasure. The usual dig uncovers broken bits of pottery, tools, eating utensils, and the remains of sleeping materials, even animal bones and food ..."

"Did you have a question?" Simon interrupted impatiently. "We don't have all day to listen to a dissertation on the field of archaeology." Some students giggled, but most of the audience sat listening quietly.

"Yes," the student replied. "I do have a question. A pretty simple one, in fact. You've said that the visitors spent some amount of time here on Earth — possibly as long as 450,000 years. My question is this: What'd they do? Clean up before they left?"

Simon looked momentarily at a loss, so the young man continued. "Everywhere on earth that people travel, they leave signs of themselves behind. In fact, they usually leave a mess. You can't convince me that an advanced race lived on this planet for almost half a million years and left no trace. We've only been a technological society for one hundred years or so, and look at the changes we've made to the planet: Highway systems, railroads, airports, dams — not to mention the damage we've done to the environment. So where are the remains? Carcasses of old spaceships? Oil cans? Silverware? Spent nuclear fuel rods? Styrofoam fast-food containers? There's an astounding lack of evidence, where there should be evidence everywhere. We might do five thousand site digs and only find a few hundred samples of pottery or art or human remains, and none of it older than around 10 or 11,000 years. Yet, if what you're saying is true, if the aliens were here just a few thousand years ago, there should be signs of them everywhere, evidence that wouldn't have decayed or been destroyed in such a short period of time. Where is any sign that there was an advanced technological society in existence on this planet for almost half a million years?"

"My theory doesn't require evidence to be true," Simon said shortly. "You have to accept that it's at least possible."

"No, that's *im*possible; in fact, it defies the very definition of archaeology! Archaeology is the study of the evidence left behind by prior civilizations. Without evidence, there's no study. With nothing to study, you can't create a hypothesis! If you make up a story with no evidence to back it up, it's just that: a story. It's not a hypothesis, and it's sure as hell not science."

Simon glared at the young man for a long beat before responding. "When I mentioned the possibility of an advanced civilization living on Earth before modern times, before the end of the last ice age, I was merely speaking of other research currently being done in this field," he said. "Personally, I'm not a big proponent of that measure. I believe that the visitors only came through once in our recorded history: At the time of the ancient Maya and Inca, when they recorded the visitor's appearance

422

and marked the time until he would return again. In such a scenario, there's no need to look for the remains of his food or cooking pot or whatever, because he wouldn't have brought it with him. He'd have used the cookware, clothing, and bedding provided by his adoptive culture, and there'd be no sign of his existence other than what was recorded in the glyphs and pictograms, which I've already detailed."

"How convenient," the young man said, taking his seat.

Simon ignored him and pointed to a tall woman near the front. "Next, please."

She stood up. "You mentioned the possibility of a pole shift that would physically switch the geographical coordinates of the Earth's magnetic poles."

"That's right," Simon said. "I can't say I subscribe to the theory fully; I don't believe the appearance of the visitors will cause much physical destruction. However, I've been advised that the rip in the fabric of our universe could have serious gravitational consequences on our planet."

"But gravity and magnetism are two different things."

Simon didn't reply. He wracked his brain for an answer, but then saw that he didn't need to expand. More hands were already up and waving, and with a broad smile, he pointed to another student, a dark haired young woman.

"Can you go into any more detail on the five ages?" she asked. Simon smiled, about to answer, glad to finally have someone on his side, when the woman continued: "Cosmology actually claims seven ages of the Universe: Quantum gravity, particle physics, nuclear physics; the ages of light, chemistry, gravity, and finally, biology — the age we're living in now. These are the actual ages the Universe passed through and continues with. You haven't actually defined your five ages – exactly what kind of ages are they?"

Simon stood up straighter, not making eye contact with the woman as he looked out and around the audience. "I *did* define them," he claimed. "Perhaps you weren't able to keep up. However, for those who were paying attention, I'm not going to bore them by reiterating. You can read my book if you want to understand it better."

"I did read your book," the woman interrupted. "All you say is that the Earth went through different phases of creation and destruction, and that each age ends with some catastrophe. But geologists know that this isn't true …"

"Please," Simon said, holding up a hand. "I believe you'll find that I have done my research and collaborated with scientists from many different fields. They didn't want their names attached to my theory — there's still a depressing prejudice in the scientific community against anyone that dares step outside their bounds. But, you'll notice —neither have they spoken against me."

He glanced over the many hands still waving, and chose another woman; a young girl who'd been gazing at him raptly from the front row throughout his presentation. He pointed to her with a beaming smile. "Go ahead, sweetheart."

"Isn't it true that your numbers are incorrect?" the woman asked. "That you can't divide them the way they're actually set up? You had to create a common divisor to get it to work, but that divisor isn't found in any of the Mayan records. Wasn't it invented by you simply to get your numbers to work the way you wanted them to?"

Simon didn't answer. Instead, he began to redden, and Dominic could've sworn he saw the man trembling. "Who the hell are you people?" Simon stormed. "Don't you have anything better to do than come out here and mock me in front of people who came to really listen? You can't discredit me. Who do you think you are?"

A figure rose to his feet, tall and dark in the shadows of the theatre.

"I'm proud to call them my students, Simon," the figure said, and he could see Simon's face freeze as he realized who was speaking. "They only want to know the truth, and they can only learn it by asking questions and getting answers. When you refuse to answer their questions, we have to wonder what you're hiding, and why you're hiding it. A real scientist puts his work out there for other scientists to test inside and out; it's the scientific process that confirms and assures that the facts are true and the results can be reproduced. When you refuse to do so, we can only assume that they can't be. And that you know it. That doesn't just make you a bad scientist, Simon. It makes you a liar."

Even from his place in the audience, Dominic could see how red Simon's face had become. He spluttered for a moment, glaring out into the audience that had so quickly turned on him, not noticing that much of the audience was also glaring at Dominic. He had won most of them over, and the antagonizing questions were unwelcome, detracting from the excitement that had enveloped the crowd.

"Well good for you," Simon finally said. "Try to shoot holes in my theory all you want, Ciriello. I'm on this stage, and you're sitting in the audience. My book has been a best seller for months. And when December comes, we'll all know who was right, won't we?"

"That we will," Dominic answered, but it was drowned out by the raucous applause that filled the theatre. Many of the students in Dominic's immediate area turned around to give him dark looks. Onstage, Simon beamed triumphantly, raising both arms over his head, victorious. This brought even more applause, and most of the crowd rose to its feet.

Simon clasped his hands over his head and shook them like a boxer, then lowered them, gave a quick bow, and strode off stage.

"At least he knows to quit when he's ahead," the student to Dominic's right said. He and Dominic exchanged a smile, and Dominic clapped him on the shoulder. He remained standing, watching the audience begin to file out, wondering if he'd have a chance to catch up with Simon backstage. He doubted the mathematician's handlers would allow him anywhere near him; after all, Simon was a celebrity now, and Dominic was dangerous. He was a little disappointed, but couldn't help but feel that he had accomplished what he'd come for. Most of the audience had come in already believing Simon's claptrap, and wouldn't have been swayed no matter what had been said. A smaller percentage would've come in open-minded, and some of them might have left as believers. He knew that his students' questions would've raised some doubts in the mind of others, though, and hoped that it would make them think.

And best of all, he had rattled Simon. Even if he hadn't changed the mind of a single person in attendance, Simon had been unsettled, and that in itself had been worth the effort.

Dominic came out of the stall, then stopped in surprise when he saw Simon at the sink. "Small world," he said, and Simon turned around.

"Well, wouldn't you know it," he said. "What are you doing, Ciriello? Following me around?"

"Not quite," Dominic said. "Don't know if it was dinner or your speech, but I suddenly didn't feel so well."

Simon turned to the sink again to shut off the water. "Must be all that jealousy and resentment you've been harboring."

He flinched at Dominic's laughter. "You're as clueless as you always were," Dominic said. "Still wrapped up in your own little world, basking in the glory of your own opinion."

"My opinion happens to be shared by scholars all over the world."

"Scholars, Simon? Come on. It's bullshit, and you know it's bullshit."

"So you say."

"Don't tell me you've actually started believing your own hype?"

"There's validity to my theory. Just because it doesn't follow accepted scientific theory doesn't mean there's nothing to it."

"'Accepted scientific theory?'" Dominic repeated. "Please, Simon … there's nothing scientific about it. It's pure speculation, nothing but rambling blather based on faulty logic and incorrect history. It's idiocy based on a fallacy."

Simon spun to face him angrily. "It's not up to you to decide whether or not my work is valid, Ciriello. Most of the world believes me."

"Jesus, Simon — *most of the world* has never heard of you. There's another of your baseless statements you just make up out of nowhere. And hell, much of the world believes in psychics, witches, demons, faith healers, and astrology, too. Just because a person believes in something, does that make it true? Majority rule has nothing to do with whether something really works, or whether a fact exists."

"At some point, majority *has* to rule. If everyone agrees on something, don't you think that maybe, just maybe they're right?"

Dominic laughed. "What the hell is this? George Orwell's *1984*? Remember the concept that freedom is being able to say that two plus two is four, even if the rest of the world insists that it's five? What happens when the entire world is telling you something that's wrong? Should we just accept it?"

"Well, now you're coming around to my way of thinking," Simon said. "Traditional world view says that history is linear; that we've started from the dawn of man and moved straight through history to today. I don't believe that world view. I believe that we've been fed a line of bull that's wrong."

Dominic shook his head, his look of amusement replaced by sadness. "I'm disappointed in you, Simon. Money really must talk, and it's said some crazy things to you. I can't believe that you now find it more rational to believe that our ancient ancestors were visited by a race of aliens that could defy the laws of physics, than to believe that the reason we've found no evidence of an advanced prior civilization is because there isn't one. You've strayed far, Simon."

Simon shrugged. "Maybe I've finally found the right path."

"So be it," Dominic said. "I felt much better about you when I thought you were just doing it for the publicity, when I thought you were chasing fame at any cost. But if you actually believe in the line you're throwing out there, then I feel sorry for you, Simon."

Simon laughed derisively. "You think I want your pity? What a joke. Here you are now, where I was years ago — teaching to a bunch of ungrateful and impressionable college students. They'll believe anything you tell them, because you're the expert. You could lie to them all year and they'd swallow it. What was the point of teaching them anything, of being a fucking expert, when they don't know you from anyone, would believe anything you tell them anyway, and probably forget it by the time grades come out anyway? I'm on top of the world now, Ciriello. Fuck teaching at the college level. Hell, I'll bet half your students skipped your class to come see me."

"Actually, all of them did," Dominic said. "I cancelled all my classes today and offered extra credit for attending your lecture. They get bonus points for turning in a report on it."

A dark look crossed Simon's face, but he didn't miss a beat. "I'm sure they learned a lot," he said. "Although, if they're your students, they're probably so close-minded and thick headed they don't recognize the truth when it hits them; they were too busy thinking up questions to try to disprove me."

Dominic stepped aside. "I don't think we have anything more to say to each other," he said. "It's interesting how much things have changed. But just as before, we'll never be able to change each others' minds. So good-bye, Simon."

"Conceding defeat again," Simon said, shaking his head. "I should've known you wouldn't have the balls to stand up to me. You know when you've lost, I'll give you credit for that much, at least."

"Any messages you want me to take back to Abby?" Dominic asked.

Simon's smile froze. "Fuck you both," he said, then pushed past Dominic and out of the room. His entourage silently followed.

Dominic smiled, crossing to the sink to wash his hands. For all the changes of opinion his old acquaintance had undergone over the last few years, Simon would never change.

12.19.19.13.6

September 18, 2012 — "Do you think we need to be there for it? I mean, if the world's going to end, or to begin, or whatever, we'll find out about it anyway. I'd like to find out about it here snug in our own home. Safe."

Dominic sighed. "Abby," he said, kneeling beside the bed. He took her hand. "You know I love you to death. You're the most important thing in the world to me. You're the only thing in the world to me. Except this.

"You're the only one who really ever understood what the Long Count meant to me, and the only one who stood by me through it all, and trusted me. You have to know how much it means to me to go there, to be there to witness it myself. To watch the changing of the guard, if that's what it'll be."

Abby smiled, then leaned forward and kissed the top of his head. She ran her fingers through his dark curls, then laid her cheek on them. "I know," she said quietly. "It's not that I don't want you to experience it, Dominic. I'm just — I don't know — uneasy. I have a lot of bad memories of that place. Losing Steve, all the fighting, the last blowout with Simon. I just get very uncomfortable when I think about going back. Like something bad is still waiting for us there."

"Sweetheart," he said, rising up to sit beside her on the bed. "I love you, but I wish you wouldn't be so pessimistic all the time. When I think about Mexico, all I can think about is you. Look at the good times we had there. The fun we had with Steve before he died. Falling in love. It wasn't all dark and stormy, Abby. It was the best time of my life."

Abby stared into his sincere, dark eyes, amazed at his simplicity. She wrapped her arms around him and held him tightly, burying her face in his strong chest. "You're unreal," she murmured, and he smiled, stroking her hair.

"Not at all," he said. "This is definitely reality, and as much as I'm looking forward to whatever is going to happen, this is a reality I don't ever want to change."

12.19.19.13.8

September 20, 2012 — "I believe I was misunderstood," Simon said, his voice dripping with false sincerity. He stopped short of making an apology. "I have always believed in a higher power; after all, this amazing world of ours can't turn on its own. Someone had to spin it into existence, and we're still playing out that grand plan. The existence of a god certainly doesn't preclude the existence of extraterrestrial intelligence. Our god isn't just the god of the Earth; He's the God of the Universe."

"Claiming to know more than God is one of the severest sins," the program host, Daniel Hall, said dispassionately.

"I couldn't agree more," Simon said smoothly. "I believe that God speaks to us in ways that he knows we'll understand. His method of communication may be different for each individual; for some, he gives signs. Others, he might speak to through prayer. I believe God and I communicate in the language of mathematics. Math, after all, is the basis for everything in the universe. It can all be understood and tied together through math; everything from music to the fabric of the cosmos can be broken down into mathematical systems. I can read these, and this is how God has chosen to provide me with the answer to the Long Count."

"Then you believe the answer to the Count came to you by divine revelation?"

"I wouldn't say that," Simon said modestly. "I don't ever want to claim to be a prophet. But I do know that many people have worked on this issue for many years, and I felt as if I was drawn to the answer by some guiding presence. I do feel that I was the person who was intended to break this story, to solve this mystery."

"Why do you feel that way?" Hall asked.

"Because I can explain it in mathematical terms to the scientific community, yet I can speak to the common people who might not follow advanced equations. I am a teacher, so I can best communicate my theory to the world."

"So when you claimed that Jesus was an alien, you didn't really mean it?"

Simon shrugged humbly. "I can't claim to know all the answers," he said. "At the time, that explanation made the most sense to me; after all, He was capable of doing the same things the Maya and Aztecs claimed that their god-men could do. It confused me; I thought, either they were all aliens, or they were all sons of God. I knew, though, that that would be blasphemy, so I dismissed it. But I consulted my spiritual advisors, and they've helped me to understand that it's not necessary for Jesus the Savior to have been an alien for my theory to still be correct. It's entirely possible that Kulkulcan and Quetzalcoatl were visitors that came through the space-time portal, at the same time that Jesus, the son of God, came to the Middle East. Maybe the events are even related; I'm not a theologian, and so I leave that to the experts to work on."

"But doesn't the mere fact of life on another planet, or life existing in another dimension, nullify the existence of God?" Hall asked. "At least, the god of the Bible, the Torah, and the Koran? After all, the holy books are based on the concept that an almighty power created the Universe, of which man – and more specifically, the Earth – is the center. We now know that the sun is the center of our solar system, and that we're only one small planet amongst billions of billions. Still, though, God created the Earth and everything that exists on it for man's usage, right? This is what gives us the right to destroy entire ecosystems, decimate the habitats of other creatures, and use up all the natural resources. After all, God put them here for man, his ultimate project, to use, correct?"

Simon smiled uneasily. "I believe you're playing the Devil's advocate."

"Maybe so, but that doesn't answer my question. Where does alien life fit into the Biblical scheme of things?"

"Well," Simon hesitated for an indiscernible moment, and then plowed on. "God is the creator of the entire Universe, not just of man. If He could create the Earth and all the life upon it, why couldn't he repeat the process elsewhere?"

"What would it mean, though, to Christianity? Christ is the savior of man, sent to ensure that we would have eternal life. Did the aliens not need saved? Do they not deserve to be saved?"

"Maybe Christ appeared in different forms on different worlds. Here he was the savior for mankind; perhaps on another planet he's the savior of giraffes, or whatever intelligent life form runs that planet." He saw the host's smile slip, and he straightened up. "Of course, I'm just speculating. I do not claim to know the mind of God. Just as we have many religions here on Earth, each of whose believers claim is the One True Faith. We all assume that we're right, and that God knows the truth. I assume religion on other planets would be the same."

"But what would that mean to our beliefs in a personal god?" Hall insisted. "Some people find it hard enough to believe in a god that would care about billions of people on this Earth, and have a hand in all their daily actions. Think about how hard they'll find it to believe in a god that doesn't just love them and look out for them, but does the same for beings on other planets."

"There are some who will say that God *doesn't* care about our daily lives," Simon said. "Unless we're living in the western world, where our biggest concern isn't dying of diphtheria or trying to find non-polluted water, or food, or avoid brutality and massacre by our own countrymen; but is instead getting out of a speeding ticket, passing an exam, getting the job we want, or our favorite team winning the World Series. We think God answers our prayers when things go our way, and we don't think about the literally millions of children dying of such simple things as hunger, or diseases we've cured among our own children decades ago."

"You sound like you don't believe it yourself."

"It's not my place to interpret the will of God," Simon said. "The Buddha himself said 'Suffering is good.' Everything plays out in God's time, on God's schedule, not ours. If He wants millions of people, including innocent children, to suffer and die; well, who are we to question it? Why should the rest of us get involved? You cannot bend the will of God."

The host looked troubled, as if he was trying to decide whether or not Simon was pulling his leg. Finally, he chose to go around the subject.

"You still haven't fully answered my question," he said. "Where does alien life fit into the Divine Plan?"

"Well, like I said, I'm not a theologian. I sure wish I had a direct line to God, but I'm as helpless as anyone else when it comes to discerning His will."

Hall frowned, beginning to get annoyed at his guest's avoidance of the subject. "The Bible says nothing about aliens. It says nothing about life on other planets."

"It says nothing about cars or DVDs, either."

"Now you're being facetious."

"I'm not," Simon insisted. "I really don't know why the Bible doesn't speak of extraterrestrial life. After all, God knows everything that ever has and ever will happen in all of creation, right? Perhaps God wrote a different book for each planet, so he didn't feel the need to mention the others to each of us."

"Perhaps you're not looking deep enough," Hall said. "Perhaps you have it backwards."

"I'm not sure that I follow."

"You've claimed that sections of the Bible, where Elijah speaks of angels, is actually talking about aliens. In the next breath, you claim that the individuals approaching our planet from another dimension are aliens, and that the Bible says nothing about them. Ignoring the contradiction for now, maybe what you think are aliens actually *are* angels."

He paused for a moment, then spoke again: "Or demons."

"No," Simon said, suddenly nervous. He didn't have enough of a religious background to delve into the subject any deeper, but he suddenly knew that he didn't want to get on the subject of demons. Bad enough the U.S. Army was wary of militant aliens; he didn't need the religious community up in arms about the arrival of the minions of Satan.

"I can't say for sure how I know it, but I'm sure they're not demons. If anything, though, you may be right with the angels. After all, in the Bible, they showed beautiful things to those who watched, right?"

"Beautiful and terrible."

"Well, they've been nothing but helpful throughout the ages. They've brought culture and civilization, and taken select few for rides on their spaceships. No one has been hurt."

"Yet," Hall said solemnly.

The interview went on, and the tone lightened and the subject matter changed to other things. Still, however, the host's words stuck in the back of Simon's mind, and although he hated to admit it, he was troubled.

12.19.19.13.19

September 31, 2012 — "Dr. Nieson, do you understand the serious nature of your claim?"

"Of course," he replied easily. "That's why I'm making it. I want the world to be prepared. Especially the United States," he added.

"You miss my point," Addison responded. "When a claim is made that the end of the world is coming, there are often dire results. Look at Heaven's Gate, at Jonestown. In 1992, a minister in Seoul announced that the rapture would occur in October of that year.

Hundreds of people — including Americans — abandoned their lives; they left their jobs, even their families. Women had abortions; people sold everything they owned, all to prepare for the upcoming rapture. In South Korea, there was mass panic."

Simon shifted uncomfortably. "What about Y2K?" he asked. "There weren't major suicides or hysteria or anything. People just stockpiled toilet paper and canned goods. January 1, they came out of their holes, and the world went on. No harm done."

The general sat silently, his hands folded on the table before him.

Simon went on, "Besides, I can't help how people react. If people are going to drop everything and panic, running around like a bunch of headless chickens, it isn't my fault. It's like blaming the Beatles for Manson's 'Helter Skelter' murders. People are going to interpret things however they want. I'm just putting the facts out there."

Addison remained impassive, and as the silence wore on, Simon found he had begun to sweat again.

"Question for you," the general finally said.

"Shoot," Simon responded, smiling at his own cleverness.

Addison ignored the attempt at humor. "You say this occurrence is supposed to happen on December 21, correct?"

"That's correct."

"Would that be the morning of the twenty-first, then? Should we gather at midnight on the twentieth, as the event will occur in the wee hours of the morning? Or do we wait all day for something to happen that night?"

Simon was floored. The thought had never occurred to him, and he wasn't sure how to answer. Luckily for him, though, the general continued on his own.

"Personally, I'd think it would be that night, am I right? It doesn't make sense that they'd count it if it was the morning of the twenty-first. They didn't measure days the same way we did, did they? Did they have 24-hour days, starting at midnight?"

Simon breathed a silent sigh of relief. "No, they didn't," he said. "The 24 hour day wasn't adopted by the western world for a couple hundred more years, and the Maya were never part of that. They'd have considered a new day starting at dawn. So for them, the twenty-first would have been from daybreak until dawn of the following day. We don't have to worry about anything happening until after dusk on the twenty-first."

Addison's expression was solemn. "That's what I thought," he said. "Okay, thank you, Dr. Nieson. We'll be contacting you again."

Simon smiled. "I appreciate that, General."

The general nodded dismissively, and Simon stood up. The military man did not offer his hand, and the professor turned and left. His heart was beating faster, and he couldn't help but feel that he had slipped out of a snare once again. Addison was onto him, he knew; on every visit Simon made to the base, the general treated him with more and more disdain. The others in the room still seemed to be looking up to him, however; still awed by his knowledge of the universe and the intricacies of his theory about the coming visitation. Lieutenant Osbourne had even asked for his autograph — when the general wasn't looking, that was.

Only Addison and another of his lieutenants, a wiry Latino named Marquez, appeared to doubt him. It didn't seem as if they were going to confront him, to out him in front of their superiors who seemed to believe, but still — Simon didn't trust the general at all. There was something about Addison's total lack of emotion that made Simon feel as if every time he stepped before the general, he was stepping further into a trap.

Simon didn't know how much farther he could push it, but he knew he'd better raise his game, or drop out entirely — this was progressing much farther than he'd intended, and he knew if he was caught out at this stage of the game, he was in some serious trouble.

12.19.19.14.1

October 3, 2012 — "We're here on location in Izapa, Mexico," the newscaster said. She was standing in front of the ballcourt, and behind her was what looked like some type of carnival.

"We're more than two months away from the End of Time, as writer and theorist Simon Thomas Nieson calls it, but already this small Mayan site in southwestern Mexico has been overrun with everyone from churches to UFO cults. The Mexican Bureau of Tourism expects hundreds of thousands of people to gather at Izapa in the next few months, and the military has already begun to set up shop to keep them under control."

She stepped aside, letting the cameras pan over the booths, tents, and tables that had been set up on the field of the ancient ballcourt. People of all races, in all manner of dress, wandered the area; it looked to Jane Lewis like a Renaissance Festival.

"Jane, do you think there's going to be trouble among all these warring factions?" the in-studio newsman asked. "After all, you have a table from the United States Presbyterian Church right next to a tent full of Wiccans. We've also heard that there are Satanists performing rituals in the nearby woods, Druids dancing on top of the temple, and the Catholic

Church housing priests to represent it in case anyone *does* arrive on the twenty-first."

"Surprisingly, things have been relatively well, Christopher," Jane Lewis replied. "There's a true spirit of togetherness here, and people have treated each other with respect. I've heard tale of a few skirmishes, but they've been nothing more than quickly dissolved shouting matches. Everyone is here to serve their own agenda, and they've kept peace among them. As far as to how long that peace will hold, there's no way to tell. The U.S. and Mexican militaries expect that relations among these opposing groups might degenerate as time wears on; not only will they get tired of sharing such a small space right beside people who might hold entirely opposite viewpoints than themselves, but the crowds are expected to grow as the time of the alignment grows nearer.

"Every year, Stonehenge brings about 20,000 worshipers during the summer solstice — Druids, spiritualists, tourists — and this event is expected to be much, much bigger than that. The summer solstice at Stonehenge occurs every year; the end of the Long Count occurs only once in … well, forever. We can't even estimate how many people will show up for it, but figures we've heard so far have been in the millions. There's much excitement now, but the month of December will bring a level of expectation never seen before. Time will only tell how capable the police and military will be at keeping the peace."

"You mentioned the United States military," the newsman said. "What are they doing in southern Mexico, down by the Guatemalan border?"

"That's a good question, Tom," she replied. "There are a lot of American citizens flooding into Izapa for this event, and the military may feel some responsibility for them. The official word is that they're helping out the Mexican government by assisting in maintaining peace and trying to avoid riots or crowd violence. It's going to take a lot of troops to police this area, especially as numbers grow, and the groups attracted to this area are going to be more and more offbeat. Right now, the mood is somewhat like visiting a fair, or even a trade show; there are different booths where you can learn about different groups and their different viewpoints on this event, pick up literature, even join them in prayer or ceremony.

"I spent much of last night with a group of astronomers from the nearby University of Chiapas, and enjoyed viewing the different planets and constellations observable in this area," she commented. "The difference between them and a group of UFO buffs set up nearby was extremely interesting. While the UFO crowd told me about the Marfa lights, giving me the background and history of them, the astronomers explained that the lights had long ago been proven to be the headlights from cars passing on a road several miles away. It was all quite fascinating; but most promising of all was how amiable they all were. Such differences of opinion could have brought out the worst in either group, but there was no fighting, and even the discussion was light-hearted. There's no way of knowing how long that will hold up, however, which is why I expect there is such a strong military presence here."

"What are they saying about the man who started all of this, Dr. Simon Nieson?"

"Well, there are many different attitudes, of course. Some groups refute him, while others claim that he's a prophet. Surprisingly, some seem to have no opinion of him at all. They don't doubt that the Long Count exists, and that it was created here at Izapa, and that it ends on December 21, 2012. However, they don't consider Dr. Nieson's interpretation to be any more probable than any other explanation that researchers have come up with over the years.

"What *is* exciting for many, though, is that Dr. Nieson is expected to show up on the twenty-first. There are already plans to construct a stage, and there will be some type of rally. I'm not altogether certain what it's all about, but it is expected to draw a crowd — Dr. Nieson's known supporters in the U.S. alone number more than one hundred thousand people."

"That would certainly help to explain the watchful eye of the Mexican army," Tom Davis replied. "I would think that at some point, though, they're going to have to shut down the area, aren't they? From my understanding, the area around Izapa won't support that many people — much of it is unexplored jungle, isn't it?"

"There is a lot of forest around here, and there is quite a concern about the animals in this area. It is extremely wild, and could be dangerous to people who've been to no place in Mexico wilder than Cancun, or Acapulco."

"Not to mention the damage the people could do to the environment in the area, correct?"

"Correct, Tom. In fact, the military has cut down a swatch of the forest surrounding Izapa, cutting deeply into the woods to set up staging areas. You can see their spotlights from here," Jane said, waving her hand back at the edge of the woods. It was daylight, so the lights weren't glowing, but the fresh tree stumps and banks of lights were clearly visible against the darker green of the forest. As she turned back to the camera, she thought she felt a slight tremble under her feet. Looking around, she didn't see anyone else who appeared to have noticed. Uneasy, she continued: "Already there are environmental groups protesting the display, and the Mexican government and cultural council are having their say about any destruction done to one of the country's most ancient sites."

"Well, it will be an interesting story as it develops, won't it, Jane?"

"That it will, Tom," she said, suddenly eager to be done and gone. "That it definitely will."

12.19.19.14.5

October 7, 2012 — "A great many stars in our own galaxy are older than the sun. Other civilizations would have a major head start," Simon stated. "We now know that the oldest planet is over thirteen and a half billion years old. Thirteen and a half billion!

"Our own earth is less than a fourth of that age, and look at how advanced we are. We think about where we'll be technologically in a hundred years, or even a thousand, and we can't imagine it. We can't imagine our advancements and evolution ten thousand years from now, or a million. Who can imagine where we'd be in another few *billion* years?"

"But that planet is long dead," the reporter replied. "Its sun burned out billions of years ago. The universe's oldest planet is dead and empty. No one from there will be coming through the fabric of the universe to visit us."

"That's not my point," Simon answered, trying to remain patient. He needed this interview; a written review by Victor Fayed would be a shot in the arm to his slumping book sales. He knew the published account would be reprinted in papers and magazines around the globe. At least in print, he'd have no one arguing with him, as the interviewers on many of the news shows had begun doing. He could do without anyone bringing in "experts" to debate him. "What I'm trying to say," he continued, "is that there are civilizations out there much older than ours; millions, if not billions of years ahead of us! We're nothing to them."

"Than why should we feel safe? If they're so far beyond us, they won't think anything of destroying us and taking the planet, will they?"

"Why would they want it?" Simon said. "Do you really think such an advanced society would want our minerals? Gold? Our water? I'd like to think that if the human race doesn't wipe itself out in the next few centuries, we'll have found a way to live in harmony with each other and with nature. If they did have some type of energy crisis, certainly they'd be capable of finding another alternative. No, there's nothing they'd want from us here."

"Then why come back? What do they want?"

Simon smiled. "Maybe to study us. To find out who we are, and what we do. After all, isn't that what we'd do if we found an extra-planetary civilization? We'd study their culture, their society. It's all in the name of science, Victor."

"So what happens when they decide to start dissecting us? Running their own laboratory experiments on us?"

Simon smiled. "Let's just hope you and I are too smart to get caught."

12.19.19.14.12

October 14, 2012 — "Did you see this article?" Abby laughed. Dominic set down the sports section and glanced over to see what she was reading.

"It's an interview he did for the New York Times, but it looks like it's been carried over both the AP and Knight-Ridder. Wow, are they tearing him apart."

"Really? Let me have a look."

Abby pushed the paper in front of him, then sat back to watch his reaction. It didn't take long before he was smiling, then laughing out loud.

"*Dr. Nieson is either a sham or a moron,*" he read aloud. "*His math seems to be deliberately in error, and his orbit speeds and distances have nothing to do with one another. He seems to have created a theory out of nothing, then rounded up anything he could find that would even remotely appear to support it. The fact that none of it actually* does *is irrelevant; Dr. Nieson continues to promote this nonsense with only one goal in mind: Making as much money as possible before the twenty-first of December.*"

"That Victor Fayed seems to have gotten right to the heart of it, anyway," Abby commented.

"That he did. Looks like Simon's days are numbered, one way or the other," Dominic replied. "Worst case scenario, people keep buying his bullshit for another two months. Best case, he drops off the face of the Earth."

Abby laughed. "We couldn't be so lucky. I guess we'd better just count on the first option."

Dominic smiled and laid down the newspaper. He reached for the sports section again. "Either way, Simon got what he went into it for — fame, notoriety, and hell, he's even amassed a small fortune. At least he'll get the world looking up at the sky on the night of the twenty-first, which is more than most astronomers have managed to do in the past year. He'll see his little joke come to completion, and then he probably *will* drop out of sight. I suppose we can put up with him until December."

"I'll be counting the days," Abby said, standing up. She cleared their breakfast dishes, still smiling as she headed into the kitchen.

October 16, 2012 — "Have you noticed how Simon has stopped responding to his critics?" Abby asked. "He hasn't done any talk shows since they've started ripping him apart on every one. He's just promoting his views through his website."

"It's safer for him," Dominic said. He didn't look up from the papers he was grading. "Someone attacks him every time he shows his face, so he's stopped coming out. He's finally learned that bullshit can only carry him so far."

"He doesn't respond to any of the scientists asking him for proof, either."

"Of course he doesn't. He's learned well." Dominic set down his pen and looked up. "He's been on the other side of the argument too much in his past; he knows how to play the game."

Abby shook her head. "There should be a law against it. Some kind of government office that investigates these things and insists any stupid claim like this be supported with evidence; if it's not, he shouldn't be allowed to sell it."

"What's he really selling, though, but his book?" Dominic asked. "It's not like he's selling some kind of fake weight loss pill or machine that doesn't work. Hell, even those are legal, as long as you don't make any claims that it actually cures anything.

"They can win a patent, because the U.S. Patent Office doesn't require proof that an invention does what you say it will, or even that it works – just that it's original. So 'inventors' will market their products and drawing in as much money as possible based on the fact that it's patented; the product doesn't legally have to do anything. There are guys that have been making the same claim on perpetual energy machines for twenty years or more, who are millionaires now from getting investors, yet still don't have a working model. They just keep trotting out the same prototype, and they won't let real scientists get their hands on it. They claim that they'll steal or destroy the technology, or something equally stupid. Yet via the internet and road shows, they can just keep on reeling in new victims."

"Well, it should be illegal. No one should be allowed to take advantage of other people that way. Just because they don't know any better doesn't give some evil asshole the right to take their money. They should be required to put it in front of an experienced team of scientists that can tell whether it works or it's just a scam. These people are jackals."

"I'm not arguing with you, Abby. And Simon is no different," Dominic said. "He refuses to allow his hypothesis to be tested, because he knows they'll find out the truth. There will always be a faction that sides with him, believing that he has the true answer. This is the same group that believes in conspiracy theories. They think that the government is trying to hide the truth from us, and they'll rally to his side, not because he has any proof, or his hypothesis makes any type of sense, but because they *want* to believe. They're prepared to believe. No matter what idiotic bullshit he throws out there, there are people that are willing to believe it, no questions asked. And the internet is the best way to find that audience."

Abby sighed. "I know you think that people can't be taken advantage of without their permission, and I agree with you. Look at how Simon treated me all those years, and I didn't just enable him, I defended him. But I can't help but feel that there should be someone to fight against it, to stand up for people who don't know any better. There's no government office that goes after frauds like this, forcing them to prove themselves. The Better Business Bureau never asks a psychic to prove she has any psychic ability, or that such an ability even exists. Any yahoo with enough money to put out an ad can claim to be psychic and swindle people out of their cash. Anyone interested in the research can find all the test results that demonstrate there's never been any proof that psychic ability exists or is even possible, but no one is stopping people from making money off of it anyway. No one asks the inventor of a perpetual energy machine to prove that they've somehow created a machine that can violate the laws of physics."

"Of course not," Dominic answered with a smile. "It comes down to the most basic element of scientific method, Abby: The burden of proof. If someone claims to have a machine that violates the laws of the universe as we know them, they're going to have to provide some pretty extraordinary evidence for it. It isn't the responsibility of detractors to prove that it isn't possible; the person claiming they can do it should have to prove it. No government agency should have to waste their time tracking down all these claims and trying to prove every one of them wrong, because anyone with a high school education should already be smarter than to fall for them.

"Let's face it, if someone invented a perpetual motion machine or proved psychic ability, it would change our view of the universe, altering or even eliminating many universal laws as we know them. It would refute Einstein's theories and laws, and destroy concepts that we've used for dozens of years of successful invention, space exploration, and manned space travel, such as the way waves travel through space. Psychic ability would change everything we know about biology and how the brain receives information, as well. Such an invention or discovery would be invaluable to science. But, we know that it shouldn't be possible, and the inventors or practitioners refuse to provide evidence or to allow it to be tested, so we have to assume that it's a fraud. Some blatantly obvious lies aren't even worth wasting manpower and money to investigate."

"Then they shouldn't be allowed to sell it, either," Abby protested.

"You're preaching to the choir, my dear," Dominic said. He picked up his pen again. "It goes back to the first rule of sales: Let the buyer beware."

"So you think it's okay to sell snake oil to people who don't know any better than to buy it?"

Dominic's smile faded. "No, I don't," he said seriously. "I think anyone that sells perpetual motion machines, tarot card readings, homeopathic medicine, and any of the like, should have to prove that it works. And if they can't, they should be subject to prosecution, just like anyone else who knowingly perpetuates a fraud and takes money for it. But they won't, Abby, because the tests have already been run. Look – there's been failed experiment after failed experiment for homeopathy. The mere concept of it is ludicrous; the idea that one molecule of an element diluted into the equivalent of sixteen Olympic size swimming pools of water will cure a disease is laughable enough, but when they claim that the water retains the 'vibration' of the element ... well, you see what we're dealing with. Not just that the water has memory, but it has some way of knowing which element it's supposed to remember, as opposed to every other element that has passed through that water since the beginning of time. There's no science whatsoever that would support such a thing. So the people selling and buying it say that there are some things *beyond* science, things that can't be tested for."

"That's insane," Abby argued. "Of course everything can be tested. Science doesn't create reality, it simply observes it. It tests and explains the world, and the universe. It defines things we don't understand in terms that we can. If something exists, then we should be able to observe it and understand the mechanism behind it."

"Again, you're not telling me anything I don't know," Dominic said. "I'm just explaining why there's no government office to fight against these things. Educated people know there's no such thing as 'alternative' medicine. There's medicine, which works; and there's the alternative, which doesn't. Once an alternative treatment is studied, tested, and proven to work, it's integrated into medicine. It's no longer considered 'alternative,' or 'complementary.' It's just medical treatment. Anything else simply doesn't work, or hasn't been subjected to rigorous scientific testing. Some of it is so ridiculous that pharmacies and scientists won't even consider it, because it's just flat out wrong. For example: the claim that all cancers are caused by some kind of invisible parasite that no physician has ever found, and would have no effect on how cells divide and become cancerous anyway, but the products this company sells can kill it. It's preposterous.

"Proponents of alternative medicine tend to believe that things can work without being repeatable in a lab environment. Why? Simply because they have a thousand anecdotes saying it worked for somebody. They don't understand why anecdotes don't count. They don't realize that many diseases go in cycles — people tend to seek treatment in the down cycles, when they feel at their worst, so when they naturally improve again, they believe it was on account of the treatment. Other diseases, including cancer, can go into remission on their own. And most of the time, the 'alternative' therapy is used in conjunction with real medical treatment, usually started after they've been undergoing conventional treatment for awhile. Sometimes real medicine takes a long time to take effect, even longer to cure, so people believe that because they got better only *after* they started the alternative therapy, that that's what caused them to improve.

"Scientific study, where all the different possibilities are removed and the therapy is studied by itself, is the only way to prove whether or not it's effective. And when it fails, then it's thrown out. People can continue to sell it after it failed laboratory testing, as long as they don't claim to be doctors, and they don't claim it will cure you. It's ridiculous, sure; but people will buy it. The government assumes people are smart enough to do their homework and check on whether anything has any evidence it works, or if all evidence is anecdotal. They can't baby-sit us all the time, or save us from everyone. At some point, people have to take responsibility for themselves."

Dominic shrugged. "I'm sorry, Abby," he said. "It's easy enough to find evidence against Simon's theory, even if you have no scientific background and don't understand what the hell he's talking about. There's been a lot of research by people who *do* understand it; even for the lay-person doing an internet search, there are plenty of websites up that refute Simon's hypothesis. There are people that will argue against his supporters in chat rooms and newsgroups, trying their damndest to convince them that he's wrong. But as long as people want to believe, they will. They'll ignore facts, they'll ignore common sense. I wouldn't worry about it too much," he said with a smile. "He only has another few months of fame, and it'll all be over. Let him sell his books and charge for his lectures. People are getting entertainment out if it, anyway; maybe not the way you or I would choose to spend our money, but not everybody values the same things. I don't think anyone's getting hurt. Anyone falling victim to Simon's idiocy is doing so willingly."

"Okay," Abby answered slowly, with some disappointment.

Dominic reached across and took her hand. "Abby, I know how you feel about it. But I think it's time to let it go."

She nodded silently. Dominic gave her a small peck on the lips, then released her hand. With an almost apologetic smile, he picked up a paper and returned to his grading.

Abby sat in silence for awhile, watching him work. Finally, she spoke up: "I want to go there."

He looked puzzled for only a moment, then the wrinkle in his forehead smoothed out. "Izapa?" he asked.

Abby nodded. "On the twenty-first."

"Okay," he responded without hesitation. "Count me in."

Abby leaned over kissed him, then stood up. "Finish your papers and come to bed."

"I'll be there in a few," he said, taking her hand. He looked up at her, his face serious. "Will you be okay, going back there?" he asked. "You know Simon will be there, probably with a mess of his followers. Will you be all right if we run into him?"

"I'll be fine," she said. "We'll just try to stay out of his way."

Dominic lifted her hand and kissed it. "Okay," he said. "I'm glad that you've changed your mind, Abby." He paused for a moment, then smiled up at her. "I'll be up in a minute. I love you."

"I love you too," she said. With a quick ruffle of his curly hair, she turned and left the room.

Dominic returned to his papers, and in a moment, Simon and Izapa were out of his mind. Abby, on the other hand, couldn't stop thinking about them. She'd decided to go back to Izapa to exorcise some demons, but she wasn't convinced she was up to the battle.

12.19.19.14.16

October 18, 2012 — He was used to speaking before crowds – scientists at NASA, crowds of reporters at press conferences, even crowds of visitors when they stopped through on the occasional tour he was required to give. Therefore, Hines was uneasy at finding himself so nervous on the way to the Pentagon. Public speaking had been the one thing that had made his nervous in the past, but he'd gotten over it long ago.

When he stepped into the conference room to face General Addison, however, he felt as if he was stepping in front of a crowded auditorium for the first time. He kept his hand from trembling as he shook hands with the large uniformed man.

"Please, sit down," the general invited him. Hines sat. He looked across the table at the other two men who stood by the door, who

442

Addison introduced as Lieutenants Marquez and Osbourne. They remained impassive, and Hines supposed they were there as security.

"Dr. Hines, I've read the results of your research on the galactic center," Addison said. "It's my understanding that there is no unusual activity in the region."

"That's correct," Hines answered. "Of course, we've had only a few months to do any careful monitoring of the area, but preliminary results imply that all is as usual in the galactic center."

"What type of signs would you be looking for, if anything was occurring there?"

"You mean if the black hole was going to spit out a contingent of aliens two months from now?"

Addison's expression didn't change. "Anything," he said.

"Well, I'm personally of the belief that such a thing is not possible. The nature of a black hole doesn't allow for space travel. Most astrophysicists agree with me. However, there are a few in my group who are intrigued by the Long Count, and who want to focus on the core to see if anything else might be occurring there. We've agreed that the only events we might be able to expect would be for our black hole to become active again, sucking in matter from the surrounding galaxy; or, an outburst or explosion from the galactic core.

"The problem with either of these, of course, is that neither are foreseeable. They couldn't be predicted unless either was on a specific cycle. We know that massive, devastating core explosions occur every thirteen to twenty-six thousand years, but it's impossible to pinpoint it to a precise date. Smaller ones occur every two thousand years or so — these smaller ones create an electromagnetic pulse. These EMPs have all occurred before we became an electronic world, but if one occurs now, it'll have the same type of effect as a solar flare — it could black out communications, fatally damage satellites, and ionize the ozone layer."

Addison didn't comment. "Has there been any evidence that one might occur?"

"That's just the problem," Hines said. "There's no warning. If there's a galactic core burst, it's going to happen instantly. We've checked for increased radiation, an increase towards infrared in the spectrum, changes in the solar wind, the cosmic dust, everything we can think of. There've been no changes from our last major study of the galactic core region."

Addison nodded and stood up. He presented his hand again, which Hines took with surprise. "Thank you for your time, Dr. Hines."

"You're certainly welcome, General," Hines replied. He rose to his feet and headed for the door.

"One more thing, Doctor," Addison said.

"Yes?" he paused between the two lieutenants and turned back. "What do you think of Simon Nieson?"

"I think he's an idiot," Dr. Hines said. Without waiting for a response from the general, he turned and left the room.

For once, Addison allowed himself a smile.

12.19.19.16.1

November 12, 2012 — Simon sat back at his desk, looking out the office window. He couldn't stop smiling; while he was waiting for his secretary to leave the room, he had to keep his mouth covered up so she wouldn't notice.

She had dropped off the month's income report: a tally of his book royalties, money from selling the books himself through his website, and money from his video sales. Not included were his lecture fees or the compensation he'd received from paid television appearances, but still, the numbers were staggering. By far, October had been his best month yet.

His smile faltered just a bit as he realized it was almost halfway through November already, and he still didn't have much of a plan to increase sales. November and December would be the end of it for him; what else could he do to win the minds —and the disposable income — of those who he had not yet won over to his side? And how could he squeeze even more out of those who had already bought his line?

Now he scowled, pushing back from the desk. Simon went to the window, his hands linked behind his back. He looked at the sidewalk and street in front of his building, recalling the religious protesters who had caused him so much irritation only three months before. In the time since, he'd managed to win over most of the moderates; those who had come out against him for his atheism had attacked him, not his theory. Some of the evangelicals were still preaching against him, but Simon was okay with that. Any press was good press; the more controversy he stirred up, he thought, the more people would look him up. The more interest in his theory he could garner, the better the chance of making more sales – especially with the end being so near.

He put his hands on the window ledge and looked out. Cars cruised by, people strolled down the sidewalk, and to Simon, every one of them looked like a pocket waiting to be picked. He frowned again, then stood straighter and slammed a hand against the glass. A man who had been walking right underneath the window startled, glancing up to see what had happened. Simon raised a hand, ready to make an obscene gesture, then lowered it again. He had his image to protect now. The Long Count was winding to a close, and his publicity would end not long after, he knew. The big question for him was deciding where to go from there.

He had been one of the most popular celebrities in America for a year now; had traveled the world as a speaker, had legions of fans supporting him, defending him, buying anything he could release as soon as he could release it.

He sat down again, looking at the paperwork on the desk in front of him. This time he frowned at it; yes, the numbers were astronomical, but for Simon, they were nowhere high enough. Not when his whole career was drawing to a close.

He had given some thought as to how he would save face when the end of the Long Count came and the portal didn't open, but he still didn't have a plan. He dreaded the first press conference after the end came and went; he had no idea what he was going to say. He knew he could maintain a fan following — people had been predicting the end of the world for decades, and every time it didn't come to pass, there was a contingent of faithful that continued to believe in the doomsayers, who continued to buy whatever the next prophecy was, to prepare for the end times.

Simon stopped. A light had gone on in his head, an idea striking him so suddenly, so quickly, and so hard, that he could swear he heard an audible click as the answer slid home.

He would start a religion. It had been done before; several con men had created fantasies and spun them out, knowingly and purposely creating their own histories and their own angels, gods, and heroes, earning the undying loyalties of millions — and the money they brought with them. All *untaxed* money; money that didn't have to be claimed or accounted for. It was the ultimate scam; the government wouldn't interfere in personal matters of faith — or in any way he could find to collect that tax-exempt cash. Even the most bizarre of cults, the most threatening and dangerous groups in society all earned constitutional protection. He knew he could tie in his failed prophecy with some future prediction, with some past history that would make him a god — or at least a living saint, or a prophet.

Freedom of religion, Simon thought. He started to smile again, a wicked smile this time that grew wider as he reached for his notebook. It was time to start writing again.

12.19.19.16.14

November 25, 2012 — "We have enough men at the location," General Addison stated. The President was silent, but the general stood his ground. His heavy face remained impassive, and it was the President who finally broke first.

"This could be the most important event known to mankind," he said. "Ever. You think that a few thousand troops are enough to maintain peace, to take control of the area if necessary."

"Sir, with all due respect, I would stake my career — even my life — on my stance that nothing will occur on the twenty-first of December."

"I've read your report, General, and while I agree with you that this theory sounds far-fetched, I don't agree that Dr. Nieson is a purposeful fraud. His credentials are too distinguished; have you seen his academic background?"

The general nodded, but remained silent.

"Graduated from high school at age sixteen. Graduated at the top of his class at Princeton; has a Master's and Doctorate from Yale. This is not a stupid man, General."

"It doesn't mean he's an honest one, sir."

"I've seen nothing in his behavior to give me reason to believe he's being dishonest," the President responded. "He may be incorrect in his calculations, and although his theory might be a little far-out, even wishful thinking on his part, I'm not ready to dismiss it full out. I want twenty-five thousand troops out there. I want them to be prepared to cordon off and quarantine the area. I want whatever comes through that portal contained."

"Yes, sir," Addison replied.

"You're dismissed, General."

Addison nodded, then turned on his heel and headed out. He had not risen to his rank by disrespecting authority, and the President was unwilling to listen. His mind had already been made up, and his eye on the prize was more focused than his eye on the research. Addison knew now he was correct in leaving out of his report the additional information he had gathered independently. He would allow the President his troops. It wasn't his place to refuse to comply with the Commander in Chief's direct order. But it wouldn't dissuade him from continuing his independent investigation, either. Not when he knew what was at stake.

12.19.19.17.18

December 19, 2012 — "How hard do you think it'll be to get in?" Abby asked. She didn't look up; instead, she was watching the ground roll by outside her airplane window, picking up speed as they headed down the runway.

"I'm not sure," Dominic replied. He wanted to tell her not to worry, but he honestly didn't know whether or not they had reason for concern. They had known there'd be a huge response to the end of the

Count, that the place would be jam-packed. He didn't know, however, if they'd be barred from attending, or simply unable to get in because of the crowd. They'd only recently found out how huge the U.S. military presence would be.

"I tried to find out as much as I could," Dominic said. "I talked to a lot of my colleagues who'd been trying to get into Izapa for the past few months, and they said the whole place has been off-limits to those without a special government permit. I guess they're afraid of end-of-the-world wackies out there destroying the place. Or of gun nuts shooting up the aliens when they come through."

"But it's open on the twenty-first, right?" Abby asked. "It'd be such tourist bonanza I can't believe they'd close it entirely. It'd be like closing the Pyramid of the Sun on the summer solstice or something."

"I know," Dominic said. "And as far as I could find out, it *will* be open. But they're not messing around, sweets. I don't know how much of it is the actual belief in Simon's foolishness, thinking that something really is going to happen, and how much is just going to be crowd control and trying to prevent acts of sabotage or terrorism."

"Maybe we're better off not going," Abby said, and Dominic smiled at her look of concern. He reached out to her, touching her forehead gently with his thumb to try to smooth the deep line between her eyebrows.

"It's a little late now, sweets," he said, motioning out the airplane window and the ground receding below.

She smiled, and he took her hand. "We'll try it, anyway," he said with a shrug. "You yourself said some of your NASA buddies were planning trips down here just to observe the sky from Izapa, checking for any actual astronomical events they hadn't predicted. If no one can get in, maybe we'll meet up with them and take them out to your clearing, or up on the mountain. They should be able to see just as easily from there."

"True," Abby said with a nod. "Although I wonder if even that will be closed off?"

Dominic shrugged. "Only one way to find out," he said. "We'll sneak down there early and try to slip in ahead of time. And if we get turned away … then screw it. We're off to Puerto Vallerta."

Abby laughed, and he squeezed her hand, then released it. Dominic reached into his carry-on bag for the book he had brought, and as he settled into it, Abby turned her gaze back to the window. The ground had fallen away from them now, the buildings mere splinters, the cars only specks. She sighed and leaned her forehead against the window, closing her eyes. She hoped for sleep to come, because she knew the next few days would not be restful. And whatever came when they got to Izapa, Abby wanted to be ready for it.

12.19.19.17.19

December 20, 2012 — "What day is it?" Abby asked, rubbing her eyes wearily.

"It's still December twentieth," Dominic said. "Don't worry, it's not here yet."

She rolled over and took him in her arms, kissing him lightly. "Good," she said. "I'm not ready to share you with the rest of the world yet."

He smiled and held her against him. "You don't have to worry about sharing me with anybody," he said. "You're the only one who would possibly put up with me."

"Good," she said. "No competition."

"None at all," Dominic responded, and his tone was serious. "There's no one on the planet that could compete with you. You're the only one I want, for now and forever."

"That's good to hear," Abby commented, "although it's easy for you to say, now that forever is only another 36 hours or so."

Dominic laughed, rolling onto his back. He ran a hand through his thick dark hair and squinted up at the ceiling, trying to block out some of the brilliant morning light that poured in through their hotel room window. "You have a point, my dear," he said. "But you know what I meant."

"Of course I did," Abby answered. She sat up, swinging her legs over the edge of the bed. "I think I'm going to go catch a shower." She felt a light touch on her back and smiled as she looked down; Dominic's hand had crept around her waist. He gave her a light tug, and she let him pull her back down onto the bed.

"We're not getting very far," she commented.

"We've got all day," he said, rolling over to take her into his arms. "And since nothing is going to happen anyway, I think I'd rather just stay in bed with you."

Abby smiled as he kissed her nose. "I'll go along with that," she agreed. "At least with you, I know what to expect."

"Oh yeah?" he countered mischievously, "That's what you think."

Abby shrieked as he rolled over onto her, and moments later, the time was forgotten, and they were lost in each other.

They spent the day in town, amazed at the number of people milling about, clogging the roads. They considered heading out a day early and camping out at their old site, but decided that the military probably had it blocked off. Dominic still held the deed to it, but he didn't think that would mean much when faced with the U.S. government.

"They never contacted you to ask if they could use the land," Abby said over lunch. "Maybe that's a good sign."

Dominic smiled. "Could mean that no one is using it; could also mean they never bothered checking who owned it. I doubt there's much left of any of the buildings, probably no sign we were ever there. If they decided to set up base camp out there, I doubt they'd come asking my permission first."

"You may be right," Abby conceded. She took a long drink of her soda before setting it back down, looking up at Dominic with a mischievous smile. "Do you have any idea how much money we could have made renting that place out to the tourists?"

Dominic laughed. "No kidding. We could have rebuilt the house — hell, we could have put up tents — and probably leased them all out every night since July."

Abby shook her head. "We were never business people, I guess."

He shrugged. "Oh well. I'd have just felt guilty about it, anyway. It's not like we have any amenities to offer. People can bring their own tents and stay there without paying for it. Land never really belongs to anyone, anyway."

"Tell my ancestors that," Abby replied. "They believed the land was free; they laughed to think the white man thought he could own it. Next thing they knew, they were crammed into reservations in the middle of nowhere, fenced in by rattlesnakes and desert."

"Quite true," Dominic said. He reached across the table and squeezed her hand. "Well, I'll do my part of reparations and give this land back to anyone that wants it. It's not like I could find a buyer for it anyway."

"A year or so ago you could have. There'd be a McDonalds and a line of hotels on it right now."

"Well, then it's a good thing I held onto it."

"Dominic," Abby said suddenly: "What if we're wrong, and Simon is right?"

He smiled. "I hope he is. I can't think of anything more exciting than that."

Abby squeezed his hand in return. "Me neither," she admitted. "I'd still hate seeing him getting the credit for it, but — man, wouldn't it be amazing?"

They finished their lunch unhurriedly, watching the people-filled streets. With the sheer numbers of human beings crammed so quickly into such a small area, they finally decided, there were bound to be restricted areas. Dominic wouldn't be surprised if the armies themselves had set up where the old house used to be; it was the most prime land in the area for miles. He and Abby finally decided to spend another night in Guatemala City; better the comfort of a soft bed than sleeping in their rented jeep if they were booted off their old land.

Later that night, Abby woke up with a nervous stomach. She glanced over at Dominic's still form beside her, breathing silently and deeply. She rolled over and curled up against him; even in his sleep, he slipped his arm around her waist. Abby took his hand in hers, then lay silently, staring up at the ceiling. They were finally at the eve of their anticipation, the long awaited event about to occur. As excited as she was about it, though, she was also scared. And she couldn't wait for it to be over.

13.0.0.0.0

December 21, 2012 — They were up early the next morning, packing quickly. Abby had woken up alone, surprised to see nothing but sunlight filling the bed next to her. After she had adjusted to her newly awakened state, she noticed that the bathroom door was half shut, and the soft sound of running water flowed from behind it. After she was up and moving about, Abby was glad Dominic was already in the shower; she didn't want him to see how her hands shook as she tried to fold their clothing. Dominic was always so calm, so in control; she thought he would be unfazed even by this, while she was a nervous wreck.

When he was out of the bathroom and dressed, however, Abby realized she didn't have reason to worry. Dominic's hurried, clumsy motions as he stuffed his small suitcase betrayed his own nervousness.

"You okay?" she asked.

He grinned over top of his open suitcase. "I'm fine," he said. "A little scared, though. I don't know of what. Scared that something is going to happen, scared that nothing will happen. I don't know. I'm just … excited."

"That makes two of us," Abby said. She reached out and tucked in a shirtsleeve that was hanging out of the side of his suitcase.

Dominic grinned and shut it, spinning the lock. "What do you say we go get some breakfast?" he asked.

"Can you eat?"

"I can always eat," he said, and Abby laughed. She did a quick check of their room to make sure they had packed everything, then flicked off the light as they headed out the door. An hour later, they were checked out of the hotel and on the road to Izapa.

"We're never going to get close enough. The crowds will be astronomical."

"We've done all right so far," Dominic said. They'd gone through two military checkpoints already, and after a quick check of their ID and their small rented vehicle, they'd been waved through.

Dominic glanced away from the road and over at her. Abby was biting her lip.

"Hey," he said, reaching a hand across to take hers. "You okay, sweetheart?"

She nodded, but didn't meet his eye.

"Abby, it'll be fine. I doubt if Simon will even be here. Seriously. He knows damn well nothing is going to happen, so he's not going to stick around to wait for failure. Can you imagine the look on his face when he's standing there with an irate crowd surrounding him?"

Abby shook her head. "You're wrong about that, Dominic. Simon will want to milk his fame for every last second he can squeeze out of it. He knows tonight is the end of it, and from what I hear, he had a stage built right in the center of Izapa. He'll be prancing around on it like he's leading a revival. And that's what it will be like — a damn circus, with him as ringleader, like a fundamentalist preacher screaming about sin, fire, and brimstone.

"And that's if he knows it's all bullshit. If he actually has started believing his own line, Dominic ... he'll be insufferable."

"He was always insufferable, sweets."

Abby shook her head again, not in denial, but refusing to discuss it. "I don't even want to be around him, honey. I really don't. I think I can probably bear watching him, but I don't want him to see me. Or you."

Dominic took his hand from hers, replacing it on the wheel as the Jeep's wheel hit a deep rut. Traffic was getting heavier, and the dirt road had not been carved out to handle such a large number of vehicles.

Abby turned to him, her golden eyes worried. "I know you think he'll never see us through the crowd, Dominic. And maybe you're right. But I want to enjoy this, just the two of us, without being in constant fear that Simon will run into us on his way to the stage, or will pick us out of the crowd. I just want to know he'll leave us alone."

Dominic smiled, then suddenly jerked the wheel hard to the left. Abby gasped and gripped the door handle harder as the Jeep bounced over the rutted field. She didn't ask where he was taking them; although it had been years since they'd seen that old familiar scenery, she knew exactly where they were going.

And she breathed a sigh of relief.

They pulled to a stop where the old driveway used to be. Dominic shut off the engine, and the two sat, surveying the land through the windshield. They were both surprised to see that the old place was desolate. It must have been too isolated, too far off-road to be of any use to the masses that now thronged around Izapa.

"Want to get out?" he asked.

Abby shook her head. "I don't think so," she said. "Are we going to stay here?"

Dominic looked around. Almost everything had been destroyed in the fire. The years that had passed since they'd abandoned the place had allowed the wild to overtake much of the property; but there were still some signs of the house and lab that had once been located on these grounds. One stone wall that had partially formed the outside of the shower house was nearly intact; a charred wooden support beam rose from the tangled undergrowth here and there, and even some broken tiles shone when the evening sun hit them, burnt reminders of where the lab once stood.

"There's not much of a view from here," Dominic finally answered. "Even if we camped here, we'll have to walk out to your clearing to get a more unobstructed view of the sky over Izapa."

Abby nodded, somewhat relieved. The scorched earth and broken timbers of their old house reminded her of the remains of a corpse.

"Can we drive out there?" she asked.

Dominic shook his head. "I don't think so. You know the gully of the lagoon runs pretty far towards the woods; there's a pretty good ditch surrounding this half of your clearing, up to the jungle. We can't go over it, or through the woods. I think we'll have to park here and walk." He glanced over at her and smiled. "I'll pull up as close to the lagoon as possible. We can hike up to the cave, if you'd like."

"I'd like that a lot," Abby said. "That cave is about the only place I ever really felt safe here. It was the only place I knew Simon didn't know about, the only place I knew we could run to if we needed to, where he'd never find us."

Dominic started the Jeep again, sliding it into gear and letting the vehicle roll slowly across the overgrown lawn. "I loved it there too," he said. "It's where I finally got up the nerve to tell you I loved you."

Abby smiled at him, but he didn't notice; he was guiding the Jeep around the sitting stones of the courtyard, careful not to catch the undercarriage on the large boulders and scattered stones. "Then I can't think of a better place to spend the rest of our lives," Abby said.

"Yeah, I keep forgetting we're waiting for the end of the world," Dominic said. He pulled the Jeep up to the edge of the lagoon and parked it, yanking on the emergency brake. They both unsnapped their seatbelts and opened their doors.

When Abby stepped onto the tangled grass, she felt more relaxed than she had inside the vehicle. The sky overhead was a bit cloudy, but the air was cool and comfortable, and the grass thick and lush.

Dominic came around the front of the vehicle and took her hand. "Looks like this place has gone wild again," he commented. They stepped onto the old path they'd carved out above the lagoon; it was well-hidden now, almost completely buried under the tangled growth of weeds.

They walked in silence for a short while, and as they reached her clearing, Abby noticed Dominic's gaze fixed on the trees between them and the ancient ruins. Trying to hide her disappointment, she smiled up at him.

"You want to go out there, don't you?" she asked.

Dominic nodded. "How can I not want to? I've been waiting my whole adult life for the end of the Long Count. Now, here it is, and here I am …"

"Sweetheart," Abby said, putting a hand to his lips. "Okay. I'm not going to keep you from it."

He smiled behind her fingertips. "Will you go with me?"

She paused, and he reached for her hand, holding them both between them. "You don't have to," he said. "You can wait for me up on the mountain. You'll be safe there. No one should bother you. If they haven't found this place, they certainly haven't found our cave."

"No," Abby said, "I'll go with you. Sitting through this alone would be like staying home on New Year's Eve while you were at a huge party right next door. No, I'll go with you."

"Great!" he replied with a wide grin. He squeezed her hand tightly, and she had to smile at his excitement.

"Come on," she said, trying to hide her reluctance. She tugged his hand, and they set off, veering to their right and heading into the jungle to the ruins beyond.

"What time is it, sweets?"

Abby checked her watch, flicking the tiny light. "Almost seven o'clock," she said.

"Things won't be in full swing yet," he commented. "Sounds like they're still getting warmed up." The noise was coming to them clearly through the trees; a combination of the murmuring crowd and a voice shouting something indecipherable over top of it. It sounded as if the voice was coming through a bullhorn.

"Halt," another voice spoke, this one from directly in front of them. Dominic and Abby stopped.

From the edge of the trees a soldier stepped out. He was clad in U.S. Army camouflage fatigues, and even in the darkness, they could see by his face that he was young, and scared.

"Who are you?" he asked. The point of his rifle was trained on Dominic.

"It's okay," Dominic said, holding his hands in front of him, palm out. Abby did the same. "We're just here to watch the show."

"Up against that tree," the soldier said, and Dominic and Abby obliged. The soldier did a quick search of them both, then picked up Dominic's pack. He undid the zipper and emptied their clothing, food, and bottled water onto the forest floor. He inspected the bag thoroughly, then handed it back to them.

"Okay," he said. "You can go on."

"Thanks," Dominic said, with no trace of sarcasm. He stuffed their things back into his pack, re-zipped it, and tossed it over one shoulder. Taking Abby's hand, they headed out towards the clearing of Izapa.

"They're not taking any chances, are they?" Abby said.

"Doesn't look like it. I wonder what they were inspecting for, though. Weapons? A bomb?"

"Either, I guess," Abby said. "A gathering like this is sure to attract loonies. But the United States Army? Here in Mexico? That doesn't make any sense."

Before Dominic could answer, they were distracted by a rise in the noise level of the crowd. Heads tilted back, and fingers began pointing up. Dominic and Abby looked up, but saw nothing but the lights of helicopters, so high above that they flickered in and out of the light cloud cover. They were too far away for any sound to reach the throng of onlookers.

"There are lights in the sky! It could be them!"

The murmur ran through the crowd. When it reached Dominic and Abby, they only laughed.

"What's so funny?" the man next to them asked. He was short and bespeckled, with wildly uncombed hair. He squinted up at Dominic in the dark.

"Have you ever seen a helicopter?" Dominic asked.

The man frowned. "They're too high up," he said. "And we can't hear the rotors. You always hear a helicopter."

"Not if it's as high as that one is," Dominic answered. "With the noise of this crowd, you would barely hear it if it was right overhead."

The spectacled man frowned more deeply. "I've seen lights in the sky," he said. "I know there are UFOs up there. You can say whatever you want. I *know*."

"Then maybe you'd know why the UFOs *have* lights?" Abby spoke up. "It's one thing I've never been able to figure out. You see, lights are unnecessary for interstellar flight. Spacecraft maneuvers are all done by computer, not by sight. They don't need lights. In fact, they're unnecessary in our atmosphere, too — it's not like aircraft need headlights to see in front of them, like cars. The only reason our aircraft have lights is for their own visibility; they use them to avoid accidents with other aircraft, and they can clearly be seen from the ground. So why would a UFO require lights? Especially if they're trying *not* to be seen?"

The man scowled. "Why wouldn't UFOs use them to signal each other?"

"I'd like to think that if a group of aliens made it all the way here from some vastly distant star, they'd have better methods of communication. Airplanes signal each other with lights because they're on different flight paths, and they don't know how many flights might be in the air at any time, and on what paths. They have lights so they don't run into each other. If there are that many UFOs up there, we're in some trouble."

"Now you understand," the man said cryptically, then quickly moved away.

"Holy hell," Dominic said. "This is one interesting crowd."

They began walking, taking in the observers as they went.

"I barely recognize the place," Abby said. Izapa had certainly changed; to one side of the main square a group praised God and thanked him for sending his angels to greet them; their opposite number, shouting about demons and the tricks of Satan, stood just a few yards away from them.

Dominic and Abby passed through the crowd, noting random people walking around in alien costumes, passing through gatherings of those in the robes of druids, and those chanting what could have been ancient Mayan prayer.

"Good lord, isn't there anyone normal here?" Abby asked. She saw a group of Raëlians, some draped in robes, others nearly naked.

"There's Simon's prime audience," Dominic said, nudging Abby and indicating the group. "They believe that human culture on Earth was brought by aliens — in fact, that humans were created by alien genetic engineering of the Neanderthals that were here on Earth at the time. Simon's ideas fall right into their line of thinking — not only do we owe everything we have to our alien visitors, but hey, they're coming back."

Abby could only shake her head as they passed. She searched the crowd, stunned by the sheer numbers, both amazed and amused by the great differences in the people who had shown up in Izapa for what they believed was the end of life as they all knew it. There did seem to be some average stargazers there, many with binoculars and guides to the ruins, but they were few and far between. The atmosphere was more like a carnival, with chanting, singing, preaching, even dancing. Interspersed among the visitors were military men and women, dressed in uniforms both Mexican and American. All were heavily armed.

Abby and Dominic stopped again for awhile in the main plaza to people-watch. While most people came and went, visiting the different booths as if they were at a county fair, many seemed to be staking out their location for the night.

"I feel kind of like I'm going to watch a parade," Abby said, "or fireworks."

"I know," Dominic said. "I guess we'd better go find a good place ourselves, or we may end up missing the show."

"The show's already started!" A young man passing in front of them had overheard their conversation, and added his own input in a strong Australian accent. "The show started thousands of years ago, my friend. We're gathering here to see the end of it."

"You really think aliens are going to come through a space portal tonight?" Abby asked, curious.

"Damn straight I do!" the man responded, pausing next to them. "They've been coming and going for years! I've seen them!"

"You've seen an alien space craft?" Dominic asked.

"A flying saucer, you got it, mate," he answered.

"Really?" Abby asked. "It was saucer shaped?"

"Damn straight it was! It looked just like all the reports!"

"That's funny," Abby said. "Did you know that the first flying saucer was reported in 1947? The pilot who claimed to see it actually reported that it was shaped like a boomerang — he said it 'skipped across the sky like a saucer.' A reporter wrote up the story, describing it as a 'flying saucer.' The next thing you know, people across the globe were reporting having seen flying saucers. Amazing. If he'd reported it as the pilot had described it, we might have had thousands of reports of flying boomerangs instead."

"Piss off," the young man said, walking off.

"Christ," Abby said, "No one is interested in education these days."

456

Dominic laughed. "I think you're wasting your breath here, sweets. Let's head over to the ballcourt and try to find a good place to sit."

They pushed their way through the crowd, past vendors selling bottled water and stuffed tortillas, and finally made their way to the far end of the site. Set up between the ancient stones was a modern stage, covered with lights and microphones.

"What are they doing, giving a concert?" Abby asked.

"I don't think so," Dominic answered. They paused a good distance away from the stage; they couldn't have gotten any closer if they'd tried. People were packed up against it as if waiting for the Beatles to come out, or the President.

The stage lights flashed, and a lackey came out to test the microphone. There was a squeal of feedback, then a steady, "Testing, one, two, three." More adjustments were made, and finally, everyone left the stage.

"You want to stick around for this?" Abby asked, and Dominic smiled.

"Why not?" he said. "We came to see the show, didn't we?"

At the stroke of eight o'clock, the lights above the stage came on again full force. There was movement offstage, and then a tall figure came out and took the mic.

"Ladies and gentlemen, welcome to the most amazing event in the history of mankind!"

"Oh brother," Abby muttered, and some people around her turned to glare. Most of the crowd's attention was riveted on the stage, however; Abby had never heard such a large group of people fall quiet so quickly.

"We've come here tonight from many different walks of life, with many different expectations. But there is one thing we've *all* been waiting for: Ladies and gentlemen, I bring you Dr. Simon Thomas Nieson!"

The crowd burst into cheering applause, drowning out whatever the emcee said next. He stood center stage, but had turned to greet the shorter figure that came ambling out to meet him. Simon shook the man's hand, then took the microphone.

"Good evening!" he shouted, and the crowd shouted back. Even from their place in the middle of the crowd, Dominic and Abby could see the expression on Simon's face. He wore the contented look of any politician who had just won an election; the charming smile that had won Abby's heart so many years ago shone forth to capture his audience. They were enthralled, and as Simon began to speak, the crowd once again fell silent.

"I can't express to you how excited I am to have you all here tonight," Simon said. "To share an evening like this with all of you fine people simply leaves me breathless. Do all of you fully understand what is going to happen here tonight?"

Half the crowd cheered, half remained silent, hanging on Simon's every word. He spoke again:

"Tonight marks not just the end of an ancient cycle that has been counting down for over five thousand years, but the beginning of the *new age* of man! We are about to make a connection with actual living, intelligent beings from a planet other than our own. We are about to meet the people – perhaps the exact same individuals – that brought culture and religion to our people. After this evening, our world, our *lives*, will never be the same!"

The crowd cheered again, and Simon launched fully into his speech. Both Dominic and Abby were surprised at how humble he sounded; he spoke mostly of the visitors that were to come, speculating on the message they would bring. They had expected him to be more self-serving, reiterating how he had come to the conclusions he had, reminding them that they were here because of him.

"I guess he doesn't want to be mocked any more than he already will be, when this is over and everyone realizes they've been had," Dominic said.

"What do you think Simon will do when it's all over and nothing has happened?" Abby asked.

Dominic shrugged. "He'll probably disappear tonight," he said. "He might hang around for a few hours, collecting some more applause and accolades, milking the attention for everything he can get out of it, and then he'll be gone. He's made a lot of money from his book, television specials, speaking engagements, and videos. At least a million dollars; maybe more. Even a man like him can live on that for awhile. Hell, he might even settle here in Mexico — with the exchange rate, he'll live like a king."

Abby nodded. "He gambled everything on this. For a man that thrives on attention, he's going to have to go into hiding, become a nobody. There'll be a lot of pissed-off people looking for him after nothing happens tonight."

"Maybe that's part of his plan too," Dominic suggested. "Hide out for awhile, then come back out with another book about how he pulled one over on the world."

"That's more like him," Abby said. "And with Simon being who he is, he can probably pull it off, too."

458

Dominic nodded, looking around at the crowd. "A lot of these people will flock to him again. They'll not only forgive him, they'll understand if he says he miscalculated, and the visitors aren't coming until 2015. Or 2020, or 2050. Or maybe there are no visitors, it was actually predicting the beginning of Armageddon or something. People will still listen, because they want to listen. They want to believe there's something more out there. Simon will have an audience as long as he wants one."

"Shhhh!" The angry shush came from a woman in front of them, who turned around and gestured for Dominic to be quiet.

Simon was winding up his speech now, and the crowd was straining to hear his big finish. Dominic smiled and squeezed Abby a little closer to him.

"So tonight, everybody, enjoy yourselves, but don't forget why you're here!" Simon shouted. "Take in these ancient ruins, bathed under the eternal light of the same stars that will shortly move aside, opening a portal for the first time in thousands of years. We don't know how long it will last, and we don't know exactly how they'll come down. The Aztec and Maya said they descended from the portals via snake chains. So keep your eyes, and your minds, wide open! Because this truly is the first day of the rest of your lives, of all of our lives! And when the sun comes up tomorrow, our world will never again be the same!"

The crowd roared, cheering and clapping, calling his name. Simon raised both hands over his head, and the audience went wild.

Dominic turned to Abby with an amused smile. "Let's get out of here," he said.

"Where are we going to go?"

He slid his arm around her. "Somewhere far above the teeming crowd. Away from these babbling fools. Where we can watch the sun come up in peace."

Abby reached for his hand. "I'm with you," she said. "Let's go."

From the edge of the stage, Simon saw the crowd part, and a deep frown crossed his face as he spotted Dominic's head above the crowd. Simon watched as they headed towards the edge of the site. The thick crowd swirled around them, and they disappeared into the darkness.

Without thinking, Simon jumped off the side of the stage and went after them. He shoved his way through the crowd, ignoring the hands upon him and the excited voices of his fans. Instead, he pushed through them, stepping up his pace as fast as he could. He caught sight again of Dominic's dark head above the surge of the crowd, and he locked onto it.

Once he had them in view again, Simon slowed down a bit, keeping an even distance between them. He didn't know where they'd headed off to all of a sudden, but he knew both of them well enough to know how well they could keep secrets. He knew nothing along the lines of his theory was going to happen here, and he'd do best to get past security and out of sight. His big moment was over, so it was time to collect his cash and run.

Besides, if Dominic and Abby knew something he didn't, he was damn sure going to find out what it was.

Just as neither Dominic nor Abby noticed Simon following them at a careful distance, neither did Simon notice when General Addison slipped into the woods behind him. The general had been keeping a close eye on him from his position near the stage while the rest of his men patrolled the site, maintaining careful watch on the speakers, exhibitors, and visitors, as well as looking out for outside threats.

Addison, however, never took his eyes off of Simon, and as soon as he disappeared into the woods, the general was on his tail. He was surprised at how well the math professor tracked Dominic and Abby, silently staying far enough behind them that they never suspected he was there. Simon's concentration was completely on keeping a far enough distance from them, but still keeping them in his sight, so any additional noise or movement made by the stocky general never caught his attention.

It had been a long time since Addison had been on the battlefield, and the years of working behind a desk had taken their toll. While still in better physical condition than most men his age, he found himself slowing down, falling farther and farther behind Simon, who moved surprising quickly. A few minutes after they started their way up the mountain, Addison had to stop to catch his breath. He braced an arm against a tree, watching Simon scale the Cliffside, following a rough path almost fully grown over. Addison thought he'd have no trouble finding it, and thought he'd rest for another minute or so before starting off again.

Just as his breath started to come back, however, the ground lurched under Addison's feet, almost knocking him down. He clung to the tree he'd been leaning on, watching as others cracked and fell over, and one huge white pine pulled completely out of the ground, the uprooted tree falling forward down the mountainside, dragging its thick roots with it. A heavy load of rocks tumbled down the mountain, bouncing off the path and rolling down the way Addison had come. The quake lasted for several long seconds, and a loud groaning noise came from deep inside the mountain.

"Holy shit," Addison breathed, looking up towards the volcano's peak, invisible in the darkness. He couldn't see any smoke rising from the mountaintop, but he'd read the seismologists reports, and knew that such a strong quake – and deep rumbling from inside Tacana – meant an eruption was imminent. It might be hours, or days, or even weeks; however, if fire and brimstone – or even clouds of hot ash – were to start raining down on the people below, he would feel responsible. He'd brought the US Army there to protect the people at Izapa, and as much as he wanted to see exactly what Simon Nieson was up to, his choice was clear.

With a heavy sigh, Addison turned and headed back down the mountain, stepping carefully, knowing there'd be aftershocks. With the amount of army personnel in Izapa – both American and Mexican – it wouldn't be a problem getting everyone out of there. They had helicopters and rescue crews; the army's unofficial duty was as an emergency response team, in case little green men stepped out of a hole in the sky and started shooting. Or even if they came in peace, there were medical labs and quarantine trucks on standby. The problem, he knew, was going to be convincing the true believers to get the hell out.

As soon as they stopped in front of the cave, Dominic dumped their bags onto the ground. "Let me just get some water, and then we'll head back down," he told Abby, who was nervously looking at the rock wall above them. Dominic had just begun to unzip his backpack when he heard a voice behind him.

"Have you two been living in this cave for the last two years?"

Abby spun around quickly; Dominic raised his head. Simon had stepped out of the darkness on the other side of the stream; he crossed it now, and the starlight that sparkled off of it showed just how rough, tired, and disheveled he was. Simon had never been much of an outdoorsman.

Dominic watched him splash across the water, and there was no surprise in his voice when he addressed his old nemesis, only anger.

"Look, Simon. I'm done with you. Just back off. You've had your time in the sun. Or under the moon, if you will. Just leave us be."

"With you fucking my fiancée? I don't think so."

"Oh, for god's sake, Simon. Leave it be," Dominic rose to his feet. "She hasn't been your fiancée for three years now. You never treated her like someone you loved anyway. She's happy now. If you care for her at all, or ever did, then just leave her be."

"It was never about her happiness," Simon said. He didn't even glance in Abby's direction.

"Of course not," Dominic said. "It's always about you. And why can't it be about you now? You're rid of her. I've seen some of the women you've paraded to your various public appearances. Hell, you've even bagged yourself a celebrity or two. You're not lacking for female attention. Let it go."

"I'm not a good loser," Simon said. "It's not something I've ever been used to, and I don't intend to start now."

He took a step closer to Dominic, up onto the bank now, closing the space between them. He still kept his distance, however, making sure the larger man couldn't reach across the gap to touch him.

"What do you want, Simon? It's all over. You've got tens of thousands of people tramping around down there, waiting for something that they think is going to happen, solely on your word. It's almost over — nothing is going to happen. What do you want?"

"My entire life, I've felt as if I was just outrunning a storm," Simon said. "It's time to quit running. Let the lightning and the rain and thunder overtake me if it will. It's time to stand in the midst of the torrent and open my arms and my soul to it. Let it come!"

"You're insane."

"Of course I'm not. Could a crazy man have published a best-selling book, been on numerous television and radio shows, and toured the country as a speaker? I made over a million dollars from sales of my book and videotapes, from my speaking engagements. I even starred in a damn prime time special, orchestrated by me, for the sole purpose of promoting my theory. What the hell have *you* done in the past couple of years? Made thirty grand as a schoolteacher?"

"Money's not important," Dominic said. "Integrity is."

Simon laughed. "So you claim. You have to; you can probably barely even make the rent each month."

"I'm touching the minds of hundreds of young people. I'm teaching them how to look at the world with a critical eye; to think for themselves, to find out the truth behind crap such as yours. They may barely remember me twenty years from now, but what I taught them will stay with them the rest of their lives. It'll affect the way they live and think; what they teach their children, how they look at the world. You? Even with your million dollars, in twenty years, no one will remember your name. You're a footnote in history, and a laughingstock at that. You'll be a joke."

"People will remember me for the charade I pulled. Hell, I have the U.S. Army stomping around out there waiting for fucking flying saucers."

"We're the only ones who know that you know it's bullshit. Everyone else will think you meant it, that you were one nutty, screwed up son-of-a-bitch. Even if you came out now and claimed it was all a big joke, you'd either get your ass murdered by one of the fanatics who have sold everything they had to come down here and wait for your visitors, or no one would believe you anyway. They'd think you were just trying to save face.

"Face it, Simon — it's over. You lost."

"Fuck you. My money and I both say fuck you. Who cares what anyone thinks of me?"

"You do, and you know it. You've probably gone through half that money already, if not more. And you're going to end up in some seriously deep shit if you get the army after you. I wouldn't be surprised to see them pursue charges, throw your ass in jail. Hell, you might even get some civil lawsuits filed against you. You're going to end up not just dirt poor, but reviled. Your good name is dirt now. And that's the one thing you can't take, isn't it?"

"Fuck you," Simon said, suddenly whipping his hand out from under his jacket. In it he held the .45, pointed directly at Dominic. There was a slight click as he cocked the hammer back. "Fuck you," he whispered, and though Dominic and Abby had suspected it all these years, they could see in his eyes for the first time that Simon really was insane.

"Look at it this way," Simon sneered. "It'll give you the chance to find the answer to life's eternal question: What happens after death?" He steadied the gun on Dominic's chest. "Isn't that what we've *really* been trying to find out this whole time? What happens when it all ends? You questioned it for months after Steve's death. 'Where is he now? Will I ever see him again?'" he mocked. "Well, now is your chance to find out."

"You killed Steve, didn't you?" Abby said, speaking up for the first time.

"Of course I did," Simon snapped, barely glancing her way. "He was getting ready to end the project. Steve didn't think anything was going to happen, that it was just a repeat of a natural event. I mean, that's pretty fucking anti-climactic, isn't it? Thanks for wasting our time? We couldn't leave yet," he said. "There had to be more to it; I just needed more time to figure out what it was. I knew that once Steve put his solution out there, you small minded people would agree with him, close up shop, and go home. I couldn't have that. There was only one way to stop him."

Abby choked back a sob, but the tears were already streaming down her face. "You could've heard him out, Simon. You could've given *us* the chance to."

"You didn't deserve the chance to. It was my project, no matter what your boy there thought. *I* was the one who was going to figure out the answer. And I did, didn't I?"

"You're insane," Abby said, and even though she'd known it for years, it was the first time she'd ever spoken it aloud, and it seemed to confirm it for her. "You're absolutely insane."

"No," he said. "I'm a genius. But I can see how someone as stupid as you could not know the difference." He lowered the gun slightly, aiming at Dominic's midsection. "I think a gutshot will suffice," he said. "Surest and most painful way to go."

"Stop it," Abby cried. "Why are you doing this? Just let us go." She glanced around for anything that she could use as a weapon, but she was kneeling in the grass close to the cave's entrance, and there wasn't so much as stone to throw.

"No way," Simon said. "I'd rather send your boy there to oblivion."

"Fine," Dominic said. He was calm; it wasn't the first time that evening he'd been at the business end of a gun. "You're right, Simon; it *is* the eternal question. I've been fascinated with death since I was a child; I always wondered if I'd get to meet my parents. At some point, we all have to find out what happens. Sooner or later; I don't suppose it makes much difference."

"Dominic!" Abby cried out. "Stop it!"

"Let him go if he wants to," Simon said. "I'll let him find out what's out there. Or not. It's the great cosmic joke, you know — people will live their whole lives adhering to some strict, non-sensical rules — I mean, really, who gives a shit what day you eat meat, or if you eat pork — or they'll sacrifice themselves and a bunch of innocent people who didn't want to go with them under the impression that their souls will live forever. Yet when they die and fade out of consciousness forever, and eternity rolls on without them, they don't even get to recognize their folly. There's just nothing there. They never know they wasted their entire life for nothing."

"Just cut the shit out, both of you," Abby said, tears streaming down her face. "Simon, you're nuts. Dominic, he's not playing around here."

"Neither am I," Dominic answered evenly. He had been standing in front of their cave, with Abby on her hands and knees beside it. As the men spoke, she'd been easing alongside the rock wall, making her way around to the back of it, trying to put the fallen rubble of boulders between her and Simon. Dominic, however, held his ground.

"What are you going to do?" Dominic asked. "Are you going to kill me? And then what?"

"I'm going to kill both of you," Simon responded. "And I'm going to leave you up here to rot. No one will ever find you. Or miss you, for that matter."

"That's where you're wrong," Dominic said, and it was only now that he began to move, circling slowly to his right, trying to move Simon's attention away from Abby. "Abby and I have families, friends, colleagues. We'll have a hundred people looking for us by mid-week. But if you drop off the face of the Earth? Who's going to notice? Everyone will just assume that you're in hiding, or that you killed yourself in shame."

The gun in Simon's hand wavered, but not from anxiety or indecision; Simon was furious. Still, Dominic saw the slight motion and knew Simon's grip would be loosened, just for a moment. He dove for the weapon, surprising all of them; Abby gave a short cry, and Simon stumbled backwards, tripping over some branch or root and going down on his back. The gun flew out of his hand, and there was a quiet splash as it hit the water of the shallow creek.

Then Dominic was on top of him, punching him hard. Simon's head struck the hard winter ground, and there was a cracking sound that was either his head, or his jaw breaking. Dominic sat back, just for a second, but it was all Simon needed. He sat up quickly, flipping the larger man off of him, and threw his own punch, connecting with Dominic's mouth. The two men wrestled, and although Dominic had his opponent outweighed, Simon had the strength of madness on his side.

They rolled over and over, throwing punches, but not a word was said; Simon could not speak with his shattered jaw, and Dominic was beyond trying to reason with him. With a sudden splash, the two rolled into the water and continued to fight.

"Stop it, damn it!" Abby shouted, running around the side of the rubble wall. She was afraid one of them would drown the other; she had lost track of the gun, until she heard the shot. It cracked loudly in the still night, and there was splashing as one of the men struggled to his feet. She could see him silhouetted under the moonlight, a thin figure balancing unsteadily in the rushing water. To her horror, Abby saw that the man standing, the man who held the gun, was Simon.

She covered her mouth to block a scream, but still he turned to her, and as he raised the gun again, there was a quick movement in the water at his feet. It happened so fast that Abby barely knew what happened: Dominic had kicked out suddenly with both legs, trapping Simon's ankle with one foot behind Simon's calf and the other braced against his shin. Simon staggered, off balance, holding his arms out to steady himself. He kicked at Dominic in the water, then lowered the gun, aiming it at the struggling shape at his feet.

There was a loud report as the sound of gunfire bounced off the rock wall behind her; Abby cried out as Simon jerked, somehow knocked off his feet, falling over backwards. He hit the water with a garbled shout, but didn't release the gun. Both Abby and Dominic heard the dull smack of Simon's head striking the water, then a crunch as it hit something hard; as he did, he reflexively squeezed off another shot. The bullet went wild, streaking into the trees away from all of them, and the gun slid out of Simon's limp hand into the water.

Dominic struggled to his feet as Abby raced up to him. "Oh my god," she said, splashing into the creek to support him. "Where are you hit?"

"I'm okay," he said, breathing out heavily. He glanced down at himself to make sure, then raised his hand to probe his chest. The bullet had caught him high, just below the shoulder, and while the damage seemed minimal, the pain was great, and he couldn't lift his left arm. He thought that along with the muscle damage, his collar bone may be broken.

"Sit down," Abby said, supporting him at the waist as he lowered himself to the ground.

"What about Simon? Is he unconscious or dead?"

Abby dragged her eyes back to Simon's limp form, motionless except for his hands, clothing, and hair waving in the streaming water. Reluctantly, she moved over to him for a better look. His eyes were gleaming in the moonlight, staring sightlessly up at the trees above him.

Abby retreated to Dominic's side; he was fighting to stand up, and she knelt beside him, a restraining hand on his shoulder. He shook her off and moved carefully in the babbling stream, keeping an eye on Simon's motionless body. He knelt carefully, then reached out for a handful of Simon's thick blond hair. He lifted up his head, and even in the dim light from the stars they could see the dark blood spooling away in the water. Underneath his head was a large sharp rock; it had knocked the life out of Simon at the speed of a bullet when his head had struck it on his way down. Dominic released his hair, and Simon's head dropped back down onto the rock with a heavy thunk.

Grimacing, he scrubbed at his hand under the running water, glad it was dark enough that he couldn't see the blood on it.

"He's dead," he said. "We can't worry about moving him right now, though -- we have to get down the mountain." Dominic tried to stand up again, and this time Abby helped him to his feet. She glanced down at Simon's body, the blond hair and his clothing floating and wavering in the current.

"Come on now," she said, tearing her eyes away. She took Dominic's uninjured arm, "we need to get you to a hospital."

Dominic was silent, and Abby turned to him, worried. "Honey, are you all right?"

He shook his head, then smiled down at her.

"So ... nothing happened."

"Did you really expect it to?" Abby asked softly.

"Not really," he answered. Dominic shrugged. "I'm a little disappointed, though. Over five thousand years of calculations and nothing to show for it."

"Well, the night's not over yet," she replied. "There's always this volcano underneath us. Come on, we really need to get the hell out of here."

Dominic smiled painfully, then sunk back down to the ground.

"Dominic!" Abby shouted, dropping to her knees beside him.

"I'll be fine," Dominic said, but his voice sounded tired. "I don't think I'm going to bleed to death or anything. Let's not rush it right now; I just need to rest."

Abby frowned, trying to study his face in the darkness. She couldn't see his eyes.

"Seriously." He reached for her with his good arm, sliding his hand on the back of her neck and drawing her closer. He kissed her lightly on the lips. Abby was alarmed to taste blood. She pulled away, putting a finger to her lips, then reaching to touch his mouth.

"It's all right," he said. "It's just from the fight. I'm not bleeding internally or anything."

"Would you tell me if you were?" she asked.

Dominic laughed. "You do know me, don't you, sweets?" He put his arm around her again. "Yes. If I thought I was going to die here on this mountain, I would tell you. I wouldn't be so unfair to you."

Abby released a sigh of relief and relaxed against him. "All right," she said. "I trust you. So if you die on me, I'm never going to forgive you for it."

He laughed again, but cut it off when the pain gripped him. "Okay, then," he said, "here's the plan. We head on down at a slow pace. I'm in no rush. I wouldn't mind a painkiller or two, but I'm not in mortal danger here. As long as I don't pick up some kind of funky jungle infection, I'm going to be fine. So, we move slowly, resting when I have to, and sometime tonight we'll make it back to the jeep."

"What about the volcano?" Abby asked worriedly, looking up again at the caldera hidden in the darkness.

"We have time," Dominic said. "It won't take us that long to get down, and I'm pretty sure it's not going to go off in the next hour or two. Of course, I could be wrong," he said with a wry smile, "but I don't think so. I told you, I'm not mortally wounded or anything, but I don't have any urge to spend a cold night up on this mountain, or to get wiped out by steam, ash, or lava, either."

Abby nodded reluctantly, then looked up at the sky with a touch of regret. "We're going to miss the end of the Count," she said.

Dominic smiled and kissed the top of her head. "Nothing is going to happen, Abby. You know that, don't you?"

Abby paused, then nodded again. "I suppose I do," she said. "Even though I could never find it, I still kept thinking there was going to be some kind of alignment. The Maya were astronomers, damn it. There had to be something. Something I was missing, that we were all missing."

"There's nothing," Dominic repeated gently.

"I know." Abby said. "There can't be any alignment. Every astronomer on the planet, both professional and amateur, would have to be missing it. Tens of thousands of people; including people who spend every day and night of their lives looking at the sky or studying the data. There's nothing. So I guess we failed."

"No, we didn't fail," Dominic said. "We didn't find out what the Long Count meant, I admit it. But maybe there's nothing to be found. Whatever the Maya had in mind, they knew what it was when they created the Count. Maybe it really *was* only a timekeeper, a system of date-keeping through the centuries. Maybe they dated it back to where they did simply as a reference point; when they recorded myths and stories, they would have to have a system of backdating, just like we say something would've happened in 2,000 B.C., for example. We'd need a point to start from, to be able to encompass all of known history. An equinox date would be an important starting point for them."

"And the end date?" Abby asked.

Dominic shrugged. "We have no way now of knowing. The date has come, and the date will go, and nothing will come to pass. There are no geological events, no astronomical alignments, no pending catastrophes, nothing. Personally, I agree with you that it may just be calculating precession. The five ages match up to the precessional cycle; most ancient cultures were focused on the heavens for signs and signals; it sounds right to me that somehow they'd figured out that a specific constellation would be rolling back around, and they counted down to it.

"Otherwise, there was nothing. No cataclysms, no alignments, no visitors from outer space. Maybe the Maya thought there would be; they could've miscalculated, or something might have changed. The fact is, whatever they intended, Abby, their purpose has been lost to the passage of time. We'll probably never know."

Abby was silent for a moment. Dominic kissed her forehead, and she looked up at him, eyes glittering under the starlight. "Then we did fail, even though it might have been through no fault of our own. We didn't set out to find out if we were going to live to see tomorrow; we set out to find out the meaning of the Count. We never did."

Dominic laughed and hugged her closer, wincing as a sharp jolt of pain shot through his shoulder and down into his chest. "Fine," he said, "we failed. We don't know what the hell they meant." He took a deep breath, and the pain lessened. "What do you say we start down the mountain?"

"If you're sure you're up to it."

"I'm not going to get any better up here," Dominic said. "The longer we sit here on this cold ground, the more I'm going to stiffen up, and the harder the trek is going to be." He glanced back towards Izapa; a haze of light rose from the area, the site illuminated by spotlights, high-wattage halogen lights, and the headlights and flashlights of the hundreds of thousands of visitors arriving, leaving, and milling about the area.

"It's probably still pretty nuts down there, and is going to be all night," Dominic commented. "It's almost midnight, and nothing has happened. Some people might start drifting away, but I think most are going to stay there all night. They want to believe, just like the guy with the helicopters and the UFOs. They're not going to give up until dawn comes up on them. Probably not even then."

He released her, and Abby stood up, helping him to his feet. He tottered for a moment, surprised at how strong the pain was whenever he moved, but steadied himself. They began walking slowly, towards the old, familiar, albeit overgrown, path. They moved along in silence for awhile, with no sound except for his heavy, ragged breathing. Finally, Abby spoke.

"Are you disappointed?"

Dominic thought for a moment. "Not really," he said at last. "It's probably better this way. The world didn't end. No aliens came. No astronomical alignments occurred that would've made the woo-woo people think the Maya were psychic. Reality is still reality, and everyone is safe — well, other than Simon, I guess."

Abby didn't speak, and Dominic stopped. "Abby, are you okay? My god, sweetheart, I didn't even think about it."

"I'm okay," she said, her voice soft. She squeezed his hand. "Simon was dead to me years ago. I'm horrified at what happened, but I feel — well, cold. I hate to say it, because any death to me is a tragedy, a truly sad, irretrievable loss ... but I feel almost relieved. It's horribly selfish, but I'm almost glad that he's gone. We don't ever have to worry about him again."

"We're going to have to answer a lot of questions," Dominic warned her. "A controversial public figure is dead, killed indirectly by my hand. There are people who are never going to believe the way it actually happened."

"Fuck 'em," Abby said, surprising him. She began to walk again, and Dominic followed. "I don't care what anyone thinks anymore. People will believe whatever they want to, and no amounts of professing the truth are going to sway them. The best we can do is put the facts out there. If people are willfully ignorant and ignore the facts, or if they try to piece the facts together to create some bizarre alternative explanation, then let them. It means nothing to me, and, I imagine, to you."

Dominic smiled. "It means absolutely nothing to me. I'll be damned if I'm going to spend the rest of my life explaining or defending it. Now," he said, slightly quickening his pace, "Let's move a little faster, if you can. The pain is getting worse, and my head is a little swimmy. It may just be from exhaustion, but either way, we're not going to make it off this mountain tonight if it gets much stronger. My whole upper body is going to be stiff and in agony before long, every step torture."

Abby looked up at him with concern. "Why don't you just stay here? You shouldn't be walking in your condition — you might make it worse. I can get back to Izapa and get help."

"I'll be fine," Dominic said. He paused for a moment, then said, "I used to love it here, Abby. Steve and I had stayed out here several times over the years before we built the lab; I loved the location — the fields, the jungle, the lagoon, this mountain. But I can't love it anymore. I lost all my old friends here, Abby. You were the only positive I got out of it, and you had an awful time here. Now we've had someone try to kill us, and with us leaving on the night the world is supposed to end, I think I'm going to close the book on Izapa. I'll be happy if we get out of here as soon as we can, and never return here again."

Abby squeezed his hand again. "I couldn't agree more," she said. "Tomorrow really will be a new day — as Simon said; the first day of the rest of our lives."

"Amen," Dominic said, and holding hands, they limped off down the path together.

They hadn't been walking much longer when Dominic stopped, clutching his injured shoulder.

"Honey, are you all right?" Abby asked.

"Fine," he said, but from the tightness in his voice she knew that he wasn't. He stopped, then suddenly sunk to his knees.

"Dominic!" Abby pulled at him frantically; realizing she'd be unable to pull him back to his feet, she helped him to the ground.

"I'm okay," he said weakly. "I just need to catch my breath."

Abby helped him to lie back against a tree, and she checked his shoulder. It was too dark for her to make out any detail, but the wound appeared to have quit bleeding. Dominic's face was pale, though, and his breathing rapid and shallow.

Abby lay down next to him, her arm across his chest. She tried to remain calm, to gently soothe and comfort him, but she thought he could hear the worry in her voice. He knew his condition better than she did, anyway, and he wasn't saying much about it.

Abby closed her eyes, hoping the bullet that had struck below Dominic's collarbone hadn't hit his lung, or severed anything that could be causing unseen internal bleeding. She thought she'd let him rest for a few minutes, and if he couldn't get up again, she would run down the mountain to the jeep, stopping the first person she saw on the road and having them call for help.

Abby couldn't remember waking up; she simply became aware that she had lost the sensation of Dominic's hand. She felt like she was looking through a thick cloud; visibility was short, and the edges of her vision were murky. The air felt thick as tar, making her movements slow and heavy.

"Dominic?" she called. She pushed forward through the haze, searching with heavily clouded eyes.

"Here."

His voice came solid and strong, a fixed point in the fog.

"Dominic?"

It didn't occur to her until later that she couldn't feel the ground under her feet. She could see the stars above, though, brilliant pinpoints of light in the black sky, floating in and out of view as the mist passed by overhead. She peered through the fog, and then saw him, standing straight and tall, unmoving.

She could barely stand to look at him, but she didn't want to look away. Abby felt as if she had to take in every detail of him, as she knew she'd never see him again.

"I love you, Abby," Dominic said quietly. "But I love it here, too. This is where I belong; where we all belong. And soon enough, you'll be with me again."

"Soon?" she questioned.

Dominic laughed, and the sound was the same as ever. "I don't mean soon by human years. Time here doesn't exist, Abby. There's no such concept. What might seem forever on earth is only a blink of the eye of eternity."

Abby was speechless for a moment, studying his face, so grateful for the final chance to see him, to speak to him. Afraid that if she didn't ıe'd fade away, Abby finally spoke: "So ... it all comes

ınew that in the beginning," he smiled.
we never knew what that meant."
ɔ," Dominic said. "We never knew." And in a heartbeat, he

Abby woke with a start, tears stinging her eyes, her heart
ding. Dominic heard her cry out, and he rolled over and took her
wardly in his arms. "What is it, sweets?" he asked.

"Oh my god," she said, burying her face in his chest. She could
arely get the words out. Her dream clung to her like reality; his death had
been so real, she could barely fathom that he was still with her. His warm,
strong arms surrounded her, holding her tightly, and she allowed him to
envelope her in his embrace like a cocoon.

"Abby, what's wrong?" he asked again. She was holding onto him
so tightly it was starting to hurt. He tried to push her away gently, afraid
his wound would begin to bleed again.

"You were dead," she finally managed. "Simon killed you, and
you were gone."

He sighed and pulled her against him again. She relaxed slightly in
his arms, and he put his chin on top of her head. "It's okay," he soothed.
"I'm still here. You can't get rid of me that easily."

"It was so real."

"But it's over."

"I know. But Dominic ... I can't bear the thought of you being
gone forever. If you had died, that would have been it. I'd never see you
again. Ever. For all of eternity."

He kissed the top of her head. "I know," he said. "Why do you
think people have such a strong belief in the afterlife? We can't live with
the thought of the ones we love being gone forever. Of having only a
limited time on this Earth, then winking out, our consciousness
dissipating into the void, forever."

"It hurts," she said, and he could tell from her voice that she was
still crying. "I can't stand the thought of it either. I want to believe that
you and I will be together, somewhere, forever. Or that we'll be
reincarnated and get to go around again, and find each other and have
another lifetime to spend together. Damn it, Dominic, I really want to
believe."

"We all do," Dominic said. "I guess no one will ever know,
though, until they get there."

472

She nodded. "It just makes me that much more dedicated to appreciating each other now, while we still can. To love you while you can receive it. To be kind and generous to others *not* because we think there'll be some reward for it in heaven, or to avoid some punishment in hell, but to do it because it's the right thing to do; to make everyone's existence, no matter how long or short, as wonderful as it can be. And for every moment we're alive on this Earth, we should love and cherish and appreciate and forgive each other, because this is all there is. We're not going to get some miraculous chance to make up for it all later when we meet up again in some big glowing city in the clouds. We need to make every minute count, now."

Dominic reached a long finger down under her chin, lifting it slightly. He put his lips on hers, kissing her for a long time. When he finally pulled away, his eyes met hers, and both of theirs were glowing with tears.

"I love you, Abby," he said. "And I do love and cherish and appreciate you. And I will forever. There won't be a moment of my life that I'm not thankful for you. Whatever dream you had, it was an awfully powerful one. But don't let it upset you. I'm all right. So are you. Simon is gone, and he's gone forever. There are no ghosts, and he won't be back to haunt us. We're finally free, and the world will go on turning as foolishly as it did yesterday.

"We don't know how much time we have, and we don't know that when it's over, it's over forever. If the Long Count taught us anything, it's that we can't predict when it'll all end. So yes, every moment counts."

Abby finally smiled, the dreaded darkness of her nightmare beginning to slip away. She kissed him back, a quick peck on the lips, then sat back and stretched. Above them, dawn was beginning to lighten the black sky over the trees that hid Izapa from the mountainside. "*Are* you all right?" she asked, concerned.

"I am," he said. "I'm stiff, and I'm going to need some stitches. I wouldn't be surprised to find out I have a cracked rib or two, either. But I'm going to live. For a damn long time, I hope."

"Me too," she said, hugging him again, but more gently this time, wary of his battered ribcage. "How do you feel about a hike down the mountain?"

He laughed, and she could see by his face how it pained him. "I think I can handle it," he said. "As long as you're not in any hurry."

"Not at all," she said. "The mountain has been quiet, and Simon's band of idiots is still tramping around down there, looking for signs of last night's 'visitation.' I'd prefer not to run into any of them."

walk slowly." He staggered to a kneeling position,
.lling him to his feet. She slid her arms around him,
As they walked, the last vestiges of her nightmare faded

' Dominic said as they began making their way through the
.u and I met down there in that ancient pile of rocks five years
g the way, we've lost several friends, including one that turned
. an enemy. We seem to finally be coming out of the darkness,
.er than a couple broken bones, some cuts and scrapes, and a
.ot wound, I don't think we're too much worse for the wear. But we
haven't figured out what the hell the Long Count meant."

"Haven't we?" she asked.

Dominic was thoughtful. "We talked about the Long Count as a beginning," he said, "a birth. But I don't know how true that is. Maybe December 22 is a new beginning for us. Maybe an ending really is an ending."

While Abby was thinking about that, Dominic turned to her with a smile. "So," he said, "do you think it was all worth it?"

"To have gotten you out of it?" Abby asked. "It was worth everything. And I think we did realize what the Long Count means, sweetheart. It's about time. It's always been about time. Counting it down to the end. The problem is that no matter what we think we know, none of us really have any idea of how much time we have left. No matter how well you treat your body, or how healthy you think you are, or even if you're given six months to live: The end can sneak up on you, or come blindsiding you out of nowhere. And no one knows what happens when it ends."

He turned to her, about to speak, when she gave him a lighthearted shrug. "So like I said before — I've realized how important it is to cherish every moment we have. Time is a fleeting thing; it moves like a snake down the pyramid of Kulkulcan. You can't get a grasp on it, and you can't always count on it being there when you need it — even when you expect it.

"I've always thought that you and I would have the next forty, fifty, sixty years together; it wasn't until tonight that it's really hit me, Dominic, that we never know how much time we really have together. Even tonight, there was the chance that it might have been our last night on Earth – but even though we'd had this date in mind, we never thought it would actually end. Simon shooting you was something I never expected. We need to just appreciate what we've got, every moment. Live every moment, with no regrets."

474

"I regret nothing," Dominic said. "Except for losing touch with Tina and Dante for so long. When we get back, we need to head out and see them down again. I miss them."

Abby nodded in agreement, and Dominic continued. "Other than that, though, no regrets. Everything we've done has brought us to where we are today. And I wouldn't change that for the world."

Abby was about to answer when they broke out of the woods into the clearing. The sky was growing lighter, and she could see the jeep parked across the way.

"Let's go home," Abby said. Dominic kissed the top of her head. He gave her a quick hug, and laughing and grateful, they limped off into the clearing, leaving behind them forever the mountain and the hidden ruins below.